CECELIA AHERN

If You Could See Me Now

HARPER

This novel is entirely a work of fiction.
The names, characters and incidents portrayed in it are the work of the author's imagination. Any resemblance to actual persons, living or dead, events or localities is entirely coincidental.

Harper
HarperCollins*Publishers*
77–85 Fulham Palace Road,
Hammersmith, London W6 8JB

www.harpercollins.co.uk

This paperback edition 2008
1

First published in Great Britain by
HarperCollins*Publishers* 2005

A catalogue record for this book is available from the British Library

ISBN: 978 0 00 783211 8

Set in Sabon by Palimpsest Book Production Limited,
Grangemouth, Stirlingshire

Printed and bound in Great Britain by
Clays Limited, St Ives plc

IF YOU COULD SEE ME NOW

Before embarking on her writing career, Cecelia Ahern completed a degree in Journalism and Media Communications. At twenty-one years old, she wrote her first novel, *PS I Love You* which instantly became an international bestseller and was adapted into a major motion picture starring Hilary Swank. Her successive novels, *Where Rainbows End*, *If You Could See Me Now*, *A Place Called Here* and *Thanks for the Memories* were also number one bestsellers. Her books are published in forty-six countries and have collectively sold over nine million copies. Cecelia has also co-created the hit ABC Network comedy series *Samantha Who?* which stars Christina Applegate. Her sixth and latest book *The Gift* is a Christmas story out now in hardback. Cecelia lives in Dublin, Ireland

To sign up for the exclusive Cecelia Ahern HarperCollins newsletter and discover all about Cecelia's books, as well as interviews, photographs and much more, log onto www.cecelia-ahern.com

For automatic updates on Cecelia Ahern, visit HarperCollins.co.uk and register for AuthorTracker.

Praise for *If You Could See Me Now*:

'A beautifully written love story.' *Closer*

'A contemporary fairytale.' *Irish Times*

'An enchanting blend of magic and whimsy.'
Daily Mail

By the same author

PS, I Love You
Where Rainbows End
A Place Called Here
Thanks for the Memories

For Georgina, who believes ...

Infinite thank yous to my family, Mimmie, Dad, Georgina and Nicky for everything – I couldn't narrow that down if I tried. To David, the best coffee-maker around – thanks for checking on me every few hours and for believing so passionately in this book. Huge thanks to the endlessly encouraging you-know-what agent Marianne for the buns, tea and advice, and thank you Pat and Vicki at the you-know-what agency for taking care of you-know-what.

Thank you Lynne and Maxine and all at HarperCollins for your faith in me and for all your hard work.

To my readers, old and new, I hope this is as good for you as it was for me – an absolute joy to work on.

Most importantly thanks to Ivan for keeping me company in my office until all hours. Do you think they will ever believe our story?

Chapter 1

It was a Friday morning in June when I first became best friends with Luke. It was 9.15 a.m., to be precise and I happen to know exactly what time it was because I looked at my watch. I don't know why I did, because I didn't need to be anywhere by any specific time. But I believe there's a reason for everything so perhaps I checked my watch at that time just so I could tell you my story properly. Details are important in storytelling, aren't they?

I was glad I met Luke that morning because I was a bit down after having to leave my old best friend, Barry. He couldn't see me any more. But it doesn't really matter because he's happier now and that's what's important, I suppose. Having to leave my best friends is all part of my job. It's not a very nice part, but I believe in finding a positive side in everything, so the way I see it is, if I didn't have to leave my best friends then I wouldn't be able to make new ones. And making new friends is my favourite part by far. That's probably why I was offered the job.

We'll get on to what my job is in just a moment but first I want to tell you about the morning I first met my best friend Luke.

I closed the gate to Barry's front garden behind me and I started walking, and for absolutely no reason at all I took the first left, then a right, then a left, went straight on for a while, took another right and I ended up beside a housing estate called Fuchsia Lane. It must have been called that because of the fuchsias growing all around the place. They grow wild here. Sorry, when I say 'here' I mean a town called Baile na gCroíthe which is in County Kerry. That's in Ireland.

Baile na gCroíthe somewhere along the line ended up being known in English as Hartstown, but as a direct translation from Irish it means the Town of Hearts. Which I think sounds nicer.

I was glad I ended up back here again; I had done a few jobs here when I was starting out but hadn't returned for years. My work takes me all over the country, sometimes even overseas when my friends take me away on holidays which just goes to show, no matter where you are, you always need a best friend.

Fuchsia Lane had twelve houses, six on each side, and all were different. The cul-de-sac was really busy with lots of people buzzing about. It was a Friday morning, remember, and June too, so it was really sunny and bright and everyone was in a good mood. Well, not *everyone*.

There were lots of children playing on the road, cycling, chasing, enjoying hopscotch, tip the can and loads of other stuff. You could hear the sounds of delighted screams and laughter coming from them. I suppose they were happy to be on their school holidays too. As much as they seemed really nice and all, I just wasn't drawn to them. You see, I can't just make friends with anyone. That's not what my job is about.

A man was cutting the grass in his front garden, and a woman tending to the flowerbed with big mucky gloves on her hands. There was a lovely smell of freshly cut grass and the sound of the lady snipping, clipping, cropping and pruning was like music in the air. In the next garden a man whistled a tune I wasn't familiar with while he pointed the garden hose towards his car and watched as the soapy suds slithered down the side, revealing a new sparkle. Every now and again he whipped round and sprayed water on two little girls who were dressed in yellow and black striped swimsuits. They looked like big bumble bees. I loved hearing them giggling so much.

In the next driveway a boy and girl were playing hopscotch. I observed them for a spell but none of them responded to my interest so I kept on moving. I walked by children playing in every garden yet none of them saw me or invited me to play. People on bicycles and skateboards, and remote controlled cars were whizzing by, oblivious to me. I was beginning to think that coming to Fuchsia Lane was a bit of a mistake, which was rather confusing because usually I was so good at choosing places and there were so many children here. I sat down on the garden wall of the last house and began to think about where I could have taken a wrong turn.

After a few minutes, I came to the conclusion that I was in the right area after all. I very rarely take wrong turns. I spun on my backside to face the house behind the garden wall. There was no action in this garden so I sat and studied the house. It had two storeys and a garage with an expensive car parked outside that glistened in the sun. A plaque on the garden wall beneath me said 'Fuchsia House', and the house had blooming fuchsia climbing up the wall, clinging to the brown bricks over the front door and reaching all the way up to the roof. It looked pretty. Fractions of the house had brown bricks and other sections had been painted a honey colour. Some of the windows were square and others were circles. It was really unusual. It had a fuchsia-coloured front door with two long windows with frosted glass in the top two panels, a huge brass knocker and letter box beneath; it looked like two eyes, a nose and a mouth smiling at me. I waved and smiled back just in case. Well, you can never be too sure these days.

Just as I was studying the face of the front door, it opened and was slammed shut rather loudly and angrily by a boy who came running outside. He had a big red fire engine in his right hand and a police car in his left hand. I love red fire engines; they're my favourite. The boy jumped off the front step of the porch and ran to the grass where he skidded to his knees. He got grass stains all down his black tracksuit bottoms, which made me laugh. Grass stains are so much fun because they never come out. My old friend Barry and I used to slide all of the time. Anyway, the little boy started crashing his fire engine against his police car and making all these noises with his mouth. He was good at the noises. Barry and I always used to do that too. It's fun pretending to do things that don't usually happen in real life.

The boy rammed the police car into the red fire engine and the head fireman, who was clinging to the ladder at the side of the truck, slid off. I laughed out loud and the boy looked up.

He actually looked at me. Right into my eyes.

'Hi,' I said, nervously clearing my throat and shifting from one foot to the other. I was wearing my favourite blue Converse runners and they still had grass stains on the white rubber tips from when Barry and I went sliding. I started to run the rubber tip against the brick garden wall to try to scrape it off and thought about what to say next. As much as making friends is my favourite thing to do I still get a bit nervous about it. There's always that scary chance that people won't like me and it gives me the collywobbles. I've been lucky so far but it would be silly to presume that the same thing will happen every time.

'Hi,' the boy replied, fixing the fireman back onto the ladder.

'What's your name?' I asked, kicking my foot against the wall on front of me and scraping the rubber tip. The grass stains still wouldn't come off.

The boy studied me for a while, looked me up and down as though trying to decide whether to tell me his name or not. This is the part of my job I absolutely loathe.

It's tough wanting to be friends with someone and them not wanting the same back. That happens sometimes but in the end they always come round because, whether they know it or not, they want me to be there.

The boy had white-blond hair and big blue eyes. I knew his face from somewhere but couldn't quite think where.

Finally he spoke. 'My name's Luke. What's yours?'

I shoved my hands deep into my pockets and concentrated on kicking my right foot against the garden wall. I was making parts of the bricks crumble and fall to the ground. Without looking at him I said, 'Ivan.'

'Hi, Ivan,' he smiled. He had no front teeth.

'Hi, Luke,' I smiled back.

I have all mine.

'I like your fire engine. My bes— my old best friend Barry used to have one just like it and we used to play with it all the time. It's got a stupid name, though, because it can't drive through fire because it melts,' I explained, still keeping my hands shoved into my pockets, causing my shoulders to hunch up past my ears. It made things a little quieter so I took my hands out of my pocket just so I could hear what Luke was saying.

Luke rolled on the grass laughing. 'You put your fire engine through *fire*?' he screeched.

'Well, it is called a *fire* engine, isn't it?' I replied defensively.

Luke rolled onto his back, kicked his feet in the air and hooted. 'No, you dummy! Fire engines are for putting *out* fires!'

I thought about that one for a while. 'Hmm. Well, I'll tell you what puts out fire engines, Luke,' I explained matter-of-factly. 'Water does.'

Luke hit himself lightly on the side of the head, screamed 'Doh!', made his eyes go cockeyed and then fell over on the grass.

I started laughing. Luke was really funny.

'Do you want to come and play?' He raised his eyebrows questioningly.

I grinned. 'Of course, Luke. Playing is my favourite!' and I jumped over the garden wall and joined him on the grass.

'What age are you?' He looked at me suspiciously. 'You look like you're the same age as my aunt,' he frowned, 'and my aunt doesn't like to play with my fire engine.'

I shrugged. 'Well, then your aunt is a boring old gnirob!'

'A *gnirob*!' Luke screamed with mirth. 'What's a gnirob?'

'Someone who's *boring*,' I said, scrunching my nose up and saying the word like it was a disease. I liked saying words backwards; it was like inventing my own language.

'Boring,' Luke repeated after me and scrunched up his nose, 'uugh.'

'What age are you anyway?' I asked Luke as I crashed the police car into the fire engine. The fireman fell off the ladder again. 'You look like *my* aunt,' I accused him, and Luke fell about the place. He had a loud laugh.

'I'm only six, Ivan! And I'm not a *girl*!'

'Oh.' I don't really have an aunt but I just said it to make him laugh. 'Well, there's nothing *only* about being six.'

Just as I was about to ask him what his favourite cartoon was, the front door opened and I heard screaming. Luke went white and I looked up to where he was faced.

'SAOIRSE, GIVE ME BACK MY KEYS!' a voice yelled desperately. A flustered-looking woman, red in the cheeks, frantic eyes, with long unwashed red hair swinging in strands around her face, came running out of the house alone. Another shriek from the voice in the house behind caused her to stumble in her platforms on the step of the front porch. She cursed loudly and reached out to the wall of the house for balance. Looking up, she stared in the direction of where Luke and I were sitting at the end of the garden. Her mouth widened into a smile to reveal a set of crooked yellow teeth. I crawled back a few more inches. I noticed Luke did too. She gave Luke the thumbs-up and croaked, 'See ya, kiddo.' She let go of the wall, wavered slightly and walked quickly to the car parked in the driveway.

'SAOIRSE!' The voice of the person inside the house screamed again. 'I'M CALLING THE GARDAÍ IF YOU SET ONE FOOT IN THAT CAR!'

The red-haired woman snorted, pressed the car keys and the lights flashed and beeped. She opened the door, climbed in, banged her head on the side, cursed loudly again and slammed the door shut behind her. I could hear the doors locking from where I was at the end of the garden. A few kids on the road stopped playing and stared at the scene unfolding before them.

Finally the owner of the mystery voice came running outside with a phone in her hand. She looked very different from the other lady. Her hair was tied back neatly and tightly at the back of her head. She wore a smart grey trouser suit, which didn't match the high-pitched, uncontrolled voice she currently had. She too was red in the face and out of breath. Her chest heaved up and down rapidly as she tried to run as quickly as she could in her high heels to the car. She danced around beside the car, first trying the door handle and, when finding it locked, threatened to dial 999.

'I'm calling the gardaí, Saoirse,' she warned, waving the phone at the window on the driver's side.

Saoirse just grinned from inside the car and started up the engine. The lady with the phone's voice cracked as she pleaded with her to get out of the car. Jumping from foot to foot, she looked like there was somebody else bubbling under her own flesh, trying to get out, like the Incredible Hulk.

Saoirse sped off down the long cobble-stoned driveway. Halfway down, she slowed the car. The woman with the phone relaxed her shoulders and looked relieved. Instead of stopping completely, the car crawled along as the window of the driver's side was lowered and two fingers appeared out of it, held up proud and high for all to see.

'Ah, she'll be back in two minutes, so,' I said to Luke, and he looked at me oddly.

The woman with the phone watched in fright as the car sped off again down the road, narrowly missing hitting a child on the road. A few hairs escaped from the tight bun on her head, as though attempting to chase the car themselves.

Luke lowered his head and quietly put the fireman back on his ladder. The woman let out an exasperated screech, threw her hands in the air and turned on her heel. There was a crack as the heel of her shoe became lodged between the cobbles of the drive. The woman shook her leg wildly, growing more frustrated by the second, and eventually the shoe flew out, but the heel remained lodged between the crack.

'FUUUUCCCK!' she yelled. Hobbling on one high heel and what was now one flat pump, she made her way back up the front porch. The fuchsia door was slammed shut and she was swallowed back up by the house. The windows, door knob and the letter box smiled at me again and I smiled back.

'Who are you smiling at?' Luke asked with a frown on his face.

'The door,' I replied, thinking it an obvious answer.

He just stared at me with the same frown, his mind evidently lost in the thoughts of what he had just seen, and the oddity of smiling at a door.

We could see the woman with the phone through the glass of the front door, pacing the hall.

'Who is she?' I asked, turning to Luke.

He was clearly shaken.

'That's my aunt,' he almost whispered. 'She looks after me.'

'Oh,' I said. 'Who was the one in the car?'

Luke slowly pushed the fire engine through the grass, flattening the blades as he went along. 'Oh, her. That's Saoirse,' he said quietly. 'She's my mom.'

'Oh.' There was a silence and I could tell he was sad. 'Seer-sha,' I repeated the name, liking how it felt when I said it; like the wind blowing out of my mouth in one big gust or how the trees sounded when they talked to one another on windy days. 'Seeeeer-ssshaaaa . . .' I eventually stopped when Luke looked at me oddly.

I picked a buttercup out of the ground and held it under Luke's chin. A yellow glow appeared on his pale skin. 'You like butter,' I stated. 'So Saorise's not your girlfriend then?'

Luke's face immediately lit up and he giggled. Not as much as before, though.

'Who's your friend Barry that you mentioned?' Luke asked, smashing into my car much harder than before.

'Barry McDonald is his name,' I smiled, remembering the games me and Barry used to play.

Luke's eyes lit up. 'Barry McDonald is in my class in school!'

Then it clicked. 'I knew I knew your face from somewhere, Luke. I used to see you everyday when I went to school with Barry.'

'You went to school with Barry?' he said, surprised.

'Yeah, school was fun with Barry,' I laughed.

Luke narrowed his eyes, 'Well, I didn't see you there.'

I started laughing. 'Well, *of course* you didn't *see* me, you silly sod,' I said matter-of-factly.

Chapter 2

Elizabeth's heart hammered loudly against her chest, as, having slipped on another pair of shoes, she paced the long maple-floored hall of her home. With the phone pressed hard between her ear and shoulder, her mind was a blizzard of thoughts as she listened to the shrill ring tone in her ear.

She stopped pacing long enough to stare at her reflection in the mirror. Her brown eyes widened with horror. Rarely did she allow herself to look so bedraggled. *So out of control.* Strands of her chocolate-brown hair were fleeing from the tight French pleat, causing her to appear as though she had placed her fingers in an electric socket. Mascara nestled in the lines under her eyes; her lipstick had faded, leaving only her plum-coloured lipliner as a frame, and her foundation clung to the dry patches of her olive skin. Gone was the usual pristine look. This caused her heart to beat faster, the panic to accelerate.

Breathe, Elizabeth, just breathe, she told herself. She ran a trembling hand over her tousled hair, forcing the wild hairs back down. She wiped the mascara away with a wet finger, pursed her lips together, smoothed down her suit jacket and cleared her throat. It was simply a momentary lapse of concentration on her part, that was all. Not to happen again. She transferred the phone to her left ear and noticed the impression of her Claddagh earring against her neck. Such was the pressure of her shoulder's grip on the phone against her skin.

Finally someone answered and Elizabeth turned her back on the mirror to stand to attention. Back to business.

'Hello, Baile na gCroíthe Garda Station.'

Elizabeth winced as she recognised the voice on the phone. 'Hi, Marie, Elizabeth here . . . again. Saoirse's gone off with the car,' she paused, 'again.'

There was a gentle sigh on the other end of the phone. 'How long ago, Elizabeth?'

Elizabeth sat down on the bottom stair and settled in for the usual line of questioning. She closed her eyes, only meaning to rest them briefly, but at the relief of blocking everything out she kept them closed. 'Just five minutes ago.'

'Right. Did she say where she was going?'

'The moon,' she replied matter-of-factly.

'Excuse me?' Marie asked.

'You heard me. She said she was going to the moon,' Elizabeth said firmly. 'Apparently people will understand her there.'

'The moon,' Marie repeated.

'Yes,' Elizabeth replied, feeling irritated. 'You could perhaps start looking for her on the motorway. I would imagine that if you were heading to the moon that would be the quickest way to get there, wouldn't you? Although I'm not entirely sure which exit she would take. Whichever is more northerly, I suppose. She could be headed north-east to Dublin, or, who knows, she could be making her way to Cork; perhaps they've a plane that can take her off this planet. Either way, I'd check the motor—'

'Relax, Elizabeth; you know I have to ask.'

'I know.' Elizabeth tried to calm herself again. She was missing an important meeting right now. Important for her, important for her interior design business. Luke's babysitter was standing in as a replacement for his nanny, Edith.

Edith had left a few weeks ago for the three months of travelling the world she had threatened Elizabeth with for the past six years, leaving the young babysitter inexperienced to the ways of Saoirse. She had rung her at work in a panic . . . again . . . and Elizabeth had to drop everything . . . again . . . and rush home . . . again. But she shouldn't be surprised that this had happened . . . again. She was, however, surprised that Edith, apart from the current trip to Australia, was still turning up to work every day. Six years she had been helping Elizabeth with Luke, six years of drama, and still after all her years of loyalty, Elizabeth expected a phone call or her letter of resignation practically every day. Being Luke's nanny came with a lot of baggage. Then again, so did being Luke's adoptive parent.

'Elizabeth, are you still there?'

'Yes.' Her eyes shot open. She was losing concentration. 'Sorry, what did you say?'

'I asked you what car she took.'

Elizabeth rolled her eyes and made a face at the phone. 'The same one, Marie. The same bloody car as last week, and the week before and the week before that,' she snapped.

Marie remained firm, 'Which is the—'

'BMW,' she interrupted. 'The same damn black BMW 330 Cabriolet. Four wheels, two doors, one steering wheel, two wing mirrors, lights and—'

'A partridge in a pear tree,' Marie interrupted. 'What condition was she in?'

'Very shiny. I'd just washed her,' Elizabeth replied cheekily.

'Great, and what condition was Saoirse in?'

'The usual one.'

'Intoxicated.'

'That's the one.' Elizabeth stood up and walked down the hall to the kitchen. Her sun trap. Her heels against the marble floor echoed loudly in the empty high-ceilinged room. Everything was in its place. The room was hot from the sun's glare through the glass of the conservatory. Elizabeth's tired eyes squinted in the brightness. The spotless kitchen gleamed, the black granite counter tops sparkled, the chrome fittings mirrored the bright day. A stainless steel and walnut heaven. She headed straight to the espresso machine. Her saviour. Needing an injection of life into her exhausted body, she opened the kitchen cabinet and took out a small beige coffee cup. Before closing the press she turned a cup round so that the handle was on the right side like all the others. She slid open the long steel cutlery drawer, noticed a knife in the fork's compartment, put it back in its rightful place, retrieved a spoon and slid it shut.

From the corner of her eye she saw the hand towel messily strewn over the handle of the cooker. She threw the crumpled cloth into the utility room, retrieved a fresh towel from the neat pile in the press, folded it exactly in half and draped it over the cooker handle. Everything had its place.

'Well, I haven't changed my licence plate in the past week so yes, it's still the same,' she replied with boredom to another of Marie's pointless questions. She placed the steaming espresso cup on a marble coaster to protect the glass kitchen table. She smoothed out her trousers, removed a piece of fluff from her jacket, sat down in the conservatory and looked out at her long garden and the rolling green hills beyond that seemed to stretch on for ever. Forty shades of green, golds and browns.

She breathed in the rich aroma of her steaming espresso and immediately felt revived. She pictured her sister racing over the hills with the top down on Elizabeth's convertible, arms in the air, eyes closed, flame-red hair blowing in the wind, believing she was free. Saoirse meant freedom in Irish. The name had been chosen by their mother in her last desperate attempt to make the duties of motherhood she despised so much seem less like a punishment. Her wish was for her second daughter to bring her freedom from the shackles of marriage, motherhood, responsibility . . . reality.

Her mother had met her father when she was sixteen. She was travelling through the town with a group of poets, musicians and dreamers, and got talking to Brendan Egan, a farmer in the local pub. He was twelve years her senior and was enthralled by her mysterious wild ways and carefree nature. She was flattered. And so they married. At eighteen they had their first child, Elizabeth. As it turned out, her mother couldn't be tamed and found it increasingly frustrating being held in the sleepy town nestled in the hills she had only ever intended to pass through. A crying baby and sleepless nights drove her further and further away in her head. Dreams of her own personal freedom became confused with her reality and she started to go missing for days at a time. She went exploring, discovering places and other people.

Elizabeth, at twelve years of age, looked after herself and her silent, brooding father and didn't ask when her mother would be home because she knew in her heart that she would eventually return, cheeks flushed, eyes bright, and speaking breathlessly of the world and all it had to offer. She would waft into their lives like a fresh summer breeze, bringing excitement and hope. The feel of their bungalow farmhouse always changed when she returned; the four walls absorbed her enthusiasm. Elizabeth would sit at the end of her mother's bed, listening to stories, giddy with delight. This ambience would last for only a few days until her mother quickly tired of sharing stories rather than making new ones.

Often she brought back mementoes such as shells, stones, leaves. Elizabeth could recall a vase of long fresh grasses that sat in the centre of the dining-room table as though they were the most exotic plants ever created. When asked about the field they were pulled from, her mother just winked and tipped her nose, promising Elizabeth that she would understand some day. Her father would sit silently in his chair by the fireplace, reading his paper but never turning the page. He was as lost in her world of words as she was.

When Elizabeth was twelve years old her mother became pregnant again and, despite the new-born baby being named Saoirse, this child didn't offer the freedom her mother craved, and so she set off on another expedition. And didn't return. Her father, Brendan, had no interest in the young life that had driven his wife away so he waited in silence for her in his chair by the fire. Reading his paper but never turning the page. For years. For ever. Soon Elizabeth's heart grew weary of awaiting her mother's return and Saoirse became Elizabeth's responsibility.

Saoirse had inherited her father's Celtic looks of strawberry-blonde hair and fair skin, while Elizabeth was the image of her mother. Olive skin, chocolate hair, almost black eyes; in their blood from the Spanish influence thousands of years before. Elizabeth resembled her mother more and more with every passing day and she knew her father found that difficult. She grew to hate herself for it, and along with making the effort of trying to have conversations with her father, she tried even harder to prove to her father and to herself that she was nothing like her mother – that she was capable of loyalty.

When Elizabeth finished school at eighteen she was faced with the dilemma of having to move to Cork to attend university. A decision that took all her courage to make. Her father regarded her acceptance of the course as abandonment; he saw any friendship she created with anyone as abandonment. He craved attention, always demanding to be the only person in his daughters' lives, as though that would prevent them from moving away from him. Well, he almost succeeded and certainly was part of the reason for Elizabeth's lack of a social life or circle of friends. She had been conditioned to walk away when polite conversation was started, knowing she would pay for any unnecessary time spent away from the farm with sullen words and disapproving glares. In any case, looking after Saoirse as well as going to school was a full-time job. Brendan accused her of being like her mother, of thinking she was above him and superior to Baile na gCroíthe. She found the small town claustrophobic and felt the dull farmhouse was dipped in darkness, with no sense of time. It was as though even the grandfather clock in the hall was waiting for her mother to return.

'And, Luke, where is he?' Marie asked over the phone, bringing Elizabeth swiftly back to the present.

Elizabeth replied bitterly. 'Do you really think Saoirse would take him with her?'

Silence.

Elizabeth sighed. 'He's here.'

The name Saoirse had brought more than something to call Elizabeth's sister by. It had given her an identity, a way of life. Everything the name represented was passed into her blood. She was fiery, independent, wild and free. She followed the pattern of the mother she could not remember, so much that Elizabeth almost felt as though she were watching her mother. But she kept losing sight of her. Saoirse became pregnant at sixteen and no one knew who the father was, not least Saoirse. Once she had the baby she didn't care much for naming him but eventually took to calling him Lucky. Another wish. So Elizabeth named him Luke. And once again, at the age of twenty-eight, Elizabeth took responsibility for a child.

There was never as much as a flicker of recognition in Saoirse's eyes when she looked at Luke. It startled Elizabeth to see that there was no bond, no connection at all. Elizabeth had never planned on having children – in fact she had made a pact with herself *never* to have children. She had raised herself and raised her sister; she had no desires to raise anybody else. It was time to look after herself. But at twenty-eight years old, after having slaved away at school and college, she had been successful in starting up her own interior design business. Her hard work meant that she was the only member of the family capable of providing a good life for Luke. She had reached her goals by being in control, maintaining order, not losing sight of herself, always being realistic, believing in fact and not dreams, and above all applying herself and working hard. Her mother and sister had taught her that she wouldn't get anywhere by following wistful dreams and having unrealistic hopes.

So now she was thirty-four years old and living alone with Luke in a house that she loved. A house she had bought, and was paying for, all by herself. A house she had made her haven, the place she could retreat to and feel safe. Alone because love was one of those feelings that you could never control. And she needed to be in control. She had loved before, had been loved, had tasted what it was to dream and had felt what it was to dance on air. She had also learned what it was to land back on the earth with a cruel thud. Having to take care of her sister's child had sent her love away and there had been no one since. She had learned not to lose control of her feelings again.

The front door banged shut and she heard the patter of little feet running down the hall.

'Luke!' she called, putting her hand over the receiver.

'Yeah?' he asked innocently, blue eyes and blond hair appearing round the doorpost.

'*Yes*, not yeah,' Elizabeth corrected him sternly. Her voice was full of the authority she had become a pro at over the years.

'*Yes*,' he repeated.

'What are you doing?'

Luke stepped into the hall and Elizabeth's eyes immediately went to his grass-stained knees.

'Me and Ivan are just playing the computer,' he explained.

'Ivan and I,' she corrected him, and continued listening to Marie at the other end of the phone arranging to send a garda car out. Luke looked at his aunt and returned to the playroom.

'Hold on a minute,' Elizabeth shouted down the phone, finally registering what Luke had just told her. She jumped up from her chair, bumping the table leg and spilling her espresso onto the glass. She swore. The black wrought-iron legs of the chair screeched against the marble. Holding the phone to her chest, she raced down the long hall to the playroom. She tucked her head round the corner and saw Luke sitting on the floor, eyes glued to the TV screen. Here and his bedroom were the only rooms in the house she allowed his toys. Taking care of a child had not succeeded in changing her as many thought it would; he hadn't softened her views in any way. She had visited many of Luke's friends' houses, picking him up or dropping him off, so full of toys lying around, they tripped up everyone who dared walk in their path. She reluctantly had cups of coffee with the mothers while sitting on teddies, surrounded by bottles, formula and nappies. But not in her home. Edith had been told the rules at the beginning of their working relationship and she had followed them. As Luke grew up and understood his aunt's ways, he obediently respected her wishes and contained his playing to the one room she had dedicated to his needs.

'Luke, who's Ivan?' Elizabeth asked, eyes darting around the room. 'You know you can't be bringing strangers home,' she said, worried.

'He's my new friend,' he replied, zombie-like, not moving his eyes from the beefed-up wrestler body-slamming his opponent on the screen.

'You know I insist on meeting your friends first before you bring them home. Where is he?' Elizabeth questioned, pushing open the door and stepping into Luke's space. She hoped to God that this friend would be better than the last little terror who had decided to draw a picture of his happy family in magic marker on her wall, which had since been painted over.

'Over there.' Luke nodded his head in the direction of the window, still not budging his eyes.

Elizabeth walked towards the window and looked out at the front garden. She crossed her arms. 'Is he hiding?'

Luke pressed Pause on his computer keypad and finally moved his eyes away from the two wrestlers on the screen. His face crinkled in confusion. 'He's right there!' He pointed at the beanbag at Elizabeth's feet.

Elizabeth's eyes widened as she stared at the beanbag. 'Where?'

'Right there,' he repeated.

Elizabeth blinked back at him. She raised her arms questioningly.

'Beside you, on the beanbag.' Luke's voice became louder with anxiety. He stared at the yellow corduroy beanbag as though willing his friend to appear.

Elizabeth followed his gaze.

'See him?' He dropped the control pad and stood up quickly.

This was followed by a tense silence in which Elizabeth could feel Luke's hatred for her emanating from his body. She could tell what he was thinking: why couldn't she just see him, why couldn't she just play along just this once, why couldn't she ever pretend? She swallowed the lump in her throat and looked around the room to see if she really was missing his friend in some way. Nothing.

She leaned down to be on an even level with him and her knees cracked. 'There's no one else but you and me in this room,' she whispered softly. Somehow saying it quietly made it easier. Easier for herself or Luke, she didn't know.

Luke's cheeks flushed and his chest heaved faster. He stood in the centre of the room, surrounded by computer keypad wires, with his little hands down by his side, looking helpless. Elizabeth's heart hammered in her chest as she silently begged, *please do not be like your mother, please do not be like your mother*. She knew only too well how the world of fantasy could steal you away.

Finally Luke exploded and, staring into space, demanded, 'Ivan, say something to her!'

There was a silence as he looked into space and then giggled hysterically. He looked back at Elizabeth and his smile quickly faded when he noticed her lack of response. 'Do you not see him?' he squealed nervously. Then, more angrily, repeated, 'Why don't you see him?'

'OK, OK!' Elizabeth tried not to panic. She stood back up to her own level. A level where she had control. She couldn't see him and her brain refused to let her pretend. She wanted to get out of the room quickly. She lifted her leg to step over the beanbag and stopped herself, instead choosing to walk round it. Once at the door, she glanced around one last time to see if she could spot the mystery Ivan. No sign.

Luke shrugged, sat down and continued playing his wrestling game.

'I'm putting some pizza on now, Luke.'

Silence. What else should she say? It was at moments like this she realised that reading all the parenting manuals in the world never helped. Good parenting came from the heart, was instinctive, and not for the first time she worried she was letting Luke down.

'It will be ready in twenty minutes,' she finished awkwardly.

'What?' Luke pressed Pause again and faced the window.

'I said it will be ready in twen—'

'No, not you,' Luke said, once again being sucked into the world of video games. 'Ivan would like some too. He said pizza is his favourite.'

'Oh.' Elizabeth swallowed helplessly.

'With olives,' Luke continued.

'But, Luke, you hate olives.'

'Yeah, but Ivan loves them. He says they're his favourite.'

'Oh . . .'

'Thanks,' Luke said to his aunt, looked to the beanbag, gave the thumbs-up, smiled, then looked away again.

Elizabeth slowly backed out of the playroom. She realised she was still holding the phone to her chest. 'Marie, are you still there?' She chewed on her nail and stared at the closed playroom door, wondering what to do.

'I thought you'd gone off to the moon as well. I was about to send a car over to your house too,' Marie chuckled.

Marie mistook Elizabeth's silence for anger and apologised quickly. 'Anyway, you were right, Saoirse *was* headed to the moon but luckily she decided to stop off on the way to refuel. Refuelling herself, more like. Your car was found blocking the main street with the engine still running and the driver's door wide open. You're lucky Paddy found it when he did before someone took off with it.'

'Let me guess. The car was outside the pub.'

'Correct.' Marie paused. 'Do you want to press charges?'

Elizabeth sighed. 'No. Thanks, Marie.'

'Not a problem. We'll have someone bring the car home to you.'

'What about Saoirse?' Elizabeth paced the hall. 'Where is she?'

'We'll just keep her here for a while, Elizabeth.'

'I'll come get her,' Elizabeth said quickly.

'No,' Marie insisted. 'Let me get back to you about that. She needs to calm down before she goes anywhere yet.'

From inside the playroom Elizabeth heard Luke laughing and talking away to himself.

'Actually, Marie,' she added with a weak smile, 'while we're on the phone, tell whoever's bringing the car to bring a shrink with them. It seems Luke is imagining friends now . . .'

Inside the playroom Ivan rolled his eyes and wiggled his body down further into the beanbag. He had heard her on the phone. Ever since he had started this job, parents had been calling him that and it was really beginning to bother him. There was nothing imaginary about him whatsoever.

They just couldn't see him.

Chapter 3

It was really nice of Luke to invite me to lunch that day. When I said that pizza was my favourite I hadn't actually intended being asked to stay to eat it. But how can you say no to the treat of *pizza* on a *Friday*? That's a cause for double celebration. However, I got the impression from the incident in the playroom that his aunt didn't like me very much, but I'm not at all surprised because that's usually the way it goes. The parents always think that making food for me is a waste because they always just end up throwing it out. But it's tricky for me – I mean, you try eating your dinner squashed in a tiny place at the table while everyone looks at you and wonders whether the food is going to disappear or not. I eventually get so paranoid that I can't eat and just have to leave the food on the plate.

Not that I'm complaining – being invited to dinner is nice but the grown-ups never quite put the same amount of food on my plate as everyone else's. It's never even half as much food as the rest and they always say things like, 'Oh, I'm sure Ivan's not that hungry today anyway.' I mean, how would they know? They never even ask. I'm usually sandwiched between whoever my best friend is at the time and some annoying older brother or sister who steals my food when no one's looking.

They forget to give me things like serviettes, cutlery, and they sure aren't generous with the wine. (Sometimes they just give me an empty plate and tell my best friends that invisible people eat invisible food. I mean, *please*, does the invisible wind blow invisible trees?) I usually get a glass of water and that's only when I ask my friends politely. The grown-ups think it's weird that I need a glass of water with my food, but they make an even bigger deal about it when I want ice. I mean, the ice is free anyway and who doesn't like a cool drink on a hot day?

It's usually the moms who have conversations with me. Only they ask questions and don't listen to the answers, or pretend to everyone else that I've said something else just to make them all laugh. They even look at my chest when they're talking to me as if they expect me to be three feet tall. It's such a stereotype. For the record, I'm six foot tall and we don't really do the 'age' thing where I'm from; we come into existence as we are and grow spiritually rather than physically. It's our brains that do the growing. Let's just say my brain is pretty big by now, but there's always room for more growth. I've been doing this job for a long, long time and I'm good at it. I've never failed a friend.

The dads always say things under their breath to me when they think no one else is listening. For example, me and Barry went to Waterford on our summer holidays and we were lying on the beach on Brittas Bay and a lady walked by in a bikini. Barry's dad said under his breath, 'Getta loada that, Ivan.' The dads always think that I agree with them. They always tell my best friends that I told them things like, 'It's good to eat vegetables. Ivan told me to tell you to eat your broccoli,' and stupid things like that. My best friends know full well that's not what I would say.

But that's grown-ups for you.

Nineteen minutes and thirty-eight seconds later, Elizabeth called Luke for dinner. My tummy was grumbling and I was really looking forward to the pizza. I followed Luke down the long hall to the kitchen, looking in every room as we passed. The house was really quiet and our footsteps echoed. Every room was all white or beige, and so spotless that I began to get nervous about eating my pizza because I didn't want to make a mess. As far as I could see, not only was there no sign of a child living in the house, there was no sign of *anyone* living in the house. It didn't have what you'd call a homely feel.

I liked the kitchen, though. It was warm from the sun and because it was surrounded by glass, it felt like we were sitting in the garden. Kind of like a picnic. I noticed the table was set for two people so I waited until told where to sit. The plates were big, black and shiny, the sun through the window made the cutlery sparkle and the two crystal glasses reflect rainbow colours on the table. There was a bowl of salad and a glass jug of water with ice and lemon in the centre of the table. Everything was resting on black marble place mats. Looking at how everything glistened, I was afraid even to get the napkins dirty.

Elizabeth's chair legs squeaked against the tiles as she sat down. She put her serviette on her lap. I noticed she'd changed into a chocolate-brown tracksuit to match her hair and complement her skin. Luke's chair squeaked and he sat down. Elizabeth picked up the giant salad fork and spoon and began to gather leaves and baby tomatoes onto her plate. Luke watched her and frowned. Luke had a slice of margherita pizza on his plate. No olives. I shoved my hands deep into my pockets and shuffled nervously from foot to foot.

'Is something wrong, Luke?' Elizabeth asked, pouring dressing over her lettuce.

'Where's Ivan's place?'

Elizabeth paused, screwed the lid on tightly and put the jar back in the centre of the table. 'Now, Luke, let's not be silly,' she said light-heartedly, not looking at him. I knew she was afraid to look.

'I'm not being silly,' Luke frowned. 'You said Ivan could stay for dinner.'

'Yes, but where *is* Ivan?' She tried to keep the soft tone in her voice while sprinkling grated cheese over her salad. I could tell she didn't want this to become an issue. She would knock it on the head straight away and there would be no more talk of invisible friends.

'He's standing right beside you.'

Elizabeth slammed her knife and fork down and Luke jumped in his seat. She opened her mouth to silence him but was interrupted by the doorbell ringing. As soon as she left the room, Luke got up from his chair and took out a plate from the kitchen press. A big black one just the same as the other two. He placed a slice of pizza on the plate, took out the cutlery and a napkin and placed it on a third place mat beside him.

'That's your seat, Ivan,' he said happily, and took a bite out of his pizza. A piece of melted cheese dribbled down his chin, looking like yellow string.

To be truthful I wouldn't have sat down at the table if it wasn't for my grumbling stomach shouting at me to eat. I knew Elizabeth would be mad, but if I gobbled the food up real fast before she returned to the kitchen then she wouldn't even know.

'Want some olives on that?' Luke asked, wiping his tomatoey face on his sleeve.

I laughed and nodded. My mouth was watering.

Elizabeth hurried back into the kitchen just as Luke was reaching up to the shelf.

'What are you doing?' she asked, rummaging through a drawer for something.

'Getting the olives for Ivan,' Luke explained. 'He likes olives on his pizza, remember?'

She looked across to the kitchen table and saw that it had been set for three. She rubbed her eyes tiredly. 'Look, Luke, don't you think it's a waste of food, putting the olives on the pizza? You hate them and I'll only have to throw it out.'

'Well, it won't be a waste because Ivan will eat them, won't you, Ivan?'

'I sure will,' I said, licking my lips and rubbing my aching tummy.

'Well?' Elizabeth cocked an eyebrow. 'What did he say?'

Luke frowned. 'You mean you can't *hear* him either?' He looked at me and circled his forefinger around his temple, signalling to me that his aunt was crazy. 'He said he sure will eat them all.'

'How polite of him,' Elizabeth mumbled, continuing to rummage through the drawer. 'But you better make sure every last crumb is gone because it'll be the last time Ivan eats with us if not.'

'Don't worry, Elizabeth, I'll gobble it all right up,' I told her, taking a bite. I couldn't face not being able to eat with Luke and his aunt again. She had sad eyes, sad brown eyes, and I was convinced that I was going to make her happy by eating every last crumb. I ate quickly.

'Thanks, Colm,' Elizabeth said tiredly, taking the car keys from the garda. She circled the car slowly, inspecting the paintwork closely.

'There's no damage done,' Colm said, watching her.

'Not to the car, anyway,' she attempted a joke, patting the bonnet. She always felt embarrassed. At least once a week there was some sort of incident involving the gardaí and although they were never anything but professional and polite about the situation, she couldn't help feeling ashamed. She would work even harder in their presence to appear 'normal' just to prove that it wasn't her fault, and that it wasn't the *entire* family that was nuts. She wiped down the splashes of dried mud with a tissue.

Colm smiled at her sadly. 'She was arrested, Elizabeth.'

Elizabeth's head shot up, now fully alert. 'Colm,' she said, shocked, 'why?' They had never done that before. They had always just warned Saoirse off and then dropped her back to wherever she was staying. Unprofessional, Elizabeth knew, but in such a small town where everyone knew everyone, they had always just kept their eye on Saoirse, stopping her before she did anything incredibly stupid. But Elizabeth feared Saoirse had been warned once too often.

Colm fidgeted with the navy-blue cap in his hands. 'She was drink driving, Elizabeth, in a stolen car, and she doesn't even have a licence.'

Hearing those words, Elizabeth shivered. Saoirse was a danger. Why did she keep protecting her sister? When would the words finally sink in and she'd accept that they were right: that her sister would never be the angel she wished her to be?

'But the car wasn't stolen,' Elizabeth stammered, 'I told her that she c—'

'Don't, Elizabeth.' Colm's voice was firm.

She had to hold her hand across her mouth to stop herself. She took a deep breath and tried to regain control. 'She has to go to court?' Her voice was a whisper.

Colm looked down at the ground and moved a stone with his foot. 'Yes. It's not just about her harming herself now. She's a danger to others.'

Elizabeth swallowed hard and nodded. 'One more chance, Colm,' she gulped, feeling her pride disintegrating. 'Just give her one more chance . . . please.' The last word pained her to have to say. Every bone in her body pleaded with him. Elizabeth never asked for help. 'I'll keep an eye on her. I promise she won't be out of my sight for a minute. She's going to get better, you know. She just needs time to work things out.' Elizabeth could feel her voice shaking. Her knees trembled as she begged on behalf of her sister.

There was a sad tone in Colm's voice. 'It's already been done. We can't change it now.'

'What will the punishment be?' She felt sick.

'It depends on the judge on the day. It's her first offence

– well, her first *known* offence. He may go lightly on her, then again he may not.' He shrugged then looked at his hands. 'And it also depends on what the garda who arrested her says.'

'Why?'

'Because if she was co-operative and gave no trouble it could make a difference, but then again . . .'

'It might not,' Elizabeth said worriedly. 'Well? Did she co-operate?'

Colm laughed lightly. 'Took two people to hold her down.'

'Damn it!' Elizabeth swore. 'Who arrested her?' She nibbled on her nails.

There was a silence before Colm spoke. 'I did.'

Her mouth dropped open. Colm had always had a soft spot for Saoirse. He was the one who was always on her side so the fact that he had arrested her rendered Elizabeth speechless. She chewed nervously on the inside of her mouth and the taste of blood slid down her throat. She didn't want people to start giving up on Saoirse.

'I'll do the best I can for her,' he said softly. 'Just try and keep her out of trouble until the hearing in a few weeks.'

Elizabeth, who realised she hadn't been breathing for the last few seconds, suddenly let her breath out. 'Thank you.' She couldn't say any more. Although she felt huge relief, she knew it was no victory. No one could protect her sister this time; she would have to face the consequences of her actions. But how was she expected to keep her eye on Saoirse when she didn't know where to begin looking for her? Saoirse couldn't stay with her and Luke – she was far too out of control to be around him – and her father had long since told her to move out and stay out.

'I'd better leave you at it so,' Colm said gently, fixed his cap back on his head, and he made his way down the cobbled drive.

Elizabeth sat on the porch, trying to rest her knocking knees, and looked at her mud-stained car. Why did Saoirse have to taint everything? Why was everything . . . every*one* Elizabeth loved chased away by her younger sister? She felt the clouds above push all that was between them and her onto her shoulders and she worried about what her father was going to do when they would undoubtedly bring Saoirse to his farm. She would give him five minutes before he rang Elizabeth complaining.

Inside the house, the phone started ringing and Elizabeth's heart sank even deeper. She rose from the porch, turned slowly on her heel and headed inside. When she got to the door the ringing had stopped and she spotted Luke sitting on the stairs with the phone pressed to his ear. She leaned against the wooden doorframe, arms folded, and watched him. A small smile crept onto her face. He was growing up so fast and she felt such a disconnection from the whole process, as though he was doing everything without her help, without the nurturing she knew she should be providing but that she felt awkward summoning. She knew she lacked that emotion – sometimes lacked emotion full stop – and everyday she wished the maternal instincts had come with the paperwork she signed. When Luke fell and cut his knee, her immediate response was to clean it and plaster his cut. To her that felt like enough, not dancing him around the room to stop his tears and slapping the ground like she'd watched Edith do.

'Hi, Granddad,' Luke was saying politely.

He paused to listen to his granddad on the other end.

'I'm just having lunch with Elizabeth and my new best friend, Ivan.'

Pause.

'A cheese and tomato pizza but Ivan likes olives on his.'

Pause.

'Olives, Granddad.'

Pause.

'No, I don't think you can grow them on the farm.'

Pause.

'O-L-I-V-E-S.' He spelled it out slowly.

Pause.

'Hold on, Granddad, my friend Ivan is telling me something.' Luke held the phone to his chest and looked into thin air, concentrating hard. Finally he lifted the phone back to his ear. 'Ivan said that the olive is a small, oily fruit that contains a pit. It's grown for its fruit and oil in subtropical zones.' He looked away and appeared to be listening. 'There are lots of types of olives.' He stopped talking, looked into the distance and then back to the phone. 'Underripe olives are always green but ripe olives are either green or black.' He looked away and listened to the silence again. 'Most tree-ripened olives are used for oil, the rest are brine- or salt-cured and are packed in olive oil or a brine or vinegar solution.' He looked into the distance. 'Ivan, what's brine?' There was silence then he nodded. 'Oh.'

Elizabeth raised her eyebrows and laughed nervously to herself. Since when had Luke become an expert on olives? He must have learned about them at school; he had a good memory for things like that. Luke paused and listened to the other end. 'Well, Ivan can't wait to meet you too.'

Elizabeth rolled her eyes and dashed towards Luke for the phone in case he said any more. Her father was confused enough as it was, at times, without having to explain the existence, or lack thereof, of an invisible boy.

'Hello,' Elizabeth said, grabbing the phone. Luke dragged his feet back to the kitchen. Irritation at the noise reared itself within Elizabeth again.

'Elizabeth,' said the stern formal voice, thick with a Kerry lilt, 'I just returned to find your sister lying on my kitchen floor. I gave her a boot but I can't figure out whether she's dead or not.'

Elizabeth sighed. 'That's not funny, and my sister is *your* daughter, you know.'

'Oh, don't give me that,' he said dismissively. 'I want to know what you're going to do about her. She can't stay here. The last time she did, she released the chickens from the coop and I spent all day getting them back in. And with my back and my hip, I can't be doing that any more.'

'I know, but she can't stay here either. She upsets Luke.'

'That child doesn't know enough about her to be upset. Half the time she forgets she's given birth to him. You can't have him all to yourself, you know.'

Elizabeth bit her tongue in rage. 'Half the time' was being overly generous. 'She can't come here,' she said more patiently than she felt. 'She was around earlier and took the car again. Colm just brought it back a few minutes ago. It's really serious this time.' She took a deep breath. 'They arrested her.'

Her father was silent for a moment and then he tutted. 'And rightly so. The experience will do her the world of good.' He quickly changed subject. 'Why weren't you at work today? Our Lord only intended us to rest on a Sunday.'

'That's the whole point. Today was a really important day for me at wor—'

'Well, your sister's come back to the land of the living and is outside trying to push the cows over again. Tell young Luke to come around with this new friend on Monday. We'll show him the farm.'

There was a click and the line went dead. Hello and goodbye were not her father's speciality; he still thought that mobile phones were some sort of futuristic alien-like technology designed to confuse the human race.

Elizabeth hung up the phone and made her way back to the kitchen. Luke sat alone at the table, holding his stomach and laughing hysterically. She took her seat and continued eating her salad. She wasn't one of those people who was interested in eating food; she only did it because she had to. Evenings spent over long dinners bored her and she never had much of an appetite – she was always too busy worrying about something or too hyper to be able to sit still and eat. She glanced at the plate directly ahead of her and to her surprise saw that it was empty.

'Luke?'

Luke stopped talking to himself and faced her. 'Yeah?'

'Yes,' she corrected him. 'What happened to the slice of pizza that was on that plate?'

Luke looked at the empty plate, looked back at Elizabeth like she was crazy and took a bite of his own pizza. 'Ivan ate it.'

'Don't speak with your mouth full,' she admonished him.

He spat the food out onto the plate. 'Ivan ate it.' He began laughing hysterically again at the mush on his plate that had been in his mouth.

Elizabeth's head began to ache. What had gotten into him? 'What about the olives?'

Sensing her anger, he waited until he swallowed the rest of his food before speaking. 'He ate them too. I told you olives were his favourite. Granddad wanted to know if he could grow olives on the farm,' Luke smiled and revealed his gums.

Elizabeth smiled back. Her father wouldn't even know what an olive was if it walked up to him and introduced itself. He wasn't into any of those 'fancy' foods; rice was about as exotic as he would get and even then he complained that the pieces were too small and that he'd be better off eating 'a crumblin' spud'.

Elizabeth sighed as she scraped the remainder of her food from her plate into the bin but not before checking through the rubbish to see if Luke had thrown the pizza and olives in. No sign. Luke usually had such a small appetite and would struggle to finish one large slice of pizza, never mind two. She presumed she would find it weeks later, mouldy and hiding at the back of a cabinet somewhere. But if he had eaten the entire thing, he would be sick all night and Elizabeth would have to clean up the mess. Again.

'Thank you, Elizabeth.'

'You're very welcome, Luke.'

'Huh?' Luke said, poking his head around the corner of the kitchen.

'Luke, I told you before, it's pardon, not huh.'

'Pardon?'

'I said you're very welcome.'

'But I haven't said thank you yet.'

Elizabeth slid the dishes into the dishwasher and stretched her back. She rubbed the base of her aching spine. 'Yes you did. You said, "Thank you, Elizabeth."'

'No I didn't,' Luke frowned.

Elizabeth felt her temper rising. 'Luke, stop playing games now, OK? We've had our fun at lunchtime, now you can stop pretending. OK?'

'No. That was Ivan who said thank you,' he said angrily.

A shiver ran through her body. She didn't think this was funny. She banged the dishwasher door shut, too fed up even to reply to her nephew. Why couldn't he, just this once, not give her a hard time?

Elizabeth rushed by Ivan with a cup of espresso in her hand, and the smell of perfume and coffee beans filled his nostrils. She sat down at the kitchen table, her shoulders sagged and she held her head in her hands.

'Ivan, come on!' Luke called impatiently from the playroom. 'I'll let you be The Rock this time!'

Elizabeth groaned quietly to herself.

But Ivan couldn't move. His blue Converse runners were rooted to the marble kitchen floor.

Elizabeth had heard him say thank you. He knew it.

He circled her slowly for a few minutes, studying her

for signs of a reaction to his presence. He snapped his fingers next to her eardrums, jumped back and watched her. Nothing. He clapped his hands and stamped his feet. The sound echoed loudly in the large kitchen but Elizabeth remained at the table with her head in her hands. No reaction at all.

But she had said, 'You're very welcome.' After all his efforts of making noise around her, he was confused to discover his deep disappointment that she couldn't sense him. After all, she was a parent and who cared what parents thought? He stood behind her and stared down at the top of her head, wondering what noise he could make next. He sighed loudly, exhaling a deep breath.

Suddenly Elizabeth sat up straight, shuddered and pulled the zip on her tracksuit top higher.

And then he *knew* she had felt his breath.

Chapter 4

Elizabeth pulled her dressing gown tighter around her body and secured it at the waist. She tucked her long legs up underneath her body and snuggled down into the oversized armchair in the living room. Her wet hair sat tower-like on the top of her head, twisted in a towel; her skin smelled fruity from her passion fruit bubble bath. She cradled a fresh cup of coffee, complete with dollop of cream, in her hands and stared at the television. She was literally watching paint dry. Her favourite house makeover show was on and she loved to see how they could transform the most run-down rooms into sophisticated, elegant homes.

Ever since she was a child she had loved giving everything she touched a makeover. She had passed the time, spent waiting for her mother to return, by decorating the kitchen table with scattered daisies, sprinkling glitter on the welcome mat by the door, causing a trail of glitter to garnish the dull stone floors of the bungalow, decorating the photo frames with fresh flowers and sprinkling the bed linen with petals. She supposed it was her fix-it nature, always wanting something better than she had, never settling, never satisfied.

She also supposed it was her own childish way of trying to convince her mother to stay. She remembered thinking that perhaps the prettier the house, the longer her mother would remain home. But the daisies on the table were celebrated for no more than five minutes, the glitter on the doormat quickly trampled on, the flowers by the photo frames could not survive without water and the petals on the bed would be tossed and float to the floor during her mother's fitful night's sleep. As soon as these were tired of, Elizabeth would immediately start thinking of something that would really grab and take hold of her mother's attention, something that she would be drawn to for longer than five minutes, something that she would love so much she would be unable to leave it. Elizabeth never considered that as her mother's daughter, she should have been that something.

As she got older she grew to love bringing the beauty out in things. She had had much practice with that at her father's old farmhouse. Now she loved the days at work when she could restore old fireplaces and rip up ancient carpets to reveal beautiful original floors. Even in her own home she was always changing things, rearranging and trying to improve. She strived for perfection. She loved setting herself tasks, sometimes impossible ones, to prove to her heart that underneath every seemingly ugly thing there was something beautiful inside.

She loved her job, loved the satisfaction it brought, and with all the new housing developments in Baile na gCroíthe and the surrounding nearby towns, she had made a very good living out of it. If anything new was happening, Elizabeth's company was the one the developers all called. She was a firm believer that good design enhanced life. Beautiful, comfortable and functional spaces were what she endorsed.

Her own living room was about soft colours and textures. Suede cushions and fluffy carpets; she loved to touch and feel everything. There were light colours of coffees and creams and just like the mug in her hand they helped clear her mind. In a world where most things were a clutter, having a peaceful home was vital to her sanity. It was her hideaway, her nest, where she could hide from the problems outside her door. At least in her home she was in control. Unlike the rest of her life, she could allow whoever she wanted in, she could decide how long they should stay and where in her home they could be. Not like a heart that invites people in without permission, holds them in a special place she never had any say in and then yearns for them to remain there longer than they plan. No, the guests in Elizabeth's home could come and go on her command. And she chose for them to stay away.

Friday's meeting had been vital. She had spent weeks planning for it, updating her portfolio, creating a slide show, gathering magazine cuttings and newspaper write-ups of the places she had designed. Her whole life's work had been condensed into a folder book in order to convince these people to hire her. An old tower standing high on the mountainside overlooking Baile na gCroíthe was to be knocked down to make space for a hotel. It had once protected the small town from approaching attackers during the Viking times, but Elizabeth couldn't see the point of it remaining there today as it was neither pretty nor of any historical interest. When the tour buses, packed full with eager eyes from all over the world, passed through Baile na gCroíthe, the tower wasn't even mentioned. No one was proud of it nor interested in it. It was an ugly pile of stones that had been allowed to crumble and decay, that by day housed the village teenagers and by night housed the village drunks, Saoirse having been among both groups.

But many of the townspeople had put up a fight to prevent the hotel from being built, claiming the tower had some sort of mythical and romantic story behind it. A story began to circulate that if the building was knocked down, all love would be lost. It grabbed the attention of the tabloids and soft news programmes, and eventually the developers saw the opportunity for an even bigger goldmine than expected. They decided to restore the tower to a version of its former glory and build around it, leaving the tower as a historical piece for their courtyard, that way keeping the love alive in the Town of Hearts. There was suddenly a huge rush of interest from believers all around the country wanting to stay in the hotel to be near the tower blessed by love.

Elizabeth would have driven the JCB through it herself. She thought it was a ridiculous story, one created by a town afraid of change and intent on keeping the tower on the mountain. It was a story kept alive for tourists and dreamers, but she couldn't deny that the job of designing the hotel's interiors would be perfect for her. It would be a small place, but one that would provide employment for the people of Hartstown. Better yet, it was only a few minutes from her home and she wouldn't have to worry about being away from Luke for long periods of time while working on the project.

Before Luke was born Elizabeth used to travel all the time. She would never spend more than a few weeks in Baile na gCroíthe and loved having the freedom to move around and work in different counties on various projects. Her last big project took her to New York, but as soon as Luke was born that had all ended. When Luke was younger, Elizabeth couldn't continue with her work around the country, never mind around the world. It had been a very difficult time, trying to set up her business in Baile na gCroíthe and trying to get used to raising a child again. She had no other choice but to hire Edith, as her father wouldn't help out and Saoirse certainly hadn't any interest. Now Luke was older and settled at school, Elizabeth was discovering that finding work within commuting distance was becoming increasingly difficult. The development boom in Baile na gCroíthe would eventually settle and she constantly worried whether the work would then dry up completely.

Her walking out of the meeting on Friday should not have happened. Nobody in her office could sell her abilities as an interior decorator better than she could. Her employees consisted of receptionist Becca, and Poppy. Becca was a timid and extremely shy seventeen-year-old, who had joined Elizabeth in her transition year while on work experience and decided not to go back to school. She was a hard worker who kept to herself, and was quiet around the office, which Elizabeth liked. Elizabeth had hired her quickly after Saoirse, who had been hired by Elizabeth to work there part time, had let her down. She had *more* than let her down and Elizabeth had been desperate to get someone in quickly. To tidy up the mess. Again. Keeping Saoirse near her during the day as an attempt to help her on her feet had only succeeded in driving her further away and knocking her right back down.

Then there was twenty-five-year-old Poppy, a recent graduate from art college, full of lots of wonderfully impossible creative ideas and ready to paint the world a colour she had yet to invent. There were just the three of them in the office but Elizabeth often called on the services of Mrs Bracken, a sixty-eight-year-old genius with a needle and thread, who ran her own upholstery shop in the town. She was also an incredible grump and insisted on being called *Mrs Bracken* and not Gwen, out of respect for her dearly departed *Mr Bracken*, whom Elizabeth didn't think had been born with a first name. And finally there was Harry, fifty-two years old and an all-round handyman, who could do anything from hanging paintings to rewiring buildings but who couldn't understand the concept of an unmarried woman with a career, not to say an unmarried woman with a career and a child not her own. Depending on people's budgets, Elizabeth would do anything from instructing painters and decorators to doing it all herself, but mostly she liked to be hands-on. She liked to see the transformation before her very eyes and it was part of her nature to want to fix everything herself.

It wasn't unusual for Saoirse to have shown up at Elizabeth's house that morning. She would often arrive drunk and abusive, and willing to take anything that she could get her hands on – anything worth selling, of course, which automatically excluded Luke. Elizabeth didn't even know if it was just the drink she was addicted to any more; it was a long time since she'd had a conversation with her sister. She had been trying to help her since she was fourteen. It was as if a switch had been flicked in her head and they had lost her to another world. She tried sending her to counselling, rehab, doctors, she gave her money, found her jobs, hired her herself, allowed her to move in with her, rented her flats. She had tried being her friend, had tried being her enemy, had laughed with her and shouted at her, but nothing would work. Saoirse was lost to her, lost in a world where nobody else mattered.

Elizabeth couldn't help thinking of the irony of her name. Saoirse wasn't free. She may have felt that she was, coming and going as she pleased, not being tied down to anyone, anything, any place, but she was a slave to her addictions. She couldn't see it, though, and Elizabeth couldn't help her see it. She couldn't turn her back completely on her sister but she had run out of energy, ideas and faith in ever believing Saoirse could be changed, and had lost lovers and friends with her persistence. Their frustration would grow as they stood by and watched Elizabeth being taken advantage of time and time again till they could no longer be in her life. But contrary to their beliefs, Elizabeth didn't feel like the victim. She was always in control. She knew what and why she was doing what she was doing, and she refused to desert a family member. She would not be like her mother. She had worked too hard all her life at trying not to be.

Elizabeth suddenly pressed Mute on the television remote control and the room was silenced. She cocked her head to one side. She thought she'd heard something again. After looking around the room and seeing that everything was as it should be, she turned the volume back up again.

There it was again.

She silenced the TV once more and stood up from the armchair.

It was 10.15 and not yet fully dark. She looked out to the back garden and in the dusk she could only see black shadows and shapes. She pulled the curtains closed quickly and immediately felt safer in her cream and beige cocoon. She tightened her dressing gown again and sat back down in her armchair, tucking her legs even closer to her body and wrapping her arms protectively around her knees. The vacant cream leather couch stared back at her. She shuddered again, turned the volume up even higher than before and took a gulp of coffee. The velvety liquid slid down her throat and warmed her insides and she tried once again to be sucked back into the world of television.

All day she had felt odd. Her father always said that when you got a chill up your spine it meant that someone was walking over your grave. Elizabeth didn't believe that but as she stared at the television, she turned her head away from the three-seater leather couch and tried to shake off the feeling that a pair of eyes was watching her.

Ivan watched her mute the television once again, quickly put her coffee cup on the table next to her and jump out of her chair as though she had been sitting on pins. Here she goes again, he thought. Her eyes were wide and terrified as they darted around the room. Once again Ivan prepared himself and pushed his body to the edge of the couch. The denim of his jeans squeaked against the leather.

Elizabeth jumped to face the couch.

She grabbed a black iron poker from the large marble fireplace and spun round on her heels. Her knuckles turned white as they tightened around it. She slowly tiptoed about the room, eyes wild with fear. The leather squeaked again underneath him and Elizabeth charged towards the couch. Ivan leaped from his seat and dived into the corner.

He hid behind the curtains for protection and watched as she pulled the cushions out of the chair while grumbling to herself about mice. After ten minutes of searching through the couch, Elizabeth put all the cushions back in place to restore its immaculate form.

She picked up her coffee cup self-consciously and made her way into the kitchen. Ivan followed closely on her heel; he was so close that strands of her soft hair tickled his face. Her hair smelled of coconut and her skin of rich fruits.

He couldn't understand his fascination with her. He had been watching her since after lunch on Friday. Luke had kept calling him to play game after game and all Ivan had wanted was to be around Elizabeth. At first it was just to see if she could hear him or sense him again, but then after a few hours he found her compelling. She was obsessively neat. He noticed she couldn't leave the room to answer the phone or front door until everything had been tidied away and wiped clean. She drank a lot of coffee, stared out to her garden, picked imaginary pieces of fluff from almost everything. And she thought. He could see it in her face. Her brow would furrow in concentration and she would make facial expressions as though she was having conversations with people in her head. They seemed to turn into debates more often than not, judging by the activity on her forehead.

He noticed she was always surrounded by silence. There was never any music or sounds in the background like most people had, a radio blaring, the window open to allow in the sounds of summer – the birdsong and the lawn mowers. Luke and she spoke little and when they did it was mostly her giving him orders, him asking permission, nothing fun. The phone rarely rang, nobody called by. It was almost as if the conversations in her head were loud enough to fill her silence.

He spent most of Friday and Saturday following her

around, sitting on the cream leather couch in the evenings and watching her watching the only programme she seemed to like on TV. They both laughed in the same places, groaned in the same places and they seemed to be completely in sync, yet she didn't know he was there. He had watched her sleeping the previous night. She was restless – she slept only three hours at the most; the rest of the time she spent reading a book, putting it down after five minutes, staring into space, picking the book up again, reading a few pages, reading back over the same pages, putting it down again, closing her eyes, opening them again, turning the light on, doodling sketches of furniture and rooms, playing with colours and shades and scraps of material, turning the light off again.

She had made Ivan tired just watching her from the straw chair in the corner of the room. The trips to the kitchen for coffee couldn't have helped her either. On Sunday morning she was up early, tidying, vacuuming, polishing and cleaning an already spotless home. She spent all morning at it while Ivan played chasing with Luke out in the back garden. He recalled Elizabeth being particularly upset by the sight of Luke running around the garden laughing and screaming to himself. She had joined them at the kitchen table and watched Luke playing cards, shaking her head and looking worried when he explained the rules of patience in extreme detail to thin air.

But when Luke went to bed at nine o'clock, Ivan read him the story of Tom Thumb quicker than he usually would, and then hurried to continue watching Elizabeth. But he could sense her getting jitterier as the days wore on.

She washed her coffee cup out, ensuring it was already spotless before putting it in the dishwasher. She dried the wet sink with a cloth and put the cloth in the wash basket in the utility room. She picked imaginary fluff from a few items in her path, picked crumbs from the floor, switched off all the lights and began the same process in the living room. She had done the exact same thing the last two nights.

But before leaving the living room this time, she stopped abruptly, almost sending Ivan into the back of her. His heart beat wildly. Had she sensed him?

She turned round slowly.

He fixed his shirt to look presentable.

Once facing him he smiled. 'Hi,' he said, feeling very self-conscious.

She rubbed her eyes tiredly and opened them again. 'Oh, Elizabeth, you are going mad,' she whispered. She bit her lip and charged towards Ivan.

Chapter 5

Elizabeth knew she was losing her mind right at that moment. It had happened to her sister and mother, and now it was her turn. For the last few days she had felt incredibly insecure, as if someone was watching her. She had locked all the doors, drawn all the curtains, set the alarm. That probably should have been enough but now she was going to go that one step further.

She charged through the living room straight towards the fireplace, grabbed the iron poker, marched out of the room, locked the door and made her way upstairs. She looked at the poker lying on her bedside locker, rolled her eyes and turned her lamp off. She *was* losing her mind.

Ivan emerged from behind the couch and looked around. He had dived behind it thinking Elizabeth was charging towards him. He had heard the door lock after she stormed out. He slumped with a disappointment he had never experienced before. She still hadn't seen him.

I'm not magic, you know. I can't cross my arms, nod my head, blink and disappear and reappear on the top of a bookshelf or anything. I don't live in a lamp, don't have funny little ears, big hairy feet or wings. I don't replace loose teeth with money, leave presents under a tree or hide chocolate eggs. I can't fly, climb up the walls of buildings or run faster than the speed of light.

And I can't open doors.

That has to be done for me. The grown-ups find that part the funniest but also the most embarrassing when their children do it in public. I don't laugh at grown-ups when they can't climb trees or can't say the alphabet backwards because it's just not physically possible for them. It doesn't make them freaks of nature.

So Elizabeth needn't have locked the living-room door when she went to bed that night because I couldn't turn the handle anyway. Like I said, I'm not a superhero; my special power is friendship. I listen to people and I hear what they say. I hear their tones, the words they use to express themselves and, most importantly, I hear what they *don't* say.

So all I could do that night was think about my new friend, Luke. I need to do that occasionally. I make notes in my head so that I can file a report for admin. They like to keep it all on record for training purposes. We've new people joining up all the time. In fact, when I'm between friends, I lecture.

I needed to think about why I was here. What made Luke want to see me? How could he benefit from my friendship? The business is run extremely professionally and we must always provide the company with a brief history of our friends and then list our aims and objectives. I could always identify the problem straight away but this scenario was slightly baffling. You see, I'd never been friends with an adult before. Anyone who has ever met one would understand why. There's no sense of fun with them. They stick rigidly to schedules and times, they focus on the most unimportant things imaginable, like mortgages and bank statements, when everyone knows that the majority of the time it's the people around them that put the smiles on their faces. It's all work and no play, and I work hard, I really do, but playing is by far my favourite.

Take, for example, Elizabeth; she lies in bed worrying about car tax and phone bills, babysitters and paint colours.

If you can't put magnolia on a wall then there are always a million other colours you can use; if you can't pay your phone bill then just write letters telling them. People forget they have options. And they forget that those things really don't matter. They should concentrate on what they have and not what they don't have. But I'm veering away from the story again.

I worried about my job a little the night I was locked in the living room. It's the first time that had ever happened. I worried because I couldn't figure out why I was there. Luke had a difficult family scenario but that was normal and I could tell he felt loved. He was happy and loved playing, he slept well at night, ate all his food, had a nice friend called Sam and when he spoke I listened and listened and tried to hear the words he wasn't saying but there was nothing. He liked living with his aunt, was scared of his mom and liked talking about vegetables with his granddad. But Luke seeing me every day and wanting to play with me every day meant that I definitely needed to be here for him.

On the other hand, his aunt never slept, ate very little, was constantly surrounded by silence so loud that it was deafening, she had nobody close to her to talk to, that I had seen yet anyway, and she *didn't* say *far more* than she did actually say. She had heard me say thank you once, felt my breath a few times, heard me squeak on the leather couch but yet she couldn't see me nor could stand me being in her house.

Elizabeth did not want to play.

Plus she was a grown-up, she gave me butterflies and wouldn't know fun if it hit her in the face, and believe me I'd tried to throw it at her plenty of times over the weekend. So I couldn't possibly be here to help her. It was unheard of.

People refer to me as an invisible or an imaginary friend. Like there's some big mystery surrounding me. I've read the books that grown-ups have written asking why kids see me, why do they believe in me so much for so long and then suddenly stop and go back to being the way they were before? I've seen the television shows that try to debate why it is that children invent people like me.

So just for the record for all you people, I'm not invisible or imaginary. I'm always here walking around just like you all are. And people like Luke don't *choose* to see me, they just see me. It's people like you and Elizabeth that choose not to.

Chapter 6

Elizabeth was woken up at 6.08 a.m. by the sun streaming through the bedroom window and onto her face. She always slept with the curtains open. It had stemmed from growing up on a farm. Lying in her bed she could see through the bungalow window, down the garden path and out of the front gate. Beyond that was a country road that led straight from the farm, stretching on for a mile. Elizabeth could see her mother returning from her adventures, walking down the road for at least twenty minutes before she reached home. She could recognise the half-hop, half-skip from miles away. Those twenty minutes always felt like an eternity to Elizabeth. The long road had its own way of building up Elizabeth's excitement, almost teasing her.

And finally she would hear that familiar sound, the squeak of the front gate. The rusting hinges acted as a welcoming band to the free spirit. Elizabeth had a love/hate relationship with that gate. Like the long stretch of road, it would tease her, and some days on hearing the creak she would run to see who was at the door and her heart would sink that it was only the postman.

Elizabeth had annoyed college room-mates and lovers with her insistence on keeping the curtains open. She didn't know why she remained firm on this; it certainly wasn't as though she was still waiting. But now in her adulthood, the open curtains acted as her alarm clock; with them open she knew the light would never allow her to fall back into a deep sleep.

Even in her sleep she felt alert, and in control. She went to bed to rest, not to dream.

She squinted in the bright room and her head throbbed. She needed coffee, fast. Outside the window a bird's song echoed loudly in the quiet of the countryside. Somewhere far away a cow answered its call. But despite the idyllic morning, there was nothing about this Monday that Elizabeth was looking forward to. She had to try to reschedule a meeting with the hotel developers, which was going to prove difficult because after the little stunt in the press about the new love nest at the top of the mountain, they had people flying in from all parts of the world willing to share their design ideas. This annoyed Elizabeth; this was her territory. But that wasn't her only problem.

Luke had been invited to spend the day with his grandfather on the farm. That bit, Elizabeth was happy with. It was the part about him expecting another six-year-old by the name of Ivan that worried her. She would have to have a discussion with Luke this morning about it because she dreaded to think of what would happen if there was a mention of an imaginary friend to her father.

Brendan was sixty-five years old, big, broad, silent and brooding. Age had not mellowed him; instead it had brought bitterness, resentment, and even more confusion. He was small-minded and unwilling to open up or change. Elizabeth could at least try to understand his difficult nature if being that way made him happy, but as far as she could see, his views frustrated him and only made his life more miserable. He was stern, rarely spoke except to the cows or vegetables, never laughed, and whenever he did decide someone was worthy of his words, he lectured. There was no need to respond to him. He didn't speak for conversation. He spoke to make statements. He rarely spent time with Luke as he didn't have time for the airy-fairy ways of children, for their silly games and nonsense. The only thing that Elizabeth could see that her father liked about

Luke was that he was an empty book, ready to be filled with information and not enough knowledge to question or criticise. Fairy tales and fantasy stories had no place with her father. She supposed that was the only belief they actually shared.

She yawned and stretched and, still unable to open her eyes against the bright light, she felt around her bedside locker for her alarm clock. Although she woke up every morning at the same time, she never forgot to set her alarm. Her arm knocked against something cold and hard and it fell with a loud bang to the floor. Her sleepy heart jumped with fright.

Hanging her head over the side of the bed she caught sight of the iron poker lying on her white carpet. Her 'weapon' also reminded her that she had to call Rentokil to get rid of the mice. She had sensed them in the house all weekend and she had felt so paranoid that they were in her bedroom the past few nights she could hardly sleep, although that wasn't particularly unusual for her.

Washed and dressed, after waking Luke she made her way downstairs to the kitchen. Minutes later, with espresso in hand, she dialled the number of Rentokil. Luke wandered into the kitchen sleepily, blond hair tossed, dressed in an orange T-shirt half tucked into red shorts. The outfit was completed with odd socks and a pair of runners that lit up with every step he took.

'Where's Ivan?' he asked groggily, looking around the kitchen as though he'd never been in the room before in his life. He was like that every morning; it took him at least an hour to wake up even once he was up and dressed. During the dark winter mornings it took even longer. Elizabeth supposed that at some point in his morning classes as school he finally realised what he was doing.

'Where's Ivan?' he repeated.

Elizabeth silenced him by holding her finger to her lips, and giving him the glare, as she listened to the lady from

Rentokil. He knew not to interrupt her when she was on the phone. 'Well, I only noticed it this weekend. Since Friday lunchtime actually, so I was wond—'

'IVAN?' Luke yelled, and began looking under the kitchen table, behind the curtains, behind the doors. Elizabeth rolled her eyes. This carry-on again.

'No, I haven't actually seen . . .'

'IVAAAAN?'

'. . . one yet but I definitely feel that they're here.' Elizabeth finished, and tried to catch Luke's eye so that she could give him the glare again.

'IVAN, WHERE ARE YOOOUUU?' Luke called.

'Droppings? No, no droppings,' Elizabeth said, getting frustrated.

Luke stopped shouting and his ears perked up. 'WHAT? I CAN'T HEAR YOU PROPERLY.'

'No, I don't have any mousetraps. Look, I'm very busy, I don't have time for twenty questions. Can't someone just come out and check for themselves?' Elizabeth snapped.

Luke suddenly ran from the kitchen and out into the hall. She heard him banging at the living-room door. 'WHAT ARE YOU DOING IN THERE, IVAN?' He pulled at the handle.

Finally Elizabeth's conversation ended and she slammed down the phone. Luke was shouting through the living-room door at full volume. Her blood boiled.

'LUKE! GET IN HERE NOW!'

The banging at the living-room door stopped immediately. He shuffled slowly into the kitchen.

'DON'T DRAG YOUR FEET!' she yelled.

He lifted his feet and the lights on the soles of his runners flashed with every step. He stood before her and spoke quietly and as innocently as he possibly could in his high-pitched voice. 'Why did you lock Ivan in the living room last night?'

Silence.

She had to put an end to this now. She would choose this moment to sit down and discuss the issue with Luke and by the end of it he would respect her wishes. She would help him see sense and there would be no more talk of invisible friends.

'And Ivan wants to know why you brought the fire poker to bed with you?' he added, feeling more confident by her failure to scream at him again.

Elizabeth exploded. 'There will be no more talk of this Ivan, do you hear me?'

Luke's face went white.

'DO YOU HEAR ME?' she shouted. She didn't even give him a chance to answer. 'You know as well as I do that there is *no such thing* as Ivan. He does *not* play chasing, he does *not* eat pizza, he is *not* in the living room and he is *not* your friend because he *does not exist*.'

Luke's face crumpled up as though he were about to cry.

Elizabeth continued, 'Today you are going to your granddad's and if I hear from him that there was one mention of Ivan, you will be in *big trouble*. Do you understand?'

Luke began to cry softly.

'Do you understand?' she repeated.

He nodded his head slowly as tears rushed down his face.

Elizabeth's blood stopped boiling and her throat began to ache from shouting. 'Now sit at the table and I'll bring you your cereal,' she said softly. She fetched the Coco Pops. Usually she didn't allow him to eat such sugary breakfasts but she hadn't exactly discussed the Ivan situation with him as planned. She knew she had a problem keeping her temper. She sat at the table and watched him pour Coco Pops into his cereal bowl and then his little hands wobbled with the weight of the milk carton. Milk splashed onto the table. She held back from shouting at him again although she had cleaned that only yesterday evening until it sparkled. Something Luke had said was bothering her and she couldn't quite remember what it was. She rested her chin on her hand and watched him eating.

He munched slowly. Sadly. There was silence apart from his crunching. Finally, after a few minutes, he spoke. 'Where's the key to the living room?' he asked, refusing to catch her eye.

'Luke, not with your mouth full,' she said softly. She took the key to the living room out of her pocket, went to the doorway in the hall and twisted the key. 'There now, Ivan is free to *leave* the house,' she joked, and immediately regretted saying it.

'He's not,' Luke said sadly from the kitchen table. 'He can't open doors himself.'

Silence.

'He can't?' Elizabeth repeated.

Luke shook his head as if what he had said was the most normal thing in the world. It was the most ridiculous thing Elizabeth had ever heard. What kind of an imaginary friend was he if he couldn't walk through walls and doors? Well, she wasn't opening the door, she had unlocked it and that was silly enough. She went back to the kitchen to gather her belongings for work. Luke finished his cereal, placed the bowl in the dishwasher, washed his hands, dried them and made his way to the living-room door. He turned the handle, pushed open the door, stepped out of the way, smiled broadly at nothing, placed a finger over his lips, pointed at Elizabeth with his other hand and giggled quietly to himself. Elizabeth watched with horror. She walked down the hall and stood beside Luke at the doorway. She looked into the living room.

Empty.

The girl from Rentokil had said that it would be unusual for mice to be in the house in June and as Elizabeth eyed the living room suspiciously, she wondered what on earth could be making all those noises.

Luke's giggling snapped her out of her trance and, glancing down the hall, she spotted him sitting at the table, swinging his legs happily and making faces into thin air. There was an extra place set and a freshly poured bowl of Coco Pops across from him.

'Boy, is she strict,' I whispered to Luke at the table, trying to grab spoonfuls of Coco Pops without her noticing. I wouldn't usually whisper around parents but as she had heard me a couple of times already over the past few days, I wasn't about to take any risks.

Luke giggled and nodded.

'Is she like this all the time?'

He nodded again.

'Does she never play games and give you hugs?' I asked, watching as Elizabeth cleaned every inch of the already sparkling kitchen countertops, moving things half an inch to the right and a half an inch to the left.

Luke thought for a while and then shrugged. 'Not much.'

'But that's horrible! Don't you mind?'

'Edith says that there are some people in the world that don't hug you all the time or play games but they still love you. They just don't know how to say it,' he whispered back.

Elizabeth eyed him nervously.

'Who's Edith?'

'My nanny.'

'Where is she?'

'On her holidays.'

'So who's going to mind you while she's on her holidays?'

'You,' Luke smiled.

'Let's shake on it,' I said, holding out my hand. Luke grabbed it. 'We do it like this,' I explained, shaking my head and my whole body, like I was having a convulsion. Luke started laughing and copied me. We laughed even harder when Elizabeth stopped cleaning to stare. Her eyes widened.

'You ask a lot of questions,' Luke whispered.

'You answer a lot,' I fired back, and we both laughed again.

Elizabeth's BMW rattled along the bumpy track leading to her father's farm. She clenched her hands around the steering wheel in exasperation as the dust flew up from the ground and clung to the side of her newly washed car. How she had lived on this farm for eighteen years was beyond her. Nothing could be kept clean. The wild fuchsias danced in the light breeze, waving their welcome from the side of the road. They lined the mile-long road like landing lights and rubbed against the windows of the car, pressing their faces to see who was inside. Luke lowered his window and allowed his hand to be tickled by their kisses.

She prayed that no traffic would come towards her as the road just about allowed her car through, leaving no room for two-way traffic. In order to let someone pass she would have to reverse half a mile back the way she'd come just to make room. At times it felt like the longest road in the world. She could see where she was trying to get to yet she would have to keep reversing in order to get there.

Two steps forward and one step back.

It was like when she was a child seeing her mother from a mile away but being forced to wait the twenty minutes it took her to dance down the road, till Elizabeth heard the familiar sound of the gate creak.

But thankfully, because they were already delayed as it was, no traffic came this time. Elizabeth's words had obviously fallen on deaf ears because Luke refused to leave the house until Ivan had finished his cereal. He then insisted on pushing forward the passenger seat in the car in order to let Ivan into the back seat.

She glanced quickly at Luke. He sat buckled up in the front seat, arm out the window, humming the same song he had been singing all weekend. He looked happy. She hoped he wouldn't keep his play-acting up for much longer, at least while he was at his granddad's.

She could see her father at the gate, waiting. A familiar sight. A familiar action. Waiting was his forte. He wore the same brown cords Elizabeth could have sworn he was wearing when she was a child. They were tucked into muddy green Wellington boots that he wore in the house. His grey cotton jumper was stitched with a faded green and blue diamond pattern, there was a hole in the centre, and the green of his polo shirt peeked through from underneath. A tweed cap sat firmly on his head, a blackthorn cane in his right hand kept him steady, and silver grey stubble decorated his face and chin. His eyebrows were grey and wild, and when he frowned they seemed to cover his grey eyes completely. His nose commanded his face with large nostrils filled with grey hairs. Deep wrinkles cracked his face, his hands as big as shovels, shoulders as wide as the Gap of Dungloe. He dwarfed the bungalow that stood behind him.

Luke stopped humming as soon as he saw his grandfather and brought his arm back into the car. Elizabeth pulled up, turned the engine off and jumped out. She had a plan. As soon as Luke climbed out of the car she shut the door and locked it before he had a chance to push the seat forward and make way for Ivan. Luke's face crumpled again as he looked from Elizabeth and back to the car.

The gate outside the bungalow creaked.

Elizabeth's stomach churned.

'Morning,' a deep voice boomed. It wasn't a greeting. It was a statement.

Luke's lower lip trembled and he pressed his face and hands up against the glass of the back seat of the car.

Elizabeth hoped he wouldn't throw a tantrum now.

'Aren't you going to say good morning to your granddad, Luke?' Elizabeth asked sternly, fully aware that she herself had yet to acknowledge him.

'Hi, Granddad.' Luke's voice wobbled. His face remained pressed against the glass.

Elizabeth contemplated opening the car door for him just to avoid a scene but thought better of it. He needed to get over this phase.

'Where's th'other one?' Brendan's voice boomed.

'The other what?' She took Luke's hand and tried to turn him away from the car. His blue eyes looked pleadingly into hers. Her heart sank. He knew better than to cause a scene.

'The young lad who knew about them foreign veg.'

'Ivan,' Luke said sadly, tears welling up.

Elizabeth jumped in, 'Ivan couldn't come today, isn't that right, Luke? Maybe another day,' she said quickly, and before it could be discussed any further, 'Right, I'd better go to work or I'll be late. Luke, have a good day with your granddad, OK?'

Luke looked at her uncertainly and nodded.

Elizabeth hated herself but she knew she was right to control this ludicrous behaviour.

'Off you go so.' Brendan swung his blackthorn cane at her as if to dismiss her and he turned his back to face the bungalow. The last thing she heard was the gate creaking before she slammed her car door shut. She had to reverse twice down the road in order to let two tractors pass. From her mirror she could see Luke and her father in the front garden, her father towering over him. She couldn't get away from the house fast enough; it was as though the flow of traffic kept pulling her back to it, like the tide.

Elizabeth remembered the moment when she was eighteen when she thrived on the freedom of such a view. For the first time in her life, she was leaving the bungalow with her bags packed and with the intention of not coming back until Christmas. She was going to Cork University, after winning the battle with her father but in turn losing all respect he had ever had for her. Instead of sharing in her excitement, he had refused to see her off on her big day. The only figure standing outside the bungalow Elizabeth could see that bright August morning as they drove away was that of six-year-old Saoirse, her red hair in messy pigtails, her smile toothless in places yet broad and wide, with her arm waving frantically goodbye, full of pride for her big sister.

Instead of the relief and excitement she always dreamed of feeling when the taxi finally pulled away from her home, breaking the umbilical cord that held her there, she felt dread and worry. Not for what lay ahead but for what she was leaving behind. She couldn't mother Saoirse for ever, she was a young woman who needed to be set free, who needed to find her own place in the world. Her father needed to step into his rightful place of fatherhood, a title he had discarded many years ago and refused to recognise. She only hoped now that as the two of them were alone, he would realise his duties and show as much love as he could for what he had left.

But what if he didn't? She continued watching her sister out the back window, feeling as if she was never going to see her again, waving as fast and as furiously as she could as tears filled her eyes for the little life and bundle of energy she was leaving behind. The red hair jumping up and down was visible from a mile away and so they both kept on waving. What would her little sister do now that the fun of waving her off had ended and the realisation set in that she was alone with the man who never spoke, never helped and never loved. Elizabeth almost asked the driver to stop the car right there and then, but quickly told herself to stay strong. She needed to live.

You do the same as me someday, little Saoirse, her eyes kept telling the little figure as they drove away. Promise me you'll do the same. Fly away from there.

With eyes full of tears, Elizabeth watched as the bungalow got smaller and smaller in her mirror until finally it disappeared when she reached the end of the mile-long road. At once her shoulders relaxed and she realised she had been holding her breath the entire time.

'Right, Ivan,' she said, looking in the mirror at the empty back seat, 'I guess you're coming to work with me so.' Then she did a funny thing.

She giggled childishly.

Chapter 7

Baile na gCroíthe was stirring as Elizabeth drove over the grey-stone bridge that served as its gateway. Two huge coaches full of tourists were currently trying to inch past each other on the narrow street. Inside, Elizabeth could see faces pressed against the windows, oohing and aahing, smiling and pointing, cameras being held up to the glass to snap the doll-like town on film. The coach driver facing Elizabeth licked his lips in concentration and she could see the sweat glistening on his brow as he slowly manoeuvred the oversized vehicle along the narrow road originally designed for horses and carts. The sides of the coaches were almost touching. Beside him, the tour guide, with microphone in hand, did his best to entertain his one-hundred-strong audience so early in the morning.

Elizabeth lifted the handbrake and sighed loudly. This wasn't a rare occurrence in the town and she knew it could take a while. She doubted the coaches would stop. They rarely did unless it was for a toilet break. Traffic always seemed to be moving through Baile na gCroíthe but never stopping. She didn't blame them; it was a great place to help you get to where you're going but not one for sticking around in. Traffic would slow down and visitors would take a good look alright, but then the drivers would put a foot down and accelerate off out the other end.

It's not that Baile na gCroíthe wasn't beautiful – it was certainly that. Its proudest moment was winning the Tidy

Town competition for the third year running, and as you entered the village, over the bridge, a display of bright blooming flowers spelled out a welcome. The flower display continued through the town. Window boxes adorned the shop fronts, hanging baskets hung from black lampposts, trees grew tall along the main street. Each building was painted a different colour, and the main street, the only street, was a rainbow of pastels and bold colours of mint greens, salmon pinks, lilacs, lemons and blues. The pavements were litter free and gleaming, and as soon as you averted your gaze above the grey slate roofs you found yourself surrounded by majestic green mountains. It was as though Baile na gCroíthe was cocooned, safely nestled in the bosom of Mother Nature.

Cosy or suffocating.

Elizabeth's office was located beside a green post office and a yellow supermarket. Her building was a pale blue, and sat above Mrs Bracken's curtain, fabric and upholstery shop. The shop had previously been a hardware shop run by Mr Bracken, but when he died ten years ago, Gwen had decided to turn it into her own store. She seemed to make decisions based purely on what her deceased husband would think. She opened the shop 'because it's what Mr Bracken would have wanted'. However, Gwen refused to go out at the weekends or involve herself in any social outings as 'it's not what Mr Bracken would have wanted'. As far as Elizabeth could see, what made Mr Bracken happy or unhappy seemed to tie in nicely with Gwen's philosophy on life.

The coaches moved past each other inch by inch. Baile na gCroíthe in rush-hour traffic; the result of two oversized buses trying to share the narrow road. Finally they were successful in their passing and Elizabeth looked on, not amused as the tour guide jumped from his seat in excitement, microphone in hand, succeeding in turning what was essentially a boring halt into an eventful bus journey on Ireland's country roads. Cue clapping and cheering on board the bus. A nation in celebration. More flashes out the window and the occupants on both buses waved goodbye to each other after sharing the morning's excitement.

Elizabeth drove on, looked in her rear-view mirror to see the excitement on the celebrating coach die down as they came face to face with another on the small bridge that led out of the town. Arms slowly went down and the flashes died as the tourists settled down for another lengthy struggle to continue.

The town had a tendency to do that. Almost as if it did it purposely. It welcomed you into its heart with open arms, showed you all it had to offer with its gleaming multicoloured florally decorated shop fronts. It was like bringing a child into a sweet shop and showing them the shelves of luminous sugar-coated, mouth-watering delights. And then while they stand there looking around with wide eyes and a racing pulse, the lids were put back on the jars and sealed tightly. Once its beauty was realised, so was the fact that it had nothing else to offer.

The bridge, oddly, was easier to drive over from outside the town. It curved in an unusual shape, making driving out of the village difficult. It disturbed Elizabeth every time.

It was just like the road leading from Elizabeth's childhood home; she found it impossible to leave in a hurry. But something about the town kept dragging her back and she had spent years trying to fight it. She had successfully moved to New York at one time. She had followed her boyfriend, and the opportunity to design a nightclub, over. She had loved it there. Loved that no one knew her name, her face or family history. She could buy a coffee, a thousand different types of coffee, and not receive a look of sympathy for whatever recent family drama had occurred. Nobody knew that her mother had left her when she was a child, that her sister was wildly out of control and that her father barely spoke to her. She had loved being in love there. In New York she could be whoever she wanted to be. In Baile na gCroíthe she couldn't hide from who she was.

She realised she had been humming to herself the entire time, that silly song that Luke was trying to convince her that 'Ivan' had made up. Luke called it 'the humming song', and it was annoyingly catchy, chirpy and repetitive. She stopped herself singing and spun her car into the empty space along the road. She pushed back the driver's seat and reached in to grab her briefcase from the back seat of the car. First things first: coffee. Baile na gCroíthe had yet to be educated on the wonders of Starbucks – in fact, it was only last month Joe's had finally allowed Elizabeth to take away her coffee, but the owner was growing increasingly tired of having to ask for his mugs back.

Sometimes Elizabeth thought that the entire town needed an injection of caffeine; it was as though some winter days the place still had its eyes closed and was sleepwalking. It needed a good shake. But summer days like today were always busy with people passing through. She entered the purple painted Joe's, which was virtually empty all the same. The concept of eating breakfast outside their own homes had yet to be grasped by the townspeople.

'Ah, there she is, the very woman herself,' boomed the singsong voice of Joe. 'No doubt spittin' feathers for her coffee.'

'Morning, Joe.'

He made a show of checking his watch and tapping the clock face. 'Bit behind time this morning, aren't we?' He raised his eyebrows at her. 'Thought maybe you were in bed sick with a bout of the summer flu. Seems like everyone's got it this week.' He tried to lower his voice but only succeeded in lowering his head and raising his voice. 'Sure didn't Sandy O'Flynn come down with it right after disappearing the other night from the pub with P. J. Flanagan, who had it the other week. She's been in bed all weekend.' He snorted. 'Walking her home me arse. I've never heard such nonsense before in my life.'

Irritation rose within Elizabeth. She didn't care for tittle-tattle about people she didn't know, especially as she was aware for so many years that her own family had been the root of all the gossip.

'A coffee, please, Joe,' Elizabeth said crisply, ignoring his rambling. 'To take away. Cream not milk,' she said sternly, even though she had the same every day, while rooting in her bag for her wallet, trying to hint to Joe that she hadn't time for yapping.

He moved slowly towards the coffee pot. To Elizabeth's utter annoyance Joe's sold only one kind of coffee. And that was the instant kind. Elizabeth missed the variety of flavours that she used to get in other towns; she missed the smooth, sweet-tasting French vanilla in a Paris café, the creamy full-bodied flavour of hazelnut cream in a bustling café in New York, the rich velvety masterpiece of the macadamia nut in Milan and her favourite, the Coco Mocha-Nut, the mixture of chocolate and coconut that transported her from a Central Park bench to a sunbed in the Caribbean. Here in Baile na gCroíthe, Joe filled the kettle with water and flicked the switch. One measly little kettle in a café and he hadn't even boiled the water. Elizabeth rolled her eyes.

Joe stared at her. He looked like he was going to say –

'So what has you so late then?'

– that.

'I'm *five minutes* later than usual, Joe,' Elizabeth said incredulously.

'I know, I know, and five minutes could be five hours for you. Sure don't the bears plan their hibernation on your time?'

That made Elizabeth smile, despite herself.

Joe chuckled and winked. 'That's better.' The kettle clicked as it boiled and he turned his back to make the coffee.

'The coaches delayed me,' Elizabeth said softly, taking the warm mug from Joe's hands.

'Ah, I saw that.' He nodded towards the window. 'Jaimsie did well to get himself out of that one.'

'Jaimsie?' Elizabeth frowned, adding a dollop of cream. It quickly melted and filled the cup to the top. Joe looked on with disgust.

'Jaimsie O'Connor. Jack's son,' he explained. 'Jack, whose other daughter, Mary, just got engaged to the Dublin boy last weekend. Lives down in Mayfair. Five kids. The youngest was arrested there last week for throwing a wine bottle at Joseph.'

Elizabeth froze and stared back at him blankly.

'Joseph McCann,' he repeated, as though she were crazy for not knowing. 'Son of Paddy. Lives up in Newtown. Wife died last year when she drowned in the bog. His daughter Maggie said it was an accident but sure weren't the family suspicious on account of the row they'd being having about not letting her run off with that troublemaker from Cahirciveen.'

Elizabeth placed her money on the counter and smiled, no longer wanting to be a part of his bizarre conversations. 'Thanks, Joe,' she said as she made her way to the door.

'Well, anyway,' he concluded his rambling, 'Jaimsie was the one driving the coach. Don't forget to bring that mug back,' he called to her, and grumbled to himself, 'Takeaway coffee, have you ever heard something so ludicrous in your life?'

Before Elizabeth stepped outside she called from the door, 'Joe, would you not think of getting a coffee machine? So you can make lattes and cappuccinos and espressos instead of all this instant stuff?' She held up her mug.

Joe crossed his arms, leaned against the counter and replied in a bored voice, 'Elizabeth, you don't like my coffee, you don't drink it. I drink tea. There's only one kind of tea I like. It's called Tea. No fancy names for it.'

Elizabeth smiled. 'Actually, there are lots of different types of tea. The Chinese—'

'Ah, be off with you.' He waved his hand at her dismissively. 'We'd all be drinking tea with chopsticks and putting chocolate and cream in our coffees like they're desserts, if you have your way. But, if you're at it, why don't I make a suggestion too then: how's about you buy yourself a kettle over there for your office and put me out of my misery?'

'And out of business,' Elizabeth smiled, and stepped outside.

The village had taken a big stretch and a yawn and was wandering sleepily from its bed to the bathroom. Soon it would be showered, dressed and wide awake. As usual she was one step ahead of it, even if she was running late today.

Elizabeth was always the first in; she loved the silence, the stillness that her office brought at that time of day. It helped her focus on what lay ahead before her noisy colleagues rattled around and before the major traffic hit the road. Elizabeth wasn't the chatty giggly type. Just as she ate to keep herself alive, she spoke to say only what she had to say. She wasn't the type of woman that she overheard in restaurants and cafés, chuckling and gossiping over what someone said someday about something. Conversations about nothing just didn't interest her.

She didn't break down or analyse conversations, glares, looks or situations. There were no double meanings with her; she meant what she said at all times. She didn't enjoy debates or heated discussions. But sitting in the silence of her small office she supposed that was why she didn't have a group of friends. She had tried to be involved before, especially during her college days with her attempts to settle in, but, just as she did then, she would quickly tune out of the mindless nattering.

Since childhood she hadn't pined for friendship. She liked her own company and liked her own thoughts, and then later, in her teens, she had Saoirse as a distraction. She liked the orderly way in which she could depend on herself and manage her time more effectively without friends. When she returned from New York she had tried to host a dinner party in her new home with the neighbours. She thought she would try a fresh beginning, try to make friendships, like most people did, but Saoirse as usual burst into the house and in one fell swoop managed to offend every single person at the table. She accused Ray Collins of having an affair, Bernie Conway of having a boob job and sixty-year-old Kevin Smith of looking at her in a sexual way. The result of Saoirse's ranting and raving was a crying nine-month-old Luke, a few red faces at the table and a burned rack of lamb.

Of course her neighbours wouldn't be as close-minded as to think that Elizabeth was responsible for her family's behaviour, but she gave up after that. She didn't desire company enough to be able to cope with the embarrassment of having to explain and apologise all the time.

Her silence was worth more to her than a thousand words. In that silence she had peace and clarity. Apart from during the night, when her own jumbled thoughts would keep her awake, sounding like a thousand voices jumping in, out and interrupting each other so much that she could barely close her eyes.

She was worried about Luke's behaviour right now. This Ivan character had been hanging around her nephew's head for too long. She had watched Luke all weekend walking, talking and playing games by himself. Laughing and giggling as though he were having the time of his life. Maybe there was something she should be doing. And

Edith wasn't there to witness his odd behaviour and deal with it in the wonderful way she always succeeded in doing. Perhaps Elizabeth was supposed to know automatically what to do. Once again the mysteries of motherhood reared their ugly head and she had no one to ask for advice. Nor had she any example to learn from. Well, that wasn't strictly true – she had learned what *not* to do, a lesson just as good as any. So far she had followed her gut instinct, had made a few mistakes along the way, but overall thought Luke had turned out to be a polite and stable child. Or maybe she was doing it all wrong. What if Luke ended up like Saoirse? What had she done so wrong with Saoirse as a child that had caused her to turn out the way she was? Elizabeth groaned with frustration and rested her head on her desk.

She turned on her computer and sipped on her coffee while it loaded. Then she went to Google, typed in the words 'imaginary friend', and hit Search. Hundreds of sites came up on her screen. Thirty minutes later she felt much better about the Ivan situation.

To her surprise she learned that imaginary friends were very common and not a problem as long as they didn't interfere with normal life. Although the very fact that having an imaginary friend was a direct interference with normal life, it didn't seem to be an issue with the online doctors. Site after site told her to ask Luke what Ivan was thinking and doing as it would be a positive way of giving Elizabeth an understanding into what Luke was thinking. They encouraged Elizabeth actually to set a place for their phantom dinner guest and that there was no need to point out that Luke's 'friend' existed only in his imagination. She was relieved to learn that imaginary friends were a sign of creativity and not of loneliness or stress.

But even so, this was going to be difficult for Elizabeth to grasp. It went against everything she believed. Her world and the land of make-believe existed on two very different plains and she found it difficult to play-act. She couldn't make baby noises to an infant, she couldn't pretend to hide behind her hands or give life or a voice to a teddy, she couldn't even role-play at college. She had grown up knowing not to do that, not to sound like her mother for fear of her father getting mad. It was instilled in her from an early age but now the experts were telling her to change all that.

She finished the last of her cold coffee and read the final line on the screen.

Imaginary friends disappear within three months, whether or not you encourage them.

After three months she would be more than glad to see the back of Ivan and return to normal life again. She flicked through her calendar and circled August with a red marker. If Ivan wasn't out of her house by then, she'd open the door and show him the way herself.

Chapter 8

Ivan laughed as he spun around in the black leather chair at the reception desk outside Elizabeth's office. He could hear her in the other room on the phone, organising a meeting using her boring grown-up voice. But as soon as she hung up the phone he heard her humming his song again. He laughed to himself. It definitely was addictive; once you got the tune in your head there was very little you could do to stop.

He swirled himself round in the chair faster and faster, doing pirouettes on wheels until his stomach danced and his head began to throb. He decided that chair spinning was his absolute favourite. Ivan knew that Luke would have loved to play the spin-the-chair game and, on picturing his sad little face pressed up against the car window from earlier that morning, his mind drifted and the chair slowed. Ivan wanted so much to visit the farm, and Luke's granddad looked like he could do with a bit of fun. He was similar to Elizabeth in that way. Two boring old gnirobs.

Anyway, at least this separation gave Ivan time to monitor Elizabeth so he could write a report on her. He had a meeting in a few days and would have to give a presentation to the rest of the team about who he was working with at the moment. They did it all the time. A few more days with her to prove that she couldn't see him would be enough and then he could get back to concentrating on

Luke. Maybe there was something he was missing with him, despite his years of experience.

As Ivan's head began to get dizzy he put his foot down on the floor to stop. He decided to leap from the whirling chair so he could pretend he was jumping from a moving car. He rolled dramatically across the floor just like they did in the movies and looked up from where he was crouched in a ball to see a teenage girl standing before him open-mouthed, watching her office chair spin out of control.

Ivan saw her look around the office to see if anyone else was present. She frowned, approached the desk as if she were walking on landmines and placed her bag on the desk ever so quietly as if afraid to disturb the chair. She looked to see if anyone was watching and then tiptoed over to study it. She held out her hands as though trying to tame a wild horse.

Ivan chuckled.

Seeing that nothing was wrong Becca scratched her head in wonder. Perhaps Elizabeth had been sitting in the chair before she came in. She smirked at the thought of Elizabeth swinging around like a child, hair tied back tightly, dressed in one of her sharp black suits with her sensible shoes dangling in the air. No, the picture didn't fit. In Elizabeth's world chairs were made to be sat on. So that's exactly what Becca did and got to work immediately.

'Good morning, everyone,' a high-pitched voice sang from the door later that morning. A plum-haired Poppy danced into the room, dressed in denim flares embroidered with flowers, platform shoes and a tie-dyed T-shirt. As usual, every inch of her body was splashed with paint. 'Everyone have a nice weekend?' She was always singing her sentences and dancing about the room, flinging her arms around with all the grace of an elephant.

Becca nodded.

'Great.' Poppy stood in front of Becca with her hands on her hips. 'What did you do, Becca, join a debating team? Go out on a date and talk the ear off some bloke? Huh?'

Becca turned the page of the book she was reading and ignored her.

'Wow, that's fabulous, sounds like a blast. You know, I really do love the banter we have in this office.'

Becca turned a page.

'Oh, really? Well, that's enough information for now, if you don't mind. What the . . . ?' She whipped her body away from Becca's desk and was silent.

Becca didn't look up from the book she was reading. 'It's been doing that all morning,' she said in a quiet bored tone.

It was Poppy's turn to remain quiet.

There was silence in the office for a few minutes while Becca read her book and Poppy stared at the sight ahead of her. In her office, Elizabeth heard the long silence between the two and stuck her head out of her door.

'Everything alright, girls?' she asked.

A mystery squeaking sound was all the reply.

'Poppy?'

She didn't move her head as she spoke. 'The chair.'

Elizabeth stepped out of her office. She turned her head in the same direction. The paint-splattered chair behind Poppy's desk, which Elizabeth had been trying to convince Poppy to get rid of for months, was flying around all by itself, the screws squeaking loudly. Poppy let out a nervous laugh. They both moved closer to examine it. Becca was still reading her book in silence as if it was the most normal thing in the world.

'Becca,' Elizabeth half laughed, 'have you seen this?'

Becca still didn't lift her eyes from the page. 'It's been doing that for the past hour,' she said softly. 'It just stops and starts all the time.'

Elizabeth frowned. 'Is it some sort of new artistic creation of yours, Poppy?'

'I wish it was,' Poppy replied, still in awe.

They all watched it spin in silence. Squeak, squeak, squeak.

'Maybe I should call Harry. It's probably something to do with the screws,' Elizabeth reasoned.

Poppy raised her eyebrows uncertainly. 'Yeah, I'm sure the *screws* are making it spin out of control,' she said sarcastically, gazing in wonder at the whirling multicoloured chair.

Elizabeth picked an imaginary piece of fluff from her jacket and cleared her throat. 'You know, Poppy, you really need to get your chair reupholstered; it's not a very positive sight for when customers come to see us. I'm sure Gwen will do it quickly for you.'

Poppy's eyes widened. 'But it's supposed to be like that. It's an expression of personality, an extension of myself. It's the only item I can project myself onto in this room.' She looked around in disgust. 'This fucking *beige* room.' She said the word like it was a disease. 'And *Mrs Bracken* spends more time gossiping with those pals of hers that have nothing else to do but drop by everyday, than actual work.'

'You know that's not true, and remember that not everyone appreciates your taste. Besides, as an interior design company we should be reflecting less . . . alternative designs and more of what people can apply to their own homes.' She studied the chair some more. 'It looks like a bird with a very bad stomach has gone to the toilet on it.'

Poppy looked at her proudly. 'I'm glad *someone* got the idea.'

'Anyway, I've already allowed you to put up that screen,' Elizabeth nodded her head at the partition Poppy had decorated with every colour and material known to man, to act as a dividing wall between Becca and herself.

'Yes, and people *love* that screen,' Poppy said. 'I've already had three requests from customers.'

'Requesting what? To take it down?' Elizabeth smiled.

They both studied the divider thoughtfully, arms folded, heads cocked to one side as though studying a piece of art in a museum, while the chair continued to spin in front of them.

Suddenly the chair leaped and the screen beside Poppy's desk went crashing to the floor. The three women jumped and each took a step back. The chair began to slow down and came to a stop.

Poppy held her hand over her mouth. 'It's a sign.' Her voice was muffled.

On the other side of the room the usually silent Becca began laughing loudly.

Elizabeth and Poppy looked at each other, stunned.

'Hmm,' was all Elizabeth could say before she turned slowly and returned to her office.

Lying on the floor of the office from where he had leaped from the chair to on top of he couldn't tell what, Ivan held his head in his hands until the room stopped spinning. He had a headache and had come to the conclusion that maybe chair spinning wasn't his favourite any more. He watched groggily as Elizabeth entered her office and pushed the door closed behind her with her foot. He leaped from the floor and dived towards it, managing to squeeze his body between the gap before it shut. She wouldn't be locking any doors on him today.

He sat in the (non-swivel) chair on front of Elizabeth's desk and looked around the room. He felt like he was in a principal's office waiting to be given out to. It had the atmosphere of a principal's office, quiet and tense, and it smelled like one too, apart from the scent of Elizabeth's perfume, which he loved so much. Ivan had been in a few headmasters' offices with previous best friends so he knew well what that feeling was like. In training they were generally taught not to go to school with their best friends. There was really no need for them to be there and the rule was introduced because children were getting into trouble and parents were being called in. Instead they hung around outside and waited in the yard until break time. And even if the children chose not to play with them in the yard, they knew they were around, which gave them more confidence to play with the other kids. This was all a result of years of research but Ivan tended to ignore all those facts and statistics. If his best friend needed him at school, he'd be there and he sure wasn't afraid of breaking any rules.

Elizabeth sat behind a large glass desk in an oversized black leather chair, dressed in a severe black suit. As far as he could see, that was all she seemed to wear. Black, brown and grey. So restrained and so very boring, boring, boring. The desk was immaculate, glistening and sparkling as though it had just been polished. All that was on it was a computer and keypad, a thick black diary and the work Elizabeth was huddled over, which looked to Ivan like some boring pieces of material cut into small squares. Everything else had been tidied away in black cabinets. There was absolutely nothing on display apart from framed photographs of rooms that Elizabeth had obviously decorated. As with the house there was no sign of a personality in the room. Just black, white and glass. He felt like he was in a space- ship. The principal's office of a space ship.

Ivan yawned. She definitely was a gnirob. There were no photographs of family or friends, no cuddly toys sitting on the computer, and Ivan couldn't see any sign of the picture Luke had drawn for her over the weekend. She had told him she would put it in her office. The only thing of interest was a collection of coffee mugs from Joe's sitting on the windowsill. He bet Joe wouldn't be happy about that.

He leaned forward in his chair, rested his elbows on the desk and stuck his face near hers. Her face was fixed in pure concentration, her forehead was smooth and no frown lines creased her skin like they usually did. Her glossy lips, which smelled to Ivan like strawberries, pursed and unpursed themselves gently. She hummed quietly to herself.

His opinion of her changed once again right then. She was no longer the headmistress he saw her as when she was among others; she had become peaceful, calm and untroubled, and unlike the way she normally was when she was thinking alone. He guessed it was because for once she wasn't worrying. After watching her for a while, Ivan's eyes drifted down to the piece of paper she was working on. Between her fingers she held a brown colouring pencil and was shading in a drawing of a bedroom.

Ivan's eyes lit up. Colouring was by far his favourite. He stood up from the chair and made his way behind her so he could get a better look at what she was doing and to see if she was any good at staying between the lines. She was left-handed. He leaned over her shoulder and placed his arm on the desk beside her to steady himself. He was so close he could smell the coconut from her hair. He breathed in deeply and felt her hair tickle his nose.

Elizabeth stopped shading for a moment, closed her eyes, leaned her head back, relaxed her shoulders, took a deep breath and smiled softly to herself. Ivan did the same and felt her skin brush against his cheek. His body tingled. For a moment he felt odd, a nice kind of odd. Like the feeling he got when embraced in a warm hug and that was good because hugging was by far his favourite. He felt light-headed and a bit dizzy but nothing like the chair-spinning dizzy. This feeling was so much better. He held onto the feeling for a few minutes until eventually they opened their eyes at the same time and stared down at her drawing of a bedroom. Her hand moved over to the brown pencil as she decided whether or not to pick it up.

Ivan groaned softly. 'Elizabeth, not brown again. Come on, go for some colour, like that lime green,' he whispered into her ear, fully aware she couldn't hear him.

Her fingers hovered over the pencil as though a magnetic force was stopping her from touching it. She moved slowly away from the chocolate-brown pencil and moved to the lime green. She smiled slightly as though amused by her choice and gingerly held the implement between her fingers as if it was for the first time. She moved it around in her fingers as though holding it felt alien to her. Slowly she began to shade in the scatter cushions on the bed, and the tassels on the curtain tiebacks, moving on to bigger pieces like the throw at the end of the bed and eventually the lounger in the corner of the room.

'Much better,' Ivan whispered, feeling proud.

Elizabeth smiled and closed her eyes again, breathing slowly and deeply.

There was suddenly a knock at the door. 'Can I come in?' Poppy sang.

Elizabeth's eyes sprang open and dropped the offending pencil from her hand as though it were a dangerous weapon. 'Yes,' she called out, sitting back in the chair, her shoulder briefly brushing off Ivan's chest. Elizabeth looked around behind her, touched her shoulder lightly with her hand and turned back to face Poppy, who was skipping into the room, eyes glistening with excitement.

'OK, so Becca just told me you've got another meeting with the love hotel people.' Her words skipped together as though she were singing a song.

Ivan sat down on the windowsill behind Elizabeth's desk and stretched out his legs. They both folded their arms across their chests at the same time. Ivan smiled.

'Poppy, please do *not* call it "the love hotel",' Elizabeth rubbed her eyes wearily. Ivan was disappointed. That gnrob voice was back.

'OK, so the "hotel", then,' Poppy exaggerated the word. 'I have some ideas. I'm thinking waterbeds in the shape of hearts, hot tubs, champagne flutes that rise from the bedside lockers.' She lowered her voice to an excited whisper. 'I'm thinking the *Romantic era* meets *art deco*. *Caspar David Friedrich* meets *Jean Dunand*. It will be an *explosion* of rich reds, burgundys and wines that make you feel like you're being embraced in a velvet-lined *womb*. Candles *everywhere*. French boudoir meets—'

'Las Vegas,' Elizabeth finished drily.

Poppy snapped out of her trance and her face fell in disappointment.

'Poppy,' Elizabeth sighed, 'we've been through this before. I really think you should stick to the profile for this one.'

'Ah,' she fell back as though she'd been shot in the chest, 'but the profile is so *boring*.'

'Hear, hear!' Ivan stood and applauded. 'Gnirob,' he said loudly into Elizabeth's ear.

Elizabeth flinched and scratched at her ear. 'I'm sorry you feel that way, Poppy, but unfortunately what you consider boring is how other people choose to decorate their homes. In liveable, comfortable, and calming environments. People don't want to return home after a hard day's work to a house that shouts dramatic statements from every beam or colours that give them a headache. With work environments so full of stress, people just want manageable, relaxing and peaceful homes.' It was a speech she delivered to all of her customers. 'And this is a *hotel*, Poppy. We need to appeal to all kinds of people and not just the few, the *very* few, in fact, that would like to reside in a velvet-lined womb,' she added, deadpan.

'Well, I don't know many people that *haven't* once resided in velvet-lined wombs, do you? I don't think it rules out anyone, on *this* planet at least.' She kept trying. 'It might spark off some comforting memories for people.'

Elizabeth looked disgusted.

'Elizabeth.' Poppy groaned her name and dissolved dramatically into the chair in front of her. 'There has to be something that you will let me put my stamp on. I just feel so constrained here, like my creative juices aren't being allowed to flow and – oooh, that's nice,' she said chirpily, leaning over to look at the page in front of Elizabeth. 'Chocolate and lime are really gorgeous together. What made *you* of all people go for that?'

Ivan returned to Elizabeth's side and crouched down beside her, studying her face. Elizabeth stared at the sketch before her as if seeing it for the first time. She frowned but then her face softened. 'I don't know, actually. It just,' she closed her eyes briefly, breathed deeply and remembered the feeling, 'it just kind of . . . floated into my head suddenly.'

Poppy smiled and nodded excitedly. 'You see, now you understand how it is for me. I can't suppress my creativeness, you know? I know *exactly* what you mean. It's such a natural instinctive thing,' her eyes glistened and her voice lowered to a whisper, 'like *love*.'

'Hear, hear!' Ivan repeated, watching Elizabeth, so close to her now his nose was almost touching her cheek, but this time it was a light whisper that blew Elizabeth's loose hair softly around her ear.

Chapter 9

'Poppy, did you call me?' Elizabeth asked from under the mound of carpet samples piled on her desk later that day.

'No, *again*,' came the dull, bored reply. 'And please refrain from disturbing me as I'm about to order two thousand pots of magnolia paint for our future projects. May as well be organised and plan ahead for the next twenty years,' she muttered, then grumbled loud enough for Elizabeth to hear, 'because it's not as if we're about to change our ideas any time soon.'

'Oh, OK,' Elizabeth smiled, giving in. 'You can order another colour in too.'

Poppy almost fell off her chair with excitement.

'Order a few hundred pots of beige as well, while you're at it. "Barley" it's called.'

'Ha ha,' Poppy said drily.

Ivan raised his eyebrows at Elizabeth. 'Elizabeth, Elizabeth,' he sang, 'did you just make a funny? I think you did.' He stared directly at her, elbows on the desk. He sighed, blowing the loose strands of her hair as he did so.

Elizabeth froze, moved her eye sockets from left to right suspiciously and then continued working.

'Oh, see how she treats me?' Ivan said dramatically, holding his hand to his forehead and pretending to faint onto a black leather chaise longue in the corner of the room. 'It's like I'm not even here,' he declared. He put his feet up and stared at the ceiling. 'Forget about being at a principal's office, this is like being at a shrink's.' He stared at the cracks in the ceiling and put an American accent on. 'You see, Doc, it all started when Elizabeth kept ignoring me,' he said loudly in the room. 'It just made me feel so *unloved,* so *alone,* so *very, very alone.* It's like I don't exist. Like I'm *nothing,*' he exaggerated. 'My life is a mess.' He pretended to cry. 'It's all Elizabeth's fault.' He stopped and watched her for a while, matching carpets with fabrics and paint charts, and when he spoke again, his voice had returned to normal and he said softly, 'But it is her fault that she can't see me because she's just too afraid to believe. Isn't that right, Elizabeth?'

'What?' Elizabeth shouted again.

'What do you mean, "what"?' shouted back an irritated Poppy. 'I didn't say anything!'

'You called me.'

'No I didn't, you're hearing voices again, and please stop humming that bloody song!' Poppy shrieked.

'What song?' Elizabeth frowned.

'Whatever that *thing* is that you've been humming all morning. It's driving me *insane.*'

'Thank you very much!' Ivan announced, standing up and taking a dramatic bow before plonking his body back down on the chaise longue. 'I *invented* that song. Andrew Lloyd Webber, eat your heart out.'

Elizabeth continued working. She started humming again, then immediately stopped herself.

'You see, Poppy,' Ivan called into the other room, 'I think Elizabeth can hear me.' He crossed his hands over his chest and twiddled his thumbs. 'I think she can hear me very well. Isn't that right, Elizabeth?'

'Christ Almighty.' Elizabeth dropped the samples onto her desk. 'Becca, is that you saying my name?'

'No.' Becca's voice was barely audible.

Elizabeth's face turned red and flustered-looking, embarrassed at appearing a fool in front of her employees. Trying to assert control again, she called out sternly, 'Becca, can you get me a coffee from Joe's?'

'Oh, by the way,' Ivan sang, enjoying himself, 'don't forget to tell her to take one of the mugs over with her. Joe will be pleased.'

'Oh,' Elizabeth snapped her fingers as though she'd just remembered something, 'you might as well bring one of these with you.' She handed Becca a coffee mug. 'Joe will be,' she paused and looked confused, 'pleased.'

'Oh, she can hear me alright,' laughed Ivan. 'She just won't admit it to herself. That self-commanding mind of hers just won't allow her to. Everything is black and white to her,' then he added, 'and beige. But I'm going to shake things up a bit around here and we are going to have some *fun*. Ever done that before, Elizabeth? Had fun?' His eyes danced with mischief.

He swung his legs off the chaise longue and jumped upright. He sat on the edge of Elizabeth's desk and glanced at the printouts of the online information about imaginary friends. He tutted and shook his head. 'No, you don't believe all that gobbledegook, do you, Lizzie? Can I call you Lizzie?'

Elizabeth's face flinched.

'Oh,' Ivan said gently, 'you don't like being called Lizzie, do you?'

Elizabeth swallowed softly.

He lay across the desk on top of all the carpet samples and rested his head on his hand. 'Well, I've got news for you,' he lowered his voice to a whisper, 'I'm real. And I'm not going anywhere until you open those eyes properly and see me.'

Elizabeth stopped fiddling with the paint charts and raised her eyes slowly. She looked around her office and then settled on staring straight ahead of her. For some reason she felt calm, calmer than she had felt in a very long time. She was stuck in a trance, staring at nothing but unable to blink or look away, feeling surrounded by warmth and security.

Suddenly the door to her office sprung open, so quickly and forcefully that the handle crashed against the wall. Elizabeth and Ivan jolted in fright.

'Oooh, well excuse me for interrupting the lovebirds,' Saoirse cackled from the door.

Ivan jumped off the desk.

Elizabeth, mystified, immediately started to tidy her desk, a natural panicked reflex to her at the unannounced arrival of her younger sister. She smoothed down her jacket and pushed her palms over her hair.

'Oh, don't tidy up on my account.' Saoirse waved her hand dismissively, chewing quickly on a piece of gum. 'You're such a fusspot, you know. Just *chill.*' Her eyes moved up and down as she examined the area beside Elizabeth's desk suspiciously. 'So aren't you going to introduce me?'

Elizabeth examined her sister through narrow eyes. Saoirse made her nervous with her neurotic behaviour and sporadic tantrums. Alcohol or no alcohol, Saoirse had always been the same – difficult. In fact Elizabeth could hardly tell when she was drunk or sober. Saoirse had never found herself; she had never grown into a personality or learned about who she was, what she wanted, what made her happy or where she wanted to go in life. She still didn't know. She was a concoction of personalities never allowed to develop. Elizabeth wondered who her sister could be if she ever managed to stop drinking. She feared it would only be one problem less on a list of many.

It was so rare that Elizabeth could get Saoirse on her own in a room to talk to her – like, as a child alone in the fields, trying to catch a butterfly in a jar. They were so beautiful to look at, brightened up a room but never settled on anything for long enough to be caught. Elizabeth was forever chasing and when she did manage to catch her sister, Saoirse would all the time be fluttering her wings in panic, wanting to get away.

When she did have Saoirse's company she tried so hard to be understanding, to treat Saoirse with the sympathy and empathy she deserved. She had learned all about it when she had sought professional help. She wanted advice from as many places as possible in order to help her sister. She needed to know the elusive magical words to say to Saoirse on the rare times that she visited. So even when Saoirse mistreated Elizabeth, she remained supportive and kind because she was afraid to lose her for good, afraid of how much further out of control Saoirse might spiral. Besides, she felt she had a duty to look out for her. But mostly it was because she was tired of seeing all the beautiful butterflies in her life fly away.

'Introduce you to whom?' Elizabeth replied gently.

'Oh, stop with that patronising tone. If you don't want to introduce me then that's fine.' She turned to the empty seat. 'She's ashamed of me, you see. She thinks I let her "good name" down. You know how the neighbours like to talk,' she laughed bitterly. 'Or maybe she's afraid I'll chase you away. Happened to the other one, you see. He—'

'OK, OK, Saoirse,' Elizabeth interrupted her play-acting. 'Look, I'm glad you dropped by because there's something I wanted to talk to you about.'

Saoirse's knee bounced up and down. Her jaw chomped on the gum.

'Colm brought the car back to me on Friday and he told me they'd arrested you. This is serious, Saoirse. You have to be really careful between now and the hearing. It's on in a few weeks and if you do anything . . . else, well, it will effect your punishment.'

Saoirse rolled her eyes, 'Elizabeth, *relax*! What are they going to do? Lock me up for years for driving two minutes down the road in my own sister's car? They can't take away my licence because I don't have one and if they prevent me from ever getting one I don't care because I don't want one. All they'll do is give me a few weeks of some community service bullshit, probably helping a few old ladies cross the road or something. It'll be fine.' She blew a bubble and it smacked against her chapped lips.

Elizabeth's eyes widened with disbelief. 'Saoirse, you didn't *borrow* my car. You took it without my permission and you don't have a licence. Come on,' her voice cracked, 'you're not stupid, you know well that's wrong.'

Elizabeth paused and tried to compose herself. This time she would succeed in talking her round. But even though it was the same situation every time, Saoirse continued to be in denial. She swallowed hard.

'Look,' Saoirse said, getting angry, 'I'm twenty-two years old and I'm doing exactly the same thing that everyone else my age is doing – going out and having fun.' Her tone turned nasty. 'Well, just because you had no life at my age it doesn't mean that I can't have one.' Her wings were fluttering wildly as if she was trapped in a jar and was running out of air.

That's because I was busy raising you, Elizabeth thought angrily. And obviously doing a terrible job of it too.

'Are you going to sit here and listen to our entire conversation or what?' Saoirse said rudely to the chaise longue.

Elizabeth frowned and cleared her throat. 'But what about what Paddy said? Whether *you* think you did nothing wrong is not important. The gardaí think that you have.'

Saoirse chewed her gum and her cold blue eyes stared back. 'Paddy couldn't organise a piss-up in a brewery. He has no reason to charge me for *anything*. Unless having fun is suddenly illegal.' Flutter, flutter.

'Please, Saoirse,' Elizabeth said softly, 'please listen to me. They really mean it this time. Just . . . just relax a bit with the, eh,' she paused, 'with the drinking, OK?'

'Oh, shut up about that,' Saoirse's face twisted. 'Shut

up, shut up, shut up, I'm fed up listening to you.' She stood up. 'My drinking's fine. It's you who's got the problem, thinking you're fucking perfect.' She opened the door and shouted so that everyone could hear, 'Oh, and you,' she nodded at the chaise longue, 'I don't think you'll be hanging around for long. They all leave eventually, isn't that right, *Lizzie*?' She spat out the name.

Elizabeth's eyes glistened with angry tears.

Saoirse banged the door loudly behind her. She had forced the jar lid open and was free to fly away once again. The noise of the bang shuddered through Elizabeth's body. The office was so silent even the fly that had been buzzing around stopped to settle on the light fitting. A moment later there was a feeble knock on the door.

'What?' she snapped.

'It's, eh, Becca,' came the quiet reply, 'with your coffee?'

Elizabeth smoothed back her hair and dabbed her eyes. 'Come in.'

As Becca was leaving the room, Elizabeth spotted Saoirse marching back through the reception area.

'Oh, by the way, I forgot to ask you for a loan of a few euros.' Her voice was gentler. It always was when she wanted something.

Elizabeth's heart sank. 'How much?'

Saoirse shrugged her shoulders. 'Fifty.'

Elizabeth rooted in her bag. 'You still staying at the B&B?'

Saoirse nodded.

She pulled out fifty euro and paused before handing it over. 'What's it for?'

'Drugs, Elizabeth, lots and lots of drugs,' Saoirse said smartly.

Elizabeth's shoulders dropped, 'I just meant—'

'Groceries – you know, bread, milk, toilet paper. That kind of thing.' She swiped the crisp note out of Elizabeth's hand. 'Not all of us wipe our arses on silk, you know.'

She lifted a swatch of material from the desk and tossed it at her.

The door banged shut behind her as Elizabeth stood alone in the centre of her office and watched the black piece of silk effortlessly drift to the white carpet.

She knew what it felt like to fall.

Chapter 10

A few hours later, Elizabeth shut down her computer, tidied her desk for the twentieth time and left her office for the day. Becca and Poppy stood together staring into space. Elizabeth turned to see what kept their attention.

'It's doing it again,' Poppy sang nervously.

They all watched the chair spinning around unaided.

'You think it's Mr Bracken?' Becca asked quietly.

Poppy imitated Mrs Bracken's voice. 'Chair-spinning isn't what Mr Bracken would have wanted.'

'Don't worry, girls,' Elizabeth said, trying not to laugh. 'I'll get Harry in tomorrow to fix it. You two head off home.'

After saying their goodbyes Elizabeth continued to stare at the chair spinning in silence. She neared it slowly, inch by inch. As she got very close to it, it stopped spinning.

'Chicken,' Elizabeth muttered.

She looked about to ensure she was alone and slowly she grabbed the handles of the chair and lowered herself into it. Nothing happened. She bounced up and down a few times, looked to the sides and under the seat and still nothing happened. Just as she was about to get up and leave, the chair began to move. Slowly at first, then gradually it began to pick up speed. Feeling nervous, she contemplated leaping off but as it spun faster and faster she began to giggle. Louder and louder she laughed, the faster it went. Her sides ached. She couldn't remember the last time she had felt so young, legs up, feet out, hair blowing in the breeze. Eventually, after a few moments, it slowed to a stop and Elizabeth caught her breath.

Her smile slowly faded and the childish laughing in her head began to die down. All she was left with was complete silence in the abandoned office. She began to hum and her eye scanned across Poppy's disorganised desk of books of material, paint sample tubs, sketches and house interior magazines. Her eye fell upon a gold photo frame. In it was a photograph of Poppy, her two sisters, three brothers and parents, all squeezed together on a couch like a football team. The resemblance between them was obvious. They had little button noses and green eyes that narrowed to slits when they laughed. In the corner of the frame was a strip of passport photos of Poppy and her boyfriend, both of them making faces to the camera in the first three of them. But the fourth was of them staring lovingly into each other's eyes. A moment between them eternally caught on camera.

Elizabeth stopped humming and swallowed. She had known that look once.

She continued to stare at the frame, trying not to remember those times but, again, she lost the battle, drowning in the sea of memories that flooded her mind.

She began to sob. Quiet whimpers at first that soon exited her mouth as pain-filled wails from the depths of her heart. She could hear her own hurt. Each tear was a call for help that had never been answered before, and that she didn't expect to be answered now. And that made her cry even more.

Elizabeth marked off another day on her calendar with a red pen. Her mother had been gone for exactly three weeks this time. Not the longest amount of time so far but long enough for Elizabeth. She hid the calendar under her bed and got into bed. She had been sent to her room by her father three hours ago as he had grown tired of her excited pacing in front of the living-room window. Since then she had been battling to keep her eyes open. She needed to fight sleep so that she wouldn't miss her mother returning. Those were the best times because her mother would be in one of her happy moods, delighted to be home, telling Elizabeth how much she'd missed her, smothering her with hugs and kisses so much that Elizabeth couldn't remember ever feeling sad.

Her mother would float through the rooms of the house almost as if her feet weren't touching the ground. Her words were big whispers of excitement, her voice so hushed making Elizabeth feel that every word her mother breathed was their big secret. Her eyes glistened and danced with delight as she told her daughter of her adventures and who she'd met along the way. Elizabeth certainly did not want to miss all that while she was sleeping.

Elizabeth jumped out of bed again and splashed ice-cold water over her face from the sink in her room. Stay awake, Elizabeth, stay awake, she told herself. She propped her pillows up against the wall and sat up straight on her bed, staring out through the open curtains and out to the dark road that led into blackness. She had no doubt that her mother would be back tonight because she had promised her. And she just had to keep that promise because it was Elizabeth's tenth birthday the next day and she wouldn't miss that. Only weeks ago she had promised her that they would eat cakes, buns and all the sweets they wanted. And they'd have balloons of all Elizabeth's favourite colours that they'd bring out into the field, let them go and watch fly away up to the clouds. Elizabeth hadn't stopped thinking of it since her mother had left. Her mouth watered for fairy cakes with pretty pink icing, and she dreamed of pink balloons attached to white ribbons floating up to the blue sky above. And the day was almost here, no more waiting!

She picked up *Charlotte's Web*, a book she had been reading at night to keep herself awake and she turned on her torch as her father wouldn't let her keep the lights on past eight. A few pages in and her eyelids grew heavy and started to droop. She slowly closed her eyes, only intending to rest them for a little while. Every night she fought sleep because it was always sleep that allowed her mother to slip away into the night and it was sleep that missed her big arrivals. Even when her mother was home she fought it, instead choosing to stay outside her door, sometimes watching her sleep, other times protecting her and guarding her from leaving. Even the rare times that she did sleep, her dreams shouted at her to wake up as though she was doing wrong. People were always commenting to her father that she was too young for the dark circles under her eyes.

The book fell away from Elizabeth's hands and she was lost to the world of sleep.

The front gate creaked.

Elizabeth's eyes shot open to the brightness of the early morning and her heart beat wildly. She heard the crunching of footsteps over gravel as they approached the front door. Elizabeth's heart did cartwheels across her chest with delight. Her mother hadn't forgotten her; she knew she wouldn't have missed her birthday.

She leaped out of bed and did a little dance around her room, not knowing whether or not to open the door for her mother or to allow her to make the grand entrance she loved doing so much. She ran out into the hall in her nightdress. She could see the blurry image of a body through the rippled glass of the front door. She hopped from foot to foot with nervousness and excitement.

Elizabeth's father's bedroom door opened. She turned to face him with a grin. He gave her a small smile and leaned against the doorframe, watching the door. Elizabeth turned her head back to the door, twisting her hem of her nightdress in her little hands. The letter box opened. Two white envelopes slid through and landed on the stone floor. The figure at the door began to fade again. The gate creaked and closed.

Elizabeth dropped the hem of her nightdress from her hands and stopped hopping. She suddenly felt the cold of the stone floor.

She slowly picked up the envelopes. Both were addressed to her and her heart quickened again. Maybe her mother hadn't forgotten, after all. Maybe she had got so caught up in one of her adventures that she couldn't make it home in time and had to explain it all in a letter. She opened the envelopes, careful not to rip the paper that could contain precious words from her mother.

Both were birthday cards from distant, dutiful relatives.

Her shoulders slumped and her heart fell. She turned to face her father and shook her head slowly. His face darkened and he stared angrily into the distance. They caught eyes again and for a moment, a rare moment, Elizabeth and he shared the same knowing feeling and Elizabeth didn't feel so alone any more. She took a step forward to give him a hug.

But he turned away and closed his door behind him.

Elizabeth's bottom lip trembled. There were no fairy cakes or buns that day. The pink balloons floating up towards the clouds remained nothing but dreams. And Elizabeth learned that imagining and fantasising did nothing but break her heart.

Chapter 11

The hissing of the water boiling over onto the cooker brought Elizabeth sharply back to the present. She raced across the kitchen to lift the pot off the hob and lowered the heat. She poked at the steamed chicken and vegetables, wondering where her head was today.

'Luke, dinner,' she called.

She had collected Luke from her father's after work, although she had been in absolutely no mood to drive down that road after sobbing in her office. She hadn't cried in years. She didn't know what was happening to her over the last few days. Her mind just kept drifting, and she never drifted. She always stayed the same, had stable, controlled thoughts and was always constant, never stopped. Nothing at all like her behaviour today at the office.

Luke shuffled into the kitchen, already dressed in his Spiderman pyjamas. He stared sadly at the table. 'You didn't set a place for Ivan again.'

Elizabeth opened her mouth to protest but stopped herself in time, remembering the advice the websites had given. 'Oh, didn't I?'

Luke looked at her in surprise.

'Sorry, Ivan,' she said, taking out a third plate. What a waste of food, she thought spooning broccoli, cauliflower and potatoes onto his plate. 'I'm sure he doesn't like chicken so this will have to do.' She placed the plate of leftover vegetables down opposite her.

Luke shook his head. 'No, he said he really does like chicken.'

'Let me guess,' Elizabeth said, cutting a corner off her own, 'chicken's his favourite.'

Luke smiled. 'He says it's his favourite kind of *poultry*.'

'Right.' Elizabeth rolled her eyes. She watched Ivan's plate, wondering how on earth Luke was going to manage to eat a second plate of vegetables. It was difficult enough trying to get him to eat his own.

'Ivan said he had fun in your office today,' Luke said, forking broccoli into his mouth, chewing quickly and making a face in disgust. He swallowed quickly and gulped back some milk.

'Did he?' Elizabeth smiled. 'What was so fun about my office?'

'He liked the chair-spinning,' he replied as he speared a baby potato.

Elizabeth stopped chewing and stared at Luke. 'What do you mean?'

Luke popped the potato into his mouth and munched. 'He says spinning around in Poppy's chair is his favourite.'

Elizabeth for once ignored the fact that he was speaking with his mouth full. 'Did you speak to Poppy today?' Luke loved Poppy and sometimes chatted to her when Edith called the office to check a detail with Elizabeth. He knew Elizabeth's office number by heart – she had insisted he learn it as soon as he learned his numbers – so it was quite possible he might have called, missing his little chats with her while Edith was away. That must have been it, she thought, relieved.

'Nope.'

'Did you speak to Becca?'

'Nope.'

The chicken suddenly tasted like cardboard in her mouth. She swallowed it quickly and put down her knife and fork. She watched Luke eat, lost in thought. Ivan's plate went untouched unsurprisingly.

'Did you speak to Saoirse today?' She studied his face. She wondered if Saoirse's little role-play in her office earlier had anything to do with Luke's new obsession with Ivan. Knowing her sister as well as she did, she would have continued to taunt her had she found out about an invisible friend.

'Nope.'

Perhaps it was just a coincidence. Perhaps Luke was just guessing about the chair-spinning. Perhaps, perhaps, perhaps. Where had all her certainties suddenly gone?

'Don't play with your vegetables, Luke. Ivan told me to tell you that they are good for you.' She may as well use the Ivan situation to her advantage.

Luke started laughing.

'What's so funny?'

'Ivan says that all mums use him to make their kids eat vegetables.'

Elizabeth raised her eyebrows and smiled. 'Well, you can tell Ivan that's because mums know best.' Her smile faded – well, *some* mums, at least.

'Tell him yourself,' Luke giggled.

'Right then.' Elizabeth faced the empty chair ahead of her. 'Where do you come from Ivan?' She leaned forward and spoke as if addressing a child.

Luke started laughing at her and she felt silly. 'He's from Ekam Eveileb.'

It was Elizabeth's turn to laugh. 'Oh, really? And where's that?'

'Far, far away,' Luke said.

'How far? Like Donegal-far?' she smiled.

Luke shrugged, already bored with the conversation.

'Hey,' Elizabeth looked at Luke and laughed, 'how did you do that?'

'Do what?'

'Take a potato from Ivan's plate?'

'I didn't,' Luke frowned. 'Ivan ate it.'

'Don't be sil—' she stopped herself.

Later that evening Luke lay on the floor of the living room, humming *that* song, while Elizabeth drank a cup of coffee and stared at the television. It was a long time since they had done that. Usually they went their own separate ways after dinner. Usually they didn't talk so much during the meal, but then *usually* Elizabeth didn't humour Luke by playing silly games. She began to regret what she had done. She watched Luke colouring with his crayons on the floor. She had put down a mat so that he wouldn't dirty the carpet and although she hated when he played with his toys outside the playroom, she was glad that he was playing with some toys that she could at least see. Every cloud and all that. She turned her attention back to her house makeover show.

'Elizabeth.' She felt the tap of a little finger on her shoulder.

'Yes, Luke?'

'Drew this for you.' He handed her a brightly coloured picture. 'It's of me and Ivan playing in the garden.'

Elizabeth smiled and studied the drawing. Luke had written their names over two matchstick men but what came to her as a surprise was the height of Ivan. He was over twice the size of Luke and was dressed in a blue T-shirt, blue jeans, blue shoes and had black hair and great big blue eyes. What looked like black stubble lined his jawline, and he held hands with Ivan with a big smile on his face. She froze, not quite knowing what to say. Shouldn't his imaginary friend be the same age as he?

'Eh, Ivan is very tall for only being six, isn't he?' Maybe he had drawn him larger than life because he was so important to him, she reasoned.

Luke rolled around the floor giggling. 'Ivan always says

there's nothing *only* about being six and, anyway, *he's* not six.' He laughed loudly again. 'He's old like you!'

Elizabeth's eyes widened in horror. *Old like her?* What kind of imaginary friend had her nephew created?

Chapter 12

Friends come in all different shapes and sizes, we all know that, so why should 'imaginary' friends be any different? Elizabeth had it all wrong. In fact Elizabeth had it *completely* wrong because as far as I could see she didn't have *any* friends. Maybe it's because she was only looking for thirty-four-year-old women that looked, dressed and acted like her. You could tell by the look on her face, she thought Luke should have found someone exactly like himself when she looked at Luke's picture of me and him. And that's no way to make friends.

The important thing is not what we *look* like but the role we play in our best friend's life. Friends choose certain friends because that's the kind of company they are looking for at that specific time, not because they're the correct height, age or have the right hair colour. It's not always the case but often there's a reason why, for example, Luke will see me and not my colleague Tommy, who looks six years old and constantly has a runny nose. I mean, I don't see any other older males interacting with Luke, do you? Just because you see 'imaginary' friends, it doesn't mean you see them all. You have the *ability* to see them all but as humans only use ten per cent of the brain, you wouldn't believe the other abilities there are. There are so many other wonderful things that eyes could see if they really focused. Life's kind of like a painting. A really bizarre abstract painting. You could look at it and think that all it is is a blur. And you can continue living your life thinking that all it is is a blur. But if you really look at it, really see it, focus on it and use your imagination, life can become so much more. That painting could be of the sea, the sky, people, buildings, a butterfly on a flower or *anything* except the blur you were once convinced it was.

After the events in Elizabeth's office I needed to call an emergency 'What IF' meeting. I've been in this job for years and I thought I'd seen it all but I obviously hadn't. Saoirse seeing me and talking to me had really stumped me. I mean, that's completely unheard of. OK, so Luke could see me – that was normal. Elizabeth had some sort of a sense of me, which was weird enough, but I was beginning to get used to it. But Saoirse seeing me? Of course it's common to be seen by more than one person on a job, but never by an *adult*, and never by *two* adults. The only friend in the company who dealt with adults was Olivia and it wasn't any kind of a rule, just what seemed to be happening all the time. I was confused, I can tell you that, so I got 'the boss' to round up all the usual suspects for an unscheduled 'What IF' meeting.

Our 'What IF' meetings were set up to discuss everyone's current situations and to knock around some ideas and suggestions for people who are slightly stuck. I've never had to call one on my behalf, so I could tell the boss was shocked when I did. The name of the meeting has a double meaning. We were all tired of being labelled as 'imaginary friends' among people and the media, so we decided to call the meeting the What Imaginary Friends meeting. I thought up that idea myself.

The six people that meet are the most senior people in the company. I arrived at the What IF room to the sound of everyone laughing and playing. I greeted them all and we sat and waited for the boss. We don't meet around long conference tables with smelly leather chairs in a boardroom with no windows. We have a more relaxed approach to it and it really has a much more positive effect because the more comfortable we all feel, the more we can contribute. We sit in a circle on comfortable seats. Mine's a beanbag. Olivia's is a rocking chair. She says it's easier for her to do her knitting that way.

The boss's not really bossy, we just call her that. She's really one of the nicest people you'll ever meet in your whole entire life. Now she's *really* seen it all: she knows everything there is to know about being a best friend. She's patient and caring, listens and hears what people don't say more than anyone I know. Opal is her name and she's beautiful. She floated into the room just then in a purple robe, her dreadlocks tied back in a half-ponytail away from her face, and they hung down past her shoulders. She had tiny sparkling beads throughout that glistened when she moved. She had daisies nestled into her dreadlocks like a tiara, a daisy chain around her neck and around her wrists. Round purple-tinted glasses sat on her nose, and when she smiled the beam was enough to guide ships into shore on a black night.

'Nice daisies, Opal,' Calendula said softly from beside me.

'Thank you, Calendula,' she smiled. 'Me and little Tara made them today in her garden. You're looking very dressed up today. What a lovely colour.'

Calendula beamed. She's been a best friend for absolute donkey's years, like me, but she only looks the same age as Luke. She is small with blonde hair that was today styled into bouncing curls, softly spoken, with big blue eyes, and was dressed in a yellow summer dress with matching yellow ribbons in her hair. She had gleaming new white shoes that swung from her hand-crafted wooden chair. The chair always reminded me of a Hansel and Gretel chair, yellow with painted hearts and candy sticks.

'Thank you, Opal.' Calendula's cheeks turned rosy. 'I'm

going to a tea party after this meeting with my new best friend.'

'Oh?' Opal raised her eyebrows, impressed. 'Very nice. Where is it?'

'In the back garden. She got a new tea set for her birthday yesterday,' she replied.

'Well, that's lovely. How are things with little Maeve?'

'Well, thank you.' Calendula looked down in her lap.

The noise from the others in the room died down and all the focus was on Opal and Calendula. Opal wasn't the type of person to ask everyone to be quiet in order to start the meeting. She always began it quietly herself, knowing that the others would soon finish their conversations and settle down in their own time. She always said that all people needed was time and then they could figure most things out for themselves.

Opal was still watching Calendula fidgeting with a ribbon on her dress.

'Is Maeve still bossing you around, Calendula?'

Calendula nodded and looked sad. 'She's still telling me what to do all the time and when she breaks things and her parents get mad, she blames it on me.'

Olivia, an old-looking best friend, who was rocking in her chair while knitting, tutted loudly.

'You know why Maeve is doing that, don't you, Calendula?' Opal said softly.

Calendula nodded. 'I know that me being around provides her with the opportunity to be in charge and she is mirroring the behaviour of her parents. I understand why she is doing it and the importance of her doing it, but that kind of treatment day in day out becomes a little disheartening at times.'

Everybody nodded in agreement. We had all been in her shoes at some stage. Most young children liked to boss us around as it was their only chance to do it without getting into trouble.

'Well, you know she won't be doing it for very much longer, Calendula,' Opal said encouragingly, and Calendula nodded, her curls bouncing up and down.

'Bobby.' Opal turned to face a little boy sitting on a skateboard with his cap turned backwards. He had been rolling back and forth while listening to the conversation. On hearing his name he stopped rolling. 'You must stop playing computer games with little Anthony. You know why, don't you?'

The little boy with the face of an angel nodded and when he spoke his voice sounded much older than his apparent six years. 'Well, because Anthony is only three and he shouldn't be forced to conform to gender roles. He needs to play with toys that allow him to take control, that are flexible and that do more than one thing. Too many of the other toys will stunt his early development.'

'What kind of things do you think you should be playing with?' Opal asked.

'Well, I'm going to concentrate on playing with, well, mostly nothing, actually, so we can do role-playing, or else use boxes, cooking utensils or empty toilet paper rolls.'

We all laughed at the last one. Toilet paper rolls are my absolute favourite. You can do so many things with them.

'Very good, Bobby. Just try to keep it in mind when Anthony tries to get you to play the computer again. Like Tommy does . . .' She trailed off, looking around. 'Actually, where is Tommy?'

'Sorry I'm late,' a loud voice called from the door. Tommy charged in with his shoulders back and arms swinging like a man fifty years older than he. There was muck all over his face, grass stains all down his knees and shins, cuts, scabs and mud on his elbows. He dived onto the beanbag, making a crashing noise with his mouth.

Opal laughed. 'Welcome, Tommy. Busy, were you?'

'Yeah,' Tommy replied cockily. 'Me and Johnno were

down in the park, digging up grubs.' He wiped his snotty nose across his bare arm.

'Uugh!' Calendula wrinkled her nose in disgust and moved her chair closer to Ivan.

'Alright, princess.' Tommy winked at Calendula, resting his feet on the table in front of him. The table had been laid out with fizzy drinks and chocolate biscuits.

Calendula looked away from him with wide eyes and concentrated on Opal.

'So John is the same as usual,' Opal stated with amusement.

'Yep, still sees me,' he replied as though that were some kind of victory. 'He's got a problem with bullies at the moment, Opal, and as he's been intimidated into secrecy, he won't tell his parents.' He shook his head sadly. 'He's afraid they'll criticise him or intervene, which will make it worse, and he's also ashamed that he allowed it to happen. All the typical emotions that goes with bullying.' He popped a sweet into his mouth.

'So what are you doing about it?' Opal asked with concern.

'Unfortunately what was happening before I came along is that John was experiencing chronic intimidation. He developed a pattern of compliance with the unfair demands of those he perceived as stronger and he was beginning to identify with the bully and become one himself. But I wouldn't let him push me around,' Tommy said toughly. 'We've been working on his posture, voice and eye contact – as you know, these communicate a lot about whether you're vulnerable. I'm teaching him to be vigilant for suspicious individuals and everyday we run over a list of possible attributes.' He sat back and rested his arms behind his head. 'We're working on him developing a mature sense of justice.'

'And you've been digging for grubs,' Opal added with a smile.

'There's always time for grub-digging, isn't there, Ivan?' Tommy winked at me.

'Jamie-Lynn.' Opal turned to a little girl in denim dungarees and dirty runners. Her hair was cut short and she balanced her behind on a football. 'How's little Samantha getting along? I hope you're both not still digging up her mother's flower garden.'

Jamie-Lynn was a tomboy and kept getting her friends into trouble, whereas Calendula mostly went to tea-parties in pretty dresses and played with Barbie and My Little Pony. Jamie-Lynn opened her mouth and began blabbering away in a mystery language.

Opal raised her eyebrows. 'So I see you and Samantha are still speaking your own language.'

Jamie-Lynn nodded.

'OK, but be careful. It's not a good idea to keep speaking like that for much longer.'

'Don't worry, I know Samantha is learning to talk in sentences and develop her memory so I won't keep it up,' Jamie-Lynn said, returning to normal language. Her voice saddened. 'Samantha didn't see me this morning when she woke up. But then she did again at lunchtime today.'

Everyone felt sad for Jamie-Lynn and we gave her our condolences because we all knew how that felt. It was the beginning of the end.

'Olivia, how's Mrs Cromwell?' Opal's voice was gentler.

Olivia stopped knitting and rocking and shook her head sadly. 'Not long for her to go now. We had a great chat last night about a day trip she had with her family seventy years ago to Sandymount beach. That put her in a great mood. But as soon as she told her family this morning that she'd been talking to me about it they all left. They think she's talking about her great-aunt Olivia that died forty years ago and are convinced she's going mad. Anyway, I'll stay with her till the end. Like I said, there isn't long for her to go and the family have only visited twice in the past month. She's not hanging on for anyone.'

Olivia always made friends in hospitals, hospices and homes for the elderly. She was good at that kind of thing, helping people reminisce to fill the time if they couldn't sleep.

'Thanks, Olivia,' Opal smiled, and then she turned to me. 'So, Ivan, how's it all going in Fuchsia Lane? What's the big emergency? Little Luke seems to be doing OK.'

I made myself comfortable on the beanbag. 'Yeah, he is OK. There are a few things we need to work on, like how he feels about his family set-up, but nothing earth-shattering.'

'Good.' Opal looked pleased.

'But that's not what the problem is.' I looked around the circle at everyone. 'His *aunt*, who adopted him, is *thirty-four* and sometimes she can feel my *presence*.'

Everyone gasped and looked at each other in horror. I knew they'd react like that.

'But that's not even the half of it,' I continued, trying not to enjoy the drama too much because, after all, it was my problem. 'Luke's *mom*, who's *twenty-two*, came into Elizabeth's office today and *saw* me and *spoke* to me!'

Double gasp – apart from Opal, whose eyes twinkled back at me knowingly. I felt better when I saw that because I knew that Opal would know what to do. She always did and I wouldn't have to feel so confused any more.

'Where was Luke when you were in Elizabeth's office?' Opal asked, a smile forming at the corner of her lips.

'On his granddad's farm,' I explained. 'Elizabeth wouldn't let me out of the car to go with him because she was afraid her dad would get mad that Luke had a friend that he couldn't see.' I was out of breath after that.

'So why didn't you walk back to Luke when you got to the office?' Tommy asked, sprawled across the beanbag with his arms behind his head.

Opal's eyes glinted again. What was up with her?

'Because,' I replied.

'Because why?' Calendula asked.

Not her too, I thought.

'How far is the farm from the office?' Bobby asked.

Why were they asking all these questions? Shouldn't the important thing be why on earth all these people were sensing me?

'It's about a two-minute drive but twenty minutes' walking,' I explained, confused. 'What's with all the questions?'

'Ivan,' Olivia laughed, 'don't act the fool. You know that when you get separated from a friend you find them. A twenty-minute walk is nothing compared to what you did to get to that last friend of yours.' She chuckled.

'Ah, come on, everyone.' I threw my hands up helplessly. 'I was trying to figure out whether Elizabeth could see me or not. I was confused, you know. This has never happened before.'

'Don't worry, Ivan,' Opal smiled, and when she spoke again her voice was like honey. 'It's rare. But it's happened before.'

Everyone gasped once more.

Opal stood up, gathered her files together and prepared to leave the meeting.

'Where are you going?' I asked in surprise. 'You haven't told me what to do yet.'

Opal took off her purple-tinted shades and her chocolate-brown eyes gazed at me. 'This is not an emergency at all, Ivan. There is no advice that I can give you. You will just have to trust yourself that when the time comes, you'll make the right decision.'

'What decision? About what?' I asked, feeling even more confused now.

Opal grinned at me. 'When the time comes, you will know. Good luck.' And with that she left the meeting, with everyone staring at me in confusion. The blank faces were enough to prevent me from asking any of them for advice.

'Sorry, Ivan, I would be just as confused as you are,' Calendula said, standing up and smoothing out the wrinkles in her summer dress. She gave me a big hug and a kiss on the cheek. 'I'd better go now too or I'll be late.'

I watched her skipping towards the door, her blonde curls bouncing with every step. 'Enjoy your tea party!' I called.

'Make the right decision,' I grumbled to myself, thinking about what Opal had said. 'The right decision about what?' And then a chilling thought occurred to me. What if I didn't make the right decision? Would someone get hurt?

Chapter 13

Elizabeth pushed herself forward gently on the swinging bench in her back garden. She cradled a warm coffee cup in her hands, wrapping her slender fingers round the limestone-coloured mug. The sun was slowly setting and a slight chill was creeping out from hiding to take its place. She stared up into the sky, a perfect vision of candy- floss clouds, pink, red and orange, like an oil painting. An amber glow rose from behind a mountain before her, like the kind of secret glow that rose from Luke's bedcovers when he was reading with a torch. She breathed in the cooling air deeply.

Red sky at night, she heard a voice inside her head say.

'Shepherd's delight,' she whispered softly.

A soft breeze blew, as if the air, like her, was sighing. She had been sitting outside now for the past hour. Luke was upstairs playing with his friend Sam, after spending the day at his grandfather's. She was awaiting the arrival of Sam's father, whom she'd never met before, to come and collect him. Usually Edith dealt with the friends' parents and so Elizabeth wasn't at all looking forward to children chitchat.

It was 9.45 p.m. and light, it seemed, was calling it a day. She had been rocking herself back and forth, fighting the tears that threatened to fall, swallowing the lump that threatened to rise in her throat, forcing back the thoughts that threatened to drown her mind. She felt that she was fighting the world that threatened to jeopardise her plans. She fought the people that invited themselves into her world without her permission; she fought Luke and his head of childish ways, her sister and her problems, Poppy and her ideas at work, Joe and his coffee shop, competitors in her business. She felt she was always fighting, fighting, fighting. And now here she sat fighting her very own emotions.

She felt as if she'd been through a hundred rounds in the ring, as if she'd taken every punch, thump and kick her opponents could throw at her. Now she was tired. Her muscles ached, her defence was falling and her wounds weren't healing so quickly. A cat leaped from the high wall that separated Elizabeth from her neighbours and landed in her garden. It glanced at Elizabeth; chin held high, eyes glowing in the darkness. It walked slowly across the grass without a care in the world. So sure of itself, so confident, so full of its own self-importance. It jumped onto the opposite wall and disappeared into the night. She envied its ability to come and go as it pleased without owing anybody anything, not even those closest, who loved and cared for it.

Elizabeth used her foot to push herself back again. The swing squeaked slightly. In the distance the mountain appeared to be burning as the sun slipped down and out of sight. On the other side the full moon awaited its final call to centre stage. The crickets continued to chatter loudly to each other, the last of the children ran to their homes for the night. Car engines stopped, car doors slammed, front doors closed, windows shut and curtains were drawn. And then there was silence and Elizabeth was once again alone, feeling like a visitor in her own back garden that had taken on a new life in the falling darkness.

Her mind began to rewind over the events of the day. It stopped and played Saoirse's visit. Played it over and over again, the volume rising at every repetition. *They all leave eventually, isn't that right, Lizzie?* The sentence repeated itself like a broken record. It kept on at her like a finger prodding her chest. Harder and harder, first grazing the skin, then breaking it, prodding and prodding until eventually it tore right through and reached her heart. The place where it hurt most. The breeze blew and stung her open flesh wound.

She shut her eyes tightly. For the second time that day Elizabeth cried. *They all leave eventually, isn't that right, Lizzie?*

It played continuously, waiting for an answer from her. Her mind exploded. *YES!* it shouted. Yes, they all eventually leave. Every single one of them, every single time. Every person that ever succeeded in brightening her day and cheering her heart disappeared as quickly as a cat in the night. As though happiness was only supposed to be some kind of weekend treat, like ice cream. Her mother had done, just as this evening's sun had done: had left her, had taken away the light and warmth and replaced it with a chill and dark.

Uncles and aunts that visited and helped moved or passed on. Friendly school teachers could only care for a school year; school friends developed and tried to find themselves too. It was always the good people that left, the people that weren't afraid to smile or to love.

Elizabeth hugged her knees and cried and cried, like a little girl who had fallen and cut her knee. She wished for her mother to come and pick her up, to carry her and rest her on the kitchen counter while she applied a plaster to her cut. And then just like she always did, she would carry her around the room, dancing and singing until the pain was forgotten and her tears had dried.

She wished for Mark, her only love, to take her in his arms, in arms so big she was dwarfed in his embrace. She wished to be surrounded by his love while he rocked her slowly and softly as he used to do, whispering hushes of assurance in her ears and running his fingers through her hair. She believed him when he said them. He made her believe that everything would be OK and, lying in his arms, she knew that it would, *felt* that it would.

And the more she wished the more she cried because she realised she was surrounded by a father who could barely look her in the eye for fear of remembering his wife, a sister who had forgotten her own son, and a nephew who looked to her everyday with big hopeful blue eyes, just *asking* to be loved and cuddled. Emotions that she felt she was never given enough of to be able to share.

And as Elizabeth sat there crying and rocking, shivering in the breeze, she wondered why it was that she allowed one sentence that had passed the lips of a girl who had never received enough kisses of love, felt warm embraces or who had never herself allowed words of love to drift over her own lips to be the one whose thump and kick sent her falling to the ground. Just as she had done with the piece of black silk in her office.

Damn Saoirse. Damn her and her hatred of life, damn her for her disregard for others and disrespect for her sister. Damn her for not trying when all Elizabeth did was try with her whole heart. What gave her the power to speak with such churlishness? How could she be so flippant with her insults? And the voice inside Elizabeth's head reminded her that it wasn't the drink talking, it was never the drink talking. It was the hurt.

Elizabeth's hurt was screaming at her tonight. 'Oh, help,' she cried softly, covering her face in her hands. 'Help, help, help . . .' she whispered through her sobs.

A light creaking at the sliding door of the kitchen caused her head to jerk up from where it was cradled in her knees. At the door stood a man, lit like an angel by the kitchen light behind him.

'Oh.' Elizabeth swallowed hard, her heart pounding at being caught. She wiped her eyes roughly and smoothed down her wild hair. She rose to her feet. 'You must be Sam's dad.' Her voice still shook from the emotion bubbling inside her. 'I'm Elizabeth.'

There was a silence. He was probably wondering what on earth he was thinking of to let his six-year-old son be minded by this woman, a woman who let her young nephew open the front door by himself at ten o'clock at night.

'I'm sorry, I didn't hear the doorbell ring.' She pulled her cardigan tighter round her waist and crossed her arms. She didn't want to step into the light. She didn't want him to see that she had been crying. 'I'm sure Luke has told Sam you're here but . . .' *But what, Elizabeth?* '. . . but I'll just give him a quick call anyway,' she mumbled. She walked across the grass towards the house with her head down, rubbing her forehead with her hand to hide her eyes.

When she reached the kitchen door, she squinted against the bright light but kept her head lowered, not wanting to make eye contact with the man. All she could see of him were a pair of blue Converse runners at the end of faded blue jeans.

Chapter 14

'Sam, your dad is here to collect you!' Elizabeth called weakly upstairs. There was no answer, just the sound of a pair of little feet running along the landing. She sighed and looked at her reflection in the mirror. She didn't recognise the woman she saw. Her face was swollen and puffy, her hair messed from being blown in the breeze and damp from rubbing her teary hands through it.

Luke appeared at the top of the stairs, sleepy-eyed and dressed in his Spiderman pyjamas that he refused to allow her to wash, instead hiding them behind his favourite teddy, George, for protection. He rubbed his eyes tiredly with his fists and looked at her confused.

'Huh?'

'Luke, it's pardon, not huh,' Elizabeth corrected him, then wondered in her current mood why the hell it mattered. 'Sam's father is still waiting so could you please tell him to hurry down?'

Luke scratched his head in a daze. 'But,' he stopped and rubbed his face tiredly.

'But what?'

'Sam's dad collected him when you were in the gar—' He stopped as his gaze was averted to over Elizabeth's shoulder.

Luke's face broke into a toothless smile. 'Oh, hello Sam's dad.' He giggled uncontrollably. 'Sam will be down in a minute,' he laughed, and ran off back down the landing.

Elizabeth had no choice but to turn slowly and face Sam's father. She couldn't continue to avoid him while he waited in her home for his son. On first glance she noticed he had a look of bewilderment as he watched Luke run back down the landing, giggling. He turned to face her, evidently worried. He was leaning against the doorframe, hands tucked into the back pockets of a pair of faded blue jeans below a blue T-shirt, and wisps of jet-black hair escaped from under his blue cap. Despite his youthful attire she presumed he was her age.

'Don't worry about Luke,' Elizabeth said, slightly embarrassed at her nephew's behaviour. 'He's just a little hyper tonight and,' she rushed her words, 'I'm sorry you caught me at a bad time in the garden.' She wrapped her arms around her body protectively. 'I'm not usually like this.' She wiped her eyes with a trembling hand and quickly clasped her hands together to hide her shaking. Her overflow of emotion had disoriented her.

'That's OK,' the soft deep voice replied. 'We all have our bad days.'

Elizabeth chewed on the inside of her mouth and tried in vain to remember her last good one. 'Edith is away at the moment. I'm sure you've had dealings with her, which is why we've never met.'

'Oh, Edith—' he smiled – 'Luke's mentioned her lots of times. He's very fond of her.'

'Yes,' she smiled weakly and wondered if Luke had ever mentioned her. 'Would you like to sit down?' She motioned towards the living room. After offering him a drink she returned from the kitchen with a glass of milk for him and an espresso for herself. She paused at the door of the living room in surprise to catch him spinning around in the leather swivel chair. The sight of him made her smile.

On seeing her at the door he smiled back, stopped spinning, took the glass from her and then moved to the leather couch. Elizabeth sat in her usual chair, so oversized it almost swallowed her up, and hated herself for hoping his runners wouldn't dirty her cream carpet.

'I'm sorry, I don't know your name,' she said, trying to brighten up the dull tone in her voice.

'My name's Ivan.'

She spluttered coffee down her top as it caught in her throat.

Ivan rushed over to pat her on the back. His concerned eyes stared right into hers. His forehead creased with worry.

Elizabeth coughed, feeling stupid, quickly broke eye contact and cleared her throat. 'Don't worry, I'm fine,' she murmured. 'It's just funny that your name is Ivan because—' She stopped. What was she going to say? Tell a stranger that her nephew was delusional? Regardless of the internet advice she still wasn't sure his behaviour could be considered normal. 'Oh, it's a long story.' She waved her hand dismissively and looked away to take another sip. 'So what is it that you do, Ivan, if you don't mind me asking?' The warm coffee ran through her body, filling her with a familiar, comfortable feeling. She felt herself coming back, slipping out of the coma of sadness.

'I guess you could say I'm in the business of making friends, Elizabeth.'

She nodded understandingly. 'Aren't we all, Ivan.'

He contemplated that idea.

'So what's your company called?'

His eyes lit up. 'It's a good company. I really love my job.'

'Good Company?' she frowned. 'I'm not familiar with it. Is it based here in Kerry?'

Ivan blinked. 'It's based everywhere, Elizabeth.'

Elizabeth raised her eyebrows. 'It's international?'

Ivan nodded and gulped down some milk.

'What is the company involved in?'

'Children,' he said quickly. 'Apart from Olivia, who

works with the elderly, but I work with children. I help them, you see. Well, it used to be children but now it seems we're branching out . . . I think . . .' He trailed off, tapped his glass with his fingernail and frowned into the distance.

'Ah, that's nice,' Elizabeth smiled. That explained the youthful clothes and playful nature. 'I suppose if you see room in another market you need to get in there, don't you? Expand the company, increase the profit. I'm always looking at ways to do that.'

'What market?'

'The elderly.'

'They have a market? Great, I wonder when it's on. Sundays, I suppose? You can always pick up a few good knick-knacks here and there, can't you? My old friend Barry's dad used to get second-hand cars and fix them up. His mom used to buy curtains and make them into clothes. She looked like something from *The Sound of Music*, good thing she lives here too because every Sunday she wanted to "climb every mountain", and because Barry was my best friend I had to do it, you see. When is it on, do you think? Not the film, I mean the market.'

Elizabeth barely heard him; her mind had slipped back into thinking mode. She couldn't stop herself.

'Are you alright?' the kind voice asked.

She stopped staring into the bottom of her coffee cup to face him. Why did he look like he cared so much? Who was this softly spoken stranger who made her feel so comfortable in his presence? Each twinkle in his blue eyes added another goose bump to her skin, his gaze was hypnotic and the tone of his voice was like a favourite song she wanted to blare and put on repeat. Who was this man who came into her house and asked her a question not even her own family could ask? *Are you alright?* Well? Was she alright? She swirled the coffee around in the cup and watched it hitting the sides and spraying up like the sea against the cliffs of Slea Head. She thought about it and came to the conclusion that if the last time she had heard those words uttered by anyone was more than a few years ago then she supposed the answer was no. She was not alright.

She was tired of hugging pillows, counting on blankets for warmth and of reliving romantic moments only in her dreams. She was tired of hoping that every day would hurry so she could get on to the next. Hoping that it would be a better day, an easier day. But it never was. Worked, paid the bills and went to bed but never slept. Each morning the weight on her shoulders got heavier and heavier and each morning she wished for night to fall quickly so she could return to her bed to hug her pillows and wrap herself in the warmth of her blankets.

She looked at the kind stranger with the blue eyes watching her and saw more care in those eyes than she had in anyone she knew. She wanted to tell him how she felt, she wanted to hear him say it would be OK, that she wasn't alone and that they would all live happily ever after and that— She stopped herself. Dreams, wishes and hopes were not realistic. She needed to stop her mind from wandering onto those paths. She had a good job and she and Luke were healthy. That was all she needed. She looked up at Ivan and thought about how to respond to his question. Was she alright?

He took a sip of his milk.

Her face broke into a smile and she started laughing, for above his lip was a milk moustache so big it reached the end of his nostrils. 'Yes, thank you, Ivan, I'm alright.'

He looked unsure as he wiped his mouth and, after a while of studying her, spoke. 'So, you're an interior designer?'

Elizabeth frowned. 'Yes, how do you know?'

Ivan's eyes danced. 'I know everything.'

Elizabeth smiled. 'Don't all men?' She looked at her watch. 'I don't know what Sam's up to. Your wife will probably think I've abducted the two of you.'

'Oh, I'm not married,' Ivan replied quickly. 'Girls, uugh!' He made a face.

Elizabeth laughed. 'I'm sorry, I didn't realise you and Fiona weren't together.'

'Fiona?' Ivan looked confused.

'Sam's mother?' Elizabeth asked, feeling foolish.

'Oh, *her*?' Ivan made another face. 'No *way*.' He leaned forward on the leather couch and it squeaked beneath his jeans. A familiar sound to Elizabeth. 'You know she makes this *awful* chicken dish. Sauce really ruins the chicken.'

Elizabeth found herself laughing again. 'That's an unusual reason not to like someone,' but funnily enough Luke had complained about it to her also, after eating dinner at Sam's over the weekend.

'Not if you like chicken, it's not,' Ivan replied honestly. 'Chicken is by far my favourite,' he smiled.

Elizabeth nodded, trying to suppress a giggle.

'Well, my favourite kind of *poultry* really.'

That did it. She started laughing again. Luke must have picked up some of his phrases.

'What?' Ivan smiled widely, revealing a set of sparkling white teeth.

'You,' Elizabeth said, trying to calm herself and control her laughter. She couldn't believe she was acting like this with a total stranger.

'What about me?'

'You're funny,' she smiled.

'You're beautiful,' he said calmly and she looked up at him in surprise.

Her face flushed. What kind of a thing was that to say? There was another silence, uncomfortable on her part as she wondered whether to be insulted or not. Rarely did people make such comments to Elizabeth. She didn't know how she was supposed to feel.

On sneaking a peak at Ivan she was intrigued to see

he didn't look at all perplexed or embarrassed. As though he said it all the time. A man like him probably did, she thought cynically. A charmer, that's all he was. Although, as much as she stared at him with forced disdain, she couldn't really bring herself to believe that. This man did not know her, had met her less than ten minutes ago, had told her she was beautiful and yet remained seated in her living room as if he were her best friend, looking around the room as if it were the most interesting place he had ever seen. He had such a friendly nature, was easy to talk to, easy to listen to, and despite telling her she was beautiful while she sat in old tattered clothes with red-rimmed eyes and greasy hair, he didn't make her feel uncomfortable. The more they sat in silence the more she realised he had simply paid her a compliment.

'Thank you, Ivan,' she said politely.

'And thank you too.'

'For what?'

'You said I was funny.'

'Oh, yes. Well, em . . . you're welcome.'

'You don't get many compliments, do you?'

Elizabeth should have stood up right there and then, and ordered him out of her living room for being so intrusive, but she didn't, because as much as she thought she should *technically*, according to her own rules, be bothered by this, she wasn't. She sighed, 'No, Ivan, I don't.'

He smiled at her. 'Well, let that be the first of many.'

He stared at her and her face began to twitch from holding his stare for so long. 'Is Sam staying with you tonight?'

Ivan rolled his eyes. 'I hope not. For a boy of only six years of age, he snores awfully loud.'

Elizabeth smiled. 'There's nothing *only* about being si—' She stopped herself and gulped back some coffee.

He raised his eyebrows. 'What was that?'

'Nothing,' she mumbled. While Ivan was looking around

the room Elizabeth stole another glance at him. She couldn't figure out how old he was. He was tall and muscular, manly but yet had a boyish charm. He confused her. She decided to cut to the chase.

'Ivan, I'm confused about something.' She took a breath to ask her question.

'Don't be. Never be confused.'

Elizabeth felt herself frown and smile at the same time. Even her face was confused by his statement. 'OK,' she said slowly, 'do you mind me asking what age you are?'

'No,' he said happily. 'I don't mind at all.'

Silence.

'Well?'

'Well what?'

'What age are you?'

Ivan smiled. 'Let's just say I've been told by one person in particular that I'm old like you.'

Elizabeth laughed. She had thought as much. Obviously Ivan hadn't been spared any of Luke's unsubtle comments.

'Children keep you young, though, Elizabeth.' His voice turned serious, his eyes deep and thoughtful. 'My job is to care for children, help them along and just be there for them.'

'You're a care worker?' Elizabeth asked.

Ivan thought about that. 'You could call me a care worker, professional best friend, guide . . .' He held out his hands and shrugged. 'Children are the ones that know exactly what's going on in the world, you know. They *see* more than adults, *believe* in more, are honest and will always, *always* let you know where you stand.'

Elizabeth nodded along with him. He obviously loved his job – as a father and as a care worker.

'You know, it's interesting,' he leaned forward again, 'children learn much more, far more quickly than adults. Do you know why that is?'

Elizabeth assumed there was some scientific explanation for it but shook her head.

'Because they're open-minded. Because they *want* to know and they *want* to learn. Adults,' he shook his head sadly, 'think they know it all. They grow up and forget so easily and instead of opening their minds and developing it they *choose* what to believe and what not to believe. You can't make a choice on things like that: you either believe or you don't. That's why their learning is slower. They are more cynical, they lose faith and they only demand to know things that will help them get by day by day. They've no interest in the extras. But, Elizabeth,' he said, his voice a loud whisper, eyes wide and sparkling, and Elizabeth shivered as goose pimples rose on her arms. She felt as if he was sharing the world's greatest secret with her. She moved her head closer. 'It's the *extras* that make life.'

'That make life what?' she whispered.

He smiled. 'That make *life*.'

Elizabeth swallowed the lump in her throat. 'That's it?'

Ivan smiled. 'What do you mean, that's it? How much more can you get than life, how much more can you ask for than life? That's the gift. Life is *everything*, and you haven't lived it properly until you believe.'

'Believe in what?'

Ivan rolled his eyes and smiled. 'Oh, Elizabeth, you'll figure it out.'

Elizabeth wanted the extras he spoke about. She wanted the sparkle and the excitement of life, she wanted to release balloons in a barley field and fill a room with pink fairy cakes. Her eyes filled again and her heart thudded in her chest at the thought of crying in front of him. She needn't have worried because he stood up slowly.

'Elizabeth,' he said gently, 'on that note, I shall leave you. It was my pleasure to spend this time with you.' He held out his hand.

When Elizabeth held out her own to touch his soft skin, he grasped it gently and pumped it hypnotically. She couldn't speak for the lump in her throat that had taken over.

'Good luck with your meeting tomorrow,' he smiled encouragingly, and with that he exited the living room. The door was closed behind him by Luke who shouted, 'Bye, Sam!' at the top of his voice, laughed loudly, and then pounded up the stairs.

Later that night Elizabeth lay in bed, her head hot, her nose blocked and her eyes sore from crying. She hugged her pillow and snuggled down into her duvet. The open curtains allowed the moon to shine a path of silver-blue light across her room. She gazed out the window at the same moon she had watched as a child, at the same stars she had wished upon, and a thought struck her.

She hadn't mentioned anything at all to Ivan about her meeting tomorrow.

Chapter 15

Elizabeth hauled her luggage out of the boot of the taxi and trailed it along behind her into the departure and arrival area of Farranfore Airport. She breathed a sigh of relief. Now she really felt that she was going home. After spending only a month living in New York she felt she fitted in there more than she ever had in Baile na gCroíthe. She was beginning to make friends; more importantly, she was beginning to *want* to make friends.

'The plane is on time at least,' Mark said, joining the small check-in queue.

Elizabeth smiled at him and rested her forehead against his chest. 'I'll need another holiday to recover from this one,' she joked wearily.

Mark chuckled, kissed the top of her head and ran his hands through her dark hair. 'You call coming home to visit our families a holiday?' he laughed. 'Let's go to Hawaii when we get back.'

Elizabeth lifted her head and raised an eyebrow, 'Of course, Mark, I'll just let you tell my boss that. You know I need to get back to that project urgently.'

Mark studied her determined face. 'You should go it alone.'

Elizabeth rolled her eyes and leaned her forehead against his chest again. 'Not this again.' Her voice was muffled in his duffel coat.

'Just listen.' He lifted her chin with his forefinger. 'You

work all the hours under the sun, rarely take time off and stress yourself out. For what?'

She opened her mouth to reply.

'For what?' he repeated, stopping her.

Again she opened her mouth to answer and he jumped in. 'Well, seeing as you're so reluctant to answer,' he smiled, 'I'll tell you what for. For *other people*. So that they get all the glory. *You* do all the work, *they* get all the glory.'

'Excuse me,' Elizabeth half laughed, 'that job pays me extremely well as you *well* know, and at the rate I'm going, by this time next year – if we decide to stay in New York, that is – I'll be able to afford that house we saw—'

'My dear Elizabeth,' Mark interrupted, 'the rate you're going, this time next year that house will be *sold* and in its place will be a skyscraper or terribly trendy bar that doesn't sell alcohol or a restaurant that doesn't serve food "*just to be different*",' he made quotation marks with his fingers, making Elizabeth laugh, 'which you will no doubt paint white, put fluorescent lights in the floors and refuse to purchase furniture for, in case it clutters the place,' he teased. 'And other people will get the credit for that.' He looked at her in pretend disgust. 'Imagine. That's *your* blank canvas, nobody else's, and they shouldn't take that away from you. I want to be able to bring our friends in there and say, "Look, everyone, Elizabeth did this. Took her three months to do, all it is is white walls and no chairs but I'm proud of her. Didn't she do well?"'

Elizabeth held her stomach from laughing so hard. 'I would *never* let them knock down that house. Anyway, this job pays me *lots* of money,' she explained.

'That's the second time you've mentioned money. We're doing fine. What do you need all this money for?' Mark asked.

'A rainy day,' Elizabeth said, her laughter dying down and her smile fading as her thoughts drifted to Saoirse and her father. A very rainy day, indeed.

'Just as well we're not living here any more then,' Mark said, not noticing her face and looking out the window, 'or you'd be broke.'

Elizabeth looked out the window to the wet day and couldn't help feeling that the week had been a complete waste of time. She hadn't exactly been expecting a welcoming committee and bunting to be hung from the shops but neither Saoirse nor her father seemed to be in the least bit interested in whether she was home or not, and what she has been up to in her time away. But she hadn't returned to share stories about her new life in New York; she had returned to check up on them.

Her father still wasn't talking to her on account of her leaving home and deserting him. Working for a few months at a time in different counties had seemed at the time the ultimate sin, but leaving the country altogether was now the mightiest sin of all. Before Elizabeth had left she had made arrangements to ensure they would both be looked after. Much to her great disappointment, Saoirse had dropped out of school the previous year and Elizabeth had had to set her up with her eighth job in two months, stocking shelves in the local supermarket. She had also arranged with a neighbour to drive her into Killarney twice a month to see her counsellor. To Elizabeth, that part was far more important than the job and she knew that Saoirse had only agreed to it as it gave her the opportunity to escape from her cage twice a month. In the unlikely event that Saoirse ever decided to talk about how she was feeling, at least there would be someone there to listen.

There had been no sign of the housekeeper Elizabeth had organised for her father, though. The farmhouse was a dusty, smelly, damp mess and after spending two days scrubbing the place Elizabeth gave up, realising there was no amount of cleaning products that would bring back the shine to the farmhouse. When her mother left, she had taken the sparkle with her.

Saoirse had moved out of the bungalow and into a house with a group of strangers she had met while camping out at a music festival. All they seemed to do was sit in a circle by the old tower near the town, lying on the grass, with long hair and beards, strumming on a guitar and singing songs about suicide.

Elizabeth had only managed to catch her sister twice during her stay. The first meeting was very brief. On the day of Elizabeth's arrival she received a phone call from the only ladies' clothes store in Baile na gCroíthe. They were holding Saoirse as they had caught her shoplifting some T-shirts. Elizabeth had gone down, apologised profusely, paid the women for the T-shirts and as soon as they had stepped outside Saoirse had headed for the hills. The second time they met was only long enough for Elizabeth to loan Saoirse some money and then organise to meet for lunch the next day, a lunch Elizabeth ended up eating alone. At least she was glad to see Saoirse had put on some weight at last. Her face was fuller and her clothes didn't seem to hang off her as they once had. Perhaps living alone was good for her.

November in Baile na gCroíthe was lonely. The young population was away at school and college, the tourists were at home or visiting hotter countries, businesses were quiet and empty, some closed, the others struggling. The village was drab, cold and dreary, the flowers not yet out to brighten the streets. It was like a ghost town. But Elizabeth was glad she had returned. Her small family may not have given two flutes whether she was home or not, but she knew with a certainty now that she couldn't live her life worrying about them.

Mark and Elizabeth moved up the queue. There was only one person ahead of them and then they would be free. Free to catch their flight to Dublin so they could go on to New York from there.

Elizabeth's phone rang and her stomach lurched instinctively.

Mark whipped around. 'Don't answer that.'

Elizabeth took the phone out of her bag and looked at the number.

'Don't answer it, Elizabeth.' His voice was steady and stern.

'It's an Irish number.' Elizabeth bit down on her lip.

'Don't,' he said gently.

'But something could be wro—' The ringing stopped.

Mark smiled, looked relieved. 'Well done.'

Elizabeth smiled weakly and Mark turned back to face the check-in desk. He took a step forward to approach the desk and as he did so her phone began ringing again.

It was the same number.

Mark was talking to the woman behind the desk, laughing and as charming as usual. Elizabeth clutched the phone tightly in her hand and stared at the number on her screen until it disappeared and the ringing stopped again.

It beeped, signalling a voicemail.

'Elizabeth, she needs your passport.' Mark swirled round. His face fell.

'I'm just checking my messages,' Elizabeth said quickly, and began rooting in her bag for her passport, phone pressed to her ear.

'Hello, Elizabeth, this is Mary Flaherty calling from the maternity ward in Killarney Hospital. Your sister, Saoirse, has been taken in with labour pains. It's a month earlier than expected, as you know, so Saoirse wanted us to call you to let you know in case you wanted to be here with her . . .' Elizabeth didn't hear the rest. She stood frozen to the spot. Labour pains? Saoirse? She wasn't even pregnant. She replayed the message, thinking maybe it was the wrong number, ignoring Mark's pleas for her to hand over her passport.

'Elizabeth,' Mark said loudly, interrupting her thoughts, 'your passport. You're holding everyone up.'

Elizabeth turned round and was greeted by a line of angry faces.

'Sorry,' she whispered, her whole body shaking, feeling stunned.

'What's wrong?' Mark said, his anger fading and concern spreading across his face.

'Excuse me,' the check-in assistant called. 'Are you getting on this flight?' she asked as politely as she could.

'Em,' Elizabeth rubbed her eyes in confusion, looked from Mark's issued ticket on the counter, to his face and back again. 'No, no, I can't.' She stepped backwards out of the queue. 'Sorry.' She turned to the few people in the queue who looked at her with softened faces. 'So sorry.' She looked at Mark standing in the queue, looking so . . . so disappointed. Not disappointed she wasn't coming but disappointed *in* her.

'Sir,' the lady called, handing him his ticket.

He took it distractedly and slowly stepped out of the queue. 'What happened?'

'It's Saoirse,' Elizabeth said weakly, a lump forming in her throat. 'She's been taken into hospital.'

'Did she drink too much again?' The concern had instantly disappeared from Mark's voice.

Elizabeth thought about that answer long and hard, and the shame and embarrassment of not having known about Saoirse's pregnancy took charge and shouted at her to lie. 'Yes, I think so. I'm not too sure.' She shook her head – trying to shake her thoughts away.

Mark's shoulders relaxed. 'Look, she probably just has to get her stomach pumped again. It's nothing new, Elizabeth. Let's just get you checked in and we can talk about it in the café.'

Elizabeth shook her head. 'No, no, Mark, I have to go.' Her voice trembled.

'Elizabeth, it's probably *nothing*,' he smiled. 'How many of these phone calls do you get a year and it's always the same thing.'

'It could be *something*, Mark.' Something that a sister in her right mind should have known, should have spotted.

Mark's hands dropped from her face. 'Don't let her do this to you.'

'Do what?'

'Don't let her make you choose her life over your own.'

'Don't be so ludicrous, Mark, she's my sister, she *is* my life. I have to look out for her.'

'Even though she never looks out for you. Even though she couldn't care less whether you were here for her or not.'

It was like a thump in the stomach.

'No, I've got you to look out for me.' She tried to lighten the mood, tried to make everyone happy as usual.

'But I can't if you won't let me.' His eyes were dark with hurt and anger.

'Mark,' Elizabeth tried to laugh but failed, 'I promise I'll be on the earliest flight possible. I just need to find out what's happened. Think about it. If this was your sister you'd be out of this airport long before now, you'd be by her side as we speak and you wouldn't have given a bit of thought to having this stupid conversation.'

'Then what are you still standing here for?' he said coldly.

Anger and tears welled in Elizabeth all at once. She lifted her case and walked away from him. Walked out of the airport and rushed to the hospital.

She did return to New York, just as she promised him. She flew over two days after him, collected her belongings from their apartment, handed in her notice at work and returned to Baile na gCroíthe with a pain in her heart so sore she almost couldn't breathe.

Chapter 16

Elizabeth was thirteen years old and had settled into her first few weeks of secondary school. This meant she had to travel further out of town to go to school so she was up and out earlier than everyone else in the morning and, because classes finished later, she returned home in the dark in the evening. She was spending very little time with eleven-month-old Saoirse. Unlike her primary school bus, the school bus dropped her at the end of the long road that led from the bungalow, leaving her to her lonely walk to the front door where nobody stood to greet her. It was winter and the dark mornings and evenings draped black velvet over the country. Elizabeth, for the third time that week, had walked down the road in the harsh wind and rain, her school skirt lifting and dancing around her legs while her school bag, laden with books, stooped her back.

Now she sat by the fire, in her pyjamas, trying to warm her body, with one eye on her homework, the other eye on Saoirse, who was crawling along the floor, putting everything she could lay her chubby hands on in her drooling mouth. Her father was in the kitchen heating up his homemade vegetable stew again. It's what they ate everyday. Porridge for breakfast, stew for dinner. Occasionally they would have a thick piece of beef or some fresh fish her father had caught that day. Elizabeth loved those days.

Saoirse gurgled and dribbled to herself, waving her hands

around and watching Elizabeth, happy to see her big sister home. Elizabeth smiled at her and made encouraging noises before turning back to her homework. Using the couch as security, Saoirse pulled herself up onto her feet as she had been doing for the past few weeks. She slowly stepped sideways, going back and forth, back and forth before turning round to Elizabeth.

'Come on, Saoirse, you can do it.' Elizabeth put down her pencil and fixed her attention on her little sister. Every day now, Saoirse had attempted the walk across the room to her sister, but had ended on her padded behind. Elizabeth was determined to be there when she finally made that leap. She wanted to make a song and dance about it like her mother would if she'd been still here.

Saoirse blew air out of her mouth, bubbles forming on her lips, and spoke in her own mysterious language.

'Yes,' Elizabeth nodded, 'come to Elizabeth.' She held her arms out.

Slowly Saoirse let go and with a determined look on her face she began to take those steps. Further and further she walked while Elizabeth held her breath, trying not to shout in excitement for fear of throwing her off. Saoirse held Elizabeth's stare all the way. Elizabeth would never forget that look in her baby sister's eyes, such determination. Finally she reached Elizabeth and she took her in her arms and danced her around, smothering her in kisses while Saoirse giggled and blew more bubbles.

'Dad, Dad!' Elizabeth called out.

'What?' he shouted crankily.

'Come here, quick!' Elizabeth called, helping Saoirse applaud herself.

Brendan appeared at the door, concern written across his face.

'Saoirse walked, Dad! Look, do it again, Saoirse; walk for Daddy!' She placed her sister on the floor and encouraged her to repeat the feat.

Brendan huffed, 'Jaysus, I thought it was something important. I thought there was somethin' wrong with ya. Don't be botherin' me like that.' He turned his back and returned to the kitchen.

When Saoirse looked up in her second attempt to show her family how clever she was and saw that her daddy was gone, her face fell, and so did she, landing on her bum again.

Elizabeth had been at work the day Luke learned to walk. Edith had called her in the middle of a meeting and she couldn't talk so had heard about it when she got home. Thinking about it now, she realised she had reacted very similarly to her dad and, once again, she hated herself for it. As an adult she could now understand her father's reaction. It wasn't that he wasn't proud or that he didn't care, it was just that he cared too much. First they walk, then they fly away.

The encouraging thought was, if Elizabeth had managed to help her sister to walk once, surely she could help her back on her feet a second time.

Elizabeth awoke with a jump, feeling cold and frozen in fear after a nightmare. The moon had finished its shift on her side of the world and had moved on, making way for the sun. The sun kept a paternal gaze on Elizabeth, keeping a close eye on her as she slept. The silver-blue light thrown across her bedclothes had been replaced by a yellow trail. It was 4.35 a.m., and Elizabeth immediately felt awake. She propped herself up on her elbows. Her duvet lay half on the floor, the other half caught up in her legs. She'd had a fitful sleep where dreams began and were unfinished before jumping into new ones, overlapping into each other to create a bizarre blur of faces, places and random words. She felt exhausted.

Looking around the room, she felt irritation seeping into her body. Although she had cleaned the house from top to bottom till it glistened two days ago, she felt the urge to do it all over again. Items were out of place and kept catching the corner of her eye. She rubbed her nose, which was beginning to itch out of frustration, and she threw off the bedclothes.

Immediately she began tidying. She had a total of twelve pillows to display on her bed, six rows of two consisting of regular pillows, with oblong-shaped and circular at the front. All had different textures, ranging from rabbit fur to suede, and were various shades of cream, beige and coffee. Once satisfied with the bed, she ensured her clothes were hanging in the correct order, from dark colours on the left to bright, although she had very little colour in her wardrobe. Wearing the slightest bit of colour felt to her as though she were walking down the street in flashing neon. She vacuumed the floor, dusted and polished the mirrors, straightened the three small hand towels in the bathroom, taking a few minutes to perfectly align the stripes through them. The taps glistened and she kept on scrubbing furiously until she could see her reflection in the tiles. By 6.30 she had completed the living room and kitchen and, feeling less restless, she sat outside in the garden with a cup of coffee while looking over her designs in preparation for that morning's meeting. She had had a total of three hours sleep that night.

Benjamin West rolled his eyes and ground his teeth in frustration while his boss paced the floor of the Portakabin and ranted in his thick New York accent.

'You see, Benji, I'm just—'

'Benjamin,' he interrupted.

'– sick and tired,' he continued, not acknowledging him, 'of hearing all the same shit from everyone. All these designers are the same. They want contemporary this, minimalist that. Well, art deco my balls, Benji!'

'It's—'

'I mean, how many of these companies have we met with over here so far?' He stopped pacing and looked at Benjamin.

Benjamin flicked through his diary, 'Em, eight, not including the woman who had to leave early on Friday, Elizabeth—'

'It doesn't matter,' he cut him off, 'she's the same as the rest.' He waved his hand dismissively and spun round to look out the window at the construction site. His thin grey plait swung with his head.

'Well, we have another meeting with her in a half-hour,' Benjamin said, checking his watch.

'Cancel it. Whatever she has to say I don't care. She's as strait-laced as they come. How many hotels have you and I worked on together, Benji?'

Benjamin sighed. 'It's Benjamin and we've worked together a lot, Vincent.'

'A lot.' He nodded to himself. 'That's what I thought. And how many of them have had as good a view as this?' He held out his hand to display the scenery out the window. Benjamin spun round in his chair, uninterested, and could barely bring himself to look past the noise and mess of the site. They were behind time. Sure it was pretty, but he'd prefer to look out that window and see a hotel standing there, not rolling hills and lakes. He'd been in Ireland for two months now and the hotel was scheduled to be finished by August, three months away. Born in Haxton, Colorado but living in New York, he thought he'd long escaped the claustrophobic feeling that only a small town could bring. Apparently not.

'Well?' Vincent had lit a cigar and was sucking on the end.

'It's a great view,' Benjamin said in a bored tone.

'It's a fucking fantastic view and I'm not gonna let some fancy shmancy interior designer come in here and make it look like some city hotel we've done a million times before.'

'What have you got in mind, Vincent?' All Benjamin had been hearing for the past two months was what he didn't want.

Vincent, dressed in a shiny grey suit, marched towards his briefcase, took out a folder and slid it down the table to Benjamin. 'Look at those newspaper articles. The place is a goddamn goldmine. I want what they want. People don't want some average hotel – it needs to be romantic, fun, artistic, none of all this clinical modern stuff. If the next person walks in here with the same shitty ideas I'll design the damn thing myself.' He turned his reddening face to the window and puffed on his cigar.

Benjamin rolled his eyes at Vincent's dramatics.

'I want a real artist,' he continued, 'a raving damn lunatic. Someone creative with a bit of flair. I'm sick of these corporate suits talking about paint colours like they're pie charts, who've never picked up a paint brush in their life. I want the Van Gogh of interior design—'

A knock on the door interrupted him.

'Who's that?' Vincent said gruffily, still red in the face from his rant.

'It's probably Elizabeth Egan, here for the meeting.'

'I thought I told you to cancel that.'

Benjamin ignored him and walked over to the door to let Elizabeth in.

'Hello,' she said, entering the room, followed by a plum-haired Poppy, spattered with paint and weighed down with folders spilling with carpet samples and fabrics.

'Hi, I'm Benjamin West, project manager. We met on Friday.' He shook Elizabeth's hand.

'Yes, I'm sorry about having to leave early,' she replied crisply, not looking him in the eye. 'It's not a regular occurrence, I can assure you.' She turned to face the struggling lady behind her. 'This is Poppy, my assistant. I hope you don't mind her sitting in with us,' she said curtly.

Poppy battled with the folders in order to shake

Benjamin's hand, resulting in a few folders crashing to the ground.

'Oh shit,' she said loudly, and Elizabeth spun round with a face like thunder.

Benjamin laughed. 'That's OK. Let me help you.'

'Mr Taylor,' Elizabeth said loudly, walking across the room with an extended hand, 'good to meet you again. Sorry about the last meeting.'

Vincent turned from the window, looked her black suit up and down and puffed on his cigar. He didn't shake her hand, but instead turned to face out the window again.

Benjamin helped Poppy carry the folders to the table and spoke to clear the awkwardness from the room. 'Why don't we all take a seat?'

Elizabeth, flushed in the face, slowly lowered her hand and turned to face the table. Her voice went up an octave. 'Ivan!'

Poppy's face crumpled into a frown and she looked about the room.

'It's OK,' Benjamin said to her, 'people get my name wrong all the time. The name's Benjamin, Ms Egan.'

'Oh, not you,' Elizabeth laughed. 'I'm talking about the man in the chair beside you.' She walked towards the table. 'What are you doing here? I didn't know you were involved in the hotel. I thought you worked with children.'

Vincent raised his eyebrows and watched her nodding and smiling politely in the silence. He began to laugh, a hearty guffaw that ended in hacking coughs.

'Are you OK, Mr Taylor?' Elizabeth asked with concern.

'Yes, Ms Egan, I'm fine. Absolutely fine. It's a pleasure to meet you.' He held out his hand.

While Poppy and Elizabeth were arranging their files, Vincent spoke under his breath to Benjamin. 'This one mightn't be too far from cutting her ear off after all.'

The door to the cabin opened and in walked the receptionist with a tray of coffee cups.

'Well, it was lovely to meet you again. Bye, Ivan,' Elizabeth called out as the door closed behind the woman.

'Gone now, is he?' Poppy asked drily.

'Don't worry,' Benjamin laughed under his breath to Poppy while watching Elizabeth in admiration, 'she's fitting the profile perfectly. You guys were listening outside the door, right?'

Poppy looked at him confused.

'Don't worry, you're not gonna get into trouble or anything,' he laughed. 'But you heard us talking, right?'

Poppy thought for a while then nodded her head slowly up and down, still looking rather confused.

Benjamin chuckled and looked away. 'I knew it. Clever woman,' he thought aloud, watching Elizabeth engrossed in conversation with Vincent.

They both tuned into the conversation.

'I like you, Elizabeth, I really do,' Vincent was saying genuinely. 'I like your eccentricity.'

Elizabeth frowned.

'You know, your quirkiness. That's when you know someone's a genius and I like geniuses on my team.'

Elizabeth nodded slowly, utterly bewildered at what he was going on about.

'But,' Vincent continued, 'I'm not too convinced on your ideas. In fact, I'm not convinced at all. I don't like 'em.'

There was silence.

Elizabeth moved uncomfortably in her seat. 'OK,' she tried to remain businesslike, 'what is it exactly that you have in mind?'

'Love.'

'Love,' Elizabeth repeated dully.

'Yes. Love.' He leaned back in the chair, fingers interlocked across his stomach.

'You have love in mind,' Elizabeth said stonily, looking at Benjamin for assurance.

Benjamin rolled his eyes and shrugged.

'Hey, *I* don't give a shit about love,' Vincent said. 'I've been married twenty-five years,' he added by way of explanation. 'It's the Irish public that wants it. Where is that thing?' He looked around the table, then slid the folder of newspaper articles towards Elizabeth.

After a moment of flicking through the pages, Elizabeth spoke. In her voice Benjamin sensed disappointment. 'Ah, I see. You want a *themed* hotel.'

'You make it sound tacky when you say that.' He waved his hand dismissively.

'I believe themed hotels *are* tacky,' Elizabeth said firmly. She couldn't forsake her principles, even for a plum job like this.

Benjamin and Poppy looked to Vincent for his response. It was like watching a tennis match.

'Elizabeth,' Vincent said with a smile twitching at the corner of his lips, 'you're a beautiful young woman, surely you should know this. Love is not a theme. It's an atmosphere, a mood.'

'I see,' Elizabeth said, sounding and looking as if she didn't see at all. 'You want to create a feeling of love in a hotel.'

'Exactly!' Vincent said, looking pleased. 'But it's not what I want, it's what *they* want.' He stabbed the newspaper with his finger.

Elizabeth cleared her throat and spoke as if addressing a child. 'Mr Taylor, it's June, what we call silly season, when there's nothing else to write about. The media simply represents a distorted image of the public's opinion – it's not accurate, you know. It doesn't represent the hopes and wishes of the Irish people. To strive for something to meet the needs of the media would be to make a huge mistake.'

Vincent looked unimpressed.

'Look, the hotel is in a wonderful location with stunning views, bordering a beautiful town with an endless amount of outdoor amenities available. My designs are about bringing the outside in, making the landscapes part of the interior. With the use of natural earthy tones like the dark greens, browns and with the use of stone we can—'

'I've heard all this before,' Vincent puffed. 'I don't want the hotel to blend in with the mountains, I want it to stand out. I don't want the guests to feel like damn hobbits sleeping in a mound of grass and mud.' He stabbed his cigar out angrily in the ashtray.

She's lost him, Benjamin thought. Too bad: this one really tried. He watched her face melt as the job slipped away from her.

'Mr Taylor,' she said quickly, 'you haven't heard *all* my ideas yet.' She was grasping at straws.

Vincent grunted and looked at his diamond-studded Rolex. 'You've thirty seconds.'

She froze for twenty of them and eventually her face fell and she looked to be in a great deal of pain as she spoke her next few words. 'Poppy,' she sighed, 'tell him your ideas.'

'Yes!' Poppy jumped up in excitement and danced around the other side of the table to Vincent. 'OK, so I'm thinking waterbeds in the shape of hearts, hot tubs, champagne flutes that rise from the bedside lockers. I'm thinking the *Romantic era* meets *art deco*. An *explosion*,' she made explosion signs with her hands, 'of rich reds, burgundy and wine that make you feel like you're being embraced in a velvet-lined *womb*. Candles *everywhere*. French boudoir meets . . .'

As Poppy rambled on and Vincent nodded his head animatedly while hanging on her every word, Benjamin turned to look at Elizabeth, who in turn had her head in her hand, wincing at every one of Poppy's ideas. Their eyes met and they both shared an exasperated look over their respective colleagues.

Then they shared a smile.

Chapter 17

'Oh, my goodness, oh, my goodness,' Poppy squealed with delight, dancing towards Elizabeth's car. 'I'd like to thank Damien Hirst for inspiring me, Egon Schiele,' she wiped an imaginary tear from her eye, 'Banksy and Robert Rauschenberg for providing me with such incredible art that helped my creative mind develop, opening delicately like a bud and for—'

'Stop it,' Elizabeth hissed through gritted teeth. 'They're still watching us.'

'Oh, they are not, don't be so paranoid.' Poppy's tune changed from elation to frustration. She turned to face the cabin on the site.

'Don't turn round, Poppy!' Elizabeth spoke as if giving out to a child.

'Oh, why not? They're not watchi— Oh, they are. BYEEE! THA-ANKSSS,' she waved her hands wildly.

'Do you *want* to lose your job?' Elizabeth threatened, refusing to turn round. Her words had the same effect as they would on Luke when she threatened to take away his PlayStation. Poppy stopped skipping immediately and they both walked in silence back to the car, Elizabeth feeling two pairs of eyes burning into her back.

'I can't believe we got the job,' Poppy said breathily once inside, hand on her heart.

'Nor can I,' Elizabeth grumbled, securing her seat belt around her body and starting up the engine.

'What's wrong with you, grumpy? You'd swear we didn't *get* this job or something,' Poppy accused, settling down in the passenger seat and drifting off to her own world.

Elizabeth thought about that. In fact she *hadn't* got the job, Poppy had. It was the kind of victory that didn't feel like a victory at all. And why had Ivan been there? He had told Elizabeth he worked with children – what had the hotel got to do with children? He hadn't even stuck around long enough for her to find out, instead leaving the room as soon as the drinks were brought without a goodbye to anyone apart from Elizabeth. She pondered this. Perhaps he was involved in business with Vincent and she'd walked in during an important meeting, which would make sense as to why Vincent had seemed so rudely preoccupied. Well, whatever it was, she needed to be informed and she was angry that Ivan hadn't mentioned it last night. She had plans to make and despised disruptions.

Separating from an overexcited Poppy, she headed over to Joe's for a coffee and to think.

'Good afternoon, Elizabeth,' Joe shouted. The three other customers jumped in their seats at his sudden outburst.

'Coffee, please, Joe.'

'For a change?'

She smiled tightly. She chose a table by the window looking onto the main street. She sat with her back to the window. She wasn't a gazer, she needed to think.

'Excuse me, Ms Egan.' The male American voice startled her.

'Mr West,' she said, looking up in surprise.

'Please call me Benjamin.' He smiled and indicated to the chair beside her. 'Mind if I join you?'

Elizabeth moved her papers out of his way. 'Would you like a drink?'

'Coffee would be great.'

Elizabeth took her mug and held it out towards Joe, 'Joe, two tall slim mango Frappaccinos, please.'

Benjamin's eyes lit up. 'You're kidding, I thought they didn't sell that he—' He was cut short by Joe dumping two mugs of milky coffee on the table. It spilled over the sides of the mugs. 'Oh,' he finished, looking disappointed.

She turned her attention to the extremely dishevelled-looking Benjamin. His thick black hair was in wavy curls around his head, and he had jet-black stubble growing from the top of his hairy chest to his cheekbones. He wore scruffy jeans streaked with muck, an identically soiled denim jacket, turf-clad sandy Caterpillar boots that had left a trail from the front door to the table, under which a small mountain of dry mud was gathering. A line of black dirt collected underneath his fingernails and as he rested his hands on the table on front of Elizabeth, she felt herself having to look away.

'Congratulations on today,' Benjamin said, seeming genuinely happy. 'It was a very successful meeting for you. You really pulled it off. You guys say *sláinte*, right?' He held up his coffee mug.

'Excuse me?' Elizabeth asked coldly.

'*Sláinte*? Isn't that right?' He looked worried.

'No,' she said with frustration, 'I mean yes, but I'm not talking about that.' She shook her head. 'I didn't "pull it off", as you say, Mr West. Getting this contract was no stroke of luck.'

Benjamin's sun-kissed skin pinked slightly. 'Oh, that's not what I meant at all and please call me Benjamin. Mr West seems so formal.' He moved uncomfortably in his chair. 'Your assistant, Poppy . . .' he looked away, trying to find the words, 'she's very talented, has lots of "out there" ideas and Vincent pretty much has the same philosophy but sometimes he gets carried away and it's up to us to talk him down from the window ledge. Look, it's my job to make sure we get this thing built on time and under budget so I plan to do what I usually do and just convince Vincent that we haven't the money to put Poppy's ideas from paper to practice.'

Elizabeth's heart quickened. 'Then he'll want a designer he can afford. Mr West, have you come here to try to talk me out of this job?' she asked coldly.

'No,' Benjamin sighed. 'It's *Benjamin*,' he stressed, 'and no, I'm not trying to talk you out of this job.' He said it in a way that made her feel foolish. 'Look, I'm trying to help you out here. I can see that you're not happy with the whole idea and truthfully I don't think the locals would be too delighted by it either.' He gestured around at the people in the room and Elizabeth tried to picture Joe going for Sunday lunch in a 'velvet womb'. No, it definitely wouldn't work, definitely not in this town.

Benjamin continued, 'I care about the projects I work on, and I think this hotel has a huge amount of potential. I don't want it to end up looking like a Las Vegas shrine to Moulin Rouge.'

Elizabeth had slid down ever so slightly in her seat.

'Now,' he said assertively, 'I came here to meet you because I like your ideas. They're sophisticated yet comfortable, modern without being too modern, and the look will appeal to a broad range of people. Vincent and Poppy's idea is too themed and will alienate three-quarters of the country immediately. However, maybe you could punch them with a bit more colour? I do agree with Vincent that your whole concept needs to look less like The Shire and more like a hotel. We don't want people feeling like they have to travel barefoot to Macgillycuddy's Reeks to drop a ring down the centre.'

Feeling offended, Elizabeth dropped her mouth open.

'Do you think,' he continued, ignoring her reaction, 'that you could work with Poppy? You know, water down her ideas . . . a lot?'

Elizabeth had been prepared once again for a stealth attack but he was here to help her. She cleared her throat that didn't need clearing and pulled at the end of her suit jacket, feeling awkward. Once she had composed herself she said, 'Well, I'm glad we're on the same page here, but.' She signalled to Joe for another coffee and thought about fusing her natural colours with Poppy's rich tones.

Benjamin shook his head wildly to Joe's offer of another coffee, still with a full untouched mug in front of him. 'You drink a lot of coffee,' he commented as Joe placed her third mug on the table before her.

'It helps me think,' she said, taking a sip.

There was a silence for a moment.

Elizabeth snapped out of her trance. 'OK, I've an idea.'

'Wow, that worked fast,' Benjamin smiled.

'What?' Elizabeth frowned.

'I said it—'

'OK,' Elizabeth interrupted, not hearing him in her rush of ideas. 'Let's say Mr Taylor is right and the legend lives on and people see this place as a place of love, blah dee blah.' She made a face, clearly not impressed by that belief. 'So there's a market there we need to cater for, which is where Poppy's ideas will work, but we'll keep them just to a minimum. Maybe a honeymoon suite and a snug thrown in here and there, the rest can be my designs,' she said happily. 'With a bit more colour,' she added with less enthusiasm.

Benjamin smiled when she'd finished. 'I'll run it by Vincent. Look, when I said earlier about you pulling it off in the meeting I didn't mean you hadn't the talent to back it up. I meant doing that whole *crazy* thing.' He circled his dirty fingers beside his temples.

Elizabeth's good mood vanished. 'Excuse me?'

'You know,' Benjamin smiled broadly, 'the whole I-see-dead-people-thing.'

Elizabeth stared at him blankly.

'You know, the *guy* at the table. The one you were talking to? Is this ringing any bells with you?'

'Ivan?' Elizabeth asked uncertainly.

'That's the name!' Benjamin snapped his fingers and bounced back in his chair, laughing. 'That's it, Ivan the very, very silent partner,' he laughed.

Elizabeth's eyebrows almost lifted off her forehead. 'Partner?'

Benjamin laughed even harder. 'Yeah, that's it, but don't tell him I said so, will you? I'd be so embarrassed if he ever found out.'

'Don't worry,' Elizabeth said drily, shocked by this information. 'I'll be seeing him later and I won't mention a word.'

'Neither will he,' Benjamin chuckled.

'Well, we'll see about that,' Elizabeth huffed. 'Although I was with him last night and he didn't say a word then either.'

Benjamin looked shocked by her. 'I don't think that kind of thing is allowed in Taylor Constructions. Office dating is strictly frowned upon. I mean, you never know, Ivan could be the reason you got the job in the first place.' He wiped his eyes wearily and his laughter calmed. 'When you think about it, isn't it amazing what we do to get jobs these days?'

Her mouth dropped.

'But it shows how much you love your job to be able to do a thing like that.' He looked at her in admiration. 'I don't think I could.' His shoulders shook again.

Elizabeth's mouth gaped even wider. Was he accusing her of sleeping with Ivan to get the job? She was rendered speechless.

'Anyway,' Benjamin said, standing up, 'it's been great meeting you. I'm glad we got the Moulin Rouge thing fixed up. I'll run it by Vincent and give you a call as soon as I know more. Do you have my number?' he asked, padding down his pockets. He reached into his front breast pocket and pulled out a leaking biro that had left a blob of ink at the bottom of his pocket. He grabbed a napkin from the dispenser and messily scrawled his name and number across the tissue.

'That's my cell number and the office number.' He handed it to her and pushed forward his leaking pen and a ripped napkin damp from his spilled coffee. 'Can I have yours? Saves me having to go through the files.'

Elizabeth was still angry and offended but reached into her bag, retrieved her leather-bound card holder and held out one of her gold-trimmed business cards. She would refrain from hitting him just this once; she needed this job. For Luke and her business's sakes, she would hold her tongue.

Benjamin flushed slightly. 'Oh right,' he retracted his torn napkin and leaking biro and took her card. 'That's a better idea, I guess.' He held out his hand to her.

She took one look at his hand stained with blue ink and with dirty fingernails, and she instantly sat on her hands.

After he had left, Elizabeth looked around in confusion, wondering if anyone else had witnessed what she had. Joe met her eyes, winked and tapped his nose as though they were sharing some sort of secret. After work she planned to collect Luke from Sam's house and although she knew Ivan and Sam's mother were no longer together she was hoping among all hopes that she would see him there.

To give him a piece of her mind, naturally.

Chapter 18

Mistake number one: going to Elizabeth's meeting. I shouldn't have done it. It's the same rule as not being allowed to go into school with our younger friends, and I should have had the sense to realise that Luke's school is the equivalent to Elizabeth's workplace. I could have kicked myself. Actually I did, but Luke thought it looked so funny that he started doing it to himself and now both his shins are bruised. So I stopped.

After I left the meeting I walked back to Sam's house, where Luke was being minded. I sat on the grass in the back garden, keeping an eye on them wrestling each other, hoping it wouldn't end in tears and also doing my favourite mental sport. Thinking.

It was constructive thinking too because I realised a few things. One of the things I learned was that I went to the meeting that morning because my gut feelings were telling me to. I couldn't figure out how my being there would possibly help Elizabeth but I had to go with my instincts and I just presumed she wouldn't see me. My meeting her the previous night had been so dreamlike and unexpected that I started the day feeling as if it was all in my imagination. And yes, I am aware of the irony there.

I was so happy she saw me. When I saw her swinging on that garden bench looking so lost, I knew that if she was ever going to see me that would be the time. I felt it in the air. I knew she needed to see me and I had prepared myself for the fact that one day she would, but I hadn't prepared myself for the shiver that ran up my spine when our eyes first locked together. It was odd because I'd been looking at Elizabeth for the past four days and I was used to her face, knew it inside out, could see it clearly even when I shut my eyes, knew that there was a tiny mole on her left temple, that one cheekbone was slightly higher than the other, that her bottom lip was larger than her top, that she had fine baby hair at the edge of her hairline. I knew it so well, but isn't it strange how different people can look when you actually look them in the eyes? They suddenly appear to be someone else. If you ask me, it's true what they say about eyes being the windows to your soul.

I had never felt that feeling before, but I put that down to not having been in the position before. I had never had a friendship with someone of Elizabeth's age and I supposed it was nerves. It was all a new experience for me but one I was immediately willing and able to take on.

There are two things that I am rarely. The first is confused and the second is worried, but while I waited in Sam's back garden on that sunny day, I was worried. And that confused me and because I was confused, that worried me even more. I was hoping I hadn't caused trouble for Elizabeth at work, but later that evening, as the sun and I were playing hide and seek, I soon found out.

The sun was trying to hide behind Sam's house, covering me in a blanket of shadow. I was moving around the garden, sitting in the very last patches of sun before they disappeared completely. Sam's mom was having a bath after doing a dance work-out video in her back room, which had been hugely entertaining, so when the doorbell rang Sam answered it. He was under strict instructions not to answer to anyone except Elizabeth.

'Hello, Sam,' I heard her say, stepping into the hall. 'Is your dad here?'

'No,' Sam replied, 'He's at work. Me and Luke are playing in the garden.'

I heard footsteps coming down the hall, the sound of heels on wood and then an angry voice as she stepped out into the garden.

'Oh, he's at work, is he?' Elizabeth said standing at the top of the garden with her hands on her hips looking down at me.

'Yeah, he is,' Sam said, confused, and ran off to play with Luke.

There was something so endearing about the sight of Elizabeth looking so bossy that it made me smile.

'Is something funny, Ivan?'

'Lots of things are,' I replied, sitting down on the only part of the grass that still had sun on it. I guess I won the hide-and-seek game. 'People getting splashed with puddles by passing cars, being tickled right here,' I gestured to my side, 'Chris Rock, Eddie Murphy in the second *Beverly Hills Cop* an—'

'What are you talking about?' She frowned, moving closer.

'Things that are funny.'

'What are you doing?' She stepped closer still.

'Trying to remember how to make a daisy chain. Opal's looked nice,' I looked up at her. 'Opal's my boss and she had them in her hair,' I explained. 'The grass is dry if you want to sit down.' I continued pulling daisies from the ground.

It took Elizabeth a moment to settle herself on the grass. She looked uncomfortable and made faces as though she was sitting on pins. After brushing invisible dirt off her slacks and attempting to sit on her hands so her bum wouldn't get grass stains, she resumed glaring at me.

'Is something the matter, Elizabeth? I sense that there is.'

'How acutely aware of you.'

'Thank you. It's part of my job but nice of you to compliment me.' I sensed her sarcasm.

'I've a bone to pick with you, Ivan.'

'A funny one, I hope.' I threaded one stalk through the other. 'There's another thing that's funny – funny bones. They hurt but they also make you laugh. Like lots of things in life, I suppose, or even life itself. Life is like a funny bone. Hmm.'

She looked at me in confusion. 'Ivan, I've come to give you a piece of my mind. I spoke to Benjamin today after you left and he told me you were a partner in the company. He also accused me of something else but I won't even get into that,' she fumed.

'You've come to give me a piece of your mind,' I repeated, looking at her. 'That phrase is really beautiful. The mind is the most powerful thing in the body, you know. Whatever the mind believes, the body can achieve. So to give someone a piece of it . . . well, thank you, Elizabeth. Funny how people are always intent on giving it to the people they dislike when it really should be for the ones they love. There's another funny thing. But a piece of your mind . . . what a gift that would be.' I looped the last stalk and formed a chain. 'I'll give you a daisy chain in return for a piece of your mind.' I slid the bracelet onto her arm.

She sat on the grass. Didn't move, didn't say anything, just looked at her daisy chain. Then she smiled and when she spoke her voice was soft. 'Has anyone ever been mad at you for more than five minutes?'

I looked at my watch, 'Yes. You, from ten o'clock this morning until now.'

She laughed. 'Why didn't you tell me that you work with Vincent Taylor?'

'Because I don't.'

'But Benjamin said that you did.'

'Who's Benjamin?'

'The project manager. He said you were a silent partner.'

I smiled. 'I suppose I am. He was being ironic, Elizabeth. I've nothing to do with the company. I'm so silent that I don't say anything at all.'

'Well, that's one side of you I've never met,' she smiled. 'So you're not actively involved with this project?'

'My work is with people, Elizabeth, not buildings.'

'Well then, what on earth was Benjamin talking about?' She was confused. 'He's an odd one, that Benjamin West. What business were you talking to Vincent about? What have children got to do with the hotel?'

'You're very nosy,' I laughed. 'Vincent Taylor and I weren't talking about any business.' Anyway, that's a good question – what do you think children *should* have to do with the hotel?'

'Absolutely nothing,' Elizabeth laughed, and then stopped abruptly, afraid she had offended me. 'You think the hotel should be child-friendly.'

I smiled. 'Don't you think everything and every*one* should be child-friendly?'

'I can think of a few exceptions,' Elizabeth said smartly, looking out to Luke.

I knew she was thinking of Saoirse and her father, possibly even herself.

'I'll talk to Vincent tomorrow about a playroom/play area kind of thing . . .' She trailed off. 'I've never designed a children's room before. What the hell do children want?'

'It will come easily to you, Elizabeth. You were a child once – what did you want?'

Her brown eyes darkened and she looked away. 'It's different now. Children don't want what I wanted then. Times have changed.'

'Not that much they haven't. Children always want the same things because they all need the same basic things.'

'Like what?'

'Well, why don't you tell me what you wanted and I'll let you know if they're the same things?'

Elizabeth laughed lightly. 'Do you always play games, Ivan?'

'Always,' I smiled. 'Tell me.'

She studied my eyes, battling with herself about whether to speak or not and after a few moments she took a deep breath. 'When I was a child, my mother and I would sit down at the kitchen table every Saturday night with our crayons and fancy paper and we'd write out a full plan of what we were going to do the next day.' Her eyes shone with the fondness of remembering. 'Every Saturday night I got so excited about how we were going to spend the next day, I'd pin the schedule up on the wall of my bedroom and force myself to go to sleep so that morning would come.' Her smile faded and she snapped out of her trance. 'But you can't incorporate those things into a playroom; children want PlayStations and Xboxes and that kind of thing.'

'Why don't you tell me what sorts of things were on the Sunday schedule?'

She looked away into the distance, 'They were collections of hopelessly impossible dreams. My mother promised me we would lie on our backs in the field at night, catch as many falling stars as we could and then make all the wishes our hearts desired. We talked about lying in great big baths filled up to our chins with cherry blossoms, tasting sun showers, twirling around in the village sprinklers that watered the grass in the summer, having a moon-lit dinner on the beach and then doing the soft-shoe shuffle in the sand.' Elizabeth laughed at the memory. 'It's all so silly, really when I say it aloud, but that's the way she was. She was playful and adventurous, wild and carefree, if not a bit eccentric. She always wanted to think of new things to see, taste and discover.'

'All those things must have been so much fun,' I said,

in awe of her mother. Tasting sun showers beat a toilet roll telescope any day.

'Oh, I don't know.' Elizabeth looked away and swallowed hard. 'We never actually did any of them.'

'But I bet you did them all a million times in your head,' I said.

'Well, there was one thing we did together. Just after she had Saoirse, she brought me out to the field, lay down a blanket and set down a picnic basket. We ate freshly-baked brown bread, still piping hot from the oven, with homemade strawberry jam.' Elizabeth closed her eyes and breathed in. 'I can still remember the smell and the taste.' She shook her head in wonder. 'But she chose to have the picnic in our cow field. There we were, in the middle of the field, having a picnic surrounded by curious cows.'

We both laughed.

'But that's when she told me she was going away. She was too big a person for this small town. It's not what she said but I know it must have been how she felt.' Elizabeth's voice trembled and she stopped talking. She watched Luke and Sam chasing each other around the garden but didn't see them, listened to their childish squeals of joy but didn't hear them. She shut it all out.

'Anyway,' her voice became serious again and she cleared her throat, 'that's irrelevant. It's got nothing to do with the hotel; I don't even know why I brought it up.'

She was embarrassed. I bet Elizabeth had never said all that aloud, ever in her life, and so I let the long silence sit between us as she worked it all out in her head.

'Do you and Fiona have a good relationship?' she asked, still not looking me in the eye after what she told me.

'Fiona?'

'Yes, the woman you're not married to.' She smiled for the first time and seemed to settle.

'Fiona doesn't talk to me,' I replied, still confused as to why she thought I was Sam's dad. I would have to have a chat with Luke about that one. I wasn't comfortable with this case of mistaken identity.

'Did things end badly between you both?'

'They never began to be able to end,' I answered honestly.

'I know that feeling.' She rolled her eyes and laughed. 'At least one good thing came out of it, though.' She looked away and watched Sam and Luke playing. She had been referring to Sam but I got the feeling she was looking at Luke and I was pleased at that.

Before we left Sam's house, Elizabeth turned to me. 'Ivan, I've never spoken to anyone about what I said before,' she swallowed, 'ever. I don't know what made me blurt it out.'

'I know,' I smiled, 'so thank you for giving me a very big piece of your mind. I think that deserves another daisy chain,' I held out another bracelet I'd made.

Mistake number two: when sliding it onto her wrist, I felt myself give her a little piece of my heart.

Chapter 19

After the day I gave Elizabeth the daisy chains . . . and my heart, I learned far more about her than just what she and her mother did on Saturday evenings. I realised she's like one of those cockles that you see clinging to the rocks down on Fermoy beach. You know by looking at it that it's loose but as soon as you touch it or get close to it, it seizes up and clings onto the rock's surface for life. That's what Elizabeth was like: open until someone came near and then she'd tense up, and cling on for dear life. Sure, she opened up to me on that day in the back garden, but then the next day when I dropped by it was as though she was mad at me because she'd talked about it. But that was Elizabeth all round – mad at everyone including herself – and she was probably embarrassed. It wasn't often Elizabeth told anybody anything about herself unless she was talking to customers about her company.

It was difficult to spend time with Luke now that Elizabeth could see me and, frankly she would have been worried if I'd knocked on her fuchsia door to ask her if Luke was coming out to play. She has a thing about friends being a certain age. The important thing, though, was that Luke didn't seem to mind. He was always so busy playing with Sam and whenever Luke decided to include me, it would make Sam frustrated because he couldn't see me, of course. I think I was getting in Luke's way of playing with Sam and I don't think Luke was bothered if I showed up or not because it wasn't him I was there for, you see, and I think he knew it. I told you kids always know what's going on, even before you know yourself sometimes.

As for Elizabeth, I think she'd go crazy if I just strolled into her living room at twelve o'clock at night. A new kind of friendship meant that there had to be new boundaries. I had to be subtle, call round less yet still be there for her at the right moments. Like an adult friendship.

One thing I definitely didn't like was the fact that Elizabeth thought that I was Sam's dad. I don't know how that started and without me even saying anything it just kept going. I never lie to my friends, ever, so I tried many times to tell her that I wasn't Sam's dad. One of the times, the conversation went like this.

'So where are you from, Ivan?'

It was one evening after Elizabeth had been at work. She had just finished a meeting with Vincent Taylor about the hotel and apparently, according to her, she just walked right up to him and told him she had been speaking with Ivan and we both felt the hotel needed a children's area to give the parents even more relaxing romantic time together. Well, Vincent laughed so much that he just gave in and agreed. She's still confused as to why he thought it was so funny. I told her it was because Vincent hadn't a clue who I was and she just rolled her eyes at me and accused me of being secretive. Anyway, because of that, she was in a good mood so she was ready to talk, for a change. I was wondering when she'd start asking me questions (other than the ones about my job, how many staff we had, what was the turnover every year. She bored me to tears with all that kind of stuff).

But she'd finally asked me where I was from so happily I answered, 'Ekam Eveileb.'

She frowned. 'That name is familiar; I've heard of it somewhere before. Where is it?'

'A million miles from here.'

'Baile na gCroíthe is a million miles from everywhere. Ekam Eveileb . . .' she allowed the words to roll off her tongue, 'what does that mean? That's not Irish *or* English, is it?'

'It's draw kcab-ish.'

'Draw Cab?' she repeated, raising an eyebrow. 'Honestly, Ivan, sometimes you're as bad as Luke. I think he gets most of his sayings from you.'

I chuckled.

'In fact,' Elizabeth leaned forward, 'I didn't want to say this to you before but I think he looks up to you.'

'Really?' I was flattered.

'Well, yes, because . . . well,' she searched for the correct words, 'please don't think my nephew is insane or anything but last week he invented this friend.' She laughed nervously. 'We had him over in the house for dinner for a few days, they chased each other around outside, played everything from football, to the computer to *cards*, can you believe it? But the funny thing is that his name was *Ivan.*'

My blank reaction started her back-tracking and she blushed wildly. 'Well, actually it's not funny at all, it's completely preposterous, *of course*, but I thought that maybe it meant that he looked up to you and saw you as some sort of male role model . . .' she trailed off. 'Anyway, Ivan's gone now. He left us. All alone. It was devastating as you can imagine. I was told that they could stay around for as long as *three* months.' She made a face. 'Thank God he left. I had the date marked off on the calendar and everything,' she said, her face still red. 'Actually, funnily enough, he left when you arrived. I think you scared Ivan off . . . Ivan.' She laughed but my blank face caused her to stop and sigh. 'Ivan, why am I the only one talking?'

'Because I'm listening.'

'Well, I'm finished now so you can say something,' she snapped.

I laughed. She always got mad when she felt stupid. 'I have a theory.'

'Good, share it with me for once. Unless it's to put me and my nephew in a grey concrete building run by nuns with bars on the windows.'

I looked at her in horror.

'Go on,' she laughed.

'Well, who's to say that Ivan disappeared?'

Elizabeth looked horrified. 'No one says he disappeared because he never appeared in the first place.'

'He did to Luke.'

'Luke made him up.'

'Maybe he didn't.'

'Well, I didn't see him.'

'You see me.'

'What have you got to do with Luke's *invisible* friend?'

'Maybe I *am* Luke's friend, only I don't like being called invisible. It's not very PC.'

'But I can see you.'

'Exactly, so I don't know why people insist on saying "invisible". If *someone* can see me then surely that's visible. Think about it – has Ivan, Luke's friend, and me ever been in the same room at the same time?'

'Well, he could be here right now, for all we know, eating olives or something,' she laughed, then suddenly stopped, realising Ivan was no longer smiling. 'What are you talking about, Ivan?'

'It's very simple, Elizabeth. You said that Ivan disappeared when I arrived.'

'Yes.'

'Don't you think that means that I'm Ivan and you just suddenly started seeing me?'

Elizabeth looked angry. 'No, because you are a real person with a real life and you have a wife and a child and you—'

'I'm not married to Fiona, Elizabeth.'

'Ex-wife then, it's not the point.'

'I was never married to her.'

'Well, far be it for me to judge.'

'No, I mean Sam isn't my son.' My voice sounded more forceful than I intended. Children understand these things far better. Adults always make things so complicated.

Elizabeth's face softened and she reached out to put her hand on mine. Her hands were delicate, with baby-soft skin and long slender fingers.

'Ivan,' she spoke gently, 'we have something in common. Luke isn't my son either,' she smiled. 'But I think it's great that you still want to see Sam.'

'No, no, you don't understand, Elizabeth. I'm *nothing* to Fiona, and I'm *nothing* to Sam. They don't see me like you do, they don't even *know* me, that's what I'm trying to tell you. I'm invisible to them. I'm invisible to everybody else but you and Luke.'

Elizabeth's eyes filled with tears and her grip tightened. 'I understand,' her voice shook. She placed her other hand on mine and clung to it tightly. She struggled with her thoughts. I could tell she wanted to say something but couldn't. Her brown eyes searched mine and after a moment's silence, looking as though she had found what she was looking for, her face finally softened. 'Ivan, you have no idea how similar you and I are, and it's such a *relief* to hear you talking like this because I sometimes feel invisible to everybody too, you know?' Her voice sounded lonely. 'I feel like nobody knows me, that nobody sees me how I really am . . . except you.'

She looked so upset that I put my arms around her. Still I couldn't help feeling so disappointed that she'd completely misunderstood me, which was odd, because my friendships aren't supposed to be about me, or what I want. And it had never been about me before.

But as I lay down alone that night and processed all the information of the day, I realised that for the first time in my life, Elizabeth was the only friend I had ever met who had completely understood me after all.

And for anyone who's ever had that connection with someone, even if it only lasted for five minutes, it's important. For once I didn't feel that I was living in a different world from everyone else, but that, in fact, there was a person, a person I *liked* and *respected*, who had a piece of my heart, who felt the same way.

You all know exactly how I was feeling that night.

I didn't feel so alone. Even better than that, I felt as if I was floating on air.

Chapter 20

The weather had changed overnight. The past week of June sunshine had burned the grass, dried the soil and brought wasps in their thousands to swarm around and annoy everyone. Saturday evening it all changed. The sky darkened and the clouds had moved in. But that was typical Irish weather: one moment a heat wave and the next, gale-force winds. It was predictably unpredictable.

Elizabeth shivered in her bed and pulled her duvet up to her chin. She didn't have the heating on and even though she needed it she refused to put it on during the summer months as a principle. Outside the trees shivered, their leaves tossed in the wind. They cast wild shadows across her bedroom walls. The fierce gusts blowing sounded like giant waves crashing against the cliffs. Inside, the doors rattled and shuddered. The bench in the garden swung back and forth, squeaking. Everything moved violently and sporadically; there was no rhythm and no sense of consistency.

Elizabeth wondered about Ivan. She wondered why she was feeling a pull towards him, and why every time she opened her mouth the world's best-kept secrets flowed out. She wondered why she welcomed him into her home and into her head. Elizabeth loved to be alone – she didn't crave companionship – but she craved Ivan's companionship. She wondered if she should take a few steps back because of Fiona living only down the road. Wouldn't her closeness to Ivan, albeit only a friendship, be disturbing for Sam *and* Fiona? She relied so much on Fiona to mind Luke at last-minute notice.

As usual, Elizabeth tried to ignore such thoughts. She tried to pretend that everything was the same as always, that there hadn't been a shift within her, that her walls weren't crumbling down and allowing in unwelcome guests. She didn't want that to happen, she couldn't deal with change.

Eventually she focused on the only thing that remained constant and unmoving in the determined gusts. And in return, the moon kept its watchful eye on her as she eventually fell into an uneasy sleep.

'Cock-a-doodle-doo!'

Elizabeth opened one eye, confused at the sound. The room was bright. She slowly opened the other eye and saw that the sun had returned and was perched low in the cloudless blue sky, yet the trees were still dancing wildly, having a disco in the back garden.

'Cock-a-doodle-doo!'

There it was again. Feeling groggy from her sleep, she dragged herself out of bed and to the window. Out on the grass in the garden stood Ivan, hands cupped to his mouth shouting, 'Cock-a-doodle-doo!'

Elizabeth covered her mouth, laughing, and pushed open the window. The wind rushed in.

'Ivan, what are you doing?'

'This is your wake-up call!' he shouted, the wind stealing the end of his words and taking them north.

'You are crazy!' she yelled.

Luke appeared at her bedroom door, looking afraid. 'What's happening?'

Elizabeth motioned for Luke to come to the window and he relaxed as he saw Ivan standing outside.

'Hi, Ivan!' Luke yelled.

Ivan looked up and smiled, removed his hand from holding down his cap to wave at Luke. His cap disappeared from his head as a sudden great big gust of wind lifted it off. They laughed as they watched him chase it across the garden, dashing to and fro as the wind's direction changed. Eventually he used a fallen branch to knock it down from a tree where it was caught.

'Ivan, what are you doing out there?' Luke yelled.

'It's Jinny Joe day!' Ivan announced, holding his arms out to display his surroundings.

'What's that?' Luke looked at Elizabeth, confused.

'I have no idea,' she shrugged.

'What's Jinny Joe day, Ivan?' Luke yelled.

'Come on down and I'll show you both!' Ivan replied, his loose clothes flapping around his body.

'We're not dressed, we're in our pyjamas!' Luke giggled.

'Well then, get dressed! Just throw anything on, it's six a.m., no one's going to see us!'

'Come on!' Luke said excitedly to Elizabeth, clambering off the windowsill, running out of her room and returning minutes later with one leg in his tracksuit bottoms, an inside-out sweater on and his runners on the wrong feet.

Elizabeth laughed.

'Come on, hurry!' he said, gasping for breath.

'Calm down, Luke.'

'No.' Luke threw open Elizabeth's wardrobe. 'Get dressed, IT'S JINNY JOE DAY!' he shouted with a toothless grin.

'But, Luke,' Elizabeth said uneasily, 'where are we supposed to be going?' She was looking for reassurance from a six-year-old.

Luke shrugged. 'Somewhere fun?'

Elizabeth thought about it, saw the excitement in Luke's eyes, felt the curiosity welling within her, went against her better judgement, threw on a tracksuit and ran outside with Luke.

The warm wind hit her as she stepped outside, taking her breath away.

'To the Bat Mobile!' Ivan announced, meeting them at the front door.

Luke giggled with excitement.

Elizabeth froze. 'Where?'

'The car,' Luke explained.

'Where are we going?'

'Just drive and I'll tell you when to stop. It's a surprise.'

'No,' Elizabeth said as if it were the most ridiculous thing she had ever heard. 'I never get into the car unless I know exactly where I'm going,' she huffed.

'You do it every morning,' Ivan said softly.

She ignored him.

Luke held the door open for Ivan and once they were all in, Elizabeth very uncomfortably set out on her journey with an unknown destination, feeling that she wanted to turn the car round at every turn and then wondering why she wasn't.

After driving for twenty minutes through winding roads, an agitated Elizabeth followed Ivan's directions for the last time and pulled up outside a field that, to her, looked the same as all the others they had passed. Except this one had a view over the glistening Atlantic Ocean. She ignored the scenery and fumed in her wing mirror at the mud splashed along the side of her shining car.

'Wow, what are they?' Luke leaped forward between the two front seats and pointed out the front window.

'Luke, my friend,' Ivan announced happily, 'they are what you call Jinny Joes.'

Elizabeth looked up. Ahead of her were hundreds of dandelion seeds, blowing in the wind, catching the light of the sun with their white fluffy threads and floating towards the three in the car like dreams.

'They look like fairies,' Luke said in amazement.

Elizabeth rolled her eyes. 'Fairies,' she tutted. 'What

books have you been reading? They're dandelion seeds, Luke.'

Ivan looked at her in frustration. 'How did I know you'd say that? Well, I got you here, at least. I suppose *that's* something.'

Elizabeth looked at him in surprise. He had never snapped at her like that before.

'Luke,' Ivan turned to him, 'they're also known as the Irish Daisy but they're not only dandelion seeds, they are what most *normal* people,' he threw Elizabeth a nasty look, 'call Jinny Joes. They carry wishes in the wind and you're supposed to catch them in your hand, make your wish and then let them go so they can deliver them.'

Elizabeth snorted.

'Wow,' Luke whispered. 'But why do people do that?'

Elizabeth laughed. 'That's my boy.'

Ivan ignored her. 'Hundreds of years ago people used to eat the green leaves of the dandelion plant because they are extremely high in vitamins,' he explained, 'which gave it its Latin name, which translates as the "official cure of all ills". So people see them as good luck and now make their wishes on the seeds.'

'Do the wishes come true?' he asked hopefully.

Elizabeth looked at Ivan angrily for filling her nephew's head with false hopes.

'Only the ones that are delivered properly, so who knows? Remember, even the post gets lost sometimes, Luke.'

Luke nodded his head, understanding. 'OK then, let's go catch them!'

'You two go on, I'll wait here in the car,' Elizabeth said, staring straight ahead.

Ivan sighed. 'Eliza—'

'I'll wait here,' she said firmly, turning on the radio and settling down to show them she wasn't budging.

Luke climbed out of the car and she turned to Ivan. 'I think it's ridiculous that you fill his head with these lies,' she fumed. 'What are you going to tell him when absolutely nothing he wishes for comes true?'

'How do you know it won't come true?'

'I have *common sense.* Something which you seem to be lacking.'

'You're right, I don't have common sense. I don't want to believe what every one else believes. I have my *own* thoughts, things that weren't taught to me or things that I didn't read in a book. I learn from experience – you, you are afraid to experience anything and so you will always have your common sense and only your common sense.'

Elizabeth looked out the window, counting to ten so that she wouldn't explode. She hated all this new-age crap; contrary to what he said, she believed it was *exactly* the kind of thing that could be learned only from books. Written and read by people who spent their life searching for something, *anything*, to take them away from the boredom that was their real life. People who had to believe that there was always more than the very obvious reason, for everything.

'You know, Elizabeth, a dandelion is also known as a love herb. Some say that to blow the seeds upon the winds will carry your love to your lover. If you blow the puff ball while making a wish and succeed in blowing off all the seeds, your wish will come true.'

Elizabeth frowned in confusion. 'Stop your gobbledygook, Ivan.'

'Very well. For today, Luke and I will settle for catching Jinny Joes. I thought you always wanted to catch a wish?' Ivan asked.

Elizabeth looked away. 'I know what you're doing, Ivan and it won't work. I told you about my childhood in the strictest of confidence. It took a lot for me to say the things I said. It wasn't so you could turn it into some game,' she hissed.

'This is not a game,' Ivan said quietly. He clambered out of the car.

'Everything is a game to you,' Elizabeth snapped. 'Tell me, how is it you know so much about dandelion seeds? What exactly is the point of all your silly information?'

Ivan leaned forward through the open door and spoke softly. 'Well, I think it's quite obvious that if you're going to rely on something to carry your wishes in the wind, you might as well know where exactly it has come from and where it intends on going.'

The door slammed shut.

Elizabeth watched them both run to the field. 'Then if that's so, where exactly are you from, Ivan?' she asked aloud. 'And where and when do you intend going?'

Chapter 21

Elizabeth watched as Ivan and Luke darted around the long grass in the field, jumping and diving to catch the dandelion seeds that floated in the air like balls of feathers.

'I got one!' she heard Luke yell.

'Make a wish,' Ivan whooped.

Luke pressed it between his hand and squeezed his eyes shut. 'I wish that Elizabeth would get out of the car and play Jinny Joes!' he roared. He lifted his podgy hand to the air, opened his tiny fingers slowly and released the ball to the wind, which carried it away.

Ivan raised his eyebrows at Elizabeth.

Luke watched the car to see if his wish came true.

As much as Elizabeth watched his hopeful little face she couldn't bring herself to do it – to get out of the car and make Luke believe in fairy tales, just a fancy word for lies. She wouldn't do it. But again she watched as Luke raced around the field, holding his arms out. He caught the seed, grasped it tightly and shouted the same wish.

Her chest tightened and her breathing quickened. They both watched her with such hope in their eyes and she felt the pressure of being relied upon. It was only a game, she tried to convince herself; all she had to do was get out of the car. But it meant more to her than that. It meant filling a child's head with thoughts and ideas that would never happen. It meant sacrificing a moment of fun for a lifetime of disappointment. She gripped the steering wheel so tightly her knuckles were white.

Again a joyful Luke jumped up and down, trying to catch another. He repeated his wish at the top of his lungs this time adding, 'Please, please, please, Jinny Joe!' Holding up his arm he looked like the Statue of Liberty and then he released the ball of seeds.

Ivan didn't do anything. He just stood still in the field observing it all with a look and presence Elizabeth felt so drawn to. She saw the frustration and disappointment growing in Luke's face as he caught another, squashed it angrily between his hands and let it go with an attempt to kick it into the air.

Already he was losing faith and she hated to be the one to be the cause of that. She took a deep breath and reached for the door handle. Luke's face lit up and immediately began chasing more. As she walked onto the field, the fuchsias danced wildly, like spectators waving their red and purple flags to welcome a player on to the field.

Driving slowly by in his tractor, Brendan Egan almost drove into a ditch at the sight he saw in a faraway field. With the sparkling sea and the sun in the background he could see two dark figures dancing around in the field. One was a woman whose long black hair was being caught by the wind and wildly draped around her face and neck. She was whooping and hollering with joy as she leaped about with a young child, trying to catch the dandelion seeds that were parachuting in the wind.

Brendan stopped the tractor and stopped breathing in shock at the familiar sight. It was as though he was seeing a ghost. His body shook as he watched in wonder and fright until a beeping behind him startled him and urged him on.

Benjamin was driving back from Killarney at 6.30 on Sunday morning, enjoying the sea view, when a tractor in the middle of the road caused him to step on the brakes. Inside the cab was an old man with a face as white as a sheet, looking into the distance. Benjamin followed his gaze. His face broke into a smile as he spotted Elizabeth Egan dancing with a young boy in a field filled with dandelions. She was laughing and cheering, bounding about. She was dressed in a tracksuit, her hair was down, loose and blowing freely instead of being tied back severely. He hadn't thought she had a son but he watched her lifting him up into the air, helping him to reach something and swinging him back down again. The little blond boy giggled with delight and Benjamin smiled, enjoying the sight. He could have watched her all morning but a beeping from behind startled him and as the tractor's engine started up and moved on, they both crawled down the road slowly, still watching Elizabeth.

Inventing imaginary men and dancing around fields at 6.30 on a Sunday morning . . . Benjamin couldn't help but laugh and admire her for her fun and energy for life. She never seemed to be afraid of what anyone thought. As he continued down the winding road his view of her became clearer. On Elizabeth's face was an expression of pure happiness. She looked like a completely different woman.

Chapter 22

Elizabeth felt giddy with delight as she drove back to town with Luke and Ivan. They had spent the past two hours chasing and catching what Ivan insisted she called Jinny Joes. Then when they were tired and out of breath they had collapsed in a heap in the long grass, breathing in the fresh early morning sea air. Elizabeth couldn't remember the last time she had laughed so much. In fact, she didn't think she had *ever* laughed so much in her life.

Ivan seemed to have boundless energy, with an appetite for all things new and exciting. Elizabeth hadn't felt excited in a very long time; it wasn't a feeling she associated with her adult life. She hadn't felt the tingle of anticipation in her stomach since she was a child; she hadn't looked forward to anything so much she felt she would burst if it didn't happen right here, right now. But being with Ivan brought all those feelings back. Time went so fast when she was with him, whether they were leaping in fields or simply sitting in each other's company in silence, as they so often did. She always wished for time to slow down when he was there, and when he left her she always felt she wanted more. She had caught many dandelion seeds that morning and among her many wishes had been for their time spent together that day to be longer and for the wind to keep up so she could hold on to the moment, with Luke too.

She likened it to a childhood crush, such strong, almost

obsessive, feelings – but *more*, it had depth. She felt attracted to everything about Ivan – the way he talked, the way he dressed, the words he used, his apparent innocence yet he was filled with a deep knowledge of wise insights. He always said the right things, even when she didn't want to hear them. The darkness lifted from the end of her tunnels and she could suddenly see *beyond*. When he breezed into the room he brought clarity and brightness with him. He was walking hope, and she could tell that things for her could be, not fantastic or wonderful or happily-ever-after, but that they could be OK. And that was enough for Elizabeth.

He filled her head every moment; she recounted conversations over and over. She asked him question after question and he was always so open and honest in his answers, but then later, while lying in bed, she would realise she knew no more about him than before, despite his replies to every question. But she sensed that they were very similar beings. Two solitary people blowing around in the breeze like dandelion seeds, carrying each other's wishes.

Of course she felt frightened by her feelings. Of course it went against the grain of her every belief, but as much as she tried, she couldn't stop her heartbeat from quickening when his skin brushed against hers, she couldn't stop herself from seeking him out when she thought he might be nearby. She couldn't prevent him from invading her thoughts. He was welcoming himself into her arms even when they weren't open; he was dropping by her home uninvited yet she couldn't stop herself from opening her door time and time again.

She was attracted to his presence, to how he made her feel, to his silences and his words. She was falling in love with him.

On Monday morning Elizabeth found herself walking into Joe's with a spring in her step, humming the same song she'd been humming for the last week and couldn't seem to get out of her head. It was 8.30 and the café was crowded with tourists who had stopped for their breakfast before heading back to their coach, which would take hours to deliver them to the next stopping place. The café was noisy with chatter in German. Joe was rushing around collecting used crockery, bringing it to the kitchen and returning with plates full of Irish breakfasts that his wife had prepared.

Elizabeth signalled to him for a coffee and he quickly nodded his head in acknowledgement, having no time for gossip today. She looked for a seat and her heart quickened at the sight of Ivan in the far corner of the room. She couldn't control the smile that broke over her face. She felt the excitement rushing around her body as she wound her way between the tables to get to him. Elizabeth was overwhelmed by the sight of him.

'Hello,' she breathed, noticing the change in her voice, and hating herself for it.

'Morning, Elizabeth,' he smiled. His voice was different too.

They both sensed it, sensed *something*, and just stared at one another.

'Kept you a table.'

'Thanks.'

Smiles.

'Can I take a breakfast order?' Joe asked her, pen and pad in hand.

Elizabeth usually didn't eat breakfast, but by the way Ivan was looking through the menu she thought she could just be a few minutes late to the office for a change.

'Can I have a second menu, please, Joe?'

Joe glared at her. 'Why do you want a second menu?'

'So I can read it,' she stated.

'What's wrong with the one on the table?' he said moodily.

'OK, OK,' she backed off, leaning closer to Ivan to share the menu.

Joe eyed her suspiciously.

'I think I'll have the Irish breakfast,' Ivan said, licking his lips.

'I'll have the same,' Elizabeth said to Joe.

'The same as what?'

'The Irish breakfast.'

'OK, so one Irish breakfast and a coffee.'

'No,' Elizabeth's forehead wrinkled, '*two* Irish breakfasts and *two* coffees.'

'Eatin' for two, are ye?' Joe asked, looking her up and down.

'No!' Elizabeth exclaimed, and turned to Ivan with an apologetic look on her face when Joe had walked away. 'Sorry about him; he acts oddly sometimes.'

Joe placed the two coffees on the table, eyed her suspiciously and hurried off to serve another table.

'Busy in here today.' Elizabeth barely even looked away from him.

'Is it?' he asked, not moving his eyes from hers.

A tingle ran through Elizabeth's body. 'I like it when the town's like this. It brings it to life. I don't know what Ekam Eveileb is like, but here you get sick of seeing the same people all the time. Tourists change the scenery, give you something to hide behind.'

'Why would you want to hide?'

'Ivan, the whole town knows about me. They practically know more about my family history than I do.'

'I don't listen to the town, I listen to you.'

'I know. During the summer, the place is like a big tree, strong and beautiful,' she tried to explain, 'but in winter, it's robbed of its leaves, standing bare, with nothing to cover you or give you privacy. I always feel like I'm on display.'

'You don't like living here?'

'It's not that. It's just it needs some livening up sometimes, a real kick in the behind. I sit in here every morning and dream of pouring my coffee all over the streets, to give it the buzz it needs to waken the place up.'

'Well then, why don't you?'

'What do you mean?'

Ivan stood up. 'Elizabeth Egan, come with me and bring your coffee cup.'

'Bu—'

'No buts, just come.' With that he walked out of the café.

She followed him in confusion, carrying her cup outside.

'Well?' she asked, taking a sip.

'Well, I think it's high time you gave this town a caffeine high,' Ivan announced, looking up and down the empty street.

Elizabeth stared at him blankly.

'Go on.' He tapped her cup slightly and milky coffee sploshed over the side and onto the pavement. 'Oops,' he said drily.

Elizabeth laughed at him. 'You're so silly, Ivan.'

'Why am I silly? You're the one that suggested it.' He hit her cup again, harder this time, sending more coffee dripping to the ground. Elizabeth let out a shout and jumped back to avoid it staining her shoes.

She attracted a few stares from inside the café.

'Go on, Elizabeth!'

It was ludicrous, preposterous, ridiculous and completely juvenile. It didn't make sense to do it, but remembering the fun in the field yesterday, how she laughed and how she floated for the remainder of the day, she craved more of that feeling. She toppled the cup to the side, allowing the coffee to fall to the ground. It first formed a pool, then she watched it flow down the cracks in the slabs of stones and run slowly down the street.

'Come on, that won't even have woken the insects up,' Ivan teased.

'Well then, stand back.' She raised an eyebrow. Ivan stepped away as Elizabeth held out her arm and spun around on the spot. The coffee shot out as though in a fountain.

Joe stuck his head out the door. 'What are you upta, Elizabeth? Did I make a bad cuppa?' He looked worried. 'You're not making me look good in front of these folk.' He nodded towards the tourists gathered at the window, watching her.

Ivan laughed. 'I think this calls for another cup of coffee,' he announced.

'Another cup?' Elizabeth asked startled.

'OK so,' Joe said, slowly backing up.

'Excuse me, what is she doing?' a tourist asked Joe as he headed back inside.

'Ah, 'tis a, eh,' Joe floundered, ''tis a custom we have here in Baile na gCroíthe. Every Monday morning we just, eh,' he looked back at Elizabeth, standing alone, laughing and twirling as she splattered coffee on the pavement, 'we like to splatter the coffee around, you see. It's good for the, eh,' he watched as it splashed over his window boxes, 'flowers,' he gulped.

The man's eyebrows rose with interest and he smiled in amusement. 'In that case, five more cups of coffee for my dear friends.'

Joe looked uncertain, then his face broke into a great big smile as the money was thrust towards him. 'Five cups on the way.'

Moments later Elizabeth was joined by five strangers who danced around beside her, whooping and hollering as they spilled coffee down the pavement. This made her and Ivan laugh even more until eventually they escaped the crowd, who were giving each other secret looks of confusion over the silly Irish custom of spilling coffee on the ground, but who were finding amusement in it all the same.

Elizabeth looked around the village in astonishment. Shopkeepers stood at their front doors watching the commotion outside Joe's. Windows opened and heads peaked out. Cars slowed down to have a look, causing the traffic behind to beep in frustration. In a matter of moments a sleepy town had woken.

'What's wrong?' Ivan asked, wiping the tears of laughter from his eyes. 'Why have you stopped laughing?'

'Are there no such things as dreams to you, Ivan? Can't some things remain only in your head?' As far as she could see he could make everything happen. Well, almost everything. She looked up into his blue eyes and her heart beat wildly.

He gazed down at her and took a step closer. He looked so serious, and older than he had previously appeared, as if he had seen and learned something new in the last few seconds. He placed a soft hand on her cheek and moved his head slowly towards her face. 'No,' he whispered, and kissed her so gently on the lips her knees almost buckled beneath her, '*everything* must come true.'

Joe looked out the window and laughed at the tourists dancing and splattering coffee outside his shop. Catching a glimpse of Elizabeth across the road, Joe moved closer to the window to get a better look. She held her head high in the air with her eyes closed in perfect bliss. Her hair, which was usually tied back, was down and blowing in the light morning breeze and she looked to be revelling in the sun shining down on her face.

Joe could have sworn he saw her mother in that face.

Chapter 23

It took Ivan and Elizabeth's mouths a while to pull away from one another but when they finally did, with tingling lips Elizabeth half skipped, half walked along the path to her office. She felt if she lifted her feet any higher from the ground she would float away. Humming as she tried to control her non-flight, she bumped straight into Mrs Bracken, who stood in her doorway, eyeing up the tourists across the road.

'Jesus!' Elizabeth jumped back in fright.

'Is the son of God, who sacrificed his life and died on the cross to spread the Lord's word and to give you a better life, so don't take his name in vain,' Mrs Bracken rattled off. She nodded in the direction of the café. 'What are those foreigners up to at all, at all?'

Elizabeth bit her lip and tried not to laugh. 'I have no idea. Why don't you join them?'

'Mr Bracken wouldn't be pleased about that carry-on at all.' She must have sensed something in Elizabeth's voice because her head shot up, her eyes narrowed and she studied Elizabeth's face intently. 'You look different.'

Elizabeth ignored her and laughed as Joe guiltily mopped up the coffee on the pavement.

'You've been spending time up at that tower?' Mrs Bracken accused her.

'Of course I have Mrs Bracken. I'm designing the place, remember? And by the way, I've ordered the fabric; it should be arriving in three weeks, which gives us two months to get everything ready. Do you think you can get some extra help here?'

Mrs Bracken's eyes narrowed suspiciously. 'Your hair's down.'

'And?' Elizabeth asked, moving into the fabric shop to see if her order had arrived.

'And Mr Bracken used to say beware of a woman who drastically changes her hair.'

'I would hardly call letting my hair down a drastic change.'

'Elizabeth Egan, for you of all people, I would call letting your hair down a drastic change. By the way,' she moved on quickly, not allowing Elizabeth to get a word in, 'there's a problem with the order that came in today.'

'What's wrong with it?'

'It's *colourful*.' She said the word as if it were a disease and, widening her eyes, she emphasised it even more: '*Red*.'

Elizabeth smiled. 'It's raspberry, not red, and what's wrong with a bit of colour?'

'What's wrong with a bit of colour, she says.' Mrs Bracken raised her voice an octave. 'Up until last week your world was brown. It's the tower that's doing it to you. The American fella, isn't it?'

'Oh, don't you start with that tower talk as well,' Elizabeth dismissed her. 'I've been up there all week, and all it is is a crumbling wall.'

'A crumbling wall is right,' Mrs Bracken said, eyeing her, 'and it's the American fella that's knocking it.'

Elizabeth rolled her eyes. 'Goodbye, Mrs Bracken.' She ran upstairs to her office.

On her entry a pair of legs sticking out from underneath Poppy's desk greeted her. They were men's legs – brown cords with brown shoes moving and squiggling around.

'Is that you, Elizabeth?' a voice shouted out.

'Yes, Harry,' Elizabeth smiled. Oddly, she was finding the two people who usually irritated her on a daily basis strangely lovable. Ivan was certainly passing the silly smile test.

'I'm just tightening up this chair. Poppy told me it was acting up on ya last week.'

'It was, Harry, thanks.'

'No problem.' His legs slithered up under the desk and disappeared as he struggled to his feet. Banging his head against the desk he finally appeared, his bald head covered by spaghetti-strings of hair brushed over from one side to the other.

'Ah, there you are,' he said, popping his head up, spanner in hand. 'It shouldn't spin on its own any more. Funny that it did that.' He gave it one last check, then looked at Elizabeth with the same expression as the one he had when examining the chair. 'You look different.'

'No, I'm still the same,' she said, walking through to her office.

'It's the hair. The hair's down. I always say it's better for a woman's hair to be down and—'

'Thank you, Harry. Will that be all?' Elizabeth said firmly, ending the conversation.

'Oh, right so.' His cheeks flushed as he waved her off and made his way downstairs, no doubt to gossip to Mrs Bracken about Elizabeth's hair being down.

Elizabeth settled at her desk and tried to concentrate on her work but found herself gently placing her fingers on her lips, reliving the kiss with Ivan.

'OK,' Poppy said, entering Elizabeth's office and placing a money box on her desk. 'See this here?'

Elizabeth nodded at the little pig. Becca stood at the door in the background.

'Well, I've come up with a plan.' Poppy gritted her teeth. 'Every time you start to hum that bloody song of yours, you have to put money in the pig.'

Elizabeth raised her eyebrows in amusement. 'Poppy, did you *make* this pig?' she stared at the papier-mâché pig sitting on her desk.

Poppy tried to hide her smile. 'It was a quiet night last night. But, seriously, it's getting beyond irritating now, Elizabeth, you've got to believe me,' Poppy pleaded. 'Even Becca is sick of it.'

'Is that right, Becca?'

Becca's cheeks pinked and she walked away quickly, not wanting to be dragged into the conversation.

'Great backup,' Poppy grumbled.

'So who gets the money?' Elizabeth asked.

'The pig. He's raising funds for a new sty. Hum a song and support a pig,' she said, quickly thrusting the pig in Elizabeth's face.

Elizabeth tried not to laugh. 'Out.'

Moments later, after they had settled down and gone back to work, Becca came charging into the office, placed the pig on the table and said with wide eyes, 'Pay!'

'Was I humming it again?' Elizabeth asked in surprise.

'Yes,' she hissed, her patience frayed, and turned on her heel.

Later that afternoon Becca brought a visitor into Elizabeth's office.

'Hello, Mrs Collins,' Elizabeth said politely, nerves forming in the pit of her stomach. Mrs Collins ran the B&B Saoirse had been staying in for the past few weeks. 'Please, sit down.' She indicated the chair before her.

'Thank you.' Mrs Collins took a seat. 'And call me Margaret.' She looked around the room like a frightened child who had been called to the principal's office. She kept her hands clasped on her lap as though afraid to touch anything. Her blouse was buttoned up to her chin.

'I've come to you about Saoirse. I'm afraid I haven't been able to pass on any of your notes and phone messages to her over the past few days,' Margaret said uncomfortably, fiddling with the hem of her blouse. 'She hasn't been back to the B&B for three days now.'

'Oh,' Elizabeth said, feeling embarrassed. 'Thank you for informing me, Margaret, but there's no need to worry. I expect she'll be calling me soon.' She was tired of being the last to know everything, of being informed of her own family's activities by complete strangers. Despite being distracted by Ivan, Elizabeth had tried to keep her eye on Saoirse as much as she could. Her hearing was on in a few weeks, but Elizabeth hadn't been able to find her anywhere. Anywhere being the pub, her dad's or the B&B.

'Well, actually it's not that. It's just that, well, it's a very busy period for us. There are a lot of tourists coming through and looking for boarding, and we need to use Saoirse's room.'

'Yes.' She sprang back in her chair, feeling foolish. *Of course.* 'That's completely understandable,' Elizabeth said awkwardly. 'I can call round after work to collect her things, if you like.'

'That won't be necessary,' Margaret smiled sweetly, then shouted, 'BOYS!'

In walked Margaret's two young teenage sons, each with a suitcase in his hand.

'I took the liberty of gathering her things together,' Margaret continued, her smile still plastered across her face. 'Now all I need is the three days' rent and that will be everything settled.'

Elizabeth froze. 'Margaret, I'm sure you'll understand that Saoirse's bills are her own. Just because I'm her sister it doesn't mean I can be expected to pay. She will return soon, I'm sure.'

'Oh, I know that, Elizabeth,' Margaret smiled, revealing a pink lipstick stain on her front tooth. 'But seeing as mine is currently the only B&B that will allow Saoirse to stay I'm sure you'll make an allow—'

'How much?' Elizabeth snapped.

'Fifteen per night,' Margaret said sweetly.

Elizabeth rooted through her wallet. She sighed. 'Look, Margaret, I don't seem to have any ca—'

'A cheque will do fine,' she sang.

After handing over the cheque to Margaret, for the first time in a while Elizabeth stopped thinking about Ivan and started worrying about Saoirse. Just like old times.

At 10 p.m. in downtown Manhattan, Elizabeth and Mark stared out of the huge black windows of the hundred-and-fourteenth-floor bar that Elizabeth had finished designing. Tonight was the opening night of Club Zoo, an entire floor dedicated to animal prints, fur couches and cushions with greenery and bamboo sporadically placed. It was everything she loathed in a design, but she had been given a brief and she had to stick to it. It was a huge success, everyone was enjoying the night, and a live performance of drummers performing jungle beats and the constant sound of happy conversation added to the party atmosphere. Elizabeth and Mark clinked their champagne glasses together and looked outside to the sea of skyscrapers, the random lights dotting the buildings like chequers and the tide of yellow cabs below them.

'To another of your successes,' Mark toasted, sipping on the bubble-filled glass.

Elizabeth smiled, feeling proud. 'We're a long way from home now, aren't we?' she pondered, looking out at the view and seeing the reflection of the party going on behind her. She saw the owner, Henry Hakala, making his way through the crowd.

'Elizabeth, there you are.' He held out his arms and greeted her. 'What is the star of the night doing in the corner away from everyone?' he asked.

'Henry, this is Mark Leeson, my boyfriend; Mark, this is Henry Hakala, owner of Club Zoo,' she introduced the two.

'So you're the person that's kept my girlfriend out late every night,' Mark joked, taking Henry's hand.

Henry laughed. 'She's saved my life. Three weeks to do all this?' He motioned at the room decorated vibrantly in zebra print on the walls, bear skins draped on the couches, leopard print lying across the timber floors, enormous plants sitting in chrome pots and bamboo lining the bar area. 'It was a tough deadline and I knew she'd do it, but I didn't think she'd do it this well.' He looked grateful. 'Anyway, the speeches are about to begin. I just want to say a few words, mention a few investors' names,' he muttered under his breath, 'thank all you glorious people that worked so hard. So don't go anywhere, Elizabeth, because I'll have all eyes on you in a minute.'

'Oh,' Elizabeth blushed, 'please don't.'

'Believe me, you'll have a few hundred more offers after I do,' he said before he made his way towards the microphone, decorated with a vine of leaves.

'Excuse me, Ms Egan.' A member of the bar staff approached her. 'You have a phone call just outside at the main desk.'

Elizabeth frowned, 'Me? A phone call? Are you sure?'

'You are Ms Egan, yes?'

She nodded, confused. Who would be ringing her here?

'It's a young woman, says she's your sister?' he explained quietly.

'Oh.' Her heart beat wildly. 'Saoirse?' she asked, shocked.

'Yes, that's it,' the young man said, sounding relieved. 'I wasn't sure I'd remembered right.'

At that moment it felt as if the music got louder, the drumming beats were pounding her head, the fur prints were all coming together in a blur. Saoirse never called her; something had to be seriously wrong.

'Leave it, Elizabeth,' Mark said rather forcefully. 'Tell the woman on the phone that Ms Egan is busy at the moment,'

Mark said to the barman. 'This is your night, enjoy it,' he added softly to Elizabeth.

'No, no, don't tell her that,' Elizabeth stammered. It must be 3 a.m. in Ireland – why was Saoirse calling so late? 'I'll take the call, thank you,' she said to the young man.

'Elizabeth, the speech is about to begin,' Mark warned her as the room began to quieten down and gather before the microphone. 'You can't miss it,' he hissed. 'This is *your* moment.'

'No, no, I can't,' she trembled, and she left him, heading in the direction of the phone.

'Hello?' she said a few moments later, the concern evident in her voice.

'Elizabeth?' Saoirse's voice sobbed.

'It's me, Saoirse. What's wrong?' Elizabeth's heart thudded in her chest.

There was silence in the club as Henry made his speech.

'I just wanted to . . .' Saoirse trailed off and was silent.

'You wanted to what? Is everything OK?' Elizabeth asked hurriedly.

Henry's voice boomed, '. . . And last but not least I'd like to thank the wonderful Elizabeth Egan from Morgan Designs for designing this place so wonderfully in such a short time. She's created something that's completely different to what's out there right now, making Club Zoo the most popular, trendy and newest club on the scene, guaranteed to have people queuing down the block to get in. She's down the back there somewhere. Elizabeth, give us all a wave, let them know who you are so they can steal you away from me.'

Everyone turned around in silence, searching for the designer.

'Oh,' Henry's voice echoed, 'well, she was there a second ago. Maybe someone's snapped her up already to do a job.'

Everyone laughed.

Elizabeth looked inside and saw Mark standing alone with two champagne glasses in his hand, shrugging at everyone who had turned to him and laughing. Pretending to laugh.

'Saoirse,' Elizabeth's voice broke, 'please tell me if there's something wrong. Have you gotten into trouble again?'

Silence. Instead of the weak sobbing voice Elizabeth had heard previously, Saoirse's voice had become strong again. 'No,' she snapped. 'No, I'm fine. Everything's fine. Enjoy your party,' and she hung up.

Elizabeth sighed and slowly hung up the phone.

Inside the speech had finished and the drums had started up again; the conversation and drinks continued to flow.

Neither she nor Mark was in the mood to party.

Elizabeth could see a giant figure looming in the distance as she drove down the road that led to her father's bungalow. She had left work early and was searching for Saoirse. Nobody had seen her for days, not even the local publican, which made a change.

It had always been difficult to direct people to the bungalow as it was so cut off from the rest of the town. The road didn't even have a name, which Elizabeth thought was appropriate; it was the road that people forgot. Postmen and milkmen new to the job always took a few days to find the address, politicians never canvassed to their door, there were no trick-or-treaters. As a child Elizabeth had tried to convince herself that her mother had simply become lost and couldn't find her way home. She remembered sharing her theory with her father, who gave a smile so small it was hardly a smile at all and replied, 'You know, you're not far wrong there, Elizabeth.'

That was the only explanation, if you could even call it that, which she got. They never discussed her mother's disappearance; neighbours and visiting family hushed when Elizabeth was near. Nobody would tell her what had happened and she didn't ask. She didn't want that uncomfortable quiet to descend on them or for her father to storm out of the house when her mother's name was mentioned. If not mentioning her mother ensured that everyone was happy, then Elizabeth was happy to oblige, as usual.

She didn't think she really wanted to know, anyway. The mystery of not knowing was more enjoyable. She would create scenarios in her head, painting her mother in exotic and exciting worlds and she would fall asleep imagining her mother on a desert island, eating bananas and coconuts and sending messages in a bottle to Elizabeth. She would check the coastline every morning with her father's binoculars for sign of a bobbing bottle.

Another theory was that she had become a Hollywood movie star. Elizabeth sat with her nose almost up against the TV screen for every Sunday matinée, searching for her mother's grand debut. But she grew tired of searching, hoping, imagining, and not asking, and eventually she no longer even wondered.

The figure didn't move from the window of Elizabeth's old bedroom. Usually her father would be waiting in the garden for her. Elizabeth hadn't been inside the bungalow for years. She waited outside for a few minutes, and when there was no sign of her father or of Saoirse she got out of the car, slowly pushed open the gate, goose pimples rising on her skin from the noise of the gate's hinges, and wobbled up the uneven stone slabs in her high heels. Weeds popped up from the cracks to study the stranger trespassing on their territory.

Elizabeth knocked twice on the green paint-flecked door and quickly pulled her fist away, cradling it as though it had been burned. There was no answer yet she knew there was someone in the bedroom to the right. She held out her hand and pushed open the door. There was a stillness inside and the familiar musty smell of what she once considered home hit her and stopped her in her tracks for a few moments. Once she had adjusted to the emotions the scent had woken inside her, she stepped inside.

She cleared her throat. 'Hello?'

No answer.

'Hello?' she called more loudly. Her grown-up voice sounded wrong in her childhood home.

She began to walk towards the kitchen, hoping her father would hear her and come out to her. She had no desire to revisit her old bedroom. Her high heels echoed on the stone floor, another sound unfamiliar to the house. She held her breath as she stepped into the kitchen and dining area. Everything and nothing was the same. The smells, the clock on the mantel, the lace tablecloth, the rug, the chair by the fireplace, the red teapot on the green Aga, the curtains. Everything still had its place, had aged and was faded with time, but still belonged. It was as though no one had lived there since Elizabeth had left. Maybe no one *had* truly lived there.

She stayed standing in the centre of the room for a while, eyeing the ornaments, reaching out to touch them but allowing her fingers only to linger. Nothing had been disturbed. She felt as though she were in a museum; even the sounds of tears, laughter, fights and love had been preserved and hung in the air like cigarette smoke.

Eventually she couldn't take it any more; she needed to talk to her father, to find out where Saoirse was, and in order to do that she needed to go to her bedroom. She slowly turned the brass door knob that was still hanging loose as it had been in her childhood. She pushed the door open, didn't step in, and didn't look around. She just looked straight at her father, who sat in an armchair in front of the window, not moving.

Chapter 24

She didn't move her eyes from the back of his head, couldn't move her eyes anywhere else. She tried not to breathe in the smell but it gathered in her throat, blocking her wind pipe.

'Hello?' she croaked.

He didn't move, just kept his head straight ahead.

Her heart skipped a beat. 'Hello?' She detected an air of panic in her voice.

Without thinking, she stepped into the room and rushed towards him. She fell to her knees and examined his face. He still didn't move and kept his eyes straight ahead. Her heart quickened. 'Daddy?' rushed out of her mouth in a panic, sounding childlike. It felt real to her then. The word meant something. She held out to touch him, placed one hand on his face and another on his shoulder. 'Dad, it's me – are you OK? Talk to me.' Her voice shook. His skin was warm.

He blinked and she breathed a sigh of relief.

He slowly turned to look at her. 'Ah, Elizabeth, I didn't hear you come in.' His voice sounded like it was coming from another room. It was gentle; gone were his gravelly tones.

'I was calling you,' she said softly. 'I drove down the road – didn't you see me?'

'No,' he said in surprise, turning back to face the window.

'Then what were you looking at?' She too turned to the window and the view took her breath away. The scene – the path, the garden gate and the long stretch of road – momentarily threw her into the same trance as her father. The same hopes and wishes of the past came back in that instant. On the windowsill sat a photograph of her mother, which had never been there before. In fact, Elizabeth thought her father had got rid of all the photographs after her mother left.

But the image of her silenced Elizabeth. It was so long since she had seen her mother; she no longer had a face in Elizabeth's mind. All she was was a fuzzy memory, more like a feeling than a picture. Seeing her was a shock. It was like looking at herself, a perfect mirror image. When she found her voice again she spoke quietly, shaken. 'What are you doing, Dad?'

He didn't move his head, didn't blink, just had a far-away look in his eye and an unfamiliar voice that came deep from within him. 'I saw her, Elizabeth.'

Palpitations. 'Saw who?' But she knew who.

'Gráinne, your mother. I saw her. At least I think I did. It's been so long since I've seen her that I wasn't sure. So I got the photo just so I can remember. So that when she walks down the road I'll remember.'

Elizabeth gulped. 'Where did you see her, Dad?'

His voice was higher pitched and slightly bewildered. 'In a field.'

'A field? What field?'

'A field of magic.' His eyes glistened, seeing it all over again. 'A field of dreams, as they say. She looked so happy, dancing and laughing just like she always did. She hasn't aged a day.' He looked confused. 'But she should have, shouldn't she? She should be older, like me.'

'Are you sure it was her, Dad?' Her whole body was shaking.

'Oh aye, 'twas her, moving in the wind like the

dandelions, sun shining on her like she was an angel. 'Twas her, alright.' He was sitting upright in the chair, two hands lying on the armrests, looking more relaxed than ever.

'She had a child with her, though, and it wasn't Saoirse. No, Saoirse's grown up now,' he reminded himself. 'It was a boy, I think. Little blond fella, like Saoirse's boy . . .' His thick caterpillar-like eyebrows furrowed for the first time.

'When did you see her?' Elizabeth asked, dread and relief both filling her body, realising it was she her father had seen in the field.

'Yesterday,' he smiled, remembering. 'Yesterday morning. She'll be coming to me soon.'

Tears filled Elizabeth's eyes. 'Have you been sitting here since yesterday, Dad?'

'Aye, I don't mind. She'll be here soon but I need to remember her face. I sometimes don't remember, you see.'

'Dad,' Elizabeth's voice was a whisper, 'wasn't there someone else in the field with her?'

'No,' Brendan smiled, 'just her and the boy. He looked so happy too.'

'What I mean is,' Elizabeth held his hand; hers was childlike next to his tough-skinned fingers, 'I was in the field yesterday. It was me, Dad, catching dandelion seeds with Luke and a man.'

'No.' He shook his head and scowled. 'There was no man. Gráinne was with no man. She's coming home soon.'

'Dad, I promise you it was me, Luke and Ivan. Perhaps you were mistaken,' she said as gently as she could.

'No!' he yelled, causing Elizabeth to jump. He faced her with a look of disgust. 'She's coming home to me!' He glared at her. 'Get out!' he finally yelled, waving his hand and knocking her small hand off his.

'What?' Her heart beat wildly. 'Why, Dad?'

'You're a liar,' he spat. 'I saw no man in the field. You know she's here and you're keeping her from me,' he hissed. 'You wear suits and sit behind desks, you know nothing of dancing in fields. You're a liar, pollutin' the place. Get out,' he repeated quietly.

She looked at him in shock. 'I've met a man, Dad, a beautiful, wonderful man who's been teaching me of all these things,' she started to explain.

He moved his face in front of hers until they were almost touching nose to nose. 'GET OUT!' he yelled.

Tears spilled from her eyes and her body shook as she rushed to her feet. Her room became a whirl as she saw everything she didn't want to see in her disoriented state – old teddies, dolls, books, a writing desk, the same duvet cover. She charged for the door, not wanting to see any more, not being able to see any more. Her trembling hands fumbled with the latch as her father's yells for her to leave got louder and louder.

She pulled the door open and ran outside into the garden, breathing the fresh air into her lungs. A knocking on the window spun her round. She faced her father, waving angrily at her to get out of his garden. She gasped for breath, her tears raced down her face and she pulled open the gate and left it open, not wanting to hear the closing creak of its hinges.

She sped down the road in her car as fast as she could, not looking in the rear-view window, not wanting ever to see the place again, not wanting ever to have to drive down the road of disappointment again.

There would be no more looking back.

Chapter 25

'What's wrong?' a voice called from the back patio door. Elizabeth was sitting at the kitchen table, head in her hands, as still as Muckross Lake on a calm day.

'Jesus,' Elizabeth said under her breath, not looking up but wondering how it was that Ivan always managed to appear at the moments when she least expected him but needed him most.

'Jesus? Has he been giving you a hard time?' He stepped into the kitchen.

Elizabeth looked up from her hands. 'It's actually his father I'm having an issue with right now.'

Ivan took another step towards her; he had the ability to overstep the boundaries but never in a threatening or intrusive way. 'I hear that a lot.'

Elizabeth wiped her eyes with a mascara-stained and crumpled tissue. 'Don't you ever work?'

'I work all the time. May I?' He gestured to the chair opposite her.

She nodded. 'All the time? So is this work for you? Am I just another hopeless case for you to deal with today?' she asked sarcastically, catching a tear halfway down her cheek with the tissue.

'There's nothing hopeless about you, Elizabeth. However, you are a case; I've already told you that,' he said seriously.

She laughed. 'A headcase.'

Ivan looked sad. Misunderstood again.

'So is that your uniform?' She indicated his attire.

Ivan looked down at himself in surprise.

'You've been wearing that outfit everyday I've seen you,' she smiled, 'so it's either a uniform or you're completely unhygienic and lack imagination.'

Ivan's eyes widened. 'Oh, Elizabeth, I don't lack imagination at all.' Not realising what he had implied, Ivan continued, 'Do you want to talk about why you are so sad?'

'No, we're always talking about me and my problems,' Elizabeth replied. 'Let's talk about you for a change. What did you do today?' she asked, trying to perk herself up. It had seemed like such a long time ago since she had kissed Ivan on the main street that morning. She had thought about it all day and had worried about who had seen her, but amazingly, for a town that learned of everything quicker than Sky News, nobody had mentioned a thing to her about the mystery man.

She had longed to kiss Ivan again, had felt scared about that longing and tried to numb herself of feeling for him but she couldn't. There was something about him so pure and untarnished, yet he was powerful and well-versed in life. He was like the drug she knew she shouldn't take but which kept coming back to feed her addiction. As her weariness set in later in the day, the memory of the kiss had become a comfort to her and the uneasiness vanished. All she wanted now was a repeat of that moment where her troubles fizzled away.

'What did I do today?' Ivan twiddled his thumbs and thought aloud. 'Well, today I gave Baile na gCroíthe a big wake-up call, kissed a very beautiful woman and then spent the rest of the day being unable to do anything but think of her.'

Elizabeth's face brightened and his piercing blue eyes warmed her heart.

'And then I couldn't stop thinking,' Ivan continued, 'so I sat down and spent the day thinking.'

'About what?'

'Apart from the beautiful woman?'

'Apart from her,' Elizabeth grinned.

'You don't want to know.'

'I can take it.'

Ivan looked uncertain. 'OK, if you really want to know,' he took a deep breath, 'I thought about the Borrowers.'

Elizabeth frowned. 'What?'

'The Borrowers,' Ivan repeated, looking thoughtful.

'The television programme?' Elizabeth said, feeling irate. She had prepared herself for whispers of sweet nothing like they did in the movies, not this unscripted loveless conversation.

'Yes.' Ivan rolled his eyes, not noticing her tone, 'if you want to refer to *that* commercial side of them.' He sounded angry. 'But I thought long and hard about them and I've come to the conclusion that they didn't borrow. They *stole*. They downright stole and everybody knows it but nobody ever talks about it. To borrow means to take and use something belonging to someone else and then eventually return it. I mean, when did they ever give anything back? I don't recall Peagreen Clock ever giving anything back to the Lenders at all, do you? Especially the food – how can you borrow *food*? You eat it and it's gone; there's no giving it back. At least when I eat your dinner you know where it's going.' He sat back and folded his arms, looking cross. 'And they get a film made about them, a bunch of thieves, while us? We do nothing but good but we get labelled a figment of people's imaginations and are still,' he made a face and made inverted commas with his fingers, '*invisible*. Please . . .' He rolled his eyes.

Elizabeth stared at him open-mouthed.

There was a long silence as Ivan looked around the

kitchen, shaking his head in anger, and then returned his attention to Elizabeth. 'What?'

Silence.

'Oh, it doesn't matter.' He waved his hand dismissively. 'I told you, you wouldn't want to know. So enough about my problems. Please tell me, what's happened?'

Elizabeth took a deep breath, the question of Saoirse distracting her from the confusing talk of the Borrowers. 'Saoirse has disappeared. Joe, the man with his finger on the pulse of Baile na gCroíthe, told me she headed off with the group of people she was hanging out with. He heard it from a family member of a guy from the group she's with but she's been gone for three days and no one seems to know where they've gone.'

'Oh,' Ivan said in surprise, 'and here I am rattling off my problems. Did you tell the gardaí?'

'I had to,' she said sadly. 'I felt like a snitch but they had to know she was gone just in case she didn't turn up for her hearing in a few weeks, which I'm almost sure she won't be at. I'll have to get a solicitor to go on her behalf, which won't look very good.' She rubbed her face tiredly.

He took her hands and cradled them in his own. 'She'll be back,' he said confidently. 'Maybe not for the hearing but she'll come back. Believe me. There's no need to worry.' His soft voice was firm.

Elizabeth stared deep into his eyes, searching for the truth. 'I believe you,' she said. But deep down Elizabeth was afraid. She was afraid of believing Ivan, afraid of believing full stop, because when that happened, her hopes were raised up the flagpole, waving and blowing in the breeze for all to see. There they would weather the storms and winds, only to be lowered, tattered and ruined.

And she didn't think she could spend any more years with her bedroom curtains open, with one eye on the road, waiting for a second person to return. She was weary and she needed to close her eyes.

Chapter 26

As soon as I left Elizabeth's house the next morning, I decided to head straight to Opal. Actually, I had decided I was going to do that long before I left Elizabeth's house. Something she said had hit a nerve – actually, everything she said hit a nerve with me. When I was with her I was like a hedgehog, all prickly and sensitive, as if all of my senses were alert. The funny thing is I thought all my senses had been alert already – as a professional best friend they should have been – but there was one emotion I hadn't experienced before and that was love. Sure, I loved all my friends but not in this way, not in the way that made my heart thud when I looked at Elizabeth, not in a way that made me want to be with her the whole time. And I didn't want to be with her for *her*, I realised it was for me. This love thing awakened a group of slumbering senses in my body that I never even knew existed.

I cleared my throat, checked my appearance and made my way into Opal's office. In Ekam Eveileb there were no doors, because nobody here could open them, but there was another reason: doors acted as barriers; they were thick, unwelcoming things that you could control to shut people in or out and we didn't agree with that. We chose open-plan offices for a more open and friendly atmosphere. Although that's what we were always taught, lately I had found Elizabeth's fuchsia front door with the smiling letter box to be the friendliest door I had ever seen, so that shot that particular theory to hell. She was making me question all sorts of things.

Without even looking up, Opal called out, 'Welcome, Ivan.' She was sitting behind a desk, dressed in purple, as usual, her dreadlocks were tied up and scattered in glitter so that with every movement she sparkled. On each of her walls were framed photos of hundreds of children, all smiling happily. They were even covering her shelves, coffee table, sideboard, mantelpiece and windowsill. Everywhere I looked were rows and rows of photographs of people Opal had worked with and become friends with in the past. Her desk was the only surface that was clear and on it sat one single photo frame. The frame had sat there for years facing Opal so that nobody ever really got a chance to see who or what was in it. We knew that if we asked she would tell us, but nobody was ever rude enough to ask. What we didn't need to know, we didn't need to ask. Some people just don't quite get the gist of that. You can have plenty of conversations with people, *meaningful* conversations without getting too personal. There's a line, you know, like an invisible field around people that you just know not to enter or cross, and I had never crossed it with Opal, or anyone else for that matter. Some people just can't even see that.

Elizabeth would have hated the room, I thought as I looked around. She would have removed everything in an instant, dusted it and polished it until it gleamed with the clinical glow of a hospital. Even at the coffee shop she had arranged the salt and pepper shakers and the bowl of sugar into an equilateral triangle in the centre of the table. She always moved things an inch to the left or an inch to the right, back and forward until it stopped nagging and she could concentrate again. Funny thing was, she sometimes ended up moving things back to exactly how they were in the first place and then convincing herself she was happy with them. That said a lot about Elizabeth.

But why did I start thinking of Elizabeth just then? I kept

on doing that. In situations that were totally unrelated to her, I would think of her and she would become part of the scenario. I would suddenly wonder, what would she think, how would she feel, what would she do or say if she was with me? That was all part of giving someone a piece of your heart; they ended up taking a whole chunk of your mind and reserving it all for themselves.

Anyway, I realised I had been standing in front of the desk not saying anything since I walked in.

'How did you know it was me?' I finally spoke.

Opal looked up and smiled one of those smiles that made her look as if she knew it all. 'I was expecting you.' Her lips looked like two big cushions, and were purple to match her robe. I thought of what it felt like to kiss Elizabeth's lips.

'But I didn't make an appointment,' I protested. I knew I was intuitive but Opal was in a whole league of her own.

She just smiled again. 'What can I do for you?'

'I thought you'd know that without having to ask me,' I teased, sitting down in her spinning chair and thinking about the spinning chair in Elizabeth's office, then thinking of Elizabeth, what it was like to hold her, hug her, laugh with her and hear the little breaths she took while she slept last night.

'You know the dress Calendula was wearing at last week's meeting?'

'Yes.'

'Do you know how she got that?'

'Why, do you want one too?' Opal asked with a glint in her eyes.

'Yes,' I replied, fidgeting with my hands. 'I mean no,' I said quickly. I took a breath. 'What I mean is, I was wondering where I could get a change of clothes for myself.' There I'd done it.

'The wardrobe department, two floors down,' Opal explained.

'I didn't know there was a wardrobe department,' I said in surprise.

'It's always been there,' Opal said, narrowing her eyes. 'May I ask what you need it for?'

'I don't know.' I shrugged. 'It's just that, Elizabeth, you see, is, um, she's *different* from all my other friends. She notices these things, you know?'

She nodded slowly.

I felt I should explain a bit more. The silence was making me uncomfortable. 'You see, Elizabeth said to me today that the reason I wore these clothes was because it was either a uniform, I was unhygienic or because I lacked imagination.' I sighed, thinking about it. 'The last thing I am is lacking in imagination.'

Opal smiled.

'And I know I'm not unhygienic,' I continued. 'And then I was thinking about the uniform part,' I looked myself up and down, 'and maybe she was right, you know?'

Opal pursed her lips.

'One of the things about Elizabeth is that she too is dressed in uniform. She wears black – the same stuffy suits all the time – her make-up is a mask, her hair is always tied back, *nothing* is free. She works all the time and takes it so seriously,' I looked up at Opal in shock, just realising something. 'That's exactly like me, Opal.'

Opal was silent.

'All this time I was calling her a gnirob.'

Opal laughed lightly.

'I wanted to teach her to have fun, to change her clothes, stop wearing a mask, change her life so she can find happiness and how can I do that when I'm the very same as her?'

Opal nodded her head lightly. 'I understand, Ivan. You're learning a lot from Elizabeth too, I can see that. She is bringing something out in you and you are showing her a whole new way of life.'

'We caught Jinny Joes on Sunday,' I said softly, agreeing with her.

Opal opened a cabinet behind her and grinned. 'I know.'

'Oh, good, they arrived,' I said happily, watching the Jinny Joes floating in a jar in the cabinet.

'One of yours arrived too, Ivan,' Opal said seriously.

I felt my face redden. I changed the subject. 'You know she got six hours of undisturbed sleep last night. That's the first time that's ever happened.'

Opal's expression didn't soften. 'Did she tell you that, Ivan?'

'No, I saw her . . .' I trailed off. 'Look, Opal, I stayed the night, I only held her in my arms till she fell asleep, it's no big deal. She asked me to.' I tried to sound convincing. 'And when you think about it, I do it all the time with other friends. I read them bedtime stories, stay with them till they sleep and sometimes even sleep on their floor. This is no different.'

'Isn't it?'

I didn't answer.

Opal picked up her fountain pen with a great big purple feather on the top, looked down and continued with her calligraphy writing. 'How much longer do you think you'll need to work with her?'

That got me. My heart did a little dance. Opal had never asked me that before. It was never a matter of time for anyone, it was always a natural progression. Sometimes you only had to spend a day with someone, other times you could be there months. When our friends were ready, they were ready, and we had never before had to put a time on it. 'Why do you ask?'

'Oh,' she was nervous, fidgety, 'I'm just wondering. As a matter of interest . . . you're the best I have here, Ivan, and I just want you to remember that there are lots more people that need you.'

'I know that,' I said rather forcefully. Opal's voice had

all sorts of tones I had never heard before, negative ones that sent blue and black colours into the air and I didn't like it one bit.

'Great,' she said, a bit too perky for her, and she knew it. 'Can you drop these by the analysis lab on your way to wardrobe?' She handed me the jar of Jinny Joes.

'Sure.' I took the jar from her. There were three Jinny Joes inside, one from Luke, one from Elizabeth and the third was mine. They sat on the floor of the jar, resting from their journey in the wind. 'Bye,' I said rather awkwardly to Opal, backing out of the office. I felt as though we'd just had an argument even though we hadn't.

I made my way down the hall to the analysis lab, holding the lid of the jar closed tightly so they wouldn't escape. Oscar was running around the lab with a look of panic on his face when I reached the entrance.

'Open the hatch!' he yelled to me while passing the door, arms out in front of him, white coat flapping like a cartoon character.

I placed the jar away from danger and hurried to the hatch. Oscar ran towards me and, at the last minute, jumped to the side, fooling what was chasing him so that it raced straight into the cage.

'Ha!' he exploded, turning the key and waving it at the cage. His forehead was glittered with perspiration.

'What on earth is that?' I asked, moving closer to the cage.

'Be careful!' Oscar shouted, and I jumped back. 'You are incorrect in asking what on earth it is because it's not.' He dabbed his forehead with a handkerchief.

'It's not what?'

'On earth,' he replied. 'Never seen a shooting star before, Ivan?'

'Of course I have.' I circled the cage. 'But not up close.'

'Of course,' he added, an overly sweet tone to his voice, 'you just see them from afar, looking so pretty and bright, dancing across the sky, and you make your wishes on them but,' his tone turned nasty, 'you forget about Oscar, who has to gather your wishes from the star.'

'I'm sorry, Oscar, I really did forget. I didn't think stars were so dangerous.'

'Why?' Oscar snapped, 'Did you think a burning asteroid millions of miles away, which is visible from earth, is going to shoot down to me and kiss me on the cheek? Anyway, it doesn't matter. What have you brought to me? Oh great, a Jinny Joe jar. Just what I needed after that ball of fire,' he shouted loudly at the cage, 'something with a bit of respect.'

The ball of fire bounced around angrily in response.

I stepped further away from the cage. 'What kind of wish was it carrying?' I found it hard to believe that this burning ball of light could be of any help to anyone.

'Funny you ask,' Oscar said, showing it wasn't funny at all. 'This particular one was carrying the wish to chase me around the lab.'

'Was that Tommy?' I tried not to laugh.

'I can only assume so,' he said angrily. 'But I can't really complain to him because that was twenty years ago when Tommy didn't know any better and was just starting out.'

'Twenty years ago?' I asked in surprise.

'It took that long to get here,' Oscar explained, opening the jar and lifting out a Jinny Joe with an odd-looking implement. 'It is, after all, millions of light years away. I thought twenty years was doing rather well.'

I left Oscar studying the Jinny Joes and made my way to wardrobe. Olivia was in there being measured.

'Hello, Ivan,' she said in surprise.

'Hi, Olivia, what are you doing?' I asked, watching as a woman measured her tiny waist.

'Being measured for a dress, Ivan. Poor Mrs Cromwell passed away last night,' she said sadly. 'The funeral's tomorrow. I've been to so many funerals my only black dress is worn out.'

'I'm sorry to hear that,' I said, knowing how fond Olivia was of Mrs Cromwell.

'Thank you, Ivan, but we must keep going. A lady arrived at the hospice this morning, who needs my help and now I must focus on her.'

I nodded, understanding.

'So what brings you here?'

'My new friend, Elizabeth, is a woman. She notices my clothes.'

Olivia chuckled.

'You want a T-shirt in another colour?' the woman who was measuring asked. She took a red T-shirt from a drawer.

'Em, no.' I shifted from foot to foot and looked around at the shelves reaching from floor to ceiling. Each of them was labelled with a name and I saw Calendula's name underneath a row of pretty dresses. 'I was looking for something a lot . . . smarter.'

Olivia raised her eyebrows. 'Well then, you'll have to be measured for a suit, Ivan.'

We agreed to make me a black suit to go with a blue shirt and tie because they were my favourite colours.

'Anything else, or will that be all?' Olivia asked me with a twinkle in her eye.

'Actually,' I lowered my voice and looked around to make sure the woman was out of earshot. Olivia moved her head closer to mine.

'I was wondering if you could teach me the soft-shoe shuffle.'

Chapter 27

Elizabeth stared at the sparse wall, dirty with dried and patchy plaster. She already felt at a loss. The wall wasn't saying anything to her. It was 9.00 a.m. on the building site, and it was already overrun by men in hard hats, drooping jeans, check shirts and Caterpillar boots. They looked like an army of ants as they rushed around carrying all sorts of materials on their backs. In the emptiness of the hotel their cheers, laughter, songs and whistling echoed around the cemented shell on top of the hill that had yet to be filled by the ideas in Elizabeth's head. Their sounds rolled down the corridors like thunder and into what was to be the children's playroom.

All it was now was a blanched and pallid canvas that would in a matter of only weeks have children frolicking in the recreation room, while outside would be a cocoon of calm. Perhaps she should have sound-proofed the walls. She had no idea what she could add to these walls to bring a smile to the children's little faces when they walked in feeling nervous and upset at being taken from their parents. She knew about chaise longues, plasma screens, marble floors and wood of every kind. She could do chic, funky, sophisticated and rooms of splendour and grandeur. But none of these things would excite a child, and she knew she could do better than a few building blocks, jigsaw puzzles and beanbags.

She knew it would be perfectly within her rights to hire

a muralist, ask the on-site painters to do the job or even ask Poppy for some guidance, but Elizabeth liked to be hands-on. She liked to get lost in her work and she didn't want to have to ask for help. Handing the brush over to someone else would be a sign of defeat in her eyes.

She laid ten tubs of primary colours in a line on the floor, opened the lids and placed the brushes next to them. She spread a white sheet on the floor and, making sure her jeans, which she wore only as work wear, wouldn't touch the dirty floor in any way, she sat crosslegged in the centre of the room and stared at the wall. But all she could think of was the fact she couldn't think of anything but Saoirse. Saoirse, who was on her mind every second of every day.

In time she wondered how long she had been sitting there. She had a vague recollection of builders entering and exiting the room, collecting their tools, watching her in puzzlement as she stared at a blank wall. She had a feeling she was suffering an interior designer's version of writer's block. No ideas would come, no pictures could be formed and, just as the ink would dry in a pen, the paint would not flow from her brush. Her head was filled with . . . nothing. It was as though her thoughts were being reflected onto that drab plastered wall and it was probably thinking the very same thing as her.

She felt someone's presence behind her and she turned round. Benjamin was standing at the door.

'I'm sorry, I would have knocked but,' he held his hands up, 'there's no door.'

Elizabeth gave him a welcoming grin.

'Admiring my handiwork?'

'You did this?' She turned back to face the wall.

'My best work, I think,' he replied, and they both looked at it in silence.

Elizabeth sighed. 'It's not saying anything to me.'

'Ah.' He took a step into the room. 'You have no idea

how difficult it is to create a piece of art that doesn't say anything at all. Someone always has some kind of interpretation but with this . . .' he shrugged, 'nothing. No statements.'

'A sign of a true genius, Mr West.'

'Benjamin,' he winced. 'I keep telling you, please call me Benjamin; you make me sound like my math teacher.'

'OK, you can keep calling me Ms Egan.'

He caught the sides of her cheeks lifting into a smile as she turned back to face the wall.

'Do you think there's any chance at all that the kids will like this room just as it is?' she asked hopefully.

'Hmm,' Benjamin thought aloud, 'the nails protruding from the skirting board would be particularly fun for them to play with. I don't know,' he admitted. 'You're asking the wrong guy about kids. They're another species to me. We don't have a real close relationship.'

'Me neither,' Elizabeth muttered guiltily, thinking of her inability to connect with Luke like Edith did. Although after meeting Ivan she found herself spending more time with him. That morning in the field with Ivan and Luke had been a real milestone for her, yet when she was alone with Luke she still couldn't let herself go with him. It was Ivan that released the child in her.

Benjamin went down on his haunches, placing his hand on the dusty floor to steady himself. 'Well, I don't believe that for a second. You've got a son, don't you?'

'Oh, no, I haven't . . .' she started, then stopped. 'He's my nephew. I adopted him but the last thing in this world I understand is children.' Everything was blurting out of her mouth today. She missed the Elizabeth who could have a conversation without revealing the tiniest part of herself but it seemed that lately the floodgates to her heart had been opened and things rushed out of it of their own accord.

'Well, you seem to have a pretty good idea what he wanted on Sunday morning,' Benjamin said softly, looking at her differently. 'I drove past you when you were dancing around that field.'

Elizabeth rolled her eyes and her dark skin pinked. 'You and the rest of the town, apparently. But that was Ivan's idea,' she said quickly.

Benjamin laughed. 'You give Ivan the credit for everything?'

Elizabeth thought about that but Benjamin didn't wait for the answer. 'I suppose in this case you just gotta sit here like you're doin' and put yourself in the position of the kids. Put that wild imagination of yours to use. If you were a kid what would you want to do in this room?'

'Other than get out and grow up quickly?'

Benjamin moved to get up.

'So how long do you plan on staying in the big smoke of Baile na gCroíthe?' Elizabeth asked quickly. She figured the longer he stayed, the more she could put off admitting to herself that for the first time in her life she had absolutely no idea of what to do with a room.

Benjamin, sensing her desire for a conversation, lowered himself to the dusty floor and Elizabeth had to ignore what she could imagine were millions of dust mites crawling all over him.

'I plan on leaving as soon as the last lick of paint is on the walls and the last nail has been hammered in.'

'You've obviously fallen head over heels in love with this place,' Elizabeth said sarcastically. 'Don't the stunning panoramic views of Kerry impress you?'

'Yeah, the views are nice but I've had six months of good views and now I could do with a decent cup of coffee, a choice of more than one shop to buy my clothes and to be able to walk around without everyone staring at me like I've escaped from a zoo.'

Elizabeth laughed.

Benjamin held his hands up. 'I don't mean to be

offensive or anything – Ireland's great – but I'm just not a fan of small towns.'

'Me neither . . .' Elizabeth's smile faded at the thought. 'So where did you escape from then?'

'New York.'

Elizabeth shook her head. 'That is not a New York accent I hear.'

'No, you got me; I'm from a place called Haxtun in Colorado, which I'm sure you've probably heard of. It's well known for a great number of things.'

'Such as?'

He raised his eyebrows. 'Absolutely nothing. It's a small town in a big dust bowl, a good strong farming town with a population of one thousand.'

'You didn't like it there?'

'No I didn't like it,' he said firmly. 'You could say I suffered from claustrophobia,' he added with a smile.

'I know how that feels,' Elizabeth nodded. 'Sounds like here.'

'It's a bit like here.' Benjamin looked out the window. He relaxed then. 'Everyone waves at you as you pass. They haven't a damn clue who you are but they wave.'

Elizabeth hadn't realised it until now. She pictured her father in the field, cap on, covering his face, holding his arm up in an L shape to passing cars.

'They wave in fields and on the streets,' Benjamin continued, 'farmers, old ladies, kids, teens, newly born and serial killers. And I've studied this to a fine art.' His eyes twinkled at her. 'You even get the one-finger wave with the index finger raised off the steering wheel as you pass traffic. Man, you'd leave the place waving at cows if you're not careful.'

'And the cows would probably wave back.'

Benjamin laughed loudly. 'You ever think of leaving?'

'I did more than think about it.' Her smile faded. 'I went to New York too but I've commitments here,' she said, quickly looking away.

'Your nephew, right?'

'Yes,' she said softly.

'Well, there's one good thing about leaving a small town. They all miss you when you're gone. They all notice it.'

Their eyes locked on one another. 'I suppose you're right,' she said. 'It's ironic, though, that we both moved to a big city where we were surrounded by more people and more buildings than we'd ever known, just so we could feel more isolated.'

'Huh.' Benjamin stared at her, not blinking. She knew he wasn't seeing her face; he was lost in his own world. And he did look lost for a moment. 'Anyway,' he snapped out of his trance, 'it was a pleasure talking to you again, Ms Egan.'

She smiled at his address.

'I'd better go and let you stare at the wall some more.' He stopped and turned at the doorway. 'Oh, by the way,' she felt her stomach turn, 'without running the risk of making you uncomfortable, I mean this in the most innocent way possible, maybe you'd like to meet up outside of work sometime? It would be nice to have a conversation with a like-minded person for a change.'

'Sure.' She liked this casual invitation. No expectations.

'Maybe you'll know some of the good places to go. Six months ago, when I just arrived, I made the mistake of asking Joe where the nearest sushi bar was. I had to tell him it was raw fish before he directed me to a lake about an hour's drive away and told me to ask for a guy called Tom.'

Elizabeth burst out laughing, the sound, which was becoming more familiar to her these days, echoing around the room. 'That's his brother, the fisherman.'

'Anyway, I'll see you again.'

The room was empty once more and Elizabeth was faced with the same dilemma. She thought of what Benjamin had said about using her imagination and putting herself in the place of a child. She closed her eyes and imagined the sounds of children hollering, laughing, crying and fighting. The noisy clatter of toys, feet pounding on the floor as they ran around, the sound of bodies falling, a shocked silence and then wails. She pictured herself as a child sitting alone in a room, not knowing anyone, and it suddenly occurred to her what she would have wanted.

A friend.

She opened her eyes and spotted a card on the floor beside her, though the room was still empty and quiet. Someone must have crept in when she had her eyes closed and left it there. She picked up the card, which had a black thumb print on the side. She didn't even need to read it to know it was Benjamin's new business card.

Maybe imagining had worked after all. It looked like she'd just made a friend in the playroom.

Sliding the card into her back pocket, she forgot about Benjamin and continued staring at the four walls.

Nope. Still nothing.

Chapter 28

Elizabeth sat at the glass table in the spotless kitchen surrounded by gleaming granite worktops, polished walnut cupboards and shining marble tiles. She had just had a cleaning frenzy and her mind still wasn't clear. Every time the phone rang, she leaped at it, thinking it was Saoirse, but it was Edith checking up on Luke. Elizabeth still hadn't heard from her sister, her father was still waiting in her old bedroom for her mother; sitting, eating and sleeping in the same chair for almost two weeks now. He wouldn't speak to Elizabeth, wouldn't even let her come as far as the front door so she had arranged for a housekeeper to call round to cook him a meal a day, and tidy up now and then. Some days he let her in, others he didn't. The young man who worked with her father on his farm had taken over all the duties. This was costing Elizabeth money she couldn't afford, but there was nothing else she could do. She couldn't help the other two members of her family if they didn't want to be helped. And she wondered for the first time if she had something in common with them after all.

They had all lived together – the girls had grown up together – but separately, and still they stayed together in the same town. They hadn't much communication with one another but when somebody left . . . well, it mattered. They were tied by an old and fraying rope that ended up being the object of tug of war.

Elizabeth couldn't bring herself to tell Luke what was

going on and, of course, he knew there was something. Ivan was right, children had a sixth sense for that kind of thing, but Luke was such a good child and as soon as he sensed Elizabeth's sadness he retreated into the playroom. Then she would hear the quiet clatter of building blocks. She couldn't bring herself to say more to him than to tell him to wash his hands, fix his speech and order him to stop dragging his feet.

She wasn't capable of holding her arms out to him, her lips couldn't form the words 'I love you', but she tried in her own ways to make him feel safe and wanted. But she knew what he really wanted. She had been in his position, knew what it was like to want to be held, cuddled, kissed on the forehead and rocked. To be made to feel safe for just a few minutes at least, to know that someone else is there looking out for you and that life just isn't in your own hands and you're stuck living it all alone in your head.

Ivan had provided her with a few of those moments over the past few weeks. He had kissed her on the forehead and rocked her to sleep, and she had fallen asleep not feeling alone, not feeling the urge to look out the window and search beyond for someone else. Ivan, sweet, sweet Ivan was shrouded in mystery. She had never known anyone have the ability to help her realise just exactly who she was, to help her find her feet, but she was struck by the irony that this man who jokingly spoke of invisibility actually did wear a cloak of invisibility. He was putting her on a map, showing her the way, yet he had no idea where he was going himself, where he came from, *who* he was. He liked to speak of her problems, help heal her, help fix her, and he never once spoke of his own. It was as though she was a distraction to him and she wondered what would happen when the distraction ended and the realisation dawned.

She got a sense that their time together was valuable, as though she needed to hold on to every minute as if it was their last. He was too good to be true, every moment spent with him magical, so much so that she presumed this couldn't last for ever. None of her good feelings had lasted; none of the people who lightened her life managed to stay. Going by her previous luck, from pure *fear* of not wanting to lose something so special, she was just waiting for the day he would leave. Whoever he was, he was healing her, he was teaching her to smile, teaching her to laugh, and she wondered what she could teach him. With Ivan, she feared that the sweet man with the soft eyes would reach a day when he would realise she had nothing to offer. That she had simply drained him of his resources and had none to give.

It had happened with Mark. She just couldn't give him any more of herself without taking away the care she had for her family. That's what he wanted her to do, of course – cut the strings that connected her to her family – but she couldn't do it, she would never do it. Saoirse and her father knew how to pull those strings and so she remained their puppet. As a result she was alone, raising a child she never wanted, with the love of her life living in America, a married man and a father of one. She hadn't heard from him or seen him for five years. A few months after Elizabeth had moved back to Ireland he visited her while on a trip home to see his family.

Those beginning months were the hardest. Elizabeth was intent on making Saoirse bring up the baby herself and as much as Saoirse protested and claimed she didn't care, Elizabeth wasn't about to let her sister throw away the opportunity of raising her son.

Elizabeth's dad couldn't hack it any more; he couldn't take the baby's screaming all night while Saoirse was out partying. Elizabeth supposed it reminded him too much of the years before when he was left holding the baby, the baby he subsequently passed on to his twelve-year-old daughter. Well, he did the same again. He threw Saoirse out of the bungalow, forcing her to arrive on Elizabeth's doorstep, cradle and all. The day that all happened was the day Mark decided to take the trip over to visit Elizabeth.

One look at the state of her life and she knew he was gone for ever. It wasn't long before Saoirse disappeared from Elizabeth's home, leaving the baby with her. She thought about giving Luke up for adoption, she really did. Every sleepless night and every stressful day she promised herself she would make that phone call. But she couldn't do it. Maybe it had something to do with her fear of giving in. She was obsessive in her strive for perfection and she couldn't give up on trying to help Saoirse. Also there was a part of her that was intent on proving she could raise a child, that it wasn't her fault for the way Saoirse turned out. She didn't want to get it all wrong with Luke. He deserved far better.

She cursed as she picked up another of her sketches, scrunched it in a ball and threw it across the room to the bin. It landed short of it and, not being able to cope with something out of place, Elizabeth walked across the room and delivered it to its rightful position.

The kitchen table was covered in paper, colouring pencils, children's books, cartoon characters. All she had succeeded in doing was drawing doodles all over the page. It wasn't enough for the playroom and it certainly wasn't the whole new world that she aspired to create. As usual, the same thing happened that always happened when she thought of Ivan: the doorbell rang and she knew it was him. She rushed to her feet, fixing her hair, her clothes, checking her reflection in the mirror. Gathering her colouring pencils and paper, she jogged on the spot in panic, trying to decide where to dump them. They slid from her hand; swearing, she dived down to pick them up. Her papers flew out of her hands and floated to the floor like leaves in an autumn breeze.

While on the floor, her eyes fell upon red Converse

runners casually crossed one another at the doorway. Her body slumped, her cheeks pinked.

'Hi, Ivan,' she said, refusing to look at him.

'Hello, Elizabeth. Have you ants in your pants?' his amused voice asked.

'How good of Luke to let you in,' Elizabeth said sarcastically. 'Funny he never actually does that when I need him to.' She reached for the sheets of paper on the floor and got to her feet. 'You're wearing red,' she stated, studying his red cap, red T-shirt and red shoes.

'Yes I am,' he agreed. 'Wearing different colours is my favourite thing now. It makes me feel even happier.'

Elizabeth looked down at her black outfit and thought about that.

'So what have you got there?' he asked, breaking into her thoughts.

'Oh, nothing,' Elizabeth mumbled, folding the pages together.

'Let me see it.' He grabbed the sheets. 'What have we got here? Donald Duck, Mickey Mouse,' he flicked through the pages, 'Winnie-the-Pooh, a racing car – and what's this?' He twirled the page round to get a better view.

'It's nothing,' Elizabeth snapped, snatching the page from his hand.

'That's not nothing – nothing looks like this.' He stared at her blankly.

'What are you doing?' she asked after a few moments' silence.

'Nothing, see?' He held out his hands.

Elizabeth stepped away from him, rolling her eyes. 'Sometimes you are worse than Luke. I'm going to have a glass of wine, would you like anything? Beer, wine, brandy?'

'A ssalg of klim, please.'

'I wish you'd stop speaking backwards,' she snapped, handing him a glass of milk. 'For a change?' she asked irritatedly, throwing her pages into the bin.

'No, that's what I always have,' he said rather perkily, eyeing her suspiciously. 'Why is that cabi net locked?'

'Em . . .' she faltered, 'so Luke can't get at the alcohol.' She couldn't say it was to keep Saoirse out. Luke had taken to hiding the key in his room whenever he heard his mother coming.

'Oh. What are you doing on the twenty-ninth?' Ivan swung himself around on the tall bar stool at the breakfast table and watched Elizabeth rooting through the wine bottles, face twisted in concentration.

'When is the twenty-ninth?' She locked the cabinet and searched through the drawer for a corkscrew.

'It's on Saturday.'

Her cheeks pinked and she looked away, giving her full concentration to opening the wine bottle. 'I'm going out on Saturday.'

'Where to?'

'A restaurant.'

'With who?'

She felt like it was Luke firing questions at her. 'I'm meeting Benjamin West,' she said, still keeping her back turned. She just couldn't face turning round right at that moment but she didn't know why she felt so uncomfortable.

'Why are you meeting him on Saturday? You don't work on Saturdays,' Ivan stated.

'It's not about work, Ivan. He doesn't know anybody here and we're going to get something to eat.' She poured the red wine into a crystal glass.

'Eat?' he asked incredulously. 'You're going to eat with Benjamin?' His voice went up a few octaves.

Elizabeth's eyes widened and she spun round, glass in hand. 'Is that a problem?'

'He's dirty and he smells,' Ivan stated.

Elizabeth's mouth dropped open; she didn't know how to reply to that.

'He probably eats with his hands. Like an animal,' Ivan continued, 'or a caveman, half man half animal. He probably hunts for—'

'Stop it, Ivan,' Elizabeth started laughing.

He stopped.

'What's really wrong?' She raised an eyebrow at him and sipped her wine.

He stopped spinning on his chair and stared at her. She stared back. She saw him swallow, his Adam's apple moving down his throat. His childishness disappeared and he appeared to her as a man, big, strong, with such a presence. Her heart beat quickened. His eyes didn't move from her face and she couldn't look away, couldn't move.

'Nothing's *wrong*.'

'Ivan, if you've got anything to say to me, you should say it,' Elizabeth said firmly. 'We're big boys and girls now.' The corner of her lips twitched at that.

'Elizabeth, would you come out with me on Saturday?'

'Ivan, it would be rude of me to cancel the appointment at such short notice – can't we go out another night?'

'No,' he said firmly, stepping off the stool. 'It has to be July the twenty-ninth. You'll see why.'

'I can't—'

'You can,' he interrupted her firmly. He took her by her elbows. 'You can do whatever you want. Meet me at Cobh Cúin at 10 p.m. on Saturday.'

'Cobh Cúin? And why so late?'

'You'll see why,' he repeated, tipped his cap and disappeared as quickly as he had arrived.

Before I left the house I called in to Luke in the playroom.

'Hey there, stranger,' I said, collapsing on the beanbag.

'Hi, Ivan,' Luke said, watching TV.

'Have you missed me?'

'Nope,' Luke smiled.

'Wanna know where I've been?'

'Smooching with my aunt.' Luke closed his eyes and did fake kisses in the air before collapsing into hysterical laughter.

My mouth dropped open. 'Hey! What makes you say that?'

'You *love* her,' Luke laughed, and continued watching cartoons.

I thought about that for a while. 'Are you still my friend?'

'Yep,' Luke replied, 'but Sam is my *best* friend.'

I pretended to be shot in the heart.

Luke looked away from the television to face me with hopeful big blue eyes. 'Is my aunt your best friend now?'

I thought about that carefully. 'Do you want her to be?'

Luke nodded emphatically.

'Why?'

'She's much better fun, she doesn't give out to me as much and she lets me colour in the white room.'

'Jinny Joe day was fun, wasn't it?'

Luke nodded again. 'I've never seen her laugh so much.'

'Does she give you big hugs and play lots of games with you?'

Luke looked at me as if that was a ridiculous idea and I sighed, worried about the small part of me that felt relieved.

'Ivan?'

'Yes, Luke.'

'Remember you told me that you can't stay around all the time, that you have to go to help other friends and so I shouldn't feel sad.'

'Yes.' I swallowed hard. I dreaded that day.

'What will happen to you and Aunt Elizabeth when that happens?'

And then I worried about the part in the centre of my chest that pained when I thought about that.

* * *

I stepped into Opal's office, hands in my pockets and wearing my new red T-shirt and a new pair of black jeans. Red felt good on me today. I was angry. I didn't like the tone in Opal's voice when she called me.

'Ivan,' she said, putting down her feather pen and looking up at me. Gone was her beaming smile that once used to greet me. She looked tired, bags hung under her eyes and her dreadlocks were down around her face and not in one of her usual styles.

'Opal,' I imitated her tone, throwing one leg over the other as I sat before her.

'What are the things you teach your students about becoming a part of your new friend's life?'

'Assist don't hinder, support don't oppose, help and listen don't—'

'You can stop right there.' She raised her voice and cut in on my bored tones. 'Assist and don't hinder, Ivan.' She allowed those words to hang in the air. 'You made her cancel a dinner reservation with Benjamin West. She could have made a friend, Ivan.' She stared at me, her black eyes like coal. Any more anger and they would have gone on fire.

'Can I remind you that the last time Elizabeth Egan made any reservations with anyone for non-business purposes was five years ago. *Five* years ago, Ivan,' she stressed. 'Can you tell me why you undid all that?'

'Because he's dirty and he smells,' I laughed.

'Because he's dirty and he smells,' she repeated, making me feel stupid. 'Then let her figure that out for herself. Don't overstep your mark, Ivan.' With that she looked back down at her work and continued writing, the feather blowing as she scribbled furiously.

'What's going on, Opal?' I asked her. 'Tell me what's really going on.'

She looked up, anger and sadness in her eyes. 'We are incredibly busy, Ivan, and we need you to work as quickly as you can and move on instead of hanging around and undoing the good work you've already done. That's what's going on.'

Stunned by her chastising I silently left her office. I didn't believe her for one minute but whatever was happening in her life was her own business. She'd change her mind about Elizabeth cancelling her dinner with Benjamin as soon as she saw what I had planned for the twenty-ninth.

'Oh, and, Ivan,' Opal called out.

I stopped at her doorway and turned. She was still looking down and writing as she spoke. 'I'll need you to come in here next Monday to take over for a while.'

'Why?' I asked with disbelief.

'I'm not going to be here for a few days. I need you to cover for me.'

That had never happened before. 'But I'm still in the middle of a job.'

'Good to hear you're still calling it that,' she snapped. Then she sighed, put down her feathered pen and looked up. She looked as if she was going to cry. 'I'm sure Saturday will be such a success you won't need to be there next week, Ivan.'

Her voice was so soft and genuine that I forgot that I was angry at her and realised for the first time that if it was any other situation, she would be right.

Chapter 29

Ivan placed the finishing touches to the dinner table, snipped a stem of fuchsia that was growing wild and placed it in the small vase in the centre. He lit a candle and watched as the flame darted in the breeze, like a dog running around the garden yet chained to his kennel. Cobh Cúin was silent, just as the name, which literally meant silent cave, suggested, christened hundreds of years ago by the locals and untouched since then. The only sound was the water gently lapping, swishing back and forth, and tickling the sand. Ivan closed his eyes and swayed to the music. A small fishing boat tied to the pier bobbed up and down on the sea, occasionally bumping the side of the pier and adding a soft drumbeat.

The sky was blue and beginning to darken with a few stray wisps of teenage clouds lagging behind the older clouds of hours ago. The stars twinkled brightly and Ivan winked back at them; they too knew what was coming. Ivan had asked the head chef at the work canteen to help him out tonight. He was the same chef responsible for catering the tea parties in the back gardens of best friends but this time he went all out. He had created the most luscious spread Ivan could have imagined. For starter was foie gras and toast cut into neat little squares, followed by wild Irish salmon and asparagus cooked in garlic, followed by a white chocolate mousse with dribbles of raspberry sauce for dessert. The aromas were being lifted by the warm gulf wind and being carried past his nose, tickling his taste buds.

He played around with the cutlery nervously, fixing all that didn't need to be fixed, tightened his new blue silk tie, loosened it again, opened the button of his navy-blue suit jacket and decided to close it again. He had been so busy all day arranging the setup that he had barely taken time to think about the feelings that were stirring inside him. Glancing at his watch and at the darkening sky, he hoped Elizabeth would come.

Elizabeth drove down the narrow winding road slowly, barely able to see past the end of her nose in the thick blackness of the countryside. Wild flowers and hedge growth reached out to brush the sides of her car as she passed. Her full headlights startled moths, mosquitoes and bats as she drove in the direction of the sea. Suddenly the inky veil lifted as she reached a clearing and the whole world was spread out before her.

Ahead were thousands of miles of ebony sea glistening under the moonlight. Inside the small cove was a tiny fishing boat tied up beside the steps, the sand was a velvety brown, the edges being licked and teased by the approaching tide. But it wasn't the sea that took her breath away; it was the sight of Ivan standing in the sand, dressed in a smart new suit, beside a small beautifully set table for two, a candle flickering in the centre, casting shadows across his smiling face.

The sight was enough to bring a tear from a stone. It was an image her mother had stamped in her mind, an image she had whispered excitedly into her ear about moonlit dinners on the beach, so much so that her mother's dreams had become her own. And there Ivan was, standing in the picture Elizabeth and her mother had painted so vividly and that had remained etched in Elizabeth's mind. She understood the phrase of not knowing whether to laugh or cry and so she unashamedly did both.

Ivan stood proudly, blue eyes glistening in the moonlight. He ignored her tears, or rather, accepted them.

'My dear,' he bowed theatrically, 'your moonlit dinner awaits you.'

Wiping her eyes and smiling a smile so big Elizabeth felt she could light the entire world, she took his extended hand and stepped out of the car.

Ivan took a sharp intake of breath. 'Wow, Elizabeth, you look stunning.'

'Wearing red is my favourite thing to do now,' she imitated him, taking his arm and allowing him to lead her to the dinner table.

After much humming and hawing Elizabeth had purchased a red dress that accentuated her slender figure, giving her curves she never even knew she had. She had taken it on and off at least five times before she left the house, feeling too exposed in such a bright colour. To prevent herself from feeling like a traffic light she had brought a black pashmina to drape over her shoulders.

The white Irish table linen flapped in the light warm breeze and Elizabeth's hair tickled her cheek. The sand was cool and soft beneath her feet, like fluffy carpet, and was protected in the cove from the sharp wind. Ivan pulled out her chair for her and she sat. Then he reached for her serviette, which had been wrapped in a stem of fuchsia, and he laid it on her lap.

'Ivan, this is beautiful, thank you,' she whispered, not feeling able to lift her voice over the peaceful lapping water.

'Thank you for coming,' he smiled, pouring her a glass of red wine. 'Now for starters we have foie gras.' He reached under the table and retrieved two plates covered in silverware. 'I hope you like foie gras,' he said, frown lines appearing on his forehead.

'I love it,' Elizabeth smiled.

'Phew.' The muscles in his face relaxed. 'It doesn't really look like grass,' he said, examining his plate closely.

'It's goose liver, Ivan,' Elizabeth laughed, spreading some on her toast. 'What made you choose this cove?' she asked, wrapping the shawl tighter around her shoulders as the breeze began to chill.

'Because it's quiet and because it's a perfect location away from streetlights,' he explained, munching on his food.

Elizabeth thought it better not to ask any questions, knowing Ivan had his own peculiar way.

After dinner Ivan turned to look at Elizabeth, who had her hands wrapped around her wine glass and was staring wistfully out to the sea. 'Elizabeth,' his voice was soft, 'will you lie with me on the sand?'

Elizabeth's heartbeat quickened. 'Yes.' Her voice was husky. She couldn't think of a better way to end the evening with him. She was longing to touch him, for him to hold her. Elizabeth made her way to the water's edge and sat down on the cool sand. She felt Ivan padding behind her.

'You're going to have to lie on your back for this to work,' he said loudly, looking down at her.

Elizabeth's mouth dropped open. 'Excuse me?' She wrapped the shawl protectively around her shoulders.

'If you don't lie back, this just won't work,' he repeated, putting his hands on his hips. 'Look, like this.' He sat down beside her and lay back on the sand. 'You have to be flat on your back, Elizabeth. It's best this way.'

'Is it now?' Elizabeth stiffened and clambered to get to her feet. 'Was all this,' she gestured around the cove, 'just to get me flat on my back, as you so beautifully phrased it?' she asked, hurt.

Ivan stared up at her from the sand, eyes wide with a flabbergasted look on his face. 'Well . . .' he stalled, trying to think of an answer, 'actually, yes,' he squeaked. 'It's just that, it's better when it peaks, for you to be flat on your back,' he stuttered.

'Ha!' Elizabeth spat and, putting her shoes back on, she

struggled through the sand to get back to her car.

'Elizabeth, look!' Ivan shouted with excitement. 'It's peaked! Look!'

'Uugh,' Elizabeth grunted, climbing the small sand dune to her car. 'You really are disgusting!'

'It's not disgusting!' Ivan said, panic in his voice.

'That's what they all say,' Elizabeth grumbled, fumbling in her bag for her car keys. Unable to see into her bag in the dark, she leaned it towards the moonlight and as she glanced up, her mouth dropped open. Above her, in the black cloudless sky, was a hive of activity. Stars glowed brighter than she had ever seen before, some darting across the sky.

Ivan lay on his back, staring up to the night sky.

'Oh,' Elizabeth said quietly, feeling foolish, glad that the darkness was hiding her skin absorbing the colour of her dress. She stumbled back down the sand dune, removed her shoes, allowed her feet to curl into the sand and took a few steps closer to Ivan. 'It's beautiful,' she whispered.

'Well, it would be a lot more beautiful if you lay flat on your back like I told you to,' Ivan huffed, crossing his arms across his chest and staring up to the sky.

Elizabeth covered her mouth with her hand and tried not to laugh out loud.

'I don't know what you're laughing at. No one accused you of being disgusting,' he said smartly.

'I thought you were talking about something else,' Elizabeth giggled, sitting down on the sand beside him.

'Why else would I be asking you to lie flat on your back?' Ivan asked in a dull tone and then he turned to her, his voice rising a few octaves, his eyes mocking. 'Oh,' he sang.

'Shut up,' Elizabeth said harshly, throwing her purse at him but letting her smile show. 'Oh, look,' she was distracted by a shooting star, 'what's going on up there tonight, I wonder.'

'It's the Delta Aquarids,' Ivan said as though that explained everything. Elizabeth's silence made him continue. 'They're meteors that come from the constellation Aquarius. The normal dates are the fifteenth of July to the twentieth of August but they peak on the twenty-ninth of July. That's why I had to take you out tonight, away from streetlights.' He turned to look at her. 'So yes, all of this was just to get you on your back.'

They studied each other's faces in comfortable silence until more action above diverted their attention.

'Why don't you make a wish?' Ivan asked her.

'No,' Elizabeth said softly, 'I'm still waiting for my Jinny Joes wish to come true.'

'Oh, I wouldn't worry about that,' Ivan said seriously. 'They just take a while to process. You won't be waiting long.'

Elizabeth laughed and stared hopefully up into the sky.

A few minutes later, sensing her sister would be on her mind, Ivan asked, 'Any word from Saoirse?'

Elizabeth gave a single shake of her head.

'She'll be home,' Ivan said positively.

'Yes, but in what condition?' Elizabeth said uncertainly. 'How is it other families manage to hold it together? And even when they've problems, how do they manage to keep it from the rest of the people in their neighbourhoods?' she asked in confusion, thinking about all the whispers she had been hearing over the past few days about her father's behaviour and her sister's disappearance. 'What's their secret?'

'See that cluster of stars right there?' Ivan asked, pointing upwards.

Elizabeth followed his hand, embarrassed to have bored him with talk of her family so much that he'd changed the subject. She nodded.

'Most meteors from a common meteor shower are parallel to one another. They appear to emerge from the same point in the sky called "the radiant" and they travel in all directions from this point.'

'Oh, I see,' Elizabeth said.

'No, you don't see.' Ivan turned on his side to face her. 'Stars are like people, Elizabeth. Just because they *appear* to emerge from the same point doesn't mean that they do. This is an illusion of perspective created by distance.' And as if Elizabeth hadn't quite understood the meaning he added, 'Not all families manage to hold it together, Elizabeth. Everyone moves in different directions. That we all emerge from the same point is a misconception; to travel in different directions is the very nature of every being and every existing thing.'

Elizabeth turned her head and faced the sky again, trying to see if what he said was true. 'Well, they could have fooled me,' she said quietly, watching more appear from the blackness every second.

She shivered and wrapped her shawl around her tighter; the sand was getting cooler with each passing hour.

'Are you cold?' Ivan asked with concern.

'A little,' she admitted.

'Right, well, the night isn't over yet,' he said, jumping to his feet. 'Time to warm up. Mind if I borrow the keys to your car?'

'Not unless you intend driving away,' she joked, handing them over.

He retrieved something from under the table once again and brought it to the car. Moments later music was softly drifting through its open door.

Ivan began to dance.

Elizabeth giggled nervously. 'Ivan, what are you doing?'

'Dancing!' he said, offended.

'What kind of dancing?' She took his extended hand and allowed herself to be pulled to her feet.

'It's the soft-shoe shuffle,' Ivan announced, dancing expertly in circles around her on the sand. 'Also called the sand dance, you'll be interested to know, which means that your mother wasn't so mad wanting to do the shuffle in the sand after all!'

Elizabeth's hands flew to her mouth, tears filled her eyes with happiness as she realised he was fulfilling yet another of her and her mother's intended activities.

'Why are you fulfilling all of my mother's dreams?' she asked, studying his face and searching for answers.

'So you don't run away like she did in search of them,' he replied, taking her hand. 'Come on, join in!'

'I don't know how!'

'Just copy me.' He turned his back and danced away from her, swinging his hips exaggeratedly.

Lifting her dress to above her knees, Elizabeth threw caution to the wind and joined in dancing the soft-shoe shuffle on the sand in the moonlight, laughing until her stomach was sore and she was out of breath.

'Oh, you make me smile so much, Ivan,' she gasped, collapsing on the sand later that evening.

'Just doin' my job,' he grinned back. As soon as the words had left his mouth his smile faded and Elizabeth detected a hint of sadness in those blue eyes.

Chapter 30

Elizabeth allowed her red dress to slide down her legs, gather at her ankles and then stepped out of it. She wrapped a warm bathrobe around her body, pinned her hair up and climbed onto her bed with a cup of coffee she had brought upstairs. She had wanted Ivan to come to bed with her tonight; despite her earlier protests she had wanted him to take her in his arms on the sand in the cove right there, but it seemed the more she felt drawn to him, the further he pulled himself away.

After they had watched the stars dancing in the sky, and then they had danced on the sand, Ivan had withdrawn into himself in the car on the journey home. He had asked her to let him out in the small town, from where he would make his own way home, wherever home was. He had yet to bring her there or introduce her to his friends and family. Elizabeth had never before been interested in meeting the others in her partners' lives. She felt as long as she enjoyed their company, whether or not she liked the company of those who surrounded him was irrelevant. But with Ivan she felt she needed to see another side to him. She needed to witness his relationships with other people so he could become a three-dimensional character to her. That was always the argument old partners had with Elizabeth and now she finally understood what it was they were searching for.

Elizabeth had watched Ivan in her mirror as she drove

away; intrigued to know what direction he would walk in. He had looked left and right down the deserted streets that were empty at the late night hour, began to walk left in the direction of the mountains and the hotel. After a few steps he stopped, turned round and walked in the other direction. He crossed the road and strode confidently toward Killarney but halted suddenly, eventually folded his arms across his chest and sat down on the stone windowsill of the butcher's.

She didn't think he knew where home was, or if he did, he didn't know his way there. She knew how he felt.

On Monday afternoon Ivan stood at the doorway to Opal's office and chuckled as he listened to Oscar ranting to Opal for a steady ten minutes. As amusing as he was to listen to, they'd have to hurry their meeting along because Ivan was due to meet Elizabeth at 6 p.m. He had twenty minutes. He hadn't seen her since the Delta Aquarids viewing on Saturday night, the greatest night of his long, long life. He had tried to walk away from her after that. He had tried to leave Baile na gCroíthe, tried to move on to someone else who needed his help, but he couldn't. He didn't feel drawn to any other direction other than Elizabeth and it was stronger than any other pull he had experienced before. This time it wasn't just his mind that was pulling him, it was his heart too.

'Opal,' Oscar's serious tones floated out to the hallway, 'I desperately need more staff for next week.'

'Yes, I understand, Oscar, and we've already arranged for Suki to help you in the lab,' Opal explained gently yet firmly. 'There's nothing more we can do for now.'

'That's simply not good enough,' he fumed. 'On Saturday night millions of people viewed the Delta Aquarids, do you know how many wishes will come shooting in here over the next few weeks?' He didn't wait for an answer and Opal didn't offer one. 'It's a dangerous procedure, Opal, and I need more hands. While Suki is extremely efficient in the administration area, she is not qualified in wish analysis. Either I'm helped out by more staff or you'll have to find a new wish analyst,' he puffed. With that he stormed out of the office, past Ivan and down the hallway mumbling, 'After years of studying to be a meteorologist I get stuck doing *this*!'

'Ivan,' Opal called.

'How do you do that?' Ivan asked, entering the office. He was beginning to think she could see through walls.

She glanced up from the desk, smiled weakly, and Ivan took a quick intake of breath. She looked very tired, with dark circles under her bloodshot eyes. She looked as if she hadn't slept for weeks.

'You're late,' she said gently. 'You were supposed to be here at 9 a.m.'

'I was?' Ivan asked, confused. 'I only called in to ask you a quick question. I have to rush off in a minute,' he added quickly. *Elizabeth, Elizabeth, Elizabeth*, he sang in his head.

'We agreed you would cover for me today, remember?' Opal said firmly, standing up from her desk and walking round to the other side.

'Oh, no, no, no,' Ivan said quickly, backing towards the door. 'I'd love to help you, Opal, really I would. Helping is one of my favourite things to do but I can't now. I've made plans to meet my client. I can't miss it, you know how it is.'

Opal leaned against the desk, folded her arms and cocked her head to one side. She blinked and her eyes closed slowly and tiredly, taking an age to open again. 'So she's your *client* now, is she?' she said wearily. Dark colours surrounded her today. Ivan could see them spreading out from all around her body.

'Yes, she's my client,' he replied less confidently. 'And I really can't miss her this evening.'

'Sooner or later you're going to have to say goodbye to her, Ivan.'

She said it so coldly, without padding or frills, that it chilled him. He gulped and shifted his weight to his other foot.

'How do you feel about that?' she asked, when he didn't answer.

Ivan thought about it. His heart thudded in his chest and he felt as if it was going to move up through his throat and out of his mouth. His eyes filled. 'I don't want to,' he said quietly.

Opal's arms lowered slowly to her sides. 'Pardon?' she asked, a little gentler.

Ivan thought about his life without Elizabeth and he raised his voice more confidently. 'I don't want to say goodbye to her. I want to stay with her for ever, Opal. She makes me feel happier than I've ever felt before in my life and she tells me that I do the same for her. Surely it would be wrong to walk away from that?' He smiled widely, recalling the feeling of being with her.

Opal's hardened face softened. 'Oh, Ivan, I knew this would happen.' There was pity in her voice and he didn't like it. He would have preferred anger. 'But I thought you of all people would have made the right decision a long time ago.'

'What decision?' Ivan's face crumpled at the thought of his having made the wrong one. 'I asked you what I should do and you wouldn't tell me.' He began to panic.

'You should have left her a long time ago, Ivan,' she said sadly, 'but I couldn't tell you to do that. You had to realise it for yourself.'

'But I couldn't leave her.' Ivan sat down on the chair before her desk slowly as the sadness and shock crept through his body. 'She kept seeing me.' His voice was almost a whisper. 'I couldn't leave until she stopped seeing me.'

'You made her keep seeing you, Ivan,' Opal explained.

'No, I didn't.' He stood up and walked away from the desk, angry at the suggestion that anything about their relationship had been forced.

'You followed her, you watched her for days, you allowed the small connection you both had to blossom. You tapped into something extraordinary and made her realise it too.'

'You don't know what you're talking about,' he spat, pacing the room. 'You have no idea how either of us is feeling.' He stopped pacing, marched up to her and looked her directly in the eye, his chin lifted, his head steady. 'Today,' he spoke with perfect clarity, 'I am going to tell Elizabeth Egan that I love her and that I want to spend my days with her. I can still help people while I'm with her.'

Opal's hands went to her face. 'Oh, Ivan, you can't!'

'You taught me that there was nothing that I couldn't do,' he snarled between gritted teeth.

'No one else will see you but her!' Opal exclaimed. 'Elizabeth won't understand. It just won't work.' She was clearly distraught by this revelation.

'If what you said is true and I made Elizabeth see me, then I can make everyone else see me too. Elizabeth will understand. She understands me like nobody else has ever done. Do you have any idea what that feels like?' He was excited now by the prospect. Before it had only been a thought, but now, now it was a possibility. He could make it happen. He looked at his watch: 6.50 p.m. He had ten minutes. 'I have to go,' he said urgently. 'I have to tell her I love her.' He strode towards the doorway with confidence and determination.

Suddenly Opal's voice broke the silence. 'I do know how you feel, Ivan.'

He stopped in his tracks, turned and shook his head. 'You can't know how this feels, Opal, not unless you've lived through this. You can't even begin to imagine.'

'I have,' she said quietly and uncertainly.

'What?' He viewed her warily with narrowed eyes.

'I have,' she said with strength in her voice this time, and crossed her hands across her stomach, clasping her fingers together. 'I fell in love with a man who saw me more than I had ever been seen in my whole entire life.'

There was a silence in the room while Ivan tried to come to terms with this. 'So that should mean that you understand me all the more.' He stepped towards her, clearly thrilled by the revelation. 'Maybe it didn't end well for you, Opal, but for me,' he smiled widely, 'who knows?' He threw his hands up and shrugged. 'This could be it!'

Opal's tired eyes stared back at him sadly. 'No.' She shook her head and his smiled faded. 'Let me show you something, Ivan. Come with me this evening. Forget the office,' she waved her hand around the room dismissively. 'Come with me and let me give you your final lesson.' She tapped his chin fondly.

Ivan looked at his watch, 'But Eliz—'

'Forget Elizabeth for now,' she said softly. 'If you choose not to take my advice you'll have Elizabeth tomorrow, the next day and everyday for the rest of her life. Nothing ventured, nothing gained.' She held out her hand to him.

Reluctantly Ivan reached out to take it. Her skin was cold.

Chapter 31

Elizabeth sat on the end of the staircase and looked out the window to the front garden. The clock on the wall said 6.50 p.m. Ivan had never been late before and she hoped he was OK. However, her sense of anger was rather more active at that moment than her worry for him. His behaviour on Saturday night gave her reason to think that his absence was due more to cold feet rather than foul play. She had thought about Ivan all day yesterday, about not meeting his friends, his family or his work colleagues, the lack of sexual contact and, in the dead of the night, as she battled to find sleep, she had realised what it was that she had being trying to hide from herself. She felt she knew what the problem was: Ivan was either in a relationship already or unwilling to enter into one.

Any niggling feeling she had along the way she had ignored. It was unusual for Elizabeth not to plan, not to know exactly where a relationship was going. She wasn't comfortable with this big change. She liked stability and routine, everything Ivan lacked. Well, she was sure that now it could never work, as she sat on the stair waiting for a free spirit, just as her father was. And she never discussed her fears with Ivan – why? Because when she was with him, every little fear dissipated. He would just show up, take her by the hand and lead her into another exciting chapter in her life, and while she was reluctant to go with him at times, often apprehensive, *with* him she was never nervous. It was when she was without him, moments like now, that she questioned everything.

She decided immediately that she was going to distance herself from him. Tonight would be the night she would discuss it with him once and for all. They were like chalk and cheese; her life was full of conflict and, as far as she could see, Ivan ran so far so fast just to avoid it. As the seconds ticked on and it moved into his fifty-first minute of being late it looked as if she didn't need to have the conversation with him after all. She sat on the stair in her new cream casual trousers and shirt, colours she would never had worn before, and she felt foolish. Foolish for listening to him, believing him, for not reading the signs properly and, even worse, for falling for him.

Her anger was hiding her pain but the last thing she wanted to do was to stay home alone and allow it to surface. She was good at doing that.

She picked up the phone and dialled.

'Benjamin, it's Elizabeth,' she said rather quickly, speaking before she had a chance to backtrack. 'How would you like to get that sushi tonight?'

'Where are we?' Ivan asked, strolling down a darkly lit cobbled street in inner city Dublin. Puddles gathered in the uneven surfaces of an area that consisted mainly of warehouses and industrial estates. One red-brick house stood alone between them all.

'That house looks funny there, sitting all on its own,' Ivan remarked. 'A bit lonely and out of place,' he decided.

'That's where we're going,' Opal said. 'The owner of this house refused to sell his property to the surrounding businesses. He stayed here while they sprung up around him.'

Ivan eyed the small house. 'I bet they offered him a fair bit. He could probably have bought a mansion in the

Hollywood Hills with what they would have paid him.' He looked down at the ground as his red Converse runner splashed into a puddle, 'I've decided cobblestones are my favourite.'

Opal smiled and laughed lightly. 'Oh, Ivan, you are so easy to love, you know that?' She walked on, not expecting an answer. Just as well, because Ivan wasn't sure.

'What are we doing?' he asked for the tenth time since they had left the office. They stood directly across the road from the house and Ivan watched Opal viewing it.

'Waiting,' Opal replied calmly. 'What time is it?'

Ivan checked his watch. 'Elizabeth will be so mad at me,' he sighed. 'It's just gone seven.'

Right on cue, the front door to the red-brick house opened. An old man leaned against the doorway, which appeared to act as a crutch. He stared outside and looked so far into the distance he appeared to be seeing the past.

'Come with me,' Opal said to Ivan, and she crossed the road and entered the house.

'Opal,' Ivan hissed, 'I can't just enter a stranger's house.' But Opal had already disappeared inside.

Ivan quickly skipped across the road and paused at the doorway, 'Em, hello, I'm Ivan.' He held out his hand.

The old man's hands remained clinging to the doorway; his watery eyes stared straight ahead.

'Right,' Ivan said awkwardly, moving his hand away. 'I'll just slide past you so, to Opal.' The man didn't blink and Ivan stepped inside. The house smelled old. It smelled as if an old person lived there with old furniture, a wireless and a grandfather clock. The clock's ticking was the loudest thing in the silent building. Time sounded and smelled to be the essence of the house, a long life lived listening to those ticks.

Ivan found Opal in the living room, looking around at all the framed photographs cluttering every surface of the room.

'This is almost as bad as your office,' he teased. 'Come on then, tell me what's going on.'

Opal turned to him and she smiled sadly. 'I told you earlier that I understand how you feel.'

'Yes.'

'I told you I knew how it felt to fall in love.'

Ivan nodded.

Opal sighed and clasped her hands together once again, almost like she was bracing herself for the news. 'Well, this is the home of the man I fell in love with.'

'Oh,' Ivan said softly.

'I still come here every day,' she explained, looking around the room.

'The old man doesn't mind us just barging in like this?'

Opal gave a small smile. 'He is the man I fell in love with, Ivan.'

Ivan's mouth dropped open. The front door closed. Footsteps slowly made their way towards them over creaking floorboards. 'No way!' Ivan hissed. 'The old man? But he's ancient – he must be at least eighty!' he whispered in shock.

The old man wandered into the room. A hacking cough stopped him in his tracks and his small frame shuddered. He winced from the pain and slowly, leaning his hands on the arms of the chair, he lowered himself into the seat.

Ivan looked from the old man to Opal and back, with a disgusted look that he tried unsuccessfully to hide from his face.

'He can't hear you or see you. We are invisible to him,' Opal said loudly. Her next sentence changed Ivan's life for good. Nineteen simple words he heard her say everyday but never in that order. She cleared her throat and there was a slight tremor in her voice as she said against the ticking of the clock, 'Remember, Ivan, forty years ago when he and I met, he wasn't ancient. He was as I am now.'

Opal watched as Ivan's face displayed many different emotions in a matter of seconds. He went from confusion, to shock, to disbelief, to pity, and then as soon as he had applied Opal's words to his own situation, to despair. His face crumpled, he paled and Opal rushed towards him to steady his swaying body. He held on to her tightly.

'That's what I was trying to tell you, Ivan,' she whispered. 'You and Elizabeth can live together perfectly happy in your own cocoon without anyone knowing but what you forget is that she will have a birthday every year and you won't.'

Ivan's body began to shake and Opal held on to him tighter. 'Oh, Ivan, I'm sorry,' she said, 'I'm so, so sorry.'

She rocked him as he cried. And cried.

'I met him in very similar circumstances to how you met Elizabeth,' Opal explained later that evening after his tears had subsided.

They both sat in armchairs in the living room of Opal's love, Geoffrey. He continued to sit in his chair by the window in silence, looking around the room and occasionally breaking into horrendous coughs that made Opal rush to his side protectively.

She twisted a tissue around in her hands, her eyes and cheeks were wet as she told her story and her dreadlocks fell around her face.

'I made every single mistake that you made,' she sniffed, and forced herself to smile, 'and I even made the one you were about to make tonight.'

Ivan swallowed hard.

'He was forty when I met him, Ivan, and we stayed together for twenty years until it became too difficult.'

Ivan's eyes widened and hope returned to his heart.

'No, Ivan,' Opal shook her head sadly and it was the weakness in her voice that convinced him. Had she spoken firmly he would have retaliated in the same manner but her voice displayed her pain. 'It couldn't work for you.' She didn't need to say any more.

'He seems to have travelled a lot,' Ivan remarked, looking around at the photos. Geoffrey in front of the Eiffel Tower, Geoffrey in front of the Leaning Tower of Pisa, Geoffrey lying on the golden sand on the shores of a faraway country, smiling and looking the picture of health, happiness at varying ages in every photo. 'At least he could move on in some way and manage to do those things alone,' he smiled encouragingly.

Opal looked at him in confusion. 'But I was there with him, Ivan.' Her forehead wrinkled.

'Oh, that's nice.' He was surprised. 'Did you take the photos?'

'No.' Her face fell. 'I'm in the photographs too, can't you see me?'

Ivan shook his head slowly.

'Oh . . .' She said studying them and seeing a different picture from Ivan.

'Why can't he see you any more?' Ivan asked, watching Geoffrey take a handful of prescribed pills and wash them down with water.

'Because I'm not who I once was, which is probably why you can't see me in the photographs. He's looking out for a different person; the connection we once had is gone,' she replied.

Geoffrey stood up from his chair, this time grabbing his cane, and made his way to the front door. He opened it and stood at the doorway.

'Come on, time to go,' Opal said, standing up from her chair and moving out to the hallway.

Ivan looked at her quizzically

'When we first started seeing each other I visited him from seven to nine every evening,' she explained, 'and seeing as I can't open doors, he used to be there waiting for me. He's been doing this every evening since we met. That's why he wouldn't sell the house. He thinks it's the only way I'll find him.'

Ivan watched his old frame wobbling on his feet as he stared out once again into the distance, perhaps thinking of that day when they had frolicked on the beach or the visit to the Eiffel Tower. Ivan didn't want that to be Elizabeth.

'Goodbye, my Opal,' his gravelly voice spoke quietly.

'Good night, my love.' Opal kissed him on the cheek and he closed his eyes softly. 'I'll see you tomorrow.'

Chapter 32

So it was clear in my mind. I knew what I had to do next. I needed to do what I was sent here to do – make Elizabeth's life as comfortable for her as possible. But now I had got so involved with her I would have to help heal old wounds *and* the new wounds that I'd foolishly caused. I was angry at myself for making a mess of everything, for getting caught up and taking my eye off the ball. My anger was overpowering the pain I felt and I was glad because, in order for me to help Elizabeth, I needed to ignore my own feelings and do what was best for her. Which was what I should have done from the start. But that's the thing about lessons: you always learn them when you don't expect them or want them. I'd have plenty of time in my life to deal with the pain of losing her.

I'd walked all night, thinking about the past few weeks and about my life. I'd never done that before – thought about *my* life. It never seemed relevant to my aim but it should always have been. I found myself back at Fuchsia Lane the next morning, sitting on the garden wall where I had first met Luke over a month ago. The fuchsia door still smiled at me and I waved back. At least that wasn't angry at me; I knew Elizabeth sure would be. She doesn't like people being late for business meetings, never mind dinner dates. I'd stood her up. Not intentionally. Not out of any malice but out of love. Imagine not meeting someone because you loved them so much. Imagine hurting someone, making them feel lonely, angry and unloved because you think it's the *best* for them. All these new rules – they were making me doubt my abilities as a best friend. They were beyond me, laws that I wasn't comfortable with at all. How could I teach Elizabeth about hope, happiness, laughter and love when I didn't know if I believed in any of those things any more? Oh, I knew they were possible, alright, but with possibility comes impossibility. A new word in my vocabulary.

At 6.00 a.m., the fuchsia door opened and I stood to attention as though a teacher had entered the classroom. Elizabeth stepped out, closed the door behind her, locked it and walked down the cobble-stoned drive. She was wearing her chocolate-brown tracksuit again, her only informal outfit in her wardrobe. Her hair was tied back messily, she had no make-up on and I don't think I'd ever seen her look so beautiful in my life. A hand reached into my heart and twisted it momentarily. It hurt.

She looked up and saw me and stalled. Her face didn't break into a smile like it usually did. The hand around my heart squeezed tighter. But at least she saw me and that was the main thing. Don't ever take for granted when people look in your eyes – you've no idea how lucky you are. Actually, forget about luck, you've no idea how *important* it is to be acknowledged, even if it is with an angry glare. It's when they ignore you, when they look right through you, that you should start worrying. Elizabeth usually ignores her problems; she usually looks right past them and never in the eye. But I was obviously a problem worth solving.

She walked towards me with her arms folded across her chest, her head held high, her eyes tired but determined.

'Are you alright, Ivan?'

Her question threw me. I expected her to be angry, to shout at me and not listen or believe my side of the story, like they do in the movies, but she didn't. She was calm, but with a temper bubbling beneath the surface, ready to erupt depending on my answer. She studied my face, searching for answers she would never believe.

I don't think I've ever been asked that question before. I was thinking about that as she was studying my face. No, it was as clear as day to me that I did not feel alright. I felt brittle, tired, angry, hungry, and there was a pain – not a hunger pain, but an ache that started in my chest and worked its way through my body and head. I felt that my views and philosophies had been changed overnight. The philosophies that I had gladly carved in stone, recited and danced upon. I felt as though the magician of life had cruelly revealed his hidden cards and it wasn't magic at all, just a mere trick of the mind. Or a lie.

'Ivan?' She looked concerned. Her face softened, her arms dropped from their folded position and she stepped forward and reached out to touch me.

I couldn't answer.

'Come on, walk with me.' She linked arms with me and we walked out of Fuchsia Lane.

They walked in silence deep into the heart of the countryside. The birds sang loudly in the early morning, the crisp air filled their lungs, rabbits bounded daringly across their path and butterflies danced through the air, waving through them as they strode along the woodlands. The sun shone down through the leaves of the dominant oaks, sprinkling light on their faces like gold dust. The sound of water trickled alongside them while the scent of eucalyptus refreshed the air. Eventually they reached an opening, where the trees held their branches out, making a grand and proud presentation of the lake. They crossed a wooden bridge, sat on a hard, carved bench and sat in silence, watching as the salmon jumped to the surface of the water to catch the flies in the warming sun.

Elizabeth was the first to speak. 'Ivan, in a complicated life, I try my best to make things as simple as possible. I know what to expect, I know what I'm going to do, where I'm going, who I'm going to meet *every single day*. In a life that is surrounded by complicated, unpredictable people, I need *stability*.' She looked away from the lake and met Ivan's eyes for the first time since they'd sat down. 'You,' she took a breath, 'you take the simplicity out of my life. You shake things around and turn them upside down. And sometimes I like it, Ivan. You make me laugh, you make me dance around streets and beaches like a lunatic and make me feel like someone I'm not.' Her smile faded. 'But last night you made me feel like someone I don't want to be. I *need* things to be simple, Ivan,' she repeated.

There was a silence between them.

Eventually Ivan spoke. 'I'm very sorry about last night, Elizabeth. You know me: it wasn't done out of any malice.' He stopped to try and figure out if and how he should explain the events of last night. He decided against it for now. 'You know, the more you try to simplify things, Elizabeth, the more you complicate them. You create rules, build walls, push people away, lie to yourself, and ignore true feelings. That is not simplifying things.'

Elizabeth ran a hand through her hair. 'I have a sister who is missing, a six-year-old nephew to mother, whom I know nothing about, a father that has not moved away from a window for weeks because he is waiting for his wife, who disappeared over twenty years ago, to return. I realised last night that I was just like him as I sat on the stairs staring out the window, waiting for a man with no surname who tells me he's from a place called Ekam Eveileb, a place that has been Googled, and searched in the damn atlas at least once a day and that I now know doesn't exist.' She took a breath. 'I care for you, Ivan, I really do, but one minute you're kissing me and the next you're standing me up. I don't know what is going on with us. I have enough worries and I have enough pain as it is and I am not volunteering myself for any more.' She rubbed her eyes tiredly.

They both watched the activities in the lake as the leaping salmon brought ripples to the surface, making soothing splashing sounds in the water. Across the lake a heron moved silently and skilfully on his stilt-like legs along the water's edge. He was a fisherman at work, watching and waiting patiently for the right moment to break the glassy surface of the water with his beak.

Ivan couldn't help but see the similarities in both their jobs at that moment.

When you drop a glass or a plate to the ground it makes a loud crashing sound. When a window shatters, a table leg breaks, or when a picture falls off the wall it makes a noise. But as for your heart, when that breaks, it's completely silent. You would think as it's so important it would make the loudest noise in the whole world, or even have some sort of ceremonious sound like the gong of a cymbal or the ringing of a bell. But it's silent and you almost wish there was a noise to distract you from the pain.

If there is a noise, it's internal. It screams and no one can hear it but you. It screams so loud your ears ring and your head aches. It thrashes around in your chest like a great white shark caught in the sea; it roars like a mother bear whose cub has been taken. That's what it looks like and that's what it sounds like, a thrashing, panicking, trapped great big beast, roaring like a prisoner to its own emotions. But that's the thing about love – no one is untouchable. It's as wild as that, as raw as an open flesh wound exposed to salty sea water, but when it actually breaks, it's silent. You're just screaming on the inside and no one can hear it.

But Elizabeth, she saw the heartbreak in me and I saw

it in her, and without having to talk about it we both knew. It was time to stop walking with our heads in the clouds, and instead, keep our feet on the harder soil of ground level we should always have been rooted to.

Chapter 33

'We should get back to the house now,' Elizabeth said, jumping up from the bench.

'Why?'

'Because it's starting to rain.' She looked at him as though he had ten heads, and flinched as another droplet of rain landed on her face.

'What is it with you?' Ivan laughed, settling down into the bench as a sign he wasn't budging. 'Why is it you're always dashing in and out of cars and buildings when it rains?'

'Because I don't want to get wet. Come on!' She looked to the safety of the trees longingly.

'Why don't you like getting wet? All it does is dries.'

'Because.' She grabbed him by the hand and attempted to pull him off the bench. She stamped her foot in frustration when she couldn't move him, like a child who couldn't get her way.

'Because why?'

'I don't know.' She swallowed hard. 'I've just never liked rain. Do you have to know all the reasons for all my little problems?' She held her hands over her head to stop the feeling of the rain falling on her.

'There's a reason for everything, Elizabeth,' he said, holding out his hands and catching the rain- drops in his palms.

'Well, my reason is simple. In keeping with our earlier

conversation, rain complicates things. It makes your clothes wet, is uncomfortable and ultimately gives you a cold.'

Ivan made a game-show noise signalling a wrong answer. 'The rain doesn't give you a cold. The *cold* gives you a cold. This is a sun shower and it's warm.' He held back his head, opened his mouth and allowed the raindrops to fall in. 'Yep, warm and tasty. And you weren't telling me the truth, by the way.'

'What?' she shrilled.

'I read between the lines, hear between the words and know when a full stop is not a full stop but more like a but,' he sang.

Elizabeth groaned and stood with her arms wrapped round herself protectively and with her shoulders hunched as though gunge were being thrown over her.

'It's only rain, Elizabeth. Look around.' He waved his hands wildly. 'Do you see anybody else here running?'

'There *is* nobody else!'

'*Au contraire!* The lake, the trees, the heron and the salmon, all getting soaked.' He threw his head back and continued tasting the rain.

Before Elizabeth headed to the trees she gave one last lecture. 'Be careful of that rain, Ivan. It's not a good idea to drink it.'

'Why?'

'Because it could be dangerous. Do you know what effect carbon monoxide has on the air and the rain? It could be acidic.'

Ivan slid off the bench while holding his throat and pretended to choke. He crawled to the edge of the lake. Elizabeth's eyes followed him but she continued lecturing him.

He dipped his hand into the lake. 'Well, there's no fatal contaminations in this, is there?' He scooped out a handful of water and threw it at her.

Her mouth fell open and her eyes widened with shock

as she stood there with water dripping from her nose. She held her arm out and pushed him roughly into the lake, laughing as he disappeared under the water.

She stopped laughing when he didn't reappear.

She began to get worried and stepped towards the edge. The only movement were the ripples caused by the heavy raindrops landing on the calm lake. The cold drops on her face no longer bothered her. A minute went by.

'Ivan?' Her voice was shaky. 'Ivan, stop playing. Come out now.' She leaned over further to see if she could see him.

She sang nervously to herself and counted to ten. Nobody could hold their breath for that long.

The glassy surface broke and a rocket shot out of the water. 'Water fight!' exploded from the water creature. It grabbed her by the hands and pulled her head-first into the lake. Elizabeth was so relieved not to have killed him she didn't even mind when the cool water hit her face and buried her.

'Good morning, Mr O'Callaghan; morning, Maur-een; hello, Fidelma; hi, Connor; Father Murphy . . .' She nodded sternly to her neighbours as she walked through the sleepy town. Silent, stunned stares followed her as her runners squelched beneath her and her clothes dripped.

'That's a good look for you,' Benjamin laughed, holding up a cup of coffee to her while he stood beside a small crowd of tourists, who were dancing, laughing and sprinkling coffee on the pavement outside Joe's.

'Thank you, Benjamin,' she answered seriously, continuing on through the town, her eyes sparkling.

The sun shone over the town, which hadn't yet received any rain that morning, and its inhabitants watched, whispered and laughed as Elizabeth Egan walked with her head held high and her arms swinging by her side as a piece of seaweed clung to her tangled hair.

* * *

Elizabeth threw another colouring pencil down; crumpled up the sheet she had been working on and tossed it across the room. It missed the bin but she didn't care. It could stay there with the other ten crumpled balls. She made a face at her calendar. A red X, which had originally signalled the end date for Ivan, Luke's invisible friend, who had long since gone, now signalled the end of her career. Well, she was being melodramatic – September was the opening date for the hotel and everything was going according to plan. All the materials had arrived on time with only the minor disasters of a few wrong orders. Mrs Bracken had her team working long hours, making cushions, curtains and duvet covers, but unusually, it was Elizabeth who was slowing things down. She just couldn't find a design for the children's playroom and was beginning to detest herself for even mentioning the idea to Vincent. She was too distracted lately.

She sat at her favourite place at the kitchen table and laughed to herself at the memory of her earlier 'swim'.

Things between her and Ivan were more unusual than ever. Today she had effectively ended their relationship and it broke her heart to do it, yet here he was, still with her in her home, making her laugh as though nothing had happened. But something had happened, something huge, and she could feel the effect of it right under her chest. As the day wore on she realised that she had never backtracked so much in a relationship with a man and yet still felt satisfied to be in his company. Neither of them was ready for more, not yet anyway, but she wished so much that he was.

Dinner with Benjamin the previous night had been pleasant. She had battled with her dislike of going out to eat, her dislike of food and her dislike of unnecessary conversations, and while she managed to put up with those things with Ivan, sometimes even enjoy them, she still found it a task. Socialising wasn't enjoyable for her, however they had much in common. They had a nice chat and a nice meal, but Elizabeth wasn't upset when it was all over and time to go home. Her mind was hugely distracted, wondering about her future with Ivan. Not like when Ivan left her.

Luke's giggles brought her out of her daydream.

Ivan spoke. '*Bonjour, madame.*'

Elizabeth looked up to see both Ivan and Luke entering the conservatory from the garden. Each had a magnifying glass held up to his right eye, causing their eyes to appear gigantic. Across each of their upper lips a moustache had been drawn in black marker. She couldn't help but laugh.

'Ah, but zis is no laffing matter, madame. Zere 'az been a mur-dare,' Ivan said gravely, approaching the table.

'A murder,' Luke translated.

'What?' Elizabeth's eyes widened.

'We're looking for clues, madame,' Luke explained, his uneven moustache wobbling up and down as he spoke.

'A ghastly mur-dare 'az taken place in your jardin,' Ivan explained, running the magnifying glass along the surface of the kitchen table in search for clues.

'That's French for garden,' Luke explained.

Elizabeth nodded, trying not to laugh.

'Forgive us for just barging into your 'ome. Allow us to introduce ourselves. I am Mister Monsieur and zis iz my foolish sidekick, Monsieur Rotalsnart.'

Luke giggled. 'It's backwards for translator.'

'Oh,' Elizabeth nodded. 'Well, it's very nice to meet you both but I'm afraid I'm very busy here, so if you don't mind . . .' She widened her eyes at Ivan.

'Mind? Of course we mind. We are in ze middle of a very serious mur-dare investigay-c-on and you are what?' He looked around, his eyes fell upon the crumpled balls of paper by the bin. He picked one up and studied it with his magnifying glass. 'You are making snowballs, as far as I can see.'

Elizabeth made a face at him and Luke giggled.

'We must interrogate you. Have you any harsh lights we can shine in your face?' Ivan looked around the room and withdrew the question on glancing at Elizabeth's face. 'Very well, madame.'

'Who has been murdered?' Elizabeth asked.

'Ah, just as I suspected, Monsieur Rotalsnart.' They paced the floor in opposite directions with the magnifying glasses still over their eyes. 'She pretends to not know so we don't suspect her. Clever.'

'Do you think she did it?' Luke asked.

'We shall see. Madame, a worm was found squished to death earlier today on the path leading from your conservatory to the clothes line. His devastated family tell us he left home when the rain had stopped in order to cross the path to the other side of the garden. His reasons for wanting to go there are not known but it's what worms do.'

Luke and Elizabeth looked at one another and laughed.

'The rain stopped at 6.30 p.m., which is when the worm left his home to cross the path. Could you tell me your whereabouts, madame?'

'Am I a suspect?' Elizabeth laughed.

'At zis stage of the investigay-c-on, everyone is a suspect.'

'Well, I returned from work at 6.15 and put the dinner on. Then I went to the utility room and emptied the damp clothes from the washing machine into the basket.'

'Then what did you do?' Ivan thrust the magnifying glass in her face and moved it around, studying her. 'I am checking for clues,' he whispered to Luke.

'After that I waited for the rain to stop and then I hung the washing on the line.'

Ivan gasped dramatically. 'Monsieur Rotalsnart, did you hear that?'

Luke's giggling revealed his gums, from where yet another tooth had fallen.

'Well then, this means you are the mur-dare-air!'

'The murderer,' Luke translated.

They both turned to her with their magnifying glasses over their eyes.

Ivan spoke. 'As you tried to keep your birthday of next week a secret from me, your punishment will be to have a party in the back *jardin* in the memory of the recently deceased Monsieur Wriggles, the worm.'

Elizabeth groaned. 'No way.'

'I know, Elizabeth,' he changed to an upper-class British accent, 'having to socialise with the village folk is so terribly frightful.'

'What folk?' Elizabeth's eyes narrowed.

'Oh, just a few people we invited,' Ivan shrugged. 'Luke posted the invites this morning, isn't he great?' He nodded to a proud and beaming Luke. 'Next week you will be the host of a garden party. People you don't know very well will be stomping through your home, possibly making it dirty. Think you can handle that?'

Chapter 34

Elizabeth sat cross-legged on the white sheet covering the dusty cement floor of the building site, with her eyes closed.

'So this is where you disappear to every day.'

Elizabeth's eyes remained closed. 'How do you do it, Ivan?'

'Do what?'

'Just appear out of nowhere exactly when I'm thinking of you?'

She heard him laugh lightly but he didn't answer the question. 'Why is this room the only room that hasn't been finished? Or started, by the looks of it.' He stood behind her.

'Because I need help. I'm stuck.'

'Well, what do you know, Elizabeth Egan is asking for help.' There was a silence until Ivan started humming a familiar song, the song she hadn't been able to get out of her head for the past two months and the song that was making her almost broke, thanks to Poppy and Becca's pig in the office.

Her eyelids flew open. 'What are you humming?'

'The humming song.'

'Did Luke teach you that?'

'No, *I* taught *him*, thank you very much.'

'Oh, really,' Elizabeth grumbled. 'I thought his *invisible* friend made it up.' She laughed to herself and then looked up to him. He wasn't laughing.

Eventually he spoke. 'Why do you sound like you're speaking with socks in your mouth? What is that on your face? A muzzle?' he chortled.

Elizabeth flushed. 'It's not a muzzle,' she spat. 'You have no idea how much dust and bacteria this building has. Anyway, you should be wearing a hard hat,' she knocked on her own. 'God forbid this place should come down on us.'

'What else are you wearing?' He ignored her moodiness and looked her up and down. 'Gloves?'

'So my hands don't get dirty,' she pouted like a child.

'Oh, Elizabeth,' Ivan shook his head and strolled comically around her, 'all the things I've taught you and you're still worrying about being clean and tidy.' He picked up a paintbrush, which was sitting beside an open pot of paint and dipped it in.

'Ivan,' Elizabeth said nervously watching him, 'what are you going to do?'

'You said you wanted help,' he grinned.

Elizabeth rose slowly to her feet. 'Ye-es, help with painting the *wall*,' her voice warned.

'Well, unfortunately you didn't quite specify that when you asked, so I'm afraid that doesn't count.' He dipped the paintbrush into the red paint, held the bristles back in his hand and released them towards Elizabeth like a catapult. Paint splattered across her face. 'Ooh, too bad you weren't wearing protective clothing on the rest of your face,' he teased, watching her eyes widen in anger and shock. 'But it just goes to show, no matter how hard you try to wrap yourself in cotton wool, you can still hurt yourself.'

'Ivan,' there was venom in her voice, 'throwing me in the lake is *one* thing but this is *ludicrous*,' she squealed. 'This is my *work*. I'm serious, I want absolutely *nothing* more to do with you, Ivan, Ivan . . . I don't even know your surname,' she spluttered.

'It's Elbisivni,' he explained calmly.

'What are you, *Russian*?' she shouted almost hyperventilating. 'Is Ekam Eveileb Russian too or does it even *exist*?' She was screaming now, and breathless.

'I'm very sorry,' Ivan said seriously, his smile disappearing. 'I can sense that you're upset. I'll just put this back down.' He slowly lowered the paintbrush back to the pot and left it back at the perfect angle it had been placed, mirroring the others. 'That was over the top. I apologise.'

Elizabeth's anger began to subside.

'The red is perhaps too much of an angry colour for you,' he continued. 'I should have been more subtle.' Suddenly another paintbrush appeared before Elizabeth's face. Her eyes widened.

'White maybe?' he grinned, and splashed the paint down her top.

'Ivan!' Elizabeth half laughed and half shouted. 'Fine,' she dived towards the pots of paint, 'you wanna play? I can play. Wearing colours is your favourite thing to do now, you say?' she grumbled to herself. She dipped a paintbrush in the pot and chased Ivan round the room. 'Blue's your favourite colour, Mr Elbisivni?' She painted a strip of blue down his face and hair, and began laughing evilly.

'You thought that was funny?'

She nodded in hysterics.

'Good,' Ivan laughed, grabbing her by the waist and pushing her to the floor, pinning her down masterfully and painting her face while she squealed and struggled to get free. 'If you don't stop shouting, Elizabeth, you'll have a green tongue,' Ivan warned.

After they had both been covered head to toe in paint and Elizabeth was laughing so much she could no longer put up a fight, Ivan turned his attention to the wall. 'What this wall needs now is some paint.'

Elizabeth removed her mouth cover and tried to regain her breathing, revealing the only normal skin colour on her face.

'Well, at least that came in handy,' Ivan noted, and turned back to face the wall. 'A little birdie told me that you went on a date with Benjamin West,' Ivan said, dipping a fresh brush into the red paint pot.

'Dinner, yes. A date, no. And may I add that I went out with him the night you stood me up.'

He didn't reply. 'You like him?' he asked.

'He's a nice man.' She still didn't turn round.

'You want to spend more time with him?'

Elizabeth began to roll up the paint-splattered sheet from the floor. 'I'd like to spend more time with you.'

'What if you couldn't?'

Elizabeth froze. 'Then I'd ask you why.'

He avoided the question. 'What if I didn't exist and you'd never met me, would you want to spend more time with Benjamin then?'

Elizabeth swallowed hard, put her paper and pens into her bag and zipped it shut. She was tired of playing games with him and his talk was making her nervous. They needed to discuss this properly. She stood up and faced him. On the wall, Ivan had written 'Elizabeth ♥s Benjamin' in big red letters.

'Ivan!' Elizabeth giggled nervously. 'Don't be such a child. What if someone was to see that!' She went to grab the brush from him.

He wouldn't let go and their eyes locked. 'I can't give you what you want, Elizabeth,' he said softly.

A coughing from the doorway caused them both to jump.

'Hi, Elizabeth,' Benjamin looked at her with curious amusement. He glanced at the wall behind her and grinned. 'That's an interesting theme.'

There was a pregnant pause. Elizabeth looked to her right. 'It was Ivan.' Her voice came out childlike.

Benjamin chuckled slightly. 'Him again.'

She nodded and he looked to the paintbrush in her

hand, dripping red onto her jeans. A red, blue, purple, green and white splashed face now turned crimson.

'Looks like it's *you* who's been caught painting the roses red,' Benjamin said, and went to take a step into the room.

'Benjamin!'

He paused mid-step, with a pained expression at the sound of Vincent's demanding voice. 'I'd better go,' he smiled. 'I'll talk to you later,' and he headed off in the direction of Vincent's shouts. 'Oh, by the way,' he called out, 'thanks for the party invitation.'

A fuming Elizabeth ignored Ivan, doubled over laughing and occasional snorting. She dipped her brush in the white pot and erased Ivan's words, trying to erase this embarrassing moment from her memory.

'Good afternoon, Mr O'Callaghan; hello, Maureen; hello, Fidelma; hi, Connor, Father Murphy,' she greeted her neighbours as she walked through the town to get to her office. Red paint dribbled down her arms, blue paint clung in strands around her hair and her jeans looked like Monet's palette. Silent, stunned stares followed her as her clothes continued to drip with paint, leaving a multi-coloured trail behind her.

'Why do you always do that?' Ivan asked, running alongside her to keep up as she marched through the town.

'Do what? Good afternoon, Sheila.'

'You always cross the road before you get to Flanagan's pub, walk on the opposite path and then cross again once you get to Joe's.'

'No I don't.' She smiled at another gawker.

'Talk about painting the town red, Elizabeth,' Joe called out to her, laughing as she left red footprints behind her as she ran across the road.

'Look, you just did it!' Ivan pointed out.

Elizabeth stopped and looked back on her track, visible by her footprints. True enough, she had crossed the road at Flanagan's, walked on the opposite path and crossed over once again to get to her office, instead of staying on the same path. She hadn't noticed that before. She looked back at Flanagan's pub. Mr Flanagan stood at the door having a cigarette. He nodded at her strangely, appearing surprised she held his stare. She frowned and swallowed the lump that had formed in her throat as she stared at the building.

'Everything OK, Elizabeth?' Ivan asked, cutting into her thoughts.

'Yes.' Her voice came out as a whisper. She cleared her throat, looked at Ivan in confusion and unconvincingly repeated, 'Yes, I'm fine.'

Chapter 35

Elizabeth passed a gobsmacked and disapproving Mrs Bracken, who was standing at the door with two other elderly women, all with pieces of fabric in their hands. They tutted as she trudged by, with paint in clumps in the ends of her hair, which was rubbing against her back and causing a beautiful multicoloured effect.

'Is she losing her marbles or what?' one of the women whispered loudly.

'No, quite the opposite.' Elizabeth could hear the smile in Mrs Bracken's voice. 'I'd say she's been on her hands and knees looking for them.'

The other women tutted and wandered away, muttering about Elizabeth not being the only one losing her marbles.

Elizabeth ignored the stare from Becca and the shout from Poppy, 'That's more like it!' and marched into her office, closing the door softly behind her. Shutting everything out. She leaned her back against the door and tried to figure out why her body was shaking so much. What had been stirred inside her? What monsters had awoken from their slumber and were bubbling away under her skin? She breathed in deeply through her nostrils and exhaled slowly, counting one, two, three times until her weak knees stopped trembling.

Everything had been fine, if not mildly embarrassing, as she walked through the town looking like she had dipped herself in a pot of rainbow-coloured paint. It had all been fine until Ivan said something. What did he say . . . ? He said . . . and then she remembered and a chill ran through her body.

Flanagan's pub. She always avoided Flanagan's pub, he said. She hadn't noticed until he brought it to her attention. Why did she do it? Because of Saoirse? No, Saoirse drank in the Camel's Hump, on the hill, down the road. She remained leaning against the door, thinking until her head was dizzy. The room spun her and she decided she needed to get home. Home to where she could control what went on, who could enter, who could leave, where things had their own place and where every memory was clear. She needed order.

'Where's your beanbag, Ivan?' Calendula asked, looking up at me from her yellow-painted wooden chair.

'Oh, I got tired of that,' I replied. 'Spinning is my new favourite thing now.'

'Nice,' she nodded with approval.

'Opal's really late,' Tommy said, wiping his runny nose along his arm.

Calendula looked away in disgust, straightened her pretty yellow dress, crossed her ankles and swung her white patent shoes and frilly socks while she hummed the humming song.

Olivia knitted in her rocking chair. 'She'll be here,' she rasped.

Jamie-Lynn reached out to the centre table to grab a chocolate Rice Krispie bun and a glass of milk, and as she coughed and spluttered, her glass of milk spilled all over her arm. She licked it off.

'Have you been playing in the doctor's waiting room again, Jamie-Lynn?' Olivia asked, glaring at her over the rim of her glasses.

Jamie-Lynn nodded, coughed again on her bun and took another bite.

Calendula wrinkled her nose in disgust and continued combing her Barbie's hair with a small comb.

'You know what Opal told you, Jamie-Lynn. Those places are full of bacteria. Those toys you like to play with are the cause of you being ill.'

'I know,' Jamie-Lynn said with food in her mouth, 'but someone's got to keep the kids company when they're waiting for the doc.'

Twenty minutes passed and eventually Opal showed. Everyone looked at each other with worry. It looked as though Opal's shadow had taken her place. She didn't float into the room like a fresh morning breeze as she usually did; it was as though every step she took she was laden down with heavy buckets of cement. The others all quietened down immediately, seeing the deep blue, almost black, colour that followed her in.

'Good afternoon, my friends.' Even Opal's voice was different, as though she was being muffled and held back in another dimension.

'Hello, Opal.' The replies were soft and hushed, as though more than a whisper would knock her to rubble.

She gave them a gentle smile, acknowledgeing their support. 'Somebody who has been a friend of mine for a great deal of time is sick. Very sick. He's going to die and I'm very sad to lose him,' she explained.

Everyone made soothing noises. Olivia stopped rocking in her chair, Bobby stopped rolling back and forth on his skateboard, Calendula's legs stopped kicking, Tommy even stopped sniffing the snot back up his nose and I stopped swinging on my chair. This was serious stuff, and the group talked about what it's like to lose people they love. Everyone understood. It happened to best friends all the time and each time it happened, the sadness was never less.

I couldn't contribute to the conversation. Every emotion I have ever felt for Elizabeth gathered and swelled in my throat like a pumping heart receiving more and more love every moment and growing bigger and prouder as a result. The lump in my throat prevented me from speaking just as my growing heart prevented me from stopping loving Elizabeth.

As the meeting was ending, Opal looked to me. 'Ivan, how are things with Elizabeth?'

Everyone looked at me and I found a tiny hole in that lump for my sound to seep through. 'I've left her until tomorrow to figure something out.' I thought of her face and my heart pumped quicker and grew, and that tiny hole in the lump in my throat closed.

And without anyone knowing my situation, they all understood it to mean 'not long now'. By the way Opal quickly picked up her files and fled the adjourned meeting, I figured it was the same case for her.

Elizabeth's feet pounded on the treadmill that faced the back garden in her home. She looked out at the hills, the lakes and mountains spread before her and ran even faster. Her hair blew behind her as she ran, her brow glistened, her arms moved with her legs and she imagined as she did every day that she was running over those hills, across the seas, far, far away. After thirty minutes of running and running yet staying in the same place she stopped, left the small gym panting and weak, and immediately began to clean, scrubbing furiously on surfaces that already sparkled.

As soon as she had cleaned the house from top to bottom, had wiped away all the cobwebs, cleared every darkened hidden corner, she began to do the same with her mind. All her life she had run from shedding light on those darkened corners of her mind. The cobwebs and dust had settled and now she was ready to start clearing them. Something was trying to crawl out of that darkness and now she was ready to help it. Enough running.

She sat at the kitchen table and stared out at the country spread before her, tumbling hills, valleys and lakes with fuchsia and montbretia lacing them all. The sky was darkening earlier now that August had arrived.

She thought long and hard about nothing and everything, allowing whatever was niggling her mind to have a chance to step out of the shadows and show itself. It was the same niggling feeling she ran from while she lay in bed trying to sleep, the feeling she fought while furiously cleaning. But now she sat at the table a surrendered woman, with her hands held high, stepping away from her weapon and allowing her thoughts to hold her under arrest. She had been like an escaped criminal on the run for so long.

'Why are you sitting in the dark?' a sweet voice called out to her.

She smiled lightly. 'I'm just thinking, Luke.'

'Can I sit with you?' he asked, and she hated herself for wanting to say no. 'I won't say anything or touch anything, I promise,' he added.

That twisted her heart – was she really that bad? Yes, she knew she was.

'Come over and sit down,' she smiled, pulling out the chair beside her.

They both sat in the darkened kitchen in silence until Elizabeth spoke. 'Luke, there are some things that I should talk to you about. Things I should have spoken to you before but . . .' She twisted her fingers, trying very carefully to decide how to word what she was saying. When she was a child, all she wanted was for people to explain what had happened, where her mother had gone and why. A simple explanation would have helped years and years of tortuous wondering.

He looked at her with big blue eyes from under long lashes, chubby cheeks that were rosy and a glistening upper lip from a runny nose. She laughed and ran a hand through his snow-white hair and left it resting on the back of his hot little neck.

'But,' she continued, 'I didn't know how to say them to you.'

'Is it about my mom?' Luke asked, his legs swinging below the glass table.

'Yes. She hasn't visited us in a while, as you've probably noticed.'

'She's gone on an adventure,' Luke said happily.

'Well, I don't know if you could call it that, Luke,' Elizabeth sighed. 'I don't know where she's gone, sweetheart. She didn't tell anyone before she left.'

'She told me,' he chirped.

'What?' Elizabeth's eyes widened, her heart quickened.

'She came to the house before she went away. She told me she was going away but she didn't know for how long. And I said that's kind of like an adventure and she laughed and said yes.'

'Did she say why?' Elizabeth whispered, surprised that Saoirse had the compassion to say goodbye to her son.

'Mm-hmm,' he nodded, kicking his feet faster now. 'She said because it was best for her and you and Granddad and me because she kept doing the wrong things and making everyone mad. She said she was doing what you always told her to do. She said she was flying away.'

Elizabeth held her breath lightly and remembered how she used to tell her baby sister to fly away when things were tough at home. She remembered how she watched her little six-year-old sister as she drove away to college and told her over and over again to fly away. All her emotions caught in her throat.

'What did you say?' Elizabeth managed to force out, running her hand through Luke's baby-soft hair and feeling and overwhelming urge to protect him more than anything for the first time in her life.

'I told her she was probably right,' Luke replied matter-of-factly. 'She said that I was a big boy now and it was my job to look after you and Granddad.'

Tears fell from her eyes. 'She did?' she sniffed.

Luke lifted his hand and delicately wiped her tear.

'Well, don't you worry,' she kissed his hand and reached out to hug him, 'because it's my job to look after you, OK?'

His reply was muffled as his head was pushed against her chest. She let go of him quickly to allow him to breathe.

'Edith will be home soon,' he said excitedly after he had taken a deep breath. 'Can't wait to see what she got me.'

Elizabeth smiled, tried quickly to compose herself and cleared her throat. 'We can introduce her to Ivan. Do you think she'll like him?'

Luke wrinkled up his face. 'I don't think she'll be able to see him.'

'We can't keep him to ourselves, you know, Luke,' Elizabeth laughed.

'Anyway, Ivan might not even be here when she gets back,' he added.

Elizabeth's heart thudded, 'What do you mean? Did he say something?'

Luke shook his head.

Elizabeth sighed. 'Oh, Luke, just because you're close to Ivan it doesn't mean he'll leave you, you know. I don't want you to be afraid of that happening. I used to be afraid like that. I used to think that everyone I loved would always go away.'

'*I* won't go away.' Luke looked at her caringly.

'And I promise you I won't go anywhere either.' She kissed him on the head, then cleared her throat. 'You know the things that you and Edith do together, like going to the zoo and the cinema, things like that?'

Luke nodded.

'Would you mind if I came along sometimes?'

Luke smiled happily. 'Yeah, that'd be cool.' He thought for a while. 'We're kind of the same now, aren't we? My mom leaving is kinda like what your mom did, isn't it?'

he asked, breathing on the glass table and writing his name in the fog with his finger.

Elizabeth's body grew cold. 'No,' she snapped, 'it's nothing like that at all.' She stood up from the table, switched on the light and started wiping down the counter. 'They are totally different people, it's not the same at all.' Her voice trembled as she scrubbed furiously. Looking up to check on Luke she caught sight of her reflection in the glass of the conservatory and froze. Gone was the composure, gone were her emotions, she looked like a possessed woman hiding from the truth, running from the world.

And then she knew.

And the memories that lurked in the dark corners of her mind began to creep ever so slowly into the light.

Chapter 36

'Opal,' I called gently from her office doorway. She seemed so brittle and I was afraid that the slightest noise would shatter her.

'Ivan.' She smiled tiredly, pinning her dreadlocks back from her face.

I could see myself in her shining eyes as I entered the room. 'We're all worried about you – is there anything we, I can do to help?'

'Thank you, Ivan, but apart from keeping an eye on things around here, there's really nothing anyone can do to help. I'm just so tired. I've been spending the past few nights at the hospital and I haven't allowed myself to sleep. He's got only days left now; I don't want to miss it when he . . .' She looked away from Ivan and to the picture frame on her desk, and when she spoke again her voice was trembling. 'I just wish there was some way I could say goodbye to him, to let him know he's not alone, that I'm by his side.' Her tears fell.

I went to her side and comforted her, feeling helpless and knowing that for once there was absolutely nothing I could do to help this friend. Or was there?

'Hold on a minute, Opal. Maybe there is a way you can. I have an idea.' And with that I ran.

Elizabeth had made last-minute arrangements for Luke to sleep over at Sam's house. She knew she needed to be alone that night. She could feel a change within her; a chill had entered her body and wouldn't leave. She sat huddled up in her bed, wearing an oversized jumper covered by a blanket, desperate to keep warm.

The moon outside her window noticed something was wrong and guarded her protectively from the darkness. Her stomach cramped with anticipation. The things that Ivan and Luke had said today had turned a key in her mind and had unlocked a chest of memories so terrifying that Elizabeth was afraid to close her eyes.

She gazed out the window through the open curtains at the moon, then allowed herself to drift . . .

She was twelve years old. It was two weeks since her mother had brought her for a picnic in the field, two weeks since she had told her she was going away, two weeks of waiting for her to come back. Outside Elizabeth's bedroom a screeching one-month-old Saoirse was held, hushed and comforted by her father.

'Hush now, baby, hush . . .' She could hear his gentle tones getting louder and then quietening as he paced the floor of the bungalow in the late night hour. Outside, the wind howled, squeezing itself through the windows and door locks with a whistling sound. It raced in and danced around the rooms, taunting, teasing and tickling Elizabeth as she lay in her bed, hands over her ears, tears falling down her cheeks.

Saoirse's cries got louder, Brendan's pleas got louder and Elizabeth covered her head with her pillow.

'Please, Saoirse, please stop crying,' her father begged, and attempted a song, a lullaby that Elizabeth's mother always sang to them. She clamped her hands over her ears harder but still could hear Saoirse's cries and her father's tuneless song. Elizabeth sat up in her bed, her eyes stinging from yet another night of tears and lack of sleep.

'You want your bottle?' her father asked gently over the roars. 'No? Ah, love, what is it?' he asked in a pained voice. 'I miss her too, love, I miss her too,' and he too began to cry. Saoirse, Brendan and Elizabeth all cried for Gráinne together, but all feeling alone, in their bungalow blown by the wind.

Suddenly headlights appeared at the end of the long road. Elizabeth leaped out of her covers and sat at the end of her bed with her stomach twisted in excitement. It was her mother – it had to be. Who else would be calling all the way down here at ten o'clock at night? Elizabeth bounced up and down at the end of her bed in delight.

The car pulled up outside the house, the car door opened and out stepped Kathleen, Gráinne's sister. Leaving the door open with the headlights still on and the wipers moving violently across the windscreen, she marched to the gate, pushed it open causing it to creak, and banged on the door.

With a screaming Saoirse in his arms Brendan opened the door. Elizabeth rushed to the keyhole of her bedroom door and looked out into the hall at the action.

'Is she here?' Kathleen demanded, without a hello or a kind word.

'Sshh,' Brendan said, 'I don't want you waking Elizabeth.'

'As if she's not already awake with all that screaming. What have you done to the poor child?' she asked incredulously.

'The child wants her mother,' he raised his voice. 'Like us all,' he added in softer tones.

'Give her to me,' Kathleen said.

'You're wet,' Brendan stepped away from her and his arms tightened around the tiny bundle.

'Is she here?' Kathleen asked again, her voice still angry. She was still standing outside the front door. She hadn't asked to come in and she hadn't been invited.

'Of course she's not here.' Brendan bounced Saoirse around, trying to calm her. 'I thought you'd taken her to that magical place that would cure her for ever,' he said angrily.

'It was supposed to be the best place, Brendan – better than the other ones, anyhow. Anyway,' she mumbled the next few words, 'she's gone.'

'Gone? What do you mean, gone?'

'She was missing this morning from her room. Nobody's seen her.'

'Has a habit of disappearing in the night, does your mother,' Brendan said angrily, rocking Saoirse. 'Well, if she's not where you sent her, you don't need to look far from here. Sure won't she be in Flanagan's?'

Elizabeth's eyes widened and she gasped. Her mother was here in Baile na gCroíthe; she hadn't left her after all.

In between their bitter exchanges, Saoirse wailed.

'For Christsake, Brendan, can you not quieten her?' Kathleen complained. 'You know I can take the children. They can live with me and Alan in—'

'They're *my* children and you won't take them from me like you did Gráinne,' he bellowed. Saoirse's wails quietened.

There was a long silence.

'Be off with you.' Brendan spoke weakly as though his earlier boom had broken his voice.

The front door closed and Elizabeth watched from the window as Kathleen banged the gate shut and got into her car. It sped off, the lights disappearing into the distance along with Elizabeth's hopes of going with her to see her mother.

A glimmer of hope remained. Her father had mentioned Flanagan's. Elizabeth knew where that was – she passed it everyday going to school. She would pack her bag, find her mother and live with her away from her screaming little sister and father, and they would go on adventures every day.

The handle on the door shook and she dived into bed

and pretended to be asleep. Squeezing her eyes tightly shut, she decided that as soon as her father had gone to bed, she would make her own way to Flanagan's.

She would sneak out into the night, just like her mother.

'Are you sure this is going to work?' Opal stood against the wall of the hospital ward, her hands trembling as they clasped and unclasped themselves against her anxiety-filled stomach.

Ivan looked at her with uncertain eyes. 'It's worth a try.'

Through the glass in the corridor they could see Geoffrey in his private room. He was hooked up to a ventilator, his mouth covered by the oxygen mask, and around him contraptions beeped while wires ran from his body into machines. In the centre of all this action, his body lay still and calm, his chest rising and falling rhythmically. They were surrounded by that eerie sound that only hospitals provided, the sound of everyone waiting, of being in between one timeless place and another.

As soon as the nurses who were tending to Geoffrey opened the door to leave, Opal and Ivan entered.

'Here she is,' Olivia spoke from beside Geoffrey's bed, as Opal entered.

His eyes shot open quickly and he began to look around wildly, searching the room.

'She's on your left-hand side, dear, she's holding your hand,' Olivia said gently.

Geoffrey attempted to speak, his sound coming out muffled from under the mask. Opal's hand flew to her mouth, her eyes filled and the lump in her throat was visible. It was a language that only Olivia could understand; the words of a dying man.

Olivia nodded as he made sounds; her eyes filled and when she spoke Ivan could no longer stay in the room.

'He said to tell you, that his heart has ached every moment you were apart, dear Opal.'

Ivan stepped out of the room through the open door and walked as quickly as he could down the hall and out of the hospital.

Chapter 37

Outside Elizabeth's bedroom window on Fuchsia Lane, the rain fell, hitting off the bedroom window like pebbles. The wind began warming its vocal chords for the night and Elizabeth, tucked up in bed, was transported back to the time she journeyed out in the late winter night to find her mother.

She had packed her schoolbag with only a few things – underwear, two jumpers and skirts, the book her mother gave her and her teddy. Her money box had revealed £4.42, and after wrapping her raincoat around her favourite floral dress and stepping into her red Wellington boots, she set out into the cold night. She climbed the small garden wall to avoid the sound of the gate alerting her father, who these days slept like the farmyard dog, with one ear pricked. She kept alongside the bushes so as not to be spotted walking up the straight road. The wind pushed and pulled the branches, scraping them against her face and legs, and wet kisses from soggy leaves brushed against her skin. The wind was vicious that night. It whipped her legs and stung her ears and cheeks, blowing against her face so hard it took her breath away. Within minutes of walking up the road, her fingers, nose and lips were numb and her body was freezing to the bone but the thought of seeing her mother that night kept her going. And on she journeyed.

Twenty minutes later she arrived at the bridge to Baile na gCroíthe. She had never seen the town at eleven o'clock at night; it was like a ghost town, dark, empty and silent, as if it were about to bear witness to something and never speak a word of it.

She walked towards Flanagan's with butterflies in her tummy, no longer feeling the lash of the cold, just pure excitement at the thrill of being reunited with her mother. She heard Flanagan's before she saw it; there, and the Camel's Hump, were the only buildings in the village with lights on. From an open window, out floated the sounds of a piano, fiddle, badhrán, and loud singing and laughter, occasional cheers and whoops. Elizabeth giggled to herself; it sounded like everyone was having such fun.

Outside, Aunt Kathleen's car was parked and Elizabeth's legs automatically moved faster. The front door was open and inside there was a small hallway, but the door to the pub, complete with stained glass, was closed. Elizabeth stood in the porch and shook the rain from her coat; hung it up alongside the umbrellas on the rack on the wall. Her black hair was soaking wet and her nose was red and running. The rain had found its way into the top of her boots, and her legs shook from the cold and her feet squelched in the ice-cold pools of water.

The piano stopped suddenly, and there was a loud roar from a crowd of men that made Elizabeth jump.

'Come on, Gráinne, sing us another one,' one man slurred, and they all cheered.

Elizabeth's heart leaped at the sound of her mother's name. She was inside! She was such a beautiful singer. She sang around the house all the time, composing lullabies and nursery rhymes all by herself, and in the mornings Elizabeth loved to lie in her bed and listen to her mother as she hummed around the rooms of the bungalow. But the voice that began in the silence, followed by the rowdy cheers of drunken men, was not the sweet voice of her mother that she knew so well.

In Fuchsia Lane, Elizabeth's eyes darted open and she sat upright in her bed. Outside, the wind howled like a wounded animal. Her heart was hammering in her chest; her mouth was dry and her body clammy. Throwing the covers off her, she grabbed her car keys from the bedside table, ran down the stairs, threw her raincoat around her shoulders and escaped the house to her car. The cold drops of rain hit her, and she remembered why she hated to feel the rain against her face: it reminded her of that night. She hurried to her car, shivering as the wind tossed her hair across her eyes and cheeks, and by the time she sat behind the wheel she was already drenched.

The windscreen wipers lashed across the window furiously as she drove down the dark roads to the town. Driving over the bridge she was faced with the ghost town. Everyone was locked safely inside, in the warmth of their houses and hostels. Apart from the Camel's Hump and Flanagan's there was no nightlife. Elizabeth parked her car and stood across the road from Flanagan's, standing in the cold rain staring across at the building, remembering. Remembering that night.

Elizabeth's ears hurt from the words of the song being sung by the woman. It was crude, the words disgusting, being sung in such crass and dirty tones. Every rude word Elizabeth was taught not to say by her father was winning the plaudits of a boozy, sozzled pack of beasts.

She stood on tiptoes to look through the red of the stained-glass windows to see what awful woman was croaking the awful tune. She was sure her mother would be sitting beside Kathleen, absolutely disgusted.

Elizabeth's heart jumped into her throat and for a moment she fought hard to breathe, for on top of the wooden piano sat her mother, opening her mouth and releasing all those awful words. A skirt she had never seen before was hitched up to her thighs and around her a handful of men taunted, teased and laughed as she threw shapes with her body Elizabeth had never seen any woman do before.

'Now, now, lads, calm down over there,' the young Mr Flanagan called from behind the bar.

The men ignored him, continuing to leer at Elizabeth's mother.

'Mummy,' Elizabeth whimpered.

Elizabeth walked slowly across the road towards Flanagan's pub, her heart beating at the memory so alive in her head. She held out her hand and pushed open the bar door. Mr Flanagan looked up from behind the counter and gave her a small smile, as though he expected to see her.

Young Elizabeth held out a trembling hand and pushed open the door to the bar. Her hair was wet and dripping around her face, her bottom lip out and trembling. Her big brown eyes looked around the room in panic as she saw a man reach out to touch her mother.

'Leave her alone!' Elizabeth shouted so loud the room was quietened. Her mother stopped singing and all heads turned to the little girl standing at the door.

Her mother's corner of the room erupted in such a loud laughter. Tears spilled from Elizabeth's terrified eyes.

'Boo hoo hoo,' her mother sang the loudest of them all. 'Let's all try to save Mummy, shall we?' she slurred. She set her eyes upon Elizabeth. They were bloodshot and dark, not the eyes Elizabeth remembered so well; they belonged to someone else.

'Shit,' Kathleen cursed, jumping up from the other side of the bar and rushing over to Elizabeth, 'What are you doing here?'

'I c-c-c-came t-t-t-to,' Elizabeth stammered in the

quietened room, looking at her mother in bewilderment, 'I came to find my mum so I could live with her.'

'Well, she's not here,' her mother shrieked. 'Get out!' She pointed a finger at her accusingly. 'Drowned little rats aren't allowed in pubs,' she cackled, knocking back her glass, but she missed her mouth, causing most of the drink to land down her chest, where it glistened on her neck and replaced the smell of her sweet perfume with whiskey.

'But, Mummy . . .' Elizabeth whimpered.

'But Mummy,' Gráinne imitated and a few of the men laughed. 'I'm not your mummy,' she said harshly, stepping down onto the piano keys and causing a disturbing sound. 'Little drowned Lizzies don't deserve mummies. They should be poisoned, the whole lot of you,' she spat.

'Kathleen,' Mr Flanagan shouted, 'what are you doing? Get her out of here. She shouldn't be seeing this.'

'I can't,' Kathleen stayed rooted to the spot. 'I have to keep an eye on Gráinne, I have to bring her back with me.'

Mr Flanagan's mouth dropped open in shock at her. 'Would you look at the child?'

Elizabeth's brown skin had paled. Her lips were blue from the cold and her teeth were chattering, a soaking wet floral dress clung to her body and her legs shook in her Wellington boots.

Kathleen looked from Elizabeth to Gráinne, caught between the two. 'I can't, Tom,' she hissed.

Tom looked angry. 'I'll have the decency to bring her home myself.' He grabbed a set of keys from under the bar and started to come round the other side to Elizabeth.

'NO!' Elizabeth screamed. She took one look at her mother, who had already become bored by this scene and was lost in the arms of a strange man, turned to face the door and ran back out to the cold night.

Elizabeth stood at the door of the bar, her hair dripping, rain rolling down her forehead and off her nose, her teeth chattering and her fingers numb. The sounds of the room weren't the same. Inside there was no music, no cheers or whoops, no singing, just the sound of an occasional clinking glass and quiet chatter. There were no more than five people in the bar on the quiet Tuesday night.

An aged Tom continued to stare at her.

'My mother –' Elizabeth called out from the door. The sound of her childlike voice surprised her – 'she was an alcoholic.'

Tom nodded.

'She came in here a lot?'

He nodded again.

'But there were weeks,' she swallowed hard, 'weeks at a time when she wouldn't leave us.'

Tom's voice was soft. 'She was what you'd call a binge drinker.'

'And my father,' she paused, thinking of her poor father who waited and waited at home every night, 'he knew this.'

'The patience of a saint,' he replied.

She looked around the small bar, at the same old piano that stood in the corner. The only thing that had changed in the room was the age of all that was in it.

'That night,' Elizabeth said, her eyes filling with tears, 'thank you.'

Tom just nodded at her sadly.

'Have you seen her since?'

He shook his head.

'Do you . . . do you expect to?' she asked, her voice catching in her throat.

'Not in this lifetime, Elizabeth.' He confirmed for her what she had always felt deep down.

'Daddy . . .' Elizabeth whispered to herself and took off out of the bar back into the cold night.

* * *

Little Elizabeth ran from the pub, feeling every drop of rain lash against her body, feeling her chest hurt as she breathed in the cold air and the water splash up her legs as she pounded in the puddles. She was running home.

Elizabeth jumped into her car and sped off out of the town towards the mile-long road that led to her father's bungalow. Approaching headlights meant she had to reverse back the way she had come and wait for the car to pass before she could continue her journey.

Her father had known all this time and he had never told her. He had never wanted her to shatter her illusions of her mother and she had always held her up on a pedestal. She had thought her a free spirit and of her father as a suffocating force, as the butterfly catcher. She needed to get to him quickly, to apologise, to make things right.

She set off again down the road only to see a tractor slowly chugging before her, unusually at this late hour. She reversed the car back to the entrance of the road again. With her impatience rising she abandoned her car and began to run. She ran as fast as she could down the mile-long road that brought her home.

'Daddy,' little Elizabeth sobbed as she ran down the road towards the bungalow. She screamed his name louder, the wind helping her for the first time that night by lifting her words and carrying them for her towards the bungalow. A light went on, followed by another, and she could see the front door open.

'Daddy!' she cried even louder, and ran even faster.

Brendan sat at the window of the bedroom, looking out to the dark night, sipping a cup of tea, hoping among all hopes that the vision he was waiting for would appear. He had chased them all away, he had done exactly the opposite to what he wanted and it was all his fault. All he could do was wait. Wait for one of his three women to appear. One, he knew for certain, would and could never return.

A movement in the distance caught his eye and he sat to attention like a guard dog. A woman ran towards him, long black hair floating behind her, her image blurring as the rain hit against the window and streamed down the glass.

It was her.

He dropped his cup and saucer to the floor and stood up, knocking his chair backward.

'Gráinne,' he whispered.

He grabbed his cane and moved as quickly as his legs would take him to the front door. Pulling the door open, he strained his eyes in the stormy night to see his wife.

He heard the sound of distant panting as the woman ran.

'Daddy,' he heard her say. No she couldn't be saying that, his Gráinne wouldn't say that.

'Daddy,' he heard her sob again.

He was taken back over twenty years by the familiar sounds. It was his little girl, his little girl was running home in the rain again and she needed him.

'Daddy!' she called again.

'I'm here,' he called, quietly at first, and then he shouted louder, 'I'm here!'

He heard her crying, saw her opening the creaking gate, dripping wet, and just as he did over twenty years ago he held out his arms to her and welcomed her into his embrace.

'I'm here, don't you worry,' he soothed her, patting her head and rocking her from side to side. 'Daddy's here.'

Chapter 38

Elizabeth's garden on the day of her birthday was like the scene of the Mad Hatter's tea party in Wonderland. She had one long table set out in the middle of the garden decorated with a red and white tablecloth. Covering every inch of the table was a huge array of plates piled high with cocktail sausages, crisps, chips and dips, sandwiches, salads, cold meats and sweets. The garden had been pruned to within an inch of its life, new flowers had been planted and the air smelled of freshly cut grass mixed with the aroma of the barbecue in the corner. It was a hot day, the sky was an indigo colour with not a cloud in sight, the surrounding hills were a rich emerald green, the sheep upon them like snowflakes, and Ivan felt the pain of having to leave such a beautiful place and the people in it.

'Ivan, I'm so glad you're here.' Elizabeth came charging out of the kitchen.

'Thank you,' Ivan smiled, swirling round to greet her. 'Wow, look at you!' His mouth dropped open. Elizabeth was wearing a simple white linen summer dress that contrasted with her dark skin beautifully; her long hair was lightly curled and hung down past her shoulders. 'Give me a twirl,' Ivan said, still taken aback by her appearance. Her features had softened and everything about her seemed gentler.

'I gave up twirling for men when I was eight. Now stop gawking at me, there's work to be done,' she snapped.

Well, not *everything* about her was gentler.

She looked around the garden, hands on her hips as though she was on patrol.

'OK, let me show you what's happening here.' She grabbed Ivan by the arm and dragged him towards the table.

'When people arrive through the side gate, they come over here first. This is where they collect their napkins, knives, forks and plates, and then they go along here.' She moved on, still clutching his arm and speaking quickly. 'When they get here, *you* will be standing behind this barbecue where you will prepare whatever they choose from *this* selection.' She displayed a side table of meats. 'On the left is soya meat, on the right is regular. *Do not* confuse the two.'

Ivan opened his mouth to protest but she held a finger up and continued, 'Then after they take their burger buns, they move on to the salad *here*. Please note that the sauces for the burgers are *here*.'

Ivan picked up an olive and she slapped his hand, causing him to drop it back into the bowl. She continued, 'Desserts are over *here*, tea and coffee *here*, organic milk in the left jug, regular milk on the right, toilets through the door on the left *only*; I don't want them traipsing through the house, OK?'

Ivan nodded.

'Any questions?'

'Just one.' He grabbed an olive and popped it into his mouth before she had a chance to steal it from his grasp. 'Why are you telling me all this?'

Elizabeth rolled her eyes. 'Because,' she wiped her clammy hands in a napkin, 'I've never done this whole *hosting* thing before, and seeing as you got me into this mess, I need you to help me.'

Ivan laughed. 'Elizabeth, you will be fine but my barbecuing food will *clearly* not help.'

'Why, don't you have barbecues in Ekam Eveileb?' she asked sarcastically.

Ivan ignored her comment. 'Look, you don't need rules and schedules today. Just let people do what they like, roam the garden, mingle with everyone and choose their food themselves. Who cares if they start at the apple pie?'

Elizabeth looked horrified. 'Start at the apple pie?' she spluttered. 'But that's the wrong end of the table. No, Ivan, you need to tell them where the queue starts and ends. I won't have time.' She rushed towards the kitchen. 'Dad, I hope you're not eating all those cocktail sausages in there,' she called.

'Dad?' Ivan's eyes widened, 'He's here?'

'Yes.' She rolled her eyes but Ivan could tell she didn't mean it. 'It's just as well you weren't here the past few days because I've been up to my eyes in family secrets, tears, break-ups and make-ups. But we're getting there,' she relaxed for a moment and smiled at Ivan. The door-bell rang and she jumped, her face contorting into panic.

'Relax, Elizabeth!' Ivan laughed.

'Come around the side!' she called to the visitor.

'Before they get here I just want to give you a present,' Ivan said, removing his arm from where it had been hiding behind his back. He held out a large red umbrella towards her and her forehead crumpled in confusion.

'It's to protect you from the rain,' Ivan explained softly. 'You could have done with this the other night, I suppose.'

Elizabeth's forehead cleared as the realisation set in. 'That's so thoughtful of you, thank you.' She hugged him. Her head shot up suddenly. 'But how did you know about the other night?'

Benjamin appeared at the gate with a bouquet of flowers and a bottle of wine.

'Happy birthday, Elizabeth.'

She spun round and her cheeks pinked. She hadn't seen him since that day in the building site when Ivan had andrewsplattered her alleged love for him in large red letters across the wall.

'Thank you,' she replied, making her way to him.

He held the gifts towards her and she struggled to find a way to take them with the umbrella in her hand. Benjamin spotted the umbrella and laughed. 'I don't think you'll need that today.'

'Oh, this?' Elizabeth reddened even more. 'This was a gift from Ivan.'

Benjamin raised his eyebrows. 'Really? You give him a hard time, don't you? I'm beginning to think there's something going on with you two.'

Elizabeth didn't allow her smile to waver. She wished. 'Actually, he's somewhere around here – maybe I can finally get to introduce the two of you properly.' She scanned the garden, wondering why it was Benjamin found her so funny all the time.

'Ivan?' I could hear Elizabeth calling my name.

'Yes,' I replied, not looking up from helping Luke put on his party hat.

'Ivan?' she called again.

'Ye-es,' I said impatiently, standing to my feet and looking at her. Her eyes passed over me and she continued scanning the garden.

My heart stopped beating; I swear I felt it stop.

I took deep breaths and tried not to panic. 'Elizabeth,' I called, my voice so shaky and distant I barely recognised myself.

She didn't turn round. 'I don't know where he's disappeared to. He was here just a minute ago.' She sounded angry. 'He was supposed to get the barbecue ready.'

Benjamin laughed again. 'How appropriate. Well, that's a subtle way of asking me but I can do it, no problem.'

Elizabeth looked at him in confusion, lost in thought. 'OK, great, thanks.' She continued looking around. I watched as Benjamin put the apron on over his head and Elizabeth explained everything to him. I watched from the outside, no longer a part of the picture. People began to arrive and I felt dizzy as the garden filled, as the volume went up, voices and laughter grew louder, the smell of food became stronger. I watched as Elizabeth tried to force Joe to taste some of her flavoured coffee as everyone else looked on and laughed; I watched Elizabeth and Benjamin's heads close together as they shared a secret and then laughed; I watched as Elizabeth's father stood at the end of the garden, blackthorn cane in one hand, cup and saucer in the other as he stared out wistfully to the rolling hills and waited for another of his daughters to return; I watched as Mrs Bracken and her lady friends stood by the dessert table, sneakily taking another slice of cake when they thought that no one was looking.

But I saw them. I saw it all.

I was like a visitor in an art museum, standing in front of a busy painting, trying to make sense of it, loving it so much and wanting to jump in and become a part of it. I was pushed further and further to the back of the garden. My head spun and my knees were weak.

I watched as Luke carried out Elizabeth's birthday cake, helped by Poppy, and led everyone in singing 'Happy Birthday to You' as Elizabeth's face pinked in surprise and embarrassment. I watched as she looked around for me and couldn't find me, as she closed her eyes, made a wish and blew out the candles like the little girl that never had her twelfth birthday party and who was living it all now. It brought back to me what Opal had said about me never having a birthday, never ageing while Elizabeth did and would this day, every year. The local crowd smiled and cheered as she blew out the candles, but for me they represented the passing of time, and as she extinguished those dancing flames, she extinguished a tiny bit of hope that was left inside me. They represented why we couldn't be together, and that stabbed my heart. The cheery mass celebrated while I commiserated and I couldn't help but be more aware than ever that with every minute that ticked by she was getting older. Me, I just felt it.

'Ivan!' Elizabeth grabbed me from behind. 'Where have you been for the past hour? I've been looking all over for you!'

I was so shocked she acknowledged me I could barely speak. 'I've been here all day,' I said weakly, savouring every second her brown eyes were locked onto mine.

'No you haven't. I've been by this way at least five times and you weren't here. Are you OK?' she looked worried. 'You're very pale.' She felt my forehead. 'Have you eaten?'

I shook my head.

'I've just heated some pizza; let me get you some, OK? What kind do you want?'

'One with olives, please. Olives are by far my favourite.'

She narrowed her eyes and studied me curiously, looking me up and down. Slowly she said, 'OK, I'll go get it but don't go disappearing on me again. There are some people I want to introduce you to, OK?'

I nodded.

Moments later she came rushing out with a huge slice of pizza. It smelled so good, my tummy screamed out with joy and I hadn't even thought I was hungry. I held my hands up to take the luscious slice from her, but her brown eyes darkened, her face hardened and she pulled the plate away. 'Damn it, Ivan, where have you gone now?' she muttered, searching the garden with her eyes.

My knees were so weak now I couldn't keep my body up any more; I just collapsed onto the grass, back up against the wall of the house, leaning my elbows on my knees.

I heard a little whisper in my ear, felt the warm breath and smelled sweets on Luke's breath. 'It's happening, isn't it?'

All I could do was nod.

This is the part where the fun stops. This part is, by far, not my favourite.

Chapter 39

Feeling every mile with every step, every stone and pebble beneath the sole of my foot, and every second that ticked by, I eventually arrived at the hospital, exhausted and totally drained. There was still one friend that needed me.

Olivia and Opal must have seen it in my face when I entered the room; they must have seen the dark colours emanating from my body, the way my shoulders were slumped, the way the entire weight of everything in the atmosphere had suddenly decided to balance itself on my shoulders. I knew from the look in their tired eyes that they knew. Of course they knew – it was all a part of our job. At least twice a year we all met special people who consumed our days and nights and all of our thoughts, and each time with each person, we had to go through the process of losing them. Opal liked to teach us that it wasn't us *losing* them; it was a matter of them moving on. But I couldn't see how I wasn't losing Elizabeth. Without having any control, any ability to make her hold on to me, to still see me, she was slipping through my fingers. What did I win? What did I gain? Every time I left a friend I was as lonely as the day before I met them, and in Elizabeth's case, lonelier, because I knew that I was missing out on the possibility of so much more. And here's the sixty-four-million-dollar question, what do our friends get out of it?

A happy ending?

Would I call Elizabeth's current situation a happy ending? Mothering a six-year-old boy she never wanted, worrying about a missing sister, a mother who had deserted her and a complex father? Wasn't her life the exact same as when I arrived?

But I guess this wasn't Elizabeth's ending. *Remember the detail*, Opal always tells me. I suppose what had changed in Elizabeth's life was her mind, the way she was thinking. All I had done was plant the seed of hope; she alone could help it to grow. And because she was starting to lose sight of me, perhaps that seed was being cultivated.

I sat in the corner of the hospital room watching Opal clinging to Geoffrey's hands as if she was hanging off the edge of the cliff. Perhaps she was. You could see in her face that she was willing for everything to be as it once was; I bet she would have done a deal with a devil right then and there if it would have brought him back. She would have gone to hell and back, she would have faced every single one of her fears just for him, right then.

The things we do to go back in time.

The things we don't do the first time round.

Opal's words were being spoken through Olivia's lips; Geoffrey could no longer speak. Tears were falling from Opal's eyes and landing on his lifeless hands, her bottom lip was trembling. She wasn't ready to let go. She had never let go of him and now it was too late, he was leaving before she had a chance.

She was losing him.

Life seemed dreary to me right then. As depressing as the cracked blue paint on the walls built to hold up a building intended to heal.

Geoffrey slowly raised a hand; you could tell he was mustering all his strength. The movement surprised everyone as he hadn't spoken in days, hadn't reacted to anything at all. No one was more surprised than Opal, who suddenly felt the touch of his hand across her face, as he wiped away her tears. Contact after twenty years. He could finally see her. Opal kissed his large hand and allowed it to cradle her small face and comfort her through her shock, relief and regret.

Geoffrey gave one last gasp, his chest rose one final time and fell, his hand dropping to the bed.

She had lost him and I wondered if Opal was still telling herself that he had merely moved on.

I decided then and there that I needed to have control of my final moment. I needed to say goodbye to Elizabeth properly, tell her the truth about me one final time so she wouldn't think I had run off and deserted her. I didn't want her to spend years being bitter about the man she once loved who broke her heart. No, that would have been too easy for her; that would have given her an excuse to never love again. And she wanted to love again. I didn't want her, like Geoffrey, to wait for ever for my return and finally die a lonely old woman.

Olivia nodded to me encouragingly as I stood up, kissed Opal on the top of her head from where she sat face down on the bed, still grasping his hand and wailing so loudly I knew it was the sound of her heart breaking. I didn't notice until I got out into the chilly air that tears were streaming down my face.

I began to run.

Elizabeth was dreaming. She was in an empty white room and she was dancing around, sprinkling and splashing colours of paint all around her. She was singing the song she hadn't been able to get out of her head for the past two months and she was so happy and free as she leaped around the room, watching the thick pulpous paint land on the walls with a splish-splosh.

'Elizabeth,' a voice was whispering.

She continued to swirl around the room. No one else was there.

'Elizabeth,' the voice whispered, and her body started to rock slightly as she danced.

'Mmm?' she responded happily.

'Wake up, Elizabeth. I need to talk to you,' came the sweet voice.

She opened her eyes slightly, spotted Ivan's worried handsome face beside her, rubbed her hand over his face and for a moment they stared deeply into each other's eyes. She revelled in the look he gave her, tried to return it but lost the battle with sleep and allowed her eyelids to flutter closed again. She was dreaming, she knew that, but she couldn't keep her eyes open.

'Can you hear me?'

'Mmm,' she responded, twirling and twirling and twirling.

'Elizabeth, I came to tell you that I have to go.'

'Why?' she murmured sleepily. 'You just got here. Sleep.'

'I can't. I'd love to but I can't. I've got to go. Remember I told you this would happen?'

She felt his warm breath on her neck, smelled his skin; fresh and sweet as though he had bathed in blueberries.

'Mmm,' she replied, 'Ekam Eveileb,' she stated, painting blueberries across the wall, reaching her hand to the paint and tasting it as though it was freshly squeezed.

'Something like that. You don't need me any more, Elizabeth,' he said softly. 'You're going to stop seeing me now. Someone else will need me.'

She ran a hand across his jawline, felt his soft stubble-free skin. She ran the length of the room, running her hand along the red paint. This tasted like strawberries. She looked down to the can of paint in her hand and spotted them – fresh strawberries piled high.

'I've figured something out, Elizabeth. I've figured out what my life is all about and it's not that different to yours.'

'Mmm,' she smiled.

'Life is made up of meetings and partings. People come into your life everyday, you say good morning, you say good evening, some stay for a few minutes, some stay for a few months, some a year, others a whole lifetime. No matter who it is, you meet and then you part. I'm so glad I met you, Elizabeth Egan; I'll thank my lucky stars for that. I think I wished for you all of my life,' he whispered. 'But now it's time for us to part.'

'Mmm,' she murmured sleepily. 'Don't go.' He was with her now in the room, they were chasing each other, splashing each other, teasing one another. She didn't want him to go; she was having so much fun.

'I have to go,' his voice cracked. 'Please understand.'

The tone of his voice made her stop running. She dropped the paint brush. It fell to the floor, leaving a red smudge on the brand-new white carpet. She looked up at him; his face was crumpled in sadness.

'I loved you the moment I saw you and I will always love you, Elizabeth.'

She felt him kiss her below her left ear, so soft and sensual she didn't want him to stop.

'I love you too,' she said sleepily.

But he did stop. She looked around the paint-splattered room and he was gone.

Her eyes flew open at the sound of her voice. Had she just said 'I love you?' She leaned up on one elbow and groggily looked around the bedroom.

But the room was empty. She was alone. The sun was rising over the tips of the mountains, night had ended and it was the start of a new day. She closed her eyes and continued dreaming.

Chapter 40

One week on from that morning and Elizabeth found herself moping around the house in her pyjamas, dragging her slipper-clad feet from room to room early on a Sunday morning. She stood at the doorway of each room, gazed inside and searched for . . . something, although she didn't quite know what for. None of these rooms offered her any solution and so she wandered on. Warming her hands on a mug of coffee, she stood still in the hallway, trying to decide what to do. She didn't usually move so slowly and her mind had never felt so clouded before, but she was a lot of things now that she never used to be.

It wasn't as though she didn't have things to do; the house was due its bi-weekly scrub from top to bottom and there was still the problem of the children's room in the hotel to be completed. Never mind completing it, it wasn't even started. Vincent and Benjamin had been on her back all week, she was losing even more sleep than usual because she had simply no idea what to do and, being the perfectionist, she couldn't begin it unless it was completely clear in her mind. To pass this on to Poppy would be a failure on her part. She was a talented professional woman, but this month she had felt like a schoolgirl again, ignoring her pencils and pens and avoiding her laptop so she didn't have to do her homework. She was looking for a distraction, a decent excuse to drag her away for once from the mindless block she found herself in.

She hadn't seen Ivan since her party last week; she hadn't received a phone call, a letter, nothing. It was as though he had disappeared off the face of the earth, and as well as being angry, she felt lonely. She missed him.

It was seven o'clock in the morning and the playroom was alive with the sounds of cartoons. Elizabeth made her way down the hall and popped her head into the room.

'Mind if I join you?' *I promise I won't say anything,* she felt like adding.

Luke look surprised but shook his head. He sat on the floor, straining his neck up to see the television. It looked uncomfortable but she chose silence instead of criticising him. She collapsed on the beanbag beside him and tucked her legs close to her body.

'What are you watching?'

'*SpongeBob Squarepants.*'

'*Sponge* what?' she laughed.

'*SpongeBob Squarepants,*' he repeated, not taking his eyes away from the television.

'What's it about?'

'A sponge called Bob who wears square pants,' he giggled.

'Any good?'

'Mm-hmm,' he nodded. 'Seen it before twice, though.' He spooned Rice Krispies into his mouth messily, spilling milk down his chin.

'Why are you watching it again? Why don't you go out into the fresh air and play with Sam? You've been inside all weekend.'

She was greeted with silence.

'Actually, where is Sam? Is he away?'

'We're not friends any more,' Luke said sadly.

'Why not?' she asked in surprise, sitting up and placing her coffee cup on the floor.

Luke shrugged.

'Did you have a fight?' Elizabeth asked gently.

Luke shook his head.

'Did he say something to make you sad?' she probed.

He shook his head again.

'Did you make him mad?'

Another shake of the head.

'Well, what happened?'

'Nothing,' Luke explained. 'He just told me one day he didn't want to be my friend any more.'

'Well, that's not very nice,' Elizabeth said gently. 'Do you want me to talk to him for you, see what's wrong?'

Luke shrugged. There was a silence between them as he continued staring at the screen, lost in thought.

'You know, I know what it's like to miss a friend, Luke. You know my friend Ivan?'

'He was my friend too.'

'Yes,' she smiled. 'Well, I miss him. I haven't seen him all week either.'

'Yeah, he's gone now. He told me so; he has to help someone else now.'

Elizabeth's eyes widened and anger welled inside her. He hadn't even the decency to say goodbye to her. 'When did he say goodbye to you? What did he say?' From the startled look on Luke's face she immediately stopped firing questions so aggressively. She needed to keep reminding herself that he was only six.

'He said goodbye to me the same day as he said goodbye to you.' His voice went up a pitch as though she was crazy. His face crumpled up and he looked at her as though she'd ten heads, and if she hadn't been so confused she would have laughed at the sight of him.

But inside she wasn't laughing. She paused and thought for a moment and then exploded. 'What! What are you talking about?'

'After the party in the garden, he came to the house and he told me that his job with us was finished, that he was going to be invisible again like he used to be but he would still be around and that meant that we were OK.' He spoke chirpily turning his attention back to the television.

'Invisible,' Elizabeth said the word like it had a bad taste.

'Yep,' Luke chirped. 'Well, people don't call him imaginary for no reason, doh!' He hit himself on the head and fell over onto the ground.

'What is he putting into your head?' she grumbled angrily, wondering if she was wrong to introduce a person like Ivan into Luke's life. 'When is he coming back?'

Luke lowered the volume on the TV and turned to her with that crazy look on his face again. 'He's not. He told you that already.'

'He didn't . . .' Her voice failed her.

'He did, in your bedroom. I saw him go in; I heard him talking.'

Elizabeth cast her mind back to that night and to the dream she had, the dream she had been thinking about all week, the dream that had been *bothering* her and suddenly realised with a sinking feeling in her heart that it hadn't been a dream at all.

She had lost him. In her dreams and in real life, she had lost Ivan.

Chapter 41

'Hello, Elizabeth.' Sam's mother opened her front door wider and welcomed her in.

'Hi, Fiona,' Elizabeth said, stepping in. Fiona had been taking Elizabeth's relationship with Ivan so well during the past few weeks. They hadn't discussed it directly but Fiona was being as polite as she always was. Elizabeth was thankful there was no awkwardness between them. Unfortunately, she was worried Sam hadn't taken it as well. 'I came round to have a chat with Sam, if that's OK. Luke is so upset without him.'

Fiona looked at her sadly. 'I know, I've been trying to talk to him all week about it. Maybe you can do a better job than me.'

'Has he told you what their falling-out is about?'

Fiona tried to hide a smile and nodded.

'Is it about Ivan?' Elizabeth asked, worried. She had always been anxious that Sam would be jealous of the amount of time Ivan was spending with her and Luke, and so she had invited him over to the house and included him in Ivan's activities as much as possible.

'Yes,' Fiona confirmed with a broad smile. 'Children can be funny at that age, can't they?' Elizabeth relaxed at finally learning Fiona hadn't a problem with the time she and Luke spent with Ivan, and was putting it down to Sam's behaviour.

'I'll let him tell you in his own words,' she continued, leading Elizabeth through her home.

Elizabeth had to fight the urge to look round to see if Ivan was there. As much as she was here to help Luke she was also trying to help herself. Finding and returning two best friends was better than one and she ached to be with Ivan so much.

Fiona pushed open the playroom door and Elizabeth entered. 'Sam, honey, Luke's mom is here to talk to you,' Fiona said gently, and for the first time, Elizabeth experienced a warm glow when she heard those words.

Sam paused the PlayStation and looked up at her with sad brown eyes. Elizabeth bit on her lip and fought the urge to smile. Fiona left them alone to talk.

'Hi, Sam,' she said gently. 'Mind if I sit down?'

He shook his head and she balanced herself on the edge of the couch.

'Luke tells me you don't want to be his friend any more, is that right?'

Unashamedly, he nodded his head.

'Do you want to tell me why?'

He took a moment to ponder that and then nodded. 'I don't like to play the same games as him.'

'Did you tell him this?'

He nodded.

'And what did he say?'

Sam looked confused and shrugged his shoulders. 'He is weird.'

A lump formed in Elizabeth's throat and she was immediately defensive. 'What do you mean, weird?'

'At first it was funny but then it just got boring and I didn't want to play any more but Luke wouldn't stop.'

'What game is that?'

'The games with his *invisible friend*.' He put on a bored voice and made a face.

Elizabeth's hands grew clammy. 'But his invisible friend was only around for a few days, and that was months ago, Sam.'

Sam gave her a funny look. 'But you played with him too.'

Elizabeth's eyes widened. 'Excuse me?'

'Ivan whatshisface,' he grumbled, 'boring old Ivan who just wants to spin on chairs all day, or have mud fights or play chasing. Every single day it was Ivan, Ivan, Ivan and,' his already squeaky voice raised a pitch, 'I couldn't even see him!'

'What?' Elizabeth was confused. 'You couldn't see him? What do you mean?'

Sam thought hard about how he could explain that. 'I mean, I couldn't see him,' he said simply, shrugging his shoulders.

'But you played with him all the time.' She ran her clammy fingers through her hair.

'Yeah, because Luke was, but I got sick of pretending and Luke wouldn't stop. He kept saying he was *real*.' He rolled his eyes.

Elizabeth placed her fingers on the bridge of her nose. 'I don't know what you mean, Sam. Ivan is your mum's friend, is he not?'

Sam's eyes widened. He had a startled expression. 'Eh, nope.'

'No?'

'No,' he confirmed.

'But Ivan minded you and Luke. He collected you and brought you home,' Elizabeth stammered.

Sam looked worried. 'I'm allowed to walk home by myself, Ms Egan.'

'But the, eh, the, em . . .' Elizabeth suddenly snapped to attention, remembering something. She clicked her fingers, making Sam jump. 'The water fight – what about the water fight in the back garden? It was you, me, Luke and Ivan, remember that?' she probed. 'Remember, Sam?'

His face paled. 'There was only three of us.'

'What?' she shouted louder than she meant to.

Sam's face crumpled up and he began to cry silently.

'Oh, no,' she panicked, 'please don't cry, Sam, I didn't mean to.' She held her hands out to him but he ran towards the door, shouting for his mother. 'Oh, I'm sorry, Sam. Please stop. Ssshhh,' she said quietly. 'Oh God,' she groaned, listening as Fiona hushed him.

Fiona entered the room.

'I'm sorry, Fiona,' Elizabeth apologised.

'It's OK.' Fiona looked a little worried. 'He's a bit sensitive about it.'

'I understand,' Elizabeth gulped. 'About Ivan,' she swallowed again and stood to her feet, 'you know him, don't you?'

Fiona's brow wrinkled. 'What do you mean by "know him"?'

Elizabeth's heart raced. 'I mean, he's been around here before?'

'Oh, yes,' Fiona smiled, 'he was here many times with Luke. We even had him over for dinner,' she winked.

Elizabeth relaxed but was unsure of how to interpret the wink. She placed her hand on her heart and it began to slow down. 'Phew, Fiona, thank God,' she laughed with relief. 'For a minute there, I thought *I* was going mad.'

'Oh, don't be silly,' Fiona placed a hand on her arm. 'We all do it, you know. When Sam was two years old, he went through the exact same thing. Rooster, he called his little friend,' she beamed. 'So, believe me, I know exactly what you're going through, opening car doors, cooking extra dinners and setting an extra place at the table. Don't worry, I understand. You were right to play along.'

Elizabeth's head was beginning to spin but Fiona's voice kept going on and on.

'When you think about it, it's *such* a waste of food really, isn't it? It just sits there through the entire meal completely untouched and, *believe* me, I know, I was keeping an eye on it. I'll have no spooky invisible men in this house, thank you very much!'

Moisture was rising to Elizabeth's throat. She grabbed the corner of the chair to steady herself.

'But like I said earlier, that's six-year-olds for you. I'm sure this so-called Ivan will disappear in time; they say they don't last for more than two months really. He should be gone soon, don't you worry.' She finally stopped talking but moved her face quizzically towards Elizabeth, 'Are you OK?'

'Air,' Elizabeth gasped. 'I just need to get some air.'

'Of course,' Fiona said hurriedly, leading her towards the front door.

Elizabeth charged outside, taking in big gulps of air.

'Can I get you a glass of water?' Fiona asked worriedly, rubbing her back as Elizabeth leaned over facing the ground, with her hands resting on her knees.

'No, thanks,' she said quietly, standing up. 'I'll be OK.' She wandered unsteadily down the path without a goodbye, leaving Fiona staring after her nervously.

Once back in her own house, Elizabeth slammed the front door behind her and slid down to the floor with her head in her hands.

'Elizabeth, what's wrong?' Luke asked worriedly, still in his pyjamas and barefoot as he stood before her.

She couldn't answer. She could do nothing but go through the past few months over and over in her mind – all her special memories and moments with Ivan, all their conversations together. Who was there with them, who had seen them, spoken to him. They had been in crowded places, people had seen them together, Benjamin had seen them, and Joe had seen them. She kept on thinking back over everything, trying to remember moments when Ivan had conversations with all of these people. She couldn't be imagining all this. She was a sane, responsible woman.

Her face was pale as she finally looked up to face Luke.

'Ekam Eveileb,' was all she could say.

'Yep,' Luke giggled. 'It's backwards language. Cool, isn't it?'

It took Elizabeth seconds to work it out.

Make Believe.

Chapter 42

'Come *on*,' Elizabeth shouted, pounding on her horn, to the two coaches inching by each other slowly on the main street of Baile na gCroíthe. It was September and the last of the tourists were passing through the town. After this the busy place would return to its usual silence, like a banquet hall the morning after a party, leaving the locals to tidy up and remember the events and people that came through. The students would be heading back to college in the neighbouring counties and towns and the locals would once again be alone to struggle with their businesses.

Elizabeth held her hand down on her horn and blasted it at the coach before her. A sea of foreign faces turned around in the back of the bus to glare at her. Beside her, the locals spilled out of the church after attending morning Mass. Taking advantage of the glorious sunny day they gathered around in groups on the street, chatting and catching up on the week's events. They too turned to stare at the source of the angry beeping but Elizabeth didn't care. She was following no rules today; she was desperate to get to Joe's as she knew Joe at least could admit to seeing Ivan and her together, putting an end to this cruel and bizarre joke.

Too impatient to wait for the coaches to pass one other, leaving the car in traffic, she jumped out and ran across the road to the café.

'Joe!' she called, charging in through the door. She couldn't keep the panic out of her voice.

'Ah, there ye are, just the woman I was lookin' for.' Joe stepped out from the kitchen. 'I want to show ye my new fancy machine. It's—'

'I don't care,' she butted in, breathlessly, 'I've no time. Just please answer me this question. You remember me being in here with a man a few times, don't you?'

Joe looked up to the ceiling in thought, feeling important.

Elizabeth held her breath.

'Aye, I do.'

Elizabeth breathed a sigh of relief. 'Thank *God*,' she laughed, a little too hysterically.

'Now could you pay attention to me new device,' he said proudly. 'It's a brand-new coffee-makin' machine. Makes these espressos and cap'chinos and all.' He picked up an espresso cup. 'Sure that would only hold a drip. Brings a whole new meanin' to the phrase "hot drop".'

Elizabeth laughed, so happy about the news about Ivan and the coffee she could have jumped over the counter and kissed him.

'So where is this man?' Joe asked, trying to figure out how to make Elizabeth an espresso.

Elizabeth's smile faded. 'Oh, I don't know.'

'Gone back to America, is he? Sure, doesn't he live there in New York? The Big Apple, don't they call it? I've seen it on the telly and if you ask me it looks nothin' like an apple at all.'

Elizabeth's heart pounded in her chest. 'No, Joe, *not Benjamin*. You're thinking of Benjamin.'

'The fella you had drinks with in here a few times,' Joe confirmed.

'No,' Elizabeth's anger rose. 'Well, yes, I did. But I'm talking about the other man who was with me here. *Ivan* is his name. I-v-a-n,' she repeated slowly.

Joe made a face and shook his head. 'Don't know an Ivan.'

'Yes you do,' she said rather forcefully.

'Listen here,' Joe took off his reading glasses and put down the manual, 'I know just about everyone in this town and I don't know an Ivan nor have I ever heard of one.'

'But, Joe,' Elizabeth pleaded, 'please think back.' Then she remembered. 'The day we splashed coffee all around outside – that was Ivan.'

'Oh.' Joe understood now. 'Part of the German crowd, was he?'

'No!' Elizabeth shouted in frustration.

'Well, where's he from?' Joe asked, trying to calm her.

'I don't know,' she said angrily.

'Well, what's his surname then?'

Elizabeth swallowed hard. 'I-I-I don't know that either.'

'Sure then how can I help you at all if you don't know his surname or where he's from? It doesn't sound much like you know him either. As far as I remember you were dancin' around out there on your own like a mad woman. Don't know what got into you that day, at all.'

Elizabeth suddenly had an idea, grabbed her car keys from the counter and ran out the door.

'But what about your hot drop?' he called as she banged the door behind her.

'Benjamin,' Elizabeth called out, banging her car door shut and running across the gravel to him. He was standing among a group of builders hunched over documents, which were spread across a table. They all looked up at her.

'Can I talk to you for a minute?' She was breathless and her hair danced around her face from the strength of the wind at the top of the hill.

'Sure,' he said, stepping away from the silent group

and leading her to a quieter area. 'Is everything OK?'

'Yes,' she nodded uncertainly, 'I just want to ask you a question, is that OK?'

He braced himself.

'You've met my friend Ivan, right?' She cracked her knuckles and shuffled from foot to foot, in anticipation of his answer.

He adjusted his hard hat, studied her face and waited for her to laugh or tell him she was joking but no smile hid behind those dark and worried eyes. 'Is this a joke?'

She shook her head and chewed nervously on the inside of her cheek, brow furrowed.

He cleared his throat. 'Elizabeth, I don't really know what you want me to say.'

'The truth,' she said quickly, 'I want you to tell me the truth. Well, I want you to tell me you've seen him, but I want that to be the truth, you see.' She swallowed.

Benjamin studied her face some more and eventually shook his head slowly.

'No?' she asked quietly.

He shook his head again.

Her eyes filled and she looked away quickly.

'Are you OK?' He reached out to touch her arm but she swayed her body away. 'I assumed you were joking about him,' Benjamin said gently, slightly confused.

'You didn't see him at the meeting with Vincent?'

He shook his head.

'At the barbecue last week?'

Another shake.

'Walking through the town with me? In the playroom that day when that, that . . . *thing* was written on the wall?' she asked hopefully, her voice full of emotion.

'No, I'm sorry,' Benjamin said kindly, trying to hide his confusion as best he could.

She looked away again, turned her back on him to face out towards the view. From this point she could see the sea, the mountains and the neat little village tucked away in the bosom of the hills.

Finally she spoke. 'He was so real, Benjamin.'

He didn't know what to say so he remained silent.

'You know when you can feel someone with you? And even though not everyone believes in that person, you know they're there?'

Benjamin thought about it and nodded understandingly even though she couldn't see him. 'My granddad died and we were close.' He kicked at the gravel self-consciously. 'My family never agreed on much – they never believed much in anything – but I knew he was there with me at times. You knew Ivan well?'

'He knew me better,' she laughed lightly.

Benjamin heard her sniff and she wiped her eyes.

'So was he a real person? Did he pass away?' Benjamin asked, feeling confused.

'I just believed so much . . .' she trailed off. 'He's really helped me over the past few months.' She looked around at the view for another moment in silence. 'I used to hate this town, Benjamin,' a tear rolled down her cheek. 'I used to hate every single blade of grass on every hill, but he taught me so much. He taught me that it's not the job of this town to make me feel happy. It's not Baile na gCroíthe's fault that I don't feel I fit in. It doesn't matter where you are in the world because it's about where you are up here,' she touched the side of her head lightly. 'It's about the other world I inhabit. The world of dreams, hope, imagination and memories. I'm happy up here,' she tapped her temple again and smiled, 'and because of that I'm happy up here too.' She held out her arms and displayed the countryside around her. She closed her eyes and allowed the wind to dry her tears. Her face was softer when she turned to Benjamin. 'I just thought it was important for you of all people to know that.' Quietly and slowly she headed back to her car.

Leaning against the old tower Benjamin watched her

walk away. He hadn't known Elizabeth as well as he'd have liked but he had an idea she'd let him in her life more than she'd let others. Likewise, he had done the same. They'd had enough conversations for him to see how similar they really were. He'd seen her grow and change and now his unsettled friend had settled. He stared out to the view Elizabeth had been looking at for so long, and for the first time in the year he'd been here he opened his eyes and saw it.

In the early hours of the morning Elizabeth sat up in her bed, wide awake. She looked around the room – saw the time, 3.45 – and when she spoke aloud to herself, her voice was firm and confident.

'To hell with you all. I *do* believe.'

She threw off the covers and jumped out of bed, imagining the sound of Ivan howling with laughter in celebration.

Chapter 43

'Where's Elizabeth?' Vincent Taylor hissed angrily at Benjamin, out of earshot of the crowd that had gathered for the opening of the new hotel.

'She's still in the kids' room,' Benjamin sighed, feeling the cement of the building wall of pressure from the last week finally dry and lay heavy on his aching shoulders.

'*Still?*' Vincent shouted, and a few people turned round from paying attention to the speech being made at the top of the room. The local politician from Baile na gCroíthe had come to open the hotel officially, and a few speeches were being made beside the original tower in the hotel grounds that had stood at the top of the mountain for thousands of years. Soon the crowd would be trampling through the hotel, looking in each room to admire the work, and the two men still didn't know what Elizabeth was up to in the playroom. The last time either of them had seen it was four days ago and it had still been a blank canvas.

Elizabeth literally hadn't come out of that room for the past few days. Benjamin had brought her some drinks and food from a vending machine and she had hastily grabbed it from him at the door and slammed it shut again. He had no idea what the interior was like and his life had been hellish all week, trying to deal with a panicking Vincent. The novelty of Elizabeth speaking to an invisible person had long since worn off on Vincent. He had never had rooms being worked on during the very moment the building was being opened, it was a ridiculous and extremely unprofessional situation.

The speeches finally finished, there was polite clapping and the crowd filed inside where they inspected the new furniture, everyone inhaling the smell of fresh paint as they were led round.

Vincent swore loudly over and over again, receiving angry glances from parents. Room by room, they got closer to the playroom. Benjamin could barely take the suspense and paced the floor behind the crowd. He recognised Elizabeth's father, looking bored while leaning on his blackthorn cane, and her nephew with his nanny, among the crowd and he hoped to God she wouldn't let them all down. Judging by their last conversation on top of the hill, he believed she would come through for them. At least he hoped so. He was due to fly back to his hometown in Colorado next week and he couldn't take having to deal with any delays on site. For once, his personal life would come before his work.

'OK, boys and girls,' the guide spoke as if she were in an episode of *Barney*, 'this next room is especially for *you* so, moms and dads, you'll have to take a few steps back to allow them through because this is a very *special* room.'

There were oohs and aahs, excited giggles and whispers as the children let go of their parents' hands, some shyly, some daringly racing to the front. The guide turned the handle on the door. It didn't open.

'Jesus Christ,' Vincent muttered, placing his hand over his eyes, 'we're ruined.'

'Eh, just a minute, girls and boys.' The guide looked questioningly at Benjamin.

He just shrugged and shook his head hopelessly.

The guide tried the door again but to no avail.

'Maybe you should knock,' one child shouted out, and the parents laughed.

'You know what, that's a very good idea.' The guide played along, not knowing what else to do.

She knocked once on the door and suddenly it was pulled open from the other side. The children slowly shuffled forward.

There was complete silence and Benjamin covered his face in his hands. They were in big trouble.

Suddenly one child let out a 'Wow!' and one by one, the hushed and stunned children gradually began calling excitedly to one another: 'Look at that!', 'Look over there!'

The children looked around the room in awe. The parents followed them in and Vincent and Benjamin looked at each other in surprise as they heard similar whispers of approval. Poppy stood at the doorway, her eyes darting about, her mouth open wide in total shock.

'Let me see this,' Vincent said rudely, pushing his way through the crowd. Benjamin followed and what he saw inside took his breath away.

The walls of the large room were covered with enormous murals of splendid bursts of colour, each wall with a different scene. One wall in particular was a familiar sight to him: three people happily jumping in a field of long grass, their arms held upward, bright smiles on their face, their hair blowing in the wind as they reached up to catch –

'Jinny Joes!' Luke exploded with excitement, his eyes popping along with those of the other children in the room. They were mostly silent as they all stood alone, looking at the detail on each wall. 'Look, it's *Ivan* in the picture!' he shouted to Elizabeth.

Stunned, Benjamin looked at Elizabeth, who was standing in the corner in scruffy denim overalls, splattered in paint, with dark circles under her eyes. But despite her apparent tiredness, she was beaming, her face alight from the visitors' reaction to the room. The pride in her shining eyes was evident as everyone pointed to each painting.

'Elizabeth!' Edith whispered, her hands flying to her mouth in shock. '*You* did all this?' She looked at her employer with both confusion and pride.

Another scene was of a little girl in a field watching a pink balloon floating up to the sky; in another a crowd of children were having a water fight, splattering paint and dancing on the sand on a beach, a little girl sat in a green field having a picnic with a cow who wore a straw hat, a group of young boys and girls climbed trees and hung from its branches, and on the ceiling Elizabeth had painted it a deep blue with shooting stars, comets and distant planets. On the far wall she had painted a man and a boy with magnifying glasses held up to their eyes and black moustaches, leaning over and studying a set of black footprints that led from the wall, all the way across the floor and up the wall on the other side. She had created a new world, a wonderland of escapism, fun and adventure but it was the attention to detail, the looks of glee on the characters' faces, the happy smiles of pure childish enjoyment, that jumped out at Benjamin. Such a face he had seen on Elizabeth when he had caught her dancing in the field and traipsing through the village with seaweed in her hair. It was the face of someone who had let go and was truly happy.

Elizabeth looked down at the floor, to a toddler who was playing with one of the many toys scattered throughout the room. She was about to bend down to talk to the little girl when she noticed that the girl was speaking to herself. Carrying out a very serious conversation, in fact, she was introducing herself to mid-air.

Elizabeth looked around the room, breathed in deeply, and tried to smell that familiar Ivan smell. 'Thank you,' she whispered, closing her eyes and imagining him with her.

The little girl continued babbling away all by herself,

looking to her right as she spoke and listening before speaking again. And then she began to hum, that familiar song that Elizabeth hadn't been able to get out of her head.

Elizabeth threw her head back and laughed.

I stood at the back wall of the playroom in the new hotel with tears in my eyes and a lump so huge in my throat I didn't think I'd ever be able to speak again. I couldn't stop looking around at the walls, at the photo album of all I had done with Elizabeth and Luke over the past few months. It was as though someone had sat in the distance and painted a perfect vision of us.

Looking at the walls, at the colour and at the eyes of the characters, I knew that she had realised and I knew that I would be remembered. Beside me, standing in a line at the back of the room, my friends joined me for moral support on this special day.

Opal placed a hand on my arm and gave me an encouraging squeeze.

'I'm very proud of you, Ivan,' she whispered, and planted a kiss on my cheek, no doubt leaving a purple lipstick stain on my skin. 'We're all here for you, you know. We will always have each other.'

'Thank you, Opal. I know that,' I said, feeling very emotional and looking to Calendula, who was on my right, Olivia, who was beside her, Tommy, who was looking around the walls in fascination, Jamie-Lynn, who had bent down to play with a toddler on the ground and Bobby, who pointed and giggled at each of the scenes before him. They all gave me the thumbs-up and I knew that I would never be truly alone as I was in the company of real friends.

Imaginary friend, invisible friend – call us what you like. Maybe you believe in us, maybe you don't. The point is, it's not important. Like most people who do truly great work, we don't exist to be talked about and praised; we exist only to serve the needs of those who need us. Maybe we don't exist at all; maybe we're just a figment of people's imaginations; maybe it's just pure coincidence that children of two, who can barely speak, all decide to start making friends with people only adults can't see. Maybe all those doctors and psychothera- pists are right to suggest that they are merely developing their imagination.

Or humour me for a second. Is there possibly another explanation that you haven't thought about for the entirety of my story?

The possibility that we do exist. That we're here to help and assist those who need us, who believe in believing and who can therefore see us.

I always look on the positive side of things. I always say that with every cloud there's a silver lining but, the truth be told – and I'm a firm believer of the truth – for a while I was struggling with my experience with Elizabeth. I couldn't figure out what I had won, all I could see was that my losing her was one big black stormy cloud. But then I realised that, as every day went by and I thought about her every second and smiled, I knew that meeting her, knowing her and above all loving her, was the biggest silver lining of all.

She was better than pizza, better than olives, better than Fridays and better than spinning and even these days when she is no longer with us – and I'm not supposed to say this – of all my friends, Elizabeth Egan was *by far* my favourite.

If you loved

IF YOU COULD SEE ME NOW

then you'll love Cecelia's latest novel

THANKS FOR THE MEMORIES

ONE

'Blood transfusion,' Dr Fields announces from the podium of a lecture hall in Trinity College's Arts building, 'is the process of transferring blood or blood-based products from one person into the circulatory system of another. Blood transfusions may treat medical conditions, such as massive blood loss due to trauma, surgery, shock and where the red-cell-producing mechanism fails.

'Here are the facts. Three thousand donations are needed in Ireland every week. Only three per cent of the Irish population are donors, providing blood for a population of almost four million. One in four people will need a transfusion at some point. Take a look around the room now.'

Five hundred heads turn left, right and around. Uncomfortable sniggers break the silence.

Dr Fields elevates her voice over the disruption. 'At least one hundred and fifty people in this room will need a blood transfusion at some stage in their lives.'

That silences them. A hand is raised.

'Yes?'

'How much blood does a patient need?'

'How long is a piece of string, dumb-ass,' a voice from the back mocks, and a scrunched ball of paper flies at the head of the young male enquirer.

'It's a very good question.' She frowns into the darkness, unable to see the students through the light of the projector. 'Who asked that?'

'Mr Dover,' someone calls from the other side of the room.

'I'm sure Mr Dover can answer for himself. What's your first name?'

'Ben,' he responds, sounding dejected.

Laughter erupts. Dr Fields sighs.

'Ben, thank you for your question – and to the rest of you, there is no such thing as a stupid question. This is what Blood For Life Week is all about. It's about asking all the questions you want, learning all you need to know about blood transfusions before you possibly donate today, tomorrow, the remaining days of this week on campus, or maybe regularly in your future.'

The main door opens and light streams into the dark lecture hall. Justin Hitchcock enters, the concentration on his face illuminated by the white light of the projector. Under one arm are multiple piles of folders, each one slipping by the second. A knee shoots up to hoist them back in place. His right hand carries both an overstuffed briefcase and a dangerously balanced Styrofoam cup of coffee. He slowly lowers his hovering foot down to the floor, as though performing a t'ai chi move, and a relieved smile creeps onto his face as calm is restored. Somebody sniggers and the balancing act is once again compromised.

Hold it, Justin. Move your eyes away from the cup and assess the situation. Woman on podium, five hundred kids. All staring at you. Say something. Something intelligent.

'I'm confused,' he announces to the darkness, behind which he senses some sort of life form. There are twitters in the room and he feels all eyes on him as he moves back towards the door to check the number.

Don't spill the coffee. Don't spill the damn coffee.

He opens the door, allowing shafts of light to sneak in again and the students in its line shade their eyes.

Twitter, twitter, nothing funnier than a lost man.

Laden down with items, he manages to hold the door

open with his leg. He looks back to the number on the outside of the door and then back to his sheet, the sheet that, if he doesn't grab it that very second, will float to the ground. He makes a move to grab it. Wrong hand. Styrofoam cup of coffee falls to the ground. Closely followed by sheet of paper.

Damn it! There they go again, twitter, twitter. Nothing funnier than a lost man who's spilled his coffee and dropped his schedule.

'Can I help you?' The lecturer steps down from the podium.

Justin brings his entire body back into the classroom and darkness resumes.

'Well, it says here . . . well, it said there,' he nods his head towards the sodden sheet on the ground, 'that I have a class here now.'

'Enrolment for international students is in the exam hall.'

He frowns. 'No, I—'

'I'm sorry.' She comes closer. 'I thought I heard an American accent.' She picks up the Styrofoam cup and throws it into the bin, over which a sign reads 'No Drinks Allowed'.

'Ah . . . oh . . . sorry about that.'

'Mature students are next door.' She adds in a whisper, 'Trust me, you don't want to join this class.'

Justin clears his throat and corrects his posture, tucking the folders tighter under his arm. 'Actually I'm lecturing the History of Art and Architecture class.'

'You're lecturing?'

'Guest lecturing. Believe it or not.' He blows his hair up from his sticky forehead. *A haircut, remember to get a haircut. There they go again, twitter, twitter. A lost lecturer, who's spilled his coffee, dropped his schedule, is about to lose his folders and needs a haircut. Definitely nothing funnier.*

'Professor Hitchcock?'

'That's me.' He feels the folders slipping from under his arm.

'Oh, I'm so sorry,' she whispers. 'I didn't know . . .' She catches a folder for him. 'I'm Dr Sarah Fields from the IBTS. The Faculty told me that I could have a half-hour with the students before your lecture, your permission pending, of course.'

'Oh, well, nobody informed me of that, but that's no problemo.' *Problemo*? He shakes his head at himself and makes for the door. *Starbucks, here I come.*

'Professor Hitchcock?'

He stops at the door. 'Yes.'

'Would you like to join us?'

I most certainly would not. There's a cappuccino and cinnamon muffin with my name on them. No. Just say no.

'Um . . . nn–es.' Nes? 'I mean yes.'

Twitter, twitter, twitter. Lecturer caught out. Forced into doing something he clearly didn't want to do by attractive young woman in white coat claiming to be a doctor of an unfamiliar initialised organisation.

'Great. Welcome.'

She places the folders back under his arm and returns to the podium to address the students.

'OK, attention, everybody. Back to the initial question of blood quantities. A car accident victim may require up to thirty units of blood. A bleeding ulcer could require anything between three and thirty units of blood. A coronary artery bypass may use between one and five units of blood. It varies, but with such quantities needed, now you see why we *always* want donors.'

Justin takes a seat in the front row and listens with horror to the discussion he's joined.

'Does anybody have any questions?'

Can you change the subject?

'Do you get paid for giving blood?'

More laughs.

'Not in this country, I'm afraid.'

'Does the person who is given blood know who their donor is?'

'Donations are usually anonymous to the recipient but products in a blood bank are always individually traceable through the cycle of donation, testing, separation into components, storage and administration to the recipient.'

'Can anyone give blood?'

'Good question. I have a list here of contra-indications to being a blood donor. Please all study it carefully and take notes if you wish.' Dr Fields places her sheet under the projector and her white coat lights up with a rather graphic picture of someone in dire need of a donation. She steps away and instead it fills the screen on the wall.

People groan and the word 'gross' travels around the tiered seating like a Mexican wave. Twice by Justin. Dizziness overtakes him and he averts his eyes from the image.

'Oops, wrong sheet,' Dr Fields says cheekily, slowly replacing it with the promised list.

Justin searches with great hope for needle or blood phobia in an effort to eliminate himself as a possible blood donor. No such luck – not that it mattered, as the chances of him donating a drop of blood to anyone are as rare as ideas in the morning.

'Too bad, Dover.' Another scrunched ball of paper goes flying from the back of the hall to hit Ben's head again. 'Gay people can't donate.'

Ben coolly raises two fingers in the air.

'That's discriminatory,' one girl calls out.

'It is also a discussion for another day,' Dr Fields responds, moving on. 'Remember, your body will replace the liquid part of the donation within twenty-four hours. With a unit of blood at almost a pint and everyone having eight to twelve pints of blood in their body, the average person can easily spare giving one.'

Pockets of juvenile laughter at the innuendo.

'Everybody, please.' Dr Fields claps her hands, trying desperately to get attention. 'Blood For Life Week is all about education as much as donation. It's all well and good that we can have a laugh and a joke but at this time I think it's important to note the fact that someone's *life*, be it woman, man or child, could be depending on you right now.'

How quickly silence falls upon the class. Even Justin stops talking to himself.

A PLACE CALLED HERE

Before embarking on her writing career, Cecelia Ahern completed a degree in Journalism and Media Communications. At twenty-one years old, she wrote her first novel *PS, I Love You*, which instantly became an international bestseller and was adapted into a major motion picture starring Hilary Swank. Her successive novels *Where Rainbows End*, *If You Could See Me Now*, *A Place Called Here* and *Thanks for the Memories* are also number one bestsellers. Her books are published in forty-six countries and have collectively sold over nine million copies. Cecelia has also co-created the hit ABC Network comedy series *Samantha Who?* which stars Christina Applegate. Her sixth and latest book *The Gift* is a Christmas story out now in hardback. Cecelia lives in Dublin, Ireland.

To sign up for the exclusive Cecelia Ahern HarperCollins newsletter and discover all about Cecelia's books, as well as interviews, photographs and much more, log onto www.cecelia-ahern.com

Praise for *If You Could See Me Now*:

'Enchanting and unexpected.' *You*

'Captivating.' *Irish Independent*

'There's more than a touch of fairytale about Cecelia Ahern's novel . . . thanks to a liberal sprinkling of magic.' *Glamour*

'A beautifully written love story.' *Closer*

'A contemporary fairytale.' *Irish Times*

'An enchanting blend of magic and whimsy.' *Daily Mail*

Also by Cecelia Ahern

PS, I Love You
Where Rainbows End
If You Could See Me Now
Thanks for the Memories

CECELIA AHERN

A Place Called Here

HARPER

This novel is entirely a work of fiction.
The names, characters and incidents portrayed in it are the work of the author's imagination. Any resemblance to actual persons, living or dead, events or localities is entirely coincidental.

Harper
An imprint of HarperCollins*Publishers*
77–85 Fulham Palace Road,
Hammersmith, London W6 8JB

www.harpercollins.co.uk

This paperback edition 2008
1

First published in Great Britain by
HarperCollins*Publishers* 2006

A catalogue record for this book is available from the British Library

ISBN 978-0-00-783209-5

Set in Sabon by Palimpsest Book Production Limited,
Grangemouth, Stirlingshire

Printed and bound in Great Britain by
Clays Ltd, St Ives plc

For you, Dad –
with all my love.

Per ardua surgo

A missing person is anyone whose whereabouts are unknown whatever the circumstances of disappearance. The person will be considered 'missing' until located and his/her wellbeing, or otherwise, established.

An Garda Síochána

1

Jenny-May Butler, the little girl who lived across the road from me, went missing when I was a child.

The Gardaí launched an investigation, which led to their lengthy public search for her. For months every night the story was on the news, every day it was on the front pages of the papers, everywhere it was discussed in every conversation. The entire country pitched in to help; it was the biggest search for a missing person I, at ten years of age, had ever seen, and it seemed to affect everyone.

Jenny-May Butler was a blonde-haired, blue-eyed beauty, who smiled and beamed from the TV screen into the living room of every home around the country, causing eyes to fill with tears and parents to hug their children that extra bit tighter before they sent them off to bed. She was in everyone's dreams and everyone's prayers.

She too was ten years old, and in my class at school. I used to stare at the pretty photograph of her on the news every day and listen to the reporters speak about her as though she was an angel. From the way they described her, you never would have known that she threw stones at Fiona Brady during yard time when the teacher wasn't looking, or that she called me a 'frizzy-haired cow' in front of Stephen Spencer just so he would fancy her instead of me. No, for those few months she had become the perfect being and I didn't think it fair to ruin that. After a while even I forgot about all the bad things she'd done because she wasn't just Jenny-May any more: she was Jenny-May Butler, the sweet missing girl from the nice family who cried on the nine o'clock news every night.

She was never found – not her body, not a trace of her; it was as though she had disappeared into thin air. No suspicious characters had been seen lurking around, no CCTV was available to show her last movements. There were no witnesses, no suspects; the Gardaí had questioned everyone possible. The street became suspicious, its inhabitants calling friendly hellos to one another on the way to their cars in the early morning but all the time wondering, second-guessing, and visualising surprisingly distorted thoughts they couldn't help about their neighbours. Washing cars, painting picket fences, weeding the flowerbeds, and mowing lawns on Saturday mornings while surreptitiously looking around the neighbourhood brought shameful thoughts. People were shocked at themselves, angry that this incident had perverted their minds.

Pointed fingers behind closed doors couldn't give the Gardaí any leads; they had absolutely nothing to go on but a pretty picture.

I always wondered where Jenny-May went, where she had disappeared to, how on earth anyone could just vanish into thin air without a trace without *someone* knowing *something*.

At night I would look out my bedroom window and stare at her house. The porch light was always on, acting as a beacon to guide Jenny-May home. Mrs Butler couldn't sleep any more, and I could see her perpetually perched on the edge of her couch, as though she was on her marks waiting for the pistol to be fired. She would sit in her living room, looking out the window, waiting for someone to call by with news. Sometimes I would wave at her and she'd wave back sadly. Most of the time she couldn't see past her tears.

Like Mrs Butler, I wasn't happy with not having any answers. I liked Jenny-May Butler a lot more when she was gone than when she was here and that also interested me. I missed her, the *idea* of her, and wondered if she was somewhere nearby, throwing stones at someone else and laughing loudly, but that we just couldn't find her or hear her. I took to searching thoroughly for everything I mislaid after that. When my favourite pair of socks went missing I turned the house upside down while my worried parents looked on, not knowing what to do but eventually settling on helping me.

It disturbed me that frequently my missing possessions were nowhere to be found and on the odd time that I did find them, it disturbed me that, in the case of the socks, I could only ever find one. Then I'd picture Jenny-May Butler somewhere, throwing stones, laughing and wearing my favourite socks.

I never wanted anything new; from the age of ten, I was convinced that you couldn't replace what was lost. I insisted on things having to be found.

I think I wondered about all those odd pairs of socks as much as Mrs Butler worried about her daughter. I too stayed awake at night, running through all the unanswerable questions. Each time my lids grew heavy and neared closing, another question would be flung from the depths of my mind, forcing my lids to open again. Much-needed sleep was kept at bay and each morning I was more tired yet none the wiser.

Perhaps this is why it happened to me. Perhaps because I had spent so many years turning my own life upside down and looking for everything, I had forgotten to look for myself. Somewhere along the line I had forgotten to figure out who and where I was.

Twenty-four years after Jenny-May Butler disappeared, I went missing too.

This is my story.

2

My life has been made up of a great many ironies. My going missing only added to an already very long list.

First, I'm six foot one. Ever since I was a child I've been towering over just about everyone. I could never get lost in a shopping centre like other kids; I could never hide properly when playing games; I was never asked to dance at discos; I was the only teenager that wasn't aching to buy her first pair of high heels. Jenny-May Butler's favourite name for me – well, certainly one of her top ten – was 'daddy-longlegs' which she liked to call me in front of large crowds of her friends and admirers. Believe me, I've heard them all. I was the kind of person you could see coming from a mile away: I was the awkward dancer on the dance floor, the girl at the cinema that nobody wanted to sit behind, the one in the shop that rooted for the extra-long-legged trousers, the girl in the back line of every photograph. You see, I stick out like a sore thumb. Everyone who passes me, registers me and remembers me. But despite all that, I went missing. Never mind the odd socks, never mind Jenny-May Butler; how a throbbing sore thumb on a hand so bland couldn't be seen was the ultimate icing on the cake. The mystery that beat all mysteries was my own.

The second irony is that my job was to search for missing persons. For years I worked as a garda. With a desire to work solely on missing persons cases, but without working in an actual division assigned to these,

I had to rest solely upon the 'luck' of coming across these cases. You see, the Jenny-May Butler situation really sparked off something inside me. I wanted answers, I wanted solutions and I wanted to find them all myself. I suppose my searching became an obsession. I looked around the outside world for so many clues I don't think that I once thought about what was going on inside my own head.

In the Guards sometimes we found missing people in a state I won't ever forget for the rest of this life and far into the next, and then there were the people who just didn't want to be found. Often we uncovered only a trace, too often not even that. Those were the moments that drove me to keep looking far beyond my call of duty. I would investigate cases long after they were closed, stay in touch with families long after I should. I realised I couldn't go on to the next case without solving the previous, with the result that there was too much paperwork and too little action. And so knowing that my heart lay only in finding the missing, I left the Gardaí and I searched in my own time.

You wouldn't believe how many people out there wanted to search as much as I did. The families always wondered what my reason was. They had a reason, a link, a love for the missing, whereas my fees were barely enough for me to get by on, so if it wasn't monetary, what was my motivation? Peace of mind, I suppose. A way to help me close my eyes and sleep at night.

How can someone like me, with my physical attributes and my mental attitude, go missing?

I've just realised that I haven't even told you my name. It's Sandy Shortt. It's OK, you can laugh. I know you want to. I would too if it wasn't so bloody heartbreaking. My parents called me Sandy because I was born with a head of sandy-coloured hair. Pity they didn't foresee that my hair would turn as black as coal. They didn't know either that those cute podgy little legs would soon stop kicking and start growing at such a fast rate, for so long. So Sandy Shortt is my name. That is who I am supposed to be, how I am identified and recorded for all time, but I am neither of those things. The contradiction often makes people laugh during introductions. Pardon me if I fail to crack a smile. You see, there's nothing funny about being missing and I realised there's nothing very different about being missing: every day I do the same as I did when I was working. I search. Only this time I search for a way back to be found.

I have learned one thing worth mentioning. There is one huge difference in my life from before, one vital piece of evidence. For once in my life I want to go home.

What bad timing to realise such a thing. The biggest irony of all.

3

I was born and reared in County Leitrim in Ireland, the smallest county in the country with a population of about 25,000. Once the county town, Leitrim has the remains of a castle and some other ancient buildings, but it has lost its former importance and dwindled to a village. The landscape ranges from bushy brown hills to majestic mountains with yawning valleys and countless picturesque lakes. But for a two mile coastal outlet on Donegal Bay, Leitrim is all but landlocked, bounded to the west by Sligo and Roscommon, to the south by Roscommon and Longford, to the east by Cavan and Fermanagh, and to the north by Donegal. When there, I feel it brings on a sudden feeling of claustrophobia and an overwhelming desire for solid ground.

There's a saying about Leitrim and that is that the best thing to come out of Leitrim is the road to Dublin. I finished school when I was seventeen, applied for the Guards and I eventually got myself on that road to Dublin. Since then I have rarely travelled back. Once every two months I used to visit my parents in the three-bedroom terraced house in a small cul-de-sac of twelve houses where I grew up. The usual intention was to stay for the weekend but most of the time I only lasted a day, using an emergency at work as the excuse to grab my unpacked bag by the door and drive, drive, drive very fast on the best thing to come out of Leitrim.

I didn't have a bad relationship with my parents. They were always so supportive, even ready to dive in front of bullets, into fires and off mountains if it meant my happiness. The truth is they made me uneasy. In their eyes I could see who they saw and I didn't like it. I saw my reflection in their expressions more than in any mirror. Some people have the power to do that, to look at you and their faces let you know exactly how you're behaving. I suppose it was because they loved me, but I couldn't spend too much time with people who loved me because of those eyes, because of that reflection.

Ever since I was ten they had tiptoed around me, watched me warily. They had pretend conversations and false laughs that echoed around the house. They would try to distract me, create an ease and normality in the atmosphere, but I knew that they were doing it and why, and it only made me aware that something was wrong.

They were so supportive, they loved me so much and each time the house was about to be turned upside down for yet another gruelling search they never gave in without a pleasant fight. Milk and cookies at the kitchen table, the radio on in the background and the washing machine going, all to break the uncomfortable silence that would inevitably ensue.

Mum would give me that smile, that smile that didn't reach her eyes, the smile that made her back teeth clench and grind when she thought I wasn't looking. With forced easiness in her voice and that forced face of happiness, she would cock her head to one side, try not to let me know she was studying me intently and say, 'Why do you want to search the house again, honey?' She always called me 'honey', like she knew as much as I did that I was no more Sandy Shortt than Jenny-May Butler an angel.

No matter how much action and noise had been created in the kitchen to avoid the uncomfortable silence, it didn't seem to work. The silence drowned it all out.

My answer: 'Because I can't find it, Mum.'

'What pair are they?' – the easy smile, the pretence that this was a casual conversation and not a desperate attempt at interrogation to find out how my mind worked.

'My blue ones with the white stripes,' I answered on one typical occasion. I insisted on bright coloured socks, bright and identifiable so that they could be easily found.

'Well, maybe you didn't put both of them in the linen basket, honey. Maybe the one you're looking for is somewhere in your room.' A smile, trying not to fidget, swallow hard.

I shook my head. 'I put them both in the basket, I saw you put them both in the machine and only one came back out. It's not in the machine and it's not in the basket.'

The plan to have the washing machine switched on as a distraction backfired and was then the focus of attention. My mum tried not to struggle with losing that placid smile as she glanced at the overturned basket on the kitchen floor, all her folded clothes scattered and rolled in messy piles. For one second she let the façade drop. I could have missed it with a blink but I didn't. I saw the look on her face when she glanced down. It was fear. Not for the missing sock, but for me. She quickly plastered the smile on again, shrugging like it was all no big deal.

'Perhaps it blew away in the wind. I had the patio door open.'

I shook my head.

'Or it could have fallen out of the basket when I carried it over from there to there.'

I shook my head again.

She swallowed and her smile tightened. 'Maybe it's caught up in the sheets. Those sheets are so big; you'd never see a little sock hidden in there.'

'I already checked.'

She took a cookie from the centre of the table and bit down hard, anything to take the smile off her aching face. She chewed for a while, pretending not to be thinking, pretending to listen to the radio and humming the tune of a song she didn't even know. All to fool me into thinking there was nothing to be worried about.

'Honey,' she smiled, 'sometimes things just get lost.'

'Where do they go when they're lost?'

'They don't *go* anywhere,' she smiled. 'They are always in the place we dropped them or left them behind. We're just not looking in the right area when we can't find them.'

'But I've looked in *all* the places, Mum. I *always* do.'

I had, I always did. I turned everything upside down; there was no place in the small house that ever went untouched.

'A sock can't just get up and walk away without a foot in it,' Mum false-laughed.

You see, just like how Mum gave up right there, that's the point when most people stop wondering, when most people stop caring. You can't find something, you know it's somewhere and even though you've looked *everywhere* there's still no sign. So you put it down to your own madness, blame yourself for losing it and eventually forget about it. I couldn't do that.

I remember my dad returning from work that evening to a house that had been literally turned upside down.

'Lose something, honey?'

'My blue sock with the white stripes,' came my muffled reply from under the couch.

'Just the one again?'

I nodded.

'Left foot or right foot?'

'Left.'

'OK, I'll look upstairs.' He hung his coat on the rack by the door, placed his umbrella in the stand, gave his flustered wife a tender kiss on the cheek and an encouraging rub on the back and then made his way upstairs. For two hours he stayed in my parents' room, looking, but I couldn't hear him moving around. One peep through the keyhole revealed a man lying on his back on the bed with a face cloth over his eyes.

On my visits in later years they would ask the same easy-going questions that were never intended to be intrusive, but to someone who was already armoured up to her eyeballs they felt as such.

'Any interesting cases at work?'

'What's going on in Dublin?'

'How's the apartment?'

'Any boyfriends?'

There were never any boyfriends; I didn't want another pair of eyes as telling as my parents' haunting me day in and day out. I'd had lovers and fighters, boyfriends, men-friends and one-night-only friends. I'd tried enough to know that anything long term wasn't going to work. I couldn't be intimate; I couldn't care enough, give enough or want enough. I had no desire for what these men offered, they had no understanding of what I wanted, so tight smiles all round while I told my parents that work was fine, Dublin was busy, the apartment was great and no, no boyfriends.

Every single time I left the house, even the times when I cut my visits short, Dad would announce proudly that I was the best thing to come out of Leitrim.

The fault never lay with Leitrim, nor did it with my parents. They were so supportive, and I only realise it now. I'm finding that with every passing day, that realisation is so much more frustrating than never finding anything.

4

When Jenny-May Butler went missing, her final insult was to take a part of me with her. I think we've established that after her disappearance there was a part of me that was missing. The older I got, the taller I got, the more that hole within me stretched until it was gaping throughout my adult life, like a wide-eyed jaw-dropping fish on ice. But how did I physically go missing? How did I get to where I am now? First question and most importantly, *where* am I now?

I'm here and that's all I know.

I look around and search for familiarity. I wander constantly and search for the road that leads out of here but there isn't one. Where is *here*? I wish I knew. It's cluttered with personal possessions: car keys, house keys, mobile phones, handbags, coats, suitcases adorned with airport baggage tickets, odd shoes, business files, photographs, tin openers, scissors, earrings scattered among the piles of missing items that glisten occasionally in the light. And there are socks, lots of odd socks. Everywhere I walk, I trip over the things that people are probably still tearing their hair out to find.

There are animals too. Lots of cats and dogs with bewildered little faces and withering whiskers, no longer identical to their photos on small-town telephone poles. No offers of rewards can bring them back.

How can I describe this place? It's an in-between place. It's like a grand hallway that leads you nowhere, it's like a banquet dinner of leftovers, a sports team made up of the people never picked, a mother without her child, it's a body without its heart. It's almost there but not quite. It's filled to the brim with personal items yet it's empty because the people who own them aren't here to love them.

How did I get here? I was one of those disappearing joggers. How pathetic. I used to watch all those B-movie thrillers and groan every time the credits opened at the early morning crime scene of a murdered jogger. I thought it foolish that women went running down quiet alleyways during the dark hours of the night, or during the quiet hours of the early morning, *especially* when a known serial killer was on the prowl. But that's what happened to me. I was a predictable, pathetic, tragically naïve early morning jogger, in a grey sweat suit and blaring headphones, running alongside a canal in the very early hours of the morning. I wasn't abducted, though; I just wandered onto the wrong path.

I was running along an estuary, my feet pounding angrily against the ground as they always did, causing vibrations to jolt through my body. I remember feeling beads of sweat trickling down my forehead, the centre of my chest and down my back. The cool breeze combined to cause a light shiver to embrace my body. Every single time I remember that morning I have to fight the urge to call out to myself and warn me not to make the same mistake. Sometimes in that memory, on more blissful days, I stay on the same path, but hindsight is a wonderful thing. How often we wish we'd stayed on the same path.

It was five forty-five on a bright summer's morning; silent apart from the theme tune to *Rocky* spurring me on. Although I couldn't hear myself I knew my breathing was heavy. I always pushed myself. Whenever I felt I needed to stop I made myself run faster. I don't know if it was a daily punishment or the part of me that was keen to investigate, to go new places, to force my body to achieve things it had never achieved before.

Through the darkness of the green and black ditch

beside me, I spotted a water-violet up ahead, submerged. I remember my dad telling me as a little girl, lanky, with black hair, and embarrassed by my contradictory name, that the water-violet was misnamed too because it wasn't violet at all. It was lilac-pink with a yellow throat but even still, wasn't it beautiful and did that make me want to laugh? Of course not, I'd shaken my head. I watched it from far away as it got closer and closer, telling it in my mind, *I know how you feel.* As I ran I felt my watch slide off my wrist and fall against the trees on the left. I'd broken the clasp of the watch the very first moment I'd wrapped it around my wrist and since then it occasionally unlatched itself and fell to the floor. I stopped running and turned back, spotting it lying on the damp estuary bank. I leaned my back against the rugged dark brown bark of an alder and, while taking a breather, noticed a small track veering off to the left. It wasn't welcoming, it wasn't developed as a rambler's path but my investigative side took over; my enquiring mind told me to see where it led.

It led me here.

I ran so far and so fast that by the time the play-list had ended on my iPod I looked around and didn't recognise the landscape. I was surrounded by a thick mist and was high up in what seemed like a pine-tree-covered mountain. The trees stood erect, needles to attention, immediately on the defensive like a hedgehog under threat. I slowly lifted the earphones from my ears, my panting echoing around the majestic mountains, and I knew immediately that I was no longer in the small town of Glin. I wasn't even in Ireland.

I was just here. That was a day ago and I'm still here.

I'm in the business of searching and I know how it works. I'm a woman who packs her own bags and doesn't tell anyone where I'm going for a straight week in my life. I disappear regularly, I lose contact regularly, no one checks up on me and I like it that way. I like to come and go as I please. I travel a lot to the destinations of where the missing were last seen, I check out the area, ask around. The only problem was, I had just arrived in this town that morning, driven straight to the Shannon Estuary and gone for a jog. I'd spoken to no one, hadn't yet checked into a B & B, nor walked down a busy street. I know what they'll be saying, I know I won't even be a case – I'll just be another person that's walked away from my life without wanting to be found; it happens all the time – and this time last week they probably would have been right.

I'll eventually belong to the category of disappearance where there is no apparent danger to either the missing person or the public: for example, persons aged eighteen and over who have decided to start a new life. I'm thirty-four, and in the eyes of others have wanted out for a long, long time now.

This all means one thing: that right now nobody out there is even looking for me.

How long will that last? What happens when they find the battered, red 1991 Ford Fiesta along the estuary with a packed bag in the boot, a missing persons file on the dashboard, a cup of, by then, cold not yet sipped coffee and a mobile phone, probably with missed calls, on the car seat?

What then?

5

Wait a minute.

The coffee. I've just remembered the coffee.

On my journey from Dublin, I stopped at a closed garage to get a coffee from the outside dispenser and he saw me; the man filling his tyres with air saw me.

It was out in the middle of nowhere, in the midst of the countryside at five fifteen in the morning when the birds were singing and the cows mooing so loudly I could barely hear myself think. The smell of manure was thick but sweetened with the scent of honeysuckle waving in the light morning breeze.

This stranger and I were both so far from everything but yet right in the middle of something. The mere fact that we were both so completely disconnected from life was enough for our eyes to meet and feel connected.

He was tall but not as tall as I; they never are. Five eleven, with a round face, red cheeks, strawberry-blond hair, and bright blue eyes I felt I'd seen before, which looked tired at the early hour. He was dressed in a pair of worn-looking blue denims, his blue and white check cotton shirt crumpled from his drive, his hair dishevelled, his jaw unshaven, his gut expanding as his years moved on. I guessed he was in his mid-to-late thirties, although he looked older, with stress lines along his brow and laughter lines . . . no, I could tell from the sadness emanating from him that they weren't from laughter. A few grey hairs had crept into the side of his temples, fresh on his young head, every strand the result of a harsh lesson learned. Despite the extra weight he looked strong, muscular. He was someone who did a lot of physical work, my assumption backed up by the heavy work boots he wore. His hands were large, weather-beaten but strong. I could see the veins on his forearms protruding as he moved, his sleeves rolled up messily to below his elbows as he lifted the air pump from its stand. But he wasn't going to work, not dressed like that, not in that shirt. For him this was his good wear.

I studied him as I made my way back to my car.

'Excuse me, you dropped something,' he called out.

I stopped in my tracks and looked behind me. There on the tarmac sat my watch, the silver glistening under the sun. Bloody watch, I mumbled, checking to see that it wasn't damaged.

'Thank you,' I smiled, sliding it back onto my wrist.

'No problem. Lovely day, isn't it?'

A familiar voice to match the familiar eyes. I studied him for a while before answering. Some guy I'd met in a bar previously, a drunken fling, an old lover, a past colleague, client, neighbour or school friend? I went through the regular checklist in my mind. There was no further recognition on either side. If he wasn't a previous fling, I was thinking I'd like to make him one.

'Gorgeous.' I returned the smile.

His eyebrows rose in surprise first and then fell again, his face settling in obvious pleasure as he understood the compliment. But as much as I would have loved to stay and perhaps arrange a date for sometime in the future, I had a meeting with Jack Ruttle, the nice man I had promised to help, the man I was driving from Dublin to Limerick to see.

Oh, please, handsome man from the garage that day,

please remember me, wonder about me, look for me, find me.

Yes, I know; another irony. Me, wanting a man to call? My parents would be so proud.

6

Jack Ruttle trailed slowly behind an HGV along the N69, the coast road, which led from North Kerry to where he lived in Foynes, a small town in County Limerick, a half-hour's drive from Limerick city. It was five a.m. as he travelled the only route to Shannon Foynes Port, Limerick's only seaport. Staring at the speedometer, he telepathically urged the truck to go faster while he gripped the steering wheel so tightly his knuckles turned white. Ignoring the advice of the dentist he had seen just the previous day in Tralee, he began to grind his back teeth. The constant grinding was wearing down his teeth and weakening his gums, causing his mouth to throb and ache. His cheeks were red and swollen, and matched his tired eyes. He'd left the friend's couch he was sleeping on in Tralee to drive home through the night. Sleep wasn't coming easily to him these days.

'Are you under any stress?' the dentist had asked him while studying the inside of Jack's mouth.

An open-mouthed Jack had swallowed a curse and fought the urge to clamp his teeth down on the white surgical finger in his mouth. *Stressed* wasn't even the word.

His brother Donal had disappeared on his twenty-fourth birthday after a night out with friends in Limerick city. After a late-night snack of burger and chips in a fast-food café he had separated himself from his friends and staggered off alone. The chipper was too packed for any particular person to be noticed; his four friends were too drunk and too distracted by their attempts to bring a female home for the night to care.

CCTV showed him taking €30 out of an ATM on O'Connell Street at 3.08 a.m. on a Friday night, and later he was caught on camera stumbling in the direction of Arthur's Quay. After that, his trail was lost. It was almost like his feet had left the earth and he'd floated up towards the sky. Jack prepared himself for the fact that in a way, maybe he had. His death was a concept he knew he could eventually accept if only there was a shred of evidence to support it.

It was the not-knowing that tortured him; the worry and fear that kept him awake every night and the inconclusive search of the Gardaí that fuelled his continuous quest. He had combined his trip to the dentist in Tralee with a visit to one of Donal's friends who had been with him the night he went missing. Like the rest of the crowd that were there that night, he was a person Jack felt like punching and hugging all at the same time. He wanted to shout at him, yet console him for his loss of a friend. He never wanted to see him again, yet he didn't want to leave his side in case he remembered something – something he'd previously forgotten that would suddenly be the clue they were all looking for.

He stayed awake at nights looking through maps, rereading reports, double-checking times and statements while, beside him, Gloria's chest rose and fell with her silent breathing, her sweet breath sometimes blowing the corners of his papers as her sleeping world crept in on his.

Gloria, his girlfriend of eight years, always slept. She had slept soundly through the entire year of Jack's horrid nightmare, and still she dreamed. Still she had hopes for tomorrow.

She had fallen into a deep sleep after hours spent at the garda station, the first day they worried about not hearing from Donal after four days of silence. She slept after the Gardaí had spent the day searching the river for his body. She slept after the day they'd spent hours attaching photos of Donal to shop windows, supermarket notice boards and lampposts. She slept the night they thought they had found his body down an alley in the town and slept the next night when they discovered it wasn't him. She slept the night the Gardaí said there was nothing more they could do after months of searching. She slept the night of his mother's funeral, after seeing the coffin of a grief-stricken mother being lowered into the dirt, to join her husband at long last after twenty years in this life without him.

It frustrated Jack, but he knew it wasn't a lack of caring that caused Gloria's lids to close. He knew this because she held his hand when they sat through the questions at the garda station that first time. She stood beside him as the wind and rain lashed at their faces, by the river, watching the divers appear on the surface of the grey murky water with faces more gloomy than when they had disappeared to the world below. She had helped him stick posters of Donal to windows and poles. She had held him tightly when he cried the day the Gardaí stopped looking and she stood in the front row of the church and waited for him while he helped carry his mother's coffin to the altar.

She cared all right, but one year on, she still slept at night during the longest hours of his life. The hours when Jack cared most about everything but the hours when, deep in her sleep, Gloria didn't and couldn't care at all. Every night he felt the distance grow between her world and his.

He didn't tell her about coming across the woman, Sandy Shortt, from the missing persons agency in the Golden Pages. He didn't tell her he had called her. He didn't tell her about the late-night phone calls all last week and the new sense of hope this woman's determination and belief had filled his head and heart with.

And he didn't tell her that they had arranged to meet on this very day in the next town because . . . well, because she was sleeping.

* * *

Jack finally managed to overtake the long vehicles, and as he neared home he found himself alone on the now quiet country road in his twelve-year-old rusting Nissan. The interior of his car was silent. Over the past year he found he was intolerant of unwanted noise; the sound of a TV or a radio in the background was merely a distraction to his pursuit of answers. Inside his mind was manic: shouting, screaming, replays of previous conversations, imaginings of future ones all leaped around his head like a bluebottle trapped in a jam jar.

Outside the car the engine roared, the metal rattled, the wheels bounced and fell over every pothole and bump in the surface. His mind was noisy in the silent car, his car clattered in the quiet countryside. It was five fifteen on a sunny Sunday morning in July and he needed to stop for air, for his lungs and for the front deflated wheel.

He pulled over at the deserted petrol station, which would be closed until later in the morning, and parked beside the air pump. He allowed the birdsong to fill his head temporarily and push out his thoughts while he rolled up his sleeves and stretched his limbs from the long journey. The bluebottle momentarily settled.

Beside him a car pulled up and parked. The population of the area was so small he could spot an alien car a mile away . . . and the Dublin licence plate gave it away too. Out of the tiny battered car, two long legs dressed in grey sweatpants appeared, followed by a long body. Jack stopped himself from gawking but from the corner of his eye he watched the curly-black-haired woman taking long strides to the coffee dispenser by the door of the shuttered garage. He was surprised that someone of her height could even fit into the small car. He noticed something fall from her hand and heard the sound of metal against the ground.

'Excuse me, you dropped something,' he called out.

She looked behind her in confusion and walked back to where the metal was glistening on the ground.

'Thank you,' she smiled, sliding what looked like a bracelet or a watch onto her wrist.

'No problem. Lovely day, isn't it?' Jack felt the pain in his swollen cheeks worsen as they lifted in a smile.

Her green eyes sparkled like emeralds against her snow-white skin and glinted as they caught the sunlight streaming through the tall trees. Her jet-black curls twirled around her face playfully, revealing parts of her features, hiding others. She looked him up and down, taking him in as though analysing every inch of him. Finally she raised an eyebrow. 'Gorgeous,' she replied, and returned the smile. She, her jet-black curly hair, the Styrofoam cup of coffee, legs and all, disappeared into the tiny car like a butterfly into a Venus flytrap.

Jack watched the Ford Fiesta drive into the distance, wanting her to have stayed, and once again he noted how things between him and Gloria, or perhaps just his feelings for her, were changing. But he hadn't time to think about that now. Instead he returned to his car and leafed through his files in preparation for his meeting later that morning with Sandy Shortt.

Jack wasn't religious; he hadn't been to church for over twenty years. In the last twelve months he had prayed three times. Once for Donal not to be found when they were searching the river for his body, the second time for the body in the alley not to be him, and the third time for his mother to survive her second stroke in six years. Two out of three prayers had been answered.

He prayed again today for the fourth time. He prayed for Sandy Shortt to take him from the place he was in and to be the one to bring him the answers he needed.

7

The porch light was still on when Jack arrived home. He insisted on it being left on all night for Donal's sake, as a beacon to guide his brother home. He turned it off now that it was bright outside and tiptoed around the cottage quietly, careful not to wake Gloria, who was enjoying her Sunday lie-in. Scouring through the linen basket of dirty clothes, he grabbed the least crumpled garment he could find and quickly changed out of one check shirt and into another. He hadn't washed as he didn't want the electric shower and ceiling fan in the bathroom to wake her. He'd even held back from flushing the toilet. He knew it wasn't his overflowing generosity that was causing him to behave that way and yet he couldn't quite summon the shame in knowing that it was exactly the opposite. He was deliberately keeping his meeting with Sandy Shortt a secret from Gloria and the rest of his family.

It was as much to help them as it was to help him. In their hearts, they were beginning to move on. They were trying their utmost to settle back into their lives after the major upheaval and upset of suffering the loss of not one but two family members in one year. Jack understood their positions, they had all reached a point where no more days off work could be taken, sympathetic smiles were being replaced by everyday greetings, and conversations with neighbours were returning to normal. Imagine, people were actually talking about other things and not asking questions or offering advice.

Cards filled with comforting words had stopped landing on his doormat. People had gone back about their own lives, employers had moved around shifts as much as possible and now it was back to business for all concerned. But to Jack it felt wrong and awkward for life to resume without Donal.

Truthfully it wasn't Donal's absence that held Jack back from joining his family in bravely carrying on with the rest of his life. Of course he missed him but, as with the death of his mother, he could and would eventually get through the grief. Instead it was the mystery that surrounded his disappearance; all the unanswered questions left question marks dotting his vision like the aftermath of flash photography.

He closed the door behind him to the cluttered one-bedroom bungalow where he and Gloria had lived for five years. Just like his father, Jack had worked as a cargo handler at Shannon Foynes Port his entire working life.

He had chosen Glin village, thirteen kilometres west of Foynes, for the meeting with Sandy Shortt as it was a place none of his family inhabited. He sat in a small café at nine a.m., a half-hour before they were due to meet. Sandy had said on the phone that she was always early and he was eager, fidgety and more than willing to give this fresh idea a go. The more time they had together, the better. He ordered a coffee and stared at the most recent photograph of Donal on the table before him. It had been printed in almost every newspaper in Ireland and seen on notice boards and shop windows for the past year. In the background of the photo was the fake white Christmas tree his mother had set up in the living room every year. The baubles caught the flash of the camera and the tinsel twinkled. Donal's mischievous smile grinned up at Jack as though he was taunting him, daring him to find him. Donal had always loved playing hide-and-seek as a child. He would stay hidden for hours if it meant winning. Everyone would become impatient and declare loudly that Donal was the winner just so that he could leave his place with a proud beaming smile. This was the longest search Jack had ever endured and he wished his brother would come out of his hiding place now, show himself with that proud smile and end the game.

Donal's blue eyes, the only similar feature between the two brothers, sparkled up at Jack and he almost expected him to wink. No matter how long and hard he had stared at the photograph, he couldn't inject any life into it. He couldn't reach into the print and pull his brother out; he couldn't smell the aftershave he used to engulf himself in, he couldn't ruffle his brown hair and ruin his hairstyle as he annoyingly had, and he couldn't hear his voice as he helped their mother around the house. One year on he could still remember the touch and smell of him, though unlike the rest of his family, to him the memory alone wasn't enough.

The photo had been taken the Christmas before last, just six months before he went missing. Jack used to call round to his mother's house once a week, where Donal was the only one of six siblings who remained living there. Apart from the habitual short casual conversations between Jack and Donal that lasted for no more than two minutes at a time, that Christmas was the last occasion Jack had spoken to Donal properly. Donal had given him the usual present of socks and Jack had given him the box of handkerchiefs his oldest sister had given him the year before. They'd both laughed at the thoughtlessness of their gifts.

That day, Donal had been animated, happy with his new job as a computer technician. He'd begun it in September after graduating from Limerick University; a ceremony at which their mother had almost toppled off her chair such was the weight of her pride for her baby. Donal had spoken confidently about how he enjoyed the work and Jack could see how much he had matured and become more comfortable after leaving student life behind.

They had never been particularly close. In the family

of six children, Donal was the surprise baby, nobody more surprised than their mother, Frances, who was forty-seven at the time she learned of the pregnancy. Being twelve years older than Donal meant that Jack had moved out of home by the time Donal was six. He lost out in knowing the secret sides to his brother that only living with someone brought, and so for eighteen years they had been brothers, but not friends.

Jack wondered, not for the first time, if he had known Donal better, whether he could have solved part of the mystery. Maybe if he'd worked harder at getting to know his little brother or had had more conversations about something rather than nothing, then perhaps he could have been out with him on the night of his birthday. Maybe he could have prevented him from leaving that fast-food restaurant or maybe he could have left with him and shared a taxi.

Or maybe Jack would have found himself in the same place as Donal was right now. Wherever that place was.

8

Jack slugged back his third cup of coffee and looked at his watch.

Ten fifteen.

Sandy Shortt was late. His legs bounced up and down nervously beneath the table, his left hand drummed on the wood and his right hand signalled for another coffee. His mind stayed positive. She was coming. He knew she would come.

Eleven a.m., he tried calling her mobile number for the fifth time. It rang and rang and finally, 'Hello, this is Sandy Shortt. Sorry I'm not available at the moment. Leave a message and I'll call you back as soon as I can.' Beep.

Jack hung up.

Eleven thirty, she was two hours late, and once again Jack listened to the voice message Sandy had left the previous night.

'Hi, Jack, Sandy Shortt here. I'm ringing to confirm our meeting tomorrow at nine thirty a.m. in Kitty's Café in Glin. I'm driving down tonight.' Her tone softened. 'As you know, I don't sleep,' she laughed lightly, 'so I'll be there early tomorrow. After all our conversations I look forward to finally speaking to you in person. And, Jack,' she paused, 'I promise you I'll do my best to help you. We won't give up on Donal.'

* * *

Twelve o'clock, Jack played it again.

At one o'clock, after countless cups of coffee, Jack's fingers stopped drumming and instead made a fist for his chin to rest on. He had felt the café owner's gaze on his back as he sat for hours waiting nervously, watching the clock and not giving up his table to a group willing to spend more money than he. Tables filled and emptied around him, his head snapped up every time the bell over the door rang. He didn't know what Sandy Shortt looked like; all she had said was that he couldn't miss her. He didn't know what to expect but each time the bell tinkled, his head and his heart both lifted with hope and then fell as the newcomer's gaze flitted past him and settled on another.

At two thirty, the bell rang once more.

After five and a half hours waiting, it was the sound of the door opening and closing behind Jack.

9

For almost two days I'd stayed in the same wooded area, jogging back and forth, trying to recreate my movements and somehow reverse my arrival here. I ran up and down the mountainside, testing different speeds as I struggled to remember how fast I'd been running, what song I'd been listening to, what I'd been thinking of and what area I was in when I first noticed the change in my location. As though any of those things had any part in what happened. I walked up and down, down and up, searching for the point of entry and, more importantly, the point of exit. I wanted to keep busy. I didn't want to settle like the personal possessions scattered around; I didn't want to end up like the backless earrings that glinted from the long grass.

Thinking you're missing is a bizarre conclusion to arrive at – I'm well aware of that – but it wasn't a sudden conclusion, believe me. I was hugely confused and frustrated for those first few hours but I knew that something more extraordinary than taking a wrong turn had occurred because, geographically, a mountain couldn't just rise from the ground in a matter of seconds, trees that had never grown before in Ireland couldn't all of a sudden sprout from the ground, and the Shannon Estuary couldn't dry up and disappear. I knew I was somewhere else.

I did of course contemplate the fact that I was dreaming, that I had fallen and hit my head and was currently in a coma, or that I'd died. I did wonder whether the anomalous nature of the countryside was pointing towards the end of the world and I questioned my knowledge of the geography of West Limerick. I did indeed consider very strongly the fact that I'd lost my mind. This was number one on the list of possibilities.

But when I sat alone for those days and thought rationally, surrounded by the most beautiful scenery I'd ever seen, I realised that I was most certainly alive, the world had not ended, mass panic hadn't taken over and I was not just another occupant of a dump yard. I realised that my searching for a way out was clouding my view of where exactly I was. I wasn't going to hide behind the lie that I could find a way out by running up and down a hill. No deliberate distractions to block out the voice of reason for me. I am a logical person and the most logical explanation out of all of the incredible possibilities was that I was alive and well but missing. Things are as they are, no matter how bizarre.

Just as it was beginning to get dark on my second day I decided to explore this curious new place by walking deeper through the pine trees. Sticks cracked beneath my trainers, the ground was soft and bouncy, covered with layers of fallen, now decayed leaves, bark, pine cones and velvet-like moss. Mist hovered like wispy cotton wool above my head and stretched to the tips of the trees. The lofty thin trunks extended up like towering wooden pencils that coloured the sky. During the day they tinted the ceiling a clear blue, shading wispy clouds and orange pigment, and now by night the charcoaled tips, burned from the hot sun, darkened the heavens. The sky twinkled with a million stars, all winking at me, sharing between them a secret of the world I could never know.

I should have been afraid, walking through a mountainside in the dark by myself. Instead I felt safe, surrounded by the songs of birds, engulfed by the scents of sweet moss and pine, and cocooned in a mist that contained a little bit of magic. I had been in many unusual situations before: the dangerous and the plain bizarre. In my line of work I followed all leads, wandered down all paths and never allowed fear to cause me to turn away from a direction that could lead me to finding someone. I wasn't afraid to upturn every stone that lay in my path or hurl them and my questions around atmospheres with the fragility of glasshouses. When people go missing it's usually under dark circumstances most people don't want to know about. Compared to the previous experiences of delving into the underworld, this new project was literally a walk in the park. Yes, my finding my way back into my life had become a project.

The sound of murmuring voices up ahead stopped me in my tracks. I hadn't had human contact for days and wasn't at all sure if these people would be friendly. The flickering light of a campfire cast shadows around the woods, and as I quietly neared, I could see a clearing. The trees fell away to a large circle where five people sat laughing, joking and singing to music. I stood hidden in the shadows of the giant conifers, but like a hesitant moth being drawn to a flame. Irish accents were audible and I questioned my ludicrous assessment of being outside the country and of being outside my life. In those few seconds I questioned everything.

A branch snapped loudly beneath my foot and it echoed around the forest. The music immediately stopped and the voices quietened.

'Someone's there,' a woman whispered loudly.

All heads turned towards me.

'Hello, there!' a jovial man called excitedly. 'Come! Join us! We're just about to sing "This Little Light of Mine".' There was a groan from the group.

The man jumped up from his seat on a fallen tree trunk and came closer to me with his arms held open in welcome. His head was bald apart from four strands of hair, which hung spaghetti-like in a comb-over style. He had a friendly moon-shaped face and so I stepped into the light and instantly felt the warmth of the fire against my skin.

'It's a woman,' the woman's voice whispered loudly again.

I wasn't sure what to say and the man who had approached me looked back to his group now uncertainly.

'Maybe she doesn't speak English,' the woman hissed loudly.

'Ah.' The man turned back to me. 'Doooo yooooou speeeeeaaaaak Eng-a-lish?'

There was a grumble from the group, '*The Oxford English Dictionary* wouldn't understand that, Bernard.'

I smiled and nodded. The group had quietened and were studying me and I knew what they were all thinking. She's tall.

'Ah, great.' His hands clapped together and remained clasped close to his chest. His face broke into an even more welcoming smile. 'Where are you from?'

I didn't know whether to say Earth, Ireland or Leitrim. I went with my gut instincts and, 'Ireland,' was all that came out of my mouth, which hadn't spoken for days.

'Splendid!' The cheery fellow's smile was so bright that I couldn't help but return it. 'What a coincidence! Please come and join us.' He excitedly led me towards the group with a hop, skip and a jump.

'My name is Bernard,' he beamed like the Cheshire cat, 'and heartiest welcome to the Irish contingency. We're frightfully outnumbered here,' he frowned, 'although it seems that the numbers are rising. Excuse me, where are my manners?' His cheeks flushed.

'Underneath that sock over there.'

I turned to look at the source of the smart comment to see an attractive woman in her fifties, tight silver hair, with a lilac pashmina draped around her shoulders. She was staring distantly into the centre of the fire, the dancing flames reflecting in her dark eyes, her comments flowing out of her mouth as though she were on autopilot.

'Who have I the pleasure of being acquainted with?'

Bernard beamed with excitement, his neck craned up to look at me.

'My name is Sandy,' I replied, 'Sandy Shortt.'

'Splendid.' His cheeks flushed again and he shook my outstretched hand. 'It's a pleasure to meet you. Allow me to introduce you to the rest of the gang, as they say.'

'As who say?' the woman grumbled irately.

'That's Helena. She loves the chat. Always has something to say, don't you, Helena?' Bernard looked at her for an answer.

The wrinkles around her mouth deepened as she pursed her lips.

'Ah.' He wiped his brow and turned to introduce me to a woman named Joan; Derek, the long-haired hippy playing the guitar; and Marcus, who was sitting quietly on the far side. I took them in quickly: they were all of a similar age and seemed very comfortable with one another. Not even Helena's sarcastic comments were causing any friction.

'Why don't you take a seat and I'll get you a drink of some sort—'

'Where are we?' I cut in, unable to take his bumbling pleasantries any longer.

All other conversation around the fire stopped suddenly and even Helena raised her head to stare at me. She took me in, a quick glance up and down, and I felt like my soul had been absorbed. Derek stopped strumming his guitar, Marcus smiled lightly and looked away, Joan and Bernard stared at me with wide frightened Bambi eyes. All that could be heard was the sound of the campfire crackling and popping as sparks sprang out and spiralled their way up to the sky. Owls hooted and there was the distant snap of branches being stepped on by wanderers beyond.

There was a deathly silence around the campfire.

'Is anyone going to answer the girl?' Helena looked around with an amused expression. Nobody spoke.

'Well, if nobody speaks up,' she wrapped her shawl

tighter around her shoulders and grasped it at her chest, 'I'm going to give my opinion.'

Voices of objection rose from the circle and I immediately wanted to hear Helena's opinion all the more. Her eyes danced, enjoying the choir of disapproval.

'Tell me, Helena,' I interrupted.

'Oh, you don't want that, trust me,' Bernard fluffed, his double chin wobbling as he spoke.

Helena lifted her silver-haired head in defiance and her dark eyes glistened as she looked at me directly. Her mouth twitched at the side. 'We're dead.'

Two words said coolly, calmly, crisply.

'Now, now, don't you mind her,' Bernard said in what I imagined was his best angry voice.

'Helena,' Joan admonished, 'we've been through this before. You shouldn't scare Sandy like that.'

'She doesn't look scared to me,' Helena said, still with that amused expression, her eyes unmoving.

'Well,' Marcus finally spoke after his long silence since I'd joined the group, 'she may have a point. We may very well be dead.'

Bernard and Joan groaned, and Derek began strumming lightly on his guitar and singing softly, 'We're dead, we may very well be dead.'

Bernard tutted, then poured tea from a china pot into a cup and handed it to me on a saucer. In the middle of the woods, I couldn't help but smile.

'If we're dead, then where are my parents, Helena?' Joan scolded, emptying a packet of biscuits onto a china plate and placing them before me. 'Where are all the other dead people?'

'In hell,' Helena said in a singsong voice.

Marcus smiled and looked away so that Joan wouldn't see his face.

'And what makes you think we're in heaven? What makes you think *you'd* get into heaven?' Joan huffed, dunking her biscuit into her tea and pulling it up before the soggy end fell in.

Derek strummed and sang gruffly, 'Is this heaven or is this hell? I look around and I can't tell.'

'Didn't anybody else notice the golden gates and the choir of angels as they entered or was it just me?' Helena smirked.

'You didn't enter through golden gates.' Bernard shook his head wildly, his neck wobbling from side to side. He looked at me and his neck continued to shake. 'She didn't enter through golden gates.'

Derek strummed, 'I didn't pass the golden gate nor felt the burning flames of hate.'

'Oh, stop it,' Joan huffed.

'Stop it,' he sang.

'I can't bear any more.'

'I can't bear any more, someone please show me the door . . .'

'I'll show you the door,' Helena warned, but with less conviction.

He continued strumming and they all fell silent, contemplating his last few lyrics.

'Little June, Pauline O'Connor's daughter, was only ten when she died, Helena,' Bernard continued. 'Surely a little angel like her would be in heaven and she's not here, so there goes your theory.' He held his head high and Joan nodded in agreement. 'We're not dead.'

'Sorry, it's over-eighteens only,' Helena said in a bored tone. 'St Peter's down at the gate with his arms folded and an earpiece in his ear, taking instructions from God.'

'You can't say that, Helena,' Joan snapped.

'I can't get in, I can't get out, St Peter, what's it all about?' Derek sang in a gravelled voice. Suddenly he stopped strumming and finally spoke. 'It's definitely not heaven. Elvis isn't here.'

'Oh, *well then*.' Helena rolled her eyes.

'We've got our own Elvis here, haven't we?' Bernard chuckled, changing the subject. 'Sandy, did you know that Derek used to be in a band?'

'How would she know that, Bernard?' Helena said,

exasperated. Bernard ignored her again. 'Derek Cummings,' he announced, 'the hottest property in St Kevin's back in the sixties.'

They all laughed.

My body turned cold.

'What was it you were called, Derek? I've forgotten now,' Joan laughed.

'The Wonder Boys, Joan, the Wonder Boys,' Derek said fondly, reminiscing.

'Remember the dances on a Friday night?' Bernard asked excitedly. 'Derek would be up there on the stage, playing the rock and roll, and Father Martin would be almost having a heart attack at him shaking his pelvis.' They all laughed again.

'Now, what was the name of the dance hall?' Joan thought aloud.

'Oh, gosh . . .' Bernard closed his eyes and tried to remember.

Derek stopped strumming and thought hard.

Helena kept staring at me, watching my reactions. 'Are you cold, Sandy?' Her voice sounded far away.

Finbar's Hall – the name jumped into my head. They had all loved going to Finbar's Hall every Friday night.

'Finbar's Hall,' Marcus finally remembered.

'Ah, that was it.' They all looked relieved and Derek's strumming continued.

Goose pimples formed on my skin. I shivered.

I looked around at the faces of the group, studied their eyes, their familiar features and I allowed all I had learned as a little girl to come flooding back to me. I could see it now as clearly as I had then, when I came across the story in the computer archives while researching a project for school. I had immediately taken interest, had followed up on the story and was more than familiar with it. I saw the young teenage faces smiling up from the newspaper's front page and I saw those same faces around me now.

Derek Cummings, Joan Hatchard, Bernard Lynch, Marcus Flynn and Helena Dickens. Five students from

St Kevin's Boarding School. They disappeared during a school camping trip in the sixties and were never found. But here they were now, older, wiser and their innocence lost.

I had found them.

10

When I was fourteen, my parents talked me into seeing a counsellor after school on Mondays. They didn't have to do much convincing. As soon as they told me I'd be able to ask all the questions I wanted and that this person was qualified enough to answer, I practically drove myself to school.

I knew they felt that they had failed me. I could tell that by their expressions when they sat me down at the kitchen table, with the milk and cookies in the centre and the washing machine going in the background as the usual distraction. Mum held a rolled tissue tightly in her hands as though she had used it earlier to dab away tears. That was the thing with my parents: they would never let me see their weaknesses but yet they would forget to get rid of the proof of them. I didn't see Mum's tears but I saw the tissue. I didn't hear Dad's anger at having failed to help me but I saw it in his eyes.

'Is everything OK?' I looked from one strong face to the other. The only time people can look so confident and as though they can face anything is when something bad happens. 'Did something happen?'

Dad smiled. 'No, honey, don't worry, nothing bad happened.'

Mum's eyebrow lifted when he said that and I knew she didn't agree. I knew Dad didn't agree with his words either but he was saying them none the less. There was nothing wrong with sending me to a counsellor, nothing wrong at all, but I knew that they had wanted to help me themselves. They had wanted their answers to my questions to be enough. I overheard their endless discussions about the correct method of dealing with my behaviour. They had helped me in every way they could and now I could feel their disappointment in themselves and I hated myself for making them feel that way.

'You know the way you have so many questions, honey?' Dad explained.

I nodded.

'Well, your mum and I –' he looked to her for support and her eyes softened immediately as she glanced at him – 'well, your mum and I have found someone that you'll be able to talk to about all of those questions.'

'This person will be able to answer my questions?' I felt my eyes widen and my heart quicken as though all of life's mysteries were about to be answered.

'I hope so, honey,' Mum answered. 'I hope that by talking to him, you won't have any more questions that will bother you. He'll know far more about all the things you worry about than we do.'

Then it was time for my quick-fire round. Fingers on the buzzers.

'Who is he?'

'Mr Burton.' Dad.

'What's his first name?'

'Gregory.' Mum.

'Where does he work?'

'At the school.' Mum.

'When will I see him?'

'Mondays after school. For an hour.' Mum. She was better at this than Dad. She was used to these discussions while Dad was out working.

'He's a psychiatrist, isn't he?' They never lied to me.

'Yes, honey.' Dad.

I think that's the moment I began to hate seeing myself in their eyes, and unfortunately it was the beginning of my dislike of being in their company.

* * *

Mr Burton's office was in a room the size of a closet, just about big enough for two armchairs. I chose to sit in the dirty olive-green velvet-covered chair with dark wooden handles, as opposed to the stained brown velvet-covered chair. They both looked like they dated from the forties and hadn't been washed or removed from the small room since. There was a little window so high up on the back wall that all I could see was the sky. The first day I met Mr Burton it was a clear blue. Every now and then a cloud passed, filling the entire window with white before moving on.

On the walls were posters of school kids, looking happy and declaring to the empty room how they had said no to drugs, spoken out against bullying, coped with exam stress, had beaten eating disorders, dealt with grief, were clever enough to not have to face teenage pregnancy because they didn't have sex, but on the off chance that they did, there was another poster of the same girl and boy saying how they used condoms. Saints, the lot of them. The room was so positive I thought I was going to be ejected from my chair like a rocket. Mr Burton the magnificent had helped them all.

I expected Mr Burton to be a wise old man with a head of wild grey hair, a monocle in one eye, a waistcoat with a pocket watch attached by a chain, a brain exploding with knowledge after years of extensive research into the human mind. I expected Yoda of the Western world, cloaked in wisdom, who spoke in riddles and tried to convince me that the force in me was strong.

When the real Mr Burton entered the room I had mixed feelings. The inquisitive side of me was disappointed, the fourteen-year-old in me positively delighted. He was more of a Gregory than a Mr Burton. He was young and handsome, sexy and gorgeous. He looked like he had just walked out of college that very day, in his jeans and T-shirt and fashionable haircut. I did my usual calculations: twice my age could work. In a few years it would be legal and I would be out of school. My whole life was mapped out before he had even closed the door behind him.

'Hello, Sandy.' His voice was bright and cheery. He shook my hand and I vowed to lick it when I got home and never wash it again. He sat on the brown velvet armchair across from me. I bet all those girls in the posters invented all those problems just to come into this office.

'I hope you're comfortable in our designer top-of-the-range furniture?' He wrinkled his nose in disgust as he settled into the chair, which had burst at the side and had foam spilling out.

I laughed. Oh, he was so cool. 'Yes, thanks. I was wondering what you would think my choice of chair says about me.'

'Well,' he smiled, 'it says one of two things.'

I listened intently.

'Firstly, that you don't like brown, or secondly that you like green.'

'Neither,' I smiled. 'I just wanted to face the window.'

'Ah-ha,' he grinned. 'You are what we call at the lab a "window facer".'

'Ah, I'm one of *those*.'

He looked at me with amusement for a second, then placed a pen and pad on his lap and a tape recorder on the arm of the chair. 'Do you mind if I record this?'

'Why?'

'So I can remember everything that you say. Sometimes I don't pick up on things until I listen back over the conversation.'

'OK, what's the pen and pad for then?'

'Doodling. In case I get bored listening to you.' He pressed record and said that day's date and time.

'I feel like I'm at a police station, about to be interrogated.'

'Has that ever happened before?'

I nodded. 'When Jenny-May Butler went missing, we were asked to give any information we had at the school.' How quickly talk had come round to her. She would have been delighted at the attention.

'Ah,' he nodded. 'Jenny-May was your friend, wasn't she?'

I thought about that. I looked at the antibullying posters on the wall and wondered how to answer. I didn't want to seem insensitive to this gorgeous man by saying no, but she wasn't my friend. Jenny-May hated me. But she was missing and I probably shouldn't speak badly of her because after all, everyone thought she was an angel. Mr Burton mistook my silence for being upset, which was embarrassing, and the next question he asked his voice was so gentle I almost burst out laughing.

'Do you miss her?'

I thought about that one too. Would you miss a slap across the face every day? I felt like asking him. Once again I didn't want him to think I was insensitive by saying no. He'd never fall in love with me and take me away from Leitrim then.

He leaned forward in his chair. Oh, his eyes were so blue.

'Your mum and dad told me you want to find Jenny-May – is this true?'

Wow. Talk about getting the wrong end of the stick. I rolled my eyes, OK enough of this crap. 'Mr Burton, I don't want to seem rude or insensitive here because I know Jenny-May is missing and everyone is sad but . . .' I trailed off.

'Go on,' he encouraged me, and I wanted to jump on him and kiss him.

'Well, me and Jenny-May were never friends. She hated me. I miss her in a way that I notice she's gone but not in a way that I want her back. And I don't want her back or to find her. Just knowing where she is would be enough.'

He raised his eyebrows.

'Now, I know you probably thought that because Jenny-May was my friend and she went missing, that every time I lose something, like a sock, and try to find it, it's like my way of finding Jenny-May and bringing her back.'

His mouth dropped open a little.

'Well, it's a reasonable assumption, I suppose, Mr Burton, but it's just not me. I'm really not that complicated. It's just annoying that when things go missing, I don't know where they go. Take, for instance, the Sellotape. Last night Mum was trying to wrap a present for Aunt Deirdre's birthday but she couldn't find the Sellotape. Now, we always leave it in the second drawer under the cutlery drawer. It's always there, we never put it anywhere else and my mum and dad know how I am about things like that and so they really do put everything in their places. Our house is really tidy, honestly, so it's not like things just get lost all the time in a mess. Anyway, I used the Sellotape on Saturday when I was doing my art homework – for which I got a crappy C today, by the way, even though Tracey Tinsleton got an A for drawing what looks like a squashed fly on a windscreen and that's considered "real art" – but I promise I put it back in the drawer. Dad didn't use it, Mum didn't use it and I'm almost certain no one broke into the house just to steal some Sellotape. So I searched all evening for it but I couldn't find it. Where is it?'

Mr Burton was silent and slowly moved back and settled into his chair.

'So let me get this straight,' he said slowly. 'You don't miss Jenny-May Butler.'

We both started laughing and for the first time ever, I didn't feel bad about it.

'Why do you think you're here?' Mr Burton got serious again after our bout of laughing.

'Because I need answers.'

'Answers like . . . ?'

I thought about it. 'Where is the Sellotape that we couldn't find last night? Where is Jenny-May Butler? Why does one of my socks always go missing in the washing machine?'

'You think I can tell you where all these things are?'

'Not specifics, Mr Burton, but a general indication would be fine.'

He smiled at me. 'Why don't you let me ask you the questions for a moment and maybe through your answers, we'll find the answers you want.'

'OK, if you think that'll work.' Weirdo.

'Why do you feel the need to know where things are?'

'I have to know.'

'Why do you feel you have to know?'

'Why do you feel you have to ask me questions?'

Mr Burton blinked and was silent for a second longer than he wanted, I could tell. 'It's my job and I get paid to do it.'

'Paid to do it.' I rolled my eyes. 'Mr Burton, you could have my Saturday job stacking toilet rolls and get paid but you chose to study for what – ten million years? – to get all of those scrolls you've hung on the walls.' I looked around at his framed qualifications. 'I'd say you went through all of that studying, all of those exams and ask all these questions for more reasons than just getting paid.'

He smiled lightly and watched me. I don't think he knew what else to say. And so there was a two-minute silence while he thought. Finally he put down his pen and paper and leaned towards me, resting his elbows on his knees.

'I like to have conversations with people, I always have. I find that through talking about themselves people learn things that they didn't know before. It's a kind of self-healing. I ask questions because I like to help people.'

'And so do I.'

'You feel by asking questions about Jenny-May, you're helping her or maybe her parents?' He tried to hide the confusion from his eyes.

'No, I'm helping myself.'

'How does it help you? Isn't *not* getting the answers frustrating you even more?'

'Sometimes I find things, Mr Burton. I find the things that have just been misplaced.'

'Isn't everything that's lost misplaced?'

'To misplace something is to lose it temporarily by forgetting where you put it. I always remember where I put things. It's the things that I *don't* misplace that I try to find; the things that grow legs and walk away all by themselves that annoy me.'

'Do you think it's possible that somebody else, other than you, moves all these things?'

'Like who?'

'I'm asking you.'

'Well, in the case of the Sellotape the answer is clearly no. In the case of the socks, unless somebody reaches into the washing machine and takes out my socks then the answer is no. Mr Burton, my parents want to help me. I don't think that they would move things and then forget about it every single time. If anything, they are more aware of exactly where they put things.'

'So what is your assumption? Where do you think these things are?'

'Mr Burton, if I had an assumption, then I wouldn't be here.'

'You have no idea then? Even in your wildest dreams, during your most frustrating times when you're vigorously searching into the early hours of the morning and you still can't find it, have you any opinion *at all* as to where you think the missing things are?'

Well, he'd clearly learned more about me from my parents than I thought, but having to answer this question truthfully I feared would mean he'd never fall in love with me. But I took a deep breath and told the truth anyway. 'At times like that I'm convinced they are in a place where missing things go.'

He didn't miss a beat. 'Do you think Jenny-May is there? Does it make you feel better to think that she's there?'

'Oh God.' I rolled my eyes. 'If someone killed her, Mr Burton, they killed her. I'm not trying to create imaginary worlds to make myself feel better.'

He tried very hard not to move a muscle in his face.

'But whether she's alive now or not, why haven't the Gardaí been able to find her?'

'Would it make you feel better to just accept that sometimes there are mysteries?'

'You don't accept that, why should I?'

'What makes you think I don't?'

'You're a counsellor. You believe that every action has a reaction and all that kind of stuff. I read up on it before I came here. Everything that I do now is because of something that happened, something somebody said or did. You believe there are answers to everything and ways of solving everything.'

'That's not necessarily true. I can't fix everything, Sandy.'

'Can you fix me?'

'You're not broken.'

'Is that your medical opinion?'

'I'm not a doctor.'

'Aren't you a "doctor of the mind"?' I held up my fingers in inverted commas and rolled my eyes.

Silence.

'How do you feel when you are searching and searching but you still can't find whatever it is that you're looking for?'

I could tell this was the weirdest conversation he had ever had.

'Have you a girlfriend, Mr Burton?'

His forehead creased. 'Sandy, I'm not sure that this is relevant.' When I didn't answer, he sighed. 'No, I don't.'

'Do you want one?'

He was contemplative. 'Are you saying that the feeling of searching for a missing sock is like searching for love?' He tried to ask the question without making me sound stupid but he failed miserably.

I rolled my eyes again. He was making me do that a lot. 'No, it's a feeling of knowing something is missing in your life but not being able to find it no matter how hard you look.'

He cleared his throat awkwardly, picked up his pen and paper and pretended to write something.

Doodle time. 'Boring you, am I?'

He laughed and it broke the tension.

I tried to explain again. 'Perhaps it would have been easier if I said that not being able to find something is like suddenly not remembering the words to your favourite song that you knew off by heart. It's like suddenly forgetting the name of someone you know really well and see every day, or the name of a group who sang a famous song. It's something so frustrating that it plays on your mind over and over again because you know there's an answer but no one can tell you it. It niggles and niggles at me and I can't rest until I know the answers.'

'I understand,' he said softly.

'Well, then, multiply that feeling by one hundred.'

He was contemplative. 'You're mature for your age, Sandy.'

'Funny, because I was hoping you'd know an awful lot more for yours.'

He laughed until our time was up.

That night at dinner Dad asked me how it went.

'He couldn't answer my questions,' I replied, slurping on my soup.

Dad looked like his heart was going to break. 'So I suppose you don't want to go back.'

'No!' I said quickly and my mum tried to hide her smile by taking a sip of water.

Dad looked back and forth from her face to mine questioningly.

'He has nice eyes,' I offered by way of explanation, slurping again.

His eyebrows rose and he looked to my mum, who had a grin from ear to ear and flushed cheeks. 'That's true, Harold. He has very nice eyes.'

'Ah, *well then*!' He threw his arms up. 'If the man has nice eyes for Christsake, who am I to argue?'

Later that night I lay on my bed and thought about

my conversation with Mr Burton. He may not have had answers for me but he sure cured me of searching for one thing.

11

I went to see Mr Burton every week while I was at St Mary's Secondary School. We even met up during the summer months when the school remained open to the rest of the town for summer activities. The last time I went to see him there was when I had just turned eighteen. I'd finished my leaving certificate the previous year and I'd found out that morning I'd been accepted into the Gardaí Síochána. I was due to move to Cork to train at Templemore in a few months.

'Hello, Mr Burton,' I said as he entered the small office that hadn't changed one bit since the first day we met. He was still young and handsome and I loved every inch of him.

'Sandy, for the hundredth time, stop calling me Mr Burton. You make me sound like an old man.'

'You are an old man,' I teased.

'Which makes you an old woman,' he said lightly, and a silence fell between us. 'So,' he became business-like, 'what's on your mind this week?'

'I got accepted into the Gardaí today.'

His eyes widened. Happiness? Sadness? 'Wow, Sandy, congratulations. You did it!' He came over and gave me a hug. We held on a second longer than we should have.

'How do your mum and dad feel?'

'They don't know yet.'

'They'll be sad to see you go.'

'It's for the best.' I looked away.

'You won't leave all your problems behind in Leitrim, you know,' he said gently.

'No, but I'll leave behind the people who know about them.'

'Do you plan on coming back to visit?'

I stared him directly in the eyes. Were we still talking about my parents? 'As much as I can.'

'How much will that be?'

I shrugged.

'They have always supported you, Sandy.'

'I can't be who they want me to be, Mr Burton. I make them uncomfortable.'

He rolled his eyes at me calling him that, at my deliberate attempts to build a wall between us. 'They just want you to be you, you know that. Don't be ashamed of how you are. They love you for who you are.'

The way he looked at me made me wonder again if we were talking about my parents at all. I looked around the room. He knew everything about me, absolutely everything, and I sensed everything about him. He was still single and living alone, despite every girl in Leitrim town chasing him. He tried to tell me week after week to accept things as they were and move on with life, but if there was one man who had put his life on hold to wait for something, or someone, it was him.

He cleared his throat. 'I heard you went out with Andy McCarthy at the weekend.'

'And?'

He rubbed his face wearily and allowed a silence to fall between us. We were both good at that. Four years of therapy, of me baring my soul, yet every new word was a word further from discussing the very thing that consumed my thoughts most moments of most days.

'So come on, talk to me,' he said softly.

Our last session and I couldn't think of anything. He still had no answers for me.

'Are you going to the fancy-dress party on Friday?' He picked up the mood of the atmosphere.

'Yes,' I smiled. 'I can't think of a better way to say

goodbye to this place than to walk out being dressed as something else.'

'What are you dressing up as?'

'A sock.'

He laughed so hard. 'Andy isn't going with you?'

'Do my socks ever come as a pair?'

He raised his eyebrows, indicating he wanted more.

'He didn't get why I turned his flat upside down when I couldn't find the invite.'

'Where do you think it is?'

'With everything else. With my mind.' I rubbed my eyes wearily.

'You haven't lost your mind, Sandy. So you're going to be a garda.' His smile was shaky.

'Worried about the future of our country?'

'No,' he smiled. 'At least I know we'll be in safe hands. You'll be questioning criminals to death.'

'I learned from the best.' I forced myself to smile.

Mr Burton turned up at the fancy-dress party that Friday night. He was dressed as a sock and I laughed so hard. He drove me home that night and we sat in silence. After so many years of talking neither of us knew what to say. Outside my house he leaned over and kissed my lips hungrily; long and hard. It was like our hello to one another and a goodbye all at once.

'Pity we're not the same pattern, Gregory. We would have made a good pair,' I said sadly.

I wanted him to tell me that we'd make the most perfect odd pair around but I think he agreed because I watched him drive away.

The more partners I had, the more I realised Gregory and I were the best pair I'd ever come across. But in my pursuit of answers to all the difficult questions in my life, I missed out on the obvious ones right in front of my very eyes.

12

Helena was watching me curiously through the amber blaze of the campfire, the shadow of the flames dancing upwards to lick her face. The other members of the group had continued with their reminiscing of Derek's rock-and-roll days, happy to move the subject away from my question about where we were. Excited chatter had resumed but I remained on the outside, though I was not alone. Finally, I lifted my eyes from the ash floor and allowed them to meet Helena's.

She waited for a silence to fall between the group before asking, 'What do you do for a living, Sandy?'

'Oooh, yes,' Joan said excitedly, warming her hands around her tea cup. 'Do tell us.'

I had everyone's attention and so I considered my options. Why lie?

'I run an agency,' I began and then stopped.

'What kind of an agency?' Bernard asked.

'A modelling agency, is it?' Joan asked in hushed tones. 'With long legs like yours I'll bet it is.' Her tea cup rested in her hands not far below her lips, her baby finger was erect and standing tall like a dog on the hunt.

'Joan, she said she *runs* the agency, not is a *member* of one.' Bernard shook his head and his chin wobbled.

'Actually, it's a missing persons agency.'

There was a silence as they searched my face and when they all looked at each other, they erupted in laughter. All except Helena.

'Oh, Sandy, that was a good one.' Bernard wiped the corners of his eyes with his handkerchief. 'What kind of agency is it really?'

'Acting.' Helena jumped in before I had a chance to answer.

'How do you know?' Bernard asked her, rather in a huff that she knew something before him. 'You're the one who asked the question in the first place.'

'She told me while you were all laughing.' She waved her hand dismissively.

'An acting agency.' Joan looked at me with wide eyes. 'How wonderful. We put on some excellent plays in Finbar's Hall,' Joan explained. 'Do you remember that?' She looked around at her friends. '*Julius Caesar*, *Romeo and Juliet* to name but two of Shakespeare's finest works. Bernard was—'

Bernard coughed loudly.

'Oh, I'm sorry.' Joan blushed. 'Bernard *is* a fantastic actor. He played quite a convincing Bottom in *A Midsummer Night's Dream*. No doubt you would love him to be in your agency.'

And they fell into their usual chatter of swapping old stories. Helena made her way round the fire and sat next to me.

'I must say, you excel in your occupation,' Helena chuckled.

'Why did you do that?' I referred to her interjection.

'Oh, you don't want to tell them that, especially Joan with her voice so hushed she feels the need to tell everybody everything just to make sure she's heard,' she teased, but watched her friend fondly. 'If anyone finds out you run a missing persons agency you'll be swamped with questions. Everyone will think you'll have come to bring us all home.' I wasn't sure whether she was joking or asking me a question. Either way, she didn't laugh and I didn't answer.

'Who else is there to tell around here?' I stared into the silent black woods. I hadn't come across any others for two days.

Helena looked at me curiously again. 'Sandy, there *are* others, you know.'

Apart from Ewoks, I found it hard to believe anybody else inhabited the dark and silent surroundings.

'You know our story, don't you?' Helena kept her voice low so that the others couldn't hear.

I nodded, took a deep breath and recited, '"Five students are missing after disappearing during a school camping trip in Roundwood, County Wicklow. Sixteen-year-olds Derek Cummings, Helena Dickens, Marcus Flynn, Joan Hatchard and Bernard Lynch from St Kevin's Boarding School for Girls and Boys in Blackrock were due to visit Glendalough but were missing from their tents that morning."'

Helena was gazing at me with such childlike intent and tear-filled eyes I felt a duty to recite the newspaper article word-perfect, tone-perfect. I wanted to express the feeling in the country during that initial week, on behalf of the country; I wanted to convey accurately the outpour of love and support complete strangers had displayed towards the missing five students. I felt I owed it to all those people who prayed for their return. I felt Helena deserved to hear it.

'"The Gardaí today said that they were following leads although they couldn't confirm ruling out foul play. They ask for anyone with any information to contact the Roundwood or Blackrock Gardaí. The students of St Kevin's have all gathered to pray for their fellow students and locals have been placing flowers near the scene."'

I was silent.

'What's wrong with your eyes, Helena?' Bernard asked worriedly.

'Oh,' Helena sniffed, 'it's nothing. Just a spark from the fire jumped into my eye, that's all.' She dabbed her eyes with the corner of her pashmina.

'Oh dear,' Joan said, moving over and peering in her eye. 'No, it looks fine to me, just red and watery. It probably just stings a bit.'

'I'm fine, thanks,' Helena dismissed them all, embarrassed by their care, and the others continued chatting amongst themselves.

'With acting like that you could join my agency,' I smiled.

Helena laughed and fell silent again. I felt I should say something.

'They never gave up looking for you, you know.'

Her mouth let out a tiny sound. A sound that was beyond her control to stop, a sound that had worked its way up straight from her heart.

'Your father championed every new Garda Commissioner and Minister for Justice that took office. He knocked on every door and searched between every blade of grass to find you. He made sure they searched the entire area with a fine-tooth comb. As for your mother, your amazing mother . . .'

Helena smiled at the mention of her mother.

'She set up an organisation to help counsel families suffering the effects of missing loved ones, named Porch Light, as many families of the missing leave their front lights on as a beacon, hoping that someday their loved ones will return. She was tireless in her charity work, setting up bases all around the country. Your parents never, ever gave up. Your mother still hasn't.'

'She's alive?' Her eyes widened and filled once again.

'Your father – I'm sorry – passed away some years ago.' I allowed her to process the information before moving on. 'Your mother is still actively involved with Porch Light. I attended their annual lunch last year and had the pleasure of meeting her and telling her how wonderful I thought she was.' I looked down at my hands and cleared my throat, the role of messenger not always proving easy. 'She told me to continue with my efforts as she wished I could find her beloved daughter for her.'

Helena's voice was barely a whisper. 'Tell me about her.'

And so I forgot about my own worries and settled down by the warmth of the campfire to do just that.

'I never wanted to go on the camping trip.' Helena was exhilarated and full of emotion after I had filled her with knowledge of her mother. 'I pleaded with them not to make me go.'

I knew all this but I listened intently, fascinated to hear the story I knew so well from one of its main characters. It was like seeing my favourite book come alive on stage.

'I'd wanted to go home that weekend. There was a boy . . .' She laughed and looked at me. 'Isn't it always about a boy?'

I couldn't relate but smiled all the same.

'A new boy had moved into the house next door to us. Samuel James was his name, the most beautiful creature alive.' Her eyes were bright, as though the fire's sparks had leaped in and set her pupils alight. 'I met him that summer and fell in love, and we had the most wonderful time together. *Sinful.*' She raised her eyebrows and I smiled. 'I'd been back at school for two months and I missed him dreadfully. I begged and pleaded with my parents to let me go home but to no avail. They were punishing me,' she said with a sad smile. 'I'd been caught cheating in my history exam in the same week I'd been caught smoking behind the gymnasium. Unacceptable, even by my standards.' She looked around the group. 'And so I was stuck going away with this lot as though separating me from my best friends would suddenly make me an angel. All the same, it turned out to be a punishment I don't think I entirely deserved.'

'Of course not,' I empathised. 'How did you get here?'

Helena sighed. 'Marcus and I made arrangements early in the evening to meet up when everyone had gone to sleep. He was the only one who had a packet of cigarettes so the other two boys went with him and, well, Joan,' Helena looked at her friend on the other side of the campfire with fondness, 'she was afraid to stay in the tent by herself so she came too. We moved away from the camp so our teachers wouldn't see the cigarettes alight or smell the smoke. We didn't walk that far at all, just a few minutes or so, but we found ourselves here,' she shrugged. 'I can't really explain it any other way.'

'That must have been terrifying for you all.'

'No more than it was for you.' She looked at me. 'And at least we had each other. I couldn't imagine going through it all alone.'

She wanted me to talk but I wouldn't. It wasn't in my nature to open up. Not unless it was with Gregory.

'You can't even have been born when we went missing. How do you know so much?'

'Let's just say I was an inquisitive child.'

'Inquisitive indeed.' She studied me again and I looked away, finding her glare intrusive. 'Do you know what has happened to everybody's family here?' She nodded at the rest of the group.

'Yes.' I looked around them all, seeing their parents' faces in each of them. 'I made it my life's work to know. I followed up on all of you every year, wanting to see if anyone came home.'

'Well, thank you for helping me feel one step closer to it now.'

A silence fell between us, Helena no doubt lost in her memories of home.

Eventually, she spoke again. 'My grandmother was a proud woman, Sandy. She married my grandfather when she was eighteen years old and they had six children. Her younger sister, who they could never seem to marry off, embarked on a mysterious affair with a man she would never name and to everybody's shock, gave birth to a baby boy,' she chuckled. 'That my grandfather's face was written all over that child was not lost on my grandmother, nor were the shillings that disappeared from their savings just as the new clothes appeared on the child. Of course, those things are entirely coincidental,' she said in a singsong voice, stretching her legs out in front of her. 'There are a great many brown-haired, blue-eyed men in the country and the fact my grandfather had a fondness for drinking would explain the dents in their savings.' Her eyes twinkled at me.

I looked at Helena in confusion. 'I'm sorry, Helena, I'm not sure why you're telling me this.'

She laughed. 'That you have ended up here with us could be one of life's great coincidences.'

I nodded.

'But my grandmother didn't believe in coincidences. And neither do I. You're here for a reason, Sandy.'

13

Helena added another log to the dying fire and its weight sent a pile of adolescent ashes racing one another down the side of the burning tower. The flames were awakened from the embers and sleepily began to climb up the log, casting out heat to Helena and me.

I had been talking to her for hours, filling her in on all the details of her family life that I knew of. An unusual feeling had stirred within me as soon as I'd realised whose company I was keeping. It washed over me in waves, each wave relaxing me, making my eyes that little bit heavier, causing my mind to tick that little bit slower, and for the tension in my muscles to relax just a little bit more. It was just a little bit, mind you, but it was something.

All of my life people had told me that my questions were irrelevant, that my over-interest in cases of missing persons unnecessary, but right there in the woods every stupid, embarrassing, irrelevant and unnecessary question I had ever asked about Helena Dickens meant the world to her. I knew there had been a reason for my endless searches, my infinite interrogations of myself and of others. And the greatest thing of all was that there wasn't just one reason for it all; sitting next to me by the campfire there were four others.

Oh, the relief. That's what the feeling was. The first sense of relief my mind had felt since I was ten years old.

The sky was growing brighter; the tips of the trees

that had been burned by the sun by day had been cooled by the night and now shaded the sky a cool blue. The birds that had been silent during the dark hours were now warming their vocal cords, like the idiosyncratic rendition of an orchestra tuning, pre-performance. Bernard, Derek, Marcus and Joan lay asleep in their sleeping bags, covered by blankets and looking how they should have the night of their school camping trip. I wondered, had they slept soundly through that night instead of venturing into the woods, would they have been back in their families' arms all those years ago, or would the secret door to this world have welcomed them in regardless?

Was it an accident that we were all here? Did we stumble upon a blip in the earth's creation, a black hole on the surface, or was this just a part of life that was unspoken throughout the centuries? Were we lost and unaccounted for, or was this where we truly belonged and our 'normal' lives the original error? Was this a place for those who felt like outsiders in life to belong, to finally feel relief? Despite my own relief, my questions kept flowing. The world around me had changed but some things remained constant.

'Were you happy?' I looked around at the others sleeping. 'Was everybody happy?'

Helena smiled softly. 'We've all asked the question of why, and there is no answer that we know of. Yes, we were happy. We were all very, very happy in our lives.' She paused. 'Sandy,' she broke the silence again, watching me with that amused expression as if enjoying a private joke, 'believe it or not we're very happy here too. We've spent more years living here than anywhere else. The past is a distant but pleasurable memory for us.'

I looked around the campfire. They had nothing. Nothing but small overnight bags packed with tea bags, unnecessary chinaware and biscuits, blankets and sleeping bags, wraps and jumpers to keep warm, all of which they undoubtedly retrieved from the piles of belongings scattered around us. These five people had slept under the stars, swathed in blankets with a fire and the sun as their only source of light and heat. For forty years. How could they be truly happy? How could they not be clawing their way back to existence, back to material belongings and craving the companionship of others?

I shook my head as I looked around.

Helena laughed at me. 'Why are you shaking your head?'

'I'm sorry.' I was embarrassed at being caught pitying a life they seemed content with. 'It's just that forty years is such a long time to settle,' I looked around at the clearing, 'well . . . here.'

Helena's face opened in surprise.

'Oh, I'm so sorry,' I backtracked. 'I didn't mean to offend you—'

'Sandy, Sandy,' she interrupted, '*this* is not our whole world.'

'I know, I know,' I backed off. 'You have each other and—'

'No.' Helena started laughing and her forehead crumpled in confusion. 'I'm sorry, I thought you knew this wasn't a permanent thing. We go camping together once a year on the anniversary of our disappearance. I thought you would recognise the date. This clearing is the first place we arrived at forty years ago – well, the first area where we *realised* we weren't at home any more. We all stay in touch during the year but we live more or less separate lives.'

'What?' I was confused.

'People go missing all the time, you know that. Wherever people gather, life begins, civilisation exists. Sandy, fifteen minutes' walk from here, the woods end and a whole new life begins.'

I was stunned. My mouth opened and closed but no words would come out.

'Interesting you should arrive here today of all days,' Helena said, deep in thought.

I scrambled to my feet. 'Come on, let's go now. Show me this place you're talking about. We won't disturb the others.'

'No.' Helena's voice was hard and her smile quickly faded. Her hand sprang up to grab my arm. I flinched and tried to pull away, not liking the contact, but this did not rattle her. I couldn't move; the force of her hold was so strong. Her face was stony. 'We do not just leave each other like that, we do not disappear from one another. We will sit here until they wake.'

She loosened her grip on my arm and wrapped her pashmina tighter around her body; retreating to the guarded woman she had been earlier in the evening. She watched her friends intently as though on duty and I realised it wasn't just me that had been keeping her awake all night. It was just her turn.

'We stay until they wake,' she repeated firmly.

Jack sat on the corner of the bed and watched Gloria sleeping with a small smile on her face. It was the early hours of Monday morning and he had just returned home. After Sandy Shortt's no-show he had spent the entire day checking B & Bs and hotels in all the nearby towns to see if she had checked in anywhere. There were so many things that could have prevented her from arriving at the café; he convinced himself her no-show that morning didn't mean it was the end of their search. She could have just overslept and missed their meeting, or got caught up in Dublin and couldn't leave for Limerick that night. There could have been a death in the family or a sudden lead in another case that took her away from Limerick. She could be heading towards him now, driving through the night to get to Glin. He had thought of the endless possibilities but not one of those theories was the idea that she could have deliberately let him down.

A mistake had been made, that was all. He would return to Glin later today in his lunch break to see if she had arrived. He had lived all week for that meeting and he wasn't going to give up now. Sandy had given him more hope in one week during a few phone conversations than anyone else had succeeded in doing over the entire year. He knew from their talks that she wouldn't let him down.

He was going to tell Gloria, he really was. He reached out to touch her shoulder and shake her gently but his hand stopped mid-air. Maybe he should hold off telling her until he made contact with Sandy again. Gloria sighed sleepily, stretched her body and turned over.

She eventually settled on her side, her back towards Jack and his outstretched hand.

14

Only a week before the no-show from Sandy, Jack had quietly closed the bedroom door adjoining the living room so as not to disturb a sleeping Gloria. The Golden Pages lying open on the couch stared back at him as he paced the far side of the room, one eye on the phone book, the other eye on the bedroom door. He stopped and traced his finger down the page until he came across the advert for Porch Light, the organisation that helped counsel friends and relatives of the missing. Jack and his sister Judith had tried to convince their mother to talk to Porch Light after Donal's disappearance, but her old Irish ways of refusing to speak her private thoughts to a stranger held her back. Below the advert was the number for Sandy Shortt's missing persons agency. He picked up his mobile and switched on the television so as to cover the sound of his voice in case Gloria awoke. He dialled the number he had memorised when he first came across the advertisement. It rang twice before a female answered.

'Hello?'

Jack suddenly couldn't remember what to say.

'Hello?' The voice was softer this time. 'Gregory, is that you?'

'No.' Jack finally found his voice. 'My name is Jack, Jack Ruttle. I got your number from the Golden Pages.'

'Oh, I'm sorry,' the woman apologised and returned to her original businesslike tone. 'I was expecting someone else. I'm Sandy Shortt,' she said.

'Hello, Sandy.' Jack paced the small cluttered living room, tripping over the unevenly rolled, mismatching rugs that adorned the old wooden floors. 'I'm sorry to call so late.' Get to the point he hurried himself, pacing faster while he watched the bedroom door.

'Don't worry. A call at this hour of the night is an insomniac's dream, pardon the pun. How can I help you?'

He stopped pacing and held his head in his hand. What was he doing?

Sandy's voice was gentle again. 'Is somebody you know missing?'

'Yes,' was all Jack could reply.

'How long ago?' He could hear her rooting for paper.

'A year.' He settled on the arm of the couch.

'What is this person's name?'

'Donal Ruttle.' He swallowed the lump in his throat.

She paused, then: 'Yes, Donal,' a tone of recognition in her voice. 'You're a relative?'

'Brother . . .' Jack's voice cracked and he knew he couldn't go on. He needed to stop now; he needed to move on like the rest of his family. He was stupid to think that an insomniac from the phone book with too much time on her hands could succeed where an entire garda search hadn't. 'I'm sorry, I'm very, very sorry. This phone call was a mistake,' he forced out. 'I'm sorry for wasting your time.' He quickly hung up the phone and fell back into the couch, embarrassed and exhausted, knocking against his files and sending pictures of a smiling Donal floating to the ground.

Moments later his mobile rang. He dived for it, not wanting the ring tone to waken Gloria.

'Donal?' he breathed, jumping to his feet.

'Jack, it's Sandy Shortt.'

Silence.

'Is that how you usually answer the phone?' she asked gently.

He was lost for words.

'Because if it is and you're still expecting your brother

to call, I don't think your phone call to me was a mistake, do you?'

His heart was hammering in his chest. 'How did you get my number?'

'Caller ID.'

'My number is blocked.'

'I find people, Jack. That's what I do. And there's a chance that I can find Donal for you.'

He glanced at all the photographs scattered around him, the cheeky smile of his younger brother staring up at him, silently daring him to seek him out as he had when he was a child.

'Are you back in?' she asked.

'I'm in,' he replied, and he headed to the kitchen for a cup of coffee in preparation for the long night ahead.

The following night at two a.m., as Gloria lay asleep in bed, Jack lay on the couch, on the phone to Sandy, his hundreds of pages of garda reports scattered around him.

'You've spoken to Donal's friends, I see,' Sandy said, and he could hear her leafing through the pages he'd faxed to her earlier in the day.

'Over and over again,' he said wearily. 'In fact, I'm going to call in to one of his friends again on Saturday while I'm in Tralee. I've got a dental appointment,' he added casually and then wondered why.

'The dentist, yuck, I'd rather have my eyes gouged out,' she murmured.

Jack laughed.

'Don't they have dentists in Foynes?'

'I've to see a specialist.'

He could hear the smile in her voice. 'Don't they have specialists in Limerick?'

'OK, OK,' he laughed. 'So I wanted to ask Donal's friend a few more questions.'

'Tralee, Tralee,' she repeated, rustling through paper. 'A-ha,' the paper rustling stopped. 'Andrew in Tralee, friend from college, works as a web designer.'

'That's him.'

'I don't think Andrew knows anything more, Jack.'

'How do you know?'

'Judging by his answers during questioning.'

'I didn't give you that file.' Jack sat upright.

'I used to be a garda. Conveniently for me, it's about the only place I managed to make friends.'

'I need to see those files.' Jack's heart raced. There was something new, something more for him to stay awake at night analysing.

'We can meet up soon,' she dismissed him politely. 'I suppose talking to Andrew again wouldn't hurt.' There was the sound of her leafing through more pages and she was silent for a long time.

'What are you looking at?'

'Donal's photograph.'

Jack picked it up from his pile and stared at it too. It was becoming too familiar to him; it was looking more like just a photograph and less like his brother every day.

'Good-looking guy,' Sandy complimented. 'Nice eyes. Do you two look alike?'

Jack laughed. 'I feel inclined to say yes after that.'

They continued studying the pages.

'You don't sleep?' Sandy asked.

'No, not since Donal went missing. What about you?'

'I've just never been a great sleeper.'

He laughed.

'What?' she asked defensively.

'Nothing. You being a light sleeper is a great answer,' he said playfully, dropping the pages onto his lap. In the deathly silence of the cottage he listened to the sound of Sandy's breathing and her voice, and tried to imagine what she looked like, where she was and what she was thinking.

After a long silence her voice was gentler. 'I've a lot of missing people on my mind. There's too much to think about, too many places to look to allow sleep to come. You can't find anyone or anything in dreams.'

Jack looked towards the closed bedroom door and agreed.

'But why I told you that, I have no idea,' she grumbled to the sound of more paper being shifted.

'Tell me honestly, Sandy, what's your success rate?'

Paper rustling stopped. 'It depends on the level of the missing case. I'll be honest with you, cases like Donal's are difficult. There has already been a large-scale search and it's rare that I have found someone under these circumstances. But with general missing cases I find people around forty per cent of the time. You should know that not all the people I find return to their families. You have to be prepared for that.'

'I am prepared. If Donal's lying in a ditch somewhere I want him back here so we can bury him and give him a proper funeral.'

'That's not what I mean. Sometimes people go missing deliberately.'

'Donal wouldn't do that,' Jack said dismissively.

'Perhaps not. But there have been situations just like this where I've learned that people just like Donal, from families just like yours, voluntarily move on from their lives without a word to anyone close to them.'

Jack digested this. It hadn't occurred to him that Donal would take off of his own free will and he found this scenario hugely improbable. 'Would you tell me where he was if you found him?'

'If he didn't want to be found? No, I couldn't tell you that.'

'Would you tell me *if* you found him?'

'It depends on how prepared you are to accept being unable to know where he is.'

'All I would want to know is that wherever he is, he's safe and happy.'

'Well, then I would tell you.'

After a long silence, Jack asked, 'Is there much work for you? On the rare occasions that people go missing, don't their families turn to the Gardaí to deal with it?'

'That's true. There aren't many severe cases for me

like Donal's, but there's always something or someone to find. There are categories of missing people that the Gardaí can't and won't investigate.'

'Like what?'

'You really want to know this?'

'I want to know everything about it.' Jack looked at the clock: two thirty a.m. 'And besides, I've nothing better to do at this time of night.'

'Well, sometimes I find people that others have merely lost contact with – long-lost relatives, old school friends or adopted children trying to find their biological parents, that kind of thing. I work quite a lot alongside the Salvation Army, trying to trace people. Then there are the more serious cases such as people who have disappeared, many of them of their own volition, and families just want to know where they are.'

'But how would the Gardaí know it was their choice?'

'Some people leave messages behind saying they don't want to return.' He could hear her unwrapping something in the background. 'Sometimes they take their personal effects with them or sometimes people have previously expressed dissatisfaction with their situation.'

'What are you eating?'

'A chocolate muffin,' she replied with her mouth full. She swallowed. 'Sorry, did you hear me properly?'

'Yeah, you're eating a chocolate muffin.'

'No, not that,' she laughed.

Jack smiled. 'So the families come to you for cases the Gardaí can't deal with.'

'Exactly. A lot of my work, using the help of other missing persons agencies in Ireland, is in specifically tracking cases that aren't classed as high risk. If a person has left home of their own accord they won't be accepted as missing but it doesn't ease the worries of their families and friends.'

'So they're just forgotten about?'

'No, a record will be made at the station but the

extent of the enquiries is left to the discretion of the garda in charge of the station.'

'What if somebody who was incredibly unhappy with his life packed his bags to be alone for a while, but then went missing? Nobody would look for him because he previously expressed a dislike of his life. And haven't we all done that at some point?'

Sandy was silent.

'Am I wrong in thinking that? Wouldn't you want to be found?'

'Jack, I can only assume that there's only one thing *more* frustrating than not being able to find someone, and that's not being found. I would want someone to find me, more than anything,' she said firmly.

They both thought it over.

'I'd better go now.' Jack yawned. 'I've to be up for work in a few hours. Will you sleep now?'

'After I go through all these files again.'

He shook his head in wonder. 'Just so you know, if you'd told me you'd never found anyone, I'd still be on this phone.'

She was quiet for a moment. 'And if I'd never found anyone, I would be too.'

15

Jack woke up earlier than Gloria, as usual. Her head rested on his chest, her long brown hair spread across his skin, tickling where it fell down alongside his ribs. He silently and very slowly moved his body from under hers and slipped out of bed. Gloria moaned sleepily and settled back down with a peaceful look on her face. He showered and dressed and left the bungalow before she had even stirred.

Every morning he left their home before she did to be at work at eight a.m. Gloria didn't start work as a guide in Foynes Flying Boat Museum until ten o'clock. The museum was Foynes' number-one tourist attraction, celebrating the era between 1939 and 1945 when Foynes was the centre of the aviation world, with air traffic between the US and Europe. Gloria, always more than willing to talk and help people, worked as a multilingual guide in the museum from March until October.

Apart from the museum, Foynes was famous for one other thing: the invention of Irish coffee. During cold and rainy weather, people waiting at the air terminal needed something stronger than coffee to keep them warm. Thus Irish coffee was born.

In a matter of days from now, Foynes would be overrun by bands playing music on the festival stage, the farmers' market in museum square, the regatta, and the children's street art would decorate the town for the Irish Coffee Summer Festival. As usual, the celebratory fireworks would be sponsored by the

Shannon Foynes Port Company, which was exactly where Jack was headed that morning.

After greeting and consulting his colleagues, Jack took his place in the gigantic metal crane and got to work loading cargo. He enjoyed his job and felt a sense of satisfaction, knowing that someone just like him, somewhere on foreign soil, would unload the gift he had helped wrap. He enjoyed placing things where they belonged. He knew everything and everyone had a place in life: every piece of cargo that lay stocked up on the docks and every man and woman who worked alongside him had a space to slot into and a part to play. Every day he had the same goal: moving things and putting them where they belonged.

He could hear Sandy's voice in his head, repeating the same sentence over and over again. *I can only assume that there's only one thing* more *frustrating than not being able to find someone, and that's not being found. I would want someone to find me, more than anything.*

He carefully placed the cargo onto the ship, lowered himself to the ground, to the surprise of his watching colleagues, took off his helmet, threw it to the ground and ran. Some watched in confusion, some in anger, but those closest to him viewed his exit with sympathy, for they guessed that even a year on, Jack could no longer sit in his perch high above the ground, so high he felt he could see the entire county and all that was in it, except his brother.

For Jack, running down to his car, all he could think about was finding Sandy, so she could bring Donal back to where he belonged.

Jack's continuous questions about Sandy Shortt to the hotels, inns and bed-and-breakfasts in Glin were beginning to raise eyebrows. Impatience was entering the voices of the once-friendly members of staff, and diversions of his phone calls to duty managers were becoming more frequent. Now, with still no clues as to where

Sandy was, Jack found himself taking deep breaths of fresh air down by the Shannon Estuary. The River Shannon had been a prominent feature in Jack's life. Ever since he was a child he had wanted to work in Shannon Foynes Port. He had loved the excitement of the bustling docks that housed the monstrous machines that roamed the river's edge like metal herons with long steely legs and beaks.

He had always felt a connection with the river and wanted to be a part of helping all it carried. His mother and father had brought the family to Leitrim on a summer holiday one year, the holiday that remained more vivid in Jack's mind than any other. Donal wasn't born and Jack hadn't yet reached ten years old. It was on that holiday he learned where and how the great river began, slowly and quietly at first in County Cavan before it picked up speed, gathering the secrets and spirit of each county with each part of soil it eroded. Each tributary was like an artery being pumped from the heart of the country, whispering its secrets in hushed and excited babbles until it eventually carried them to the Atlantic where they were lost with the rest of the world's whispered hopes and regrets. It was like Chinese whispers, starting out small but eventually growing and becoming exaggerated, from the freshly painted wooden boats that bobbed on the surface in Carrick-on-Shannon, to finally carrying steel and metal ships alongside cranes and warehouses that was the grand excitement of Shannon Foynes Port.

Jack rambled aimlessly down a quiet road along the Shannon Estuary, grateful for the peace and quiet. Glin Castle disappeared behind the trees as he walked further down the track. A splash of bright red glowed from behind the greenery in an area that had long ago been used as a car park but was now overgrown and merely used as a walk for ramblers and birdwatchers. The gravel was uneven, the white lines had faded and weeds grew from between every crack. There sat an old red Fiesta, battered and dented, its gleam long ago rubbed away. Jack stopped in his tracks, immediately recognising the car as the Venus flytrap that had captured the long-legged beauty from the garage the previous morning.

His heart quickened as he looked around to find her but there was no sight or sound of any other presence. A coffee-filled Styrofoam cup sat on the dashboard, newspapers piled up on the passenger seat alongside a towel, which led Jack's overactive imagination to believe she was jogging nearby. He moved away from the car in fear she would return to find him peering through the windows. The coincidence of them meeting once again in another deserted area filled him with far too much curiosity for him to walk away. And saying hello to her again would be a welcome joy to a day lacking in results.

After forty-five minutes of waiting around, Jack began to feel bored and foolish. The car looked like it had been abandoned years ago in the forgotten area, yet he knew for sure that he had seen it being driven yesterday morning. He moved closer and pressed his face against the glass.

His heart almost stopped. Goose bumps rose on his skin as a shiver ran through his body.

There on the dashboard, beside the cup of coffee and a mobile phone with missed calls, was a thick brown file with 'Donal Ruttle' written in neat handwriting across the front.

16

I tapped my shoe against the plate that once held the chocolate digestives, causing a loud tinkling sound to echo through the clearing. Around me the four sleeping bodies were lazily stretched out on the forest floor, and Bernard's snores seemed to get louder with every minute that passed. I sighed loudly, feeling like a pesky hormonal teenager who couldn't get her way. Helena, whom I hadn't spoken to for an hour, raised her eyebrows at me, trying to show her lack of amusement although I knew well that she was enjoying every second of my torture. Over the past hour I had 'accidentally' knocked over the china, dropped a packet of biscuits on Joan and had a rather loud bout of coughing. Still they slept and Helena refused to lead or even direct me out of the woods to the other life she had spoken of.

Hearing laughter, I had attempted to make my own way out but, finding my way blocked by thousands of identical leering pines, I decided that getting lost once was enough, to get lost a second time in already unusual circumstances would be just plain stupid.

'How long do they usually sleep for?' I asked loudly in a bored tone, hoping my voice would disturb them.

'They like to get a good eight hours.'

'Do they eat?'

'Three times a day; usually solids. I walk them twice a day. Bernard in particular loves the leash.' She smiled into the distance as though remembering. 'And then they partake in the occasional personal grooming,' she finished.

'I meant do they eat here?' I looked around the clearing in disgust, no longer caring if I insulted their annual camping resort. I couldn't help my agitation but I hated to be pinned down. Usually I came and went in my life as I pleased, in and out of others'. I never even succeeded in staying in my own parents' house for very long, usually grabbing my bag by the door and running. But here, I had no place to go.

Laughter echoed in the distance once again.

'What is that noise?'

'People call it laughter, I think.' Helena settled down in her sleeping bag, looking snug and smug at the same time.

'Have you always had an attitude problem?' I asked.

'Have you?'

'Yes,' I said firmly, and she laughed. I let go of my frown and smiled. 'It's just that I've been sitting in these woods for two entire days now.'

'Is that an apology?'

'I don't apologise. Not unless I really need to.'

'You remind me of me when I was young. Young*er*. I'm still young. What has you so irritable at such a young age?'

'I'm not a people person.' I looked around as I heard another bout of laughing.

Helena continued talking as though she hadn't even heard it. 'Of course you're not. You've just spent the guts of your life working to find them.'

I registered her statement but decided not to respond to it. 'Do you not hear these sounds?'

'I grew up beside a train station. When friends stayed over they'd be kept awake all night by the noise and the vibrations. I was so used to it I couldn't hear a thing, yet the creaking on the stairs when my parents went to bed woke me every time. Are you married?'

I rolled my eyes.

'I'll take that as a no. Do you have a boyfriend?'

'Sometimes.'

'Have you got children?'

'I'm not interested in children.' I sniffed the air. 'What is that smell? And who is laughing? Is there somebody nearby?'

My head whizzed round like a dog trying to snap at a fly. I couldn't discern where the sounds were coming from. They had seemed to be coming from behind me but when I'd turned round the noise appeared to be louder in the other direction.

'It's everywhere,' Helena explained lazily. 'What the new people here compare to a surround-sound system. You probably understand that more than I.'

'Who's making that noise and is someone smoking a cigar?' I sniffed the air.

'You ask a lot of questions.'

'And you didn't when you first arrived here? Helena, I don't know where I am and what's going on, and you're not being much help.'

Helena at least had the decency to look embarrassed. 'I'm sorry. I'd forgotten what it's like.' She stopped and listened to the sounds. 'The laughter and these smells are just entering our atmosphere now. So far, what do you know about people who come here?'

'That they're missing.'

'Exactly. So the laughter, cries and scents that arrive are missing too.'

'How can that be?' I asked, utterly confused.

'Sometimes people lose more than just socks, Sandy. You can forget where you put them first of all. Forgetting things is just parts of your memory missing, that's all.'

'You can remember again, though.'

'Yes, but you don't remember *all* things and you don't find *all* things. Those things end up here, like the touch and smell of someone, the memory of their exact face and the sound of their voice.'

'That's bizarre.' I shook my head, unable to take it all in.

'It's really very simple if you remember it like this. Everything in life has a place and when one thing moves, it must go somewhere else. Here is the place that all those things move to.' She held her hands up to display our surroundings.

A thought suddenly occurred to me. 'Have you ever heard your own laughter or cries?'

Helena nodded sadly. 'Many times.'

'*Many* times?' I asked in surprise.

She smiled. 'Well, I had the great privilege of being loved by many people. The more people who love you, the more people you have out there to lose memories. Don't make that face, Sandy. It's not as desperate as it sounds. People don't intend to lose memories. Although there are always some things that we would rather forget.' She winked. 'It could be that the real sound of my laughter has been replaced by a new memory, or that, when a few months after I went missing my scent left my bedroom and my clothes, the scent they tried so hard to remember was altered. I'm sure the image I have of my own mother's face is very different from how she actually looked but, forty years on and no reminder, how is my mind to know, exactly? You can't hold on to all things for ever, no matter how hard you grip them.'

I thought of the day I'd hear the sound of my own laughter drifting overhead, and I knew it would only happen once because there was only one person who knew the true sound of my laughter and cries.

'All the same,' Helena looked up to the now bright sky with tears in her eyes, 'you do sometimes feel like catching them and throwing them back to where they came from. Our memories are the only contact we have. We can hug, kiss, laugh and cry with them over and over again in our minds. They're very precious things to have.'

Chuckles, hisses, snorts and giggles filtered through the air, floating by our ears on the wind, the light breeze carrying the faint scents like the forgotten smell of a childhood home; a kitchen after a day's baking. There's a mother's forgotten smell of her baby, now grown up: baby powder, Sudocrem, candy-smelling skin. There are older, musty smells of favourite grandparents: lavender for Grandma, cigar, cigarette and pipe smoke for Granddad. There are the smells of lost lovers: sweet perfumes and aftershaves, the scent of sleepy morning lie-ins or simply the unexplainable individual scent left behind in a room. Personal smells as precious as the people themselves. All the aromas that had gone missing in people's lives had ended up here. I couldn't help but close my eyes and breathe in those scents and laugh along with the sounds.

Joan stirred in her sleeping bag and I snapped out of my trance. My heart began to race in anticipation of finally seeing beyond the woods.

'Good morning, Joan,' Helena sang so loudly she succeeded in waking Bernard too. He awoke with a start, raising his head and revealing his spaghetti strips hanging to the wrong side. He looked around sleepily, his hand feeling for his glasses.

'Good morning, Bernard,' Helena said so loudly she succeeded in waking both Marcus and Derek.

I stifled a laugh.

'Here you go, a nice hot drop of coffee to wake you up.' She thrust steaming mugs in their faces.

They looked at her sleepily in confusion. As soon as they'd taken their first sip of coffee Helena threw off her blanket and rose to her feet.

'Well, that's enough hanging around now. Let's go, everybody.' She started folding her blanket neatly and packing away the utensils.

'Why are you talking so loudly and what's the rush?' Joan held her messy bed head and whispered as though she was suffering a hangover.

'It's a brand-new day so let's drink up and we'll head back as soon as you're all done.'

'Why?' Joan asked, sipping quickly.

'What about breakfast?' Bernard moaned like a child.

'We'll have that when we get back.' Helena grabbed his mug from him, threw the remainder of the coffee over her shoulder and packed the mug in a bag. I had to look away out of fear of laughing.

'What's the rush?' Marcus asked. 'Is everything OK?' He watched her intensely, still unsure of my presence.

'Everything's fine, Marcus.' She placed a hand on his shoulder caringly. 'Sandy just has some work to do.' She smiled at me.

I did?

'Oh, how lovely. Are you staging a play? It's been such a long time since we've done a play,' Joan said excitedly.

'I do hope you give us notice of the auditions well in advance because we'll need time to prepare. It's been a while,' Bernard said worriedly.

'Don't worry,' Helena jumped in, 'she will.'

My mouth dropped open but Helena held a hand up to stop me from protesting.

'Have you ever thought of doing a musical?' Derek asked, packing away his guitar. 'There would be huge interest in taking part in a musical.'

'That's a very strong possibility.' Helena spoke as though dismissing a child.

'Will they be group auditions?' Bernard asked, a little panicked.

'No, no,' Helena smiled, and I finally knew what she was up to. 'I think Sandy will want to spend a little time with everyone alone. Well,' she lifted Bernard's blanket from off his shoulders and began folding it while he watched open-mouthed, 'let's get ourselves ready so we can show Sandy around. She'll need to find a good venue for the show.'

How quickly Bernard and Joan got ready.

'By the way, I meant to ask you,' Helena whispered, 'were you working when you arrived here?'

'What do you mean exactly?'

'Were you on a job or following the trail of somebody

at the time you arrived here? It's such an important question but I forgot to ask it.'

'Yes and no,' I replied. 'I was jogging by the Shannon Estuary when I found myself here but my reason for being in Limerick was work-related. I had just taken on a new case five days beforehand.' I thought back to the phone call that I'd received from Jack Ruttle late one night.

'The reason I ask is because I wonder what it was about *that* person out of all the missing people you've searched for, that brought you here. Had you a strong link to him?'

I shook my head but knew I wasn't quite telling the truth. The late-night phone calls with Jack Ruttle had been very different from all my other cases. They were phone calls I enjoyed receiving, he was someone I could talk with about other things besides business. The more I spoke to the likeable Jack, the harder I worked trying to find his brother. There was only one other person in my life who could allow me to feel similarly.

'What was the missing person's name?'

'Donal Ruttle,' I said, remembering the playful blue eyes from the photograph.

Helena thought about it. 'Well, we might as well start now. Anyone here know a Donal Ruttle?' She looked around.

17

Jack paced alongside the red Ford Fiesta, feeling a mixture of impatience, frustration and anxiety. Occasionally he would stop, stare in the passenger window and will the door to open so he could grab the file and hungrily scoff the information on the pages. Then he'd calm down and pace again. He looked around, not wanting to venture far from the car in case Sandy Shortt returned and drove off without him.

He couldn't believe Sandy Shortt was the woman from the petrol station. They had passed by each other as though they were strangers but just as when he'd been speaking over the phone, he had felt something when he saw her, a bond that linked them. At the time he had thought it was because they were the only two in the place so early in the morning, but now he knew that connection was more. And now, here again, he had come across her in a hidden place. Something was drawing him to her. What he'd give to go back to that moment so he could talk to her about Donal. So she had come to Glin after all. He knew she wouldn't have let him down, and she had driven through the night just as she'd promised. Finding her car in this desolate spot only raised more questions than he already had. If she was in Glin, where had she been on Sunday when they were due to meet?

He looked at his watch. Three hours had passed since he'd come across the car and there was still no sign of her. A more important question reared its ugly head: where was she now?

He sat down on the dilapidated kerb by the car and did what he had become accustomed to doing over the past year. He waited. And he wasn't going to budge an inch until Sandy Shortt came back to her car.

I followed the group through the trees, my heart beating so loudly I could barely hear Bernard, who was chatting to me constantly about his previous years' acting experience. I nodded now and then when I felt his eyes on me. Disappointingly, there had been no reaction to Donal's name when asked; just shrugged shoulders and mumbles of 'I don't know'. But a reaction had stirred within me as soon as Helena mentioned his name to the others because hearing it made it all become real to me. I would be seeing people I had been searching for, for years.

I felt as though all my life's work led up to this moment. Nights of no sleep, distancing myself from possible friends and caring parents had left me living a solitary life I had been content with, but it was a life haunted by friendships and relationships with people I'd never met. I knew everything about them: their favourite colours, their best friends' names, their favourite bands, and I felt that with every step I took I was closer to meeting my long-lost friends, my missing parents, uncles, aunts and family. Recognising these emotions alerted me to the island I had become. None of those missing people I thought of so fondly would even know me. When their eyes fell upon me they would see a stranger, yet my eyes would see anything but. Though we had never met, family photos of past Christmases, birthdays and weddings, first days of school, debutante balls were firmly imprinted in my memory. I had sat with crying parents and been shown photo album after photo album, yet I couldn't remember a day when I had shared a couch with my own family and done the same. The people I lived for didn't even know of my existence and I hadn't acknowledged that of the people who lived for me.

I could see up ahead where the trees ended. The stillness of the woods was dissipating and instead there was lots of movement, noise and colour. So many people. I stopped walking with the group and shakily held out my hand to hold on to the trunk of a pine.

'Sandy, are you OK?' Bernard asked, stopping beside me.

The group stopped walking and turned to look at me. I couldn't even smile. I couldn't pretend everything was OK. The master of lying was caught in a web of lies I'd weaved myself. Helena pushed her way from the front of the group and rushed over to me.

'Go ahead, all of you. We'll meet you later on,' she dismissed them, and when they didn't move: 'Go on!' Slowly they turned round and reluctantly left the shade for the light.

'Sandy.' Helena softly placed her hand on my shoulder. 'You're trembling.' She put her arm round my shoulders and held me to her. 'It's OK, you've nothing to fear here. It's perfectly safe.'

It wasn't the safety of the place my body shook for. It was the fact that I had never felt as if I belonged anywhere. I had spent my life detaching myself from anyone who wanted to be close, dissociating myself from friends and lovers because they never answered my questions or tolerated or understood my searches. They made me feel like I was wrong and, without them knowing it, maybe even a little crazy, but I had a passion to just *find*. Finding this place was just one big answer to a life-long question that had caused me to sacrifice everything. I'd hurt so many people that loved me in order to help those that I couldn't see and now as I was just about to see them I was afraid to let them in too. I used to think that I was a saint, just like Jenny-May Butler on the nine o'clock news; I thought I was Mother Teresa with a missing persons file, making sacrifices to help others. In reality I'd sacrificed nothing. My behaviour suited me and only me.

The people in this place were the people I had clung to. When I grabbed my bag by the door of my family home in Leitrim it was for these people. When I ended relationships and turned down invitations to nights out it was for these people.

But now that I'd found them, I had no idea what to do.

18

Helena and I stepped out of the darkness of the shaded woods and entered a world of colour. I held my breath at the sight before me. It was as though grand red curtains had parted to welcome a production on such a grand scale I could barely focus on one thing for long enough. What welcomed my eyes was an entire bustling village of nations gathering. Some people were walking alone, others gathering in twos, threes, groups and in crowds. Sights of traditional costumes, sounds of combined languages, scents of cuisine from all over the world. It was rich and alive, bursting at the seams with colour and sound as though we'd followed the path of a pulse to reach the heart of the woods. And there it pumped, people flowing here, there and everywhere.

Sophisticated wooden buildings lined the street, with doors and windows decorated with ornate carvings. Each building was constructed from a different timber, the varying shades and grains camouflaging the village so that it and the woods were combined and almost one. Solar panels lined the roofs – hundreds of roofs into the distance. All around were wind turbines, up to one hundred feet tall, with blades going round and round in the blue skies, their dark shadows circling on rooftops and roadways. The village was nestled among the trees, among mountains, among wind machines. Before me, hundreds of people, dressed in traditional costumes from all eras, *lived* in a lost place that looked real and smelled real, and when I held out my hand

and felt the fabric of someone rush by, it felt real. I fought with myself to believe it.

It was a scene I was familiar yet unfamiliar with all at the same time because everything I could see was composed of recognisable elements from home, but used in such very different ways. We hadn't stepped back or forward, we had entered a whole new time. A great big melting pot of nations, cultures, design and sound mixed to create a new world. Children played, market stalls decorated the road and customers swarmed around them. So much colour, so many new sounds, unlike any country I'd been in. A sign beside us said 'Here'.

Helena linked my arm, a gesture I would have shrugged off had I not physically needed her to prop me up. I was stunned. I was Ali Baba who'd stumbled across the cave of treasures, Galileo after his discoveries through the telescope. More importantly, I was a girl of ten years old who had found all her socks.

'Every day is market day,' Helena explained softly. 'Some people like to trade whatever bits they've found for other things of value. Sometimes they're of no value at all but it's become a bit of a sport now. Money has no value – all we need is found readily on the streets – so there is no need to work for pay to provide for ourselves. There is, however, a requirement to work to help the village, age, health and other personal reasons permitting. Our occupations are more of a community service rather than for self-gain.'

I looked around in awe. Helena continued talking softly in my ear, holding my arm as my body shook.

'The turbines are something you will see throughout the land. We have many wind plants, most of them among the mountain gaps that produce wind funnelling. One wind machine can produce enough electricity for up to four hundred homes a year, and the solar panels on the buildings also help generate energy.'

I listened to her but barely heard a word. My ears were tuned into the conversations around me, to the sounds of the monstrous wind turbine blades breaking through the air. My nose was adjusting to the crisp freshness that seemed to fill my lungs with cool air in one small breath. My attention turned to the market stall closest to us.

'It's a mobile phone,' a British gentleman explained to an elderly stall owner.

'What use have I for a mobile phone?' the Caribbean stall owner dismissed him, laughing. 'I've heard those things don't even work here.'

'They don't, but—'

'But nothing. I have been here forty-five years, three months and ten days.' He held his head high. 'And I don't see how this music box is a fair trade for a phone that doesn't work.'

The customer stopped fuming and appeared to view him with more respect. 'Well, I've been here only four years,' he explained politely, 'so let me show you what phones can do now.' He held the phone up in the air, pointed it at the stall owner and it made a clicking sound. He showed the screen to the salesman.

'Ah!' He started laughing. 'It's a camera! Why didn't you say?'

'Well, it's a camera *phone* but, even better, look at this. The person who owned it took a whole pile of photos of themselves and whatever country they live in.' He scrolled down the phone.

The stall owner handled it gently.

'Somebody here might know these people,' the customer said softly.

'Ah, yes, mon,' the salesman replied gently, nodding. 'This is very precious indeed.'

'Come on, let's go,' Helena whispered, leading me by the arm.

I began to move as though on autopilot, looking around open-mouthed at all the people. We passed the customer and stall owner; they both nodded and smiled. 'Welcome.'

I just stared back.

Two children playing hopscotch stopped their game

on hearing the men's salutation. 'Welcome.' They both gave me toothless grins.

Helena led me through the crowd, through the choruses of welcomes, the nods and smiles of well-wishers. Helena acknowledged them all politely for me. We walked across the street towards the large wooden two-storey building with a decked porch across the front. An intricate carving of a scroll and theatrical feathered pen decorated the door. Helena pushed the door open and the scroll and feather halved as though bowing and holding out their arms to make way for us.

'This is the registry. Everyone comes here when they first arrive,' Helena explained patiently. 'Everybody's name and details are logged in these books so that we can keep track of who is who and how many people are here.'

'In case anybody goes missing,' I said smartly.

'I think you'll find that nothing goes missing here, Sandy.' Helena was serious. 'Things have no place else to go and so they stay here.'

I ignored the chill of her implication and instead tried unsuccessfully to inject humour into the situation. 'What will I do with myself if I've nothing to look for?'

'You'll do what you've always wanted; you'll seek out those you searched for. Finish the job you started.'

'Then what?'

She was silent.

'Then you'll help me get home, right?' I asked rather forcefully.

She didn't respond.

'Helena,' a cheery fellow called out from where he was sitting behind a desk. On the desk a series of numbers was displayed. Beside the main door there was a board with all the countries of the world, their associated languages, some I'd never even heard of, and their corresponding numbers. I matched one of the numbers on his desk to a familiar one on the board. 'Country: Ireland. Languages: Gaelic, English.'

'Hello, Terence.' Helena seemed glad of the interruption to our conversation.

It was then I looked around the room for the first time. There were dozens of desks in the large room. Each desk had a series of numbers and behind each desk sat a person of a different nationality. Queues had formed before the tables. The room was quiet and filled with the tension of hundreds of people who had just arrived, who couldn't yet comprehend their situation. They each looked around the room nervously with wide terrified eyes as they hugged their own bodies for comfort.

I noticed Helena had joined Terence at his desk.

He looked up as I approached them. 'Welcome,' he smiled softly. I sensed sympathy in his voice and his accent revealed his Irish roots.

'Sandy, this is Terence O'Malley. Terence, this is Sandy. Terence has been here for . . . oh gosh, how many years has it been now, Terence?' Helena asked him.

Eleven years, I thought.

'Almost eleven years now,' he replied with a smile.

'Terence worked as a—'

'Librarian in Ballina,' I cut in before even thinking about it. Ten years on, he was still recognisable as the single, fifty-five-year-old librarian who had disappeared on his way home from work eleven years ago.

Helena froze and Terence looked confused.

'Oh, yes, I told you that before we came in,' Helena jumped in. 'Silly me. I must be getting old, repeating myself like that,' she laughed.

'I know the feeling,' Terence laughed, pushing his sliding spectacles back up his nose.

I'd always thought his nose was exactly like his sister's. I studied it some more.

'Well,' Terence began to fidget under my glare and he turned to Helena for backup, 'let's get down to business now, shall we? If you wouldn't mind taking a seat, Sandy, I'll help you go through this form. It's very simple really.'

As I took a seat before the desk I looked at the queues around me. To my right a woman was helping a young boy onto the chair before her desk.

'Permettimi di aiutarti a sederti e mi puoi raccontare tutto su come sei arrivato fin qui. Avresti voglia di un po' di latte con biscotti?'

He looked at her with big brown eyes, as lost as a puppy, and nodded. She nodded to someone behind her, who disappeared through a door behind the desk and returned moments later with a glass of milk and a plate of cookies.

To my right, a bewildered-looking gentleman stepped up to the top of the queue. The man at the desk, name tag revealing 'Martin', smiled at him encouragingly. *'Nehmen Sie doch Platz, bitte, dann helfe ich Ihnen mit den Formularen.'*

'Sandy.' Terence and Helena were calling me, trying to get my attention.

'Yes, what, sorry,' I snapped out of my trance.

'Terence was asking you where you are from.'

'Leitrim.'

'Is that where you lived?'

'No. Dublin.' I looked around as more people were led into the room, looking dazed.

'And you went missing in Dublin,' Terence confirmed.

'No. Limerick.' My voice was quiet as all the thoughts in my head got louder and louder.

'You know Jim Gannon . . . Leitrim town . . . ?'

'Yes,' I replied, watching a young African woman draping her ochre-coloured blanket tighter around her body as she looked about her strange surroundings in fear. Armbands of copper, weaved grasses and beads decorated her skin. We locked eyes for a moment before she quickly looked away and I continued speaking to Terence as though I wasn't really there. 'Jim owns the hardware store. His son taught me geography.'

Terence laughed happily about it being a small world.

'A lot bigger than I thought,' I replied, my voice

sounding like it was coming from somewhere else.

Terence's voice came and went in my head as I looked around at all the faces, all the people who had one moment ago been on their way to work, or walking to the shop and who had suddenly found themselves here.

'. . . for a living?'

'She's involved in theatre, Terence. She runs an acting agency.'

Some more mumbling as I tuned out.

'. . . is that right, Sandy? You run an agency of your own?'

'Yes,' I said absentmindedly, watching as the little boy beside me was led by the hand through a door behind the Italian registry desk.

He watched me with big worried eyes all the way. I smiled at him and his frown softened. The door was closed behind him.

'Where does that door lead?' I asked suddenly in the middle of one of Terence's questions.

He stopped. 'Which door?'

I looked around the room and noticed for the first time there was a door behind each desk.

'All of them. Where do they all lead to?' I asked faintly.

'That's where people are briefed on what we know, where we are and what happens here. There's counselling services and employment opportunities, and we arrange for somebody from here to come to greet them so that they can guide them around for however long they're needed.'

I looked at the large solid oak doors and didn't say anything.

'As you have already met Helena, she will be your guide,' Terence said gently. 'Now we'll just get through the last of these questions and then you can get out of here, which I'm sure you're looking forward to do.'

The main door opened and sunlight filled the room again. Everyone looked up to see a young girl, no older than ten years old, with soft bouncing blonde curls and big blue eyes, walk into the room. She sniffled and wiped her eyes, following the guide who led her into the room.

'Jenny-May,' I whispered, my head becoming dizzy again.

'And your brother's name?' Terence asked, working his way down the form.

'No, hold on a minute. She doesn't have a sister,' Helena interrupted. 'She told me earlier she was an only child.'

'No, no,' Terence sounded slightly agitated, 'I asked her if she had any sisters and she said Jenny-May.'

'She mustn't have heard you correctly, Terence,' Helena said calmly, and the rest of their sentences turned to murmuring in my ears.

My eyes continued to follow the little girl as she was led through the room; my heart beat faster just as it always had when Jenny-May Butler was within a few feet of me.

'Maybe you could clear this up.' Terence looked at me. His face appeared and faded from my vision.

'Maybe she's not well, Terence. In fact, she looks very pale.' Helena's voice was close to my ear now. 'Sandy, would you like to—'

That's when I passed out.

19

'Sandy . . .'

I could hear my name being called and felt a warm breath on my face. The smell was familiar: sweet coffee, which sent my heart into its usual flutter, fanning my body and causing excited chills to chase one another just below the surface of my skin.

Gregory's hand softly brushed back strands of hair from my face as though gently brushing away sand on an excavation site to reveal something far more precious than me. But that's what he was, my excavator, the one who unearthed all that was buried beneath to discover my hidden thoughts. One hand was placed at the back of my neck as though I was the most fragile thing he'd ever held; the other softly traced the line of my jaw, occasionally running up my cheeks and through my hair.

'Sandy honey, open your eyes,' the voice whispered close to my ear.

'Move back, everybody!' a louder and more aggressive voice shouted nearby. 'Is she OK?' His voice got louder, closer.

The comforting hand moved from my hair to my hand and grasped it tightly, his thumb soothingly stroking my skin as he spoke quietly. 'She's not responding. Call an ambulance.' His voice was distorted and it echoed in my head. My head hurt.

'Oh, Mother of Jesus,' the voice muttered.

'Sean, get the kids back into the school. Don't let them watch this,' my saviour said calmly.

Sean, Sean, Sean. I knew that name. Knew that voice.

'Where's that blood coming from?' he panicked.

'Her head. Get the kids away.' My hand was held tighter.

'He hit her hard, the bastard.'

'I know, I saw. I was watching her from the window. Call the ambulance.'

Sean's shouts to the kids to go inside moved further away and I was left in the echoing silence with the angel. I felt soft lips on my hand.

'Open your eyes, Sandy,' he whispered. 'Please.'

I tried to but they felt like they were glued together, like a lotus nestled in the mud, forced to open its petals ahead of time. My head was heavy, my thoughts clumsy and slow as it throbbed and pulsated repeatedly with abnormally strong force in the protective hand that cradled it. The ground felt cold and rough beneath me. Concrete. Why was I on the ground? I struggled to get up but my body resisted the action, and still my eyes wouldn't open.

I heard the ambulance in the distance and I fought to open my eyes. They opened just a slit. Ah. Mr Burton. My saviour. He held me in his arms, looking down at me as though he'd just discovered gold in the Leitrim tarmacadam. He had blood on his shirt – was he hurt? His eyes looked hurt as they searched my face. I suddenly remembered the great big spot on my chin that I wished all day I'd popped that morning. I tried to move my hand to cover it but it felt like my hand had been dipped in concrete and left to dry.

'Oh, thank God,' he whispered, his hand holding mine tighter. 'Don't move yet. The ambulance is almost here.'

I had to cover my spot. I was finally this close to Mr Burton after four years and I looked a mess. My seventeen-year-old's hormones were ruining the moment I'd been dreaming of. Hold on, he'd said, ambulance. What had happened? I tried to speak and a croak passed my lips.

'It's going to be OK,' he hushed, his face close to mine.

I believed him and forgot my pain for a moment while I once again self-consciously felt for my spot.

'I know what you're trying to do, Sandy, so stop it.' Gregory attempted to laugh lightly while carefully removing my arm from my face.

I groaned, words still not coming to me.

'He's not so awful, you know. His name is Henry, he's been keeping me company while you've been so rudely passed out. Henry, meet Sandy; Sandy, meet Henry, although I don't think you're a very welcome guest here.' He ran his finger across my chin, lightly brushing the spot as though it were the most beautiful thing about me.

So there I was with blood running from my head, a spot named Henry on my chin and a face so aflame it could have powered the entire town. I began to close my eyes again. The sky seemed so bright it pierced my pupils and sent spears of pain through my sockets and into my already throbbing head.

'Don't close your eyes, Sandy,' Gregory said more loudly.

I opened them and caught the worry in his face before he had a chance to hide it.

'I'm tired,' I finally whispered.

'I know you are.' He held me tighter. 'But stay awake with me for a while. Keep me company until the ambulance gets here,' he pleaded. 'Promise me.'

'Promise,' I whispered, before shutting them again.

A second siren arrived on the scene. A car pulled up nearby. I could feel the vibrations on the concrete near my head and I feared the tyres would run over me. Doors opened and slammed.

'He's over there, Garda.' Sean was back, shouting. 'He drove straight into her, wasn't even looking,' he panicked. 'This man here saw it.'

Sean was quietened down, I heard a man crying. Heard garda voices trying to comfort, radios crackling and beeping, Sean being led away. Footsteps came closer to me, there was a mumbling above my head of concerned voices. All the time Gregory whispered in my ear words that sounded pretty, the vowels easy in my ringing ears. The sounds shut out the sirens, the cries of fear, the shouts of panic and anger, the feel of the cold concrete and the sticky wet trickling down my ear.

As the ambulance sirens got louder, Gregory's tones became more urgent as I began to drift away in his arms.

'Welcome back.'

I awoke to see a worried Helena wafting a fan in my face.

I groaned and my hand flew to my head.

'You've got a nasty bump so I'd advise you not to touch it,' she said gently.

My arm kept moving.

'I said don—'

'Ouch.'

'Serves you right,' she said haughtily, and walked away.

I squinted around the unfamiliar room, feeling the egg-sized bump that had formed above my temple. I was on a couch; Helena was at a sink facing a window. The light was bright and illuminated her, blurring her around the edges as though she were a holy vision.

'Where are we?'

'My home.' She didn't turn around, continued rinsing a cloth.

I looked around. 'Why do you have a couch in the kitchen?'

Helena laughed lightly. 'Of all the questions you could have asked, that is the first one you chose.'

I was silent.

'It's not a kitchen, it's a family room,' was her reply. 'I don't cook here.'

'I don't suppose you have electricity.'

She grunted. 'Once you get a chance to look around

outside you'll see we have a system of what we call *solar panels*.' She dragged out the words as though I was slow. 'They're similar to the ones found on pocket calculators and they generate electricity from the sun. Each house has its own power voltage system,' she said excitedly.

I lay back on the couch, feeling dizzy, and closed my eyes. 'I'm aware of how solar panels work.'

'They exist there too?' She was surprised.

I ignored her question. 'How did I get here?'

'My husband carried you.'

My eyes flew open and I winced with the pain. Helena still didn't turn around and the water still flowed.

'Your husband? You can get married here?'

'You can get married anywhere.'

'Not technically true,' I protested meekly. 'My God, electricity *and* marriage? This is too much for me,' I mumbled, the ceiling beginning to swirl above me.

Helena sat beside me on the couch and held a cold face cloth over my forehead and eyes. It was soothing on my throbbing, burning head.

'I had the most awful dream that I was in a bizarre place where all the missing things and people in the world go,' I grumbled. 'Please tell me that was a dream or at least a nervous breakdown. I can handle a nervous breakdown.'

'Well, if you can handle *that* then you can handle the truth.'

'What is the truth?' I opened my eyes.

She was silent as she stared at me, then sighed. 'You know the truth.'

I closed my eyes and fought the urge to cry.

Helena grabbed my arm, squeezed it and leaned in with urgency in her voice. 'Hang in there, Sandy. It will make sense to you after a while.'

I didn't think that possible.

'If it makes you feel better, I haven't told anybody else what you've told me. *No one*.'

It did make me feel better. I could figure out whatever it was I had to do in my own time.

'Who is Jenny-May?' Helena asked curiously.

I closed my eyes and groaned, remembering the scene at the registry. 'Nobody. Well, not nobody, she's somebody. I thought I saw her in the registry, that's all.'

'It wasn't her?'

'Not unless she stopped ageing the day she arrived here. I don't know what I was thinking.' Frowning, I reached to my pounding head again.

There was a light tap on the door and it was gently opened by a man so tall and broad he filled the doorframe. White light impatiently squeezed itself through the small spaces he didn't fill, shooting into my eyes like spears of fire direct from the sun. He was of similar age to Helena, with shining ebony skin and intense black eyes. He stood well over my own six foot one height and for that reason alone I immediately liked him. His figure dominated the room yet brought with it a feeling of safety. A small smile revealed snow-white teeth, while eyeballs like purified sugar melted around pupils of black coffee. He was hard, but softened around the edges. His cheekbones sat high and proud on his face, his jaw square yet, above it, cushioned lips for his words to bounce from and launch themselves into the world.

'How is our kipepeo girl doing?' The rhythmic sound of his words revealed his African roots.

In confusion I looked to Helena, who was looking at the man in surprise, the surprise I could tell, not for his sudden presence but for the words he had spoken. She knew this man and I assumed knew his words. I didn't know what the words meant but I guessed the speaker of them to be her husband. We locked eyes and I felt drawn to his gaze, trapped in his and he trapped in mine as though a magnet drew us together. He held a plank of wood in his large hands; sawdust covered his white linen clothes.

'What does "kipepeo" mean?' I asked the room. The room didn't answer, but knew.

'Sandy, this is my husband, Joseph,' Helena introduced us. 'He's a carpenter,' she added, referring to the plank of wood in his hand.

My unusual introduction to Joseph the carpenter was interrupted by a little girl who entered the kitchen through Joseph's legs, giggling while her curly black hair bounced with each childish skip. She ran to Helena and grabbed her leg.

'And who's this, the immaculate conception?' I asked, the little girl's shrieks sounding like wails in my pounding head.

'Almost,' Helena smiled. 'She's our daughter's immaculate conception. Say hello, Wanda.' She ran her hand through the little girl's hair.

A toothless smile greeted me before she shyly ran out of the room under her grandfather's legs. I looked up from where she had disappeared to Joseph's eyes again. He was still watching me. Helena looked from him and back to me, not with suspicion but with . . . I couldn't quite figure it out.

'You must sleep.' He gave a single nod.

Under the gaze of Helena and Joseph, I placed the face cloth over my eyes and allowed myself to drift. For once I was too tired to ask questions.

'Ah, there she is now.' My father's voice greeted me as though I was suddenly pulled up out of the water. Muffled sounds gradually became audible, faces eventually recognisable. It was as though I was reborn into the world, facing my loved ones from a hospital bed once again.

'Hello, honey.' My mother rushed to my side and took my hand. Her face appeared close to mine, too close for me to focus and so she remained a lavender-scented blur with four eyes. 'How do you feel?'

I hadn't yet had time to feel before I was asked and so concentrated on it before answering. I didn't feel very good.

'OK,' I responded.

'Oh, my poor baby.' Her cleavage dominated my view as she leaned over to kiss my forehead, glossy lips leaving my skin sticky and ticklish. I looked around the room after she'd moved and saw my father, scrunched cap in hand and looking older than I remembered. Perhaps I had been underwater longer than I'd thought. I winked, he smiled, relief written all over his face. Funny how it was the job of the patient to make the visitors feel better. It was as though I was on stage and it was my turn to entertain. The walls of the hospital had rendered everyone speechless and awkward as though we had met that day for the very first time.

'What happened?' I asked after sipping water through a straw from a cup that had been thrust at me by a nurse.

They looked nervously at one another. Mum decided to do the honours.

'A car hit you, honey, just as you were walking across the road from the school. He came around the corner . . . he was just a young lad, only on his provisional licence. His mother didn't know he'd taken the car, bless her heart. Luckily Mr Burton saw it all happen and could give the Gardaí a full witness report. He's a good man, is Mr Burton,' she smiled. 'Gregory,' she added to me a bit more quietly.

I smiled too.

'He stayed with you all the way into the hospital.'

'My head,' I whispered, the pain suddenly entering my body as though hearing the story had reminded it it needed to do its job.

'Your left arm is broken.' Mum's glossy lips glistened in the light as they opened and closed. 'And your left leg,' her voice shook lightly, 'but apart from that you're very lucky.'

It was only then I noticed my arm in a sling and my left leg in a cast, and found it amusing that they thought I was lucky even after being hit by a car. I started to laugh but the pain stopped me.

'Oh, yes, and you've a cracked rib,' my father added

quickly, looking apologetic for the lack of warning.

When they had left, Gregory rapped lightly on the door. He looked more gorgeous than ever with his tired concerned eyes and messy hair that I could imagine he ruffled as he paced with worry. He always did that.

'Hi,' he smiled, walking in, and kissed me on the forehead.

'Hi,' I whispered back.

'How are you feeling?'

'Like I've been hit by a bus.'

'Nah, it was only a Mini. Stop looking for attention.' A smile tickled the sides of his lips. 'You've heard the bad news, I assume?'

'That I have to do my Leaving Cert exams orally?' I lifted up the cast covering my left arm. 'I think the Guards will still accept me,' I smiled.

'No,' he said seriously, and took a seat on the bed. 'We lost Henry in the ambulance. I think it's the oxygen mask that took him out.'

I started laughing but had to stop.

'Oh shit, sorry.' He immediately stopped joking around at seeing me in pain.

'Thanks for staying with me.'

'Thanks for staying with me,' he replied.

'Well, I did promise,' I smiled, 'and I'm not planning on disappearing anywhere anytime soon.'

20

Jack sat on the gravel surface beside what he assumed to be the now abandoned car. His overactive mind contemplated every possible scenario as to where Sandy Shortt was, why her car was in the middle of the trees in an old car park, why she hadn't turned up to their meeting the previous day and why she hadn't returned to her car for the entire day. Nothing made sense to him any more. He hadn't moved from the car's vicinity all day. A quick search of the surroundings showed no sign of her – or of any other life, for that matter. It was late now. The forest area was black, the only lights being those from distant ships out at sea and Glin Castle in the distance behind the tall pines. Jack could barely see past the end of his nose. The blackness of the night was thick and engulfing, yet he was afraid to leave in case he missed her, in case somebody towed the car away, which in turn would take away Donal and all possible traces of him.

The file sat on the dashboard. The mobile phone beside it was the only immediate source of light, flashing every few seconds to signal a dying battery. If Sandy wasn't going to arrive at her car anytime soon, Jack needed to get his hands on that phone to see her recent call list and, with luck, trace somebody from her phone book who would help find her. If her battery went dead it was possible he wouldn't be able to switch it back on without a pin code.

His own mobile phone rang again: Gloria looking

for him, no doubt. It was eleven o'clock and he couldn't bring himself to answer; he didn't know what he could possibly say to her. He didn't want to lie, so lately he had avoided conversation with her altogether, leaving the house before she woke, arriving home after she had fallen asleep. He knew his behaviour would most definitely be upsetting her – sweet, patient Gloria, who never nagged as friends of his claimed their partners did. She always gave him the space he needed and felt secure enough in herself to know that he wouldn't betray her. But he was – he was betraying her patience now and perhaps even driving her away. Maybe that's what he wanted. Maybe it wasn't. All he knew was that Donal's disappearance had brought an end to talks of family and marriage that had previously seemed so important to him, to them both. Right now he was putting their relationship aside and focusing on finding his missing brother. Somehow he felt that by finding Sandy, he would be one step closer to finding Donal, or perhaps that was just another excuse, another obsession to delay moving on with life, to delay confronting Gloria over a relationship he no longer knew how he felt about.

He did the only thing he could think of. He picked up his phone and rang Graham Turner, the guard Jack and his family had been dealing with during the search for Donal.

'Hello?' Graham answered. The background was noisy with shouts, chatter and laughter. Pub noises.

'Graham, it's Jack,' Jack shouted in the silent wooded area.

'Hello?' Graham shouted again.

'It's Jack,' he raised his voice even higher, startling whatever animals had taken refuge in the nearby trees.

'Hold on, I'm going outside,' Graham shouted. The voices and noise grew louder as the phone was carried through the pub. Finally there was silence. 'Hello?' Graham said more quietly.

'Graham, it's Jack.' He kept his voice down now. 'Sorry to call you so late.'

'No problem. Is everything OK?' Graham asked with concern, used to Jack's late-night calls over the past year.

'Yeah, things are OK,' Jack lied.

'Any news on Donal?'

'No, no news. Actually I was calling you about something else.'

'Sure, what's up?'

How on earth was he going to explain this? 'I'm just a bit worried about someone. I was due to meet them yesterday morning in Glin but they didn't show up.'

Silence.

'I see.'

'A message on my answer phone was left before leaving Dublin to let me know they were on their way down but they never showed and the car is parked down by the estuary.'

Silence.

'Yeah.'

'I'm just starting to get worried, you know?'

'Yeah, yeah, I know. You're bound to under the circumstances.'

That one statement suddenly made Jack feel like a raving paranoid lunatic. Maybe he was.

'I know it sounds like nothing but I think it's something, you know?'

'Yeah, yeah, of course,' Graham said hurriedly. 'Sorry, hold on one minute.' The phone was covered as voices became muffled. 'Yeah, another pint. Cheers, Damian. I'll be in as soon as I finish my smoke,' he said, and then came back on the line. 'Sorry about that.'

'No problem. Look, I know it's late and you're out. I apologise for calling.' Jack held his head in his hands, feeling like a fool. His story had sounded stupid and his concern for Sandy unnecessary as soon as he had vocalised them, but he knew deep down that things weren't right.

'Don't worry about it. What do you want me to do? What's the guy's name and I'll ask around?'

'Sandy Shortt.'

'*Sandy* Shortt.' Yep, the guy was a woman.

'Yeah.'

'Right.'

'And you were to meet her . . . ?'

'In Glin yesterday. We passed one another at Lloyds station, you know the one on—'

'Yeah, I know it.'

'Yeah, well, we met there at about five thirty a.m. but she didn't show up later that morning.'

'She didn't say where she was going when you met her?'

'No, we hardly spoke.'

'What does she look like?'

'Very tall, curly black hair . . .' He trailed off, realising he had no idea what Sandy Shortt looked like, he had no reason to believe that the woman he had passed at the petrol station was even Sandy Shortt. The only proof he had was a file on the dashboard with Donal's name on it. The driver could have been anyone. He had allowed all the pieces to fit together nicely without even questioning its sense, which right now seemed like none at all.

'Jack?' Graham was calling him.

'Yeah.'

'She's tall with curly black hair. Know anything else? Her age or where she's from or anything?'

'No. I don't know, Graham. I'm not even sure what she looks like. We only ever spoke over the phone. I don't even know if that was her at the station.' He suddenly had a thought. 'She used to be a garda. In Dublin. She quit four years ago. That's all I know.' He gave up.

'OK, right, well, I'll make a few phone calls and get back to you.'

'Thanks.' Jack felt humiliated; his story was full of holes. 'You'll keep this between us, won't you?' he asked quietly.

'Will do. All well with Gloria?' The tone was accusing. Or maybe it wasn't – it was possible Jack was misjudging everything these days.

'Great, yeah.'

'Good. Send her my regards. You've got a saint there, Jack.'

'Yeah, I know,' he replied defensively.

Silence. Then pub atmosphere.

'I'll get back to you, Jack,' Graham shouted. The line went dead.

Jack thumped his head, feeling like an idiot.

At midnight, as he ran a finger up and down the side of the cold metal car as he paced, his phone rang. He had already texted Gloria to let her know he would be home late, and so he knew it wasn't her when he answered.

'Jack, it's Graham here.' His tone was gentler than before. 'Listen, I made a few calls, asked around the lads to see if any of them knew a Sandy Shortt.'

'Go on.' His heart thumped.

'You should have told me, Jack,' Graham said softly.

Jack nodded in the darkness, though Graham couldn't see him.

Graham continued, 'Seems you shouldn't worry about her. A good few of the lads knew her,' he laughed, and stopped himself. 'They said she disappears all the time without letting anyone know. She's a hermit, keeps to herself and comes and goes as she pleases but always comes back within a week or so. I wouldn't worry about her, Jack. This seems to be in keeping with her usual behaviour.'

'But what about her car?'

'A 1991 red Ford Fiesta?'

'Yeah.'

'That's hers all right. Don't worry about it; she's probably around the area checking out the place. The lads say she's a keen jogger, so she probably parked there and went for a run earlier or maybe the car wouldn't start or something simple as that. Anyway it's been a little over twenty-four hours since you were supposed to meet. There's no need to panic.'

'I thought the first twenty-four hours were supposed

to be the most important,' Jack said through gritted teeth.

'In missing cases they are, Jack, but this Sandy Shortt isn't missing. She likes to disappear all the time. The way it sounds, from speaking to her ex-colleagues, is that she'll contact you within a few days. Apparently that's the way she works. I was told that even her own family never know where she is. They called the guards on three occasions years ago but they don't bother any more. She comes back.'

Jack was silent.

'There's not much I can do. There's nothing to go on, nothing to suggest she's in any danger.'

'I know, I know.' Jack rubbed his eyes wearily.

'As a word of advice, be careful of those kinds of people. Agencies like Sandy Shortt's are just out to make money, you know? I wouldn't be surprised if she's done a runner. There's nothing that they can do that we haven't already done. There aren't any more places to search that we haven't already searched.'

Sandy hadn't asked for a cent, knowing that Jack hadn't got a cent to give.

'I had to do something,' was all he replied. He didn't like how Graham was referring to Sandy. He didn't believe she was crooked, he didn't believe she had gone wandering on an investigation without her phone, her file, her diary and her car, or was still jogging at midnight. Nothing Graham said made sense, yet nothing Jack said aloud seemed to make sense either. He was going entirely by instinct alone, instinct that had been affected by Donal's disappearance and a week of nightly phone calls to a woman he had never met.

'I understand,' Graham responded. 'I'd probably do the same myself if I was in your shoes.'

'What about my stuff that's locked in her car?' Jack bluffed.

'What stuff?'

'I sent her Donal's file and a few other things. I can see them sitting in the car. If she's going to take my money and run, I'd at least like my things back.'

'I can't help you out in that area, Jack, but I wouldn't be asking any questions if by morning your belongings are back in your possession.'

'Thanks, Graham.'

'Anything at all to help.'

A few hours later, as the sun was rising over the estuary, casting orange hues on black ripples, Jack found himself sitting in Sandy's car, leafing through Donal's file and through all the pages of garda reports that only Sandy had been able to retrieve through her contacts. Her diary revealed a plan to go to Limerick city that day to visit one of Donal's friends, Alan O'Connor, who had been out with Donal the night of his disappearance. Hope returned at the possibility of meeting her there. The cramped car smelled sickeningly sweet of the vanilla air freshener that hung from the dashboard mirror, mixed with the tinge of stale coffee from the Styrofoam cup balanced below it. There was nothing about the car that gave him any more clues as to the type of person Sandy was. There were no wrappers left behind, no CDs or cassettes revealing her taste in music. Just an old, cold car with work and cold coffee left behind.

It had no heart; she had taken that part with her.

21

I awoke I wasn't sure how many hours later, to a little girl with wild black frizzy hair perched next to me on the arm of the couch, watching me with the same intense black eyes as her grandfather.

I jumped.

She smiled. Dimples dented her yellow skin and her eyes softened to a dark brown.

'Hi,' she chirped.

I looked around the room that was now almost pitch-black save for the orange light creeping under the kitchen door, lighting the floor just enough for me to be able to make out my surroundings and the little girl half-lit before me. The sky outside the window over the sink was black. Stars, the same stars I never paid the slightest bit of notice to at home, hung above like Christmas lights decorating a toy village.

'Well, aren't you going to say hi?' the little voice chirped happily.

I sighed; I had never had time for children and had even despised being one myself.

'Hi,' I said with disinterest.

'See? That wasn't so hard, was it?'

'Excruciating.' I yawned and stretched.

She hopped off the arm of the sofa and bounced onto the end, joining me but crushing my feet in the process.

'Ouch,' I moaned, tucking my legs closer to my body.

'That can't have hurt.' She lowered her head and viewed me doubtingly.

'How old are you, one hundred and ninety?' I asked, pulling my blanket around me tighter as though it would protect me from her.

'If I was a hundred and ninety, I'd be dead.' She rolled her eyes.

'And what a shame that would be.'

'You don't like me, do you?'

I thought about that. 'Not really.'

'Why not?'

'Because you sat on my feet.'

'You didn't like me before I sat on your feet.'

'True.'

'Most people think I'm cute,' she sighed.

'Really?' I asked in mock surprise. 'I don't get that impression.'

'Why not?' She didn't seem to be insulted, just more interested.

'Because you're three feet tall and you have no front teeth.' I closed my eyes, wishing she'd go away, and rested my head against the back of the couch. The throbbing in my head had dissipated but the chirping at the end of the couch would no doubt bring it back in full force.

'I won't be like this for ever, you know,' she said, trying to please me.

'I hope so, for your sake.'

'Me too,' she sighed, and rested her head on the back of the couch, imitating me.

I stared at her in silence, hoping she'd take the hint and go away. She smiled at me.

'Most people's impression of me is that I don't want to talk to them,' I hinted.

'Really? I don't get that impression,' she imitated me, saying the words with difficulty in her toothless mouth.

I laughed. 'What age are you?'

She held up her hand, displaying four fingers and a thumb.

'Four fingers and a thumb?' I asked.

She frowned and looked at her hand again, her lips moving as she counted.

'Is there a special school kids go to, to learn to do that?' I asked. 'Can't you just say "five"?'

'I can say "five".'

'So what, you think holding up a hand is cuter?'

She shrugged.

'Where is everyone?'

'Asleep. Did you used to have a television? We have televisions here but they don't work.'

'Bummer for you.'

'Yeah, bummer,' she sighed dramatically, but I don't think she cared. 'My grandma says I ask a lot of questions but I think you ask more.'

'You like to ask questions?' I was suddenly interested. 'What kind of questions?'

She shrugged. 'Normal questions.'

'About what?'

'Everything.'

'You keep on asking them, Wanda, maybe you'll get out of here.'

'OK.'

Silence.

'Why would I want to get out of here?'

Not such normal questions after all, it appeared. 'Do you like it here?'

She looked around the room. 'I prefer my own room.'

'No, this *village* place,' I pointed out the window, 'where you live.'

She nodded.

'What do you do all day?'

'Play.'

'How tiring for you.'

She nodded. 'Sometimes it is. I start school soon, though.'

'There's a school here?'

'Not in here.'

She still couldn't get past this room. 'What do your parents do all day?'

'Mama works with Granddad.'

'She's a carpenter too?'

She shook her head. 'We don't have a car.'

'What does your dad do?'

She shrugged again. 'Mama and Daddy stopped liking each other. Have you got a boyfriend?'

'No.'

'Ever had one?'

'I've had more than one.'

'At the same time?'

I didn't answer.

'Why aren't you with any of them now?'

'Because I stopped liking them.'

'*All* of them?'

'Almost all of them.'

'Oh, that's not very nice.'

'No . . .' My mind wandered. 'I suppose it's not.'

'Does it make you sad? It makes Mama sad.'

'No, it doesn't make me sad.' I laughed awkwardly, not feeling comfortable with her gaze or loose tongue.

'You look sad.'

'How can I look sad when I'm laughing?'

She shrugged again. That's why I hated children; there were so many empty spaces in their minds and not enough answers, the exact reason why I'd hated being one myself. There was always a lack of knowledge about what was going on and seldom did I come across an adult who could enlighten me.

'Wanda, for someone who asks a lot of questions you don't know a lot of answers.'

'I ask different questions than you do,' she frowned. 'I know lots of answers.'

'Like what?'

'Like . . .' she thought hard, 'the reason Mr Ngambao from next door doesn't work in the fields is because he has a sore back.'

'Where are the fields?'

She pointed out the window. 'That way. That's where

our food grows and then everyone goes to the eatery three times every day to eat it.'

'The entire village eats together?'

She nodded. 'Petra's mama works there but I don't want to work there when I'm older, or in the fields. I want to work with Bobby,' she said dreamily. 'My friend Lacey's dad works in the library.'

I searched for the importance of her sentence and found none. 'Does anybody ever think of spending their time more wisely, like trying to get the hell out of here?' I asked smartly, more to myself.

'People try to leave,' she said, 'but they can't. There's no way out, but I like it here so I don't mind.' She yawned. 'I'm tired. I'm going to bed. Night.' She climbed down off the couch and made her way to the door, dragging a torn blanket behind her. 'Is this yours?' She stopped, bending over to pick up something from the floor. She held it up and I saw it shine as the light seeping in from under the door hit it.

'Yes,' I sighed, taking my watch from her hands.

The door opened, orange light filled the room, forcing me to close my eyes, and then I heard it shut again and I was alone in the darkness with the words of a five-year-old ringing in my ears.

People try to leave but they can't. There's no way out . . .

That was the other thing I hated about kids: they always said the exact things that deep down you already knew, would never admit, and most certainly never wanted to hear.

22

'So Joseph is a carpenter. What is it that you do, Mary?' I asked Helena as we strolled along the dusty path of the village.

Helena smiled.

We had walked through the village and now wandered beyond, passing fields of glorious golds and greens, dotted with people of all nationalities, who stooped and rose as they worked the farm, growing anything and everything I had ever and never heard of. Dozens of greenhouses speckled the landscape, the villagers taking every opportunity to grow what they could. Like the diverse people, the weather had arrived in this place in all its fiery yet vital forms. Already in just a few days I'd experienced the sweltering heat, a thunderstorm, a spring breeze and a winter chill, inconsistent weather I presumed to be the explanation for the unusual array of plants, trees, flowers and crops that all managed to successfully live together in the same environment. The explanation for the humans, I hadn't yet learned. But it seemed there were no rules regarding nature in this place. Four seasons in one day was accepted, welcomed and adapted to. It was warm again now as we strolled side by side, me feeling revitalised after sleeping more hours in one night than I had since I was a child. Since Jenny-May.

'Since Jenny-May *what*?' Gregory would always ask me. 'Since she went missing?'

'No, just *since Jenny-May* full stop,' I would reply.

That morning I encountered someone I had been searching for for twelve years. Helena had urged me onwards, snapping shut my gaping gob and clicking fingers before my goggling eyes. I was overwhelmed by her presence and I was never overwhelmed. I was dumbfounded, and I was never dumbfounded. I suddenly felt lonely, and I was never lonely. But lately I was a lot of things I never was. After so many years of looking, it was near impossible to remain as serene as Helena when the faces I saw in my dreams passed me in waking hours.

'Stay calm,' Helena had murmured more than once into my ear.

Robin Geraghty was the first of my ghosts to float by. We had been seated at the 'eatery', a stunning timber build on two levels, with a balcony around four sides from which the views of forestry, mountains and fields were displayed to perfection. It wasn't a crammed work canteen, as I had imagined, it was a beautiful building that housed the local villagers for breakfast, lunch and dinner; a scheme created to help ration the food they collected and grew. Money, I learned, had no value here, not even when wallets filled with it arrived on their doorsteps. 'Why spend money on something that arrives in abundance daily?' Helena had asked by way of explanation.

On the front of the building, ornate hand-crafted timber decorated the entrance as it did the registry. Owing to the many languages of the village, Helena explained, these carvings were the most productive and attractive methods of exhibiting the use of the building. Oversized vine of grapes, wine and bread decorated the front, looking so delectable even in its lumber form that I had to run my hand along the smooth curve of the berry.

I was returning from my trip to the buffet-style counter when I saw Robin, causing me almost to drop my tray of doughnuts and frappacino. (It appeared that a box of food had gone missing from a Krispy Kreme delivery van and had arrived on the outskirts of the village that morning, much to my delight. I had visions of a delivery man, clipboard in hand, ignoring the insults of a stressed-out store manager, as he scratched his head in wonder and recounted the contents of his van, parked up on a busy loading bay outside a downtown New York store while I, and a line of hungry people behind me, dived into the basket in a long-lost place.) The appearance of Robin almost caused me to scald myself, it was as though my frappacino got a fright too, wavering slightly in its stance.

Robin Geraghty had disappeared at the age of six. She had gone out to play in her front garden in the suburbs of North Dublin at eleven a.m. but was gone when her mother checked on her at 11.05. Everyone – and I mean *everyone* – the family, the country, the Gardaí, which at that time included me, all thought she had been abducted by the next-door neighbour. Fifty-five-year-old Dennis Fairman, an odd man, a loner, spoke to nobody but Robin each time he passed her, much to her parents' concern.

He said he didn't do it. He swore to me he didn't do it; he kept on repeating that she was his friend and that he couldn't and wouldn't hurt her. Nobody believed him – *I* didn't believe him – yet we didn't have the proof of his guilt. We didn't even have a body. The man became so tormented by his neighbours, by the media, by the constant garda questioning that he ended his own life, a sure sign to the parents and everybody else of his guilt. But as a nineteen-year-old Robin walked by me and made her way to the counter, I felt ill.

Although Robin had disappeared at the age of six, I knew it was her the moment I lifted my ogling eyes from the Krispy Kreme to see the young woman walk by. A computer-generated image of her had been made public and updated every few years. I had memorised it, had used it every day as part of my mind checks when I came across familiar faces. And that face was all of a sudden coming towards me. The computer image hadn't been far off, though her face was fuller, her hair was darker, there was a swing in her hips and a knowledge in her eyes as all she had seen and done had altered all but their colour. All the things a picture couldn't convey. But it was her.

I'd been unable to eat my breakfast; instead I sat at the table with Helena's family in a daze, while Wanda studied me and impersonated my every move. I ignored her and her constant babbling about somebody called Bobby, unable to stop myself from watching Robin while trying to figure out how I felt about seeing this young woman living life as she had done for the past twelve years. My feelings were mixed, my happiness bittersweet, because although all the people I yearned to find surrounded me, it was also the moment I realised that I had spent a colossal portion of my life looking in all the wrong places. It's that moment when you meet your idol, when all your wishes come true; there's a feeling of secret disappointment.

Helena and I stopped walking at an uncultivated multicoloured field filled with bright yellow Bermuda buttercups, blue and mauve milkwort, daisies, dandelions and long grasses; the sweet smell reminding me of the last few breaths I had taken in Glin.

'What's up ahead?' I spotted more buildings peeking out behind a gathering of silver birch, the oak visible against the peeling, papery black and white bark of the trunk.

'That's another village,' Helena explained. 'There are so many new arrivals every day, we couldn't possibly fit into this tiny town. Also, there are so many cultures that wouldn't and couldn't settle for living in environments like this. Their homes are out there.' She nodded towards the faraway trees and mountains.

I hadn't even contemplated that. 'So there are more people I've searched for, over there?'

'Possibly,' she agreed. 'They would have registry offices just as we have here so all the names will be logged, although I'm not sure they'll release the information as it's usually deemed private except in the case of emergencies. Hopefully we won't have to go looking for them. They'll find you.'

I smiled at the irony. 'What exactly is this plan you're hatching?'

'Well,' she smiled and her eyes sparkled mischievously, 'thanks to the list you provided me with, Joan is now taking bookings for private auditions for a new Irish play in about,' she lifted my hand and looked at my watch, 'two hours' time.'

I felt anxious about meeting people like Robin but Helena's plan made me laugh. 'Surely there could have been an easier way to do this.'

'Of course.' Helena threw her lemon pashmina over her right shoulder. 'But this is so much more fun.'

'What makes you think that any of the people on my list will come to these auditions?'

'Are you joking?' She looked surprised. 'Didn't you see Bernard and Joan? Most people here really love to get involved in activities, especially ones held by people from home.'

'Won't the non-Irish communities be jealous?' I half-joked. 'I wouldn't want them to think I'm omitting them from my grand production.'

'No,' Helena laughed, 'everyone will have a laugh at our expense come show time.'

'Show time? You mean we're actually staging a play?' My eyes widened.

'Of course!' Helena laughed. 'We're not dragging twenty people to the auditions just to tell them there's no play, but what exactly that play will be we've yet to decide.'

My headache returned. 'As soon as I start talking to them today they're going to realise the likelihood of my running an acting agency is no more than Bernard's chances of landing a lead role.'

Helena laughed again. 'Don't worry, they won't suspect a thing, and even if they do they won't mind. People tend to reinvent themselves here; they use this experience as a second chance in life. If what you were at home was not an acting agent, it doesn't mean that you're not one here. The longer you're here the more you'll notice that there really is a good atmosphere among everyone.'

I had noticed. The atmosphere was relaxed; people were peaceful and went about their daily duties efficiently yet without rushing or panic. There was room to breathe, space to think, time to spend wisely and lessons to be learned. People who were once lost took time to reflect, to love, to miss and to remember. Belonging was important, even if it meant joining a hopeless play.

'Won't Joseph mind that he can't take part?'

'Oh, I don't think that will worry him in the slightest,' Helena said.

'Joseph is from Kenya?'

'Yes.' We began walking back towards the village. 'Along the coast of Watamu.'

'What was it he called me yesterday?'

Helena's expression changed and I knew she was feigning ignorance. 'What do you mean?'

'Come on, Helena, I saw your face when he called me it. You were surprised. I can't remember the word, Kalla . . . Kappa something, what does it mean?'

Her forehead wrinkled in pretend confusion, 'Sorry, Sandy, I've no idea. I honestly can't remember.'

I didn't believe her. 'Did you tell him what I do for a living?'

Her face changed to that same intrigued look from yesterday. 'He knows now, of course, but he didn't then.'

'He didn't *when*?'

'When he met you.'

'Of course he didn't. I don't expect him to be psychic, I just want to know what he said.' I stopped walking out of frustration. 'Helena, please be straight with me. I can't take riddles.'

Her face pinked. 'You'll have to ask him, Sandy, because I don't know. Whatever it was, it must have been in his local Kiswahili language and I'm far from being an expert.'

I was convinced she was lying and so we walked in silence. I looked at my watch again, anxious that I would soon be sharing messages from family members at home. Messages they sent off in their prayers every night to land here and be told. I questioned my ability to transmit their sentiments accurately. What I had said to Helena the previous day was true: I *wasn't* a people person, finding them didn't mean wanting to spend time with them. Wondering where Jenny-May went didn't mean I wanted to go there or wished she'd return.

Helena, as usual, in her own instinctive way picked up on my feelings. 'It was nice being able to tell Joseph about my family at long last,' she said gently. 'We spoke about them until my lids closed and I dreamed about them until the sun came up. I dreamed about my mother and her organisation, about my father and his searching for me.' She closed her eyes. 'I woke up in this place this morning hardly knowing where I was after spending hours in my dreams where I grew up.'

'I'm sorry if I upset you,' I apologised. 'I'm not quite sure how to tell people what it is their families would want me to say.' I played with the watch around my wrist as we walked, wanting to turn back the time that kept ticking on.

Helena's eyes opened and I could see a layer of tears settling on her lower lashes, building up in an invisible reservoir. 'Don't think that about yourself, Sandy. I felt soothed by your words – how could I not be?' Her face brightened. 'I woke up *knowing* I had a mother out there still minding me. Today I feel protected, like I'm swaddled in an invisible blanket. You know, you're not the only one whose life-long questions have been answered. I now have photographs in my mind that I never had before. An entire catalogue has been filed and stored, all in one night.'

I just nodded. There was nothing to say.

'You will be fine with these people; I know you will

be *more* than fine. The people on the list you have given will be arriving in how long?'

I looked at my watch. 'An hour and a half.'

'Right, in ninety minutes, they'll all be there with the full intention of spending a short while of their lives calling Romeo from a balcony or re-enacting the great escape through the art of mime.'

I laughed.

'Anything more you tell them will be a bonus, no matter how you phrase it.'

'Thank you, Helena.'

'No problem.' She gave my arm a comforting pat and I tried to stop myself from stiffening.

I looked down at my clothes. 'There's just one more problem. I've been wearing this tracksuit for days and I would really love a change of clothes. Is there anything you have that I could borrow?'

'Oh, don't worry about that,' Helena said, walking off in the direction of the trees. 'You wait here; I'll be back in a minute.'

'Where are you going?'

'Just a minute . . .' Her voice disappeared, along with her short salt-and-pepper hair and billowing lemon pashmina, into the darkness.

I tapped my foot impatiently, wondering and worrying about where she'd gone. I couldn't lose Helena now. Up ahead I spotted the towering figure of Joseph leaving the woods, carrying logs in one hand, an axe in the other.

'Joseph!' I called.

He looked up and waved with the axe, a motion that wasn't particularly heart-warming, and he made his way towards me. His bald head shone like polished marble, his flawless skin making him appear younger than his years.

'Everything OK?' he asked with concern.

'Yes, I think so. Well, I don't know,' I added with confusion. 'Helena just disappeared into the woods and—'

'What?' His eyes darkened.

'I don't mean *disappeared*.' I realised my error. 'She walked, *walked* into the woods a few minutes ago.' Disappearing from here was impossible, so no wonder Joseph was alarmed. 'She told me to wait here for her.'

He set the axe down and watched the woods. 'She will return, kipepeo girl.' His voice was gentle.

'What does that mean?'

'It means she will come back,' he smiled.

'Not *that* – what does the Kenyan word mean?'

'It is what you are,' he said lazily, his eyes not moving from the trees.

'Which is?'

Before he had a chance to answer the question, Helena reappeared, tugging what appeared to be luggage behind her. 'Found this for you. Oh, hi, sweetheart. I thought I heard you tapping away at the trees. Name on the bag says Barbara Langley from Ohio. Hope, for your sake, Barbara from Ohio has long legs.' She dropped the bag by my feet and dusted off her hands.

'What is this?' I asked open-mouthed, studying the baggage ticket on the handle. 'This was bound for New York over twenty years ago.'

'Great, you'll have a nice retro look,' Helena joked.

'I can't wear someone else's clothes,' I protested.

'Why not? You were going to wear mine,' Helena laughed.

'But I know you!'

'Yes, but you wouldn't have known the person who wore them before me,' she teased, heading off before me. 'Come now, how much time have we left? We're going to the auditions now,' she explained to Joseph, who nodded solemnly and picked up his axe again.

I looked at my wrist. My watch was gone.

'Oh damnit,' I grumbled, dropping the bag back down on the ground and searching around my legs.

'What's wrong?' Helena and Joseph stopped walking and turned round.

'My watch fell off my wrist again,' I grumbled, standing back and scouring the ground.

'Again?'

'The fastener on it is broken. Sometimes it just opens and falls onto the ground.' My voice was muffled as I went down on my knees and searched closer to the ground.

'Well, you were wearing it just a minute ago so it can't have gone far. Just lift the bag,' Helena said calmly.

I looked under the bag.

'That's funny.' Helena came over to where I stood and leaned in to get a closer look at the ground. 'Did you go anywhere when I went into the trees?'

'No, nowhere. I was waiting *right* here with Joseph.' I climbed down onto my knees and began crawling around the dusty floor.

'It can't have gone missing,' Helena said, not at all worried about the situation. 'We'll find it, we always do, here.'

We all stood still as we looked around the small area I hadn't moved from for over five minutes. There was nowhere else it could have fallen. I shook out my sleeves, emptied my pockets, and checked the bag to see if the watch had got caught up. Nothing, no sign, nowhere.

'Where on earth did it roll to?' Helena muttered, examining the ground.

Joseph, who had barely said a word since he'd joined us, stood still in the same place he had been standing all along. His eyes, as black as coal, appeared to have absorbed all light from around him. They were on me the whole time.

Just watching.

23

I spent the next half-hour searching the road for my watch, retracing my steps over and over again in my usual obsessive way. I combed the long grass by the sides of the uncultivated fields and dug my hands deep into the soil lining the forest. The watch was nowhere to be seen, but this brought a strange kind of comfort to me. My mind instantly erased where I was and all that had happened, and for those few moments I was me again with one goal. Finding. As a ten-year-old I would hunt for a single sock as though it had the value of the rarest diamond in the world but this time it was different; the watch was worth far more.

Joseph and Helena watched over me worriedly as I uprooted grass, followed by sods, in order to find the precious jewel that had clung to my wrist for thirteen years. Its inability to remain where it should have been for too much of that time pretty much tallied with the inconsistency of the relationship with the person who had given it to me. But even those times when it released itself from my clutches and flew off, drawn in the opposite direction to the one I was heading, I always looked out for it and wanted to be near it. That way too, exactly like the relationship.

Helena and Joseph didn't pretend, as my parents used to when I had a hunting episode. They looked worried and they were right to, because for people who said nothing could or ever had gone missing in this place, they were finding it difficult having to munch on and digest their own words. At least that's what the obsessive side of me thought. The rational side of me reckoned the more obvious cause for their concern may have just been me, on my hands and knees, covered in dust, dirt, grass stains and muck.

'I think you should stop looking now,' Helena said with a hint of amusement on her face. 'You have lots of people to meet at the Community Hall, not to mention now needing a shower and change of clothes.'

'They can wait,' I said, clawing my way through the grass, feeling soil gathering beneath my fingernails.

'They've waited long enough,' Helena said forcefully, 'and frankly so have you. Stop trying to avoid the inevitable and come with me now.'

I stopped clawing. There was the word I was so used to hearing from Gregory's mouth. 'Avoid'. *Stop avoiding things, Sandy . . .* Was that what I was doing? How I could be avoiding things by concentrating fully on one thing and refusing to leave it, had always been beyond me. Surely avoidance meant walking in the other direction. It was people like Gregory, my parents and now Helena and Joseph who were avoiding dealing with the fact that something had gone missing and couldn't be found. I looked up at Helena, who looked doll-like beside Joseph's huge frame. 'I really need to find that watch.'

'And you will,' she said so easily that I believed her. 'Things *always* show up here. Joseph said he would keep an eye out for you, and maybe Bobby will know something.'

'Who's this Bobby that I keep hearing about?' I asked getting to my feet.

'He works in Lost and Found,' Helena explained handing me the luggage I had abandoned in the middle of the road.

'Lost and Found,' I laughed, shaking my head.

'I'm surprised you didn't end up in the front window,' Helena said gently.

'That's Amsterdam you're thinking of,' I smiled.

Her forehead wrinkled. '*Amsterdam?* What are you talking about?'

Dusting myself off, I left the search scene behind me. 'Helena, you have so much to learn.'

'A wonderful piece of advice, coming from someone who spent the last thirty minutes on her hands and knees trawling through muck.'

We left Joseph standing in the middle of the road, hands on his hips, logs and axe by his feet, surveying the dusty path.

I arrived at the Community Hall dressed as Barbara Langley from Ohio. Her legs, it seemed, were far from long, and she had a penchant for mini skirts and leggings I didn't even dare try on. The other items she unfortunately missed out on wearing on her New York trip were stripy sweaters with shoulder pads that brushed my earlobes and jackets covered with badges of peace signs, Yin and Yang emblems, yellow smiley faces and American flags. I had hated the eighties the first time round; I had no intention of reliving it.

Helena had laughed when she saw me in skin-tight stone-washed jeans that stopped above my ankles, white socks, my own trainers, and a black T-shirt with a yellow smiley face.

'Do you think Barbara Langley was in *The Breakfast Club*?' I asked, trudging out of the bathroom like a child who had been forced to replace her play clothes with a dress and tights for Sunday dinner of green vegetables aplenty.

Helena looked confused. 'I have no idea what clubs she was a member of although I do see others wearing those kinds of clothes here.'

I ended up doing what I had been convinced I would never resort to: grabbing marginally more decent items of clothing lying alongside the roads as we made our way to the village.

'We can go to Bobby's afterwards,' Helena had tried to cheer me up. 'He has a huge collection of clothes to choose from or else there are a few clothes makers around.'

'I'll just get some second-hand clothes,' I preferred. 'I won't be here by the time they finish making me a wardrobe.'

She snorted at that, much to my annoyance.

The Community Hall was a magnificent oak building with a large double-door entrance similar to the others. On it were larger-than-life carvings of people gathered together, arms and shoulders touching and hands holding, while their hair and clothes flapped in a breeze trapped in the walls of wood. Helena pushed open the twelve-foot-tall doors and the crowd parted for us.

A stage stood at the top of the forty-foot-long hall. Around it on three sides were rows of solid oak chairs, and the same above on a second gallery level. A red velvet curtain parted and was held back on both sides by a thick golden rope. On the entire length of the back wall on the stage was a canvas covered in black paint handprints. They were all of different sizes, representing ages from babies to the elderly as they lined up in a row of at least one hundred across and one hundred down. Above it were words written in many languages but reading the English I saw they were 'Strength and Hope'. It was so familiar to me.

'They are the handprints of each person that lives and has lived here over the past three years. Each village has the same in its community hall. I suppose it's our emblem now for here.'

'I recognise it,' I said, thinking aloud.

'Oh, no, you couldn't.' Helena shook her head. 'The Community Hall is the only place you'll see this in the village.'

'No, I recognise it from home. There is a national monument just like it in the grounds of Kilkenny Castle. Each hand was cast from the actual hand of a relative of a missing person. Beside it is a stone with an inscription of the words –' I closed my eyes and recited the inscription I had run my finger over so many times –

'"This sculpture and area of reflection is dedicated to all missing persons. May all relatives and friends who visit find continuing strength and hope." The cast of your mother's hand is there.'

Helena looked as though she was holding her breath as she searched my face, waiting for me to somehow announce that I was joking. I didn't and she exhaled slowly.

'Well, I don't know what to say.' Her voice shook and she turned to look at the mural. 'Joseph thought it would be a nice idea for everyone to do that.' She shook her head in disbelief. 'Wait until he hears what you've told me.'

'Wow,' I said, looking around the rest of the building. It was more like a theatre than a community hall.

'This seats twenty-five hundred people,' Helena explained, moving on from what I had told her, though understandably seeming somewhat distracted. 'The chairs are taken out if we need to hold more but it's very rare that the entire community will attend anything. It's used for lots of different things such as a ballot hall, a discussion forum between the elected council and the community, art galleries, debates, even a theatre for the rare occasions that plays are staged. The list goes on.'

'Who is on the elected council?'

'A representative from each nation in the village. We have over one hundred nations in this village alone and every village has its own council. There are dozens of villages.'

'So what happens at these council meetings?' I asked with amusement.

'The same as everywhere else in the world; everything that needs discussion and decision is discussed and decided.'

'What are the crime levels here?'

'Minimal.'

'How is it kept that way? I don't recall seeing the long hand of the law patrolling the streets on our way here. How is everyone kept on the straight and narrow?'

'There has been a judicial system in place for hundreds of years. We have a courthouse, a rehabilitation institute and a security council, but getting every nation to abide by the same rules isn't always easy. The council at least encourages talk and debate.'

'So this is the sounding house? Do they actually have any power?'

'The power that we have vested in them. Everybody gets one of these in their information pack when they arrive.' Helena took a pamphlet from a display on the wall. 'You should have one too if you bothered to look through your folder. There are voting guidelines.'

I flicked through the pamphlet, reading aloud: '"Vote for those with the ability to listen and to make decisions on behalf of the people in a manner reflecting consensus and serving the wellbeing of all,"' I laughed. 'What else is preached – two legs good, four legs bad?'

'They are the basics of good leadership.'

'Well, does this pamphlet for how to elect a leader work?' I smirked.

'I should think so.' She made her way over to Joan, who was on the far side of the room. 'Seeing as Joseph is on the council.'

My mouth dropped as I watched her cross the room. '*Joseph*?'

'You seem surprised.'

'Yes, well, I am surprised. He seems so . . .' I searched for the correct way to explain without offending her. 'He's a carpenter,' I eventually settled on.

'Those on the council are ordinary people with their own day jobs. He's merely called on to voice decisions when decisions need voicing.'

I couldn't stop smiling. 'I just get the feeling that everybody here is playing "house", you know? It's hard to take seriously,' I laughed. 'Come on. I mean, we're in the middle of *nowhere* and you have councils and courthouses and who knows what else.'

'You think it's funny?'

'Yes! Everywhere I look everyone's playing dress-up

in other people's clothes. How can this place, wherever this place is,' I stressed, 'have any kind of order or rules at all? It exists completely without *logic*. It lacks all sense of *practicality*.'

Helena seemed offended at first but then became sympathetic, which I hated. 'This is *life*, Sandy, *real life*. Sooner or later you'll discover that nobody's playing any games here. We're all just getting on with life and doing what we can to make it as normal as possible, just like everybody else, in every other country, in every other world.' She approached Joan. 'How did you get on with Sandy's list?' she asked, ending our conversation.

Joan looked up in surprise. 'Oh, hello. I didn't hear you both coming. You look,' she gave my eighties outfit the once-over, 'different.'

'Did you get in touch with everyone on the list?' I asked, ignoring her disapproving gaze.

'No, not all of them,' she said, glancing down at her page.

'Let me see.' I grabbed her notepad, my body surged with a sudden rush of adrenalin. My eyes scanned through the list of thirty names I had provided her with: fewer than half of them had ticks beside them. Joan continued talking as I read through the names so quickly I was barely able to take them in. My heart beat wildly, and skipped a beat each time my eyes registered a name and I realised that person was alive and well, and that soon we would be meeting.

'As I was saying,' Joan spoke, angry I had jumped ahead of her story, 'Terence at the registry was no help because he couldn't give out any information unless someone from the council requested it for official reasons.' She eyed Helena warily. 'So I had to just ask around the village. But you'll be pleased to know, Sandy, the Irish community here is so small that everyone knows everyone anyway.'

'Go on,' Helena urged.

'Well, I got in contact with quite a lot of people,

twelve in total,' she continued. 'Eight are interested in auditioning, the other four said they'd take part in the production in some way but definitely not on stage. But I didn't get the likes of, let me see . . .' She put her glasses on and lifted the page.

'Jenny-May Butler,' I finished the sentence for her, my heart plunging into the depths of my stomach.

Helena looked at me, obviously recognising the name from the time of my collapse.

'Bobby Stanley,' I read another name, my hopes dashed. I continued, 'James Moore, Clare Steenson . . .' The list of untraceable people went on.

'Well, just because they're not here doesn't mean they're not in the next village,' Joan tried reassuring me.

'What are the chances of that?' I asked, feeling hopeful again.

'I won't lie to you, Sandy. The majority of the Irish community are in this village,' Helena explained. 'Five to fifteen people, at most, arrive each year, and because there are so few of us we tend to stick together.'

'So Jenny-May Butler must be here,' I said forcefully. 'She has to be here.'

'What about the others on the list?' Joan said in a quiet voice.

I scanned it quickly, Clare and Peter, Stephanie and Simon . . . I had sat with their relatives long into the night, thumbed through photo albums and wiped tears through promises of finding their children, brothers, sisters and friends. If they weren't here then it meant I could only suspect the worst.

'But Jenny-May . . .' I started digging into the facts of the case I'd stored in my brain. 'There was no one else. Nobody saw anything or anybody.'

Joan looked confused; Helena sad.

'She has to be here. Unless she's hiding, or else she's in another country; I didn't look into other countries,' I rambled on to myself.

'OK, Sandy, why don't you just take a seat now? I think you're burning up,' Helena interrupted.

'I'm not burning up.' I swatted her hand away. 'No, she's not hiding and she can't be in another country. She's my age now.' I looked to Joan and everything was clear. 'You have to find Jenny-May Butler, tell everyone that she's my age. She's thirty-four years old. She's been here since she was ten, I know it.'

Joan nodded her head quickly, almost afraid to say no. Helena held out her hands towards me, afraid to touch me yet afraid to move away. I noticed the faces of the two women as they watched me. Worried. I quickly sat down and drank from a glass of water Helena had thrust into my hands.

'Is she OK?' I heard Joan ask Helena as they moved away.

'She's fine,' Helena said calmly. 'She just really wanted Jenny-May for the play. Let's do our best to find her, shall we?'

'I don't think she's here,' Joan whispered.

'Let's look anyway.'

'Can I ask why I was given a list of thirty to find? How does Sandy know they can act? When I contacted them all, they were very surprised. Most of them have never been involved in amateur dramatics. What about all the others who are interested in taking part? They're still allowed to audition, aren't they?'

'Of course everyone's allowed,' Helena fobbed her off. 'The people on the list were just special, that's all.'

Of the two thousand people reported missing in Ireland every year, between five and fifteen will never be found. The thirty people I had chosen were the ones I had spent my entire working life obsessed with finding. Others I had found, others I could give up looking for, knowing something sinister was involved, that harm had sadly come to them or that they'd merely walked away of their own accord. But these thirty on the list – they were the ones that had disappeared without a trace and without reason. These were the thirty that haunted me, the thirty without a crime scene to examine or witnesses to question.

I thought of all their relatives and of how I'd promised I'd find their loved ones. I thought of Jack Ruttle, of how only last week I had made that promise. I thought of how I had failed to show up at our meeting in Glin and how now I had once again failed.

Because according to the list, Donal Ruttle wasn't here.

24

On Tuesday morning, exactly two days since Sandy's no-show, Jack, who had not long returned home with Sandy's file on Donal, stepped out into the fresh July morning air and closed the door to the cottage quietly behind him. Around the town, preparations were being made for the pending Irish Coffee Festival. Banners were rolled up beside telegraph poles, ready to be hung, and the back of a lorry had been opened up as a makeshift stage for the outdoor trad-band performances. The town was quiet now, though, everybody still in the comfort of their beds, dreaming of other worlds. Jack started his engine, the noise of it loud enough in the quiet square to wake the entire town, and he made his way into Limerick city where he would hopefully meet Sandy at Donal's friend Alan's home. He also wanted to pay a visit to his sister Judith.

Judith was the closest of his siblings. Married with five kids, she was a mother from the moment she arrived kicking and screaming into this world. Eight years older than Jack, she had practised her skills of obedience training and nurturing on every doll and every child that lived nearby. The common joke on the street was that there wasn't a doll in the city that didn't sit up straight and shut up when Judith was around. As soon as Jack was born, she turned her attention to him, a real baby whom she could mother and often smother from that day until now. She was the one he ran to for advice and she always found time between school runs, nappy changing and breastfeeding to lend an ear.

As he pulled up outside her terraced house, the front door opened and the wail of a thousand banshees flew past his ears, almost blowing his hair.

'Daaa-deee,' a banshee yelled.

The banshee's father appeared at the door in an off-white creased shirt with an open top button and a loosened tie in an uneven knot. He held in one hand a mug that he clung to for dear life and gulped on with bulging eyes. His other hand gripped a tattered briefcase while the banshee with white-blonde hair, Power Rangers pyjamas and Kermit the Frog slippers clung to his leg.

'Dooon't gooooo,' she yelled, wrapping her limbs around one of his legs as though her life depended on his staying.

'I have to go, sweetie. Daddy has to work.'

'Nooooooo.'

An arm appeared from inside the door, thrusting a slice of toast in Willie's direction. 'Eat,' said Judith's voice over more wails from a second source.

Willie took a bite, slugged down some more coffee and shook Katie from his leg gently. His head disappeared from the doorway, kissed the owner of the arm, shouted, 'Bye, kids!' and the door was slammed. The screams were still audible yet Willie kept a smile on his face. It was eight a.m. and he'd already been through an hour or two of what Jack would consider pure torture. Yet he smiled.

'Hiya, Jack.' His moon-shaped face beamed.

'Good morning, Willie,' Jack said, noticing how his shirt buttons strained at his gut, a coffee stain decorated his shirt pocket and there was toothpaste on his paisley tie.

'Sorry. Can't talk. Escaping,' he chuckled, patting Jack on the back and squeezing into his car. The exhaust let out a bang and off he sped.

Jack looked around the housing estate of tightly packed grey houses and noticed a similar scene occurring on each doorstep.

He opened the door tentatively, hoping the madhouse wouldn't swallow him whole. He stepped inside and saw fifteen-month-old Nathan running off down the hall, with a bottle hanging from his lips and naked but for a bulging nappy. Jack followed him. Four-year-old Katie, who had only seconds ago clung to her father as though her world was going to end, was sitting a foot away from the television, cross-legged on the floor, a bowl of cereal spilling onto the already stained carpet, completely captivated by dancing bugs singing about the rainforest.

'Nathan!' Judith called pleasantly from the kitchen. 'I have to change your nappy. Come back in here, please!'

She had the patience of a saint, while around her chaos ensued. Toys cluttered every surface, scribbles and drawings were either pinned to the walls or drawn directly *on* the walls. There were baskets of dirty clothes, baskets of clean clothes, clothes horses with drying clothes lining the walls. The television was blaring, a baby was wailing, pots and pans were being banged. It was a human zoo: three girls and two boys, a ten-year-old, an eight-year-old, a four-year-old, a fifteen-month-old and a three-month-old, all running riot and demanding attention, while Judith sat at the kitchen table, dressed in her stained robe, hair wild and unwashed, *things* just everywhere, cluttering every surface and her face a picture of serenity.

'Hi, Jack.' She looked up in surprise. 'How did you get in here?'

'The door was open, and I followed your doorman in.' He nodded at Nathan, who had taken his position on the floor, stinky nappy and all, and had resumed banging pots with a wooden spoon. Three-month-old Rachel was shocked into silence, her eyes widened and her lips parted ready to release bubbles. 'Don't get up.' Jack leaned over Rachel in her cot to kiss Judith.

'Nathan honey, I told you not to unlock the door without Mammy saying so,' Judith explained calmly.

'He keeps turning the lock,' Judith explained to Jack.

Nathan stopped banging and looked up at her with big blue eyes, a double chin with drool dripping from it. 'Dada,' he gurgled in response.

'Yes, you do look like your daddy,' Judith replied, getting to her feet. 'Can I get you anything, Jack? A cup of tea, coffee, toast, earplugs?'

'Tea and toast, please. I've had enough coffee,' Jack replied, rubbing his face wearily as the saucepan banging became almost unbearable.

'Nathan, stop,' Judith said firmly, flicking the switch on the kettle. 'Come on, let's change your nappy.'

She lifted him onto a nappy-changing facility in the kitchen and got to work, giving Nathan her house keys to amuse himself with.

Jack looked away, no longer feeling hungry.

'So why aren't you at work?' Judith asked, holding two podgy legs together at the ankles as though she was about to stuff a turkey.

'I took the day off.'

'Again?'

He didn't answer.

'I spoke to Gloria yesterday. She said you'd taken the day off,' Judith explained.

'How did she know?'

Judith pulled a baby wipe from a container. 'Now is not the time to start thinking your intelligent partner of eight years is stupid. Oh, what's that I hear?' She held her hand to her ear and looked off into the distance. Nathan stopped jangling the keys and watched her. 'Oh, no, I don't hear it any more but I used to hear the sound of wedding bells and the pitter-patter of tiny feet.'

Nathan laughed and continued jangling his keys. Judith popped Nathan back on the floor again, the sound of his feet on the tiles like a duck stepping in puddles.

'Gee, Jack, you've gone awful quiet,' she said sarcastically, washing her hands in the kitchen sink, he noted, over a pile of dirty dishes and cups.

'It's not the right time,' Jack said tiredly, taking the wooden spoon from Nathan, who in turn started screaming, which woke Rachel, who started screaming, which caused Katie to turn up the volume of the television instantly in the living room. 'Besides, this place alone is enough of a contraceptive for me.'

'Yes, well, when you marry a man with the name Willie you pretty much know what you're getting.' In less than one minute Judith had calm again, a cup of tea and a slice of toast on the table before Jack. She finally sat down, removed Rachel from her cot, moved her dressing gown to one side and began breastfeeding while Rachel's tiny fingers opened and closed in mid-air, playing an invisible harp with her eyes closed.

'I've taken the week off work,' Jack explained. 'Arranged it on the way here this morning.'

'You've what?' Judith took a sip of tea. 'They let you have more time off?'

'With a bit of persuasion.'

'That's good. You and Gloria need to spend more time together.' But she could tell by his face that that wasn't the intention. 'What's going on, Jack?'

He sighed, wanting so much to tell her the story but afraid to do so.

'Tell me,' she said gently.

'I came across someone,' he began. 'An agency.'

'Yes?' Her voice was low and questioning like it used to be when he came home from school after being in trouble and was forced to explain such things as why they'd stripped Tommy McGovern naked and tied him to the goal posts in the yard.

'It's a missing persons agency.'

'Oh, Jack,' she whispered, hand flying to her mouth.

'Well, what harm could it do, Jude? What's the damage in one more person having a look?'

'*This* is the damage, Jack. *You*, taking one more week off from work, *Gloria* ringing me, looking for you.'

'She rang?'

'Ten o'clock last night.'

'Oh.'

'So go on, tell me about the agency.'

'No.' He leaned back in his chair, frustrated. 'No, I couldn't be bothered now.'

'Jack, don't be such a child and tell me.'

He waited to cool down before speaking again. 'I came across the ad in the Golden Pages and I gave her a call.'

'Who?'

'Sandy Shortt. I explained the case to her and she told me she'd solved cases like this before. We spoke on the phone until late every night last week. She used to be a garda and she got her hands on a few reports we'd never seen.'

Judith raised her eyebrows.

'She wasn't asking for a penny, Judith, and I believed her. I believed she wanted to help and I believed she could find Donal. She was legit, there's no doubt about it.'

'Why are you speaking about her like she's dead?' she smiled, and then stopped, looking alarmed. 'She's not dead, is she?'

'No,' Jack shook his head, 'but I don't know where she is. We arranged to meet on Sunday morning in Glin. We passed one another at a petrol station but I didn't know it was her until after.'

Judith's forehead wrinkled.

'We'd only ever spoken on the phone, you see.'

'So how do you know it was her?'

'I found her car down by the estuary.'

Judith looked even more flummoxed.

'Look, we were supposed to meet and she left a voice message the night before saying she was on her way over from Dublin but she didn't show up. So I looked around the town, asked for her in all the B & Bs, and when I couldn't find her, I went for a walk by the estuary. That's when I found the car.'

'How can you be sure it was her car?'

Jack opened the bag beside him. 'Because this was

on the dashboard.' He placed the file on the kitchen table. 'So was this,' he placed her diary down, 'and this,' her charged mobile phone. 'She labels *everything*, absolutely everything. I went through her bag – all her clothes, her socks, *all* labelled. It's like she's afraid of losing things.'

Judith was quiet. 'You went through her bag?' She shook her head, confused. 'But how did you get these from the car? Maybe she was just taking a walk, Jack. What if she returns to her car and all her stuff is missing? Are you crazy, taking all this?'

'Then I'll have some apologising to do but it's been *two* whole days. That's a long walk.'

Silence while they both remembered how their mother had been desperately worried after two days of Donal's silence.

'I rang Graham Turner.'

'What did he say?' Hands buried her face. The same scenario all over again.

'He said that as it had only been over twenty-four hours and because it was in keeping with her usual behaviour that he didn't think there was any cause to worry.'

'Why, what's her usual behaviour?'

'That she comes and goes as she pleases, keeps to herself and doesn't tell anyone where she's going,' Jack rattled off tiredly.

'Oh.' Judith looked relieved.

'But that doesn't mean you park your car in the middle of trees by the estuary and desert it for two days. That's slightly different from coming and going as she pleases.'

'So let me get this straight,' Judith said slowly. 'The missing persons person is missing?'

Silence.

Judith allowed that thought to roll around in her head, shifting it until it found a place it was comfortable to settle in. She looked contemplative as she moved her jaw from side to side.

Then she snorted and burst out laughing.

Jack sat back in his chair and folded his arms, feeling offended as Judith shook uncontrollably before him. Rachel stopped suckling and watched her bouncing mother, who was now wiping tears from her eyes. Nathan stopped playing with his blocks, stood to his feet to watch his mother. His face broke into a gummy smile and he began laughing, clapping his podgy hands and bouncing his body with delight from the knees up. Eventually Jack felt the corners of his lips tickle and he joined in, laughing deliriously at the ridiculousness of the situation and feeling such relief to let go after so long, even if only momentarily. Once they'd settled down Judith began rubbing Rachel gently on her back, so soothingly it made Jack's eyes feel heavy.

'Look, Judith, maybe Graham is right. Maybe she did just walk away. Maybe she just thought, to hell with all this, and left her car, left her phone, her diary, her life, and gave up. Maybe she's this mad, loony woman who does it all the time with the intention of coming back after a while. Maybe she walked away completely, but *I'm* going to find her, *she's* going to find Donal and *then* she can quit. *Then* I'll let her walk away.'

'You really think this woman could find Donal?' Judith was contemplative.

'She believed she could.'

'What do you think?'

He nodded.

'So if you find her, you'll be helping to find Donal.' She was deep in thought. 'You know, Willie and I were going through the photo album last night with the kids and Katie pointed to Donal and asked who he was.' Her eyes filled. 'Neither Katie or Nathan remember him – they'll *never* have a memory of him – and Rachel,' she looked down at her baby in her arms, 'she doesn't even know he existed. Life is going on without him and he's missing all this.' She shook her head.

Jack couldn't think of anything to say, didn't think

there was anything *to* say. The same thoughts ran through his head every second of every day.

'What makes you so sure that a woman you've never even met, a woman you don't know anything about, has the ability to find Donal?'

'Blind faith,' he smiled.

'Since when did you ever have that?'

'Since I spoke to Sandy on the phone,' he replied earnestly.

'There was nothing . . .' she paused and decided to ask anyway, 'there was nothing between you two was there?'

'There was something, but it was nothing.'

'When is something ever nothing?'

He sighed and decided to avoid the question. 'Gloria doesn't know about Sandy – not that there's anything to know – but I don't want her or the rest of the family knowing about the agency.'

Judith didn't look happy.

'Please, Jude.' He grabbed her hand. 'I don't want to bring everyone through all this again. I just want to try by myself. I need to.'

'OK OK.' She let go, holding it up in defence. 'So what are you going to do now?'

'Simple.' He put the file, diary and phone back into his bag. 'I'm going to start looking for her.'

25

I was sixteen years old, in Mr Burton's office. I was sitting on one of the burst velvet chairs, the same since the day I'd arrived over two years ago, but for the extra foam on display. I was staring at the same posters on the walls of the cramped room. The bricked walls had been clumsily painted white, some holes still black and naked of paint, others holding clumps of white. It was all or nothing in this room, never even. Blu-Tack clung to parts of the walls, corners of old posters still hung on to the Blu-Tack. Somewhere in the school I imagined a room fully stocked with corner-less posters.

'What are you thinking about?' Mr Burton finally spoke.

'Corner-less posters,' I replied.

'Ah, that old chestnut.' He nodded. 'How was your week?'

'Crap.'

'Why crap?'

'Nothing very exciting happened.'

'What did you do?'

'School, ate, slept, school, ate, slept, multiplied by five more times and to be multiplied by a million more weeks in my life. My future looks bleak.'

'Did you go out at the weekend? You were saying last week that you'd been asked out by a group of people.'

He always wanted me to make friends. 'Yeah, I went out.'

'And?'

'And it was OK. There was a house party. Johnny Nugent's parents were away, so we all went there.'

'Johnny Nugent?' He raised his eyebrows.

I didn't answer but my cheeks pinked.

'Were you able to forget about Mr Pobbs and enjoy yourself?'

He asked it so seriously, I studied the Blu-Tack again, feeling slightly embarrassed. I'd had Mr Pobbs since I was a baby – a grey, fluffy, one-eyed teddy in blue striped pyjamas, who slept in my bed, and any other bed I stayed in, every night. My parents and I had been away for the week a short time before and as soon as we'd returned I had repacked to go stay with my grandparents for the weekend. Somewhere in changing over my clothes I'd misplaced Mr Pobbs. It had upset me deeply all the time I was at my grandparents', and I'd taken to a two-week-long search of the house on my return, much to my parents' dismay. Last week we had discussed my not wanting to go out with Johnny Nugent at the weekend because I'd have preferred to find Mr Pobbs, my trusted friend, no matter how ridiculous it sounded. It had been difficult leaving the house to go out for the night, knowing that somewhere in there, Mr Pobbs lay hidden.

'So you went out with Johnny Nugent?' Mr Burton went back to the question.

'Yes, I did.'

He smiled awkwardly. He'd obviously heard the rumours too. 'Is everything . . . are you . . . ?' He stopped talking and instead made trumpeting noises with his lips while he thought how to rephrase his question. It was rare to see him awkward as he always seemed to be in control. He was in this room, anyway; other than the small hints of personal information he revealed unwittingly during our, at times, candid talks, I knew nothing of his life outside of these four walls. I also knew not to ask any questions, because he wouldn't answer and because I didn't want to know.

Not knowing, asking and him not answering reminded me that we were strangers in a way. Only inside this room were we familiar. We had created our own world, had rules to follow and had a line between us that, although couldn't be passed, could be danced upon on playful days.

I jumped in and stopped his trumpeting lips from launching into an orchestra of brass instruments. 'Mr Burton, if you're wondering if I'm OK then, please, don't worry. For once in my life I've lost something and I've no intention of searching for it or expect it to come back. I think I'm cured.'

We laughed. And laughed. And when there was an uncomfortable silence while I fantasised about him curing me too, we laughed again.

'Will you see him again? And by that I mean, did you enjoy the company of others? Did you enjoy going out, did you relax, could you forget about all the things that are missing?' He started laughing again. 'Did they manage to reach Scathach's island?'

While my head was banging against the headboard in Johnny Nugent's parents' bed, I'd had an epiphany. I'd remembered where I thought I'd put Mr Pobbs aside before packing my clothes. I had called my gran the next day and expected Mr Pobbs to be found, lying under the bed staring with his one eye at the broken springs beneath. But he wasn't and we had arranged for my search of my grandparents' house the following weekend. Even though Johnny Nugent had asked me out. I was going to explain all this when I was pulled up short. 'Wait a minute, what's Scathach's island?'

Mr Burton laughed. 'Sorry, that just slipped out. It's a bad analogy.'

'Explain!' I smiled, watching his face redden.

'I didn't mean to say it. It just popped out. Never mind, let's move on.'

'Hold on a minute, you don't let me get away with that! I have to repeat *everything* I mumble,' I laughed, watching him squirm for the first time in my life.

He composed himself. 'It's an old Celtic story, and it was a stupid comparison.'

I motioned for more.

He rubbed his face. 'Oh, I can't believe I'm telling you this. Scathach was a great warrior woman who trained many heroes of the time. Legend tells us that it was almost impossible to reach her island, so that anyone who did was considered worthy to be trained in martial arts.'

My mouth dropped. 'You're comparing me to a warrior woman who trains men in martial arts?'

He laughed again. 'The point is that she was a woman that was hard to reach.' He stopped laughing when he saw my face. He leaned forward and grabbed my hand. 'I think you've taken that the wrong way.'

'I hope so,' I said, slowly shaking my head.

He groaned and thought fast. 'It's just that only the strongest, bravest and most worthy people could reach her.'

I relaxed a little, liking the sound of this. 'How would they reach her?'

He relaxed a little too. 'First they would have to cross the Plain of Ill Luck where they would be pierced by razor-sharp grass blades.' He paused while he studied my face to see whether he should go on or not. Happy that I wasn't about to punch him, he continued, 'Then they would face the Perilous Glens with devouring beasts. Their final task was the Bridge of the Cliff, which was a bridge that tilted upwards whenever anyone tried to cross.'

I pictured the people in my life that tried to approach me, that tried to befriend me, that tried to connect with me. I pictured me knocking them back.

'Only real heroes would get across,' he finished.

Goose bumps formed on my skin. My hairs stood up and I hoped he didn't notice.

He ran his hands through his hair and shook his head. 'That wasn't part of the . . .' *job*, he almost said. 'I shouldn't have said that. Sorry, Sandy.'

'It's OK,' I decided, and he looked relieved. 'Just tell me one thing, where are you on this journey?'

Those gorgeous blue eyes bored into mine. He didn't even need to think about it, didn't even look away. 'I'd say I've just passed over the Plain of Ill Luck right this minute.'

I pondered that. 'I'll go easy with my devouring beasts if you promise to just let me know when you've passed the Bridge.'

'You'll know,' he smiled, reaching for my hand and squeezing it. 'You'll know.'

Jack pulled up beside Alan's flat and flicked through Sandy's diary. She had also made an appointment for yesterday for one o'clock at a place with a Dublin number, and he needed to know if she had kept it. He was hoping whoever she was to meet would be able to help him. Though Sandy had made this appointment for yesterday in Dublin, yet she had planned to visit Alan in Limerick today. It must have been an important appointment in Dublin in order for her to make the journey over and back.

With shaking hands he dialled the Dublin number Sandy had written. A woman answered quickly, sounding distracted as other phones rang in the background.

'Hello, Scathach House.'

'Hi, I am wondering if you can help me,' Jack said politely. 'I have your phone number written down in my diary and I can't remember why I've made a note to call you.'

'Of course,' she said politely. 'Scathach House is the office of Dr Gregory Burton. Maybe you wanted to make an appointment?'

I woke up in my Dublin bedsit to the shrill sound of a telephone ringing in my ear. I put the pillow over my head and prayed for the noise to stop. I had a terrible hangover. I peeked over the side of my bed and caught a glimpse of my crumpled garda uniform lying in a ball on the ground. I'd worked a late shift and then gone for a few drinks. A few had clearly turned into a few too many and I had absolutely no memory of coming home. The ringing finally stopped and I breathed a sigh of relief, although it echoed in my head for a few seconds longer. And then it started again. I grabbed the phone from the side of the bed and brought it back under the pillow to my ear.

'Hello,' I croaked.

'Happy birthday to yoooou, happy birthday to yoooou, happy birthday, dear Sandeeeee, happy birthday to yooou.' It was my mother singing so sweetly as though she was in a church choir.

'Hip, hip . . .'

'Hooray!' That was Dad.

'Hip, hip . . .'

'Hooray!' He blew a party blower down the receiver, which I instantly held far away from my ear, allowing my arm to hang off the bed. I could still hear them celebrating from under the pillow as I drifted off again.

'Happy twenty-first, honey,' Mum said proudly. 'Honey? Are you there?'

I put the phone back to my ear. 'Thanks, Mum,' I mumbled.

'I wish you'd have let us throw you a party,' she said wistfully. 'It's not every day my baby girl is twenty-one.'

'It is actually,' I said tiredly. 'I have three hundred and sixty-four more days of being twenty-one, so we've lots of time to celebrate.'

'Oh, you know it's not the same.'

'You know what I'm like at those things,' I said, referring to the party idea.

'I know, I know. Well, I want you to enjoy your day. Would you think about coming home for dinner at all? At the weekend, maybe? We could just do a small thing, just me, you and your dad. We won't even mention the birthday word,' she tried.

I paused. 'No, I can't this weekend, sorry. Things are really busy at work,' I lied.

'Oh, OK, well, what about if I come to Dublin for a few hours? I won't even stay over; we can have a coffee or something. A quick chat and I'll be gone, I promise.' She gave a nervous laugh. 'I just want to mark the day with you in some way. I'd love to see you.'

'I can't, Mum, sorry.'

There was a silence. For far too long.

Dad came on the phone cheerily. 'Happy birthday, love. We understand you're busy so we'll let you get back to doing what you were doing.'

'Where's Mum?'

'Oh, she, eh, had to answer the door.' He was as bad at lying as I was.

She was crying, I knew it.

'OK, well, have a great day, honey. Try to enjoy yourself, OK?' he added softly.

'OK,' I said quietly, and the phone clicked and went dead.

I groaned, hung the phone back up on my bedside locker and threw the pillow off my head. I allowed my eyes to adjust to the bright light my cheap curtains were incapable of keeping out. It was ten a.m. on a Monday morning and I finally had a day off. What I was going to do with it, I had no idea. I would have preferred to work on my birthday, although I would busy myself with working on a missing case that had recently run into a dead end. A little girl named Robin Geraghty had disappeared while playing in her front garden. All the signs were implicating her middle-aged neighbour next door in Robin's vanishing. However, no matter how hard we'd dug into this case we weren't hitting the treasure chest at the bottom. Recently I had started following up on such cases by myself, unable to switch off when the file was locked away in a cabinet.

I turned to lie on my back and noticed from the corner of my eye a lump beside me in the bed. The lump was on its side, a tousle of dark brown hair lying on the pillow. I jumped, gathering my bedclothes and wrapped them around me tighter. The lump began to move to face me, his eyes opened. Bloodshot tired eyes.

'I thought you were never going to answer that phone,' he said croakily.

'Who are you?' I asked in disgust, clambering out of bed and taking the covers with me, leaving him lying on the bed spread-eagled and naked. He smiled, rested his hands behind his head sleepily, and winked.

I groaned. It was meant to be a silent, inward groan but it forced its way out of my mouth. 'I'm going to the bathroom and when I get back you will be gone.' I picked up what I assumed were his clothes and threw them onto the bed. I picked up my own stray clothes that were resting on a chair, hugged them close to me and banged the door shut. Almost immediately I returned and grabbed my wallet, much to his disgust. I wasn't about to leave that there.

Not after the last time.

I stayed in the bathroom for as long as I could until Mr Rankin from next door began pounding on the door and telling me and everyone else in the building how he was going to burst an area of his body that I didn't care to think much about. I opened the door immediately and went back to my bedsit, hoping the hairy stranger had vanished. No such luck. He was closing the door behind him.

I walked towards him slowly, not knowing what to say. He didn't seem to know either, but nor did he care, his smirk still on his face.

'Did we . . . ?' I asked.

'Twice.' He winked and my insides churned. 'By the way, before you throw me out of your building, some guy called by when you were in the bathroom. I told him he could wait if he wanted, but you probably wouldn't recognise him when you saw him.' He grinned again.

'What guy?' I racked my brain.

'See, I told him you wouldn't remember him.'

'Is he in there?' I looked to the closed door.

'No, I guess he didn't feel like hanging around a bedsit with a naked hairy man.'

'You answered the door naked?' I asked angrily.

'I thought it was you,' he shrugged. 'Anyway, he left this card for you.' He handed me the business card. 'I don't suppose there's any point in me giving you my number?'

I shook my head, took the card from his hand. 'Thanks, eh . . .' I began weakly.

'Steve.' He held out his hand.

'Nice to meet you,' I smiled, and he laughed. He was kind of cute but still I watched him walk down the stairs.

'We met before, by the way,' he called up, not turning around as he made his way down the steps.

I was silent while I tried to remember.

'At Louise Drummond's Christmas party last year?' He stopped and looked up hopefully.

I frowned.

'Ah, it doesn't matter.' He waved his hand dismissively. 'You didn't remember the next morning then, either.' He smiled and was gone.

There was a moment of guilt until I remembered the business card in my hand and the bad feelings vanished. My knees went weak when I saw the name.

It seemed Mr Burton had set up a clinic in Dublin – Scathach House on Leeson Street. Wait a minute – *Dr* Burton; he'd passed his exams at last.

I danced around excitedly on the spot. I heard the toilet flush and Mr Rankin left the toilet with a paper in his hand and caught me dancing.

'You need to go again? I wouldn't go back in there for a while.' He wafted the newspaper.

I ignored him and went back into my bedsit. Mr Burton was here now. He'd found me three years after I'd moved away and that's all that mattered. At last one odd sock had showed up.

26

'Oh, Dr Burton.' Jack sat up in the car seat and pressed the phone closer to his ear. 'I remember why I'd made a note of it now. Actually, it's not me that I'm enquiring about. It's about a friend of mine who had an appointment yesterday with Dr . . .' He stopped, already forgetting the surname.

'Burton,' the secretary finished for him and he could hear another phone ringing in the background. 'I'm sorry, could you just hold for a moment, please, sir?'

'Yes.' Jack waited and listened to Duran Duran playing over the phone while he tried to formulate some sort of a plan. He scribbled Dr Gregory Burton's name and address into his notebook. Later he would go through Sandy's missed calls, received calls and dialled numbers that her phone had recorded over the last few days and he would try to piece together where she had gone, even if it meant ringing everyone in her phonebook.

The secretary returned on the line. 'I'm sorry, it's very busy here today. How can I help you?'

'I was wondering if you could tell me whether my friend Sandy Shortt showed up for her appointment yesterday?'

'I'm sorry, Mr . . . ?'

Jack thought fast. 'Le Bon.' Not fast enough. *Le Bon?*

'I'm sorry, Mr Le Bon, but we can't give out information about our clients.'

'Oh, of course you can't, I understand that, but I'm not looking for any personal information. My friend has been terribly sick lately but she has been afraid to do anything about it in case it's more serious than she anticipates. It's her stomach; it's been giving her trouble for months. I made an appointment for her and she says she went to Dr Burton yesterday but I'm afraid she's lying to us all. The family are all so worried. Could you at least just let us know if she arrived for the appointment? I'm not asking for any personal details.'

'You're enquiring about Sandy Shortt?'

He sat back relieved. 'Yes, Sandy,' he replied happily. 'Her appointment was for one o'clock.'

'I see, well, I'm afraid I can't help you as this is not a medical clinic, Mr Le Bon. It's a counselling centre, so you can't have made the appointment for her regarding stomach problems. Is there anything else I can help you with?' Her voice was firm, angry even.

'Em,' Jack's face was red with embarrassment, 'no.'

'Thank you for calling.' She hung up.

He stared in embarrassment at the appointment made for one o'clock in Sandy's diary. Suddenly Sandy's mobile phone began ringing and the name 'Gregory B' flashed up on the screen. Jack's heart thumped like a drum. He ignored the ring tone, relieved when it finally stopped and beeped to signal a message. He picked up the phone and dialled into her messaging service.

'Hi, Sandy. Gregory here. I've tried calling you a few times but there's no answer. I presume you've gone wandering the deep abyss again. I was just calling to let you know that a man named . . .' he moved his mouth away from the phone, 'Carol, what was his name?'

Jack heard the secretary's voice saying, 'Mr Le Bon.'

'Right, yeah.' Gregory came back on the phone. 'A Mr Le Bon – I assume that's not his real name –' he laughed, 'rang our offices looking for you. He was wondering if you'd made your appointment yesterday for your *stomach* problem?' His voice got quieter. 'Just be careful, OK? I don't suppose there's any chance you've considered getting a real job yet, waitressing or something. There's little chance nuts would be chasing you then. You could go door-to-door, selling bibles; in fact a nice woman dressed head to toe in tweed called to my door last night, which quite obviously made me immediately think of you, so I took her card. Think about calling her. It's a fine uplifting card with Our Lord looking miserable on the Cross. And it's recycled paper, so she really must care,' he laughed again. 'Anyway, if you don't think you could endure the tweed, get a nine-to-five. I don't know if you've heard of it, it's this thing that people do. It allows them to have a life outside of work hours. That's "life", L-I-F-E; you can look it up in your dictionary when you get the chance. Anyway . . .' he sighed and was quiet for a while as if deciding what to say, or more likely he knew exactly what to say and was deciding whether to say it or not. Jack knew that silence well. 'Right,' his voice suddenly got louder and more businesslike. 'Talk to you soon.'

Knuckles rapping loudly on the glass of the passenger side of the car caused Jack to jump and drop the phone. He looked up to see Alan's mother, a round-faced frump of a woman, glaring in the window. He leaned over and rolled down the window.

'Hello, Mrs O'Connor.'

'Who's that?' She scrunched up her face and stuck her head in the window. Wiry hairs escaped from her jawline. Her false teeth unclamped themselves from her gums and moved around in her mouth as she spoke. 'Do I know you?' she shouted, spit landing on Jack's lip.

'Yes, Mrs O'Connor.' He wiped his lip and raised his voice, knowing she had bad hearing. 'I'm Jack Ruttle, Donal's brother.'

'Merciful hour, baby Donal's brother. What are you doing sitting out here? Get out and let me have a look at you.'

She shuffled away in maroon-coloured velvet

slippers, her jaw moving as she looked him up and down, teeth sloshing around in her mouth. She was dressed in the same outfit she appeared to have been wearing since the forties. 'Make Do and Mend' had always been a part of the O'Connors' way of life, recycling textiles around the house to clothe the twelve children she had reared without their father, who came for one thing and left when he got it. Jack remembered Alan coming on a day out with Donal when they were kids, wearing white shorts made from pillowcases. Donal never seemed to care, refusing to mock his friend as the other kids did. Not that Alan endured the taunts, instead choosing to knock the bejaysus out of anyone who even looked at him the wrong way. But he protected Donal from everyone, and his friend's disappearance had hit him particularly hard.

'Com'ere to me, aren't ya all grown up?' She rubbed Jack's hands and tousled his hair as though he had just reached adolescence that very day. 'You're the image of your father, God rest his soul,' she blessed herself.

'Thank you, Mrs O'Connor. You look great too,' he lied.

'Ah, I don't,' she waved her hand dismissively and began to shuffle back towards her ground-floor flat in the high-rise building. Two bedrooms and twelve kids – he wondered how she had managed it. No wonder Alan had spent so much time in the Ruttles' house, being satiated with food by Jack's mother.

'Is Alan here? I came to talk to him.'

'No he's not. He finally moved in with that young wan. In a house now, wouldn't you know. He's only with her because of the house but she only gets it because of her kid, mind you. Fancy houses they get nowadays, the single mothers. I had nothin' like it in my day – not that I was single but I was as good as and all the better for it,' she continued, shuffling to her door.

Jack laughed. Alan was always involved in something, landing on his feet no matter what the circumstances. Donal had named him 'The Cat'.

'I won't disturb you, Mrs O'Connor. I'll go over to Alan at the house, if that's OK.'

'You think he done something wrong?' She looked worried.

'Not to me, anyway,' Jack smiled, and she nodded, relief written all over her hard face.

Alan must have received a phone call from his mother as he was outside in the driveway waiting. He looked thin – thinner than usual – and his face was pale and drawn, paler and more drawn than usual. But didn't they all; hadn't everyone and everything been affected by Donal's disappearance? It was as if, when he left the chipper that night, bumping against the doorframes in his drunken state, he had managed to bump the earth off its axis, causing it to swirl at top speed in the wrong direction on the wrong path. Everything felt out of place.

They greeted one another with a hug. Alan immediately began to cry and Jack fought the urge to join him. Instead he stiffened, allowing the younger man to weep on his shoulder, swallowing back the swelling in his throat, blinking back the tears and trying to focus on everything around him that was real and that he could touch, everything except Donal.

They sat in the living room. Alan's hands shook as he tapped ash from his cigarette into one of the empty beer cans piled alongside the couch. The room was deathly silent; Jack wished they could put on the television as a background distraction.

'I came here to see if a woman had called by today. She's helping me out with looking for Donal.'

Alan's face brightened. 'Yeah?'

'She just wanted to ask you questions about the night – you know, go back over everything again.'

'I've been through that a million times with the guards, and a million times every day with myself.' Alan inhaled deeply on his cigarette and his nicotine-stained fingers rubbed his eyes wearily.

'I know, but it's good to have a fresh eye and ear go

over everything again. Maybe there's something they missed.'

'Maybe,' he said in a small voice, but Jack doubted he believed that. He doubted there was any moment of that night that Alan hadn't analysed, over-analysed and then dissected all over again. To tell him there might be something he was forgetting must surely be an insult.

'She didn't call by?'

Alan shook his head. 'I've been here all day, was here all day yesterday and I'll be here all day tomorrow too,' he said angrily.

'What happened to that last job of yours?'

He made a face and Jack knew not to ask any more questions.

'Do me a favour will you?' Jack handed Alan his phone. 'Ring this number and make an appointment for me with Dr Burton. I don't want them to recognise my voice.'

Alan being Alan didn't ask any questions. 'Hi, I want to make an appointment with Dr Burton,' he said, opening another beer can.

He raised his eyebrows and looked at Jack. 'Yeah, for a counselling session.'

Jack nodded.

'When do I want the appointment?' he repeated the secretary's question, looking at Jack.

'As soon as they can,' Jack whispered.

'As soon as you can,' Alan repeated. He listened and looked at Jack. 'Next month?'

Jack shook his head wildly.

'No, I need it sooner than that. My head is really messed up, you never know what I might do.'

Jack rolled his eyes.

Seconds later he hung up. 'You got a cancellation for noon on Thursday.'

'Thursday?' Jack asked, jumping up from his chair as though moving now would get him there on time.

'Well, you said as soon as possible,' Alan said, handing him back the phone. 'Has that got anything to do with finding Donal, by any chance?'

Jack thought about it. 'In a way, yeah.'

'I hope you find him, Jack.' His eyes filled up again. 'I keep going back over that night again and again, wishing I'd left with him. I really thought he'd be OK getting a taxi down that way, you know?' His eyes looked tortured and his hand shook. Around his feet on the floor lay sprinkles of ash he constantly flicked off with his nicotine-stained thumb.

'You weren't to know,' Jack comforted him. 'It's not your fault.'

'I hope you find him,' Alan repeated, opening another can of beer and slugging it down.

Jack left him sitting there in the silence of the empty house, staring into space, knowing he was rethinking and reliving that night all over again, looking for the vital piece of evidence they had all missed. It was all they could do.

27

Missing person number one, Orla Keane, entered the great Community Hall, the light shining in from the open door spotlighting her presence. She stopped at the entrance, trying to get her bearings, looking like Alice in Wonderland who had just swallowed an 'Eat Me' beside the monstrous oak door. I cleared my throat nervously and its amplified sound bounced off the walls, raced to the ceilings and back down again like a ping-pong ball let loose. She turned to where I had made the noise and began to make her way towards me, high heels on the wooden floor echoing loudly.

Joan and Helena had set up a table for me to sit behind on the far side of the room and, much to Joan's disappointment, they stepped outside to give me privacy. As Orla walked towards me, I felt star struck. I couldn't believe that this person had stepped out of my 'Missing' photographs and was now a living, breathing person walking directly towards me.

'Hello,' she smiled, her Cork accent still strong, despite her time here.

'Hello.' My voice came out as a whisper. I cleared my throat and tried again. I looked down at the list of names on the table before me. I would have to do this twelve times today, and then again with Joan and Bernard. The thought of seeing all these people thrilled me but the idea of having to discuss such delicate topics so subtly, was draining me already. I had asked Helena earlier once again why on earth it was that I couldn't just let everybody know without having to carry out this charade.

'Sandy,' she had said so firmly that I needn't have even heard a reason. 'When people want to get home they get desperate. For them to learn that you found your way here while looking for them would cause them to believe that they can leave with you. Life wouldn't be worth living here with a few hundred people trailing your every move.'

She had a point. So here I was, playing the role of casting agent and owner of an acting agency, about to wind a conversation about every member of their family and friends into a Hamlet soliloquy.

I had had one more question for Helena. 'Do you think that I *can* lead the people out of here and bring them home?' I had been wondering if that was my purpose for being here, because I was convinced I wasn't staying. The typical victim belief: this can't happen to me, not me of all people.

She smiled sadly and once again I needn't have heard her response because her face said it all. 'Sorry, Moses, I don't think so.' But before I dissolved completely she quickly added, 'But I think you are here for a reason and that reason is, right now, to share your stories with everyone, to tell them about their families and how much they're missed. That's your way of bringing them home.'

I looked up at Orla, who was sitting before me, anxiously awaiting my next move. It was time to bring her home.

She was twenty-six years old now and she looked like she'd hardly changed at all. Nearly six years had passed since she had gone missing. Six years I'd spent looking for her. I knew her parents' names were Clara and Jim and they had divorced two years ago. I knew she had two sisters, Ruth and Lorna, and a brother, James. Her best friends were Laura, and Rebecca, who was also known as 'Fly' due to her regular forgetfulness to zip up her fly. Orla was studying art history at

Cork University when she went missing. Her debs dress was purple, and the scar across her left eyebrow was from when she'd fallen off her bike on holiday in Bantry when she was eight. She lost her virginity when she was fifteen at a house party, to Niall Kennedy, the guy who worked at the local video store, and she secretly crashed her parents' car when they were away for a week in Spain but had it repaired on time and they still don't know it to this day. Her favourite colour is lilac, she loves pop music, played the piano until she was fourteen, had secretly dreamed of becoming a ballet dancer since the age of six yet never once took a class, and she had been here for five and three-quarter years.

I looked at her and didn't know where to start. 'So, Orla, tell me a bit about yourself.'

I watched her as though in a trance, watched as the lips I'd seen only in photographs opened and closed, her face animated, *alive*, and I listened to her words. The singsong tone of her Cork accent, the way her long blonde hair moved as she spoke. I was enthralled.

When she got to the part about studying in college I saw my chance to jump in. 'Art history in Cork University?' I repeated. 'I know someone who studied the same year as you.'

'Who?' She almost jumped off her seat.

'Rebecca Grey.'

Her mouth dropped open. 'No way! Rebecca Grey is one of my best friends!'

'Really?' I noticed everything was still in the present. Rebecca was still her best friend.

'Yeah! That's so weird, how do you know her?'

'Oh, I met her brother Enda a few times. He's friends with friends of mine – you know how it is.'

'What's he doing now?'

'Actually, last time I saw him was at his wedding a few months ago. I think I may have met your mum and dad there too.'

She was silent for a moment and when she spoke

again her voice was hushed and shaking. 'How are they?'

'Oh, they were in great form, I was talking to one of your sisters – Lorna, I think.'

'Yes, Lorna!'

'She was telling me that she got engaged.'

'To Steven?' She bounced up and down on her seat, clapping her hands excitedly.

'Yes,' I smiled, 'to Steven.'

'Oh, I knew she'd take him back,' she laughed with tears in her eyes.

'Your older sister was there with her husband. She was heavily pregnant, I noticed.'

'Oh.' A tear fell from her eye and she quickly wiped it away. 'What else? Who else did you see? Did my mum and dad say anything? What did they look like?'

And so I brought her home.

A half-hour had passed and Joan coughed rather loudly to let me know another audition applicant had arrived. We hadn't even noticed Joan enter the hall and I looked at my wrist to check the time, forgetting that my watch was still lying somewhere on the road leading out of the village. The familiar feeling of irritation scratched at my body as I thought of it being somewhere yet not being able to find it. I looked up to see the next person I was due to meet – Carol Dempsey, nervously wringing her hands as she stood by Joan – and my irritation disappeared. I became scared all over again.

'I'm sorry, our time is up,' I said to Orla.

Her face fell and I knew she had all of a sudden been whisked away from home and transported and plonked back to the reality of where she was.

'But I haven't even auditioned,' she panicked.

'It's OK, you've got the part,' I whispered, and winked.

Her face lit up as she stood, leaned over and grasped my hand in both of hers. 'Thank you, thank you so much.'

I watched her leave with Helena, Orla's head awash with a million new thoughts of stories from home. So much to think about now: new thoughts and new memories all raising new questions and a new longing for home.

Carol sat before me. A mother of three, housewife, from Donegal, forty-two years old and a member of the local choir, who went missing while on her way back from choir practice four years ago. She had passed her driving test a week before her disappearance, her husband had celebrated his forty-fifth birthday with the family the night before and her youngest daughter's school play was opening the following week. I looked at her mouse-like face, timid and shy, her brown limp hair tucked behind pink ears, a purse clasped in her hands on her lap, and I instantly wanted to take her home.

'So, Carol,' I said gently, 'why don't we start off by you just telling me a bit about yourself?'

Later in the day we all sat around in a circle in the grand Community Hall. I faced the stage and the thousands of handprints decorating the backdrop. 'Strength and Hope', I repeated to myself. Strength and hope had got me through today; I was still on a high from meeting my idols but knew I would quickly become drained. As usual, as soon as everybody had taken their places, I had chosen to stand back and observe, outside of the circle. Old habits die hard. Helena had called out to me and the chorus of fifteen other voices joined in, coercing me to sit down. I took a seat, aware that I was joining a group, something I had run from doing all of my life. I slowly sat down, all the time battling with my legs, which wanted to run out of the door, and my mouth, which wanted to make an excuse to leave.

After I had spoken to everybody individually, Helena had come up with the idea of everybody getting to know one another better by sharing the experiences of where and when they had gone missing. She was calling it a team-building workshop all to help the production but I knew she was really doing it for me, to help me with my continuous search for understanding where we all are and how we got here.

One by one the people explained how they had arrived here. It was an emotional experience. Some had been here only a few years, others over a decade, yet the realisation of never returning home was still raw. There were tears from many, as usual, but none from me. It was as though by the time my tears worked their way from my heart to my eyes, they had evaporated and drifted into the air as sad vapours instead. I was fascinated to hear what had happened after they left the scenes that I had examined so many times and arrived here. It was all so simple. I had followed unnecessary routes, suspected all the wrong people, scrutinised every single inch of the road they were last seen on. It was pointless because all they did was wander off here.

While it was painful for the missing, knowing that they wouldn't be returning home, it was a lot better than the alternative. I wished Jenny-May Butler was here, I wished Donal Ruttle was here, I wished the others on my list and the thousands of others that go missing every year were here. I prayed that harm hadn't come to Jenny-May. I prayed that, if it had, it had been quick and painless. But mostly I prayed that she was here.

I was captivated as I watched all of these people. I was a stranger to them but they were best friends to me. I had so many stories of theirs I wanted to tell them, that I knew and understood and had laughed at and could identify with. There were so many people they knew that I wanted to tell them I'd met and laughed with. There were situations that I knew they'd been in that I wanted to tell them I shared. The complete opposite to how I was in life. I wanted to join in, swap stories and belong.

There was a silence and I realised all eyes were on me.

'Well?' Helena asked, adjusting her lemon pashmina around her shoulders.

'Well, what?' I asked, looking around in confusion.

'Aren't you going to tell us your story of arriving here?'

I felt like telling them I'd been here long before them all. But I didn't. Instead I politely excused myself from the hall.

Later that night I sat in the eatery at a quiet table with Helena and Joseph. Candles flickered on every table, bird-of-paradise flowers sat in small tin buckets in the centre. We had just finished a starter of wild mushroom soup and piping hot brown bread, and I sat back in my chair, already full, and awaited my main course. The eatery was quiet on this Wednesday night, people choosing to go to bed before their early starts at work the next day. Each of the people taking part in the production had been granted time off from their work, their involvement in the arts seen by the council to be enough. We were to spend all day every day rehearsing in order to meet the deadline of next Sunday, when Helena had already assured the cast and community the dress rehearsal would be. This was a task that seemed highly ambitious and entirely unrealistic in my eyes, yet Helena assured me that people here threw themselves into their work and were highly productive. But what did I know?

I looked at my wrist for the millionth time since I'd lost my watch and sighed with frustration.

'I have to find my watch.'

'Don't worry,' Helena smiled. 'It's not like being at home, Sandy; things don't just go missing.'

'I know, I know, you keep telling me that, but if that's so, well then, where is it?'

'Wherever you dropped it,' she laughed, and shook her head at me like I was a child.

Joseph, I noticed, didn't smile but changed the subject altogether. 'What kind of play will you do?' he asked in his deep soothing tones.

I laughed, 'We have no idea. Helena managed to steer the conversation away from talk of what the actual play would be every time someone asked. I don't mean to rain on your parade but I think a week is an entirely implausible amount of time to rehearse and perfect a play.'

'It will be a short one,' Helena said defensively.

'What about scripts and costumes and whatever else is needed?' I asked, suddenly realising the extent of what we would have to do.

'Don't worry about all of that, Sandy.' She turned to Joseph. 'There's the belief at home that old theatres are haunted because costumes and make-up are always reported or rumoured to go missing. Well, it's true, they do go missing but it's not due to ghosts, not of the pilfering kind, anyway, because the finest costumes show up here daily. Bobby will have everything we need,' she said calmly.

'She has thought this all through.' Joseph smiled affectionately at his wife.

'Oh, the thinking is all finished, dear. It has already been decided. We are going to stage *The Wizard of Oz*,' Helena said grandly and proudly, swirling her red wine and taking a sip.

I started laughing.

'Why is it funny?' Joseph asked, amused.

'It's *The Wizard of Oz*,' I stressed. 'It's not a play, it's a musical! It's what children do in school shows. I thought you'd come up with something a bit more cultured, like a Beckett play or O'Casey,' I argued. 'But *The Wizard of Oz . . .* ?' I wrinkled my nose.

'My, my, I think we have a snob on our hands.' Helena tried not to smile.

'I'm not aware of this *Wizard of Oz*.' Joseph looked confused.

I gasped. 'Neglected child.'

'It's not something that was shown all the time in Watamu,' Helena reminded me. 'And if you hadn't left rehearsals so early today, Sandy, you would have learned that we are not doing a musical version. It is an adaptation written many years ago by Dennis O'Shea, a fine Irish playwright who has been here for two years. He heard about what we were doing and brought it to me this morning. I thought it was perfect and so it has already been cast and the first few scenes blocked. Mind you, I had to tell them that it was you that had made the decision.'

'You cast them in *The Wizard of Oz*?' I said, totally unimpressed.

'What is it about?' Joseph asked, intrigued.

'Sandy, you do the honours,' Helena said.

'OK, well, it's a *children*'s movie,' I stressed to Helena, 'made in the thirties about a little girl called Dorothy Gale who is swept away in a tornado to a magical land. Once there she embarks on a quest to see the wizard, who can help her return home. It's ridiculous to ask a group of adults to do it,' I laughed, but realised no one was laughing with me.

'And this wizard, does he help her?'

'Yes,' I said slowly, feeling it odd the story was being taken so seriously. 'The wizard helps her and she learns that she could have returned home all the time, all she had to do was tap her ruby heels together and say, "There's no place like home, there's no place like home."'

He still didn't laugh. 'So she returns home in the end?'

There was a silence and I finally understood why. I nodded slowly.

'And what does she do while she's in this magical land?'

'She helps her friends,' I said quietly.

'It doesn't seem such a silly story to me,' Joseph said seriously. 'One the people here will very much like to see.'

I thought about that. In fact, I thought about it all night, until I was dreaming of ruby slippers and tornadoes and of talking lions and houses that fell on witches, until the phrase 'There's no place like home' was echoing so loudly and continuously in my head that I woke up saying it aloud and I was afraid to go back to sleep.

28

I stared up at the ceiling, at the point right above my head where the white paint had bubbled and cracked over the wood. The moon was sitting perfectly framed in the window of the family room I was sleeping in. Blue light cast through the glass, causing an exact reflection of its window squares to appear on the chunky wooden table. There was no moon in the window on the table, I noticed, just a ghostly reflection of pale blue.

I was wide awake now. I felt for my wrist to check the time and remembered again my watch was gone. My heart started to pound as it always did when something of mine was missing; I would immediately become restless and ache to start looking. My hunts were like an addiction, the feeling pre-search like a craving. A part of me was possessed and became obsessed with not resting until my belongings were found. There was very little anybody could do when I was in that mode, there was very little that could be said or done to cause me to screech in my tracks. The people with me always used to tell me it was lonely for them when I left them like that all of a sudden. Everybody I was with was always the victim; didn't they know that it was lonely for me too?

'But the *pen* is not your missing object,' Gregory would always say to me.

'Yes it is,' I would grumble, while rooting in my bag, nose practically touching the bottom.

'No it's not. When you search you are trying to fulfil

a *feeling*. Whether you have the pen or not is completely irrelevant, Sandy.'

'It is not irrelevant,' I would shout back. 'If I have no pen, well then, how can I write down what you are about to tell me?'

He reached into the inside pocket of his jacket and handed me a pen. 'Here.'

'But that isn't *my* pen.'

He would sigh and smile as he always did. 'This idea of searching for lost things is a *distraction*—'

'Distraction, distraction, distraction, distraction. Never mind me; *you* are obsessed with saying that word. You saying the word "distraction" is *your* distraction from saying anything else,' I spluttered angrily.

'Let me finish,' he said sternly.

I stopped rooting immediately and listened to him, feigning interest.

'This idea of searching for lost things is a distract—' he stopped himself, 'is a way of avoiding dealing with something else that's lost in your life *within you*. Now shall we start searching for what that is?'

'A-ha!' I smiled, happily extracting my pen from the bottom of my bag. 'Found it!'

Unfortunately for Gregory, the craving never reared its ugly head anytime we would try to search within me.

If there had been a ten-foot wall surrounding the house I would have scaled it. There was no barrier to my search scenes; all they did was become invisible hurdles. Gregory did have one good thing to say about my searching and that was that he had never seen stamina and determination quite like it. And then he ruined the compliment by saying what a pity it was that I didn't pump that energy into other areas of my life. Still, somewhere in his comment I sensed praise.

The clock on the family-room wall read 03.45. I threw back the covers in the deathly silent house and began rummaging through Barbara Langley's suitcase of eighties nightmare clothes. I settled on a black and white sailor-style top, black drainpipe jeans and flat black pumps. All I needed was an armful of bracelets, hoop earrings and backcombed hair and I'd be dancing to 'The Time Warp'. But then, I already was.

Joseph and Helena seemed so sure that my watch wasn't lost, they seemed so confident that nothing could leave this place. I had to find out. I slipped out of the house silently so as not to wake the family. Outside, the weather was mild. I felt as if I was walking around a toy village in the snowy mountains of Switzerland: little wooden chalets with window boxes, and candles in the windows to help light the way and welcome new wanderers. All was quiet outside. The crackling and the snapping of branches could be heard from the forest as people made their way to the village for the first time. People who'd probably found themselves there during an innocent walk to the shop or a stroll home from the pub. I felt safe in the village, protected by people intent on picking up from where they left off and moving on.

I walked out of the village, following the dusty road that led alongside the fields. The sun was rising over the trees in the distance, casting orange hues over the blue light, like a giant orange squeezing its colourful juice over the villages, the trees, the mountains and fields, and allowing the liquid light to flow like a stream down the pathways.

In the distance I saw a figure rising and stooping in the centre of the road. He stood up and his height and physique revealed him to be Joseph. His figure was jet-black against the rising sun, which was the giant orange sitting at the top of the road, looking like it was about to roll down to us, squashing all in its path. I was just about to approach him when he got down on his hands and knees and began brushing the dusty floor. I jumped into the woods and hid behind a tree, watching him. He'd beaten me to it; I realised he was searching for my watch.

Torchlight flashed through the trees and made its way towards me. I quickly ducked, wondering where on earth it was coming from. Joseph stopped what he was doing to look up at the light. It disappeared, he continued searching and I continued to watch him, wanting to see what he would do when he came upon the watch. But he didn't find it. After an hour of very determined searching, I think Gregory would agree, Joseph finally rose to his feet, placed his hands on his hips, shook his head and sighed.

A chill ran through me. It wasn't there, I *knew* it.

Before Jack went home on Wednesday night he returned to the estuary to see if Sandy's car had upped and gone over the past twenty-four hours.

Gloria had been delighted to learn that he was planning on seeing a psychiatrist, although she was a little confused to say the least as to why he had to travel to Dublin for a session. Still, he hadn't seen her so happy in a long time and it showed him how bad he must have been lately. He could almost hear her thinking and planning wedding, babies, christenings and who knows what else, as he told her. However, she was misguided in thinking the counselling was directly for him. He had no intention of wanting to be cured of wanting to find his brother. To him it was no sickness.

It was dark outside, pitch-black among the trees down by the Shannon Estuary, where owls hooted and creatures moved around in the undergrowth. He took his emergency flashlight out of his car and, as he switched it on, he saw various startled glowing eyes freeze and then dash back into the bushes. Sandy's Ford Fiesta was in its place, untouched since he'd last been there. He shone the light around the trees, at the laneway that led further along the estuary. A pleasant walk for bird-watchers and nature lovers or a jogging path for Sandy? He walked towards it, deeper into the forest where he had looked so many times over the last few days. His inexperience had previously led him to look out for footprints, as if they would be any help to him. He walked further, enjoying seeing creatures leap out of the line of the light into the distance, and he shone the light up into the trees and watched as it found its way up to the sky.

A trail appeared on his left. He stopped walking and immediately stopped trying to work out what was niggling at him. He'd never noticed that trail before. He shone the light up the trail: more trees and blackness were at the end. He shuddered and moved the light away again with the intention of returning in the light of day to wander up the track. As he shone the torch in another direction, shining metal caught his eye and disappeared again. He quickly searched around with the light, afraid whatever it was would vanish. His eye fell upon a silver watch, lying among the long grass beside the trail to his left. He bent to pick it up with his heart thumping in his chest, an image suddenly appearing in his mind.

It was the memory of Sandy bending to pick up her watch in the garage a few mornings ago.

29

'Hello. I hope I've called the correct number for Mary Stanley.' Jack spoke to the answer-phone service. 'My name is Jack Ruttle. You don't know me but I've been trying to get in touch with Sandy Shortt, whom I know you were recently in contact with. I know this seems like a strange phone call but if you hear from her or have any idea where she has gone, could you please contact me on the following number . . .'

Jack sighed and tried another number. All around him on this sunny day in Dublin, people were lying out on the grass of St Stephen's Green. Ducks were waddling around his bench, searching for bits of bread people had dropped while feeding them. They quacked, pecked and hopped back into the glistening water, distracting him momentarily. After spending over an hour trying to find his way around Dublin city's one-way system, and then being stuck in traffic jams, he'd finally managed to find a parking space around St Stephen's Green. He had an hour to spare before his session with Dr Burton, something he was growing increasingly nervous about. Jack wasn't good at discussing his feelings with anyone at the best of times, never mind an entire hour of searching his brain for pretend worries with a psychiatrist, all just to find information about Sandy Shortt. Columbo he was not, and he was growing tired of trying to find backward ways of getting answers.

He had been ringing through the list on Sandy's phonebook all morning, leaving messages with all those who had contacted her over the past few days and those she had made appointments with in previous weeks. He wasn't getting anywhere. So far he'd left six voice messages, he'd spoken to two people who were extremely guarded about giving any information out, and he'd listened for far too long to her fuming landlord, who seemed more upset about not being paid yet that month than where Sandy was.

'Let me warn you now, sonny, before she breaks your heart,' he'd growled, 'unless you want to be hanging around for days on end, waiting for her, then I suggest you cut your ties with her now. You're not the only one, I can tell you that.' He'd laughed heartily. 'Don't be fooled by her. She brings them back all the time, thinking none of us hear her. I'm right above; I hear her comings and goings, if you'll pardon the pun. You mark my words; she'll turn up here in a few days wondering what all the fuss was about, probably thinking she was gone for two hours instead of two weeks. She does it all the time. But if you do see her before then, tell her to get that money to me a.s.a.p. or she'll be turfed out on her arse.'

Jack sighed. If he was going to give up, now was the time to do it. But he couldn't. Here he was in Dublin, a few minutes away from meeting someone he imagined knew more about what went on in Sandy's head than anybody else. He didn't want to pack it all in and head home to . . . nothing. His idea of Sandy was changing. Through their conversations on the phone he had painted a picture of her in his mind: organised, businesslike, in love with her job, chatty, personable. The more he dug around into her life the more that image of her altered. She was still all of those things, but more. She was becoming more real to him. This wasn't a phantom he was chasing; she was a real, complex, layered person, no longer just the helpful stranger he'd spoken to on the phone. Maybe Garda Turner was right, maybe she'd just had enough and was hiding from the world for a while, but that was something her counsellor would surely know.

Just as he was about to dial another number, his phone rang.

'Is that Jack?' a woman asked quietly.

'Yes,' he replied. 'Who is this?'

'This is Mary Stanley. You left a message on my phone about Sandy Shortt.'

'Oh, yes, Mary, hello. Thank you so much for returning my call. It was a peculiar message, I know.'

'Yes . . .' She was guarded, just as the others had been; unsure of this strange man who was looking for their friend without any viable reason whatsoever.

'You can trust me, Mary. I mean no harm to Sandy. I don't know how well you know her, if you're a relative or friend, but let me explain myself first.' He told the story of how he contacted Sandy, arranged to meet her, passed her at the petrol station, and since had lost contact with her. He left out the reason for his meeting her, feeling that wasn't relevant. 'I don't want to raise any alarm bells,' he continued, 'but I've been ringing around people she seems to have maintained close contact with, just to see if they've seen or heard from her lately.'

'I received a phone call from a Garda Graham Turner this morning,' Mary said, and Jack wasn't sure if it was a question or a statement. It was probably both.

'Yes, I contacted him. I'm concerned for Sandy.' Jack had called Garda Turner that morning and told him about discovering Sandy's watch, hoping that would make him sit up and take notice. It obviously had.

'I'm worried too,' Mary said, and Jack's ears pricked to attention.

'How did he know to call you?' Jack asked, meaning, who are you? How do you know Sandy?

'Who else was on your call list?' she asked, ignoring his question, sounding lost in thought.

He flicked open his notepad. 'Peter Dempsey, Clara Keane, Ailish O'Brien, Tony Watts – do you want me to keep going?'

'No, that's enough. You got your hands on a list of Sandy's?'

'She left her phone and diary behind. They were the only ways I could look for her.' Jack tried not to sound guilty.

'Did somebody you know go missing?' Her tone wasn't soft but it wasn't harsh either. He was taken aback by the question, asked so directly, as though missing people happened all the time.

'Yes, my brother Donal.' A lump swelled in Jack's throat every time he mentioned his brother.

'Donal Ruttle – yes, that's right. I remember reading that in the paper,' she said, and was quiet again in thought. 'All those you've mentioned are people whose family members have gone missing,' Mary explained, 'including me. My son, Bobby, has been gone for three years.'

'I'm very sorry,' Jack said softly. It would make sense that all of Sandy's recent contacts were work-related; he had yet to come across any friends of hers.

'Oh, don't be sorry. It's not your fault. So let me get this straight: we all enlisted Sandy to help us find our loved ones and now you're enlisting us to help you find Sandy?'

Even though Jack was on the phone, his face pinked. 'Yes, I guess so.'

'Well, whether the others have replied to you yet or not, I don't care. I'll speak for them. You can count us all in. Sandy's very special to us all; we'll do everything we can to help find her. The quicker we find her, the quicker she can find my Bobby.'

They were Jack's thoughts exactly.

Unable to sleep for the remainder of the night, I lay awake pondering the whereabouts of my watch. My head was dizzy with possibilities, for after finding myself here, there were now a plethora of places I could imagine it inhabiting. Just as I was picturing a world where watches ate, slept and married one another, with grandfather clocks as heads of state, pocket watches as the intellects, waterproof watches that inhabited the waters, diamond watches the aristocracy, and digital watches the mere workers, Joseph's creeping into the house stopped me. I had observed him for what I guessed was a further hour walking up and down the road, looking wide-eyed and fierce in his attempts to find my watch. I now knew what I looked like during my searches, focused and in the zone, completely unaware of all life around, particularly oblivious to a person hiding behind a tree not far away.

A half-hour after I'd returned to my bed, Joseph made his way quietly, but not quietly enough, into the house. I pressed my ear to the wall as I tried to hear the mumblings between him and Helena in the room next to me. The timber was warm against my cheek and I closed my eyes momentarily, hit by a pang of homesickness and a longing for the warm heaving chest I used to rest my head upon in bed. Then there was silence and, feeling like a caged lion, I decided to slip out of the house before anybody stirred again.

Outside, the market stalls were being set up for another busy day of trading. There was the colourful sound of banter mixed with birdsong, laughter, shouting as crates and boxes were being unpacked and stacked. I closed my eyes, hit by my second longing for home that day, and imagined myself as a child walking hand in hand with my mother through the organic farmers' markets in the Market Yard in Carrick-on-Shannon, the scintillating smell of the fruit and vegetables, so ripe and colourful, enticing everybody to touch, smell and taste. I opened my eyes again and was back here.

I arrived outside the Lost and Found building and noticed how the carvings on this building were more colourful and playful: two odd socks, one yellow and pink polka dot and the other purple and orange stripes. I stood thinking of Gregory and me at my final goodbye dance at school, and I laughed. A face appeared in the window, a very familiar face, and I immediately stopped laughing, feeling as though I'd seen a ghost. He was young – nineteen by now, if I calculated correctly. He gave me a cheeky grin, waved and disappeared from the window, and appeared at the now open door like the Cheshire cat. So this was the Bobby from Lost and Found that Helena and Wanda had mentioned.

'Hello.' He leaned against the doorframe with his shoulder, crossed one leg over the other and held out his two hands. 'Welcome to Lost and Found.'

I laughed. 'Hello, Mr Stanley.'

His eyes narrowed at my knowing his name, but his smile widened. 'And you are?'

'Sandy.' I'd heard he was a character, always acting the joker. I had watched countless home videos of him performing for the camera from age six all the way up to sixteen just before his disappearance. 'You were on my list,' I explained, 'for auditions yesterday, and you didn't show up.'

'Ah!' Realisation dawned on him yet he still continued to study me curiously. 'I've heard about you.' He stopped leaning against the doorframe and coolly made his way down the steps with his hands in his pockets. He stopped directly in front of me, folded his arms, then placed one hand to his chin and began to circle me slowly.

I laughed. 'What have you heard about me?'

He paused behind me and I twisted my upper body around to him. 'They say you know things.'

'They do?'

'They do,' he repeated, and continued strolling around me. When he had come full circle he stopped and folded his arms again, twinkles dancing in his blue eyes. He was everything his mother had boasted. 'They say you're the soothsayer of Here.'

'Who are *they*?' I asked.

'The . . .' he looked around to make sure nobody was listening; he lowered his voice to a whisper, '*auditionees*.'

'Ah.' I nodded, smiling. 'Them.'

'Yes, *them*. We have a lot in common,' he said mysteriously.

'We do?'

'We do,' he repeated. 'They say – *they* being,' he looked left and right again before whispering, 'the *auditionees* – say you're the person to go to if you want to know things.'

I shrugged. 'Maybe I know some things.'

'Well, I'm the person to go to if you want to *get* things.'

'Well, that's why I'm here,' I smiled.

He became serious. I think. 'Which one? You're here to get something or to let me know something?'

I thought about that but didn't answer aloud. 'Aren't you going to let me inside?'

'Of course,' he smiled and dropped the act. 'I'm Bobby,' he held out his hand, 'but you already know that.'

'I do,' I smiled. 'I'm Sandy Shortt.' I took his hand and shook it. It felt limp and I looked up to see that his face had paled.

'Sandy *Shortt*?' he asked again.

'Yes.' My heart beat nervously. 'Why, what's wrong with that?'

'Sandy Shortt from Leitrim, Ireland?'

I let go of his limp hand and swallowed. I didn't answer. It seemed that I didn't need to. Bobby took me by the arm and led me to the shop. 'I've been expecting you.' He looked over his shoulder to see that no one was watching one last time before dragging me inside and closing the door.

Then he closed the shop.

30

Leading away from St Stephen's Green, Leeson Street was a fine Georgian street largely intact. The buildings, once grand homes housing the aristocracy, now mainly housed businesses: hotels, offices, and the basements were home to Dublin's 'Strip', a chain of thriving night-clubs and strip clubs.

A brass plate beside the grand black Georgian door announced the building to be Scathach House. Jack took the seven concrete steps up to the door and came face to face with a brass lion's head with a ring clasped between his teeth. He was just about to grasp it and rap it against the door when he noticed a collection of buzzers to the right of the door: modern day's ugly invention mingled with the old. He looked up Dr Burton's clinic; it was on the second floor, a PR agency at the bottom, a solicitor's office at the top. He was buzzed upstairs where he waited in an empty reception area. The receptionist smiled at him and he felt like shouting, 'I'm not here for *me*, there's nothing wrong with *me*, I'm *investigating*!'

But he smiled back instead.

Magazines adorned the table, some a few months old, others a year old. He picked up one and self-consciously flicked through the pages, reading about a member of the royal family of an obscure country who lay across beds, couches, kitchen tables and pianos in the favourite rooms of her house.

The door to Dr Burton's office opened and Jack quickly disposed of the magazine.

Dr Burton was younger than Jack had imagined, mid-to-late forties. He had a tight beard, light brown, speckled with silver in places. He had piercing blue eyes, was five eleven, Jack guessed, and was dressed in jeans and a tan corduroy jacket.

'Jack Ruttle?' he asked, looking at him.

'Yes.' Jack stood up and they greeted one another with a handshake.

The office was busy, the style of furniture and design eclectic with a packed bookshelf, a full desk, a line of filing cabinets, a wall of academic achievements, non-matching rugs, a chair and a couch. The place had character. It suited the man that sat before him in the chair taking his personal details.

'So, Jack.' Dr Burton finished filling out the form and crossed his legs, focusing all his attention on Jack. Jack fought the urge to run out of the building. 'Why is it that you have come here today?'

To find Sandy Shortt, he wanted to say, but instead shrugged and shifted uncomfortably in his seat. He wanted to just get this all over and done with right now. How on earth was he going to find out about Sandy through making up lies about himself? He hadn't fully thought this through, assuming that everything would fall into place as soon as he'd walked into Dr Burton's office. What was it they said in the movies when the shrinks asked them questions? *Think Jack, think*. 'I'm under a lot of pressure,' he said a bit too confidently, pleased with himself for answering a question.

'What kind of pressure?'

What *kind*? Was there more than one kind? 'Just normal kind of pressure.' He shrugged again.

Dr Burton frowned and Jack feared he'd got the question wrong. 'Is it due to work or—'

'Yeah,' he jumped in, 'it's work. It's really . . .' he searched his brain, 'pressurising.'

'OK.' Dr Burton nodded. 'What is it that you do?'

'I'm a stevedore in Shannon Foynes Port Company.'

'And what brings you to Dublin?'

'You.'

'You came all the way to see me?'

'I had to visit a friend too,' he said quickly.

'Oh, OK.' Dr Burton smiled. 'So what is it about work that you find so pressurising? Talk to me about it.'

'Uh, the hours.' Jack made an under-pressure face that he thought was convincing. 'The hours are so long.' He was silent then and he clasped his hands together on his lap and nodded and looked around the room.

'How many hours do you work a week?'

'Forty.' He spoke before thinking.

'Forty hours aren't more than average, Jack. Why is it you feel that you can't cope with these?'

Jack's face pinked.

'It's OK to feel that way, Jack. Perhaps we can get to the root of why work is bothering you, if it is indeed work that is bothering you . . .'

Dr Burton continued talking while Jack tuned out and looked around the room for signs of Sandy, as if she would have scribbled her name across the wall before she left. Jack realised Dr Burton was staring at him in silence.

'Yes, I think that's it,' Jack said, nodding, and looked at his hands, hoping he had said something suitable.

'And what's her name?'

'Whose name?'

'Your partner, the person at home you're having difficulties with?'

'Oh, Gloria,' he said, thoughts switching to her at home and how delighted she was that he was here today, spilling his heart out, when in reality he wasn't even listening. The more he thought about it, the angrier he began to feel inside.

'Do you talk to her about your feelings of stress and pressure?'

'Oh, no,' Jack laughed. 'I don't talk to Gloria about that kind of thing.'

'Why not?'

'Because she always has an answer, she always has a way to fix me.'

'You don't want that?'

'No,' he shook his head. '*I* don't need to be fixed.'

'What needs to be fixed?'

He shrugged, not wanting to be dragged into this discussion.

Dr Burton left a long silence and Jack felt the pressure to fill it. 'It's what's going on around us that needs to be fixed,' he finally answered.

Dr Burton waited for more.

'And . . .' he stalled, 'so that's what I'm trying to do.'

'You're trying to fix what's going on around you,' he repeated.

'That's what I just said.'

'And Gloria's not happy with this.'

Dr Burton was being paid an extortionate amount of money for this, Jack thought incredulously. 'No,' he shook his head, 'she thinks I should move on and forget about everything.' He hadn't actually meant to say any of that, but it hadn't hurt and he still hadn't given anything away.

'What does she want you to forget about?'

'Donal,' Jack said slowly, not sure whether to continue or not. Maybe if he explained, Dr Burton would agree with him and he would finally have someone on his side. 'The rest of the family are the same. They want to forget him, let him go, leave him behind. Well I don't think like that, you know? He's my brother. Gloria looks at me like I'm crazy when I try to explain.'

'Did your brother Donal pass away?'

'No, he didn't,' Jack said as though that was ludicrous, 'but you would think he had. He's only missing. *Only*,' he laughed angrily, rubbing his face tiredly. 'I sometimes think it would be easier if I knew he was dead.'

There was a silence and Jack felt the need to fill it

again. He thumped his fist against his hand with every point he delivered. 'He went missing last year on the night of his twenty-fourth birthday.' *Thump*. 'He took cash out of the ATM on O'Connell Street at 3.08 a.m. on Friday night.' *Thump*. 'He was seen on Arthur's Quay at 3.30 a.m.' *Thump*. 'And after that no one saw him again. How can you let that go?' he asked. 'How can you decide to keep on living life when your brother is somewhere out there and you don't know where he is or if he's hurt and needs you? How the hell is everything supposed to become normal?' He became angry now. 'How does anybody expect you to be bothered to do forty hours of pointless work a week, putting cargo on a ship? Boxes I don't even know what's in them, and send them to places I've never been and never will be in. Why is that more important than finding my brother? How can you *not* look around you in all directions, trying to find him every time you're outside? Why is it everywhere I go and everyone I ask I'm met with the same answers?'

His voice raised even louder now. 'Nobody *saw* anything, nobody *heard* anything, nobody *knows* anything. There are *five million* people in this country, there are 175,000 of them living in Limerick, 55,000 of whom are living in Limerick city. How the hell didn't *somebody*, even *one* person, see my brother, *somewhere*?' He stopped shouting now, out of breath, his throat sore and his eyes full of tears he was adamant he wouldn't let fall.

Dr Burton allowed the silence to lengthen. He allowed Jack to gather himself and his thoughts and ponder all that he had blurted out. He went to the water cooler and returned with a plastic cup for Jack.

Jack sipped the water and thought aloud. 'She sleeps a lot, you see. The times when I need her, she's asleep.'

'Gloria?'

Jack nodded.

'Do you have difficulty sleeping?'

'I've so much going on in my head, I've so many

papers to look through and reports to go over. Things people said go through my head over and over again, and I just can't switch off. I have to find him. It's like an addiction. It eats away at me.'

Dr Burton nodded understandingly – not in the patronising way that Jack had thought would be the case, but as if he had a *real* understanding. It was as though Jack's problem was now *their* problem, and it was time for them to figure it out together.

'You're not the only person that feels like this and lives like this, you know, Jack. This is exactly the kind of behaviour expected after a trauma such as yours. Were you advised to speak to a counsellor after your brother's disappearance?'

Jack crossed his arms. 'Yeah, the guards mentioned something, and every day leaflets and fliers landed on my hall floor about joining groups of other "sufferers", they called them.' He waved his hand dismissively. 'Not interested.'

'It's not just a waste of time, you know. You would realise that there are many people in your position suffering from the same effects of losing someone,' and he added, more to himself, 'or even suffer from losing *things*.'

Jack looked at Dr Burton with confusion. 'No, no, you've got me wrong. I can deal with losing *things*, absolutely fine, it's missing family members that I've the problem with. My siblings have lost a brother too and not one of them feels the way I do. I can't imagine anything worse than sitting in a group and having the same conversations as I do at home.'

'Gloria seems supportive of you – you should appreciate that. I'm sure it's been difficult for her to lose Donal, but remember not only has she lost him, she's lost you too. Show that you appreciate her. I'm sure that would mean a lot to her.' Real emotion slipped into Dr Burton's voice and he stood up and walked over to the other side of the room to get himself a cup of water. When he came back, he was back to his cool self.

'Do you love her?'

Jack was silent, then shrugged. He didn't know any more.

'My mother used to say listen to what your heart tells you,' Dr Burton laughed, lightening the mood.

'Was she a psychiatrist too?' Jack smiled.

'As good as,' he laughed. 'You know, you remind me of someone, Jack, someone I know very well.' He smiled lightly, sadly, and then returned to his former self. 'So what are you going to do?' He checked his watch. 'Bearing in mind we only have a few minutes left to tell me.'

'I've already started to do something about it.' Jack suddenly remembered why he was here and saw a way in.

'Talk to me.' Dr Burton leaned forward, resting his elbows on his thighs.

'I found someone in the Golden Pages, an agency, a *missing persons* agency,' he stressed.

Dr Burton didn't flinch. 'Yes?'

'I got in touch with this woman and we spoke at length about her helping me to find Donal. We arranged to meet last Sunday in Limerick.'

'Yes?' He leaned back in his chair, slowly, poker-faced.

'Funny thing is, we passed one another at a petrol station on the way and then she never turned up at the meeting point.' He shook his head. 'I really believed and still believe this person has the ability to find him.'

'Really?' Dr Burton's tone was dry.

'Yes, really. So I started looking for her.'

'The missing persons person?' he stated, deadpan.

'Yes.'

'And did you find her?'

'No, but I found her car and I found my brother's files in her car, and her phone, her diary, her wallet and a bag full of labelled clothes all with her name on them. She labels everything.'

Dr Burton began to fidget in his chair.

'I was so worried about her – I am *still* worried about her – because I believe this woman has the ability to find my brother.'

'So you're fixing your obsession onto this other woman,' Dr Burton said a bit too coldly.

Jack shook his head. 'She said to me on the phone once that the one thing that would be more frustrating than not being able to find someone would be not being found. It's her wish to be found.'

'Perhaps she just wandered off for a few days.'

'The garda I contacted said the very same thing.' Dr Burton's eyebrows rose at the mention of involving the police. 'I contacted a lot of people who know her and they also said the same thing,' Jack shrugged.

'Well, then, you should listen to those people. Leave it alone, Jack. Try to concentrate on dealing with your brother's disappearance before you start worrying about another one. If she's been gone a few days and hasn't been in touch, maybe it's for a reason.'

'I wasn't bothering her, Doctor, if that's what you're implying. There are a few of us that are worried so we've arranged to meet up and do something about it.'

'Maybe she does this a lot,' Dr Burton said. 'Maybe there's nothing at all wrong with her and she's gone off on her own for a few days.'

'Yeah, maybe. But it's been four days since I've seen her and more days since anybody else has, unless I find somebody that tells me differently. If that's the case, then I'll back off and get on with my own life, but I don't think she's *wandering*, as so many people have said,' he said gently. 'I just would really love to find her, to thank her for the encouragement she's given me, for the hope of finding Donal that she has helped me to feel. That hope she's given me has allowed me to realise that I could find her too.'

'What makes you think that she's missing?'

'I'm listening to my heart on this one.'

Dr Burton smiled grimly at having his words thrown back in his face.

'And in case my heart isn't proof enough for you, there's also this.' Jack reached into his pocket and gently placed Sandy's silver watch on the table.

31

It had been three years since I'd seen Mr Burton. From a distance I could tell that time had aged him well. From a distance it appeared that time hadn't aged either of us. From a distance everything was perfect and nothing was altered.

I had changed my clothes six times before leaving the bedsit. Feeling mildly pleased with my appearance, I had made my way to Leeson Street for the fourth time that month. I had danced in the halls when I had received his business card. I had skipped down the stairs like the fourteen-year-old on a Monday morning, knowing what and who lay ahead of me that day. I had run from Harold's Cross to Leeson Street, I had taken the steps up to the grand Georgian door in twos, and I had then frozen as my finger hovered above the intercom button and had quickly retreated to the other side of the road. Close up, it was a completely different picture.

I was no longer the schoolgirl coming to him for help. Now I didn't know who I was, running *from* help. I sat across the road on two more occasions, unable to cross over, instead watching as he arrived in the mornings, left in the evenings and everything else in between.

I sat on the concrete steps on the fourth visit, elbows on my knees, fists under my chin, staring at all the feet and legs rushing by on the sidewalk. A pair of tan shoes beneath a pair of blue jeans crossed the road. They walked towards me. I expected them to pass me by and enter through the door behind me but they didn't. One step, two step, three steps up they stopped and sat down beside me.

'Hi,' the voice said softly.

I was afraid to look up but I did. I came face to face with him, blue eyes as bright as the day I first laid mine on him.

'Mr Burton,' I smiled.

He shook his head. 'How many times do I have to tell you not to call me that?'

I was about to call him Gregory when he said, 'It's *Doctor* Burton now.'

'Congratulations, *Doctor* Burton,' I smiled. I examined his face, taking all of him in.

'Do you think this week you could move away from these steps and make it inside the building? I was getting tired of watching you from a distance.'

'Funny, I was just thinking that sometimes it's easier to see things from a distance.'

'Yes, but it's impossible to hear.'

I laughed.

'I like the name of the building.' I looked over at the brass plate with the 'Scathach House' engraving.

'I came across it advertised for rental in the paper. I thought it was perfect. A good luck sign, perhaps.'

'Perhaps. I don't suppose you're any closer to that Bridge we discussed.'

He smiled and searched my face, took all of me in, and shivers ran through me.

'If you let me take you out for lunch, we could see where we are. That's if your boyfriend doesn't mind.'

'Boyfriend?' I asked, confused.

'The follicley unchallenged young male who answered the door to your place a few weeks back.'

'Oh, him.' I shook my head. 'That was just . . .' I paused, unable to remember his name, 'Thomas,' I lied. 'We're not together.'

Mr Burton laughed, stood up and held out his hand to help me up. 'My dear Sandy, I think you'll find his name was Steve, but not to worry. The more men's names you forget, the better it is for me.' He placed his hand lightly on the small of my back and I felt a jolt of electricity race through my body. He guided me across the road. 'Can we go into my office for just a moment? There's something I want to give you first.'

He introduced me proudly to his receptionist, Carol, and brought me into his office. It smelled of him, it looked like him, everything about it was Mr Burton, Mr Burton, oh, Mr Burton. I felt like I was wrapped in a gigantic hug, embraced in his arms as soon as I stepped in and sat on his couch.

'It's a bit better than the one we used to have, isn't it?' he smiled, retrieving something from a desk drawer and bringing it over.

'It's beautiful.' I looked around and breathed in his scent.

Suddenly he was nervous. He sat opposite me. 'I was supposed to give this to you last month when I called round, for your birthday. I hope you like it.' He slid the box across the veneer cherry table. The box was long, red and velvet. I took it in my hands as though it were the most fragile thing I'd ever held, and I rubbed my fingers along the soft furry velvet. I looked at him; he was nervously eyeing the box. I opened it slowly and held my breath. A silver watch glistened inside.

'Oh, Mr Bur—' I started and he grabbed my hand, stopping me.

'*Please*, Sandy. It's Gregory now, OK?'

It's Gregory now. It's *Gregory* now. It's Gregory *now*. A choir of cherubs sang in my ear.

I nodded, smiling. I took the watch from the box and wrapped it around my left wrist, fiddling with the clasp, still stunned by the unexpected gift.

'If you look at the back, you'll see your name is engraved.' With shaking hands he helped me turn it over. There it was, 'Sandy Shortt'. 'May it never go missing.'

We smiled.

'Don't force it,' he warned, watching me trying to close it. 'Here, let me help you,' he said just as the clasp made a snapping sound between my fingers.

I froze. 'Did I break it?'

He moved to the couch beside me, all fingers and thumbs as he tried to fix it, his skin brushing against mine and everything, *everything*, melting inside of me.

'It's not broken but the clasp is loosened. I'll have to take it back and get it fixed.' He tried to keep the disappointment from his voice but failed miserably.

'No!' I stopped him from taking it off me. 'I love it, I want to keep it on.'

'It's too loose, Sandy. It may open and fall off.'

'No, I'll keep my eye on it. I won't lose it.'

He looked unsure.

'Just for today at least, let me wear it.'

'OK.' He stopped fiddling with it and we both finally stayed still and looked at one another.

'I'm really giving you this to help you with your time-keeping. Three years without contact are not allowed to pass again.'

I looked down and twisted the watch around my wrist, admiring the links of the wristband, the mother-of-pearl face. 'Thank you, Gregory,' I smiled, loving how the word felt in my mouth, on my tongue as I said it. 'Gregory, Gregory,' I repeated a few more times as he laughed, loving every moment of it.

I let him take me out for lunch and we saw where we were.

Lunch was as close to a disaster as it could possibly have been. We consumed enough Food for Thought to last us our lifetimes. If either of us had any ridiculous notions that this could be the beginning of something special – and we most certainly did – we were brought to earth by the realisation that we were right back where we finished off. Or very possibly right back to Gregory having to walk over razor-sharp grass blades. I was Scathach and my heart was on Scathach's island in all her and its fierce extremities. I had worsened by the years.

Yet I didn't ever, not for one day, take my watch off. There were times when it fell, but we all do that. It was put back where it belonged, where I felt and knew it to belong. That watch symbolised an awful lot. The positive side to our learning lunch was that it confirmed that we felt inextricably linked to one another, as if there was an invisible umbilical cord joining us both, allowing us to feed off one another, helping us to grow and give one another life.

Inevitably, there was the flip side: that we could tug on the cord whenever we liked, twisting it and knotting it, not caring enough that our twisting and knotting had the ability to choke and suffocate one another slowly.

From a distance everything was great, close up things were completely different. We couldn't fight the effects of time; how it alters us, how with each year an extra layer is glazed upon us, how every day we are something more than we were. Unfortunately for me and for Gregory, it was glaringly obvious that I was something and somebody far less than who I once was.

32

Bobby closed the door of Lost and Found quietly behind us, as though the sound would bring the stall owners outside to a stunned silence. I wasn't sure if this carry-on was just another of his dramatics but I sensed with a mild panic that it wasn't. Bobby let go of my clammy hand and scuttled off into an adjoining room without a word, closing the door over behind him. Through the slit I could see his shadow flickering as he darted by the light, furiously rooting around; moving boxes, scraping furniture across the floor, clinking glasses, making every possible sound, each introducing a new conspiracy theory in my suspicious mind. Finally I averted my eyes from the doorway and looked around the room.

I was faced with walnut shelves floor-to-ceiling high, like in the old grocery stores of decades ago. Baskets were filled to the brim with knick-knacks: Sellotape, gloves, pens, markers and lighters. Others were filled with socks with a handwritten sign excitedly announcing the sale of actual *pairs*. There were dozens of clothes rails lining the centre of the shop, the men's and women's sections separated, everything colour-co-ordinated, styles, eras labelled with dates from the fifties, sixties, seventies and up. There were costumes, traditional clothing and wedding dresses (who loses a wedding dress?). On the opposite wall there was a selection of books, and before that there was a counter displaying jewellery: backs of earrings, single earrings, some pairs Bobby had matched up despite the difference in their appearances.

There was a musty smell in the shop, everything was second-hand; used, had a history. Thin T-shirts had depth, had layers glazed upon them. There wasn't the same atmosphere as in a shop of shiny new things. Nothing was squeaky clean and young and innocently ready to learn. There were no books unread, no hats not yet worn, no pens not yet held. The gloves had held the hand of an owner's loved one, the shoes had walked distances, scarves had wrapped, umbrellas had protected. These objects knew things, knew what they were supposed to do. They had experience of life and lay in baskets, folded on shelves and hung on rails ready to teach those who wore them. Like most of the people here, these objects had tasted life and then seen it slip away. And like most people here, they waited until they could taste it again.

I couldn't help but wonder about who was looking for them now, who was tearing their hair out to find their favourite earrings. Who was grumbling and searching in the bottom of their bag for another lost pen? Who was on their cigarette break only to find their lighter was missing? Who was already late for work and couldn't find their car keys that morning? Who was trying to hide from their spouse the fact their wedding ring had disappeared? They could look and look till their eyes were sore but they would never find. What a time for me to have such an epiphany. Here in Aladdin's cave of lost possessions far away from home. *There's no place like home* . . . the phrase taunted me again.

'Bobby,' I called, inching closer to the doorway, and shutting out the voice in my head.

'Just a minute,' came his muffled reply, followed by a bang, followed by a profanity.

Despite my nerves I smiled. I ran my finger along a walnut display cabinet, the kind you'd expect to contain good silverware and crockery. Here it contained hundreds of photographs of smiling faces from all over the world, over the decades. I picked up one of a couple standing in front of Niagara Falls and studied it. It looked like it was taken in the seventies; it had the yellowy tint that could only be obtained by being dipped in time. Two forty-something-year-olds in wide flares and raincoats, one second caught and contained among a lifetime of seconds. If they were alive now, they too would be in their seventies with grandchildren looking on and waiting patiently as they leafed through their photo albums, looking for the picture to recall their trip to Niagara. Secretly wondering if they had imagined it all, whether that second among a lifetime of seconds had been true at all, while grumbling to themselves, 'I know I have it here somewhere . . .'

'Nice idea, isn't it?'

I looked up to see Bobby watching me from the doorway. After all his rummaging in the next room, he had nothing in his hands.

'Last week, Mrs Harper found a wedding photo of her cousin Nadine, whom she hadn't seen for five years. You wouldn't believe her reaction when she came across the photo. She sat there all day just staring at it. It was a group photo of all at the wedding, you see. Her entire family were there. Imagine not seeing your family for five years and then suddenly coming across a recent photo of them. She only came in looking for socks.' He shrugged. 'It's times like that when I feel useful around here.'

I put the frame of the couple down. 'You said you were expecting me.' I said it more harshly than I meant to, but I was scared.

He unfolded his arms and placed his hands in his pockets. I thought he was finally going to take something out of them and give it to me but instead he left them there. 'I've been here for three years now.' He had the same haunted face as everyone else had when they recalled the memory of arriving here. 'I was sixteen years old. Two years to go till I finished school, ten years to go till I planned on growing up. I had no idea what I wanted to do with my life. I figured I'd still be at home annoying Mum until she forced me out and made me get a proper job. In the meantime I was happy being the joker at school and having my boxers washed and ironed. I didn't take many things seriously,' he shrugged. 'I was only sixteen,' he repeated.

I nodded, not knowing where this was going. Wondering why on earth he said he'd been expecting me.

'I didn't know what to do when I first arrived here. I spent most of the time on the other side of the woods, trying to find a way out. But there's none.' He took his hands out of his pockets and made a clear signal. 'I'll tell you that now, Sandy, there's *no* way out of here and I've seen people drive themselves demented trying to find a way.' He shook his head. 'I soon realised I had to start life here. I had to, for once in my life, take something seriously.' He shifted uncomfortably in his stance. 'It happened when I was looking for some clothes to wear. I was rummaging through all the gear outside, feeling like a homeless man at a junk site. I came across a sock that was bright orange, glowing from under a business file I imagine someone was fired that morning for losing. It was so bright I couldn't help but wonder how on earth someone had managed to lose something so luminous, something that so clearly stood out from the crowd. But the more I looked at it, the better it made me feel about myself turning up here, because before, I thought it was my fault. I thought it was my complacency that led me to wind up here. I thought that if I'd paid more attention in school and had stopped messing around so much, that I could have prevented myself from coming here.'

I nodded. I knew that very same feeling.

'The sock made me feel better because it was the brightest thing I'd ever seen,' he laughed. 'It was even *labelled*, for Christsake, and I just knew that it was bad luck and *only* bad luck on both our parts for ending up here! There was nothing I could have done to avoid ending up here, no more than the sock could have done. I felt sorry for the person who'd labelled it, put their address on it, who'd basically done everything to avoid it going missing. So I kept it to remind myself of that feeling, of that day I stopped blaming myself and everybody else. A *sock* made me feel better.' He smiled. 'Follow me.' He went back into the adjoining room.

The next room was much the same as the shop, with walls lined with shelving units, though it was much smaller and was piled high with cardboard boxes, by the looks of it, used for storage.

'Here's the sock.' He gave it to me and I held it in my hands. It was small, that of a child, and was of towelling material. If Bobby thought the sock was going to have the same effect on me as it did on him, he was wrong. I still wanted out of here and blamed myself and everybody else for putting me here.

'After a few weeks of being here, I found myself helping newcomers to find clothes and anything else they needed when they arrived. So I eventually opened this place up. Mine is the only store in this village where you can get everything all under one roof,' he said proudly. My lack of enthusiasm caused his smile to disappear and to continue his story. 'Anyway, as part of owning and running this place, I have to go out every day and collect as many useful things as possible. I pride myself on being the only place that sells actual pairs of shoes, socks, matching outfits and such like. Other people just gather what they find and display them. I search for the other half, kind of like a matchmaker,' he grinned.

'Go on,' I urged, sitting on an old torn chair that reminded me of my first sessions with Mr Burton.

'Anyway, the orange sock wasn't much of a big deal at all until I found this.' He leaned over and took a T-shirt from a box beside him. Again, it appeared to be that of a child. 'And *that* wasn't even a big deal until I found this.' He placed another odd sock on the floor before me and studied my face.

'I don't get it,' I shrugged, throwing the orange sock down to the floor.

He continued to take out the contents of the cardboard box in silence and laid them out on the floor before me while my mind worked overtime trying to decipher the code.

'I thought there was more in this one, but anyway, that's the lot,' Bobby said finally.

The floor was almost covered in items of clothing and accessories and I was about to stand up and demand he start talking sense when I finally recognised a T-shirt. And then I recognised a sock, a pencil case . . . and then handwriting on a piece of paper.

Bobby stood by the empty box, excitement flashing in his eyes. 'You get it now?'

I couldn't speak.

'They're all labelled. The name "Sandy Shortt" is written on every single thing you see before you.'

I held my breath, looking furiously from one item to another.

'That's just *one* box. They're all yours too,' he said excitedly, pointing to the corner of the room where five more boxes were stacked up. 'Every time I saw your name I collected the item and stored it. The more things of yours I found, the more I became convinced that it was only a matter of time before you would come to collect them yourself. And here you are.'

'Here I am,' I repeated, looking at everything on the floor. I got down on my knees and ran my hand across the orange sock. Although I couldn't remember it, I could imagine my frantic searches that night while my poor parents watched. That was the beginning of it all. I took my T-shirt in my hands and saw my name written on the label in my mother's handwriting. I felt the ink with my fingertips, hoping that in some way I was connecting with her. I moved on to the piece of paper with my messy teenage handwriting. Answers to questions on *Romeo and Juliet* from school. I remember doing that homework and being unable to find it in class the next day. The teacher hadn't believed me when I couldn't find it in my school bag. He'd stood over me in a silent class and watched me root in my school bag, my frustration clearly growing, yet his failure to recognise that genuine frustration had meant punishment homework. I felt like grabbing the page and running back to Leitrim, bursting in on that teacher's class and saying, 'Here, look, I told you I had done it!'

I touched every item on the floor, the memory of wearing them, losing them and searching for them coming to mind. After I'd seen every item from the first box, I raced over to the next on the top of the stacked pile in the corner. With shaking hands I opened the box. Staring up at me with his one eye was my dear friend Mr Pobbs.

I took him out of the box and held him close to me, inhaling him, trying to get the familiar scent of home. He had long lost that and was musty, like the rest of the belongings here, but I clung to him and squeezed him to my chest. My name and phone number were still visible on his tag, the blue felt pen of my mother's writing blurred now.

'I told you I'd find you, Mr Pobbs,' I whispered, and I heard the door behind me gently close as Bobby stepped out of the room, leaving me alone with a head and a room full of memories.

33

I don't know how long I'd been in the storeroom – I had lost track of all time. I looked out the window for the first time in hours, feeling cross-eyed and tired from concentrating on my possessions for so long. My *possessions*. I actually had belongings in this place. They brought me that bit closer to home, momentarily linking the two worlds and blurring the boundaries so that I didn't feel so lost as I touched and held things I had once held in my place near the people I loved. Especially Mr Pobbs. So much had happened since I'd seen him. Johnny Nugent and a thousand other Johnny Nugents had happened. It seemed the night Mr Pobbs disappeared from my bed, an entire team of Mr Wrongs had taken his place.

Joseph walked by the window and I sat back and watched as he strode confidently in his white linen shirt with sleeves rolled to just below his elbows and trousers rolled above the ankles of his sandalled feet. He always stood out from the crowd to me. He looked like somebody important, who oozed dominance and power. He spoke little, yet when he did he chose his words carefully. When he spoke, people listened. His words moved from whispers to songs, never anything in between. Despite the strength of his physical demeanour, he spoke softly, which made him all the more superior.

The bell on the shop's front door rang again. The door squeaked and closed.

'Hello, Joseph,' Bobby said cheerfully. 'Did my Wanda not want to see me today?'

Joseph laughed lightly and I *knew* Bobby was funny to have made him laugh, 'Oh, that girl is so in love with you. Do you think she wouldn't be here if she knew I was here?'

Bobby laughed. 'How can I help you?'

Joseph's voice lowered as though he knew I was here and I immediately pressed my ear against the door.

'A watch?' I heard Bobby repeat loudly. 'I have lots of watches here.'

Joseph's voice was lowered to inaudible again and I *knew* it was terribly important for his voice to be so hushed. He was talking about *my* watch.

'A silver watch with a mother-of-pearl face,' I heard Bobby say, and I was thankful for his habit of repeating people. Their footsteps on the walnut floor got louder and I prepared to move away from the door in case it was opened.

'What about this one?' Bobby asked.

'No, it would have been one you had found yesterday or this morning,' Joseph said.

'How do you know?'

'Because it went missing yesterday.'

'Well, I don't know how you could know that,' Bobby laughed awkwardly. 'Unless you've been talking to someone from the other world, which I'm highly doubtful of.'

There was silence.

'Joseph, this watch is exactly what you've described.' I could hear the confusion in Bobby's voice.

'It's not the one I want,' Joseph said.

'Did you see it somewhere? On somebody? Perhaps you could tell them to visit me so I get an idea of what you're looking for. If I come across it, I'll save it for you.'

'It is the very watch I saw somebody wearing that I'm looking for.'

'Someone from Kenya? Years ago?'

'No, from Here.'

'Here?' Bobby repeated.

'Yes, Here.'

'Did somebody from Here give it to me?'

'No, it went missing.'

Silence.

'It can't have. They must have misplaced it.'

'I know but I saw it with my own eyes.'

'You saw it *disappear*?'

'I saw it on her wrist and she didn't move an inch from her place, and then I saw that it was gone from her wrist.'

'It must have fallen off her.'

'Yes, it did do that.'

'So it's on the ground.'

'That's the funny thing,' Joseph said drily, and I *knew* it wasn't funny at all.

'But it can't ha—'

'It did.'

'And you thought it would show up here?'

'I thought you may have found it.'

'I didn't.'

'I can see that. Thank you, Bobby. Speak of this to no one,' he warned, giving me a chill. Footsteps began to move away.

'Hold on, hold on, Joseph. Don't go yet! Tell me, who lost it?'

'You don't know her.'

'Where did she lose it?'

'Halfway between here and the next village.'

'No,' Bobby whispered.

'Yes.'

'I'll find it,' Bobby said determinedly. 'It has to be there.'

'It's not.' Joseph raised his voice to a normal tone but for him it was loud. From the way that he said it I *knew* that it was not.

'OK, OK.' Bobby backed down, still not sounding like he believed it. 'Does the person who lost it know that it's gone? Maybe she knows where it is.'

'She's new here.' That said it all. That meant *she doesn't understand a thing*, and he was right, I didn't, but I was learning fast.

'She's new?' The tone in Bobby's voice had changed. I recognised that and was sure Joseph would too. 'Maybe I can talk to her and get the exact description.'

'I have given you the exact description.' Yes, he noticed it. Footsteps moved towards the door again, the door squeaked and the bell rang.

'Was there a name on the watch?' Bobby called out at the last minute, and the squeak of the front door stopped, it closed again, and footsteps got louder as they neared me again.

'Why do you ask?' Joseph's voice was firm.

'Because sometimes people engrave names, dates or messages on the backs of watches.' Bobby sounded nervous.

'You asked me if there was a name – why did you specifically ask about a name?'

'Some watches have names engraved on them.' His voice went up an octave in defence. 'I should know.' He tapped on glass and I guessed it was the jewellery cabinet.

There was an odd atmosphere outside. I didn't like it.

'Let me know if you find the watch. Be quiet about it, you know how people would react if they found out that things from Here were going missing.'

'Of course, I understand it might give them hope.'

'Bobby . . .' Joseph warned, and a chill ran through me.

'Yes, sir,' Bobby said smartly.

The door squeaked, the bell rang and it was closed again. I waited a while to make sure Joseph didn't come back in. Bobby was silent outside. I was about to stand up when Joseph walked by the window again, closer this time, staring at the building suspiciously. I quickly ducked and lay flat on the floor, wondering why on earth I was suddenly hiding from Joseph.

Bobby opened the door and looked down at me. 'What on earth are you doing?'

'Bobby Stanley,' I sat up brushing the dust off me, 'you have a *lot* of explaining to do.'

He took me by surprise and folded his arms across his chest. 'And so have you,' he said coolly. 'Want to know why I wasn't at your auditions? Because nobody told me about them. Want to know why? Because around here everybody knows me as Bobby *Duke*. Ever since the day I arrived here, I haven't told *anybody* that my name is Bobby Stanley. So how did you know?'

34

'Mr Le Bon, I assume,' Dr Burton addressed Jack, leaning back in his chair and folding his arms.

Jack reddened but he was determined not to back down or be dismissed from Dr Burton's company as a raving lunatic. He leaned forward. 'Dr Burton, there are *many* of us who are trying to find Sandy—'

'I don't need to hear any more.' He pushed his chair back, grabbed Jack's file from the coffee table and got to his feet. 'Our time is up, Mr Ruttle. You can settle the fee outside with Carol.' He spoke with his back turned as he made his way to his desk.

'Dr—'

'Goodbye, Mr Ruttle.' His voice rose.

Jack took the silver watch in his hands and stood. He spoke quietly but quickly while he had the chance. 'Can I just say that a garda by the name of Graham Turner may contact—'

'Enough!' Dr Burton shouted, slamming the file down on the desk. His face reddened and his nostrils flared. Jack froze and was immediately silenced.

'You obviously haven't known Sandy very long *or* intimately. Taking that into consideration, it's glaringly obvious that it's absolutely no business of yours to go snooping around in her life.'

Jack opened his mouth to protest but he was beaten to it again.

'But,' Dr Burton continued, 'I believe that you and your group are genuine and so I will tell you this before you take things any further with the police.' He battled visibly with his anger. 'I'll tell you what the Gardaí will tell you if they start ringing around. I'll tell you what Sandy's own family will tell you,' his anger rose again and he ground his back teeth. 'And what every single person who knows her will tell you and that is this: that *this*,' he threw his arms up helplessly in the air, 'is what Sandy does.'

Jack tried to speak again.

'*All* of the time,' he shouted. 'She floats in and floats out, leaves things behind, sometimes she collects them, sometimes she doesn't.' He placed his hands on his hips, his chest heaving with anger. 'But the point is, she'll come back again. She always comes back.'

Jack nodded and looked down at the ground. He started to cross the room to leave.

'You can leave her things here,' Dr Burton added. 'I'll make sure she gets them and thanks you on her return.'

Jack slowly lowered the rucksack of her belongings to the ground by the door and quietly stepped out, feeling like a scolded schoolboy, but at the same time feeling sympathy for the schoolmaster who had chastised him. It wasn't Jack he was angry at. It was the breeze that came and went, blowing sporadic gusts of hot and cold air from puckered lips, kisses that tickled and air that smelled sweet, but who at the snap of her fingers inhaled it all back in an instant. It was Sandy he was mad at. And himself, for his eternal wait.

Jack left Dr Burton, hands on hips, staring out the Georgian window, grinding his jaw. Jack closed the door softly behind him, locking the atmosphere inside. It was far too precious to allow to creep into the reception for the awaiting people to sense. It would remain locked in the office, hovering around Dr Burton while he took the time to process it, deal with it, allow it to cool, and then eventually dissipate.

The receptionist, Carol, looked at Jack with worry, not sure whether to be frightened of him or sorry for him at the screaming she had heard inside. Jack placed his credit card on the counter and reached down to her desk to pass her a piece of paper.

'Could you please tell Dr Burton that if he changes his mind, here's my phone number and the address of the meeting point later today?'

She read the note quickly and nodded, still defensive of her boss.

He entered his pin code into the machine and retrieved his credit card. 'Oh, and please give him this too.' He placed the silver watch on the counter. Her eyes narrowed as he walked away.

'Mr Le Bon?' he heard her say as he reached the door. A man reading a car magazine looked up at the mention of the peculiar name.

Jack froze and turned to her slowly. 'Yes?'

'I'm sure Dr Burton will be in contact soon.'

Jack laughed lightly. 'Oh, I'm not too sure about that.' He moved to leave again and she cleared her throat, trying to get his attention. He walked back to her desk.

She leaned forward and lowered her voice. The man took the hint and went back to reading his magazine.

'It's usually just a few days each time. The longest was almost two weeks but that was at the beginning. This is by far the longest in a while,' she whispered. 'When you find her, tell her to come back to . . .' she looked sadly at the door to Dr Burton's office, 'well, just tell her to come back.'

As quickly as she'd spoken, she stopped, took the watch from the counter, placed it in a drawer and carried on typing. 'Kenneth,' she called, ignoring Jack now. 'Dr Burton will see you now. Go right in.'

It's difficult beginning a relationship with someone you were never allowed to know anything about.

Our relationship to date had been based on me and I was finding it hard to make the transition to it suddenly being about the both of us. Every week our meetings were centred on how *I* was feeling, what *I* had done that week, what *I* thought and what *I'd* learned. He was allowed to access my mind whenever he wanted. That was the reason alone for our relationship; for him to delve into my mind and try to figure me out. And to try to stop me from trying to figure him out.

A more serious relationship, a more *intimate* relationship was proving to be the opposite. I had to remember to ask him about him and to remember that he couldn't now know everything that was inside my head. Some things had to be held back, for safe-keeping, for self-preservation, and in a way I lost my confidant. The closer we got, the less he knew about me, the more I learned about him.

An hour a week had been intensified and roles had been reversed. Who'd have thought Mr Burton had a life beyond the four walls of the old school? He knew people and did things that I never knew about. Things that I was suddenly allowed to know about but wasn't sure of whether I wanted to. How could a person historically incapable of sharing a bed *and* a head not need to run from all of that? Sure I went missing for days at a time.

No, the age gap didn't matter, it had never mattered. The years weren't the problem; it was the time that was the fault. This new relationship existed without a ticking clock. There was no long hand to dictate the end of a conversation; I could not be saved by the proverbial bell. He could access me at all times. Of course I ran.

There's a fine line between love and hate. Love frees a soul and in the same breath can sometimes suffocate it. I walked that tightrope with all the gracefulness of an elephant, my head weighing me to the side of hate, my heart hoisting me to the side of love. It was a wobbly journey and sometimes I fell. Sometimes I fell for long periods of time but never for too long.

Never for as long as this.

I'm not asking to be liked. I've never yearned to be

liked, nor am I asking to be understood; I've never been that either. When I behaved that way, when I left his bed, let go of his hand, hung up the phone and closed his door behind me, even *I* had difficulty liking me, understanding me. But it's just how I was.

How I *was*.

35

Bobby stood at the door of the stockroom, arms folded across his chest, a scowl on his face.

'What?' I scrambled to my feet and towered over him. He didn't seem so confident now that I'd risen to my full six foot one. He dropped his hands by his sides and looked up at me. 'Your name *isn't* Bobby Stanley?'

'No, according to everybody else here, my name is Bobby Duke,' he said defensively, accusingly, childishly.

'Bobby *Duke*?' I rubbed my face in frustration. 'What?' I repeated. 'The guy from the cowboy movies? Why?'

'Never mind the *why*.' His face reddened. 'I think the issue here is that you are the only one who knows my real name. How?'

'I know your mother, Bobby,' I said softly. 'There's no great mystery. It's as simple as that.' The past few days had consisted of secrets, mysteries and little white lies. It was time to stop all that, for now anyway. All I wanted to do was meet the people I had been searching for, tell them all that I knew and then bring them home. That is what I would do. While contemplating all this I suddenly noticed that Bobby had gone completely silent and had whitened ever so slightly.

'Bobby?' I said.

He didn't speak, just backed away a little from the doorway.

'Bobby, are you OK?' I asked a little more gently.

'Yeah,' he said, not looking at all OK.

'You're sure?'

'I kind of knew that,' he said quietly.

'What?'

'I kind of knew that you knew my mum. Not just when I first opened the shop door this morning and you called me Mr Stanley, and not just when everybody from the auditions told me that you knew so much, but I kind of knew when I kept finding all of your things.' He looked beyond me to my lost life scattered on the floor. 'When you're on your own, you look for signs. Sometimes you make them up, sometimes they're actually there, but most of the time you can't tell the difference between the two. I believed in this one the most.'

I smiled. 'You're exactly as she said you'd be.'

His lower lip trembled and he tried to stop it. 'Is she OK?'

'Apart from missing you like crazy, she's OK.'

'Ever since Dad left it was always just her and me. She's on her own now. I hate that she's on her own.' His voice went up and down as he tried to control it.

'She's never alone, Bobby; she has your uncles, aunts and grandparents. Besides, she brings anyone and everyone who'll listen into her home and goes through photo albums and home videos of you. I don't think there's one person in Baldoyle who hasn't seen you score against St Kevin's in the finals.'

He smiled. 'We could have won that match had it not been . . .' he trailed off.

I continued for him, 'Had it not been for Gerald Fitzwilliam getting injured in the second half.'

He raised his head and looked at me, light in his eyes. 'It was Adam McCabe's fault,' he tutted, and shook his head.

'He should never have been put in midfield,' I said, and he laughed. He laughed that loud, cartoon laugh that I'd heard so many times in the home videos, the laugh that his family spoke about so much. The high-pitched, addictively funny sound that instantly made me giggle.

'Wow,' he breathed, 'you know her *well*.'

'Bobby, believe me, you don't need to know your mother well to know that.'

Jack sat in Mary Stanley's home, drinking coffee and watching home videos of her son, Bobby.

'See this bit here.' Mary inched forward suddenly in her chair, coffee spilling over the side of her mug and falling onto her blue jeans. 'Ah,' she jumped back, making a face, and Jack leaped forward, thinking she'd burned herself. 'That's where it all went wrong,' she said angrily.

Jack realised she was still referring to the television and he sat back on the couch.

'See him?' She pointed at the TV, spilling coffee again.

'Watch yourself,' Jack warned her.

'I'm fine.' She rubbed her leg without looking. 'This is where it all went wrong. We could have won that match had it not been for him,' she pointed again, 'Gerald Fitzwilliam, getting injured right there in the second half.'

'Mmm,' Jack replied, sipping his coffee and watching the amateur footage of the match jumping up and down on the screen. Most of the time all he could see was a blur of green followed by close-ups of Bobby's head.

'It was Adam McCabe's fault,' she tutted and shook her head. 'He should never have been put in midfield.'

Bobby brought me up a small winding staircase, which led to his residence above the shop. I sat waiting for him in his living room on an impressive leather couch I imagined somebody had impatiently waited for, for longer than the average four-to-six-week period. He brought me in a glass of orange juice and a croissant and my ravenous stomach gurgled in thanks.

'I thought everybody was supposed to eat in the eatery,' I said, attacking the fresh croissant, which flaked in my hands.

'Let's just say the chef has a soft spot for me. She has a son my age back home in Tokyo. She slips me food every once in a while and I occasionally tease her, disgust her and do other son-like things.'

'Charming,' I murmured, face covered in pastry.

Bobby was staring at me, his food untouched on his plate.

'Whapft?' I said with a mouthful of food. He continued staring and I quickly swallowed. 'Is there something on my face?' I felt around.

'I want to hear more,' he said sombrely.

I looked sadly to the remainder of food on my plate, wanting so much to finish it but knowing by the look on Bobby's face that I owed it to his mother to start talking fast.

'You want to know about your mum?' I washed down the crumbs with orange juice.

'No, I want to know about you.' He got comfortable on the couch while I watched him, suddenly uncomfortable, with my mouth agape.

'I was told you ran an acting agency – was it through the agency that you became friends with my mum?'

'No, not really.'

'I didn't think so.'

'What do you mean by that?'

'You don't run an acting agency, do you? You don't seem like the type.'

My mouth dropped open and I felt oddly insulted. 'Why, what *type* of person usually runs an acting agency?'

'People that aren't like you,' he smiled. 'What do you really do?'

'I search,' I smiled. 'I hunt.'

'For talent?'

'For people.'

'For talented people?'

'I suppose everybody I look for has a talent of some sort, although I'm not too sure about you.' Bobby looked confused and I decided to drop the awkward humour and place my trust in him. 'I run a missing persons agency, Bobby.'

At first he looked shocked. Then, as the realisation hit him, he began to smile, the smile grew into a grin, the grin worked its way into laughter, laughter became the addictively funny sound I knew so well, and then I was laughing too.

Suddenly he stopped. 'Are you here to bring us all home or are you just visiting?'

I looked at his hopeful face and immediately felt sad. 'Neither. I'm stuck here too, unfortunately.'

At moments when life is at its worst there are two things that you can do: 1) break down, lose hope and refuse to go on while lying face down on the ground banging your fists and kicking your legs, or 2) laugh. Bobby and I did the latter.

'OK, here's what you have to do. *Do not* tell anybody else this news,' Bobby said.

'I haven't. Apart from Helena and Joseph, nobody else knows.'

'Good. We can trust them. The idea for the play was Helena's?'

I nodded.

'Clever move.' His eyes glistened mischievously. 'Sandy, you really need to be careful. People were talking this morning at the eatery.'

'People don't usually talk at the eatery?' I joked, tucking into the remainder of my croissant.

'Come on, this is serious. They were talking about you. The group of auditionees must have told their friends and their families here about what you'd told them, who in turn told a few other people, and now *everybody's* talking.'

'Is it really that bad that they know? I mean, what harm will it do if they all know I used to look for missing people?'

Bobby's eyes widened. 'Are you crazy? The vast majority of people here are settled and wouldn't go back to their old ways if you paid them, and not just because money has absolutely no use for them here. But there are a number of people – the kind of people that are how I was when I arrived. These people haven't found their feet yet because they are still trying to find their way out. Those people will latch on to you like you don't know what, and you'll be wishing you'd never opened your mouth.'

'Helena said the very same thing to me. Did that happen before?'

'*My God*, did it happen before! Well, not *exactly* the same circumstances.' He waved his hand dismissively and dropped the dramatics. 'Years ago before I even arrived here, some old guy claimed that some of his things kept going missing. If you ask me it was his mind more than anything. Well, as soon as people heard, there wasn't a toilet he could go to without company. He was followed absolutely *everywhere*. When he went to the eatery, people flocked to his table; they followed him to the shops and even waited outside his home. It was madness. Eventually he had to give up his job because huge numbers would shadow him.'

'What was his job?'

'He was a postman.'

'A postman? Here?' I screwed up my face.

'What's so odd about that? We need postmen here more than anywhere. People need to get letters, messages and packages to others in surrounding villages, as even though we have telephones, televisions and computers, there's no network or service on any of them, just static and a lot of fuzz. Anyway, he couldn't keep cycling into villages with a trail of people behind him. Villagers were giving out about it but the people who followed him thought he was miraculously going to find his way out of here.'

'And what happened?' I asked, now on the edge of my seat.

'They all drove him crazy, even more crazy than he already was. There was nowhere he could go in privacy.'

'Where is he now?'

'I dunno.' Bobby appeared suddenly bored by the story. 'He disappeared. He's probably a few towns away or something. Joseph would know as they were very close. You should ask him.'

A chill entered my body and I shivered.

'Are you cold in here?' Bobby asked, incredulous. 'It's always so hot upstairs, I find. I'm absolutely sweating.' He picked up our plates and glasses.

He may have acted cool, but I saw him. I saw him from the corner of my eye, giving me a long, long look before he exited the room. He wanted to see if his seed had been planted. He needn't have worried. It had.

36

'Come on, we can walk and talk at the same time,' Bobby said, standing and grabbing my hand to pull me up.

'Where are we going?'

'To rehearsals, of course. Now more than anything, you have to keep up this play lark. People will be keeping their eyes on you whether you notice it or not.'

I got chills again and shuddered. Once downstairs, Bobby started throwing clothes at me.

'What are you doing?'

'People will take you a lot more seriously if you stop dressing like Sinbad the Sailor.' He handed me a pair of grey pinstripe trousers and a blue shirt.

'These are the correct sizes,' I said, looking through the tags, impressed.

'Yes, but I did not take into account the very long legs.' He bit his lip looking down at me.

'The bane of my life.' I rolled my eyes, handing the trousers back.

'No problem, I've got just the thing!' He ran off down the end of the shop. 'This entire rail is for people with very long legs.' He rooted through the hangers, while I looked at the clothes like a kid in a sweetshop. Never, *never* had I come across such a luxury.

'My God, I think I might be happy here after all.' I ran my fingers along all the clothes.

'Here you go.' He handed me what looked like

exactly the same trousers, but longer. 'Put them on quick. We don't want to be late for rehearsals.'

We stepped outside into the bright sunny day, my eyes aching after being hidden away in the darkness of the musty walnut building. It was noisy with the business of trade going on. People were shouting, bargaining, laughing and calling out in all different languages, some I had never heard before. A small group of four women turned to stare at Bobby and me as he locked up the shop. I stood on the porch in my new clothes, feeling on show as they whispered to one another.

'There she is,' I heard one whisper very loudly, so loudly I wonder how on earth she thought I wouldn't hear her. One nudged another and she was pushed forward, stumbling towards us as we made our way down the steps.

'Hi.' She stopped us in our tracks.

Bobby went to move around her but she stepped to the left, blocking us again.

'Hi,' she repeated, looking at me and ignoring Bobby.

'Hi,' I responded, aware that the group she had emerged from were watching.

'My name is Christine Taylor?'

Was that a question?

'Hi, Christine.'

Silence.

'I'm Sandy.'

Her eyes narrowed as she searched my face, hunting for my recognition of her.

'Can I help you?' I asked politely.

'I've been here for two and a half years?' she asked again.

'Oh, I see. That's,' I looked to Bobby, who raised his eyes to heaven in response, 'well, that's quite a while, isn't it?'

She studied me again. 'I used to live in Dublin?'

'Really? Dublin's a very nice city.'

'I have three brothers and one sister?' She tried to

refresh my memory. '*Andrew* Taylor?' Eyes searched my face. '*Martin* Taylor?' Silence. '*Gavin* Taylor?' Silence. 'My sister is *Roisín* Taylor?' Searched again. 'She's a nurse in Beaumont Hospital?'

'I see . . .'

'Do you know any of them?' she asked hopefully.

'No, I'm sorry, I don't.' I really didn't. 'It was nice to meet you, though.' We started to move away when she grabbed my arm. 'Hey!' I yelped, trying to shake her off. Her grip tightened.

'Hey, let go of her,' Bobby stepped in.

'You know them, don't you?' she said, moving closer to me.

'No!' I said, stepping back, her grip tightening on my arm.

'My mam and dad are Charles and Sandra Taylor.' She spoke more quickly now. 'You probably know them too. Just tell me ho—'

'Get *off* me!' I pulled my arm violently away from her as the crowd around us quietened and turned to stare.

That stopped her talking and she turned to her friends, who stared back, assessing me.

'I'm sorry, but we're late for the rehearsals. We have to go now.' Bobby took me by the sore arm and pulled me away. In shock I allowed him to pull me along, half running, half walking through the crowd, feeling eyes boring into me as we passed.

We finally reached the Community Hall and there was a small queue forming at the door.

'Sandy!' one person called out. 'There she is! Sandy!' Others began to call out and swarmed around me. I felt Bobby tugging me again, I was pulled backwards and the door to the Community Hall slammed behind me. The cast of the play, who sat in a circle, all turned to stare at me and Bobby, who stood panting, with our backs pressed up against the door.

'Well,' I said, catching my breath, and my voice echoed around the hall, 'is this the bloody twilight zone or what?'

Helena jumped up. 'Said Dorothy as she landed in Oz. Thank you, Sandy, for sharing her first line with us,' she said quickly as horrified faces transformed to understanding nods. 'It will be a modern twist on an old story,' Helena explained. 'Thank you, Sandy, for sharing that with us *so* dramatically.'

Mary finally pressed Stop as Bobby's first class school play ended and she ejected the videotape Jack had secretly fantasised about burning for the last two hours. He knocked back the remainder of his cold coffee in a bid to stay awake.

'Mary, I really have to get back to Limerick tonight,' he hinted, looking at his watch. In all the time he had spent in her company, there hadn't been one mention of Sandy. He felt he was being broken in first, being inducted into Mary's life before they could move on to other matters. All around him in the living room framed photographs cluttered every surface. Bobby as a new-born baby, Bobby as a toddler, Bobby on his first bike, Bobby on his first day of school, Bobby on the day of his Holy Communion, his Confirmation, decorating a Christmas tree, Bobby freeze-frame, leaping into a swimming pool on a sun holiday. From bald, to bleach blond, to mousy-brown hair. No teeth, to missing teeth, to metal train tracks. There were no clocks in this room, time was imprinted in every picture and suspended as if forbidden to tick on from the last photograph; Bobby and Mary on his sixteenth birthday.

Thirty-eight-year-old Mary lived in an apartment above her charity shop, which consisted of clothes, shoes, books, knick-knacks, home accessories and everything else you could imagine. The shop was musty from the smell of second- or third-hand clothes, dusty books that had been well thumbed and old toys that had been outgrown and outlived. Above was the space that Mary had shared with Bobby all of his sixteen years.

Mary stood up. 'More coffee?'

'Please.' Jack followed her to the kitchen where he found more photographs dotting the walls, lining the window sill. 'Aren't any of the others I called coming to the meeting?' Jack had been expecting a small gathering.

'They can't make it on such short notice. Peter lives in Donegal with his two young children and Clara and Jim live in Cork although they've recently divorced so the chances of getting them in the same room will be slim. It's sad really. Their daughter, Orla, has been missing for six years. I think it's that that drove them apart.' She poured more coffee. 'Things like this, huge dramatic changes in life have the magnet effect. They either drive people apart or bring them together. Unfortunately the latter happened in their case.'

Jack immediately began thinking of Gloria and how this magnetic event had repelled them apart.

'I've no doubt everybody will pitch in to help, though, once we need them for something specific.'

'Sandy helped all of these people?'

'Sandy *helps*, Jack. She's not gone yet. She's a Trojan worker. I know you didn't get the benefit of quite seeing her in action but she keeps in touch with us every week. Even after all these years, she gives us a weekly call to let us know if there's any news. Most of the time, and particularly more lately, the phone calls have been to see how we are.'

'Did anybody hear from her this week?'

'Nobody.'

'And that's unusual?'

'Not *entirely* unusual.'

'I've been told by a few people that it's not unusual for her to lose contact and just disappear for a while.'

'She disappeared all the time, but she'd still ring us from her hiding places. If there's one thing Sandy is committed to it's her work.'

'It sounds like it's the only thing.'

'Yes, I wouldn't be surprised if that's true,' Mary nodded. 'Sandy gave – *gives* –' she corrected herself, 'very little away. She's a pro at not talking about herself. She never mentions family or friends. *Not once*, and I've known her for three years.'

'I don't think she has any,' Jack said, sitting at the kitchen table with a fresh mug.

'Well, she has us.' Mary joined him. 'You didn't get anywhere with Garda Turner?'

Jack shook his head. 'I spoke to him today. There's really nothing he can do if relatives and friends are saying that this is normal behaviour. Sandy's not a danger to herself or others, and there's nothing suspicious about her disappearance.'

'There's nothing suspicious about a deserted car with all her belongings left inside?' Mary asked in surprise.

'Not if it's what she does all the time.'

'But what about the watch you found?'

'The link on it was broken. She apparently often drops it.'

Mary tutted and shook her head. 'That poor girl is going to be punished for all her previous odd behaviour.'

'I'd love to talk to her parents, see what they think about the whole thing. I have such a hard time dealing with the fact that five days without hearing from a family member isn't something to be worried about.' Jack knew inside that this was all entirely possible. He wasn't particularly close to Donal, or with the rest of his family, for that matter. Apart from Judith, they would often go for weeks without hearing from one another. It was his mother that raised the alarm bells after three days.

'I have their address, if you want.' Mary left the table to rummage around in a kitchen cabinet. 'Sandy quite surprisingly asked me to send something to her there.' Her voice was muffled from inside the press. 'I think she was stranded with the family for Christmas one year and was desperately looking for some work to save her,' she laughed. 'But isn't that what Christmases are all about? Here it is.' Her head finally emerged.

'I can't just drop in unannounced,' Jack said.

'Why not? The worst they can do is not talk to you, but it's worth a try.' She handed him the Leitrim address. 'You can stay here tonight, if you like. It's far too late for you to be travelling to Leitrim and then on to Limerick.'

'Thanks, I might even stay in Dublin a bit longer tomorrow to see if Sandy shows up to another appointment she made.' Jack smiled, looking at a photo of a young Bobby dressed as a dinosaur for Hallowe'en. 'Does it get any easier?'

Mary sighed. 'Never easier but a little less hard, perhaps. It's always at the forefront of my mind, every single waking and sleeping moment. The hurt begins to . . . not quite disappear, but it's as though it evaporates so that it's always there in the air around me, ready to rain down when I least expect it. Then when the hurt goes, anger takes its place, when the anger runs out of steam, loneliness steps in to take over. It's a neverending circle of emotions; every lost emotion being replaced by another. The same isn't so for sons, unfortunately,' she smiled wryly. 'I used to love the great mysteries of life, the uncertainties, the not knowing. I always thought it was so necessary to our journey,' she smiled sadly. 'I'm not so enthusiastic about that any more.'

Jack nodded and they both got lost in thought for a while.

'Anyway, it's not all doom and gloom,' Mary perked up. 'Hopefully Sandy will do what she always does and return home in the morning.'

'With Bobby and Donal in tow,' Jack added.

'Well, here's hoping.' Mary raised her mug and clinked it with Jack's.

37

Jack slept in Bobby's box bedroom that night, surrounded by posters of sports cars and half-naked blondes. On the ceiling were miniature stars and spaceships that once illuminated brightly in the dark but, like Bobby's presence, now merely emitted a faint glow. Stickers that had been stuck to the door and the discoloured wallpaper had been torn off, leaving He-Man without his sword, Bobby Duke without his cowboy hat and Darth Vader without his helmet. The earth's solar system was displayed on the navy-blue duvet cover, every planet and place to be seen but the one Bobby was in.

A writing desk was piled high with CDs, a CD player, speaker phones and magazines containing yet more cars and women. Few school books were piled up in the corner, their place of importance low on the scale. Above the desk, shelves burst with more CDs, DVDs, magazines and football medals and trophies. Jack doubted anything had been altered since the day Bobby had left this room and never come back. Jack placed his hands on as few items as possible and tiptoed on the carpet, not wanting to leave his imprint behind. Everything in this room was precious and existed only as a museum.

Peeking out from between the posters of cars and naked glamour models was *Thomas the Tank Engine* wallpaper. Just beneath the surface lay childhood with only a thin layer to separate it from adolescence. It was the room of someone no longer a boy but not yet a man; of someone in a place between innocence and realisation, on the path of discovery.

Jack once again felt as he had earlier while in the house. He felt trapped in a time that wasn't allowed to move on. The door plate reading '*Bobby's Room: KEEP OUT!*' had been heeded and the door had been firmly shut, leaving everything inside, all the treasured items locked away as though the boxroom were a safe. Jack wondered whether Bobby was elsewhere now, living his life, whether he had moved on from the image Mary was fighting to hold on to or whether his journey had ended. Was he forever to exist in time as no longer a boy and not yet a man, in an in-between place as an in-between person with nothing fully whole, nothing fully realised?

He thought of his own refusal to let go of Donal and what Dr Burton had said to him about replacing one search, which had reached a dead end, with another. He supposed in theory he was, but he was adamant that it wasn't due to an unwillingness and inability to move on. He shook away the thought that he was in any way similar to Mary, hanging on to memories and being stuck eternally in a moment that had long since passed. He pulled the duvet over his head and hid from the stars on the ceiling and galaxy above him. Realistically, his search for Sandy wouldn't find Donal, but something in his heart, in his mind, was driving him forward.

Tomorrow would be Friday, and Sandy, if she didn't wander back into her life, would have been missing for six days. He needed to make the decision now whether it was the moment to pull back, to open the door of his life and allow the trapped time and memories to escape, to move on and catch up on all it had missed. Or he could go full steam ahead with this search, peculiar and out of the ordinary though it might be. He thought about Gloria at home, at the nothingness he felt towards her, his life and their future, and he decided that he, like the Bobby that still inhabited the room he lay in, was embarking on a journey of discovery. He heard Mary switching off the television and unplugging appliances in the kitchen. A gap in the curtains welcomed a sudden light through into the bedroom, shining a ruler of yellow light onto a poster of a red Ferrari. Realising it was the porch light, Jack was engulfed by a strange sort of calm and he watched the light on the wall until his eyes became heavy.

He awoke at eight forty-five the following morning to the sound of his phone ringing.

'Hello?' he croaked, eyes looking around and momentarily thinking he'd travelled back in time to his teenage years and was waking up at home in his mother's house. His mother . . . he felt a pang of loneliness for her.

'What the hell are you doing?' his sister Judith asked angrily. In the background he heard babies crying and dogs barking.

He groaned. 'Waking up.'

'Yeah?' she said sarcastically. 'Beside whom?'

Jack turned to his right and looked at the blonde wearing not much more than a cowboy hat and boots. 'Candy from Houston, Texas. She likes horse-riding, homemade lemonade and taking her dog Charlie for walks.'

'What?' she shrieked, and a baby cried louder.

Jack started laughing. 'Relax, Jude. I'm in the box bedroom of a sixteen-year-old boy. There's no need to worry.'

'You're *what*?'

Could he hear gunshots?

'JAMES, TURN THAT TV DOWN!'

'Ouch.' Jack moved his head away from the phone.

'I'm sorry, did that noise from *hundreds of miles away* disturb you?' she huffed.

'Judith, why are you so tetchy today?'

She sighed. 'I thought you were only going to Dublin to meet with the doctor.'

'I was but I thought I'd ask around a bit more before I head home.'

'This is still about the missing persons woman?'

'Sandy Shortt, yes.'

'What are you doing, Jack?' she asked softly.

He rested his head back against Babs from Down Under's nether regions. 'I'm putting my life back together.'

'By tearing it apart first?'

'Remember when we used to do the Humpty Dumpty jigsaw together every Christmas?'

'Oh dear, he's lost his mind,' she sang.

'Humour me. Do you remember?'

'How can I forget? The first year it took us till March to finish it and all because Mum cleared it off the good room's dining table in a panic when Father Keogh paid one of his surprise visits.'

They both laughed.

'After Father Keogh had left, Dad came in to help us start again, remember? He taught us to separate all the pieces, turn them all face up first *and then* get to work putting them together.'

'And they said, "All the king's horses and all the king's men",' she sighed. 'So you're gathering all your pieces.'

'Exactly.'

'My philosophical baby brother. What happened to trips to the pub and fart jokes?'

He laughed. 'They're still inside me somewhere.'

She turned serious. 'I understand what you're going through and I understand what you're doing, but do you have to do it all on your own without telling anybody anything? Can't you at least make it back home for the festival this weekend? I'm going tonight with Willie and the kids. There's an outdoor band playing and some games for the kids with the usual firework display on Sunday night. You've never missed one before.'

'I'll try to get there,' Jack lied.

'I don't know where Gloria gets her patience from. She seemed so cool about you staying on, but you're certainly testing her. Are you deliberately trying to push her away?'

Jack was about to launch into another defence of himself but stopped and thought about it for a change. 'I don't know,' he sighed. 'Maybe. I don't know.'

'Good morning,' Mary sang, knocking on the door.

'Come in,' Jack called out, wrapping the bedclothes around him.

There was a rattle and a few clinks as the handle lowered and Mary pushed open the door with a tray filled with breakfast.

'Wow,' Jack said, eyeing the food hungrily.

Mary laid the tray down on the writing desk. She didn't move any magazines or CDs, preferring to allow the tray to rest dangerously on the edge of the desk. Nothing was to be touched. Jack was surprised she had allowed him to sleep in the bed at all.

'Thanks, Mary, everything looks great.'

'You're very welcome. I used to love treating Bobby occasionally to breakfast in bed.' She looked around the room, wringing her hands together. 'Did you sleep well?'

'Yes, thanks,' he replied politely.

'Liar,' Mary said, moving towards the door. 'I haven't slept through one single night ever since Bobby disappeared. I bet you're the same.'

Jack just smiled, grateful to hear he wasn't the only one.

'I have to open the shop now, but take your time. I've left a towel in the bathroom for you.' She smiled, took one more haunted look around the room and was gone.

Jack was glad he'd made a note of all of Sandy's future appointments before handing her diary over to Dr Burton. For today she had written, 'YMCA Aungier Street. 12 Noon – Room 4.' There was no mention at all of what the occasion was, but he noted that she had attended it, or at least made a note of it, once every month. He decided it was best not to call ahead but to go straight there.

He entered the building ten minutes after twelve, thanks to Dublin's dire traffic he had yet to account for in his travel time. There was no one behind the counter at reception. He leaned over the desk, looking left and right, and called out but to no avail. He was faced with many doors and notice boards advertising fitness classes, childcare, computer classes, counselling services and youth work programmes. What was behind door number four, he wondered. He seriously doubted it was another counselling service, but whatever it was he hoped it wasn't a fitness class. Computers he hoped for; he could do with learning about computers. He rapped lightly on the door, looking for signs of what was inside and hoping, *hoping* it was Sandy.

The door opened and a lady with a kind face answered.

'Hello,' she smiled, her voice almost a whisper.

'Sorry to interrupt,' Jack whispered. Whatever was going on behind the door, it was certainly being done quietly. Yoga – he hoped it wasn't yoga.

'Don't worry, people are welcome regardless of the time. Do you want to join us?'

'Em, yes . . . I was actually looking for Sandy Shortt.'

'Oh, I see. Did she recommend this to you?'

'Yes.' He nodded emphatically.

She opened the door wider and a circle of people turned to stare. No mats, he thought with relief, no yoga. His heart beat wildly as he looked for Sandy, wondering if she could see him before he'd spotted her. And if she was looking at him now, would she recognise him? Would she be angry he had found her, hiding in her burrow, or would she be thankful, relieved someone had noticed her absence?

'Welcome, come and take a seat.' The woman held her arm out towards the circle while somebody unstacked a chair from the side of the small room and brought it to the circle. Jack walked towards them, searching from face to face for a sign of Sandy. The circle grew larger as he neared, the movement like an umbrella being opened slowly. He sat down with trepidation. Sandy wasn't there.

'As you can see, Sandy unfortunately isn't with us today.'

'Yes, I see that.' He ground his back teeth together and the familiar pain began to throb at the back of his mouth.

'I'm Tracey,' the woman smiled.

'Hello.' Jack cleared his throat nervously as heads turned to stare at him, assess him, study him, analyse his every awkward move. 'I'm Jack.'

'Hello, Jack,' they all responded in unison and he paused, his eyes widening in surprise at the hypnotic tone of their voices. There was a long silence as he shifted uncomfortably in his seat, not at all sure what it was he was supposed to be here for.

'Jack, would you prefer it if the others spoke first this week, and maybe next week you can tell us your story?'

His *story*? He looked at everybody else; some had notepads and pens in their laps. To one side of the room was a whiteboard with the words 'Written Assignment' circled at the top of the board. From that circle stemmed the words: 'Feelings', 'Thoughts', 'Concerns', 'Ideas', 'Language', 'Expression', 'Tones' among so many others he couldn't take them all in, and finally came to the conclusion that it was more than likely he was in a creative writing class.

'Sure,' he replied with relief. 'I'd like to listen to everyone else first.'

'OK. Richard, can you start off for us by letting us know how you got on this month.'

'Here, I find that this helps,' a woman beside Jack whispered, and handed him a pamphlet.

'Thank you.' He left it on his lap and decided to

wait until Richard had finished his story before reading through it. Richard's story was a rather absurd tale about an instantly dislikeable man and his constant fear of acting on violent impulses. He droned on, painfully and miserably reciting the tale of how an equally painfully miserable man constantly felt overly responsible for the safety of others, to the point he was afraid to drive, out of fear he would run over someone with his car. At times Jack shook his head and laughed out loud, thinking it an obvious, however slightly dark, comedy, but he quickly stopped after receiving numerous odd looks from the group.

Minutes, which felt like hours, later, the room was still echoing to the incessant droning of Richard's story, each word sounding twice in Jack's ears, which were already bored from hearing them the first time. As the story moved towards being just plain depressing, with the main character's behaviour the cause of the loss of his wife and child, Jack finally tuned out and began to read the pamphlet scrunched beneath his clammy hands.

His relaxed body stiffened as he finally concentrated on the cover of the thin glossy booklet. Hot waves of colour spread from his neck all the way to the top of his strawberry-blond head within seconds as he read 'Welcome to Obsessive Compulsive Anonymous'.

Jack sat quietly through the remainder of the meeting, feeling embarrassed to be there and generally ashamed by his earlier behaviour during Richard's story. Keeping his head down when the hour was up, he filed out of the room, hiding amongst the rest of the members.

'Jack!' Tracey called out, and he froze. He stopped walking and allowed everyone to file past him, watching their faces as they prepared to leave their safety net and battle the world and all its demons alone. He also saw Dr Burton, who was waiting outside the room, arms folded and a face like thunder. Jack took a few steps back into the room towards Tracey.

Tracey caught up to him and held out her hand to

shake his. 'Thank you for coming today,' she smiled. 'You know you coming here was the first step in helping to heal yourself. It's a rocky journey, it will be difficult, but please know that we are all here to help you through it.' Jack heard Dr Burton laugh mirthlessly. 'The twelve steps that we mentioned earlier, as originated by Alcoholics Anonymous, and adapted for OCA *can* bring relief. I've seen that they can reduce and even eliminate our obsessions and compulsions, so do come again next month.' Tracey patted his arm encouragingly.

'Thanks.' He cleared his throat awkwardly, feeling like an impostor.

'Do you know Sandy well?' she asked.

He winced, disliking being asked the question in Dr Burton's company. 'Kind of,' he said uncomfortably, clearing his voice.

'If you see her, tell her to come back to us. It's unusual for her to miss a meeting.'

Jack nodded again and felt glad now that Dr Burton was within earshot. 'I'll do my best.'

'Hear that?' he said to Dr Burton as soon as Tracey was out of earshot. 'She says it's unusual for Sandy not to be here. I wonder where she is.'

38

I went to the OCA meetings every month. I went because every month that I was there I knew it was another month of deserving to be with Gregory.

'Sandy!' I could hear Gregory calling my name. I was downstairs in his house, half-naked at ten past two in the morning, rooting through my overnight bag that I'd placed, as usual, by the front door when I'd walked in.

'Sandy!' he called again.

There was a thump and the floorboards above me creaked as he climbed out of bed and crossed the bedroom. My heartbeat quickened and my search became more frenzied. Feeling a pressure now that Gregory was making his way towards me, I turned my bag upside down and spilled the contents to the floor. I picked items up, tossed them aside, shook out all my clothes, went through the pockets, laid them flat on the floor and ironed each point firmly with the palm of my hand, trying to feel for the hidden lump.

'What are you doing?' His voice was suddenly behind me and I jumped. My heart thudded and adrenalin raced through me as I felt like I'd been caught in the act, as though I'd been doing something criminal like stealing, or immoral like cheating on him. I hated that he made me feel what I was doing was wrong. It was that same look in his face that I had run from in others, the look that, strangely, hadn't chased me away from him yet. Not completely, anyway, although I had run a few times.

The aftershave I bought for him each of the six Christmases we had been together filled the room. I didn't respond to him. I just laid my navy-blue garda uniform out on the carpet, feeling each point for unusual bumps.

'Hello?' he sang. 'I was calling you.'

'I didn't hear you,' I replied.

'What are you doing?'

'What does it look like?' I replied calmly, running my hand down the length of the navy-blue nylon trouser leg.

'It looks like your clothes are being given a deep massage.' I felt him move further into the room and he sat down before me on the couch, wrapped in the robe I'd bought for him this Christmas, wearing tartan slippers I'd bought for him the previous. 'I'm rather jealous,' he murmured, watching me smoothing down the pockets.

'I'm looking for my toothbrush,' I explained, emptying the contents of my washbag onto the floor.

'I see.' He watched me. He just sat there quietly and watched me, yet this made me feel uncomfortable. His disapproving eyes on me made me feel like I was sitting on the floor doing drugs instead of merely looking for something. A few minutes passed of my searching without results.

'You know that you have a toothbrush upstairs in the bathroom already?'

'I bought a new one today.'

'The old one won't do?'

'The bristles are too soft.'

'I thought you liked soft bristles.' He ran his hand through his tight beard.

I smiled for his sake.

He watched me for a little while longer.

'I'm going to make a cup of tea, do you want one?' He had the same method as my parents; they too used to keep an easy tone in their voices to pretend to me that everything was all right, to stop me from picking up negative vibes and panicking because something was lost. When I was younger that's what I thought. Now that I was older, I had learned from Gregory that it wasn't me he was trying to lighten the atmosphere for, it was himself. I stopped searching and watched him moving around the adjoining kitchen as though he made cups of tea at two o'clock every morning. I watched him playing house and pretending that his on/off girlfriend was perfectly normal and correct to be sitting on the carpet half-naked while emptying her bag for a toothbrush she already had sitting in a cup holder upstairs. I watched him pretending to himself, smiling as I fell in love with another flaw I never knew existed within him.

'Maybe it fell out in the car,' I said, more to myself.

'It's raining, Sandy. You don't want to go out now, do you?'

He needn't have asked, he knew the answer, but he was still playing along with his own game. Pretending now that his full-time, eternally faithful girlfriend was going to risk running out into the wet night to look for something. How unusual, how frightfully odd, how attractively kooky. Such fun.

I looked around the living room for a jacket or blanket to throw on. There was none. In this state, although I appear calm on the outside, inside I'm running around screaming, shouting, looking in all directions, anxious to go, go, go. To run upstairs and throw some clothes on would take too long, would take precious minutes away from finding. I looked at Gregory, who was pouring the boiling water into a witty mug I'd got him for the previous Christmas. He obviously saw the desperate search in my eyes, the silent longing for help. He played it cool as usual.

'OK, OK,' he held his hands up in surrender, 'you can have the robe.'

I actually hadn't thought of his robe.

'Thanks.' I got to my feet and walked to the kitchen.

He undid the belt and coolly shrugged it off his

shoulders, and handed it to me, standing dressed now in only his tartan slippers and the silver chain I had given him for his fortieth birthday the previous year. I laughed and took it from him, but he held on to it, the robe firmly in his grasp. He turned serious.

'Please don't go outside, Sandy.'

'Gregory, don't,' I mumbled, tugging on the robe, not wanting this discussion again, not wanting to go through the same thing all over again, fighting about it, talking in circles, resolving nothing and apologising for nothing but the insults fired between the main issues.

His face crumpled. 'Please, Sandy, *please* can we just go back to bed? I'm up in four hours.'

I stopped tugging on the robe and looked at him, standing before me naked but revealing more in the look on his face alone. Whatever it was about that face, about the way he looked at me, the way he yearned for me not to leave him, the way it seemed so important that I be with him rather than away, something inside me stopped fighting.

My grip relaxed on the robe. 'OK.' I gave in. *I gave in*. 'OK,' I repeated, more to myself this time, 'I'll go to bed.'

Gregory looked surprised, relieved and confused all in one glance, but he didn't push it, didn't question it. He didn't want to ruin the moment, spoil the dream and chase me away again. Instead he held my hand and we went back upstairs to bed, leaving the clutter of my scattered clothes and washbag on the floor by the door. It was the first time I'd turned my back on the situation and headed in the other direction. It was apt that it was Gregory leading me.

In bed I laid my head on his warm heaving chest, felt his heartbeat beneath my cheek and his breath on the top of my head. I felt loved and secure, and thought everything in my life couldn't possibly be any more perfect and wonderful. Before he fell asleep, he whispered to me to remember that feeling. At the time I thought he was referring to us being together, but as the night slowly moved on for me and the niggling returned, I knew he had meant for me to remember the feeling of walking away and the reason that led to that decision. I needed to hold on to that, store it in my memory and call upon it whenever the moment raised its ugly head.

I was restless that night. I only meant to go back downstairs and tidy my belongings away. And then when I had done that, I only meant to go out into the wet night to search my car. But then when it wasn't there, I forgot the feeling that I'd tried to hold on to while in Gregory's arms and Gregory's bed.

He woke up alone that morning and it pains me to imagine his thoughts when he felt around the bed and his hand rested on the cold sheets. Meanwhile, while he was asleep in his bed, pretending in his dreams that I was alongside him, I had returned to a cold bedsit to find my toothbrush still in its packet, lying on the table. For once I got no solace from finding. I was emptier after finding the toothbrush than I had been before. It seemed the more things I found when I was with Gregory, the more I lost inside. I was alone in bed at five in the morning after leaving the warm bed of a man I loved, and who loved me. Of a man who would, as a result, no longer take my calls. A man who after thirteen years of wanting to learn all there was to learn about me had finally given up and wanted to know me no longer.

For a while, I gave up on him too, until I became too lonely, too tired, and my heart became too sore from pretending I cared more about a whole series of nothings with nobodies rather than a single episode of *something* with somebody. I told myself that morning to hold on to that feeling, to remember the foolishness of leaving warmth to walk alone in the cold, the ridiculous loneliness of leaving something for nothing.

He took me back on one condition. That I recognise my problems and attend a monthly meeting called the OCA. The first thing you learn while in OCA, is that you can't be in OCA for anybody else but yourself. It was a lie from the very beginning. Every extra month I attended the meeting was another month spent with Gregory, a happier Gregory, who was content knowing I was taking steps, twelve to be precise, to recover. He pretended to himself again because it was obvious to everyone that there had been no change in my behaviour. I knew in my heart that I wasn't the same as the others in the class. I felt it absurd that he think I was among the likes of those who scrubbed and cleaned themselves for hours at night before going to bed until they almost bled, and hours in the morning before going to work. Or the woman who made tiny slits with a blade on her own arms, or the man who touched, counted, arranged and hoarded every little thing that came into his path. I wasn't like them. My *dedication* was confused with obsession. There was a difference. *I* was different.

Years and years of going to the meetings and I was still the same as the twenty-one-year-old who sat on the concrete steps opposite Dr Burton's office building every week, with my elbows on my knees, chin rested on my hands, watching the world pass by as I waited to cross the road.

Every single time, Gregory crossed over for me and met me on my side. I realise now, I don't think I ever met him in the middle. And I don't think I ever once said thank you for that.

But I'm saying sorry now. I shout it a thousand times a day from this place that he can't hear me from. I say thank you and sorry and I scream it through the trees, over the mountains, pour my love into the lakes and I blow kisses in the wind, hoping that they will reach him.

I went to the OCA meetings every month. I went because every month that I was there I knew it was another month of deserving to be with Gregory.

I missed it this month.

39

After returning from an afternoon rehearsal at the Community Hall, Helena, Joseph, Bobby and I sat around the pine table in their home. Wanda sat opposite me, her head of messy black curls just about visible over the table, and her arms pulled up in a giant effort to clasp her hands together, imitating how I was seated. Joseph had just announced that the council had called a meeting for tomorrow night, which for reasons known only to the others around the table was a cause to become quiet and allow an atmosphere of impending doom to fall over us.

I don't know why, but I found the day-to-day running of this place comical. I didn't and couldn't take their world and their issues seriously, however important they were. I hid my smile beneath my hand as I watched them worriedly looking at one another. I was completely detached from the problem, thankful that whatever was happening was happening to them and not me. It was as though their problems weren't mine because I was an outsider, of my own choosing, and I would do my utmost to remain in that position. Anything to avoid having to deal with the harsh reality of settling here. There seemed to be very little choice involved in that reality. So my feeling while I sat at the table was that my time here would be too short-lived to have to care about whatever it was that affected their world. *Their* world, not mine. Nobody had spoken for a while so I tried to break the frosty atmosphere.

'So what's such a big issue that would cause a meeting to be called?'

'You,' Wanda said perkily, and I could tell her legs were swinging under the table from the way her shoulders rocked.

A chill went through me. I chose to ignore her, annoyed that a child was allowed to sit in on our conversation without being silenced, annoyed that she had transformed me from black sheep to piggy by snatching me from the outside where I felt comfortable and plonked me right in the middle of the equation. I looked to the faces around the table, still glancing worriedly at one another but still not speaking. The only one willing to look me in the eye was Wanda.

'What makes you say that?' I questioned the five-year-old, taking that nobody had corrected her, either because it was the general consensus or they were ignoring her because she was bonkers. I hoped for the latter.

'From the way that everyone was staring at you when we walked from the Community Hall to here.'

'That's enough now, sweetheart,' Helena said gently.

'Why?' Wanda looked up at her grandmother. 'Didn't you see how they all stopped talking and made way for her? It was like she was a fairy princess.' She revealed her gummy smile. Yep, bonkers.

'OK,' Helena patted her on the arm to signal her to stop. Wanda was quiet and I could tell her legs were still.

'The meeting is being called about me.' I absorbed this. 'Is this true, Joseph?' I very rarely, if at all, got nervous for anything and, at the idea of this, curiosity was the only emotion that stirred within me. And yet it was still mixed with the bizarre feeling of thinking it was all very cute and twee. A funny little happening in a funny little place.

'We don't know that it's about you.' Bobby leaped to my defence. He looked at Joseph. 'Do we?'

'I have been told nothing.'

'Do people regularly call meetings about new arrivals? Is that normal?' I asked. I squeezed the stone that was Joseph, for water.

'Normal,' he threw his hands up in the air. 'What do we know of normal? What does our world and the old world, the world who thinks it knows it all, really know of normal?' He stood up and loomed over us.

'Well, do I need to be worried?' I asked, hoping now that he could at least reassure me.

'Kipepeo, one never *needs* to be worried.' He placed his hand on my head and I felt his warmth soothe my pounding headache. 'We will be at the Community Hall at seven p.m. tomorrow. We shall test our understanding of normality then.' With a small smile he drifted out of the room. Helena followed him.

'What did he just call you?' Bobby asked, confused.

'Kipepeo,' Wanda sang, her legs swinging wildly again.

I leaned into the table and Wanda momentarily looked startled. 'What does that mean?' I asked rather aggressively but I was anxious to know.

'Not telling you,' she pouted and crossed her arms across her chest. 'Because you don't like me.'

'Don't be silly. Of course Sandy likes you,' Bobby said.

'She *told* me she didn't.'

'I'm sure you misheard her.'

'She didn't,' I explained, 'I told her directly.' Bobby looked shocked so I made an attempt to wave the white flag. 'Well, tell me what kipepeo means and I might like you.'

'Sandy!' Bobby exclaimed.

I shushed him. Wanda mulled it over. Slowly but surely her face began to crumple. Bobby kicked me in the leg and I leaned forward. 'Wanda, don't worry about it.' I tried to soften my voice as much as I could. 'It's not your fault that I don't like you.' In the background Bobby tutted and sighed. 'If you were ten years older, it's very possible that I could like you.'

Her eyes lit up. Bobby shook his head at me. 'What age will I be then?' she asked, kneeling excitedly on her chair and leaning forward on her elbows on the table to get closer to me.

'You'll be fifteen.'

'Nearly the same age as Bobby?' She was hopeful.

'Bobby is nineteen.'

'Which is four years older than fifteen,' Bobby explained politely.

Wanda seemed delighted by this and gave him a shy gummy smile.

'But I'll be twenty-nine when you're fifteen,' Bobby explained and I saw her face fall. 'Every time you get older, I get older,' he laughed. He was confusing her fallen face with a lack of understanding, and he continued, 'I'll always be fourteen years older than you, you see.' As I watched her face falling along with the penny in her mind, I signalled for him to stop.

'Oh,' she whispered.

Your heart can break at any age. I think that's when I started liking Wanda.

I hated going to sleep in the place they called Here. I hated the sounds at night that drifted into the atmosphere from home. I hated to hear the laughter, I wanted to block my nose to the smells, close my eyes to the people wandering in from the woods for the first time. I was afraid each noise would be me, I was afraid each sound would be a part of me forgotten. Bobby and I shared that fear. We stayed up late into the night, talking about the world he had left behind: music, sport, politics and everything in between, but mostly we spoke about his mother.

Jack returned to Mary Stanley's house after leaving Dr Burton at the OCD meeting. Once again angry words had been shared between them, with the doctor firing threats of stalking charges and everything he could think of to make Jack back off from his search. After wandering around Dublin city for the afternoon, he had left a voicemail on Gloria's phone, telling her he wouldn't be home for another few days; that it was complicated but that it was important. He knew she would understand. He had postponed his trip to Leitrim to visit Sandy's parents after being warned off by Dr Burton. Instead he hoped to share his thoughts and concerns with Mary before he moved on with his search. He needed to know whether to continue or not. He needed to know if he was chasing his own shadow, whether there was any purpose to him searching for Sandy if those who knew her well weren't concerned.

Mary had welcomed Jack to stay with her for another night and they sat in her living room, once again watching a video of Bobby performing in his sixth class school play of *Oliver*. He noticed Bobby had an unusual laugh, a loud chuckle that came from deep inside him, causing everyone around him, including the audience, to smile. Jack found himself with a grin on his face as Mary turned off the tape.

'He seemed like a happy lad,' Jack commented.

'Oh, yes,' she nodded enthusiastically, sipping on her coffee. 'He was that, indeed. He was always cracking jokes, always acting the class clown and letting his words get him into trouble and his laugh get him out of it. People loved him.' She smiled. 'That laugh of his . . .' She looked at a photograph on the mantelpiece, Bobby's face a picture of delight, his mouth wide open mid-laughter. 'It was infectious, just like his grandfather's.'

Jack smiled and they studied the photo.

Mary's smile faded. 'I have a confession to make, though.'

Jack was silent, not sure he wanted to hear it.

'I don't hear that laugh any more.' Her voice was almost a whisper, as though if she said it any louder it would make it true. 'It used to fill the house, it used to fill my heart, my head, all day, every day. How can I not hear it any more?'

From the faraway look in her eye Jack could tell she wasn't asking him for a reply.

'I remember how it used to make me *feel*. I remember the atmosphere just one simple giggle would evoke in a room. I remember people's reactions. I can see their faces and the impact the sound made on them. I can hear it on the videos when I play it back, I can see it on his face in photographs, I hear versions of it, I suppose, echoes of it in other people's laughter. But without all those things, without the photographs, videos and echoes, when I'm lying in bed at night, I can't remember it. I don't hear it and I try to but my head becomes a jumble of the sounds I've made up and the sounds I've recalled from memory. But as much as I search and search, my memory of it is missing . . .' she trailed off. She looked over at the photo on the mantel again, cocked her ear as though listening for the sound. Then her body seemed to collapse into itself as she gave up.

Bobby and I were both tucked up on the couch in Helena's home. Everybody had gone to bed, apart from Wanda, who had sneaked back in and was hiding behind the couch, overexcited by the fact her dear Bobby was staying the night in her house. We knew she was there but ignored her, hoping she would get bored and go to sleep.

'Are you worried about the meeting tomorrow night?' he asked.

'No, I don't even know what reason I have to be worried. I don't see what I've done wrong.'

'You haven't done anything wrong but you know things – you know too much about people's families for everybody's comfort. They will want to learn how and why.'

'And I'll tell them I'm a hugely sociable person. I move around the Irish social scene talking to friends and family of missing people,' I said drily. 'Come on, what are they going to do to me? Accuse me of being a witch and burn me at the stake?'

Bobby smiled lightly. 'No, but you don't want your life being made difficult.'

'They couldn't possibly make it any more difficult. I'm living in a place where lost things go. How bizarre is that?' I rubbed my face wearily and muttered, 'I'm definitely going to need some serious counselling when I get back.'

Bobby cleared his throat. 'You're not going back. You need to get that out of your head, for a start. If you say that at the meeting you'll definitely be asking for trouble.'

I waved him off, not interested in hearing that again.

'Maybe you could start writing your diaries again. It looked like you enjoyed doing that.'

'How do you know I wrote diaries?'

'Well, because of the diary in one of your boxes back at the shop. I found it down by the river just at the back of the shop. It was dirty and damp but when I saw your name written on it I brought it back to the shop and spent a lot of time restoring it,' he said proudly. On my lack of reaction he quickly lied, 'I promise I didn't read it.'

'You must be thinking of somebody else.' I forced a yawn. 'There wasn't a diary there.'

'There was.' He sat up. 'It was purple and . . .' he trailed off, trying to remember it.

I began to pull on a thread on the hem of my trousers.

He snapped his fingers and I jumped in fright, feeling Wanda behind the couch jumping too. 'That's it! It was purple, kind of a suede material which was ruined because of the damp but I cleaned it up as much as I could. Like I said, I didn't read it but I did open up the first few pages and there were doodles of love hearts all over it.' He thought again. '"Sandy loves . . ."'

I pulled on the thread more.

'Graham,' he continued. 'No, it wasn't Graham.'

I tightly wrapped the fine filament around my baby finger, watching my skin squeezing through, watching the blood being caught.

'Gavin or Gareth . . . Come on, Sandy, you must remember. It was written so many times I don't know how you could forget the guy.' He kept on thinking while I kept on pulling the thread, wrapping it tighter and tighter.

He snapped his fingers again. 'Gregory! That's it! "Sandy loves Gregory." It was written all over the inside of the book. You must remember it now.'

I spoke quietly. 'It wasn't in the boxes, Bobby.'

'It was.'

I shook my head. 'I spent hours going through everything. It's definitely not there. I would have remembered it.'

Bobby looked confused and irritated. 'It was bloody well there.'

With that, Wanda gasped from behind the couch and jumped up.

'What's wrong with you?' I asked, seeing her head popping up between mine and Bobby's.

'You've lost something else?' she whispered.

'No I haven't,' I denied, but felt a chill again.

'I won't tell anyone,' she whispered, her eyes wide. 'I promise.'

There was a silence. I fixed my eyes on the black thread that kept on coming. Suddenly and completely inappropriately, I heard Bobby laugh loudly, one of his finest, loudest laughs I had heard from him yet.

'The situation is hardly very funny, thanks, Bobby.'

Bobby didn't reply.

'Bobby . . .' Wanda's childish whisper ran down my back.

I looked up at Bobby, noticed the deathly pale of his face, his mouth hung open as though the words that had run from his vocal cords had chickened out last minute, refused to jump and instead stood on his lips in fear. Tears formed in his eyes and his bottom lip trembled and I realised the laughter hadn't come from his mouth at all. It had floated from there to Here, carried on the wind, over the tree-tops and into this place, landing somewhere amongst us. While I attempted to process all this, the door to the living room was pushed open and Helena appeared sleepy-eyed in her dressing gown, her hair tousled and her face a picture of worry. She froze at the door while she studied Bobby, making sure she had heard correctly. His look said it all and she charged at him, holding her arms out. Plonking herself on the couch, she held his head to her chest and rocked him as though he were a baby while he cried and mumbled through his tears how he'd been forgotten.

I sat on the other end of the couch and kept on pulling the thread. It kept on coming, unravelling more and more with every minute spent in this place, unable to stop detaching itself from the seams.

40

I have found that the many imbalances within our individual lives result in an overall more worldly balance. What I mean is that no matter how unfair I think something is, I need only look at the bigger picture to see how, in a way, it fits. My dad was right when he said that there was no such thing as a free meal: *everything* comes at a cost to others, most of the time at a cost to ourselves. Whenever something is gained, it has been taken from another place. When something is lost, it arrives elsewhere. There are the usual philosophical questions: why do bad things happen to good people? Within every bad thing I see good, and likewise, within every good thing I see bad, however impossible it is to understand it or see it at the time. As humans we are the epitome of life, in life there is always balance. Life and death, male and female, good and bad, beautiful and ugly, win and lose, love and hate. Lost and found.

Apart from the Christmas turkey my dad won at the Leitrim Arms pub quiz when I was five years old, my dad had never won anything in his life. The day Jenny-May Butler went missing was the day that my dad won £500 on the lotto scratch cards. Maybe he had a good thing owed to him.

It was a summer day. There was only one week left before we were to go back to school and I was dreading even the thought of it, but apart from the anxiety for the week ahead, without having to get up every morning for school over the past few months, I had lost all sense of time. Weekdays were the same as weekends. For a few months a year, the dreaded Sunday nights were the same as Friday and Saturday nights. This night was a Sunday night but, unusually for this time of year, it was a dreaded one. It was six forty p.m., still bright, the cul-de-sac was busy with kids playing, just like me, forgetting what day it was but knowing that whatever day it was, it sure was a great one because tomorrow would be exactly the same. My mother was in the front garden with my grandma and granddad, getting the last few warm evening sunrays. I was sitting at the kitchen table anxiously waiting for the doorbell to ring. I was drinking a glass of milk and watching the clothes in the washing machine go round and round, trying to identify each garment that flashed by, just to occupy my mind.

My dad had eyed me warily as he came back and forth from the TV room to the kitchen, grabbing food he wasn't supposed to be eating while on his new diet. I didn't know whether he was trying to suss me out or whether he was eyeing me to see if I had noticed him stealing food. Either way, he'd asked me three times already what was wrong, and I'd just shrugged and told him nothing. It was one of those occasions when telling someone wouldn't make it any better. He checked on me from time to time, noticing how I'd jumped when the doorbell rang (only my mum, who had forgotten to put the door on the latch). He made a few faces at me to try to make me laugh, cramming a few biscuits into his mouth all at once to pretend he was entertaining me and not his stomach. I smiled for his sake, he seemed happy enough with that and then moved into the TV room again, this time with a Jaffa cake up his sleeve.

You see, I was waiting for Jenny-May to call around.

She had challenged me to a game of King/Queen. It was a game we used to play on the road with a tennis ball. Each person stood in the boxes that were drawn on the tarmac with chalk and then the idea was to bounce the ball first in your own box before passing it into someone else's. They had to do the same and if they missed it, if it failed to bounce in their own box first or if the ball went outside the lines, they were out. The idea was to try to make it to the box at the top, which was the King's box, which was where Jenny-May was for the duration of the game. Everybody used to always say how wonderful she was at playing the game, how amazing and brilliant and talented and fast and precise and how gag, gag, make me puke, she was. My friend Emer and I used to watch the games from our wall. We were never allowed to play because Jenny-May wouldn't allow us. I merely commented to Emer one day that one of the reasons Jenny-May always won was because she always *started* in the top box. This meant that she didn't have to work her way up like everybody else did.

Well, somebody somewhere overheard and word got back to Jenny-May what I'd said and the next day when Emer and I were sitting on the wall kicking our heels against the bricks and flicking ladybirds from the pillars to see how far they'd go, Jenny-May marched up to us with her hands on her hips, surrounded by her posse, and demanded I explain myself, which I did. Red-faced and flustered at being answered back at, she challenged me to a game of King/Queen. As I said, I'd never played this game before and I knew all too well that Jenny-May was good. All I'd meant was that she wasn't *as* good as people were saying. There was something about Jenny-May that made people see more in her than there actually was. I've come across a few people like that in my life and they always make me think of her.

She was clever, though. She made sure that everyone knew that if I didn't show up then she would automatically become the champion, and I suddenly wished my dreaded visit to Aunty Lila was a day early.

Word spread among everyone in the road that Jenny-May had challenged me to a game. They were all going to turn out and sit on the kerb to watch, including

Colin Fitzpatrick, who was way too cool to hang out on our road. He used to go skateboarding with the people around the corner that no one else had the privilege of hanging out with. Word was that even the skateboard gang were all coming to watch.

I barely slept a wink the night before. I got out of bed, put my runners on with my nightdress and went outside to practise King/Queen up against the garden wall. It wasn't much use because the ball kept hitting against the stippled back wall, which sent it flying in all the wrong directions. Plus it was so dark I could hardly see it. Eventually Mrs Smith from next door opened her bedroom window and stuck her head out, which was covered in hair-curlers, which I thought was odd because the next morning her hair was straight, and she sleepily asked me to stop. I went back to bed but didn't sleep much and when I did, I dreamed of Jenny-May Butler being lifted onto everyone's shoulders wearing a crown, while Stephen Spencer, who was on a skateboard, pointed a nail-varnished finger at me and laughed. Oh, and I was naked.

It was my challenge with Jenny-May that alerted her parents to the fact she was missing. During the summer months we all had complete freedom. We stayed outside together all day playing, rarely going inside and sometimes having lunch in one another's house. So I don't blame her parents for not noticing she hadn't been around all day. Nobody blamed them because I knew they all understood. They all knew deep down that it could have happened to them too, that it could have been their child no one had noticed not being around for a few hours that day.

Jenny-May's house and mine were directly opposite each other. Mum and my grandparents had come back inside now that the sun had finally disappeared behind the Butlers' house. I knew everybody was gathering on the kerb waiting for me and Jenny-May to leave our houses and meet in the middle. I saw my dad look out the front window and then back at me. I think he finally understood what was wrong and gave me a small smile. Then he put biscuits on the table and sat with me, munching away.

Eventually, as it struck seven p.m., everybody outside began chanting. Some voices called for me but they were drowned out by chants for Jenny-May. Maybe it was equal but I seemed to hear only her name. All my life, I've heard her name louder than my own. Suddenly there was a big cheer and I assumed Jenny-May had left her house. Then the cheering stopped, there was chattering, then it got quieter and then it was completely silent. Dad looked at me and shrugged. The doorbell rang. I didn't jump this time because something didn't feel quite right. Dad patted my hand. I heard Mum answer the door, as usual her voice friendly and chirpy. Then I heard Mrs Butler's voice, not so friendly, no singsong tone. Dad recognised it too and left the table to join them in the hall. Voices turned to concerned tones.

I don't know why, but I couldn't leave the table. I just sat there thinking of ways to get out of the challenge, but at the same time having the strange feeling that I wouldn't need an excuse. The atmosphere had changed, for the worse, I sensed, but I had that relieved feeling like arriving at school to find out the teacher's sick and not for one second worrying about the teacher. A few minutes later the kitchen door opened and Dad, Mum and Mrs Butler came in.

'Honey,' Mum said softly, 'do you, by any chance, know where Jenny-May is?'

I frowned, confused by the question even though it was perfectly straightforward. I looked back and forth to all their faces. Dad was looking at me with concern, Mum was nodding at me encouragingly and Mrs Butler looked like she was going to cry. She looked like her entire life depended on my answer. I suppose it did, in a way.

When I didn't answer immediately, Mrs Butler spoke quickly. 'The kids outside haven't seen her all day. I thought maybe she would be with you.'

I knew it was wrong but I felt the sudden urge to laugh at the idea that Jenny-May would have spent the day with me. I just shook my head. Mrs Butler called around to all the neighbours to see if they'd seen her daughter. The more doors she knocked on, the more I could see how her face changed from embarrassment to steely determination and then to fear.

I've seen mothers' faces in shopping centres when they turn round and notice their child isn't with them. I studied their faces so intently, completely fascinated by it, because I don't recall ever seeing that look on my mum's face. Not because she didn't love me, of course, but because I was always so tall and out of place there was no way she could lose me. I used to try to get lost sometimes, just to see her face. I would close my eyes, spin around and choose a direction to head in. Other times I deliberately waited for her to turn the corner into the next aisle in the supermarket. I would shiver by the frozen food and count to twenty until I felt she was far enough away but most of the time I would turn the corner and there she would be, studying the calorie content on the back of food packets, not having even noticed my absence. If she ever did notice the lack of my shuffling, lanky body trailing behind her, no more than five minutes would pass before she found me. She only needed to look up and she'd see my head above the clothes rails, or look down to spy my awkward oversized feet poking out from behind a shelf.

From viewing other mothers, I see how the first casual glance over their shoulder changes to panic, how their movements become quicker, head, eyes, limbs darting around, then their abandoning shopping trolleys in search for the only thing that truly feeds their soul. The fear, the panic, the dread, the drive. They say a mother has the strength to lift a car if it means saving her child. I think that week Mrs Butler could have lifted a bus just to find Jenny-May. As it got into the second month she looked as though she could barely lift her own eyes above ground level. Jenny-May had taken a big chunk of her with her too.

It turned out that I was one of the last to see her. When Grandma and Granddad arrived at noon that day, I opened the door to welcome them in and Jenny-May cycled past. She turned to me and gave me a look. One of her looks that I hated so much. A look that could wither you instantly, a look that said I'm better than you and you are going to lose today at King/Queen and then Stephen Spencer will know what an incompetent lanky idiot you are. I looked over my grandmother's shoulder as I hugged her and watched Jenny-May cycling down the road with her head held high, her chin and nose up in the air and her blonde hair falling to the small of her back. I did what anyone in my situation would have done. I wished she would disappear.

That day my dad won £500 in the lotto scratch cards. He was so delighted, I could tell. He sat down in the kitchen with me and tried not to smile but I could see the corners of his lips curling. We could hear Mrs Butler crying in the next room with my mother. He placed his hand over mine and I knew he was thinking right then that he was so lucky, what a lucky father to win money in the lotto and still have his daughter when people like Mr and Mrs Butler were suffering so much. I, in turn, was glad that I hadn't gone missing, and due to Jenny-May's no-show I was now the undisputed champion of King/Queen. I'd also made some new friends now that Jenny-May wasn't around to tell them not to. Things were going great for my family and life couldn't possibly be any worse for Mr and Mrs Butler. My parents stayed up late those nights, talking and thanking God how they had been blessed.

But something inside me felt different. Jenny-May's last stolen glance had taken a part of me with it. That day, Mr and Mrs Butler weren't the only parents to lose a child.

Like I said, there's always balance.

41

Despite Dr Burton's threats and protestations, Jack had decided to continue with his mission and make the journey to Leitrim after all. Another night spent in young Bobby's room had awoken the drive within him to find Donal – not that it had needed much of an awakening. It was the part of him that was constantly wide-eyed and alert, searching around for answers, clues and meaning with every beat of his heart. He was still clinging to the idea that finding Sandy was his way out. She was the medicine his overworked mind needed in order to rest. Why exactly, he didn't know, but he had rarely felt such instincts for something in his life. It was as though the part of him that had been lost along with Donal had been replaced by a strengthened sense. He was like a blind man being led by his heightened sense of smell, by touch he could orientate himself, by sound he could listen to his heart. When Jack had lost Donal he had lost his vision but he'd gained a new sense of direction in his life.

He didn't know what he was going to say to Sandy's parents when he saw them, if indeed they were home or if they would even give him the time of day. He just kept on following the invisible internal compass that had replaced Donal. At noon he found himself sitting in his car around the corner from the housing estate where they lived, taking deep breaths. It was a Saturday, but the small cul-de-sac was quiet. He got out of the car and strolled down the street, trying to look inconspicuous but feeling and knowing he was completely out of place on the tranquil road, the only moving piece on a chessboard.

He stopped outside number four where there was a small two-door silver car in the drive that glistened to within an inch of its life. The front garden was immaculate and was a hive of activity for bees and birds. All the summer flowers were out in their glory, colours of every shade, sweet honey scents, jasmines and lavenders. The grass was an even inch in height all around, the border where it met the soil a razor-sharp line that looked like it could cut any petal that dared to fall. A hanging basket overflowing with petunias and geraniums hung from outside the porch door. An umbrella stand sat inside, Wellington boots and fishing gear beside that. By the entrance a gnome hid under a willow tree, holding a sign saying 'Welcome'. Jack relaxed slightly. Here were not the boarded-up windows, barking dogs and burned-out car from his worst-case-scenario fears.

He opened the lemon-coloured gate, which matched the front door and windowframes, like a perfectly edible candy house. There was no creak, just as he'd suspected. He walked up the even flagstones, not a weed peeking between them. He cleared his throat and pressed the doorbell, its tinkling sound also non-threatening. He heard footsteps, saw a shadow through the obscured glass. Despite the friendly appearance of the woman he assumed to be Sandy's mother, the arrival of a strange man on her doorstep demanded the porch's sliding door remain closed.

'Mrs Shortt?' Jack smiled, giving her the least threatening face he could.

She seemed to relax a bit and stepped into the porch area, the sliding door still a barrier. 'Yes?'

'My name is Jack Ruttle, I'm very sorry to disturb you at home but I was wondering if Sandy was here?'

Her eyes moved fleetingly over him, quickly surveying the man who looked for her daughter, and then she slid the porch door open. 'You're a friend of Sandy's?'

Saying no would probably result in the closing of the door once again. 'Yes,' he smiled. 'Is she here?'

She smiled back. 'I'm sorry, Mr . . . what did you say your name was?'

'It's Jack Ruttle, but just call me Jack.'

'Jack,' she smiled pleasantly. 'She's not here. Is there anything I can help you with?'

'I don't suppose you could tell me where she is?' He kept smiling, knowing it had the potential to be far more of an awkward moment, a perfect stranger interrogating a mother on the whereabouts of her child.

'Where is she?' she repeated thoughtfully. 'I don't know, Jack. Would she want me to tell you where she is?'

They both laughed and Jack shifted uncomfortably. 'Well, I'm not sure how I could possibly convince you of that.' He held his hands out, admitting defeat. 'Look, I don't know what I was expecting when I got here but I just thought I'd take a chance. I'm very sorry for bothering you. Could I leave a message for her? Could you tell her that I'm looking for her and that,' he paused and tried to think of something that could convince Sandy to crawl out of her hiding place if she was in that house listening to him right now, 'could you tell her that I can't do this without her. She'll know what I'm talking about.'

Sandy's mother nodded, studying him all the while. 'I'll pass the message on.'

'Thank you.' There was a pause and Jack prepared to wrap it up.

'You're not a Leitrim boy, by the sounds of it?'

He smiled. 'Limerick.'

She mulled that over. 'She was going to visit you last week?'

'Yes.'

'The one thing I do know about my daughter, she rang me on her way to Glin, was it?' she smiled and it faded quickly. 'She was looking for someone of yours?'

Jack nodded, feeling like a teenager faced by a nightclub bouncer and hoping his silence would allow him in.

Mrs Shortt was quiet while she pondered what to do. She looked up and down the road. A neighbour across the road raised a garden glove to her and she waved back. Perhaps feeling less threatened, she made her decision. 'Come inside,' she motioned to him, and moved away from the door, heading back down the hall.

Jack looked up and down the road. The neighbour watched him reluctantly step into the house. He smiled awkwardly. He could hear Mrs Shortt in the kitchen, clattering cups and plates. He heard the kettle go on. The inside of the house was as immaculate as the outside. The front door led directly into the living room. It smelled of furniture polish and fresh air, as though all the windows had been left open for the scents of the garden to rush inside. There was no clutter. The carpet was vacuumed, silver and brasses gleamed, wood shone.

'I'm in here, Jack,' Mrs Shortt called out as though they were life-long friends.

He went through to the unsurprisingly gleaming kitchen. The washing machine was running, RTE Radio 1 was on in the background and the kettle was building up its crescendo to boiling point. From the kitchen there were French doors that led out to the back garden, and it was as well maintained as the front, with a large birdhouse, currently accommodating a greedy-looking robin singing between each peck at the seeds.

'You have a lovely home, Mrs Shortt,' Jack said, taking a seat at the kitchen table. 'Thank you for the kind invitation.'

'You can call me Susan, and you're welcome.' She filled the teapot with boiling water, covered it with a tea-cosy and waited. Jack hadn't had tea like that since his mother used to make it. Despite welcoming him into her home Susan was still on guard and stood by the counter with one hand on the tea-cosy, the other fiddling with a tea bag. 'You're the first friend of Sandy's to call by since she was a teenager.' She looked deep in thought.

Jack didn't know how to respond to that.

'Everybody after that knew better,' she smiled. 'How well do you know Sandy?'

'Not well enough.'

'No,' she said more to herself, 'I didn't think so.'

'Every day that I search for her, I learn something new about her,' he added.

'You're searching for her?' She raised her eyebrows.

'That's why I'm here, Mrs Shortt—'

'Susan, please.' She looked pained. 'I look around for Harold's mother and the scent of cabbage when I hear that name. Everything was cabbage, cabbage, cabbage with that woman,' she laughed at the memory.

'Susan,' he smiled. 'The last thing I came here to do is worry you, but I was due to meet with Sandy last week, as you mentioned. She didn't show up and since then I've done everything to try and contact her.' He deliberately left out the details about finding her car and phone. 'I'm sure she's fine,' he insisted, 'but I really want,' he started again, 'I really *need* to find her.' Sending Sandy's mother into a panic was the very opposite of his intention and he held his breath, awaiting her response. He was relieved if not a little shocked to see a tired smile crawl onto her face but it gave up, collapsing in a sad heap, before reaching her eyes.

'You're right, Jack, you certainly don't know our Sandy well enough.' She turned her back to him to pour the tea. 'Now let me teach you another thing about my daughter. I love her very much but she has the ability to hide as expertly as a sock in a washing machine. No one knows where it goes just as no one knows where she goes, but at least when she decides to come back, we're all here, waiting for her.'

'I've heard that from everyone this week.'

She whisked around. 'Who else did you speak to?'

'Her landlord, her clients, her doctor . . .' he trailed off guiltily. 'I really didn't want to have to call on you about this.'

'Her doctor?' Susan asked, not minding at all that she had been left until last. She was more interested in the mention of her daughter's doctor.

'Yes, Dr Burton,' Jack said slowly, not sure whether to reveal Sandy's private information to her mother.

'Oh!' Susan tried to hide a smile.

'You know him?'

'Do you know by any chance if it's *Gregory* Burton?' She tried to hide her excitement but failed miserably.

'That's him, but he isn't so keen on me, in case you're talking to him.'

'Indeed,' Susan said thoughtfully, not hearing what he'd said. 'Indeed,' she repeated with her eyes alight, answering a question Jack wasn't privy to. She was clearly delighted but, remembering Jack was in the room, she composed herself, intrigue taking the place of a mother's excitement. 'Why is it that you want to find Sandy so much?'

'I was worried about her when she didn't turn up to meet me in Glin, and then I was unable to contact her, which made me even more concerned.' It was partly true but it sounded lame and he knew it.

Susan appeared to know it too. She raised her eyebrows and spoke in a bored tone. 'I've been waiting for three weeks for Barney the plumber to come and fix my sink but I haven't yet planned on visiting his mother.'

Jack looked absentmindedly at her sink. 'Well, Sandy *is* looking for my brother. I even got in touch with a member of the Gardaí in Limerick.' He felt his face flush as Susan let out a sound of surprise. 'Graham Turner is his name, in case he calls.'

Susan smiled. 'We called the police on three occasions at the beginning but we've learned not to now. If Garda Turner asks around he'll know not to continue with his investigations.'

'He's already done that,' Jack said grimly and then he frowned. 'I don't understand all this, Susan. I can't understand where she's gone. I can't fathom how she can disappear so cleverly without anyone knowing where she is, without anyone *wanting* to know where she is.'

'We each have our hiding places and we each put up with the little quirks of the people we love.' She rested her head on her hand and seemed to study him.

He sighed. 'That's it?'

'What do you mean?'

'That's it? Just let people vanish? No more questions asked? Come and go as you please? Flutter in and out. Disappear, reappear and disappear again? No problem!' he laughed angrily. 'Nobody worry about a thing! Don't bother caring about all the people at home that love you and that are worrying themselves sick about you.'

There was silence.

'You love Sandy?'

'What?' he screwed his face up.

'You said . . .' she trailed off. 'Never mind.' She sipped her tea.

'I've only ever spoken to Sandy on the phone,' Jack said slowly. 'There was no . . . relationship between us.'

'So by finding my daughter, you find your brother?' He didn't have time to answer the question. 'Do you think your brother's hiding place is the same as Sandy's?' she asked boldly.

And there it was. Said by a complete stranger, someone who had met him no more than ten minutes before had summed up the ridiculous notion behind his frantic search in one question. Susan allowed a few moments to pass before offering, 'I don't know the circumstances of your brother's disappearance, Jack, but I know he's not in the same place as Sandy. Here's another lesson,' she said softly, 'a lesson Harold and I have learned over the years. No one ever finds the other sock in the washing machine, not through actively looking, anyway.' She waved her hand dismissively.

'Things just turn up. You can drive yourself crazy trying to find them. It doesn't matter how neat and tidy you keep your life, it doesn't matter how organised things are.' She paused and laughed sadly. 'I'm a hypocrite. I pretend to myself that a tidy house will make Sandy come home more often. I think, if she can just *see* everything, if she can see that everything is in order and has its place then she won't have to worry about things going missing.' She looked around the spotless kitchen. 'Anyway, it doesn't matter how much, how often or how closely you keep an eye on things, you can't control it. Sometimes things and people go,' she waved her hand through the air, 'just like that.' Then she placed a comforting hand over his. 'Don't destroy yourself trying to find out where.'

They said their goodbyes at the door and Susan, trying to hide her embarrassment, said, 'Talking about things turning up, if you do come across Sandy before we do, tell her I found her purple diary with the butterflies. It was in her old bedroom, unusual because I've cleaned out that wardrobe dozens of times but never came across it,' she frowned. 'Anyway, it would be important for her to know.'

She looked up and waved again across the road and Jack turned to see a woman of similar age to Susan. 'That's Mrs Butler,' she said, although it was of no importance to Jack. 'Her daughter, Jenny-May, went missing when she was ten years old, the same age as Sandy. Such a lovely little girl, an angel, everyone said.'

Jack, suddenly interested, studied the woman some more. 'Did they find her?'

'No,' Susan said sadly, 'they never did but she has left that porch light on every single night for twenty-four years hoping she'll come home. She'll barely go away on holiday, she's so afraid she'll miss her.'

Jack slowly walked back to his car, feeling odd, different, as though he had switched bodies with the man who had only an hour ago entered the Shortt household. He stopped walking, looked to the sky and contemplated all that he had learned through meeting Sandy's mother. He smiled. And he cried as relief washed over him like a waterfall raining down. Because for the first time in a year, he felt like he could finally stop.

And start living again.

42

Bobby was in no mood to discuss hearing his laughter enter this atmosphere the previous night but he needn't have spoken a word because it was clear that the air had been let out of his once ballooned spirit and all that was left was its deflated shell. It broke my heart to see him that way, to see a bird that had once soared now lie defeated on the ground, a broken wing stopping his flight. The few times I had attempted to raise the issue the more still he lay. There wasn't a whimper, there wasn't a tear; it was his silence that screamed the words he couldn't or wouldn't voice. It appeared he was going to concentrate on my problems until he felt fit to deal with his own – not an altogether alien method of dealing with life, for me.

'Why do you always leave your bag by the door?' Bobby spoke for the first time as we entered his shop.

I looked to where Bobby was staring to see my bag or, dare I say, Barbara Langley's bag, that had been quite absentmindedly placed beside the door. Like a cowboy in a Western who parked his horse up by the saloon door, it was to enable a swift departure from any situation. To help ease the feelings of claustrophobia I would feel in the rooms and company of those I wasn't altogether comfortable with, my parents included. Gregory included. My own home included. Rarely were there places I would keep my bag on my person. I would look to the door, see my bag, and feel secure knowing there was a way out and there, as proof, were my belongings not far from that exit to freedom.

I shrugged. 'Just habit.' How all of my life's complications and complex idiosyncrasies could be reduced to a shrug and two words. How nothing words could be.

Bobby wasn't in the mood to question me any further and we returned to the storeroom containing my boxes of belongings.

'So,' I broke the silence and looked to Bobby, who was staring as though lost, as though he had never before encountered this room, 'what are we doing back here?' I asked.

'We're going to empty your boxes.'

'Why?'

He didn't respond; not because he was ignoring me but because I think he didn't hear me. There was so much more for him to hear now. He began emptying the top box, placing Mr Pobbs very carefully on the floor. He lined up each item in a row from wall to wall, then moved to the next box and did the same. I helped him, though I didn't understand why. After twenty minutes, my belongings from Here were lined neatly in six rows across the walnut floor. I looked down at each item and couldn't help smiling. Each one, from the impersonal, the stapler, to the personal, Mr Pobbs – all opened the doors to previously locked-away memories.

Bobby was looking at me.

'What?'

'Do you notice anything?'

I looked back to the floor, running my eyes along the rows. Mr Pobbs, stapler, T-shirt, twenty odd socks, engraved pen, work file I got in trouble for losing . . . Was I missing the point? I turned to him questioningly.

'What about the passport?' he stated lifelessly.

I looked back to the floor, smiling already. When I was fifteen years old my parents had arranged for us to go to Austria on a hiking holiday but the night before we were due to travel, my passport was nowhere to be found. I hadn't wanted to go away at all. I had been complaining about the trip for months. A week away had meant missing two sessions with Mr Burton but not only that, any fear, any irrational phobia, tends to affect normal daily life. I stopped enjoying trips away due to my fear of losing things, and if something was lost in a place like Austria, a place I had never been to, a place I would more than likely never return to again, well then, how on earth was I supposed to find anything again? The night I lost my passport I had a quick change of heart. The two sessions with Mr Burton were forgotten – all of a sudden I wanted to find the passport and I wanted to go on the trip. Anything that meant not missing another possession in my life.

The trip was cancelled as it was too late to get a replacement or temporary passport but for once, my parents were genuinely as flummoxed as I was, and had searched as frantically as I had. Finding it here after all those years, tattered and worn and complete with gawky photograph of me aged eleven, had been an incredible moment. But as I looked around the floor my smile faded. It was no longer there.

I stepped over the rows of items, kicking some in my rush to get to the cardboard boxes where I frantically searched. Bobby left the room to give me my space, or so I thought, but he returned with a Polaroid camera. He motioned for me to step aside, which I did without question. He pointed the camera at the ground, took a photograph, extracted the square photo, shook it, examined it and then slid it into a plastic folder.

'I found this camera years ago,' he explained, sadness echoing in his words. 'It's difficult to find the cartridges that go with it. I don't even know if they make them any more, but now and again I come across boxes of the right ones. I have to be careful with the photographs I take; I can't waste them. I don't mind being careful but it's difficult to know which second among a lifetime of seconds is more special. Often when you realise how precious those seconds are, it's too late for them to be captured because the moment has passed. We realise too late.' He was silent for a moment, lost in thought, frozen as though his batteries had run out. I touched his arm and he looked up, surprised to see me in the room. He looked down at the camera in his hands, surprised to see it there too. Then he rebooted, the light returned behind his eyes and he continued, 'This is how you refill it. Take photos of these items on the floor every morning from now on.' He handed it to me and added before walking away, 'And then I suggest you start taking the other photos.'

'What other photos?'

He stopped at the doorway and suddenly looked even younger than his nineteen years, like a little lost boy. 'I don't know much about what goes on around here, Sandy. I don't know why we're all here, how we all got here or even what we're supposed to be doing. I never knew that when I was at home with my mum either,' he smiled. 'But as far as I can see, you followed all your belongings here and now, day by day, items disappear. I don't know where they're going, but wherever that is, I suggest that when you find yourself there, you have proof that you were ever here. Proof of us.' His smile weakened. 'I'm tired now, Sandy. I'm going to go to bed. See you at seven for the council meeting.'

43

Barbara Langley hadn't much in the way of clothes suitable for community meetings, most likely because the doomed New York holiday, which resulted in the loss of her luggage over twenty years ago, didn't call for being put on trial by an entire community. But then again, you never know.

I chose to stay away from rehearsals at the Community Hall, knowing that my presence there later would be enough and that Helena had all under control the play I really wasn't interested being involved in. I passed the day by covering the shop for Bobby, who had quite understandably decided to stay in bed the entire day. I busied myself; I *pleasured* myself rooting around the long-legged people's section, diving into bargain buckets with all the ferocity of a bear that had stumbled upon a picnic park. Excitedly I pulled out outfits I dreamed of having at home. Ecstasy-fuelled purrs escaped my lips as I tried on shirts with sleeves that reached my wrists, T-shirts that covered my belly button and trousers with hems that fell to the floor. A tingle rushed through my body each time the feel of fabric covered an area of skin so used to being bare and exposed. What a difference an inch of fabric made. Particularly on a cold morning standing at the bus stop, stretching the sleeves of a favourite jumper just so it covered a racing angry pulse. That small inch, insignificant to most, everything to me, was the difference between a good day and a bad, between internal peace and outward loathing, denial and the realisation of an overwhelming, albeit temporary, desire to be like everyone else. A few inches shorter, a few inches happier, richer, content, warmer.

Every once in a while the bell over the door sounded and just like the end of my playtime at school, the climax would come to an abrupt end. The majority of shoppers that day had come to the shop with one goal in mind: to have a look at me, the one they had heard about, the one who knew things. People from all nations would lock eyes with me, hoping for recognition, and when there wasn't any, would leave, disappointment weighing heavy on their shoulders. Each time the bell rang and another pair of eyes bored into mine, I became more nervous for the evening ahead, and no matter how hard I wanted to prevent the many clocks on the wall from ticking, the hands raged on and the night was suddenly upon me.

It seemed the entire village had decided to attend the council meeting at the Community Hall. Bobby and I pushed our way through throngs of people slowly filing towards the giant oak door. News of somebody with the capacity to know all about families at home had caused people of all nationalities, races and creeds to flock in their thousands to the building. The hot orange sun was disappearing behind the pines trees, giving the effect of strobe lighting as we walked briskly alongside them. Above us, hawks circled low in the sky, dangerously skimming the tree-tops. Around me, I felt eyes on me, watching, waiting to pounce.

The carvings of people shoulder to shoulder, upon the giant doors, parted and bodies began to file in. The theatre had been transformed from the informal arrangement of rehearsal hours. I felt deceived, realising it was more than it had originally appeared to be, capable of more than it had shown itself to me, and now here it was elegantly dressed, standing upright and proud; royalty when I had thought it a servant. Hundreds of rows of seats led from the stage, the red velvet curtains pulled back by a chunky golden twist with tassels bowing, their overturned heads of hair skimming the ground. On stage rows of representatives sat on tiered seating, some wearing their countries' traditional costumes, others choosing modern dress. There were three-piece suits next to embroidered dishdash, sequined jellabahs, silk kimonos, kippas, turbans and jilbab, bead, bone, gold and silver jewellery, women in elaborately patterned khanga, upon them Swahili proverbs offering pearls of wisdom I could not understand, and men in fine hanbok. There was everything from khussa shoes to Jimmy Choos, Thousand Mile sandals and flip-flops to polished leather lace-ups. I spotted Joseph in the second row wrapped in a purple gown with gold trimming. The vision was stunning, the mixture of fine cultured clothes side by side a treat. Despite my feelings on the evening ahead, I lifted the Polaroid camera and took a photo.

'Hey!' Bobby grabbed the camera from my hands. 'Stop wasting the cartridges!'

'Wasting?' I gasped. 'Look at that!' I pointed to the stage of representatives from all nations, sitting grandly overlooking the sea of villagers, who watched them expectantly, desperately awaiting news of the old world they had left behind. We sat in seats halfway up the auditorium to ensure I wasn't in the first row for the firing line. We spotted Helena towards the front of the room, desperately scouring the crowds with an alarming look of concern or fear – I couldn't tell which. Assuming it was us she was looking for, Bobby waved at her wildly. I couldn't move. My body sat frozen in this new fear I was experiencing, in a theatre that had very quickly become full with the noise of thousands of people becoming louder and louder in my ears. I glanced over my shoulder. Dozens more stood at the back of the hall, blocking the exits, unable to find seats. The banging shut and locking of the gigantic doors reverberated around the room and everybody instantly fell silent. The breathing of the man behind me was loud in my ears, the whispering of the couple in front of me like a loudspeaker. My heart began a drumbeat of its own. I looked at Bobby for reassurance I didn't get. The harsh lights from above didn't allow anybody or their reactions to hide. Everyone and everything was revealed.

Helena had been forced to take her seat when the door had shut and silence had ensued. I tried my best to keep thinking that this was a silly little place, a figment of my imagination. It was all a dream, unimportant, not real life. But no matter how much I pinched myself and tried to zone out, the atmosphere pulled me back in, leaving me with the foreboding sense that this was as real as the beating of my heart.

A woman walked up the outside aisle with a basket of earphones. They were taken by the person at the end seat and passed along the rows like a church collection. I looked to Bobby questioningly and he demonstrated, plugging the headphone set into a socket in the chair in front. He placed them over his ears as a man stood before the microphone on stage. He began speaking Japanese, a word of which I could not understand but was so transfixed by the scene before me I failed to remember to put my earphones on. Bobby elbowed me and I jumped, quickly placing them over my ears. A heavily accented English voice offered the translation. I had missed the beginning of his announcement.

'. . . this Sunday evening. It's rare that so many of us all gather together. Thank you for the wonderful turnout. There are a few reasons why we are here tonight—'

Bobby elbowed me again and my headphones came off. 'That's Ichiro Takase,' he whispered. 'He's the Rep President. It changes person every few months.'

I nodded and the headphones went back on again.

'. . . Hans Liveen wishes to speak to you about the plans for the new mill scheme but before we address that we will deal with the reason why so many of you have attended this meeting. Irish Representative Grace Burns will speak to you about this.'

A woman who appeared to be in her fifties stood from her seat and made her way to the microphone. She had long wavy red hair, her features were pointed as though chiselled from a rock and she was dressed in a sharp black business suit.

I removed my headphones.

'Good evening, everybody.' Her accent placed her from the north of Ireland, Donegal. Many of the non-Irish English speakers put their headphones back on for the translation. 'I'll make this brief,' she said. 'I was approached this week by many people from the Irish community with news that a newcomer from Ireland had information on various villagers' families. Despite the rumours, this of course isn't unusual, given Ireland's size. I was also told that an item belonging to this person – I understand that it's her watch – has gone missing,' she said in her matter-of-fact tones.

People that understood English immediately gasped, although the majority of them were surely aware of this rumour already. A few seconds later, there was a second gasp as the interpreters translated. Murmuring began in the hall and the Irish Representative held her arms up to silence everyone. 'I understand this news has had an effect on the entire village. News like this disrupts our attempts at normal living and we are keen to put the rumours to rest.'

My heart began to beat a little less dramatically.

'We've called the meeting tonight to assure you that the matter is in hand and it will be dealt with. As soon as it is, we will immediately inform the community, as we always do, as to the outcome. I believe this newcomer is among us tonight,' she announced, 'and so I wish to address this person.'

Instantly my heart began to palpitate again. People around me looked about, murmuring, jabbering excitedly in foreign tones and eyeing one another suspiciously, accusingly. I looked to Bobby in shock. He gaped back at me.

'What will I do?' I whispered. 'How do they know about the watch?'

The nineteen-year-old in him shrugged back, eyes wide.

'We all think it's best to deal with this privately and quietly so that the person can remain anonymous—'

There was a heckling of boos from the crowd, some people laughed and my skin crawled.

'I see no need for dramatics,' Grace continued in her official, no-nonsense tone. 'If the newcomer could just present us with the alleged missing item then this will be dropped and forgotten once and for all so that the congregation can get back to spending their valuable time in their usual greatly productive ways.' She smiled cheekily and there were chuckles from around the room. 'If the person in question could familiarise themselves with my office tomorrow morning and bring the watch with them, then this can be dealt with swiftly and privately.'

More boos by members of the audience.

'I'll take a few questions on this and then we will move on with the more important matter of the plans to build further past the wind farm.' I could tell she was being deliberately blasé about the whole thing. An entire village had turned out to hear about me, about how I knew intimate details of people here and their family members. In a few sentences she had brushed it all under the carpet. People looked around at each other unhappily and I sensed a storm brewing.

Many people raised their hands and the representative nodded to one. A man stood. 'Ms Burns, I don't think it's fair that this matter be dealt with privately. I think it's clear from the turnout tonight that this issue is more important than the manner of how you have chosen to address it, which is a deliberate attempt at playing down the significance.' There were a few claps. 'I put forward that the person in question, whom I know to be a woman, show us the watch right *now*, right here *tonight*, so that we can see it with our own eyes and therefore allow the matter to be dropped and for our minds to be put at rest.'

There was a healthy applause to this suggestion.

The representative looked uncomfortable, she turned to look at her colleagues. Some nodded, some shook their heads, others looked bored, some shrugged and left it up to her.

'I'm concerned only with the welfare of the person in question, Mr O'Mara,' she addressed him. 'I hardly see it fair that she has arrived here only this week and is also faced with this. Her anonymity is vital. Surely you can appreciate that.'

This wasn't so strongly supported by people, but there was a light round of clapping from a few dozen and I silently thanked them and cursed Grace for confirming my sex.

An elderly woman standing beside the man speaking from the audience shot up out of her seat. 'Ms Burns, our wellbeing is more important, and the wellbeing of all the villagers. Isn't it more important that if once again we have heard rumours of somebody's belongings going missing we have a right to know if it's true?'

There were noises of support from among the crowd. Grace Burns held her hand up to her forehead to block the harsh stage lights in order to see the person belonging to the voice. 'But, Catherine, it *will* be revealed to you tomorrow after the person has come to me. Whatever the outcome it will be dealt with appropriately.'

'This doesn't just affect the Irish community,' a southern American male voice called out. Everybody looked around. The voice came from a man standing at the back. 'Remember what happened the last time there were rumours of things going missing?'

There were mumbles of agreement and nods.

'Everybody here remember a guy called James Ferrett?' he shouted now, addressing the hall.

There were loud murmurs of 'yes' and heads nodded.

'A few years ago he told of the very same thing happening to him. The representatives did the same thing then as they are doing now,' he addressed the crowd who were unfamiliar with the story. 'Mr Ferrett was encouraged to follow the same procedure as our anonymous woman tonight and instead he disappeared. Whether it was to join the rest of his belongings or whether it was the work of the reps we will never know.'

There was uproar at this but he shouted over the noise. 'At least let us deal with it now before the person in question has a chance to escape once again without us learning about what is happening. It's not as though any harm will come to her, and it's our duty to know!'

There was huge applause to this. The entire community erupted. They didn't want another opportunity of finding a way back to go by. The rep was quiet for a while as the hall chanted around her. She made a motion for silence and the crowd died down.

'Very well,' she said loudly into the microphone and those two words bounced around my heart until I thought I would faint or laugh, which one I wasn't sure.

I looked to Bobby. 'Please pinch me,' I smiled, 'because this is all so ridiculous I feel as though I'm in one of those awful nightmares you laugh about the next day.'

'It's not funny, Sandy,' he warned. 'Don't tell them anything.'

I tried to hide a smile yet my heart pounded.

'Sandy Shortt,' the representative announced, 'could you please stand up?'

44

After Jack had left Sandy Shortt's family home, he drove to the Leitrim Arms, the local bar in the small village. Despite the early hour the pub was dark, lit by too few dusty wall lights, natural light blocked out by dark burgundy stained-glass windows. The floor was uneven, flagged with stones, and the wooden benches were covered with paisley cushions with foam spilling from the sides. There were a total of three men in the bar: two at opposite ends of the counter, pints in hand, necks craning to see the horseracing on the small television suspended from a bracket from the ceiling. The barman held court behind the counter, arms resting on the taps, head up, eyes glued to the race. There was anxious expectation painted on each of the men's faces, a monetary interest in the outcome obvious. The commentator's thick Cork accent speedily documented a second-by-second account of the race, speaking so fast, everybody couldn't help but hold his breath, adding to the atmosphere of suspense.

Catching the barman's attention, Jack ordered a pint of Guinness and chose to sit in the quiet snug at the far end of the bar, away from everyone. He had something important to do.

The barman took his gaze away from the television, choosing profession over obsession, and gave his pouring of the perfect pint his complete attention. He held the glass at a forty-five-degree angle close to the spout, preventing large bubbles from forming in the head. He pulled the tap fully open and filled the glass seventy-five per cent full. He placed the pint on the counter, allowing the stout to settle before filling the rest of the glass.

Jack took Donal's police file out of his bag and placed it on the table before him, spreading out the pages one last time. This was his goodbye. This was the end, the final glance at all he had studied every day for the past year. The end of the search, the beginning of the rest of his life. He wanted to raise a glass to his brother one final time, one last drink together. He ran his eyes over the police reports, the long hours of dedicated police time, each page reminding him of the ups and downs, the hopes and disappointments of the previous year. It had been long and hard. He laid out the witness statements in a row, the reports from all of Donal's friends who had been with him that night. The anguish and tears, lost sleep and despair that had gone into trying to remember every last blurred detail of the night.

Jack placed Donal's photograph on the tall stool opposite him. One final pint with his brother. He smiled across at him. *I've done my best, Donal; I promise you I've done my best.* For the first time he believed it. There was no more he could do. With that thought came great relief. He looked down again at the pages before him. Alan O'Connor's face stared back at him from the passport photo attached at the corner. Another broken man, another life almost destroyed. Alan was far from reaching the point Jack had arrived at that day. Jack had lost his brother, a brother he didn't know as well as he should have but Alan had lost his greatest friend. He glanced at the statement he'd read a thousand times, if not more. Alan's full, detailed account of the doomed night matched Andrew, Paul and Gavin's accounts and those of the three girls they had met at the fast-food restaurant, though they had trouble barely remembering the beginning of their night, never mind the early hours of the next morning. The language of the report was awkward, stilted and foreign. It lacked emotion, relayed only the facts of the matter, times and places, who was there and what was said. No feelings to convey the fact a group of friends had been torn apart by the incident of this one night. The one night that changed a lifetime of nights.

Andrew, Paul, Gavin, Shane, Donal and I left Clohessy's on Howley's Quay at approximately 12.30 on Friday night. We went to the nite club, 'The Sin Bin' in the same building . . . Jack skipped the details of what happened inside the club. *Andrew, Paul, Gavin, Donal and I left the club at approximately 2 a.m. and walked two blocks to SuperMacs on O'Connell Street. Shane had met a girl in the nite club that none of us knew and went home with her . . .* He skipped a few lines. *All of us sat down in a booth on the right-hand side of the chipper closest to the counter, to eat our burgers and chips. We got talking to three girls who were also in the chipper. We asked them to join us and we all sat in the booth. There were eight of us: me, Andrew, Paul, Gavin, Donal, Collette, Samantha and Fiona. Donal sat on the outside, on the edge of the seat beside Fiona, and opposite me. We made plans to go back to a party at Fiona's house . . .* Jack skipped to the most important part. *I asked Donal if he was going to the party and he said yes and that was the last conversation we had that night. He didn't tell me he was leaving the chipper. I started talking to Collette and when I turned around Donal was gone. That was at 3 a.m. approximately.*

They had all relayed the same story. It was just a normal lads' Friday night out. Pub, night club, chipper, nothing out of the ordinary for them to remember; just the fact that their best friend went missing. Each of Donal's friends relayed different final conversations, nobody noticed him leave the chipper apart from the girl named Fiona, who was sitting beside him and only noticed that he was not beside her when she turned around and saw him walking out of the chipper. She said he had fallen against the doorframe as he left and a few girls by the door had seen him and laughed. Later, none of these girls could offer any more information than that. The chipper was full of people all thrown out of night clubs at the same time, and the CCTV in the chipper did not film the booth that Donal had been seated at. The queues forming at the counter and the pockets of people standing around unable to get a table blocked the booths. Still, there was nothing to see but Donal walking out of the chipper, bumping his shoulder on the doorframe as everyone had witnessed. CCTV filmed him at the nearby ATM where he withdrew €30, he was seen again stumbling down Arthur's Quay, and then his trace was lost.

Jack thought back to the last time he had spoken to Alan and felt guilty for putting him under such pressure to try to remember more. Alan had clearly already been squeezed for every last drop of detail of the night by the Gardaí. Jack had felt that in some way his brother going missing was his fault, that as an older brother there was something that he should have done, was supposed to do to make it right. His mother died feeling that same responsibility. Was there anyone that didn't blame themselves? He recalled his conversation with Alan, how only a few days ago he had admitted the same.

I hope you find him, Jack. I keep going back over that night again and again, wishing I'd left with him.

On the counter, the creamy head of the Guinness began to separate from the dark body. It was still foggy but was becoming clearer.

I keep going back over that night again and again, wishing I'd left with him.

Jack's heart caught in his throat. He fumbled through the pages to find Alan's statement again. *We all made plans to go back to a party at Fiona's house. I asked Donal if he was going to the party and he said yes and that was the last conversation we had that night. He didn't tell me he was leaving the chipper.*

The barman topped off the pint by pushing the tap

forward slightly, allowing the head to rise just proud of the rim.

Jack sat up straight, focused his mind, didn't lose his head. Thoughts began to rise to the top and he felt close to something. He kept reading and rereading the police report while simultaneously going over in his mind the conversation with Alan from only days ago.

The stout didn't overflow or run down the glass.

Jack controlled his breathing and kept his fear contained.

The barman delivered the pint to the snug and hesitated at the entrance, unsure of where to put the Guinness with the table a mess of papers.

'Just put it down anywhere,' Jack said. The barman made a circular motion with the pint in the air, trying to decide where to plant it and finally brought it down to the table, rushing back to where the men were shouting at the television, urging their horse on. Jack's eyes moved down the ruby-black belly of the body of the pint, right down to the base of the glass. The barman had placed it on Alan's statement, next to the sentence he had read over and over again. Everything was drawing him back to that sentence. *I asked Donal if he was going to the party and he said yes and that was the last conversation we had that night. He didn't tell me he was leaving the chipper.*

Jack was trembling but he didn't know why. He raised the shaking glass into the air and smiled wobbily at his brother's photo. He put the glass to his lips and took a big slug of the thick liquid. At the same time the warm stout slid down his throat, the memory of Alan's next sentence fired itself at him.

I really thought he'd be OK getting a taxi down that way, you know?

The Guinness caught in his throat and he began to cough, leaning away from the table to hack it up.

'You OK?' the barman shouted over.

'Yes! Go on, ya boya!' The two men in the bar

celebrated the victory of their horse, clapping their hands and cheering, giving Jack a fright.

Jack's mind ran through a million excuses, defences, mistakes and whether he'd misheard. He thought of Sandy's diary entry to visit written in red capital letters, he thought of the worried face of Mrs O'Connor – *You think he done something wrong?* She knew. She had known all along. Chills ran through him. Anger fired through his veins. He slammed the pint down on the table, the white ring left on the inside of the glass. His legs went weak as rage and fear took over his body.

He didn't remember leaving the pub, he didn't remember calling Alan and he didn't remember driving back to Limerick in record time to meet him. Looking back on those hours there was very little he knew about that night other than what people told him. The one thing he did recall was Alan's forlorn voice, now ringing constantly in his head: *I keep going back over that night again and again wishing I'd left with him. I really thought he'd be OK getting a taxi down that way, you know?* The contradicting voice from his statement shouted even louder: *I asked Donal if he was going to the party and he said yes and that was the last conversation we had that night.*

The last conversation we had.

He had lied. And why would he do that?

45

I stood up from my chair and the eyes of thousands of people turned to look at me, study me, form opinions, judge, hang me, and burn me at the stake. I spotted Helena in the front row, clearly distressed by how this was all playing out. Her hands were clasped tightly to her chest as though in prayer and her eyes glistened with welling tears. I smiled at her, feeling sorry for her. For *her*. She nodded at me encouragingly. Joseph, on the stage, did the same. I wasn't sure what to fear and I suppose that's why I didn't. I didn't understand what was going on, why it mattered so hugely that something of mine had gone missing, why something that seemed so positive could be turned into something so negative. The one thing I did understand was that those who had been here longer than me were fearful for me, and that was enough. Already over the last few days, life had been even more uncomfortable for me with people following me around, questioning me as to whether I knew their families. I wasn't keen on it getting any worse.

The representative fixed her eyes on me. 'Welcome, Sandy. I know it doesn't seem fair to do this so publicly but you have witnessed the reason for having to do it this way.'

I nodded.

'I must ask you, this rumour of your belongings going missing,' she paused, clearly not wanting to ask the question for fear of the answer, 'could you please confirm how this isn't true?'

'You're leading her!' one man shouted out, and others hushed him.

'This is not a courtroom,' the rep said angrily. 'Please allow Ms Shortt to speak.'

'The rumour,' I looked around to the thousands of faces, some of which were listening to the translation of my words in their headphones, 'is most definitely not true.' There was a babble of voices again so I raised my voice. 'Though I do understand where it has come from. I was waving to somebody and my watch flew from my wrist and landed in the nearby field. I enlisted some people to help me find it. It's really not a big deal.'

'And they found it?' Grace Burns said, unable to hide the relief from her voice.

'Yes,' I lied.

'Show it to us!' one man shouted out and a few hundred more agreed.

Grace sighed. 'Are you wearing this watch now?'

I froze and looked down at my bare wrist. 'Em . . . no, because the clasp broke as it fell to the ground and it hasn't been fixed yet.'

'Bring the watch!' a woman shouted.

'No!' I shouted back, and everyone quietened. I felt Bobby look at me in surprise. 'With respect to you all, I feel that this whole thing is no more than a ludicrous witch-hunt. I have given you my word that my watch has not gone missing and I refuse to continue with this charade by bringing it here to masquerade around the hall. I haven't been here long enough to understand why it is exactly you are all behaving this way but if you all wish to welcome me here as you should, then please, allow my word to be enough.'

That didn't go down well.

'Please, Ms Shortt,' Grace said worriedly. 'I suggest the best thing for you to do is to leave the hall and retrieve the watch. Jason will accompany you.' A man dressed in a black suit, lean and slenderly built, with a posture so perfect it could only have come from the army, arrived at the end of my row. He held his arm out towards the door.

'I don't know this man.' I grasped at straws. 'I'm not going with him.'

Grace looked confused first, and then wary. 'Well, you have to bring the watch to us whether you like it or not so who would the best person be to accompany you?'

I thought quickly. 'The man beside me.'

Bobby jumped to attention.

Grace strained her eyes to see, there was a flash of recognition, and she nodded. 'Very well, they will both go with you. We will move on with the session while you're gone.'

The Dutch Representative took to the stage to talk about the plans for more mills but nobody took any notice of him. All eyes were on us as we walked down the long aisle of the hall. People who stood at the back parted for us and we were swallowed up through the huge doors. Once outside, Bobby gave me big eyes, not wanting to speak in front of our companion.

'We have to collect my watch from Bobby's shop,' I explained calmly to Jason. 'He was supposed to fix the clasp for me.'

Bobby nodded, finally understanding.

We arrived outside the door of the Lost and Found shop, the brightly coloured odd socks decorating the front. It was dark outside now, the village like a ghost town with everybody in the Community Hall waiting for me, waiting for news of whether it was possible to leave Here or not.

'I'd like to wait here for Bobby.' I stopped walking and stayed on the veranda looking out to the black forest. Jason didn't say anything, but stood back with his hands joined before him and waited with me.

'What are you, secret service?' I teased, looking him up and down. He didn't smile, just looked away. 'Matrix bad guy? Man in black? Johnny Cash über fan?' He didn't answer. I sighed. 'Are you here to make sure I don't run away?' I asked him.

He didn't answer.

'Would you shoot at me if I did?' I said smartly. 'Asking you to accompany me,' I tutted. 'What do they think I am, a criminal?' I turned to him. 'Just for the record, I don't appreciate you being here.'

He stared straight ahead.

Bobby interrupted the uncomfortable silence, banging the door behind him. 'Right, got it.'

I took it from his hand and examined it.

'Is that yours?' Jason spoke for the first time, studying my face.

It was silver with a mother-of-pearl face but that's where the similarities ended. Instead of a linked bracelet it was chunky; instead of a rectangular face, this was round.

'Yep,' I said confidently. 'That's my watch all right.'

Jason took it in his hands and wrapped it around my wrist. It was hugely oversized even for my wrist. 'Bobby,' Jason rubbed his eyes wearily, 'get her another watch. One that fits, this time.'

We both looked at him in surprise.

'*That's* what I'm here for,' he said smartly, returning to his spot on the veranda.

Bobby quickly headed back to the shop and Jason called after him, 'Oh, and make sure the clasp is broken. You said you weren't wearing it because it was broken, right?'

I nodded, still silent.

'Well, that shut you up,' he said, looking back out to the forest.

Jason, Bobby and I walked back quickly to the Community Hall in silence, me holding the watch tightly in my hands. Just before Jason pulled open the door, I stopped him.

'What happens now?' I asked, anxiety building up inside me.

'Well, I assume you go in there and,' he thought about it and finally shrugged his shoulders, 'lie.' He pulled the door open and thousands of faces turned to look at us.

The Dutch Representative's speech immediately quietened and Grace Burns moved forward to the microphone. Anxiety was written all over her face. Bobby and Jason stayed at the door, Bobby nodded encouragingly and I began to walk forward up the long aisle to the stage at the top. If I hadn't been so uneasy I would have laughed at the irony of it. Gregory would have done anything to get me up the aisle, and his gift of the watch had finally succeeded.

I reached the top and handed the watch to Grace. She studied it, but I questioned how on earth she was to know whether it was my watch or not. It all seemed so ridiculous. It was all an act. To make those who were unsettled here feel more secure so they wouldn't rise up and demand to find a way out.

'How do we know it's her watch?' one person shouted out, and I rolled my eyes.

'Her name is engraved on the back!' someone shouted, and my blood turned cold. There were only a few people who knew that. I looked immediately to Joseph, but from the look on his face I knew it wasn't him. He was looking angrily at Helena, who was looking even more angrily to . . . Joan. Joan sat in the front row, with a red face, beside the man who had shouted out. She must have overheard. She looked apologetically to Helena and me. I looked away, not knowing how to feel, not truly knowing what any possible outcome could be.

'Is this true?' The representative looked at me.

'I assure you it's true,' the man shouted out again.

My face said it all, I'm sure.

She turned the watch over to look for my name at the back. She seemed pleased. 'Sandy Shortt is engraved on the back.'

There was a loud sigh and more talk within the audience.

'Sandy, thank you for co-operating. You may leave

now and enjoy your life here with us. I hope people will be more welcoming towards you from now on,' she smiled warmly.

Stunned, I took the watch, unable to believe that Bobby had managed to engrave my name in such a short space of time. I quickly walked back down the aisle while people clapped and smiled at me, some apologising, others still not convinced but probably never would be. I grabbed Bobby by the hand and led him out of the hall.

'Bobby!' I laughed once we were a safe distance away from the Community Hall. 'How the hell did you manage that?'

Bobby looked horrified. 'Manage what?'

'To engrave my name so quickly!'

'I didn't,' he said in shock.

'What?' I turned the watch over. A clear metallic back stared back at me.

'Come on, let's get inside,' Bobby said, unlocking the door to the shop while looking around him uncertainly.

In the shadows there was a noise and Jason stepped out.

I jumped.

'Sorry to startle you,' he said in his robot-like tone. 'Sandy,' emotion slipped into his voice and his body loosened as he stepped into the light of the porch, 'I just wondered if you knew my wife, Alison?' he asked awkwardly. 'Alison Rice? We're from Galway. Spiddal.' He swallowed hard, his aggressive appearance softened and vulnerable, concern written all over his face.

Still taken by surprise at his sudden appearance, I ran the name through my mind a few times. Not familiar with it, I shook my head slowly. 'Sorry.'

'OK.' He cleared his throat and straightened up, the hardness returning as though the question had never passed his lips. 'Grace Burns wanted me to tell you that she requests a meeting with you in her office first thing in the morning.' And he disappeared back into the darkness.

46

Jack felt the anger pumping through his veins. The muscles in his face twitched as they jumped around under his skin, psyching themselves up for the big fight as he tried to control his breathing, control his temper. His back teeth felt like they'd been ground to the bone on the drive there. His cheeks were hot, and throbbed along with the rest of his body. He clenched and unclenched his fists while walking through the crowded Limerick city pub.

He spotted Alan sitting alone at a small table with a pint before him, a stool sat in front of him, waiting for Jack. Alan looked up and waved, a smile stretched across his face and in that face Jack could see the ten-year-old that used to call round to their house every day. He prepared to fire himself at Alan but stopped. Instead he diverted to the toilet, where he stood at the sink, splashing water on his face, panting as though he'd run a marathon. It was all he could do to stop himself reaching out and wanting to kill Alan himself.

What had he done? What on earth had Alan done?

47

The week that Jenny-May Butler went missing, the Gardaí came to Leitrim National School. We were all especially excited because it was rare that our principal graced our humble selves with his presence, particularly in our classrooms. As soon as we caught sight of his stern, accusing face, butterflies fluttered in everyone's stomachs, each of us instantly hoping we weren't in trouble even though we knew we'd done nothing wrong. But such was his power. Our main reason for excitement was due to him disrupting our religion lesson to whisper loudly into Ms Sullivan's ear. Loud whispering in the classroom by teachers always meant something important was happening. We were allowed to abandon our studies that morning and told to queue in single file at the door with our fingers on our lips. For teachers, our placing our fingers on our lips didn't usually have the desired effect, the finger not being a suitable silencer as it was indeed a finger, not a zip, and it was, more importantly, our own finger, which we had the ability to remove at any stage. But that day when we entered the school hall, none of us said a word, because at the top of the very unusually silent room were two members of the Gardaí Síochána. One woman and one man, dressed head to toe in navy blue.

We sat on the floor in the middle of the hall with the other fourth-classers. Up the front were junior and senior infants, the older you were, the further back you were allowed to be. The sixth-classers always coolly took their places in the back row. Very quickly the hall was filled. The teachers lined up against the walls on the outside aisles like prison wardens, and every now and then clicked their fingers with an angry face at someone who was whispering or who was trying to make themselves more comfortable on the cold and slightly dirty gym floor, but who was seen to be fidgeting too much.

Our principal introduced the two guards to us, explaining that they were from the local garda station and were here to talk about a very important issue. He told us that we would be asked questions later in class about what they had said by our teachers. I looked over at our teachers when he announced this and noticed a few suddenly straightening themselves up to listen. Then the male garda began talking, he introduced himself as Garda Rogers and his colleague Garda Brannigan, and while he slowly walked the width of the top of the room with his hands behind his back he explained how we shouldn't trust strangers, how we shouldn't get into their cars, not even when they tell us that our parents have told them to collect us. That made me think of refusing to get into my uncle Fred's car on Wednesday afternoons when he collected me and I almost laughed out loud. He told us that we should always speak up if we notice someone getting friendlier than they should. If someone approaches us or we witness anybody else being approached we should tell our parents or teachers straight away. I was ten years old and I remember thinking about when I was seven and I saw Joey Harrison being collected by a weird man at school. I told my teacher at the time and she gave out to me because it was his dad and she thought I was being rude.

Also at ten years of age, almost eleven, this safety talk was old news. But I supposed that particular safety talk was especially for the five- and six-year-olds, who sat in the front rows of the hall, picking their noses, scratching their heads, looking at the ceiling. A front row of little grasshoppers. At that point I had no desire to join the Guards. It wasn't that day's free lesson in safety that set off my ambition; it was the odd socks. I also knew the talk was due to Jenny-May's disappearance that week. Everybody had been acting weirdly about it all week. Our teacher had even left the classroom in tears a few times whenever her eyes fell upon Jenny-May's empty seat. I was secretly delighted, which I knew was wrong but it was the first week of peace I'd gotten at school for years. For once I didn't feel Jenny-May's balls of paper hitting my head as she blew them through a straw, and whenever I answered a question in class I didn't hear sniggers behind me. I *knew* that a really terrible and sad thing had happened but I just couldn't *feel* sad.

We said a prayer in class every morning for the first few weeks after she went missing, praying for Jenny-May's safety, praying for her family and praying that she would be found. The prayer got shorter and shorter as the weeks went by and then suddenly one Monday, when we came back after the weekend, Ms Sullivan just left out that prayer without mentioning a thing. Everybody's desks were rearranged in a different shape in the room and, bam!, everything went back to normal. I found that even weirder than Jenny-May going missing in the first place. I spent the first few minutes of that day looking at everybody reciting their poem like they were crazy, but the teacher gave out to me for not learning the poem I had spent two hours learning the night before and she picked on me for the rest of the day.

After Garda Rogers had finished his safety talk, it was Garda Brannigan's turn to talk more specifically about Jenny-May. She spoke in softer tones about how, if anybody knew anything or had any information about something they saw over the last few weeks or months, they should go to room four beside the staffroom as she and Garda Rogers would be there for the day. My face burned because I felt like she was talking directly to me. I looked around, paranoia, feeling as though this entire event had been staged for me just to confess all that I knew. No one looked at me oddly apart from James Maybury, who picked a scab on his elbow and flicked it at me. Our teacher clicked her fingers at him, which had little effect as the damage had already been done and he wasn't afraid, nor did he care much about clicking fingers.

When the talk was over we were once again encouraged by our teachers to go to room four to talk to the Gardaí and then we were given our lunch break, which was a stupid idea because nobody was going to bother missing time playing in the yard by going to the guards. As soon as we got back into our classroom and Ms Sullivan told us to take our maths books out, hands suddenly shot into the air. People just suddenly seemed to remember vital evidence. But what else could Ms Sullivan do? And so the Gardaí found themselves with a very long queue of students of all ages outside their door, some of whom had never even met Jenny-May Butler.

Room four was nicknamed the interrogation room, and the story of what went on inside became more and more exaggerated with each pupil that left and rejoined their friends. There were so many pupils with alleged information that the guards had to come back the next day, but not without a stern announcement to each class that although everybody's help was very much appreciated, garda time was very precious and students should only go to room four if they had something very important to tell them. By the second day, I had already been refused access to room four by my teacher twice on account of the first request to go taking place during the history lesson and the second during Irish.

'But I like Irish, miss,' I protested.

'Good, then you'll be happy to stay,' she snapped, before ordering me to read an entire chapter aloud from the book.

I had no alternative but to raise my hand during art

class on Friday afternoon. *Everybody* loved art class. Ms Sullivan looked at me in surprise.

'Can I go now, miss?'

'To the toilet?'

'No, to room four.'

She looked surprised but finally took me seriously and I was given permission to leave art class to the sound of 'oooooooh' from everybody else.

I knocked on the door to room four and Garda Rogers opened the door. He must have been six foot tall. At ten years old I was already very tall at five foot five and I was happy finally to see someone tower over me, even if he was intimidating, dressed in a garda uniform, and I was about to confess to him.

'Another maths class?' he smiled broadly.

'No,' I said so quietly I could barely hear myself. 'Art.'

'Oh.' He raised his thick caterpillar-eyebrows with surprise.

'I'm responsible,' I said quickly.

'Well, that's good, but I don't think missing one maths class makes you irresponsible, although don't tell your teacher I said that.' He touched his nose.

'No,' I said, taking a deep breath. 'I mean I'm responsible for Jenny-May going missing.'

This time he didn't smile. He opened the door wider. 'Come on in.'

I looked around the room. It was nothing like the rumours that had been going around the last two days. Jemima Hayes said that someone told her friend that someone told her that someone hadn't been allowed to leave the room to go to the toilet and had to wee in his pants. The room was non-threatening, with a couch up against one wall, small table in the centre and a plastic school chair opposite that. There was no sign of a wet chair.

'Sit down there.' He pointed to the couch. 'Make yourself comfortable. What's your name?'

'Sandy Shortt.'

'You're tall for your age, though, aren't you, Miss Shortt?' he laughed, and I smiled politely even though I'd heard it a million times. He stopped himself laughing. 'So, tell me, what makes you think you were responsible for Jenny-May's disappearance, as you called it?'

I frowned. 'What do you call it?'

'Well, we don't know for sure if . . . I mean there's nothing to suggest . . .' He sighed. 'Just tell me why you think you're responsible.' He motioned for more.

'Well, Jenny-May didn't like me,' I began slowly, suddenly becoming nervous.

'Oh, I'm sure that's not true,' he said kindly. 'What makes you think that?'

'She used to call me a lanky slut and throw stones at me.'

'Oh.' He fell silent.

I took a breath. 'Then last week she found out that I told my friend Emer that I didn't think she was as good at King/Queen as everybody thought she was and she got really angry and stormed over to me and Emer and challenged us to a game – well, not us actually, because she didn't say anything to Emer, just me. She doesn't like Emer either but she doesn't like me more, and I was the one that said it so we were supposed to play this game the next day, me and Jenny-May, and whoever won meant that they were the undisputed champions and nobody could say that they weren't good because the fact that they'd won would prove it. She also knew that I fancied Stephen Spencer and she always used to shout stuff at me just so he wouldn't like me, but I knew that she liked him too. Well, it was obvious because they French-kissed in the bushes at the end of the road a few times for dares but I don't think that he really liked her and maybe he's happy she's gone now too, so he'll be left alone, but I'm not saying I think he did anything to make her disappear. Anyway, the day we were supposed to play King/Queen I saw Jenny-May Butler cycling past my house down the road and she gave me a bad look and I knew she was going to beat me that day at King/Queen and that things would be even worse than they already were and—' I stopped talking and pursed my lips, not sure whether to say what I felt next.

'What happened, Sandy?'

I gulped hard.

'Did you do something?'

I nodded and he moved in, shuffling his backside closer to the edge of his chair.

'What did you do?'

'I . . . I . . .'

'It's OK. You can tell me.'

'I wished her away,' I said it quickly, like pulling a plaster from my skin, quick and easy.

'I'm sorry, you what?'

'I wished her away.'

'Whisht? Is that a weapon of some—'

'No, *wished*. I *wished* that she'd disappear.'

'Ah.' Realisation dawned and he sat back slowly in his chair. 'I understand now.'

'No, you're just saying that you do but you don't really. I really did wish for her to be gone, much more than I've ever wished for anything to be gone in my whole entire life, even more than when my uncle Fred stayed over in our house for a month after he split up from Aunt Isabel and he smoked and drank and stunk the place out and I really wanted him gone but not as much as I wanted Jenny-May gone, and a few hours after me wishing that, Mrs Butler came over to our house and told us she was missing.'

He leaned forward again. 'So you saw Jenny-May a few hours before Mrs Butler came over to your house?'

I nodded.

'What time was this at?'

I shrugged.

'Is there anything that could remind you of what time it was? Think back – what were you doing? Was there anybody else around?'

'I had just opened the door to my grandma and

granddad. They came over for lunch and I was giving Grandma a hug when I saw her cycling by. That's when I made the wish.' I winced.

'So this was lunchtime. Was she with anyone?' He was on the edge of his seat now, ignoring my concern over my wishing her away. He asked question after question about what Jenny-May was doing, who she was with, how did she look, what was she wearing, where did it look like she was going – lots of questions over and over again until my head hurt and I could barely think what the answers were any more. It turned out that I was such a good help to them because I was the last person to see her, that I was allowed to go home early that day. Another benefit to Jenny-May's disappearance.

A few nights before the Gardaí came to the school I had begun to feel guilty about Jenny-May disappearing. I watched a documentary with my dad about how one hundred and fifty thousand people in Washington DC all arranged to think positive thoughts at the same time and the crime rate went down, which proved that positive and negative thinking had a real effect. But then Garda Rogers told me that it wasn't my fault Jenny-May Butler was gone, that wishing for something to happen didn't actually make it happen, and so I became a lot more realistic after that.

And there I was, standing outside the office of Grace Burns twenty-four years later, about to knock on the door and feeling exactly the same as when I was ten. I had that same feeling of being responsible for something beyond my control but I also held the belief in some childish way that ever since I was ten years old, I had been secretly, silently and subconsciously wishing I'd discover a place like this.

48

'Jack, is everything OK?' Alan asked, as soon as Jack had taken his seat opposite him at the low bar table. Concern was written all over his face and doubt crept in on Jack again.

'I'm fine,' Jack replied, putting down his drink, settling on the stool, trying to keep the anger out of his voice, feeling confused.

'You look like shit.' His eyes dropped to Jack's leg, which was bouncing away steadily.

'Everything's OK.'

'You're sure?' Alan narrowed his eyes.

'Yeah.' He took a slug of Guinness, his mind going back to the memory that had hit him with his last taste. Alan's lie.

'So what's up?' Alan said. 'You sounded like there was a fire, on the phone. Something important to tell me?'

'No, no fire.' Jack looked around, avoiding eye contact, doing everything he could do to stop himself from throwing a punch. He needed to approach this properly, and tried to relax. His leg stopped bouncing, he leaned in to the table and stared into his pint. 'It's just this past week I've been looking for Donal, and it's brought everything back, y'know?'

Alan sighed and stared into his pint too. 'Yeah, I know. I think about it every day.'

'About what?'

Alan looked up quickly. 'What do you mean?'

'I mean what kind of things do you think about every day?' Jack tried to take the interrogative tone out of his voice.

'I don't know what you mean. I think about the whole thing,' Alan frowned.

'Well, *I* think about how I wish I'd been there that night, how I wish I'd known Donal better because if I had then maybe . . .' Jack held his hands up, 'maybe, maybe, maybe. Maybe I'd know where to look, maybe I'd know the places or people he went to for safety or for privacy. Anything like that, you know? Maybe there were some people he was running from, people he got involved with. We didn't talk much about private things and every day I think about the fact that if I'd been a better brother maybe I'd have found him. Maybe he'd be sitting right here beside us having a pint.'

They both naturally looked to the empty stool beside them.

'Don't think stuff like that, Jack. You were a good bro—'

'Don't,' Jack interrupted, raising his voice.

Alan stopped in surprise. 'Don't what?'

Jack looked him directly in the eyes. 'Don't lie.'

Fear, uncertainty entered Alan's face and Jack knew his intuition was correct. Alan looked around the room anxiously but Jack stopped him. 'You don't need to tell me I was a good brother because I know I wasn't. Don't lie to make me feel better.'

Alan seemed relieved by this answer. 'OK, you were a shit brother,' he smiled, and they both laughed.

'As much as I've been giving myself a hard time for not being there that night, deep down I know that even if I'd been there, the same thing probably would have happened. Because I know you had his back, you've always had his back.'

Alan smiled sadly into his pint.

'Last time we talked, you blamed yourself for not leaving with Donal that night.' Jack picked up a soggy beer mat and began peeling the outer label off slowly.

'I know what it's like to blame yourself: it's not good. I've been going to see some people, to help sort my head out.' He scratched his head awkwardly. 'They told me all this stuff about blaming yourself was normal. I thought it'd be important to tell you that. Over a pint.'

'Thanks,' Alan said quietly, 'I appreciate that.'

'Yeah, well . . . at least you got to have a conversation with him before he left, right?'

Alan's face said he wasn't sure where this was going, but Jack's voice was still non-threatening and he'd managed to calm himself completely now, to ignore what he guessed.

'You're lucky. The rest of the lads didn't notice him leave.'

'I didn't either.' Alan began fidgeting.

'No, you did,' Jack said. 'You said so last week.' He took another slug of Guinness and looked around, trying to keep the conversation casual. 'Busy here, isn't it? Didn't think it would be, so early in the evening.' He looked at his watch: six p.m. It felt like days since he had met Sandy's mother, not hours. 'Last week you said you wished you'd left with him and you thought he'd be safe getting a taxi down that way.'

Alan looked uncomfortable. 'I didn—'

'You did, man,' Jack interrupted and laughed. 'I may be losing my mind but I do remember that. I was happy to hear it, though.'

'Yeah?'

'Yeah,' Jack nodded happily, 'because it meant that he didn't just wander off, you know? He let someone know and it also makes sense what he was doing walking in that direction. That must make you feel better. The other lads, they're frustrated with themselves for not noticing. They blame themselves for not seeing him leave. At least you don't have that on your head.'

Alan was fidgeting. 'Yeah, I suppose so.' He took his bag of tobacco out of his shirt pocket. 'I'm going outside for a smoke. I'll be back in a minute.'

'Hang on a minute,' Jack said. 'I'll finish off this pint and go out with you.'

'You don't smoke.'

'I took it back up,' Jack lied. The last thing he wanted was for Alan to disappear. He would only get one chance to do this. 'Why is it so busy this evening?' he said, looking around.

Alan relaxed. 'I dunno.' He took out the skins and began to sprinkle the tobacco inside. 'It's a Saturday, I suppose.'

'Should we get a taxi down by Arthur's Quay tonight?' Jack asked casually. 'I left the car at home.'

'What do you mean?'

'That's where you told Donal to go for a cab, isn't it?'

Alan snorted and swallowed, cleaning his nostrils, making a sound but not answering the question. He slowly rolled the cigarette between his hands; Jack could see he was thinking. Trying to work it all out in his head.

'It's probably not such a good idea to recommend it to anyone now,' Jack said a little too angrily.

Alan stopped playing with his cigarette and looked at Jack. 'What's going on, Jack?'

'There are a few things running through my mind.' He scratched his forehead with his thumb and noticed his fingers tremble with anger. Alan looked up and saw them too. His eyes narrowed. 'I lost contact with the woman who was helping me look for Donal,' Jack explained, hearing his voice shaking but having no control over it. 'And that's driven me half insane. But mostly what's bothering me,' he spoke through gritted teeth, 'is the fact you told the guards and my family and everyone that would listen that you hadn't noticed Donal leave. Then last week you told me that you *had* noticed him leave. In fact you'd even spoken to him, in fact you'd even told him which way to go for a taxi.'

Alan's eyes got wider and wider as he spoke. His hands began to fidget more, he moved uncomfortably in his seat and a bead of sweat formed above his top lip.

'It doesn't make sense, Alan. And it might not even be a big deal but can you tell me why you lied for an entire year about the fact you told my brother, your best friend, to walk to an area for a taxi that would cause him to disappear?' The anger began to rise, and the volume of his voice with it.

Alan started to tremble. 'I had nothing to do with it.'

'With what?'

'With Donal going missing. I had nothing to do with it.' He went to stand up but Jack reached out and pushed him down by the shoulder. The bag of tobacco spilled to the carpet. Jack kept his hand there firmly, holding him down.

'Well then, who did?' he said angrily.

'I don't know.'

Jack dug his fingers into Alan's shoulder blade. He was just skin and bone.

'Jesus Christ, do we have to do this here?' Alan said in pain, trying to squirm out of Jack's grasp but failing.

Jack leaned in. 'Do what here? Is there some place else you'd like to go? The garda station maybe?'

'I didn't do anything,' Alan hissed. 'I swear.'

'Then why did you lie?'

'I didn't lie,' he said with big wide eyes, which looked like they'd never told the truth in his life. 'I don't exactly have a clean sheet as it is. I thought the guards would think I'd something to do with it.'

Their faces were only inches apart now. 'Tell me the truth.'

'I have.'

'He was your best friend, Alan, he was always there for you—'

'I know, I know,' he interrupted, holding his trembling nicotine-stained fingers to his head. Tears began to form in his eyes and he stared down at the table, his whole body shuddering.

'You can either tell me and make me understand, or I go to the guards,' Jack threatened.

It felt like hours before Alan built up the nerve to speak again. 'Donal got involved in something,' he said so quietly Jack had to move his head even closer. Their heads were practically touching now.

'You're a liar.'

'I'm not a liar.' Alan's head shot up, and Jack could see for once he was telling the truth. 'I was working for these lads—'

'What lads?'

'I can't say.'

Jack reached across and grabbed his collar. 'Who are they?'

'I'm helping you as much as I can, Jack,' Alan croaked, colour rising quickly in his face.

Jack loosened his grip slightly, enough for Alan to be able to breathe, and listened.

'They brought Donal in to program some stuff onto their computer. I suggested him as he'd got his degree and all, but he saw and heard a few things he shouldn't have and they got angry. I told them he wouldn't say a word but Donal was threatening to talk.'

'About what?' Anger was firing through Jack. He couldn't believe after one year of searching, the answer was right here at home, the truth lying with his brother's best friend.

'I can't tell you that,' Alan said through gritted teeth, spittle spilling from the sides of his mouth. 'I couldn't talk Donal out of snitching. He was trying to get me on the straight and narrow but he didn't understand how serious they were. He wouldn't listen.' His entire body trembled and Jack's eyes filled as he waited. Alan's voice broke and the shame was evident as he whispered, 'They were only supposed to knock him around a bit, warn him off, give him a scare.'

It was as though red powder fell before Jack's eyes. The anger pumped violently within him. 'And you walked him straight into it.' His voice was hoarse. Jack jumped out of his chair, pushed his hand up against Alan's throat and forced him off his chair. He fell back against the wall and the mirror behind Alan's head smashed with the force. The pub was silenced and people leaped out of the way of the two men. Jack threw Alan's head hard against the wall again. 'Where is he?' he hissed, his face up against Alan's.

Alan made choking sounds and Jack squeezed his grip tighter. Alan tried to speak and Jack remembered himself and loosened his grip. 'Where is his body?'

When he got his answer, he let go of Alan's throat and backed away, dropping him from his grip as if he was a dirty rag. He allowed Garda Graham Turner, who had been sitting nearby, to take over, and Jack left the pub to find his brother. This time he could say goodbye properly. This time the brothers would both finally be at rest.

49

'Hello, Sandy.' Grace Burns smiled at me from behind her desk. Her office was a boxroom at the back of a planning office. Inside were models of buildings and layouts of future plans for the surrounding lands.

I took a seat before her desk. 'Thank you for saving me from the angry mob last night,' I joked.

'No problem.' But her smile quickly faded. 'Tell me what's really happening, Sandy. Is your watch missing?'

After talking to Joseph, Helena and Bobby late into the night about what was the best thing do, they all agreed that I should lie. I didn't agree.

'Yes, it's missing,' I responded. Her eyes widened and she sat up straight in her chair. 'But the last thing I want to do is make a big deal of it,' I warned. 'I cannot explain how it disappeared, just as I can't explain how I arrived here. No amount of questions from your colleagues or scientists or people who consider themselves to be experts can help this situation. I don't want that GI Joe following me around any more either. I don't know anything. You must give me your word that you won't spread this news because I will not be co-operative.'

'I understand,' she said. 'In the time that I've been here there have been a few people I know of that have reported the same thing but we have been unable to learn anything, just as all of our studies have had little success in discovering how we arrived here. The people I knew of either moved town because word got out and life became too difficult under the gaze of everybody in the village, or else it was a false alarm and they found whatever it was they thought they'd lost. The two people that we did actually have the opportunity to work with closely just couldn't provide us with anything solid to work on. They knew nothing about why and how it was happening and most of us have realised that it's an impossible thing to understand.'

'Where are they now?'

'One passed away, another is living in another village. You're definitely sure your watch is gone?'

'It's gone,' I assured her.

'Is this the only thing that has disappeared?'

This is where I chose to lie. I nodded. 'And believe me, there's no better person at searching than me.' I looked around her room while she studied me.

'What is it that you do back home, Sandy?' She rested her chin on her hand and gazed intently at me, trying to solve the puzzle in her own mind.

'I run a missing persons agency.'

She laughed, but her smile faded when she realised she was laughing alone. 'You search for missing people?'

'And help people reunite, find long-lost relatives, adopted children's biological parents, that kind of thing,' I rattled off.

Her eyes widened with each example. 'So your case is certainly very different from the others I spoke about.'

'Or it's coincidental.'

She mulled that over but didn't comment. 'So that's how you know so much about the people here.'

'Only some people. Only the people in the play. By the way, the dress rehearsal is on tonight. Helena wanted me to invite you.' I remembered how Helena had hammered it into my head before I left the house that morning. 'It's *The Wizard of Oz* but it's not a musical, Helena is stressing to everybody. It's just her and Dennis O'Shea's interpretation,' I laughed. 'Orla Keane is playing the role of Dorothy. I'm actually quite looking forward to it,' I realised for the first time. 'The idea for the play was initially just my way of having a chance to talk to the potential cast without raising suspicions. We thought it would be far cleverer than knocking on doors and relaying stories of home, but perhaps we should have put a bit more thought into it. I didn't realise how quickly people talk here.'

'Word gets around fast,' Grace replied, still in a daze. She leaned in further. 'Were you looking for someone in particular when you arrived here?'

'Donal Ruttle,' I said, still hoping I'd find him.

'No.' She shook her head. 'The name isn't familiar.'

'He's now twenty-five years old, from Limerick, and would have arrived here last year.'

'He's definitely not in this village anyway.'

'I don't think he's here at all, I'm afraid,' I thought aloud, feeling instant sympathy for Jack Ruttle.

'I'm from Killybeggs in Donegal – I don't know if you know it . . .' Grace leaned forward again.

'Of course I do,' I smiled.

Her face softened. 'I'm married here but my maiden name is O'Donohue. My parents were Tony and Margaret O'Donohue. They have passed away now. I saw my dad's name in the obituaries in a newspaper I found six years ago. I've kept it.' She glanced over at her wall cabinet. 'Carol Dempsey,' she started up again, 'you know Carol? She's in the play too, I believe. Well, she's a Donegal woman too, as you'll know, and she informed me of my mother's death when she arrived a few years ago.'

'I'm sorry to hear that.'

'Yes, well . . .' she said gently. 'I'm an only child,' she explained, 'but I have an uncle Donie who moved to Dublin a few years before I arrived here.'

I nodded along with her, waiting for the story to begin but she fell silent and watched me. I shifted uneasily in my chair realising she was giving me information about her life to refresh my memory.

'I'm sorry, Grace,' I said softly. 'That might have been before I set up the agency. How long have you been here?'

'Fourteen years.' I must have looked at her with such pity because she quickly explained, 'I love it here, don't get me wrong. I have a wonderful husband and three gorgeous children and I wouldn't go back in a heart-beat, but I was just wondering . . .' she trailed off. 'I'm sorry.' She sat upright again and composed herself.

'It's OK, I'd want to know too,' I said gently, 'but I'm not familiar with the people you've mentioned. I'm sorry.'

There was a silence and I thought I'd upset her but when she spoke again she seemed fine.

'What made you want to find missing people? It's such an unusual career.'

I laughed. 'Now there's a question.' I thought back to when it all began. 'Two words,' I smiled. 'Jenny-May Butler. She lived across the road from me when I was a child in Leitrim, but she went missing when she was ten.'

'Yes,' Grace smiled, 'Jenny-May is as good a reason as any. What a character.'

It took me a moment to catch what she'd said. My heart leaped into my throat with the surprise. 'What? What did you say?'

50

'Come on, Bobby!' I yelled, poking my head in the door of Lost and Found.

'What?' he shouted from upstairs.

'Bring the camera, get your keys, lock up and let's go. We've got to go!' I allowed the door to swing shut and I paced up and down the veranda, Grace's words still ringing in my ears. She knew Jenny-May. She had given me directions. I had to go to her *now*. My excitement had gone way past boiling point and was overflowing, spilling from me as I waited impatiently outside for Bobby. I needed him to show me the way to Jenny-May's home in the forest, yet I didn't have the patience to explain what it was I wanted.

Bobby arrived at the door, looking bewildered. 'What the hell are you doing—' He stopped as soon as he saw the look on my face. 'What happened?'

'Get your things, Bobby, quick.' I pushed by him into the shop. 'I'll explain on the way. Bring the camera.' I hopped around him as he clumsily tried to gather his things, trying to keep up with the speed with which I was barking my orders. By the time he had finished locking up I was power-walking down the dusty street, aware that even more eyes were on me now, after the community gathering last night.

'Wait, Sandy!' I heard him panting behind me. 'What the hell happened to you? It's like you've a rocket shoved up your ass!'

'Maybe I have,' I smiled, racing on.

'Where are we going?' He jogged alongside me.

'Here.' I thrust the page of directions at him and kept walking.

'Hold on. Slow down,' he said, trying to read it and run alongside me at the same time. One of my strides equalled two of his but I kept walking none the less. 'Stop!' he shouted loudly in the market area, and others turned to stare. I finally stopped. 'If you want me to read this properly you have to tell me what the hell is happening.'

I spoke faster than I had ever spoken before in my life.

'OK, I think I got all that,' Bobby said, still slightly confused, 'but I've never been in this direction before.' He studied the map again. 'We'll have to ask Helena or Joseph.'

'No! We've no time! We have to go *now*,' I whined like an impatient child. 'Bobby, I've been waiting for this moment for the past twenty-four years of my life. Please do not delay me now when I'm so close.'

'Yes, Dorothy, but it will take a bit more than following the yellow brick road,' he said sarcastically.

Despite my frustration I laughed.

'I understand your haste but if I try to bring you to this place it will be another twenty-four years before we get there. I don't know this part of the woods, I have never heard of this Jenny-May person, and I don't have any friends who live that deep. If we get lost, we're in big trouble. Let's just go to Helena for help first.'

Although he was almost half my age, the boy made sense and so I grudgingly stomped my way to Helena and Joseph's house.

Helena and Joseph were sitting on the bench outside the front of their house, enjoying the relaxing atmosphere of Sunday lunchtime. Bobby, sensing my urgency, rushed straight to Helena and Joseph while Wanda jumped up from the ground where she was playing to run to me.

'Hi, Sandy,' she said, grabbing my hand and skipping alongside me as I walked towards the house.

'Hi, Wanda,' I said in a bored tone, but tried to hide my smile.

'What's that in your hand?'

'It's called Wanda's hand,' I said.

She rolled her eyes. 'No, the *other* hand.'

'It's a Polaroid camera.'

'Why?'

'Why is it a camera?'

'No. Why do you have it?'

'Because I want to take a photograph of somebody.'

'Who?'

'A girl I used to know.'

'Who?'

'A girl called Jenny-May Butler.'

'Was she your friend?'

'Not really.'

'Well then, why do you want to take a photograph of her?'

'I don't know.'

'Is it because you miss her?'

I was about to say no when I stopped myself. 'Actually I did miss her, very much.'

'And are you going to see her today?'

'Yes,' I smiled, grabbing Wanda under her armpits and swinging her around, much to her delight. 'I am going to see Jenny-May Butler *today*!'

Wanda began laughing uncontrollably and sang a song she pretended to know about a girl called Jenny-May, which she clearly was making up on the spot, much to my amusement.

'I'm going to come with you,' Helena said, breaking into Wanda's song, giving her a kiss on the top of her head. I took a photo of the two of them when they weren't looking.

'Stop wasting the cartridges,' Bobby barked at me, and I snapped his face too.

'No, Helena, I don't expect you to come.' I waved

the photos in the air to dry before placing them in my shirt pocket. 'You've got the dress rehearsal tonight. That's more important. Just explain to Bobby where it is.' I began to get jittery again.

She looked at her watch and I had a pang of longing for mine. 'It's just after one. The dress rehearsal isn't until seven; we'll be back in time. And besides, I want to go with you.' She touched my chin lightly and winked. 'This is far more important, plus I know exactly where we're going. This clearing is not much further on from where you and I met last week.'

Joseph made his way to me. He held out his hand. 'Safe trip, kipepeo girl.'

I took his hand with confusion. 'I'm coming back, Joseph.'

'I should hope so,' he smiled, and placed his other hand on my head. 'When you get back I shall tell you what a kipepeo girl is,' he smiled.

'Liar,' I said, narrowing my eyes.

'Right, let's go,' Helena said, throwing a lime-green pashmina over her shoulder.

We set off in the direction of the woods, Helena leading the way. At the edge of the woods a young woman appeared, looking dazed and confused as she gazed around the village.

'Welcome,' Helena said to her.

'Welcome,' Bobby said happily.

She looked with confusion from their faces to mine. 'Welcome,' I smiled, pointing her towards the registry office.

The routes Helena chose were cleared and well-travelled trails. The atmosphere reminded me of the first few days I had spent alone in these woods, wondering where I was. The scent of pine was rich, mixed with moss, bark and damp leaves. There was the foul smell of rotting leaves mixed with the sweet floral scents of the wild flowers. Mosquitoes hovered in small areas, darting in circular motions together. Red squirrels bounced from branch to branch, and occasionally

Bobby stopped to pick up an item of interest in our path. We couldn't walk fast enough as far as I was concerned. Yesterday I had thought the prospect of finding Jenny-May an impossibility; today I was going back the way I had come to actually see her.

Grace Burns had explained that Jenny-May had arrived in the village with an elderly Frenchman, who had been living deep in the woods for years. She had knocked on his door, seeking help when she had first arrived all those years ago. Seldom in the forty years he had lived Here had he ventured to the village, but twenty-four years ago he arrived at the registry office with the ten-year-old girl named Jenny-May Butler who insisted on him being her guardian, the only person she trusted. Despite his desire for solitude, he agreed to care for her, choosing to remain in his home in the woods but making sure Jenny-May went back and forth to school every day and formed and maintained friendships. She became fluent in French, choosing to speak it when in the village, meaning few of the Irish community were aware of her true roots. Jenny-May cared for her guardian until his dying day fifteen years ago, and she decided to remain in the home he made hers, outside of the village, rarely venturing to the village herself.

After twenty minutes we passed the clearing where I had met Helena and she insisted on stopping for a break. She drank from the canteen of water she had carried with her, and passed it to Bobby and me. I didn't feel the heat or the thirst on this hot day though. My mind was focused on Jenny-May. I wanted to keep moving, keep walking until we reached her. After that I had no idea what would happen.

'God, I've never seen you like this before,' Bobby said, staring at me oddly. 'It's as though you've ants in your pants.'

'She's always like that.' Helena closed her eyes and fanned her perspiring face.

I paced up and down beside Helena and Bobby, hopping around, kicking leaves and trying desperately to channel the adrenalin that was rushing through me. Feeling more anxious with every second they spent with me, they finally felt under pressure to move again, which I was glad of but felt guilty about.

The next part of the journey was further than Helena had thought. We walked for another thirty minutes before seeing a small wooden cabin in a clearing in the distance. Smoke was puffing from the chimney, following the direction of the tall pines until it overtook them, going where they couldn't go, up and out in the cloudless sky.

We stopped walking as soon as we saw the cabin in the distance. Helena was red in the face and tired, and I felt more guilty for bringing her on such a journey on this hot day. Bobby was looking at the cabin rather disappointedly, probably hoping for something far more luxurious than this. I, on the other hand, was more pumped up than ever. The sight of the humble home before me took my breath away. It was the home of a girl who had always boasted about wanting so much more, yet to me the sight of it was a dream, a perfect pretty little picture. Just like Jenny-May.

Tall pines stood protectively on two sides of the house. In front, there was a little garden amidst the large clearing, with small bushes, pretty flowers and what looked from afar to be a vegetable patch or herb garden. Mosquitoes and flies, when hit by the sun, looked like symbiotic creatures circling in the air, pockets of them scattered throughout the area. Streams of sunlight shone down through the trees, spotlighting centre stage.

'Oh, look,' Helena said, handing the water to Bobby as the front door of the cabin opened and out of it streamed a little girl with white-blonde hair. Her laughter echoed around the clearing and was carried over to us on the warm breeze. My hand went to my mouth. I must have made a sound, though I didn't hear it, because Bobby and Helena immediately looked to me. Tears welled in my eyes, as I watched the little girl, no older than five, exactly like the little girl I began my first day of school with. Then a female voice called from the house and my heart thudded.

'Daisy!'

Then a male voice: 'Daisy!'

Little Daisy ran around the front garden, giggling and twirling, her lemon dress floating around her on the wind. Then from the front door a man stepped out and began to chase her. Her giggling turned to screams of delight. He made terrifying noises behind her, teasing how he was going to catch her, which made her scream with laughter even more. Finally he caught her and spun her around in the air while she screamed for, 'More, more, more!' He stopped when both were out of breath and he carried her in his arms back towards the house. Just outside the door he stopped and turned around slowly to look straight at us.

He called into the house. We heard the female voice again but not her words. He stood there looking directly at us.

'Can I help you?' he called, holding his hand to his forehead to shield the sun from his eyes.

Helena and Bobby looked to me. I stared at the man and the child in his arms, speechless.

'Well, yes, thank you. We're looking for Jenny-May Butler,' Helena called politely. 'I'm not sure if we're at the right place.'

I had no doubt we were at the right place.

'Who is looking for her?' he asked politely. 'I'm sorry, I can't see you from here.' He began to take a few steps forward.

'Sandy Shortt is here for her,' Helena called.

Immediately a figure appeared at the door.

I heard my large intake of breath.

Long blonde hair, slim and pretty. The same but older. My age. The child in her was gone. She wore a loose-fitting white cotton dress and was barefoot. She held in her hand a tea cloth, which fell to the floor when she held her hand to her forehead to block out the sunlight and her eyes fell upon me.

'Sandy?' Her voice was older but the same. It quivered and was uncertain, displaying fear and joy all at the same time.

'Jenny-May,' I called back, hearing exactly the same tone in my voice.

Then I heard her cry as she slowly started to walk towards me and I heard myself cry as I took steps towards her. And I saw her arms reaching out and felt mine do the same. The distance between us grew smaller, the idea of her being before me becoming more real. Her tears were loud, mine too I was sure. We cried like children as we walked towards one another, studying faces, hair, bodies, and remembering: good things and bad. And then we were within each other's grasp and we fell into each other. Crying and hugging, moving to look at each other's face, wiping tears from one another's cheek and then holding on again. Never wanting to let go.

51

'Jack,' Garda Graham Turner said with surprise, 'what are you doing back here? We won't have results back from forensics for another few days and I promise you we'll contact you with the news.'

Time had got to Donal's body before them and had spared it no mercy. He had yet to be officially identified although Jack and his family knew in their hearts it was Donal. Fresh and decaying flowers were found on the site that Alan had visited each week of the year. He had confessed his true story to police the previous night but had refused to give the names of the gang involved. Over the next few months he would stand trial, and Jack was glad his mother wasn't around to see the man she helped raise take part of the blame for the murder of her baby.

After discussing the night's events with his family, it was the early hours of the morning before Jack returned to Foynes. The town was still celebrating the festival with all the energy of its opening hours. He ignored the sounds of music and singing, and went into the bedroom to find Gloria lying asleep in bed. He sat on the bed beside her and watched her, her long black lashes resting on the tops of her rosy cheeks. Her mouth was slightly open, soft sounds of her breath causing her white chest to heave gently up and down. It was that hypnotic sound and sight that compelled him to do what he hadn't done for a year. He reached out to her, placed his hand on her shoulder and gently woke her from her slumber, finally inviting her into his world. When they had talked all night about the past year and all he had learned in past week, he finally felt tired and joined her in her sleep at last.

'I'm not here about Donal,' Jack explained, sitting down in the station on Sunday evening. 'We need to find Sandy Shortt.'

'Jack,' Graham rubbed his eyes wearily. His desk and the surrounding desks were covered in paperwork and phones rang all around him. 'We've been through this.'

'Not in enough detail. Now listen to me. Maybe Sandy got in touch with Alan and he panicked. You never know. Maybe they arranged to meet and he got nervous she was getting close to the truth and maybe he did something. I don't know what. I'm not even talking about murder. I know Alan's not capable of that but,' he paused, 'actually,' his pupils dilated with anger, 'maybe he did, maybe he got desperate and—'

'He didn't,' Graham interrupted. 'I've been through it over and over again with him. He doesn't know anything about her, he had never even heard of her. He had no clue about what I was talking about. All he knew was what you told him: that some unknown woman was helping you find Donal. That's all.' He looked Jack in the eyes and softened his tone. 'Please, Jack, give up on this.'

'Give up? Like everyone told me to when I was looking for Donal?'

Graham shifted in his seat uncomfortably.

'Alan was Donal's *best friend* and he lied about what happened to him for *one year*. He's in enough trouble already – do you think he's going to bother telling us about what he could have done to some woman he cares nothing about? Was I not right about Alan the first time?' Jack raised his voice.

Graham was silent for a long time, biting down on his already non-existent nail as he quickly made a decision. 'OK, OK.' He closed his tired eyes and focused. 'We'll start searching the site where her car was left.'

52

I have thought about that moment with Jenny-May long and hard for many hours, days and nights but I have no words for the time that we spent together that day. It was far too big for words. It was more important than words; it had more meaning than just words.

We stole away from the cabin, leaving Bobby, Helena, Daisy and Jenny-May's husband, Luc, to chat among themselves. We had a lot to say to one another. To explain our conversations would not do the moment justice because we talked about nothing. To explain how I felt, watching an older version of the pretty photo embedded in my memory come alive, would fall short of the enormity of my delight. Delight – not good enough a word. Relief, joy, pure ecstasy – still not even close.

I filled her in on local people she once knew who were doing things of no interest to anybody but her. She told me about her family, her life, all that she had done since I had seen her. I told her of mine. Not once did we speak about her treatment of me. Does that seem odd? It didn't then. It wasn't important. Not once did we mention where we both were. Does that seem odd too? Perhaps, but that wasn't important either. It wasn't about then, or where, it was just about now. This moment, today. We didn't notice the hours go by, we barely saw the sunset and the moonrise. We didn't feel the heat leave our skin and the evening breeze cooling it. We felt nothing, heard nothing, saw nothing but the stories, sounds and visions of our own minds, which we filled one another with. It is nothing to others but so much to me.

But it is perhaps enough to say that a part of me was set free that night, as, I sensed, was the case for Jenny-May. We never said it to one another, of course. But we both knew.

53

Helena called to us that she had to get back to the village for the dress rehearsal and so while they said their goodbyes, Jenny-May and I put our heads together and looked up to the camera in my hand and smiled. I took the photo and slid it into my shirt pocket. Jenny-May turned down her invitation to see the play, preferring to stay home with her family. We said we would meet again but we made no arrangements. Not out of any badness between us, but because I felt it had all been said, or not said but understood, and she probably did too. To know she was there was enough, and for her to know I was around probably was too. Sometimes that's all people ever really need. Just to know.

We borrowed a flashlight from Jenny-May as the sun was hiding behind the trees, leaving us bathed in blue light. Helena led the way back to the village. Eventually I could see the lights in the distance. Feeling dizzy with happiness, I took the photos from my pocket to study them once more while walking. I retrieved two and felt around for the third. It was gone.

'Oh, no,' I moaned, and stopped walking, immediately looking to the ground.

'What's wrong?' Bobby stopped walking and called to Helena to stop.

'The photograph of me and Jenny-May is gone.' I started to walk back the way I had come.

'Hold on, Sandy.' Bobby followed me, looking at the

ground. 'We've been walking for almost an hour now. It could be anywhere. We really have to get back to the Community Hall for the play; we're late as it is. You can take another photo with her tomorrow when it's bright.'

'No I can't,' I whinged, straining my eyes to see the ground in the evening light.

Helena, who so far hadn't said a word, stepped forward. 'You dropped it?'

That made me stop and look up at her. Her face was serious, her tone grave.

'I assume so. I doubt it leaped out and ran away on its own.'

'You know what I'm talking about.'

'No, I definitely dropped it. My pocket is open, see?' I showed them the shallow breast pocket. 'Why don't you two just go on ahead and I'll look around here for a little while.'

They looked unsure.

'We're less than five minutes away. I can see the pathway back we're so close,' I smiled. 'Honestly, I'll be OK. I have to find this photo and then I'll go straight to the Community Hall to see the play. I promise.'

Helena was looking at me oddly, obviously torn between helping me and helping the cast prepare for their dress rehearsal.

'I'm not leaving you on your own,' Bobby said.

'Here, Sandy, you take this torch. Bobby and I will be able to see our way from here. I know it's important for you to find it.' She handed over the torch and I thought I saw tears in her eyes.

'Helena, stop worrying!' I laughed. 'I'll be OK.'

'I know you will, sweetheart.' She leaned over and, taking me by surprise, planted a quick kiss on my cheek and gave me a quick tight hug. 'Be careful.'

Bobby smiled at me over Helena's shoulder. 'She's not going to die, you know, Helena.'

Helena slapped him playfully over the head. 'Come on with me. I need you to bring all the costumes over from the shop a.s.a.p., Bobby! You promised I'd have them yesterday!'

'Well, that was before David Copperfield here was called to the Community Hall!' he defended himself.

Helena glared at him.

'OK, OK!' He backed away from her. 'Hope you find it, Sandy.' He winked at me before following Helena back down the path. I heard them nagging and teasing one another for a while until the sounds of their voices disappeared and they entered the village.

I turned around and immediately started scanning the ground. I could pretty much remember the way we had come. It seemed to be one main pathway, very rarely did we come across a choice of others, and so with my eyes peeled to the floor, I made my way back deeper into the forest.

Helena and Bobby rushed around backstage, fixing costumes, last-minute broken zips and sewing tears, going over lines with nervous cast members and giving final pep talks to a panicked crew. Helena hurried out to her seat in the auditorium beside Joseph before the performance began and finally relaxed for the first time in the last hour.

'Is Sandy not with you?' Joseph asked, looking around.

'No,' Helena said, staring straight ahead, refusing to look at her husband. 'She stayed behind in the forest.'

Joseph took his wife's hand and whispered, 'Along the Kenyan coast where I come from, there is a forest called the Arabuko-Sokoke Forest.'

'Yes, you've talked about it,' Helena acknowledged.

'There, there are kipepeo girls, butterfly farmers who help keep the forest preserved.'

Helena looked up at him, finally learning the meaning of the nickname.

He smiled. 'They are known as guardians of the forest.'

'She stayed in the forest to find a photograph of her

and Jenny-May. She thinks she dropped it.' Helena's eyes began to fill and Joseph squeezed her hand.

The curtains on stage parted.

At times I thought I saw the white of the photograph glowing in the moonlight and I would wander off the track to search among the weeds and undergrowth, chasing small birds and creatures away with my flashlight. After half an hour I was sure I should have reached the first clearing by now. I shone the torch all around me, looking for something familiar but it was just trees, trees and more trees. But then again I had been walking far slower and so it would take me longer to get there. I decided to keep walking in the same direction. It was black now, and around me owls hooted and creatures moved in their natural habitat, startled to find me where I didn't belong. I didn't plan on being there much longer. I shivered, the cool evening now turning to cold. I shone the torch straight ahead, deciding that I'd dropped the photograph closer to Jenny-May's house than I thought.

'Where am I?' Orla Keane stepped onto the stage as Dorothy Gale, looking around the community hall that for the night was a grand theatre. Thousands of faces stared back at her. 'What is this strange land?'

Thirty minutes later, sweating, panting and dizzy from jogging around in different directions, I recognised the first clearing up ahead. I stopped running and leaned over to hold on to a tree, to steady myself and catch my breath. I breathed a sigh of relief and was taken aback by the realisation I'd been more anxious about being lost than I'd thought.

'I need a heart,' Derek sang. 'I need a brain,' Bernard announced theatrically. 'And I need courage,' Marcus said quietly in his bored tone. The audience laughed as they all hopped off with Dorothy stage right, arm in arm.

* * *

It was brighter in the clearing, the moon shining down without the trees acting as a shield. The floor of the clearing was blue and in the centre I could see a small white square sheet glistening. Despite my tiredness and the pain in my chest, I began to run towards the photograph. I knew I was out longer than I had intended to be and I had promised Helena I would be there for her. A mixture of emotions rushed through me as I felt such pressure to find the photograph and be there for Helena and my new friends. I wasn't concentrating as I stupidly ran at top speed in the dark, in Barbara Langley's heeled shoes. I landed unevenly on a rock and felt my ankle twist. The pain shot up my leg, forcing me off balance. The ground came up to meet me quickly before there was anything I could do to stop it.

'You mean I had the power inside myself to go home all the time?' Orla Keane said innocently. The audience laughed.

'Yes, Dorothy,' Carol Dempsey, dressed as the good witch Glinda, said in her usual gentle tones. 'Just click your heels together and say the words.'

Helena grabbed Joseph's hand tighter and he squeezed back.

Orla Keane closed her eyes and began to click her heels together. 'There's no place like home,' she said, pulling everyone into her mantra. 'There's no place like home.'

Joseph looked across at his wife and saw a tear roll down her face. He raised a thumb to stop it from dropping from her chin. 'Our kipepeo has flown.'

Helena nodded and another tear fell.

I felt everything go from under me, my head smashed violently against something hard. I felt the pain shoot down my spine and everything went black.

* * *

On stage Orla Keane tapped her ruby slippers together one last time before disappearing in a puff of smoke, compliments of Bobby's firecrackers. 'There's no place like home.'

54

'I don't think she's here.' Graham walked towards Jack in the wooded area of Glin. In the distance fireworks were going off over Foynes as the village celebrated the last few moments of the Irish Coffee Festival. They both stopped to look up.

'I have a feeling you might be right,' Jack finally admitted. They had spent the last few hours searching the scene where Sandy had deserted her car and, despite the fact it had fallen dark mid-search Jack had insisted they continue. They were not practical searching conditions and he could see the others checking their watches. 'Thanks for letting me try,' Jack said as they walked along the pathway back to the car.

Suddenly there was a loud crash; a sound as though a tree had come down. A thud and a female cry. The men both froze and each looked at the other.

'Which way did that come from?' Graham asked, spinning around, shining his flashlight in every direction. They heard groaning coming from further up on their left and all involved rushed to find her. Jack's flashlight fell upon Sandy, lying on her back, her leg looking dislocated, blood on her hand and staining her clothes.

'Oh my God.' Jack rushed forward and kneeled down by her side. 'She's here!' he called to the others, and they hurried over, crowding around her.

'OK, let's move back, give her space.' Graham radioed for an ambulance.

'I don't want to move her. Her head is bleeding

heavily and it looks like her leg's broken too. Oh God, Sandy, talk to me.'

Her eyes fluttered open. 'Who are you?'

'I'm Jack Ruttle,' he said, relieved she'd opened her eyes.

'Keep her talking, Jack,' Graham said.

'Jack?' Her eyes widened in surprise. 'Are you missing too?'

'What? No,' he frowned. 'No, I'm not missing.' He looked at Graham worriedly. Graham made motions to keep her talking.

'Where am I?' she asked in confusion, looking around. She tried to move her head and called out in pain.

'Don't move. An ambulance is on its way. You're in Glin, in Limerick.'

'Glin?' she repeated.

'Yes, we were supposed to meet here last week, remember?'

'Am I home?' Her eyes filled with tears, which quickly fell over her mud-streaked face. 'Donal,' she said suddenly, stopping her tears, 'Donal wasn't there.'

'Donal wasn't where?'

'I was in this place, Jack. Oh my God, this place where all the missing people were. Helena, Bobby, Joseph, Jenny-May, oh my God, Helena's play – I'm missing her play.' Tears fell quickly now. 'I need to get up,' she struggled to move. 'I have to go to the dress rehearsal.'

'You have to wait for the ambulance to come, Sandy. Don't move.' He looked back to Graham. 'She's delusional. Where the hell is the ambulance?'

Graham radioed again. 'On its way.'

'Who did this to you, Sandy? Tell me who did this and we'll get them, I promise.'

'Nobody did.' She looked confused. 'I fell. I told you I was in the place . . . where's my photograph, I've lost a photograph. Oh, Jack, I've something to tell you,' she said softly now. 'It's about Donal.'

'Go on,' he urged.

'He wasn't there. He wasn't in . . . the place with everyone else. He's not missing.'

'I know,' Jack said sadly. 'We found him this morning.'

'I'm so sorry.'

'How did you know?'

'He wasn't there, with all the missing people,' she mumbled, her eyes fluttering closed.

'Stay with me, Sandy,' Jack said with urgency in his voice.

My eyes opened to bright white, and my lids felt heavy. I looked around but to move my sockets was sore. My head pounded. I groaned.

'Sweetheart . . .' My mum's face appeared from above.

'Mum.' I instantly began crying and she reached out her arms to hold me.

'It's OK, sweetheart, it's OK now,' she said soothingly, while smoothing down my hair on my head.

'I've missed you so much,' I cried into her shoulder ignoring the pulsing pain around the rest of my body.

Her patting stopped when I said that, the shock of my words freezing her, and then it slowly began again. I felt Dad kiss the top of my head.

'I missed you, Dad,' I continued crying.

'We've missed you too, love.' His voice shook as he spoke.

'I found the place,' I said excitedly, the sounds and visions around me still blurred and faraway. My own voice was muffled. 'I found the place where all the missing things go.'

'Yes, sweetheart, Jack told us,' Mum said in a worried tone.

'No, I'm not mad, I didn't imagine it. I was really there.'

'Yes,' she hushed me, 'you need to rest, sweetheart.'

'The photographs are in my shirt pocket,' I explained,

trying to explain all the details clearly, but it felt muddled in my head. 'It's not my shirt pocket, it's Barbara Langley from Ohio's. I found it. I put them in my pocket.'

'The guards didn't find anything, honey,' Dad said quietly, not wanting anyone else to hear. 'There aren't any photographs.'

'They must have fallen out,' I mumbled, getting tired of trying to explain. 'Is Gregory here?' I asked.

'No, shall we call him?' my mother asked excitedly. 'I wanted to call him but Harold wouldn't let me.'

'Call him,' was the last thing I remember saying.

I awoke in my childhood bedroom and stared at the same floral wallpaper I was forced to look at all throughout my teens. I had hated it then, I couldn't wait to see the back of it, but now it gave me a strange sense of comfort. I smiled, feeling delighted to be home for the first time in my life. There was no bag by the door, no feeling of claustrophobia or fear of losing things. I had been at home now for three days, catching up on sleep and resting my injured and weary body. I had broken my leg, twisted my ankle and had stitches on the crown of my head but I was home and I was happy. I often thought of Helena, Bobby, Joseph and Wanda, and felt a longing to be with them but knew that they would understand what had happened, and wondered if they perhaps understood the entire time.

There was a knock on the door.

'Enter,' I called.

Gregory peeked his head around, then entered with a tray of food in his hands.

I groaned. 'Not more food. I think you're all trying to fatten me up.'

'We're trying to make you well again,' he said sombrely, placing the tray on the bed. 'Mrs Butler brought you the flowers.'

'That's so sweet of her,' I said gently. 'Do you still think I'm crazy?' I asked.

I had told him about where I had been as soon as I had felt well enough to explain it properly. My parents had also obviously asked him to talk to me about it as it was issue number one on the agenda, although he was keen not to take the role of counsellor. Not any more. That was then, this is now.

He avoided the question. 'I spoke to Jack Ruttle today.'

'Good. I hope you apologised.'

'I definitely apologised.'

'Good,' I repeated, 'because if it wasn't for him I would literally be lying in a ditch somewhere. My own partner didn't care enough to join the search party,' I huffed.

'Honestly, Sandy, if I joined a search party every time you disappeared . . .' he trailed off. He had meant it as a joke but it changed the mood.

'Well, it won't be happening again.'

He looked unsure.

'I promise, Gregory. I've found what I was looking for.' I reached out to touch his cheek.

He smiled but I was sure it would take time before he'd truly believe me. The past few days I had questioned whether I believed myself.

'What did Jack say on the phone?'

'That he went back to the place where he'd found you to look for the photographs you've been talking about and he didn't find anything.'

'Does *he* think I'm crazy?'

'Probably, but he still loves you because he's convinced you and your mum helped him find his brother.'

'He's a sweet guy. If it wasn't for him . . .' I repeated, trailing off just to annoy Gregory.

'If you didn't already have a broken leg, I'd break it for you,' he threatened, but then became serious again. 'You know how your mum received a phone call from the Sheens? The people who bought your grandparents' house all those years ago?'

'Yes.' I tore the crust off a slice of toast and put it in my mouth. 'I thought that was weird. I can't believe they were ringing to tell her they were moving.'

Gregory cleared his throat. 'Actually, well, that's not why they called; your dad concocted that story.'

'What? Why?' I put the toast down, no longer hungry.

'He didn't want to worry you.'

'Tell me, Gregory.'

'Well, your parents may not agree with me but I think it's important you know that they'd actually called to say that they'd found a teddy bear belonging to you. A Mr Pobbs, lying underneath a bed in the spare room with your name engraved on his striped pyjamas.'

I gasped. 'Everything's turning up again.'

'They found this particularly unusual because they had used that room as storage for a number of years and only turned it back into a bedroom last month. They had never noticed the teddy bear before.'

'Why didn't anyone tell me?'

'Your parents didn't want to upset you again, with you talking about this missing place and—'

'It's not a missing place, it's a place where missing people and things go,' I said angrily, realising once again how stupid it sounded.

'OK, OK, calm down.' He ran his fingers through his hair and leaned his elbows on his knees.

'What's wrong?'

'Nothing.'

'Gregory, I know when something's wrong with you. Tell me.'

'Well,' he wrung his hands together, 'after their phone call I gave further thought to your . . . theory.'

I rolled my eyes with frustration. 'What disorder do you think I have now?'

'Let me finish,' he raised his voice and an angry silence fell between us. After a while he spoke again. 'When I was emptying your hospital bag I found this in your shirt pocket.'

I held my breath as he removed something from his top pocket.

The photograph of me with Jenny-May.

I took it from his hands as though it were the most fragile thing in the world. Trees framed the photograph.

'Do you believe me now?' I whispered, running my finger over her face.

He shrugged. 'You know how my mind works, Sandy. For me this kind of thinking is nonsensical.' I looked to him angrily. '*But*,' he said firmly before I had a chance to snap, 'this is very difficult to explain.'

'That's good enough for now,' I accepted, holding the photograph close to me.

'I'm sure Mrs Butler would want to see that,' he said.

'Do you think?' I was unsure.

He thought about it. 'I think she's the only woman you could show it to. I think she's the only woman you *should* show it to.'

'But how could I explain it?'

He looked at me, spread his hands apart and shrugged. 'This time, you're the one with the answer.'

55

Sometimes, people can go missing right before our very eyes. Sometimes, people discover you, even though they've been looking at you the entire time. Sometimes, we lose sight of ourselves when we're not paying enough attention.

Days later, when I was feeling fit enough to venture outside on my crutches, under the gaze of Gregory and my parents, I hobbled my way across the road to Mrs Butler's house with the photograph of her daughter in my pocket. The lantern-shaped porch light provided a warm orange glow above the door and drew me in, like a moth to a flame. I took a deep breath and knocked on the door, once again feeling a responsibility and knowing that I'd wished for this moment my entire life.

We all get lost once in a while, sometimes by choice, sometimes due to forces beyond our control. When we learn what it is our soul needs to learn, the path presents itself. Sometimes we see the way out but wander further and deeper despite ourselves; the fear, the anger or the sadness preventing us returning. Sometimes we prefer to be lost and wandering, sometimes it's easier. Sometimes we find our own way out. But regardless, always, we are found.

Huge thank you (and farewell) Maxine Hitchcock for all you've done on my first four books – I'll miss you for the rest of the journey, but hope our paths will cross again sometime.

Thanks Lynne Drew, Amanda Ridout and the HarperCollins team for the fantastic support.

Thank you Marianne Gunn O'Connor for continuing to inspire and motivate me.

Also thanks to the incredibly supportive Pat Lynch and Vicki Satlow and thank you to Dermot Hobbs and John-Paul Moriarty.

Special thanks to David, Mimmie, Dad, Georgina, Nicky and all my family; Kellys, Aherns, Keoghans, and of course, the Witches of Eastwick – Paula Pea, Susana and SJ.

Thank you to all those who read my books – for the greatest motivation of all.

WHERE RAINBOWS END

Before embarking on her writing career, Cecelia Ahern completed a degree in Journalism and Media Communications. At twenty-one years old, she wrote her first novel *PS, I Love You*, which instantly became an international bestseller and was adapted into a major motion picture starring Hilary Swank. Her successive novels *Where Rainbows End*, *If You Could See Me Now*, *A Place Called Here* and *Thanks for the Memories* are also number one bestsellers. Her books are published in forty-six countries and have collectively sold over nine million copies. Cecelia has also co-created the hit ABC Network comedy series *Samantha Who?* which stars Christina Applegate. Her sixth and latest book *The Gift* is a Christmas story out now in hardback. Cecelia lives in Dublin, Ireland.

To sign up for the exclusive Cecelia Ahern HarperCollins newsletter and discover all about Cecelia's books, as well as interviews, photographs and much more, log onto www.cecelia-ahern.com

Praise for *Where Rainbows End*:

'A winner.' *Glamour*

'Heartwarmingly good.' *Heat*

'A heartwarming, completely absorbing tale of love and friendship.' *Company*

Praise for *PS, I Love You*:

'A sensational debut novel that proves true love never dies.' *Cosmopolitan*

'A wonderfully life-affirming, witty debut.' *Company*

'Like an Irish *Sleepless in Seattle.*' *In Style*

'A wonderfully warm and witty debut from a terrific new writer . . . This exceptional novel about bereavement, friendship and lost love is both heartbreaking and uplifting.' *Express*

'Everything she writes comes from the heart.'
Sunday Tribune

'A deeply touching story full of "maybes" and "what ifs" . . . a page-turner that makes you evaluate your own life, and urges you to do the things that you really want to, and to live life to the full.'
Woman's Way

'An irresistible page turner . . . warm, fun and cosy.'
Evening Echo

By the same author

PS, I Love You
If You Could See Me Now
A Place Called Here
Thanks for the Memories

CECELIA AHERN

Where Rainbows End

HARPER

This novel is entirely a work of fiction.
The names, characters and incidents portrayed in it are the work of the author's imagination. Any resemblance to actual persons, living or dead, events or localities is entirely coincidental.

Harper
HarperCollins*Publishers*
77–85 Fulham Palace Road,
Hammersmith, London W6 8JB

www.harpercollins.co.uk

This paperback edition 2008
1

First published in Great Britain by
HarperCollins*Publishers* 2004

A catalogue record for this book
is available from the British Library

ISBN 978 0 00 7832101

Set in Sabon by Palimpsest Book Production Limited,
Grangemouth, Stirlingshire

Printed and bound in Great Britain by
Clays Ltd, St Ives plc

For Mimmie

PART ONE

Chapter 1

To Alex

You are invited to my 7th birthday party on Tuesday the 8th of April in my house. We are having a magician and you can come to my house at 2 o'clock. It is over at 5 o'clock. I hope you will come.

From your best friend Rosie

To Rosie

Yes I will come to your brithday party on Wensday.

Form Alex

To Alex

My birthday party is on Tuesday not Wednesday. You can't bring sandy to the party because mum says so. She is a smelly dog.

From Rosie

To Rosie

I do not care wot your stupid mum says sandy wants to come.

Form Alex

To Alex

My mum is not stupid you are. You are not aloud to bring the dog. She will brust the baloons.

From Rosie

To Rosie

Then I am not going.

Form Alex

To Alex

Fine.

From Rosie

Dear Mrs Stewart,

I just called by to have a word with you about my daughter Rosie's birthday on the 8th of April. Sorry you weren't in, but I'll drop by again later this afternoon and maybe we can talk then.

There seems to be some sort of little problem with Alex and Rosie lately. I think they're not quite on talking terms. I hope you can fill me in on the situation when we meet. Rosie would really love if he came to her birthday party.

I'm looking forward to meeting the mother of this charming young man!

See you then,

Alice Dunne

To Rosie

I would be happy to go to your brithday party next week. Thank you fro inviting me and sandy.

Form Alex your frend

To Rosie

Thanks for the great day at the party. I am sorry sandy brust the baloons and ate your cake. She was hungry because mum says dad eats all our leftovers. See you at skool tomorrow.

Alex

To Alex

Thanks for the present. Its ok about what sandy did. Mum says she needed a new carpet anyway. Dad is a bit mad though. He said the old one was fine but mum thinks the house smells of poo now, and its not baby Kevin.

Look at Miss Casey's nose. It is the biggest nose I have ever seen. Ha ha ha.

Rosie

To Rosie
I no and she has a big snot hanging down too. She is the ugliest alien I have ever seen. I think we should tell the police we have an alien as a teacher who has a really smelly breath and—

Dear Mr and Mrs Stewart,
I would like to arrange a meeting with you to discuss how Alex is progressing at school. Specifically, I would like to talk about the recent change in his behaviour along with the problem of his note writing during class. I would appreciate it if you called the school to arrange a suitable time to meet.
Yours sincerely,
Miss Casey

To Alex
I hate that we dont sit together anymore in class. I'm stuck beside stinky Steven who picks his nose and eats it. It is gross. What did your mum and dad say about Miss Big nose?
From Rosie

To Rosie
Mum did not say much because she kept laffing. I dont no why. It is reall boring up the front of the class. Smelly breath Miss Casey keeps on lucking at me. Have to go.
Alex

To Alex
You always spell know wrong. It is KNOW not NO.
From Rosie

To Rosie
Sorry miss prefect. I no how to spell it.
Form Alex

Hello form Spain! The weather is really nice. It is hot and sunny. There is a swimming pool with a big slide.

It is cool. Met a freind called John. He is nice. See you in 2 weeks. I broke my arm coming down the slide. I went to the hopsital. I would like to work in a hopsital like the man that fixed my arm because he wore a white coat and had a chart in his hand and was really nice and he helped me to feel better. I would like to make people feel better and wear a white coat. My freind john signed my cast. You can too when I get home if you like. Alex

To Alex. Hello from Lundin. My hotel is the one in the picture on the front. My room is the one that is 7 up from the ground but you cant see me in the post card. I would like to work in a hotel when I grow up because you get free chocolates everyday and people are so nice that they tidy your room for you. The buses here are all red like the toy ones you got last Christmas. Everyone talks with a funny voice but are nice. Have met a frend called Jane. We go swimming together. Bye. Love from Rosie

To Alex

Why amnt I invited to your birthday party this year? I know all the boys from the class are going. Are you fighting with me?

Rosie

Dear Alice,

I'm sorry about Alex's behaviour this week. I know that Rosie is upset about not going to the party and she doesn't understand why she hasn't been invited. To be honest I can't quite understand it myself; I have tried to talk to Alex but I'm afraid I can't get inside the mind of a ten-year-old boy!

I think it's just a case of his not being able to invite her because the other boys don't want a girl to go. Unfortunately, he seems to be at that age . . . Please give my love to Rosie. It seems so unfair and when I spoke to her last week after school I could see how hurt she was.

Perhaps George and I can take the two of them out some other evening during the week.

Best wishes,

Sandra Stewart

To Rosie

The party was not very good. You did not miss anything. The boys are stupid. Brian threw his pizza in Jameses sleeping bag and when James woke up he had tomato and cheese stuck in his hair and everything and my mum tried to wash it and it would not go away and then Jameses mum gave out to Brians mum and my mum went real red and my dad said something I didn't here and Jameses mum started to cry and then everyone went home. Do you want to go to the cimena on Friday and go to McDonalds after? My mum and dad will bring us.

Alex

To Alex

Sorry about your party. Brian is a weirdo anyway. I hate him. Brian the Whine is his name. I will ask my mum and dad about the cinema. Look at Miss Casey's skirt it looks like my grannys. Or it looks like sandy puked up all over it and the—

Dear Mr and Mrs Dunne,

I was hoping to arrange a meeting with you to discuss Rosie's recent behaviour in school and her note writing during class. How does Thursday at 3 p.m. sound?

Miss Casey

Alex,

My mum and dad won't let me go to the cinema tonight. I hate not sitting beside you. It's so boring. Frizzy Lizzys hair is blocking my view of the blackboard. Why does this happen to us all the time?

Rosie

TO ALEX
HAPPY VALENTINE'S DAY!
MAY THERE BE SEX IN YOUR LIFE AND . . .
LIFE IN YOUR SEX!
LOVE FROM YOUR SECRET ADMIRER XXX

To Rosie
You wrote that card didn't you?
From Alex

To Alex
What card?
From Rosie

To Rosie
Very funny. I no it was you.
From Alex

To Alex
I really don't know what you're talking about. Why would I send you a Valentine's card?
From Rosie

To Rosie
Ha ha! How did you no it was a Valentine's Card! The only way you could no is if you sent it. You *love* me, you want to *marry* me.
From Alex

To Alex
Leave me alone I'm listening to Mrs O'Sullivan. If she catches us passing notes again we're dead meat.
From Rosie

To Rosie
What happened to you? You've turned into such a swot.
Alex

Yes Alex and that's why I'll go places in life, like going to college and being a big successful business person with loads of money . . . unlike you.
From Rosie

Chapter 2

Dear Mr Byrne,

Alex will be unable to attend school tomorrow, the 8th of April, as he has a dental appointment.

Sandra Stewart

Dear Ms Quinn,

Rosie will be unable to attend school tomorrow, the 8th of April, as she has a doctor's appointment.

Alice Dunne

Rosie,

I'll meet you round the corner at 8.30 a.m. Remember to bring a change of clothes. We're not wandering around town in our uniforms. This is going to be the best birthday you ever had, Rosie Dunne, trust me! I can't believe we're actually getting away with this!

Alex

PS. Sweet 16 my arse!

St James's Hospital
10 April

Dear Mr and Mrs Dunne,

Enclosed is the medical bill for Rosie Dunne's stomach pumping on 8 April.

Yours sincerely,

Dr Montgomery

Rosie,

Your mum is guarding the door like a vicious dog

so I don't think I'll get to see you for the next ten years or so. The kind big sis you love so much (not!) has agreed to pass this on to you. You owe her big time . . .

Sorry about the other day. Maybe you were right. Maybe the tequila wasn't such a good idea. The poor barman will probably be closed down for serving us. Told you that fake ID my mate got would work, even though yours did say you were born on the 31st of February!

Just wondering if you remember anything that happened the other day . . . write to me. You can trust Stephanie to pass it on. She's mad at your mum for not letting her drop out of college. Phil and Margaret have just announced that they're having another baby so it looks like I'll be an uncle for the second time round. At least that's taking the attention off me, which makes for a change. Phil just keeps laughing at what you and me did because we remind him of himself ten years ago.

Get well soon, you alco! Do you no I didn't think it was possible for a human being to go *so* green in the face. I think you have finally found your talent, Rosie, ha ha ha ha.

Alex/Mr Cocky,

I FEEL AWFUL. My head is pounding, I have never had such a headache, I have never felt so ill before in my life. Mum and Dad are going ape shit. Honestly, you never get any sympathy in this house. I'm gonna be grounded for about thirty years and I'm being 'prevented' from seeing you because you're 'such a bad influence'. Yeah right, whatever.

Anyway, it doesn't really matter what they do because I'm gonna see you at school tomorrow, unless they 'prevent' me from going there too, which is absolutely fine by me. Can't believe we have double maths on a Monday morning. I would rather get my stomach pumped again. Five times over. See you on Monday then.

Oh by the way, in answer to your question, apart from my face smashing against that filthy pub floor, flashing lights, loud sirens, speeding cars and puking, I can't remember anything else. But I bet that just about covers it. Anything else I should know about?

Rosie

To Rosie

Glad to hear everything is as normal as usual. Mum and Dad are driving me crazy too. I can't believe I'm actually looking forward to going to school. At least no one will be able to nag us there.

From Alex

Dear Mr and Mrs Dunne,

Following the recent actions of your daughter Rosie, we request a meeting with you at the school immediately. We need to discuss her behaviour and come to an agreement on a reasonable punishment. I have no doubt you understand the necessity of this. Alex Stewart's parents will also be in attendance.

The scheduled time is Monday morning at 9 a.m.

Yours sincerely,

Mr Bogarty

Principal

From Rosie
To Alex
Subject Suspended!

Holy shit! I didn't think that old bogey would go ahead and suspend us! I'd swear we were axe murderers from the way that he was carrying on! Oh, this is the best punishment *ever*. I get to stay in bed for a whole week nursing a hangover instead of going to school!

From Alex
To Rosie
Subject I'm in hell

Glad life is going so wonderfully for you these days. I'm emailing you from the worst place in the world. An office. I have to work here with Dad for the entire week, filing shit and licking stamps. I swear to God I am NEVER EVER going to work in an office in my life.

The bastards aren't even paying me.

A very pissed off Alex

From Rosie
To Alex
Subject A very pissed off Alex

Ha ha ha ha ha ha ha ha ha em . . . I've forgotten what I was going to write . . . oh yeah . . . ha ha ha ha ha ha ha ha ha ha ha ha ha ha ha ha ha.

Lots of love from an extremely comfy, snuggy, warm and happy Rosie typing from her bedroom.

From Alex
To Rosie
Subject Lazy

I don't care. There is an absolute babe working in this office. I am going to marry her. Now who's laughing?

From Rosie
To Alex
Subject Don Juan

Who is she?

From a non-lesbian so am therefore NOT jealous.

From Alex
To Rosie
Subject To non-lesbian

I will for the time being humour you by calling you that although I have yet to see any evidence to suggest otherwise.

Her name is Bethany Williams and she is seventeen (older woman!), blonde, has a massive pair of boobs and the longest legs I have ever seen.

From the sex god

From Rosie
To Alex
Subject Mr Sex God (puke puke gag vomit)

She sounds like a giraffe. I'm sure she is a really nice person (not!). Have you even said hello to her or has your future wife yet to acknowledge your existence? (Apart from handing you memos to photocopy, of course.)

You have an instant message from: ALEX.
Alex: Hey there, Rosie, got some news for you.
Rosie: Leave me alone, please. I'm trying to concentrate on what Mr Simpson is saying.
Alex: Hmmm wonder why . . . could it be those beautiful big blue eyes all you girls are always going on about?
Rosie: Nope, I have a great and growing interest in Excel. It's so exciting – I could just sit in and do it all weekend.
Alex: Oh, you're turning into such a bore.
Rosie: I WAS JOKING, YOU IDIOT! I hate this crap. I think my brain is turning to mush from listening to him. But go away anyway.
Alex: Do you not wanna hear my news?
Rosie: Nope.
Alex: Well, I'm telling you anyway.
Rosie: OK, what's the big exciting news?

Alex: Well, you can eat your words, my friend, because virgin boy is no longer.
Alex: Hello?
Alex: You still there?
Alex: Rosie, c'mon, stop messing!
Rosie: Sorry, I seem to have fallen off my chair and knocked myself out. I had an awful dream you said you are no longer virgin boy.
Alex: No dream.
Rosie: I suppose that means you won't be wearing your underwear over those tights any more.
Alex: I have no need for underwear at all now.
Rosie: Uuuugh! So who's the unlucky girl? Please don't say Bethany please don't say Bethany . . .
Alex: Tough shit. It's Bethany.
Alex: Hello?
Alex: Rosie?
Rosie: What?
Alex: Well?
Rosie: Well what?
Alex: Well say something.
Rosie: I really don't know what you want me to say, Alex. I think you need to get yourself some male friends because I'm not gonna slap you on the back and ask for gory details.
Alex: Just tell me what you think.
Rosie: To be honest, from what I hear about her, I think she's a slut.
Alex: Oh, come on, you don't even no the girl, you've never even met her. You call anyone who sleeps with anyone a slut.
Rosie: I've seen her around and, eh, SLIGHT exaggeration there, Alex. I call people who sleep with different people every day of the week sluts.
Alex: You no that's not true.
Rosie: You keep spelling KNOW wrong. It's KNOW not NO.
Alex: Shut up with the 'know' thing. You've been going on about that since we were about five!

Rosie: Yeah, exactly, so you think you would listen by now.
Alex: Oh forget I said anything.
Rosie: Oh, Alex, I'm just worried about you. I know you really like her, and all I'm saying is that she's not a one-man kind of girl.
Alex: Well, she is now.
Rosie: Are you two going out with each other?!
Alex: Yes.
Rosie: YES?????
Alex: You sound surprised.
Rosie: I just didn't think Bethany went out with people, I thought she just slept with them.
Rosie: Alex?
Rosie: OK, OK, I'm sorry.
Alex: Rosie, you need to stop doing that.
Rosie: I no I do.
Alex: Ha ha.
Mr Simpson: You two, get down to the principal's office now.
Rosie: WHAT??? OH, SIR, PLEASE, I WAS LISTENING TO YOU!
Mr Simpson: Rosie, I haven't spoken for the last fifteen minutes. You are supposed to be working on an assignment now.
Rosie: Oh. Well, it's not my fault. Alex is an awful influence on me. He just never lets me concentrate on my school work.
Alex: I just had something really important to tell Rosie and it just couldn't wait.
Mr Simpson: So I see, Alex. Congratulations.
Alex: Eh . . . how do you know what it was?
Mr Simpson: I think you two would find it interesting sometimes if you listen to me every now and again. You can really learn some useful tips, like how to keep an instant message private so everyone else can't see.
Alex: Are you telling me other people in the class can read this?
Mr Simpson: Yes I am.

Alex: Oh my God.
Rosie: Ha ha ha ha ha ha ha ha ha ha ha ha ha ha ha
Mr Simpson: Rosie!
Rosie: Ha ha ha ha ha ha ha
Mr Simpson: ROSIE!!!
Rosie: Yes, sir.
Mr Simpson: Get out of the class now.
Alex: Ha ha ha ha ha ha ha
Mr Simpson: You too, Alex.

Chapter 3

From Rosie
To Alex
Subject Julie's house party

Hiya, long time no see . . . I hope they're not working you to death down there at 'the office'. I've hardly seen you at all this summer. There's a party at Julie's house tonight so was just wondering if you wanted to go. I don't really want to go on my own. Anyway, I'm sure you're busy doing whatever it is you do so just ring me when you get a chance or email me back.

From Alex
To Rosie
Subject Re: Julie's house party

Rosie, this is just quick email. Real busy. Can't go out tonight, promised Bethany would go to cinema. Sorry! You go and have fun.

Rosie, hello from Portugal! Weather here really hot. Dad got sunstroke and all Mum does is lie by the pool, which is really boring. Not much people here my age. Hotel quiet (on front of postcard) and it's right on the beach, as you can see. You would love to work here! I'm bringing home a collection of those little shampoos and shower caps and stuff that you love. The bathrobe is too big to fit into my bag. See you when I get back. Alex

From Rosie
To Alex
Subject Catching up?

How was the holiday? Haven't heard from you since you've been back. Fancy going out tonight to catch up?

From Alex
To Rosie
Subject Re: Catching up?

Sorry have been so busy since I got back. Got you pressie. Can't go out tonight but will drop your pressie by before I head out.

From Rosie
To Alex
Subject Re: Catching up?

Didn't see you last night. I want my little shampoos, ha ha.

From Alex
To Rosie
Subject Re: Catching up?

Heading to Donegal for the weekend. Beth's parents have a little 'hideaway' there. Will drop your pressie by when I get back.

To the most inconsiderate asshole of a friend

I'm writing you this letter because I know that if I say what I have to say to your face I will probably punch you.

I don't know you any more. I don't see you any more. All I get is a quick text or a rushed email from you every few days. I know you are busy and I know you have Bethany, but hello? I'm supposed to be your best friend.

You have no idea what this summer has been like. Since we were kids we pushed away every single person that could possibly have been our friend until there was only me and you. It's not that we didn't *want* anyone else, it's just that we didn't *need* them. You always had me. I always had you. Now you have Bethany and I have no one.

Sadly it looks like you don't need me any more. I feel like those other people that used to try to become our friends. I know you're probably not doing it deliberately just as we never did. Anyway, I'm not moaning on about how much I hate her, I'm just trying to tell you that I miss you. And that, well . . . I'm lonely.

Whenever you cancel nights out I end up staying home with Mum and Dad watching TV. Stephanie's always out and even Kevin has more of a life than I do. It's so depressing. This was supposed to be our summer of fun. What happened? Can't you be friends with two people at once?

I know you have found someone who is extra special, and that you both have a unique 'bond', or whatever, that you and I will never have. But we have another bond: we're best friends. Or does the best friend bond disappear as soon as you meet somebody else? Maybe it does, and I just don't understand that because I haven't met that 'somebody special'. I'm not in any hurry to either. I liked things the way they were.

In a few years' time if my name ever comes up you will probably say, 'Rosie. Now there's a name I haven't heard for ages. We used to be best friends. I wonder what she's doing now; I haven't seen or thought of her in years!' You will sound like my mum and dad when they have dinner parties with friends and talk about old times. They mention people I've never even heard of when they're talking about some of the most important days of their lives. How could Mum's bridesmaid of twenty years ago be someone she doesn't even ring up now? Or in Dad's case, how could he not know where his own best friend from school lives?

Anyway, my point is (I know, I know, there is one), I don't want to be one of those easily forgotten people, *so* important at the time, *so* special, *so* influential and *so* treasured, yet years later just a vague face and a distant memory. I want us to be best friends for ever, Alex.

I'm happy you're happy, really I am, but I feel like I've been left behind. Maybe our time has come and gone. Maybe your time is now meant to be spent with Bethany. And if that's the case I won't bother sending you this letter. And if I'm not sending this letter then what am I doing still writing it? OK, I'm going now and I'm ripping these muddled thoughts up.

Your friend,
Rosie

From Alex
To Rosie
Subject Buttercup!!

Hey, Buttercup, you OK? (Haven't called you that for a *long* time!) I haven't heard or seen you in a while. I'm sending you this email because every time I call by your house, you're either in the bath or not there. Should I begin to take this personally? But knowing you, if you had a problem with me you wouldn't be too shy to let me know all about it!

Anyway, once the summer is over we'll see each other every day. We'll be sick of the sight of each other then! I can't believe this is our last year in school. It's crazy! This time next year I'll be studying medicine and you will be hotel manager woman extraordinaire! Things at work have been frantic. Dad kind of gave me a promotion so I've more to do than just filing and labelling. (I answer phones now too.) But I need the money and at least I get to see Bethany everyday. How's your job as chief dish-washer at The Dragon? I'm amazed you turned down baby-sitting for that. You could have stayed in all night and watched TV instead of turning your hands to prunes while you scrape egg noodles from woks. Anyway, email me or call me back or something.

From Rosie
To Alex
Subject Moonbeam!

It's not because I hate Bethany that I'm not seeing much of you (although I do hate her) it's just that I think Bethany dislikes me just a little. It could have something to do with the fact that a friend of hers told her what I wrote about her in that (not so) private instant messaging thingy in computer class last year. But I suppose you already know that. I don't think she liked being called a slut, I don't know why . . . some women are just funny like that. (Speaking of computer class, you know Mr Simpson got married this summer? I'm gutted. I'll never look at Excel in the same way again.)

Anyway it's your birthday soon! You will have finally reached the grand old age of eighteen! Want to go out and do some legal celebrating (well, legal for you, anyway)? Let me know.

PS. Please STOP calling me Buttercup!

From Alex
To Rosie
Subject 18th Birthday

Good to hear you're alive after all. I was beginning to worry! I would love to celebrate my 18th with you but Bethany's parents are taking me and my parents out for dinner to the Hazel. (How posh is that?) It's so we can all get to know each other. Sorry, another night definitely.

~~Dearest Alex,~~

~~Well whoopdeedoo for you.~~

~~Fuck Bethany.~~

~~Fuck her parents.~~

~~Fuck the Hazel.~~
~~And fuck you.~~
~~Love your best friend Rosie~~

From Rosie
To Alex
Subject Happy Birthday!

OK then. Well, enjoy the meal. Happy birthday!

From Rosie
To Alex
Subject DISASTER!

I can't believe this is happening! I was just talking to your mum; called over for a chat and she told me the bad news. This is the *worst* news *ever*! Please call me when you can. Your boss keeps telling me you can't take calls during working hours – QUIT, Mr I never EVER want to work in an office.

This is so terrible. I feel awful!

Chapter 4

Dear Mr Stewart,

We are delighted to inform you that you have been accepted to fill the position of Vice President of Charles and Charles Co. We are thrilled that you will be joining the team over here and we look forward to welcoming you and your family to Boston.

I hope the relocation package we are offering is to your satisfaction. If there is anything further that Charles and Charles Co. can do for you, please do not hesitate to ask. Maria Agnesi, personnel executive, will call you to discuss a suitable date for you to begin work.

We look forward to seeing you at the office.

Welcome to the team!

Yours sincerely,

Robert Brasco

President, Charles and Charles Co.

From Alex
To Rosie
Subject Re: DISASTER!

I'll call you when I get home. It's true. Dad was offered a job doing something that sounds incredibly boring . . . I don't really know, I wasn't listening when he told me exactly what. I can't understand why he has to go all the way over to Boston to do a boring job. There's plenty of them right here. He can have mine.

I'm so pissed off. I don't want to go. I only have a year left in school. This is such the wrong time to leave. I don't want to go to a stupid American high school. I don't want to leave you.

We can talk about it later. We have to think of a way that I can stay. This is really bad, Rosie.

From Rosie
To Alex
Subject Stay with me!

Don't go! Mum and Dad said that you could stay here for the year! Finish school in Dublin and then we can both decide what to do after that! Please stay! It will be so brilliant, us living together. It'll be just like when we were young and we used to keep each other up all night with those walkie-talkies! We used to hear more static than our voices but we thought we were so cool! Remember that time on Christmas Eve absolutely *years* ago when we had a 'Santa' watch? We planned it for weeks, drawing little diagrams of the road and maps of our houses just so we could cover every angle and not miss him. You were on the 7–10 p.m. watch and I was on the 10 p.m.–1 a.m. watch. You were *supposed* to wake up and take over from me, but – surprise, surprise – you didn't. I stayed awake all night, screaming down into that walkie-talkie, trying to wake you up! Ah well, it was your loss. I saw Santa and you didn't . . .

If you stay with us, Alex, we'll be able to talk all night! It would be so much fun. When we were kids we always wanted to live together. Now's our chance.

Talk to your mum and dad about it. Convince them to say yes. Anyway, you're eighteen so you can do what you like!

Rosie,

I didn't want to wake you so your mum said she would pass this on to you. You no I hate goodbyes, but anyway, it's not goodbye because you're going to come over and visit all the time. Promise me. Mum and Dad wouldn't even let me stay with Phil, never mind you. I couldn't convince them. They want to keep their eye on me for my final year of school.

I have to go . . . I'll miss you. Ring you when I get there.

Love,

Alex

PS. I told you, I *was* awake that Christmas Eve. My battery just went dead on my walkie-talkie . . . (and I did see Santa, I'll have you no).

Alex,

Good luck, little brother. Don't worry, you'll enjoy yourself once you get there and I can't wait to come and visit. Despite having Margaret and the kids, I still feel like moving over with the lot of you. I'll miss you all. It won't be the same without you. Stop worrying about Rosie. Her life's not going to fall apart just because you're in different countries. But if it'll make you feel any better I'll look out for her for you – she does almost seem like my little sister. By the way, if Sandy doesn't learn how to control her bladder in this house then I'm sending her over to you on a plane.

We'll miss you,

Phil (+ Margaret, William and Fiona)

From Rosie
To Stephanie
Subject Urgent sisterly advice needed

I can't believe he's gone, Steph. I can't believe you're gone. Why is everyone leaving me? Surely you could have 'found yourself' a little closer to home? But France? Alex left only a few weeks ago but I almost feel like he's dead . . .

Why did he have to break up with Slutty Bethany just two weeks before he left? Then I wouldn't have gotten used to him being around so much again. Things really got back to normal, Steph. It was brilliant. We spent every second together and had so much fun!

Brian the Whine threw a going-away party for Alex just last week; I think it was just an excuse for Brian the Whine to get permission from his parents to have a party, to be honest, because the two of them *never* liked each other. Not since that pizza in James's hair incident. But anyway, Whine held the party in his house and invited all of his friends, and me and Alex knew hardly anyone in the entire place! The people we did know we can't stand, so we left and headed into town. You know O'Brien's where we held your surprise 21st? Well, we went there and Alex had the bright idea of standing outside the pub door and pretending to be the bouncer. (There was none on the door that night because it was only a Monday.) Well, he pulled it off anyway because he's really tall and muscly – you know Alex! Anyway, we stood there for ages turning people away; I don't think he let one person in. Eventually we got bored and headed inside to the empty pub. Of course, the more drinks we had, the more me and Alex ended up getting all weepy about him moving away . . . Apart from that the night was brilliant. I miss the times we had, just us together like that.

You can't imagine how lonely it is at school these days. I'm just short of getting down on my hands and knees and begging for someone to be my friend. How pathetic. No one really cares. I spent the last few years ignoring them so they don't feel like they really have to talk to me. I think some of them are even enjoying it. The teachers are loving it. Mr Simpson called me back after class to congratulate me on how well I'm doing lately. It's shameful; Alex would be appalled if he found out I was actually working at school. I'm horrified that things have gotten so bad that I actually pay attention to the teachers. They're the only people who even talk to me from one day to the next. How depressing.

I wake up in the morning and I feel like I'm missing something. I know that there's something not right, and it takes me a while to remember what it is . . . then I remember. My best friend is gone. My only friend. It was silly of me to rely so much on one person. It's all coming back on me now.

Anyway, sorry for whinging on and on all the time. I'm sure you have enough problems of your own to worry about. Tell me how my sophisticated big sis is doing over in France. Strange you're over there – you always hated French class. At least it's only for a few months, right? And then you're coming back? Dad's still not happy about you dropping out of college. Why you had to go away to find yourself is beyond me. Just look in the mirror. What's the restaurant like? Have you dropped any plates yet? Are you going to work there for long? Any nice men? There must be; French men are yummy. If there are any spare men that you don't want, send them my way.

Love,

Rosie

PS. Dad wants to know if you have enough money and if you've found yourself yet. Mum wants to know if you are eating properly. Little Kevin (he is so tall now you wouldn't believe!) wants to know if you'll send him some video game or other over. I don't know what he's talking about so just ignore him.

From Stephanie
To Rosie
Subject Re: Urgent sisterly advice

Hello, my darling little sister.

Don't worry about Alex. I've thought long and hard about it and I've come to the conclusion that it's a good idea he's not there for your final year of school because at least for the first year EVER you may not get suspended. Think of how proud you would make Mum and Dad. (Oh, by the way, tell them I'm broke, starving and currently looking for myself in an internet café in Paris.)

I definitely know how you feel right now. I'm alone here too, but just stick the year out and when you're finished maybe Alex will move back to Ireland, or you can go to college in Boston!

Aim for something, Rosie, I know you don't want to hear it, but it will help. Aim for what you want and the year will all make sense. Go to Boston if that will make you happy. Study hotel management like you've always wanted.

You're only young, Rosie, and I know that you absolutely hate to hear that but it's true. What seems tragic now won't even be an issue in a few years' time. You're only seventeen. You and Alex have the rest of your lives to catch up together. After all, soulmates always end up together. Silly Bethany won't even be remembered then. Ex-girlfriends are easily forgotten. Best friends stay with you for ever.

Take care. Tell Mum and Dad I said hi and that I'm still looking for myself but may have found someone else in the process. Tall, dark and handsome . . .

Chapter 5

Dear Ms Rosie Dunne,

Thank you for your application to study Hotel Management with us at Boston College. We are delighted to inform you that you were successful in your application . . .

From Rosie
To Alex
Subject Boston here I come!

I GOT IN!! Boston College, here I come!!!
WAHOOO! The letter arrived just this morning and I am soooo excited! You'd better not move a muscle, Mr Stewart, because I am finally coming to see you. It'll be great, even though you and I won't be studying at the same college. (Harvard is far too distinguished for the likes of me!) But I think it's just as well because I don't think we can really afford to get suspended again . . .

Email or call me as soon as possible. I'd call you but Dad put a block on long-distance calls, as you know, after the last bill. Mum and Dad are so proud, they're phoning all the family to tell them. I think they're hoping I'll be the first Dunne child to go to college and actually finish the course. Dad keeps warning me not to go trying to 'find myself' anywhere like Stephanie did. By the way, it doesn't look like Steph is coming home anytime soon. She met some chef that works at the restaurant she's waiting at, and she's officially 'in love'.

The phone hasn't stopped ringing all day with congratulations! Honestly, Alex, the house is buzzing! Paul and Eileen from across the road sent over a bunch of flowers for me, which was really nice. Mum's getting the house ready for a get-together tonight, just a few sandwiches and cocktail sausages, that kind of thing. Kevin is happy I'm leaving so he can be even more spoiled than usual. I'll miss the brat even though he never talks to me. I'll miss Mum and Dad even more, but right now everyone is just so excited I've been accepted to think about the fact that I won't be living here any more. I suppose the enormity of it will hit me the day I wave goodbye, but in the meantime we'll continue to celebrate!

PS. One of these days I can run a hotel and you can be the doctor-in-the-house who saves the lives of the guests I poison in the restaurant, just like we always planned. Oh, this has all worked out wonderfully . . .

From Alex
To Rosie
Subject Re: Boston here I come!

This is *brilliant* news! I can't wait to see you too! Harvard isn't too far away from Boston College (well, in comparison to being a whole ocean apart – can you believe Harvard accepted me? It must be the intellects' idea of a hilarious joke). I'm too excited to type – just get over here. When are you coming?

From Rosie
To Alex
Subject September

I won't be over till September, only a few days before the semester starts, because I have got so many things to sort out you wouldn't believe!

The debs are at the end of August – will you come over for them? Everyone would love to see you, and I need someone to go with! We will have so much fun and we can annoy all our teachers, just like old times . . . Let me know.

From Alex
To Rosie
Subject Re: Debs

Of course I'll come home for our debs. I wouldn't miss it for the world!

From Rosie
To Alex
Subject Where r u???

I'm at the internet café at the airport. Me & Dad have been here for hours. I tried your house phone and mobile. Don't know where else to call. Hope everything's ok.

From Alex
To Rosie
Subject Sorry!

Rosie, I am so sorry. This whole day has been an absolute nightmare. There was a foul-up with the flight. I don't no what happened, but my name wasn't in the system when I went to collect my ticket. I've been here all day trying to get another flight. They're all booked because of people flying home from holidays and students returning home, etc. I'm on standby, but so far there's been nothing. I'm just hanging around the airport waiting for a flight. This is a nightmare.

From Rosie
To Alex
Subject Flight tomorrow

Dad's talking to the lady at Aer Lingus ticket desk. She says there's a flight that leaves Boston tomorrow at 10.10 a.m. It takes five hours to get here so that will make it 3 p.m., then we're five hours ahead, which will make it 8 p.m. We could collect you from airport and go straight to ball? Or maybe you'd prefer to go to my house first? You can't wear your tux on the plane because you'll get all crumpled. What do you think?

From Alex
To Rosie
Subject Flight

Rosie, bad news. That flight is fully booked.

From Rosie
To Alex
Subject Flight

Shit. Think, think, think. What can I do? It seems that we can get you here every other bloody day except tomorrow. Somebody up there really doesn't want you to get on that plane. Maybe it's a sign?

From Alex
To Rosie
Subject My fault

It's my fault, I should have double-checked with the airline yesterday – they always say you should reconfirm your flights but whoever does? I no I've messed up your night but please go to the debs anyway. You still have the whole day to find someone else to go with you. Take loads of photos for me, and enjoy yourself. Sorry, Rosie.

From Rosie
To Alex
Subject Re: My fault

It's not your fault. I'm disappointed but let's be realistic, it's not the end of the world. I'm gonna be in Boston in a little over a month and we'll be seeing each other EVERY DAY! Make sure you get your money back for that flight, the eejits. We'll have a brilliant time. I better go searching for a man now . . .

From Alex
To Rosie
Subject Manhunt

Any luck finding a man?

From Rosie
To Alex
Subject Man found

What a stupid question!! Of course I found a man. I'm insulted you even needed to ask . . .

From Alex
To Rosie
Subject Mystery man

Then who is it?

From Rosie
To Alex
Subject Secret man

That would be absolutely none of your business.

From Alex
To Rosie
Subject Invisible man

HA! You didn't find a date!! I knew it!

From Rosie
To Alex
Subject Big strong man

Yes I did.

From Alex
To Rosie
Subject No man

No you didn't.

From Rosie
To Alex
Subject Yes, man!

Yes I did.

From Alex
To Rosie
Subject What man?

THEN WHO IS IT?

From Rosie
To Alex
Subject Almost a man

Brian.

From Alex
To Rosie
Subject Brian?

BRIAN? BRIAN THE WHINE?

From Rosie
To Alex
Subject Re: Brian?

Maybe . . .

From Alex
To Rosie
Subject HA HA!

Ha ha ha ha ha ha, you're going to the debs with Brian the Whine?! Talk about scraping the barrel! Brian who lifted your skirt when you were six, in front of everyone in the school yard, to reveal your knickers? The Brian you were stuck sitting beside for all of second class, who ate fish sandwiches every day for lunch and picked his nose while you ate your sandwiches? The Brian who followed us home from school everyday singing 'Rosie and Alex up a tree, K-I-S-S-I-N-G?' and made you cry and ignore me for a week? The Brian who spilled his beer all down your new top at my going-away party? The Brian you absolutely can't stand and was the one person you actually hated all throughout school? And now you're going to the last school dance ever, *with Brian*?

From Rosie
To Alex
Subject No, the other Brian

Yes, Alex, *that* Brian. Now may I ask that you please stop emailing me as my darling mother is currently tying knots in my head trying to make me look half decent? She has also been reading your emails and wants you to know that Brian the Whine won't be lifting up my skirt tonight.

From Alex
To Rosie
Subject Re: Brian

Well, it won't be for lack of trying. Have fun! May I suggest that you wear your beer goggles tonight?

From Rosie
To Alex
Subject Re: Beer goggles

The beer goggles will be well and truly on! Brian was the only person I could get last minute, thanks to you. All I have to do is stand in with him for the photos so that Mum and Dad can have lovely memories of their daughter going to the debs all dressed up with a man in a tuxedo. The tables seat ten so I won't even have to talk to him at dinner. You're enjoying this, aren't you, Alex?

From Alex
To Rosie
Subject Re: Re: Beer goggles

Not really. I'd love to be there instead. Don't do anything that I wouldn't do . . .

From Rosie
To Alex
Subject Re: Re: Re: Beer goggles

Well, that doesn't rule out much. Hair's done now, have to get the rest of me ready. I'll let you know how it went tomorrow.

From Alex
To Rosie
Subject Debs

How were the debs last night? No doubt you're nursing a hangover. I'll wait to hear from you tomorrow but I'll wait no longer! I want to know *everything*!

From Alex
To Rosie
Subject Debs

Did you get my last email? I keep calling and there's no answer. What's up? I hope you're busy preparing for the big move over to me!
Email me soon, please.

Steph: Rosie, stop avoiding Alex and tell him how the debs went. Alex is even emailing me wondering what happened, and I'm certainly not going to tell him! The poor guy missed out and all he wants to know is who did what, where and when.
Rosie: Well, I certainly won't be telling him who did who.
Steph: Ha ha.
Rosie: It's not funny.
Steph: I think it's hilarious. Come on, it's been three weeks now!
Rosie: Are you sure it's three weeks?
Steph: Yeah, why?
Rosie: Holy shit.
Rosie has logged off.

From Alex
To Rosie
Subject Hello??

Rosie, are you there? Are you having problems with your email? Please reply. You should be getting on a plane soon to come over here – you'll miss the start of term.

From Alex
To Rosie
Subject Please, Rosie?

Are you mad at me? I'm sorry I couldn't go to the debs ball, but I thought you understood. Things with whiny Briany can't have gone that badly, can they? What have you been doing all month? This is ridiculous. Why doesn't anyone answer the phone at your house when I call?

Answer me,
Alex

Dear Alice,

Hi, it's Alex here. I'm just writing to see if Rosie's OK. I haven't heard from her and I was getting a bit worried, to tell you the truth. It's unusual for me to not hear from her in so long. Every time I call the house it just goes on to answering machine. Are you getting my messages? Maybe you've all gone away? Please let me no what's happening, and tell Rosie to call.

Best wishes,
Alex

Dear Sandra,

Alex has been leaving messages with us all week and he's terribly concerned about Rosie. I know you're worried about him worrying about Rosie so I'm just writing to let you know the situation . . .

From Alex
To Rosie
Subject You're not coming to Boston?

My mum told me today that you're not coming to Boston. Please tell me what's happening. I'm so worried. Did I do something wrong? You no that I am always here for you when you need me.

Whatever it is, Rosie, I will understand and will always be here to help you. Please let me no what is happening. I'm going out of my mind here. If you don't get in touch with me, I'm booking a flight back to Ireland to see you myself.

Love,
Alex

From Stephanie
To Rosie
Subject I'm coming over

Rosie, my sweetie, don't worry. Just take deep breaths and try to relax. Everything happens for a reason. Maybe this is the correct path for you; perhaps Boston wasn't. I'm booking a flight and I'll be home as soon as I can. Hang in there, little sis.

Love,
Stephanie

Dear Miss Rosie Dunne,

Thank you for your recent letter. Boston College acknowledges that you will not be accepting your position this year.

Yours sincerely,
Robert Whitworth

Rosie, can't believe this is the decision u have made. You know I am not in support of it. I'm moving away as I had already planned. Hope everything works out well 4 u.

From Rosie
To Alex
Subject Help

Oh God, Alex, what have I done?

Chapter 6

Alex,

It was good to see you again. Please don't be a stranger – I'm really going to need all the friends I can get right now. Thank you for being so supportive last week. I honestly think I would go mad without you sometimes.

Life is funny, isn't it? Just when you think you've got it all figured out, just when you finally begin to plan something, get excited about it and feel like you know what direction you're heading in, the paths change, the signs change, the wind blows the other way, north is suddenly south, and east is west and you're lost. It is so easy to lose your way, to lose direction.

There aren't many sure things in life, but one thing I do know is that you have to deal with the consequences of your actions. You have to follow through on some things.

I always give up, Alex. What have I ever had to do in my life that really *needed* to be done? I always had a choice, and I always took the easy way out – *we* always took the easy way out. A few months ago, the burden of double maths on a Monday morning and finding a spot the size of Pluto on my nose was as complicated as it ever got for me.

This time round I'm having a baby. A baby. And that baby will be around on the Monday, the Tuesday, the Wednesday, Thursday, Friday, Saturday *and* Sunday. I will have no weekends off. No three-month holidays. I can't take a day off, call in sick or get Mum to write a note. *I* am going to be the mum now. I wish I could write myself a note.

I'm scared, Alex.

Rosie

From Alex
To Rosie
Subject Baby talk

No, it's not double maths on a Monday morning. It will be *far* more exciting than that. Double maths on a Monday morning is boring: it makes you sleep and gives you headache. You will learn masses more from this experience than a maths class can ever teach you.

I am here for you for whenever you need me. College can wait for you, Rosie, because you have far more important work to do now.

I no you will be just fine.

From Rosie
To Alex
Subject Re: Baby talk

You KNOW I will be fine. Watch the spelling, Mr Stewart!

From Alex
To Rosie
Subject Re: Re: Baby talk

Rosie, you're already acting like a mother – you're going to be fine! Take care. Alex

You have received an instant message from: ALEX.
Alex: I thought you said you'd keep an eye on her for me, Phil.
Phil: I told you, if she didn't learn to control her bladder she'd be out of here. She's fine in the garden.

Alex: Not the *dog*, Phil, I'm talking about *Rosie*.
Phil: What about Rosie?
Alex: Stop pretending you don't no. I heard Mum and Dad tell you over the phone.
Phil: How do you feel about it?
Alex: Everyone keeps asking me that and I have no idea. It's weird. Rosie is pregnant. She's only eighteen. She can barely take care of herself, let alone a baby. She smokes like a chimney and refuses to eat greens. She stays awake till 4 a.m. and sleeps till one o'clock in the day. She chose to take a job washing pots and pans at the Chinese takeaway for less money than her neighbours were offering for baby-sitting because she couldn't stand the hassle. I don't think she's changed a nappy in her life. Apart from when Kevin was tiny, I don't think she's ever held a baby for more than five minutes. What about college? What about working? How the hell is she going to manage? How will she ever meet someone? How will she make friends? She's just trapped herself into a life that's her worst nightmare.
Phil: Believe me, Alex, she'll learn. Her parents are supporting her, aren't they? She won't be alone.
Alex: Her mum and dad are great but they will be at work all day, Phil. She's an intelligent person, I no that. But as much as she tries to convince me, I'm not quite sure she's convinced herself that when the crying starts, she can't hand this one back. If only I'd gotten on that flight and made it to the debs . . .

Dear Stephanie,

Let me help you find yourself. Allow my words of wisdom, from the sister who greatly loves and respects you and wishes for nothing but happiness and great fortune in your life, to rain down on you and shower you with knowledge. Please take my advice. Never get pregnant. Or *enceinte*, as you would say over there. Look at the word, say it out loud, familiarise yourself with it, repeat it in your head and learn to *never ever* want to be it.

In fact, never have sex. Might as well try to completely eradicate the odds.

Trust me, Steph, pregnancy is not pleasant. I'm not feeling at all at one with nature, I'm not radiating any sort of magical motherly signals, I'm just fat. And bloated. And tired. And sick. And wondering what on earth I am going to do when this little one is born and looks at me.

Glowing, my bum. Smouldering is more like it. Alex has started his wonderful life in college, people who were at school with me are out tasting what the world has to offer and I'm just expanding by the second, wondering what I have got myself into. I know it's my own fault but I feel like I'm missing out on so much. I've been going to these antenatal classes with Mum where they teach me how to breathe. All around me I'm surrounded by couples, and they're all at least ten years older than me. Mum tried to start me chatting with them but I don't think any of them are too interested in becoming friends with an eighteen-year-old just out of school. Honestly, it's like being back at playgroup and Mum trying to teach me how to make friends. She told me not to worry because they were just jealous of me. I don't think the two of us have laughed so much for months.

I'm not allowed to smoke and the doctor says I have to start eating properly. I'm going to be a mother yet I'm still being spoken to like a child.

Lots of love,
Rosie

Mr Alex Stewart,

You are invited to the christening of my beautiful baby daughter, Katie. It's on the 28th of this month. Buy a suit and try and look presentable for a change, seeing as you're the godfather.

Lots of love,
Rosie

From Alex
To Rosie
Subject Re: Christening

It was great to see you. You look amazing! And you are NOT fat! Little Katie was a girl of few words but I am already besotted with her. I almost felt like stealing her and bringing her back over to Boston.

In fact that's a lie. I really felt like staying in Dublin. I almost didn't get back on that flight. I love it here in Boston and I love studying medicine. But it's not home. Dublin is. Being back with you felt so right. I miss my best friend.

I've met some great guys here, but I didn't grow up with any of them playing cops and robbers in my back garden. I don't feel like they are *real* friends. I haven't kicked them in the shins, stayed up all night on Santa watch with them, hung from trees pretending to be monkeys, played hotel or laughed my heart out as their stomachs were pumped. It's kind of hard to beat those sorts of experiences.

However, I can see that I have already been replaced in your affections. Little Katie is your whole world now. And it's easy to see why. I even loved her when she threw up on my (new and very expensive) suit. That must mean something. It's weird to see how much she looks like you. She has your twinkling blue eyes (I sense trouble ahead!) and jet-black hair and a little button nose. Though her bum is slightly smaller than her mother's. Just joking!

I no that you are incredibly busy at the moment but if you ever need a break from it all, you're welcome to come over here and relax. Let me no when you want to come – the invitation is always open. I realise things are tricky for you financially so we could help out with the cost of the flights. Mum and Dad would love you to come over too. They've got photos of you and Katie from the christening all around the house already.

There's also somebody I would like you to meet when you come over. She's in my class in college. Her name is Sally Gruber and she's from Boston. You would both get along.

College is a lot tougher than I thought it would be. There's just so much studying to do; so much reading. I barely have a social life. I've got four years here in Harvard altogether, then I've to do about five to seven years in a general surgical residency so I'm estimating that I'll be fully qualified in my specialised field (whatever that will be) by the time I'm one hundred years old.

So that's all I do here. I wake up at 5 a.m. and study. Go to college, come home and study. Every day. Not much more to report really. It's great that Sally and I are in class together. She takes away from the feeling of dread I get every morning at having to face another day of study, study, study. It's tough, but then I don't need to tell you that. I bet it's a hell of a lot easier than what you're doing right now. Anyway, I'm going to sleep now, I'm shattered. Sweet dreams to you and baby Katie.

Note to self:

Do not bounce Katie on knee after feeding.

Do not breast-feed beside football pitch.

Do not inhale when changing nappy. In fact, allow Mum and Dad or even random strangers to change nappy as often as possible if they so wish.

Do not push buggy by old school for Miss Big Nose Smelly Breath Casey to see.

Do not laugh when Katie falls on her bum after attempting to walk.

Do not try to have conversation with old friends from school with whole lives ahead of them, as this will result in huge frustration.

Stop crying when Katie cries.

Bonjour Stephanie!

How's my beautiful sister doing? Sitting in a café drinking a *café au lait*, wearing a beret and a stripy top while stinking of garlic, no doubt! Oh, who says stereotypes are dead and gone?

Thanks for the present you sent Katie. Your goddaughter says she misses you very much, and she sends lots of drool and sloppy kisses your way. I think I could make those words out of the screaming and wailing bellowing out of her tiny little mouth, anyway. Honestly, I don't know where all the noise comes from. She is the tiniest and most fragile little thing I have ever seen, so that sometimes I'm afraid to hold her, *but then* she opens her mouth and all hell breaks loose. The doctor says she's colicky. All I know is that she doesn't stop screaming.

It's amazing how something so small can be *so* smelly and *so* noisy. I think she should go into the *Guinness Book of Records* for being the smelliest, noisiest, smallest thing ever. What a proud mother I would be.

I'm so knackered, Stephanie. I feel like a complete zombie. I can barely read the words I'm writing (apologies for mashed banana on bottom of page, by the way – small breakfast-time accident). Katie just cries and cries and cries through the night. I have a constant headache. All I do is wander around the house like a robot, picking up teddy bears and toys that I trip over. It's hard to bring Katie anywhere because she just screams wherever we are; I'm afraid people think I'm kidnapping her or being a terrible mother. I still look like a balloon. All I wear are the most unflattering tracksuits. My bum is huge. My stomach is covered in stretch marks; there's all this flab that just won't seem to go away, no matter how much I shout at it, and I've had to throw all my belly tops out. My hair is dry and feels like straw. My tits are HUGE. I don't look like me. I don't feel like me. I feel like I'm about 20 years older. I haven't been out since the christening. I can't remember the last time I had a drink. I can't remember the last time a member of the opposite sex even looked my way (except the people who glare at me angrily in cafés when Katie starts to scream). I can't remember the last time I even cared about a member of the opposite sex not staring at me. I think I am the world's worst mother. I think that when Katie looks at me she knows that I haven't a clue what I'm doing.

She's almost walking now, which means I'm running around saying, 'NO! KATIE, NO! Katie, do not touch that! NO! Katie, Mummy says NO!' I don't think Katie cares about what Mummy thinks. I think Katie is a girl who sees something she wants and she goes for it. I dread the teenage years! But time moves so fast that she'll be grown up and moving out before I know it. Maybe then I'll have some rest. But then again that's what Mum and Dad thought.

Poor Mum and Dad, Steph. I feel so bad. They have been so fantastic. I owe them so much and I don't just mean money. Although, there's another depressing situation. I get benefits and all, and I'm paying them as much as I possibly can each week for our keep but it never feels like enough and you know the situation, Steph – things were always tight for us as it was. I don't know how I'm ever going to move out *and* work *and* look after Katie. Dad and me are going to some clinic during the week to talk to some guy about putting me on a list so I can get a place of my own. Mum keeps saying that I can stay with her and Dad, but I know Dad's just trying to help me get some sense of independence.

Mum has been fabulous. Katie loves her. Katie listens to her. When Mum says 'NO, KATIE!' Katie knows to stop. When I say it, Katie laughs and keeps going. When will I ever feel like a proper mum?

Alex has met someone over in Boston, she's the same age as me and has enough brains to be studying medicine at Harvard. But is she *really* happy I ask myself? Anyway, I have to go. Katie is wailing for me.

Write soon.

Love,

Rosie

To Rosie

I'm glad all is well with Katie; the photos you sent of her on her third birthday are beautiful. I framed them and they're on our mantelpiece in the house. Mum and Dad were delighted to see you when they visited Dublin last month. They can't stop talking about you and Katie. We're all so proud of you at having created such a perfect child.

Hope you had a happy 22nd birthday. Sorry I couldn't make it home to celebrate with you, but things have been crazy at college. Because it's my final year here there's just been so much work to do. I'm dreading the exams. If I fail I don't no what I'll do. Sally was asking after you. Although you've never met, she feels like she nos you from me talking about our old times so much.

From Alex

To Alex

~~Katie's teething is not as bad as it was.~~

~~Katie is starting playschool soon.~~

~~Katie said five new words today.~~

It was Dad's birthday last weekend and we splashed out and went out for dinner to the Hazel restaurant where I believe you went with slutty Bethany and her rich parents all those years ago for your 18th. It was good to be able to let my hair down and relax without Katie. I hired a baby-sitter so that was my treat for the weekend.

Rosie

From Alex
To Rosie
Subject (none)

Ah come on, Rosie! You're letting the side down!
You better have something wild to tell me about next time!

From Rosie
To Alex
Subject 3-year-old child

In case you didn't know, I have a three-year-old child, which makes it rather difficult for me to go out and drink myself silly, otherwise I wake up with an awful headache and a screaming child who needs me to look after her and NOT to be sticking my head down the toilet.

From Alex
To Rosie
Subject Sorry

Rosie, I'm sorry. I didn't mean to come across as insensitive. I just meant that you should remember that you need to enjoy life too. Look after yourself and not just Katie.
Sorry if I hurt you.

From Rosie
To Stephanie
Subject A moment to whinge

Oh, Stephanie, sometimes I just feel like the walls are closing in on me. I love Katie. I'm glad I made the decision I made, but I'm tired. So bloody tired. All of the time.

And that's how I feel with Mum and Dad helping me. I don't know how I'm going to cope on my own. And I'm going to have to do that eventually. I can't live with Mum and Dad for ever. Although I really want to.

But I wouldn't want Katie depending on *me* so much when *she's* older. Of course, I want her to know that I'm here for her always and that my love is absolutely unconditional, but she needs to be independent.

And I need to be independent. I think it's time for me to grow up now, Steph. I've been putting it off, running away from it for so long. Katie will be starting school soon. Imagine! It's all happened so quickly. Katie will be meeting new people and beginning her life and I have left mine behind. I need to pick myself up and stop feeling so sorry for myself. Life is hard – so what? It's hard for everyone, isn't it? Anyone who says it's easy is a liar.

As a result of all that, there's this huge divide between me and Alex right now because I feel like we're living in such different worlds, I don't know what to talk about with him any more. And we used to be able to talk all night. He phones once a week and I listen to what he's been up to during the week and try to bite my tongue every time I launch into another Katie story. Truth is, I have nothing other than her to talk about and I know it bores people. I think I used to be interesting once upon a time.

Anyway, I've decided I'm finally going to visit Boston. I'm going to finally face up to what my life could have been like had Alex gotten on that plane and made it to the debs with me instead of . . . well, you know who. I could have a degree by now. I could have been a career woman. I know it seems silly to put all that's happened down to the fact that Alex couldn't make it to the debs, but if he had come then I wouldn't have gone with Brian. I wouldn't have slept with Brian and there would be no baby. I think I need to face what I could have been in order to understand and accept what I am.

All my love,
Rosie

Chapter 7

Stephanie,

Honey, Mum here. I was wondering if you would be able to get in touch with Rosie and maybe have a word with her. She just returned from Boston a week earlier than we expected and she seems upset about something, though she won't say what it is. I was afraid this would happen. I know she feels that she has missed out on huge opportunities. I just wish she could see the positive side to what she has now. Will you get in touch with her? She always loves hearing from you.

Love you, sweetheart,
Mum

You have an instant message from: STEPH.
Steph: Hey, you, you're not answering your phone.
Steph: I know you're there, Rosie. I can see that you've logged online!
Steph: OK, I'm going to stalk you until you reply.
Steph: Hellooooo!
Rosie: Hi.
Steph: Well, hello there! Why do I get the feeling I'm being ignored?
Rosie: Sorry, I was too tired to speak to anyone.
Steph: I suppose I can forgive you. Everything OK? How was the trip to Boston? Was it as beautiful as it looks in the photos Alex sent us?
Rosie: Yeah, the place is really gorgeous. Alex showed me around everywhere. I hadn't a minute to spare while I was over there. He really took care of me.

Steph: As he should. So where did you go?
Rosie: He showed me around Boston College so I could see what it would have been like for me to study there, and it is so magical and beautiful and the weather was just fabulous . . .
Steph: Wow, it sounds great. I take it you liked it then?
Rosie: Yeah, I liked it. It was even better than the photographs I saw of it when I was applying. It would have been a nice place to study . . .
Steph: I'm sure it would have been. Where did you stay?
Rosie: I stayed in Alex's parents' house. They live in a very posh area, not at all like around here. The house is really lovely: Alex's dad is obviously making loads of money in that job.
Steph: What else did you two get up to? I know there has to be some exciting story here! There's never a dull moment when you two are involved!
Rosie: Well, we went looking round the shops, he brought me to a Red Sox game in Fenway Park and I hadn't a clue what was going on but I had a nice hotdog, we went out to a few clubs . . . sorry I've nothing that interesting to tell you, Steph . . .
Steph: Hey, that's a hell of a lot more interesting than what I did all week, believe me! So how is Alex? How does he look? I haven't seen him for ages. I wonder if I'd even recognise him!
Rosie: He looked really well. He's got a slight American accent although he denies it. But he's still the same old Alex. As lovable as usual. He really spoiled me for the entire week, he didn't let me pay for a thing, he brought me out somewhere new every night. It was good to feel free for a while.
Steph: You are free, Rosie.
Rosie: I know that. I just don't feel it sometimes. Over there I felt like I hadn't a care in the world. Things felt so good and it was almost as if every muscle in my body relaxed the moment I landed

there. I haven't laughed so much in years. I felt like a twenty-two-year-old, Steph. I haven't felt like that much lately. I know this probably sounds weird but I felt like the me that I could have been.

I liked that I didn't have to look out for somebody else while I walked down the street. I didn't have the fifty near heart attacks per day that I usually get when Katie goes missing or puts something in her mouth that she shouldn't. I didn't have to dive onto the road and hold her back just in time from being hit by a car. I liked that I didn't have to give out, correct people on their pronunciation or make threats. I liked laughing at a joke without my sleeve being tugged at and being asked to explain. I liked having adult conversations without being interrupted to cheer and applaud a silly dance or the learning of a new word. I liked that I was just me, Rosie, not Mammy, thinking just about me, talking about things I liked, going places I liked to go without having to worry about what Katie was touching, or putting in her mouth, or sleepy-head tantrums. Isn't that awful?

Steph: It's not awful, Rosie. It's good to have time to yourself but it's good to be back with Katie, isn't it? And if things were so great then why did you come home so early? You weren't supposed to return for another week. Did something happen?

Rosie: Not really worth mentioning.

Steph: Oh, come on, Rosie. I know when something is bothering you, and you can tell me.

Rosie: It was just time to go, Steph.

Steph: Did you and Alex have a fight or anything?

Rosie: No, too embarrassing to explain.

Steph: Why, what do you mean?

Rosie: Oh, I just made a show of myself one night.

Steph: Don't be silly. I'm sure Alex didn't mind! He's seen you make a show of yourself plenty in your lifetime.

Rosie: No, Steph, this was a different kind of making

a show of myself. Trust me. Not the usual kind of Alex and Rosie thing to do. I kind of threw myself at him and the next day I was mortified.

Steph: WHAT? Do you mean that . . . ? *Did you and Alex . . . ?*

Chapter 8

Rosie: Calm down, Stephanie!
Steph: I can't! This is too bizarre! You two are like brother and sister! Alex is like my little brother! You can't have!
Rosie: STEPHANIE! WE DIDN'T!
Steph: Oh.
Steph: Then what happened?
Rosie: Well, I'm hardly going to tell you now, Ms Overreactor.
Steph: Just stop trying to wind me up and tell me!
Rosie: OK, I realise that this was a very silly thing for me to do and I am extremely embarrassed so don't go mental at me . . .
Steph: Go on . . .
Rosie: Well, it's really far more innocent than you think but equally embarrassing. I kissed Alex.
Steph: *I knew it!* And what happened?
Rosie: He didn't kiss me back.
Steph: Oh. And did you mind that?
Rosie: The unsettling thing is that yes, I did.
Steph: Oh, Rosie, I'm so sorry . . . but I'm sure Alex will come round. He was probably just shocked. Oh, I'm sure he feels the same!! This is so exciting! I always knew something would happen between you two someday.
Rosie: I've been lying on my bed, staring at the ceiling ever since I got home, trying to figure out what came over me. Was it something I ate that made me feel light-headed and impetuous? Was it something he said that I could have misunder-

stood? I'm trying to convince myself that it was more than just the silence of the moment that changed my heart.

At first we had so much to catch up on we were talking a hundred words a second, barely even listening to the ends of one another's sentences before moving on to the next. And there was laughing. Lots of laughing. Then the laughing stopped and there was this silence. This weird comfortable silence. What the hell was it?

It was like the world stopped turning in that instant. Like everyone around us had disappeared. Like everything at home was forgotten about. It was as if those few minutes on this world were created just for us and all we could do was look at each other. It was like he was seeing my face for the very first time. He looked confused but kind of amused. Exactly how I felt. Because I was sitting on the grass with my best friend Alex, and that was my best friend Alex's face and nose and eyes and lips, but they seemed different. So I kissed him. I seized the moment and I kissed him.

Steph: Wow. And what did he say?

Rosie: Nothing.

Steph: Nothing?

Rosie: Nope. Absolutely nothing. He just stared at me.

Steph: So how do you know he didn't feel the same?

Rosie: At that very moment, Sally came bounding over. We had been waiting for her before going out. She was all excited. Wanted to know whether Alex had told me the good news or not. He didn't seem to quite hear her the first time. So she snapped her fingers in front of our faces. Then she repeated, 'Alex, honey, did you tell Rosie the good news?'

He just blinked so she wrapped her arms around him and she told me herself. They're getting married. So I came home.

Steph: Oh, Rosie.

Rosie: But what the hell was that silence?
Steph: It sounds like something I'd like. It sounded nice.
Rosie: It was.

Phil: What kind of a silence?
Alex: Just a weird silence.
Phil: Yeah, but what do you mean by 'weird'?
Alex: Unusual, not normal.
Phil: Yeah, but was it good or bad?
Alex: Good.
Phil: And that's bad?
Alex: Yes.
Phil: Because?
Alex: I'm engaged to Sally.
Phil: Did you ever have 'the silence' with her?
Alex: We have *silences* . . .
Phil: So do Margaret and I. You don't always have to talk, you know.
Alex: No, this was *different*, Phil. It wasn't just a silence, it was a . . . oh, I don't no.
Phil: Bloody hell, Alex.
Alex: I no. I'm all over the place.
Phil: OK, so don't marry Sally.
Alex: But I love her.
Phil: And what about Rosie?
Alex: I'm not sure.
Phil: Well then, I don't see a problem here. If you were in love with Rosie and not sure about Sally *then* you'd be in trouble. Marry Sally and forget about the goddamn silence.
Alex: Once again, you've put my life into perspective, Phil.

Dear Rosie,

I am so sorry about what happened. You didn't have to leave Boston so soon; we could have worked this out . . . I'm sorry I didn't tell you about Sally before you got here but I was waiting until you met her and had got to know her – I didn't want to tell you over the phone. Maybe I should have . . .

Please don't distance yourself from me. I haven't heard from you in weeks. It was wonderful seeing you . . . please write soon.

Love,
Alex

To Alex, or should we say Dr Alex!
CONGRATULATIONS!
GIVE YOURSELF A BIG PAT ON THE BACK . . .
YOU MADE IT!! WE KNEW YOU COULD DO IT!
Congratulations on graduating from Harvard, you genius!!
Sorry we couldn't be there,
Love Rosie and Katie

You have an instant message from: ALEX.

Alex: Rosie, I wanted you to be the first person to no that I've decided to become a heart surgeon!

Rosie: Great, does it pay well?

Alex: Rosie, it's not about the money.

Rosie: Where I come from, it's *all* about the money. Probably because I don't have any. Working part time at Randy Andy Paperclip Co. isn't really as financially rewarding as it sounds.

Alex: Well, in my world it's all about the lives you save. So what do you really think? Do you approve of my choice of employment?

Rosie: Hmmm . . . my best friend, the heart doctor. You have my approval.

From Alex
To Rosie
Subject Thank you!

The last time we spoke I forgot to thank you for the congrats card you and Katie sent me. It's about the only thing I actually have here in the new apartment. Sally and I just moved in a few weeks ago. You and Katie are very welcome to come over and see it whenever you like. It can be Katie's first time on a plane to visit her godfather in Boston! There's a nice park directly across the road and it's got a playground for kids. Katie would love it.

The apartment is small but because I've such long shifts at the hospital, I hardly get to be here anyway. I've got another life-long sentence here at Boston Central Hospital before I can actually call myself a heart surgeon. In the meantime I'm being paid a pittance and slaving away till all hours.

Anyway, that's enough about me. I seem to be just talking about myself these days. Please write to me and let me no how things are going for you. I don't want there to be any awkwardness between us, Rosie.

Keep in touch,
Alex

To Alex

Merry Christmas!

May the festive season be filled with love and joy for you and your loved ones.

Love Rosie & kAtIe

Rosie and Katie,

HAPPY NEW YEAR!

May this year bring you lots of fun, love, and happiness!

Love,
Alex and Sally

Dear Stephanie,

You will not believe the card that just arrived through my door this morning. I was almost sick. I was just cleaning up the mess Mum and Dad made after their annual New Year party when it made its grand entrance on the doormat. I'm surprised the sound of trumpets didn't accompany it! 'Da da da! Announcing the arrival of the extremely sad coupley card!' (Our wonderful Uncle Brendan was at the party, by the way, and was looking down my top as usual. He was asking for you

. . . lots. God, he's so creepy.) There was about ten million bottles of wine rolling around the floor when I came downstairs and I nearly tripped over a game of Trivial Pursuit (yes, it was one of those nights). There were those stupid paper hats strewn around the living room, hanging from the light bulbs, dangling in the gravy dish, looking extremely unappealing. There were Christmas crackers pulled apart with their crappy little miniature toys falling out that no one could possibly ever use, like little torches the size of your thumbnail and jigsaws with about two pieces, lying in the leftover food. *The place was a mess!*

Honestly, Steph, whenever Mum and Dad went away we held the *craziest* parties, but at least we still managed not to behave like farmyard animals. Plus they were screaming and singing (well, *trying* to sing) and dancing (or stamping their feet in some sort of crazy people ritual) *all night*. Poor Katie was terrified of all the noise (she obviously can't be my daughter!), and she spent the night in tears so I let her share my bed and she elbowed me in the face about ten times. Eventually everyone started to leave the house at about 6 or 7 a.m., and I was starting to fall asleep when I was jerked awake by a little monster jumping on me and demanding food.

So anyway, I think what I'm *trying* to say is that I wasn't in the greatest mood for what arrived on my doorstep. I had a pounding headache, I was so tired and after cleaning the mess downstairs (which is fine because it is Mum and Dad's house, after all, and they are kindly letting me stay rent free so I'm not complaining about them) I just wanted peace and quiet and a bit of sleep.

But the card came.

On the front was a lovely little picture of Alex and Sally all wrapped up warmly in their winter coats and hats and gloves, etc. They were standing outside in a park that was covered in snow with their arms wrapped around . . . a snowman. A bloody snowman.

They looked so sickeningly happy. Two little happy

Harvard-heads. Uugh. How sad is it to send a photo of yourself and your boyfriend building a snowman??? Very, very, very sad. That's how sad. And to send it to me, especially!! The cheek! I should have sent them a photo of me and . . . me and . . . George (the lollipop man and the only fellow I seem to speak to these days), standing outside in the freezing cold, jumping in puddles. That's how pointless that would have been to them!

Oh God, I'm rambling. Sorry. I have to go before Katie finishes the last of that red wine in the bottle on the floor.

Oh, by the way, it was great to meet Pierre after all this time. He's a really nice guy. You two should come home more often. It was fun speaking to people closer to my age for a change.

Happy New Year. Whoever thought of that expression?

Love, your festive and extremely joyous younger sister, Rosie

To Rosie

Happy Birthday, my friend!

Welcome to the world of twenty-six-year-olds! We are getting old, Rosie!

Write to me more often!

Love, Alex

TO ALEX

YOU ARE IVNITED TO MY 7TH BIRTHDAY PARTY ON THE 4TH OF MAY IN MY HOWSE. WE ARE HAVING A MAJICIN. I CANT WAIT. IT IS ON AT 2 O'CLOCK AND YOU CAN LEAVE AT 5 O'CLOCK.

LOVE KATIE

Dear Katie,

I'm sorry I can't come to your birthday party. The magician sounds like he will be lots of fun. You will have so many friends you won't even no I'm not there!

I have to work at the hospital so they won't let me take a holiday. I told them it was your birthday but they still wouldn't listen!

However, I have sent you a little something so I hope you like it. Happy Birthday, Katie, and take care of your mummy for me. She is very special.

Lots of love to you and Mum,

Alex

To Alex

Thank you for my brithday present. My mummy cried when I opened it. I never had a locket before. The photographs of you and Mummy are very small.

The majicin was good but my best freind Toby said he new he was cheating and showed everyone where the man hid the cards. The man was not very happy and he got mad at Toby. Mummy laffed so loud I do not think the majic man liked her eether. Toby likes Mum.

I got lots of nice presents but Avril and Sinead got me the same notepad. Mummy and me are moving howse soon. I will miss Grandma and Granddad so much and I no Mummy is sad because I heard her crying last night in bed.

But we are not moving too far away. You can get the bus form Grandma and Granddad to our new house. It does not take too long and we are nearer to all the shops in town so we can walk.

It is much smaller than the howse we are in now. Mummy is funny she calls it a shoe box! There are 2 bedrooms and the kitchen is tiny. Just a place to eat and watch telly. We have a balcony and it's nice but Mum wont let me stand on it on my own.

I can see the park. Mummy says the park is our garden and that we have the biggest garden in the world.

Mummy said that I can paint my room whatever colour I want. I think I'll paint it pink or purple or blue. Toby says we should paint it black. He is funny.

Mummy has a new job. She works only a few days

a week so sometimes she can collect me from skool and other times she cant. I play with Toby until she comes home. His mum always brings him and collects him because they say we are too young to get the bus. I don't think Mum likes her job. She is always tired and crying. She said she would perfer to be back in skool doing dubble matts. I don't no what she means. Me and Toby hate skool but he always makes me laff. Mummy says she is tired of having to keep going back to my teacher Miss Casey. Grandma and Granddad think it is funny. Miss Casey has the biggest nose ever. She hates me and Toby. I do not think she likes Mum eether because they always fight when they see each other.

Mum has a new freind. They work in the same building but not in the same office. They met outside in the cold because they have to smoke outside. Mum says she is the best freind she has had for ages. Her name is Ruby and she is real funny. I like when she comes over. She and Mum are always laffing. I like it when Ruby is here because Mum doesn't cry.

It is real sunny now in dublin. Me and Mum have been to Portmarnock Beach a few times. We get the bus out and it's always full of people in their swimsuits, eating ice creams and with loud music. Upstairs in the bus is my favourite. I sit in the front and pretend to drive and Mum loves looking out the window at all the water on the way. I am learning to swim. But I have to keep my armbands on in the sea. Mum says she wants to live on the beach. She says she would like to live in the sea shells!

When are you coming to see us? Mummy says you are getting married to a girl named Bimbo. That's a funny name.

Love,
Katie

Chapter 9

You have an instant message from: RUBY.
Ruby: Hey, you, happy Monday.
Rosie: Oh, great. Hold on while I get the champagne.
Ruby: What did you do over the weekend?
Rosie: Oh, *wait* till you hear this! I was just *dying* to tell you all morning, it's *so* exciting! You'll *never* believe it, I—
Ruby: I sense sarcasm here. Let me guess: you watched TV.
Rosie: Introducing Ruby . . . and her psychic powers!! I had to listen to it with the volume blaring just to drown out the loving couple next door screaming their ears off. Some day they're going to kill each other. I can't wait. Poor Katie didn't know what was going on so I sent her down to stay at Toby's house.
Ruby: Honestly, don't some people understand the meaning of the word DIVORCE?
Rosie: Ha ha, well, it's a magic word for you.
Ruby: I would appreciate it if you wouldn't make fun of a devastatingly difficult time in my life that left me feeling shattered and emotionally distraught.
Rosie: Oh, please! Getting that divorce was the happiest day of your life! You bought the most expensive bottle of champagne, we got pissed, went out clubbing and you snogged the ugliest man in the world.
Ruby: Ah well, people have their different ways of grieving . . .
Rosie: Have you finished typing up all that crap Randy Andy gave us?

Ruby: No, I haven't. Have you?
Rosie: No.
Ruby: Good. Let's take a coffee break as a reward. We really shouldn't overwork ourselves. I hear it's quite dangerous. Will you bring your fags? I forgot mine.
Rosie: Yep, meet you downstairs in five minutes.
Ruby: It's a date. Gosh, how exciting. Neither of us has been on one of them for a while.

You have an instant message from: RUBY.
Ruby: Where the hell were you? I waited for you in the café for half an hour! I had to force myself to eat *two* chocolate muffins *and* a slice of apple pie.
Rosie: Sorry about that. Randy Andy here wouldn't let me leave the office.
Ruby: Oh, he is such a slave driver! You should complain to Head Office, get the asshole fired.
Rosie: He is Head Office.
Ruby: Oh yeah.
Rosie: Well, in all fairness, Ruby, he may be a prick but we did just take a break an hour ago . . . and it was our third one in less than three hours . . .
Ruby: You are turning into one of THEM!
Rosie: Ha ha. I have a child to feed.
Ruby: As do I.
Rosie: That child feeds himself, Ruby.
Ruby: Ah, leave my little fatso alone. He's my baby and I love him regardless.
Rosie: He's seventeen.
Ruby: Yes, and old enough to have a baby of his own, going by your standards . . .
Rosie: Well, he'll be fine as long as he doesn't go to his school ball with the most uninteresting man in the world, with the ugliest face. That way he won't have to drink a sickening amount of alcohol to trick the brain into thinking that man is beautiful and funny and . . . well, you know the rest.
Ruby: Are you suggesting that my son could perhaps have a gay relationship at his debs?

Rosie: No! I was just saying—
Ruby: Oh, I know what you were saying, except I think that my poor darling son may be the exact person that girls will have to drink excess amounts of alcohol just to love.
Rosie: RUBY!! You can't say that about your son!!
Ruby: Why not? I love him with all my heart but, bless him, he wasn't born with his mother's looks. Anyway, so when are you going to *ever* go out with *someone*, *anyone*?
Rosie: Ruby, we are *not* having this conversation again. Everyone you have tried to set me up with has been a complete weirdo! I don't know where you meet these men and in fact I don't think I even *want* to know, but after last weekend I can assure you that I'm never going to Joys again. Anyway, you can't talk. When exactly was the last time you went out on a date?
Ruby: Ah, that's a very different matter altogether! I'm a woman ten years your senior who has just been through a very difficult divorce from a selfish little bastard of a man and I have a seventeen-year-old son who only communicates with me in monosyllabic grunts. I think he is the son of an ape (actually, I know he is). I have no time for a man!
Rosie: Well, neither do I.
Ruby: Rosie honey, you're twenty-six years old, you've got at least ten years of your life left before it's over. You should get out there and enjoy yourself, stop letting the weight of the world rest on *your* shoulders; that's my job. And stop waiting for him.
Rosie: Stop waiting for who?
Ruby: For Alex.
Rosie: I don't know what you're talking about! I am *not* waiting for Alex!
Ruby: Yes you are, my dear friend. He must be some man because nobody can ever measure up to him. And I know that's what you do every time you

meet someone: compare. I'm sure he's a fabulous friend and I'm sure he always says sweet and wonderful things to you. But he's not here. He's thousands of miles away, working as a doctor in a great big hospital and he lives in a fancy apartment with his fancy doctor fiancée. I don't think he's thinking of leaving that life anytime soon to come back to a single mother who's living in a tiny flat working in a crappy part-time job in a paperclip factory with a crazy friend who emails her every second. So stop waiting and move on. Live your life.

Rosie: I am not waiting.

Ruby: Rosie—

Rosie: I have to get back to work now.

Rosie has logged off.

Dear Rosie and Katie Dunne,

Shelly and Bernard Gruber proudly invite you to the marriage ceremony of their loving daughter, Sally, to Alex Stewart.

From Stephanie
To Rosie
Subject Re: No way in the world I'm going to that wedding!

I am so angered by your last letter! You cannot miss Alex's wedding! That would be completely unthinkable!

This is *Alex* we're talking about! Alex, the boy who used to sleep on a sleeping bag on your floor, the boy who used to sneak into my room and read my diary and look through my underwear drawer! Little Alex who you used to chase down the road and shoot at with a banana for a gun! Alex who sat beside you in class for twelve years!

He was there for you when you had Katie. He was so supportive throughout the entire thing when I'm sure it was difficult for him to adjust to the fact that little Rosie, who had slept in a sleeping bag on *his* floor, was having a *baby*.

Go over to him, Rosie. Celebrate this with him. Share in his happiness and excitement. Share it all with Katie. Be happy! Please! I'm sure he needs you right now. This is a huge step for him and he needs his best friend by his side. Learn to get to know Sally too, as she is an important person in his life now. Just as he has learned to get to know Katie – the most important person in your life. I know you don't want to hear it, but if you don't go you will be ending what was once and what still is one of the strongest bonds of friendship that I have ever seen.

I know you are embarrassed by what happened a few years ago when you visited, but swallow your pride, hold your chin up. You are going to be at that wedding because Alex *wants* you to be there for *him*; you are going to be there because you *need* to be there for *yourself*.

Make the right decision, Rosie.

Dear Rosie,

Hey there! I have no doubt you have received our wonderful wedding invitation that took Sally about three months to choose. Why, I don't know, but it seems that a cream-coloured invite with a gold border was so much more different than a white invite with a gold border . . . you women . . .

I don't no if I should be worried or not, but Sally's mom hasn't seemed to have received a reply yet! Now I no I don't need one from you because I'm just *presuming* you will be there!

The reason why I am writing and not ringing is because I want to give you time to think about what I'm asking you. Myself and Sally would be honoured if you would allow Katie to be our flower girl at the wedding. We would need to no quite soon so that Sally and Katie can pick out a dress.

Whoever thought this would be happening, Rosie? If someone had told us ten years ago that *your daughter* would be a flower girl at *my wedding* we would have just laughed at the ridiculousness of it all. Even though it has taken Sally and me so long to get round to actually getting married – what with doctors' mad schedules ruling our lives!

The second question I have to ask you is the one I'm sure you will need to think about. You are my best friend, Rosie; that goes without saying. I have no best friend over here, no one that measures up to what you mean to me, therefore I have no best man. Will you be my best woman? Will you stand beside me at the altar? I no I will definitely need you there! And I trust you will organise a better stag night than any of my male friends over here!

Think about it and let me no. And say yes!

Love to you and Katie,

Alex

You have an instant message from: ROSIE.

Rosie: You won't fucking believe it.

Ruby: You got a date.

Rosie: No, more unbelievable than that. Alex has asked me to be his 'best woman'.

Ruby: I don't suppose that means you'll be standing to the left of him in the church?

Rosie: Eh, no . . . to the right.

Ruby: What about his brother?

Rosie: He's an usher or something.

Ruby: Wow, so he really is going ahead with it?

Rosie: Yep. Looks like it.

Ruby: I think you should stop waiting for him now, honey.

Rosie: I know. I probably should.

Chapter 10

My 'best woman' speech.

Good evening, everyone. My name is Rosie and, as you can see, Alex has decided to go down the non-traditional route of asking me to be his best woman for the day. Except we all know that today that title does not belong to me. It belongs to Sally, for she is clearly his best woman.

I could call myself the 'best friend', but I think we all know that today that no longer refers to me either. That title too belongs to Sally.

But what *doesn't* belong to Sally is a lifetime of memories of Alex the child, Alex the teenager and Alex the almost-a-man that I'm sure he would rather forget but that I will now fill you all in on. (Hopefully they will laugh.)

I have known Alex since he was five years old. I arrived on my first day of school teary-eyed and red-nosed and half an hour late. (I am almost sure Alex will shout out, 'What's new?') I was ordered to sit down at the back of the class beside a smelly, snotty-nosed, messy-haired little boy who had the biggest sulk on his face and who refused to look at me or talk to me. I hated this little boy.

I know that he hated me too, him kicking me in the shins under the table and telling the teacher that I was copying his school work was a tell-tale sign. We sat beside each other every day for twelve years, moaning about school, moaning about girlfriends and boyfriends, wishing we were older and wiser and out of school, dreaming of a life where we wouldn't have double maths on a Monday morning.

Now Alex has that life and I'm so proud of him. I'm so happy that he's found his best woman and his best friend in perfect little brainy and annoying Sally.

I ask you all to raise your glasses and toast *my* best friend, Alex, and his new best friend, best woman and wife, Sally, and to wish them luck and happiness in the future.

To Alex and Sally!

OR SOMETHING TO THAT EFFECT. WHAT DO YOU THINK, RUBY?

You have an instant message from: RUBY.
Ruby: Gag gag puke puke puke. They'll all love it.

Good luck, Rosie. No tears and DO NOT drink.

Dear Rosie,

Greetings from the Seychelles! Rosie, thank you so much for last week! I had such a good time. I never really thought I could actually enjoy my wedding day but you made it so much fun. Don't worry, I don't think anyone noticed you were drunk for the entire ceremony (maybe they did for the speech – but it was funny), but I don't think the priest was too impressed when you hiccuped just as I was about to say 'I do!'

I can't quite remember the stag night but I hear it was a great success. The boys just keep going on and on about it. I think Sally is a little angry that she had to marry a man with one eyebrow and I don't care what anybody says, I no it was you who did it! All the wedding photos are of the left side of my face but it doesn't matter because Sally says it's my best side. Unlike you, who say my best side is the back of my head.

The wedding went really well, didn't it? I thought I was going to be a bundle of nerves all day but you just made me laugh so much I think it helped to get rid of the nervous energy. Although we shouldn't really have laughed when the wedding photos were being taken, I doubt we'll find any decent shots where my face and yours aren't distorted from laughter. Sally's family thought you were really terrific. They weren't really keen on the idea of me having a best woman, to be honest, but Sally's dad thought you were great. Is it true you made him knock back a shot of tequila?!

My mum and dad were *so* glad to see you and Katie. I'm glad Katie wore the locket I gave her on her last birthday. It's funny; Mum says Katie is exactly how you looked when you were seven. I think she kind of kept hoping that it *was* you and that I was that age again too. She was very teary that day! But they just wouldn't stop going on and on about how beautiful you looked in that dress! It's as if you were the bride!

But you did look beautiful, Rosie. I don't think I've ever seen you in a dress before (not since you were Katie's age, anyway). Well, I suppose I would have seen you in one had I made it to the debs all those years ago. God, listen to me. I sound like an old man reminiscing on years gone by!

Everyone agreed your best woman speech was brilliant. I think all my friends have a crush on you. And no, you can't have their phone numbers. By the way, Rosie, you *were* my best woman that day and you still are my best friend. Always will be. Just to let you no.

Married life is going well so far. We've only been married ten days so we've only had, let's see . . . ten fights. Ha ha. I'm sure somebody told me that was healthy in a relationship . . . I'm not worried. The place we're honeymooning in is fabulous, which I'm glad about because it's costing us an absolute fortune. We're staying in this little wooden hut-type building on stilts high up over the water. It's beautiful. The water is that turquoise-green colour that you can see through right down to the multicoloured fish below. It's paradise; you would love it. Now *this* is the hotel you should work at, Rosie. Imagine your office being the beach . . .

I would just love to laze on the beach and drink cocktails all day, to be honest, but Sally always has to be doing something so every second I'm being dragged into the sea or I find myself flying in the sky hanging out of some odd contraption. I wouldn't be surprised if she decides that we should have lunch underwater while scuba-diving.

Anyway, I've bought you and Katie presents so I hope they arrived at your house safely and that they weren't crushed in the post. They're supposed to be a kind of good-luck charm over here and I no you always loved collecting shells on the beach when we were kids so now you can wear the prettiest ones around your neck.

Well, I better go. Apparently people aren't even supposed to send postcards while they're on their honeymoon, never mind writing novels for letters (according to Sally – so I must go). I think she wants to do something crazy like be dragged around on water-skis by a dolphin.

God help me, what have I gotten myself into?!

Love,

Alex

PS. I miss you!

You have an instant message from: RUBY.

Ruby: I spotted you out the window coming into work – what the hell are you wearing around your neck? Is it shells?

Rosie: It brings luck.

Ruby: Uh-huh. Any luck yet?

Rosie: I didn't miss my bus this morning.

Ruby: Uh-huh.

Rosie: Oh, piss off.

Rosie has logged off.

From	Rosie
To	Ruby
Subject	You'll never believe this.

I'm faxing you over a letter Sally sent Katie. Let me know what you think.

Dear Katie,

Thank you for being my flower girl at my wedding last week. Everybody said that you looked beautiful, just like a real little princess.

Myself and Alex are now on holiday in a place called the Seychelles, just where your mummy wants to live. Tell her it is lovely, very hot and sunny, and you can show her the photograph of me and Alex lying on the beach so she can see what it looks like here. We are very happy and very much in love.

I am enclosing a photograph of you, me, and Alex on our wedding day so you can frame it and put it up in your house. I hope you like it.

Ring us soon.

Love,

Sally

You have an instant message from: RUBY.

Ruby: Sounds like the bitch is just pissing around her man to mark her territory.

Rosie: By sending a letter to a seven-year-old little girl??!!

Ruby: Well, she obviously knew that it would get into your hands. That's cruel alright. Don't let Sally worry you. She's just trying to let you know who the woman is in Alex's life now. Anyway, why is she doing this? Did you do anything to make her feel threatened?

Rosie: No way! As if!

Ruby: Rosie?

Rosie: Oh, OK then, maybe she felt just a little threatened by the fact that Alex and I had a better time at her wedding than she did.

Ruby: Bingo!

Rosie: Yes, but that's the way we always are, Ruby. It wasn't flirting, it wasn't anything. It was just happiness. However, she did not crack one smile for the whole day. She just kept sucking her cheekbones in and pouting at everyone.

Ruby: OK, I believe you, but millions wouldn't. Anyway, don't rise to her, just ignore it.

Rosie: Oh, don't worry, I won't respond. I'm just sorry that the stupid woman didn't have the common sense to leave my daughter out of her insecurities.

Ruby: Katie will be fine; she's a smart girl. Just like her mother.

Dear Sally,

Thank you for your letter. I'm glad you liked my dress, but if I were you I would have worn a pretty dress like my mum's for my wedding day. Everyone said that it matched Alex's tuxedo really well. They looked so nice together, don't you think? I showed Mum and Toby (my best friend) the photograph of you and Alex on the beach and Toby says that he hopes that your sunburn doesn't hurt too much. It looks really sore.

That's all for now. I have to go now because Mum's new boyfriend is coming to the flat soon. Tell Alex that me, Mum and Toby said hi.

Love from Katie xxx

Chapter 11

From Alex
To Rosie
Subject Secret boyfriend

Back home from my honeymoon; you sly little lady, you never told me about this new boyfriend of yours! Sally couldn't wait to tell me, which I thought was rather sweet. I didn't realise Katie and Sally were writing to each other, did you?

Anyway, why didn't you say a word about this guy at the wedding? You usually tell me everything. So come on! What's he like? What's his name? Where did you meet him? What does he look like? What does he do for a living? I hope he earns loads of money and that he's treating you well, or else I'm coming over to throttle him.

I'll have to get back to Dublin to meet this guy; make sure he gets the best friend approval. Anyway, let me no all the details (maybe not *all* of them).

Hi Stephanie,

Just writing to see how you are, love, and to share a bit of good news with you. I'm sure Rosie hasn't told you this already because she's keeping pretty quiet about it, but she's met someone! We are all so delighted. She seems so happy, those big blue eyes don't look so sad any more and there's a spring in her step again. More like the Rosie we used to know.

Anyway, she brought him over to the house yesterday for dinner and I have to say he really is a charming man. His name is Greg Collins and he's a bank manager for AIB in Fairview.

He's a little taller than Rosie with a cute little face. He's thirty-something, I would guess, and he is absolutely wonderful with Katie. They spent the day teasing each other, which was very funny. It's been difficult, as you know, for Rosie to meet someone who she likes herself as well as taking into account that it has to be somebody that Katie feels comfortable with too. But there should be no compromises I keep telling her. Too often she ended up on dates with those other men just because Katie liked them. Anyway, as I said, Katie adores Greg. I'm so pleased Rosie seems to have found a nice fellow at last.

Anyway, how's work? Busy as always? Don't work yourself too hard in that restaurant, love; you need to enjoy life too. Your dad and me were thinking of coming over to you for a little holiday soon – would that be OK? Let us know when you're free and we'll work around it. Say hello to Pierre for us. Looking forward to seeing you.

Love,
Mum

From Rosie
To Alex
Subject Re: Secret boyfriend!

Oops, my little secret is out now, thanks to Katie and her big mouth! Well, I didn't say anything about Greg (that's his name) at your wedding, because at that stage we hadn't even gone out yet! We met in the Dancing Cow nightclub (it's a very long story!) just before I went over to you in Boston, and he took my number and asked me out but I said no! So I must have gone all gushy after your wedding because when I came back I rang him up and asked him out!

Oh, Alex, I've been wined and dined like never before! He's taken me to restaurants I've only read about in magazines and he's terribly romantic, but you said not to give you *all* the details so I won't tell you about our weekend away down the country . . . OK, so you wanted to know all about him, here goes. He is thirty-six, works at the bank in Fairview. He's not exactly tall (my height), which isn't exactly small either, but . . . OK if he was to stand beside you, you would have a fantastic view of his scalp. But he has sandy-coloured hair and wonderful twinkling blue eyes.

He is always bringing Katie little gifts when he comes, which I know he shouldn't do, but I love seeing her being spoiled, especially as I haven't exactly been able to do that myself over the years. I can't believe I have finally met a man who doesn't mind that I have a daughter; all the others looked at me like I was diseased when I told them, and would suddenly think of a great excuse to have to leave the dinner table. I also can't believe that Katie and I have finally agreed on the same man. She seemed only to like the young, pretty ones that she fancied herself, probably. We need to be realistic here, though. I can hardly afford to be picky!! Her idea of a great partner for me was someone who would play games with her all the time, pull silly faces, put on unattractive voices and wear brightly coloured clothes that should only be worn on Saturday morning TV.

Anyway, I seem to have found him. He is a very generous, caring and thoughtful man, and I think I am very lucky to have met him. It may not last for ever but I'm enjoying myself, Alex. I know I've been such a misery guts for the past, oh, I don't know . . . ten years or so (!) but now I have realised that Katie and I are a team and if they can't love us both then they can get lost.

But I *think* I may have met a man who does. Fingers crossed.

PS. I notice you have stopped referring to Ireland as home. Your heart must finally be in Boston now.

From Alex
To Rosie
Subject Oooh Rosie's in love!

Oooooh! Rosie sounds like she's in love!

With a bank manager who goes clubbing in a place called the Dancing Cow? What kind of bank manager (or any man, for that matter) goes to the Dancing Cow? Fair enough, you and your friend Ruby seem to have gone off the rails altogether, so therefore I wouldn't expect anything more from you. But I don't no, I'm not yet convinced this man is the right one for you.

And I have to say I was slightly insulted by your last letter. What do you mean by the statement, 'I have finally met a man who doesn't mind that I have a daughter'? I think that I have always been supportive of you and Katie – in fact I no I have. Whenever I can, I visit you and bring you out to all your favourite restaurants and bring my goddaughter presents.

Anyway, I'd better go. Just worked a double shift at the hospital so I'm feeling really tired.

From Rosie
To Alex
Subject Thanks, Mr Supportive

Well, thank you, Mr Supportive, for being so happy for me. In case you haven't noticed, you and I are not involved in a romantic relationship. Yes, you are a wonderful friend (supportive and generous), but you are not here every day with me. I'm sure you will understand when I say that finding a friend and finding a partner are two very different things. You accept me warts and all, some men don't. But you're not here.

OK, well, that's all. Hope married life is going wonderfully!

You have an instant message from: RUBY.
Ruby: Katie told Sally what??
Rosie: I know, it's crazy, isn't it? And Katie wrote that letter after I had only been on *one* date with Greg!
Ruby: Wow, she must really like him to be telling people about him so soon. Ah well, maybe Sally won't feel like you're trying to get your grubby little mitts on her husband now.
Rosie: Ah, who cares anyway? I have my Greg!
Ruby: Ugh, you make me sick. You've turned into one of those sickening couples that we hate. You two are carrying on like love-struck teenagers; I think I'll have to find a new single friend so that I don't feel like a *complete* gooseberry the next time we go out.
Rosie: You're such a liar! You were having a great time with all those guys every time I looked at you. You were the centre of attention!
Ruby: Oh, a girl does what she has to . . . Anyway, you must have spotted me only on the rare occasion you detached your lips from Greg's. Oh, by the way, that guy called me last night so I'm thinking of—

You have an instant message from: GREG.
Greg: Hello, gorgeous. How's your day going?
Rosie: Oh, hello! Oh, it's the same as usual . . . better now, though!
Ruby: Hello? Are you still there or has Randy Andy attacked you?

Rosie: Sorry, Greg, just a second. I'm chatting to Ruby online too!
Greg: Do you two ever do any work?!
Rosie: Enough to keep ourselves from getting fired.
Greg: I'll try you again later.
Rosie: No, no! Don't be silly! I'm perfectly capable of carrying on two conversations at the same time. Besides, I want to chat to you and if I tell that to

Ruby she'll be even more angry at me for becoming one of *them* . . .
Greg: Who's 'them'?
Rosie: Part of the secret couple élite.
Greg: Oh, *them*! Of course, silly me . . .

Rosie: Sorry, Ruby, Greg is messaging me too, so bear with me for a few minutes.
Ruby: Can you two not live without each other for a few hours?
Rosie: No!
Ruby: Oh, I miss Rosie. Who are you and what have you done to my man-hating friend?
Rosie: Don't worry, she's still here, just taking a well-deserved break. So what were you saying about this guy you met the other night?
Ruby: Oh yeah, his name is Ted (a real teddy bear), he's overweight but then again so am I so who cares; we can bounce off each other. He's a truck driver and he seemed like a nice guy because he kept buying me drinks, which puts him up pretty high on my Decent Man scale. Plus he was the only person who wasn't ignoring me in the pub that night.
Rosie: Oh, I'm so sorry, but you know what it's like when you meet someone new: you want to get to know *everything* about them.
Ruby: No, I don't quite want to know everything about Ted . . . I don't want to be put off him.

Rosie: So, Greg, what are you doing tonight?
Greg: Rosie, my dear, I am all yours! Why don't we get a bottle of wine, some takeaway and stay in? We can get Katie a DVD or something.
Rosie: Yep, that sounds like a great idea! And Katie will be really excited to see you.

Ruby: So should I call him?
Rosie: Call who?
Ruby: TED!

Rosie: Oh, yeah, of course! Ask him out. I can get Kevin to baby-sit and then we can all go on a double date. I've always wanted to do that!
Ruby: Oh, please, the innocence of the young and inexperienced. Ted and Greg will have absolutely nothing in common. They're like chalk and cheese: a bank manager and a possible bank robber. They will hate each other, the atmosphere will be awkward, no one will talk, all you'll hear is the munching of food in our mouths over the deafening silence like some kind of weird Chinese torture, we'll all refuse dessert, skip the coffee, pay, leg it out the door and feel relieved and promise ourselves never to meet up again.
Rosie: How does next Friday sound?
Ruby: Friday's fine.

Greg: I hope Ruby is OK with us after the other night; we were kind of in a world of our own.
Rosie: Don't be silly, she didn't mind at all. She met some guy called Teddy Bear. Oh, and by the way, are you free to go out on a double date thingy for dinner on Friday night? That's if I can get a babysitter for Katie.
Greg: A dinner date with Ruby and a man named Teddy Bear. Sounds interesting.

Rosie: Greg said he's free for dinner on Friday.
Ruby: Well, that's all very well but I haven't asked Ted yet. What did Alex say about you and Greg being *in love*?
Rosie: Well, I didn't say I was *in love*, Ruby! Greg and I haven't even said that to *each other* yet! But Alex sent me some weird letter telling me that he thinks that Greg sounds like a freak of nature and that he's insulted that I don't think that he's supportive of me and Katie. He just went on a bit of a rant, to be honest, but I won't take any notice because he had worked all night at the hospital and he was tired.

Ruby: Uh-huh.
Rosie: What's that supposed to mean?
Ruby: This is just as I suspected. He's jealous.
Rosie: Alex is *not* jealous!
Ruby: Alex is jealous of your relationship with Greg; he feels threatened.

Greg: So what time should I call over to you tonight? Seven or eight?

Rosie: No, Alex is *not* jealous of my relationship with Greg! Why should he be? He's married to perfect pretty little Sally – happily, might I add (at least according to Sally) – *and* I have a lovely photograph of the two of them lying on the beach together looking *very* much in love just to prove it. I gave him a chance to be part of Katie's life and mine and he chose to remain my friend, which I have now come to terms with. It's fine. Now I am in a relationship with Greg, he's wonderful and I no longer care about Alex in that way *at all whatsoever*! So that's all I have to say about that, thank you very much! I am over Alex, he is not interested in me and now I am in love with Greg! So there!
Greg: Well . . . thank you for sharing all that with me, Rosie. I can't tell you enough how thrilled I am to hear that you are no longer in love with a man named Alex '*at all whatsoever*', as you so articulately put it.

Rosie: Oh my God, Ruby!! I just sent Greg the message that was supposed to be for you!! Fuck fuck *FUCKETY FUCK!* I TOLD HIM I *LOVED* HIM!!!!
Greg: Em . . . that, eh . . . went to me again, Rosie. Sorry . . .

Rosie: Oh . . .
Ruby: Oh what?

Chapter 12

Rosie: OK, so that has to be the singularly *most embarrassing* thing that has ever happened to me, without any doubts, NO exceptions!!!

Ruby: What about the time you wore that white dress out to a club with no underwear on, and someone spilled water all over you and it was suddenly completely see-through?

Rosie: OK, so that was pretty embarrassing.

Ruby: And what about the time you were in the supermarket and you grabbed another little girl's hand by mistake and started dragging her out to the car while Katie waited inside crying her eyes out?

Rosie: That little girl's mother said it was fine and she dropped the charges.

Ruby: And what about the time—

Rosie: OK, that's enough, thank you! Maybe it was not *the* most embarrassing thing ever, but it's pretty much up there with the all-time classics. The number-one embarrassing moment being the time I kissed Alex.

Ruby: Ha ha ha ha ha ha ha

Rosie: Oh, come on, you're supposed to make me feel better.

Ruby: Ha ha ha ha ha ha ha ha

Rosie: The joy of having supportive friends. I'm going now; Randy Andy is glaring at me like a schoolmaster over the rim of his incredibly sexy brown-rimmed spectacles.

Ruby: Maybe he wants you to be the naughty schoolgirl.

Rosie: Well, he's just a few years too late for that. I think he wants to kill me. His nostrils are flaring and he's breathing quite heavily.
Ruby: Are his hands above the desk?
Rosie: Uuugh! Ruby, stop!
Ruby: What? You don't think they call him Randy Andy for nothing, do you?
Rosie: I hate open-plan offices. He can see me from every corner of this room, and my legs underneath the desk. Oh my, now he's staring at my legs.
Ruby: Rosie, you really need to get out of that office. It's not healthy.
Rosie: I know, I'm working on it, but I can't quit until I get another job and that's proving to be rather difficult. Apparently no one really cares about whether or not you work as a secretary in a paperclip factory.
Ruby: How odd . . . and it *sounds* so glamorous.
Rosie: Oh my God, he has now moved his chair over so he can get a better look. Hold on a minute while I send him a message. I've had enough!
Ruby: Don't!
Rosie: Why not? I'll just send him a polite message asking him to stop looking at me because I find it distracting while I'm trying to work.

You have an instant message from: ROSIE.
Rosie: Stop staring at my tits, you pervert.

Rosie: OK, Ruby, I sent it.
Ruby: Oh, you are so fired. Randy Andy doesn't take too kindly to brash young ladies who stick up for themselves.
Rosie: Screw him! He can't fire me for that!

Ms Rosie Dunne,

Andy Sheedy Paperclip & Co. will no longer be requiring your services, which means that your contract will therefore not be up for renewal next month as was previously discussed.

You are, however, entitled to remain as an employee of Andy Sheedy Paperclip & Co. until the end of the month, i.e. 30 June.

Andy Sheedy Paperclip & Co. thanks you for the work you have put into the company over the past few years and we wish you luck in the future.

Yours sincerely,

Andy Sheedy

Owner of Andy Sheedy Paperclip & Co.

You have an instant message from: ROSIE.

Rosie: I faxed the letter over, did you see it?

Ruby: Ha ha ha ha ha ha.

Rosie: Do you know what? The more I read it, the more I'm glad that I'm leaving. The name Andy Sheedy Paperclip & Co. says it all really, doesn't it? I wonder who wrote the letter for him, seeing as I'm his secretary and that's my job. I probably did it myself and didn't even realise it. Ah well, so what do you think?

Ruby: This is the best way to leave. Rosie Dunne, you will go down in history in this building as the woman who told Randy Andy to eff off. I will spread the word, Rosie; you being fired will not have been in vain. I'll miss you! Where will you go?

Rosie: I have absolutely no idea.

Ruby: Why don't you apply for a job in a hotel? Ever since I met you you've been going on and on about hotels.

Rosie: I know. I have a slight obsession with them. Before I had Katie all I ever wanted to do was run a hotel. I don't think that will ever happen now but we all need dreams. We all need hope, that something more than what we have is possible to achieve.

Perhaps it's the huge furniture that makes me feel so safe in hotels, like oversized vases the size of people, and couches that wouldn't fit in my

living room and kitchen put together. I feel like Alice in Wonderland in hotel lobbies. At least I have a month to find somewhere. It shouldn't be *that* hard. I'd better start writing up my CV.
Ruby: That shouldn't take long then.

From Rosie
To Alex
Subject Is my CV OK?

Attachment: CV.doc
Please, please, please help me with my CV or my poor daughter and I will starve to death. How do I make all my crappy jobs look impressive? Help! Help! Help!

From Alex
To Rosie
Subject Re: CV

Attachment: CV.doc
As you can see (by the attached document) I have been over your CV. The one you sent me was practically perfect as it was, of course, but I just fixed the grammar and a few spelling mistakes . . . you no how great at spelling I am!

By the way, Rosie, you haven't been doing a 'crappy job', as you so nicely phrased it. I don't think you understand the difficulty of what you are doing. You are a full-time *single* mum who has a job as a personal secretary to a very successful businessman. I only changed the words around; I didn't alter the truth in any way. What you have been doing day after day is incredible. When I come home from work I'm so shattered that I just collapse; I barely take care of myself, never mind another person.

Don't underestimate yourself, Rosie; don't play down what you do. When you go into your interviews keep your head held high and feel confident that you are an incredibly hard worker (when you want to be), you have the wonderful ability to work with other people as you are always well liked (except that time when we had to do a group project in school on the planets and you insisted on drawing little men on Mars and little women on Venus over Susie Corrigan's picture that took her weeks to do in art class, which ended up causing everyone in the group to walk out in protest, leaving just the two of us having to start another one all by ourselves. God, what is it about you and me being together that makes everyone hate us?). You are wonderful, beautiful, smart, and intelligent, and if you knew anything about coronary heart diseases I'd hire you myself.

I've suggested adding that you were offered a place in Boston College, which is impressive, so everything will be fine. Just be yourself and they'll love you.

Just one more thing. I *strongly* suggest that you apply for a job that you actually *like* this time. You would be surprised at how easy it is to get out of bed in the morning when you're going to do something that doesn't make you want to jump off the top floor of the bus (I was a bit worried when I got that email). How about finally trying to find a place in a hotel? You've wanted to do that since you stayed in the Holiday Inn in London when you were seven, remember?

Go for it and let me no how you get on.

Chapter 13

From Alex
To Rosie
Subject Boston visit?

Just taking a sneaky break from performing 'lobotomies' to send a quick email to see how you're getting on with the job search. You have one week left till Randy Andy throws you out of his paperclip empire, so there's still plenty of time, and if by any chance something hasn't caught your eye by then, I can send a cheque to help tide you over for a while (but only if you *want* my help).

I would love to go home right now and go to bed, I am so tired. I've worked a double shift so I don't have to get my hands bloody tomorrow; I have the day off, such bliss . . . The problem is that when I get home Sally will be getting ready to go on her shift. We don't have the most sociable hours in the world – well, not unless you count talking to people who are rolling around in agony on hospital beds. Sorry, that wasn't funny.

I'm just tired, and Sally and I don't really get to spend a lot of time together, and when we do we're usually so tired we just pass out.

Here's a good idea. If you come over with Katie and whatshisname then I'll take a few days off and we can see all the sights, eat out, enjoy ourselves and I can *sleep*. And I'll finally get to meet whatshisname. I've had a lousy few weeks; I really need your comic relief! Work your magic, Rosie Dunne, and make me laugh.

From Rosie
To Alex
Subject Rosie is here!

Hello there, misery man. Have no fear, Rosie is here! Sorry things have been shit for you lately. I think life likes to do that every now and again: it does a dip and when you feel like you can't take any more it smooths out again. But until then, my dear friend, I will try to humour you by explaining the events of my life.

OK, firstly you are a bad, bad influence on me. After I read the masterpiece that was my CV, and after I read your letter I felt so motivated and hyped up that I donned my tracksuit, headband, wristbands and jogging shoes (not really) and I raced around Dublin city like a woman on a mission.

You horrible, horrible man. You made me feel like I could do anything, like I could take on the world (never *ever* do that again) so I proceeded to drop my CV into every single hotel I've ever wanted to work in but was always too afraid to try. Shame on you for giving me strength, because it quickly disappeared and I found myself faced with a million billion interviews with a million billion snotty companies that hated me and my cheek for even *thinking* I could work for them.

So let's see, which embarrassing interview should I tell you about first? Hmm . . . there are so many to choose from. Well, let's start with the most recent, shall we? Yesterday I had an interview to work at the reception in the Two Lakes Hotel – you know, that really posh one in the city? The front of the building is made entirely of glass so you can see the big bright glistening chandeliers dripping down from miles away. At night-time the building looks like it's on fire, it's so bright. The restaurant is on the top floor so that you can look out over the entire city. It really is very beautiful.

But it's also one of those places where there's a guy (actually, more of a gentleman) dressed in one of those cloak things and a top hat who stands at the door and refuses to let anyone in. It must have taken me about ten minutes just to get inside the door. He just wouldn't listen, just kept saying that I needed to be a resident. Honestly, how could anybody ever get to be a resident if they don't let you in the door? Anyway, finally he let me in and I nearly slipped on the marble floor that was *so* shiny.

The place was so quiet you could hear a pin drop. No, I mean it literally: the woman at reception actually *did* drop a pin. I heard it. Well, I suppose the hotel wasn't *that* quiet: there was the tinkling sound of a piano filtering out from the lounge, there was a water fountain trickling down through the lobby area – the sounds were just so calming. It even had all those giant pieces of furniture that I always loved as a child, like huge mirrors, gigantic chandeliers, doors the length of my apartment wall. When I stepped onto the carpets I thought I was going to bounce up to the balcony, they were so spongy.

I was seated at The Longest Table Ever for the interview. Two men and a woman sat at one end – at least I think that's what they were; I was so far away I could barely see (I almost felt like asking them to pass the salt).

So I thought that I would try and make myself sound interested in the company, just like you told me to, so I asked them how the hotel got its name as I wasn't aware of any lakes in that part of the city. The two men started laughing and introduced themselves as Bill and Bob Lake. They own the place. How embarrassing.

So I basically just kept talking about what you told me to say: how I like working as part of a team, that I'm good with people, how I'm very interested in the running of a hotel and about how I'm such a hard worker and always put my mind to working on tasks and always finishing off what I start . . . bla bla bla.

And then I waffled on for what felt like an hour about how I've loved hotels since I was a child and have always wanted to work in one. (Well, the luxury is in *staying* in one but we both know I can't afford *that*.)

And then they go and spoil it all by saying something stupid like: 'So, Rosie, from the time you spent working at Andy Sheedy Paperclip & Co. what have you learned that you think you can bring to the table here at the Two Lakes?'

Please, like that's even worth asking.

OK, I have to go now, actually, because Katie just got home from school with the look of evil on her face and I haven't made dinner yet.

From Alex
To Rosie
Subject Two Lakes Hotel

It's a shame you had to rush off. I was enjoying that email. Glad to hear your interviews are going so well – it's cheered me right up!

But I'm dying to no, what was your answer to that question they asked you?

From Rosie
To Alex
Subject Re: Two Lakes Hotel

Alex, isn't it obvious?

Paperclips!

(They just laughed so I got myself out of that one easily.) OK, so I'm really going now. Katie is shoving pictures that she drew in school in my face. Oh, by the way, she drew one of you . . . you look like you've lost a bit of weight. I'll scan it to you . . .

Dear Ms Rosie Dunne,

It is our pleasure to inform you that we are offering you the position of head receptionist at the Two Lakes Hotel.

On a more personal note, we are very excited about having you here following the success of your interview last week. You come across as a bright, intelligent and witty young woman; the kind of person we like to have working at the hotel.

We take pride in hiring people we ourselves would like to be greeted by in a hotel and we have great faith that the smiles you brought to our faces when we met will also be brought to the customers of the hotel when they arrive at reception. We are pleased to have you as a member of the team, and hope our working relationship will develop successfully over many years in the future.

We ask that you get in touch with Shauna Simpson at reception with regard to your work uniform.

Yours sincerely,

Bill Lake   Bob Lake

PS. We would also appreciate it if you would bring those paperclips with you – office supplies are rather low!

You have an instant message from: ROSIE.

Rosie: My God, Ruby, could it be possible that I'm actually going to have a *nice* boss/bosses? I think everything is finally falling into place.

Ruby: And then she goes ahead and jinxes herself. She will never learn . . .

From	Rosie
To	Stephanie
Subject	Congratulations

I'm delighted to hear that you and Pierre got engaged! I know we spoke on the phone for hours last night but I wanted to send you this email too. Congratulations! By the way, have you heard from Kevin lately? He never calls or emails me – I think he's afraid I'm going to ask him to baby-sit again.

Something rather bizarre is happening in my life, Stephanie. I have a boyfriend who loves me, and who

I love back, I'm about to start work in the hotel of my dreams, Katie is beautiful and healthy and funny, and I finally feel like a good mum. I feel happy. I want to enjoy this feeling and revel in my good fortune but there's something niggling at me in the back of my mind. There's a little voice whispering to me, 'Things are too perfect.' It almost feels like the calm before the storm.

Is this how normal life is supposed to be? Because I'm used to drama, drama, drama. I'm used to things refusing to go my way. I'm used to having to struggle, moan and whinge my way into getting something that's not exactly what I want but that will *just do*.

This is not something that will 'just do', this is perfect; this is exactly what I wanted. I wanted to feel loved by someone, I wanted Katie to stop wondering if it was all her fault that she didn't have a daddy like all the other kids, I wanted to feel that the two of us not only belong together but that someone else would accept us in his life too, I wanted to feel important, I wanted to feel like *somebody*, I wanted to know that if I called in sick to work that I would be *missed*. I wanted to stop feeling so sorry for myself, and I have.

Things are going great. I'm feeling really good about myself and I'm not quite used to that. This is the new Rosie Dunne. Young and confused Rosie is gone. Phase two of my life now begins . . .

PART TWO

Chapter 14

Dear Ms Dunne,

I am hoping that you can come to the school to discuss Katie's rapidly deteriorating behaviour in class.

How does Wednesday after school sound? You can reach me at the school. You know the number.

Miss Casey

To Katie

What do you mean, your mum just laughed?

From Toby

From	Rosie
To	Alex
Subject	Flight details

Hey there, OK our flight is landing at 1.15 p.m. – flight number is EI4023. I'll be the woman dragging a terrified-looking man by the hair through arrivals, carrying a hyperventilating child by the other arm and pulling twenty suitcases along by my toes. (Greg hates flying, Katie is so excited I'm really very concerned that she's going to explode, and I couldn't decide what to bring with me so I've packed my entire wardrobe.)

Are you sure Sally knows what she's got herself into, allowing me and my mad family to stay with you?

From Sally
To Alex
Subject Re: Rosie's stay

Of course it's not OK, Alex. You couldn't have chosen a worse time to invite her and you know it.

From Alex
To Rosie
Subject Re: Flight details

Of course Sally doesn't mind. I can't wait to see you and Katie, and to meet whatshisname. I'll be waiting at arrivals for you.

Dear Alex,

Thank you so much for the holiday! I had such a fantastic time. Boston was even more beautiful than I remembered, and I'm glad I didn't have to run home early in embarrassment this time round. Katie just loved the whole experience, and the child will just not stop talking about you!

Greg really enjoyed it too. I'm glad you finally got to meet him and also learn that his face isn't usually the greenish colour that it was when he first got off the plane. It was such a treat to finally have my two favourite men in the same country, never mind in the same room! So what do you think of him? Does he get the best friend seal of approval?

So apart from the fact that your wife absolutely hates me, everything else was very comfortable and enjoyable. But I actually don't mind, Alex; I'll just accept it. It just makes it official and confirms what I've already thought: for some unknown reason, any girlfriend or wife of yours will forever hate me. And that's fine with me. I'm over it.

I just hope she lets me see your son or daughter when he or she is born. Now there's something else I never imagined would happen! Alex Stewart is going to be a daddy! Every time I think about it I just have to laugh out loud. God love your child to have a father like you! Just joking – you know I'm thrilled! Although I can't believe you kept it a secret from me for so many months. Shame on you.

By the way, I'm really sorry Katie spilled her drink over Sally's new dress. I don't know *what* got into her; she's usually not so clumsy! I've told her to write a letter of apology to Sally. Hopefully she won't hate us all so much then.

Anyway, my few weeks of fun are over now; it's back to reality again. I start work at my new job on Monday. All my life I've wanted to work in a hotel and I've put the thought away, with the rest of my dreams. I just hope it isn't hell, or all my little dream bubbles will burst in an instant.

There's one more thing I forgot to tell you. Greg has asked me and Katie to move in with him. I'm not quite sure how I feel about it. Things are going so well at the moment between us but it's not just me that I have to think about. Katie really likes Greg, and she loves to spend time with him (it may not have been that obvious in Boston because she was so excited to see you), but I don't know if she would be ready for such a huge change in her life. We're only in the flat together less than two years now and we're learning to live our lives with just the two of us. I'm not sure if uprooting her *again* would be the right thing. What do you think?

Well, I suppose all I need to do is ask her. But what if she says no? Do I say to Greg, 'Eh . . . sorry, I love you and all, but my eight-year-old daughter doesn't want to live with you?' Do I tell Katie, 'Tough luck you're moving house,' or do I do what she wants? I clearly can't just do what *I* want because there's two other people involved. I'm going to think about it for the next while anyway.

Thanks again for the break. I really needed it. I'll make sure Katie sends on that letter to Sally.

Love,
Rosie

Dear Rosie,

Welcome to your first day at the Two Lakes. I hope everyone has helped you to settle in so far. I'm sorry I'm not there to greet you but I am currently in the States finalising a few things at our new Two Lakes Hotel in San Francisco.

In the meantime, Amador Ramirez, the hotel assistant manager is there to show you the ropes. Let me know if you have any problems.

Once again, welcome!

Bill Lake

You have an instant message from: RUBY.

Ruby: Remember me?

Rosie: I'm sorry, Ruby, it's just that I don't get to spend much time on the computer like the last job. It's a bit difficult to pretend I'm doing work here.

Ruby: I give you one month . . .

Rosie: Thank you for your support; it's always very much appreciated.

Ruby: No problem. So how's life with Greg?

Rosie: Great thanks.

Ruby: So you don't hate each other yet?

Rosie: No, not yet.

Ruby: I give you one month . . .

Rosie: And once again, thank you.

Ruby: Just doing my duty as a friend. Any news with you?

Rosie: Well, actually I have a bit. I've told only Alex so far, but you're not allowed to tell anyone.

Ruby: Ooh, I love it! The most magical words you'll ever hear in a sentence. What is it?

Rosie: Well, a few weeks ago when I came home from work Greg had a beautiful dinner cooked, the dining table was set, candles were lit and the music was playing . . .

Ruby: Go on . . .

Rosie: Well, he asked me—

Ruby: To marry you!

Rosie: No, actually, he asked me if I was interested in moving in with him.

Ruby: Interested?

Rosie: Yeah.

Ruby: Were those his exact words?

Rosie: Eh, yeah, I think so. Why?

Ruby: You think that's romantic, do you?

Rosie: Well, he went to a lot of trouble to cook the meal, and set the table and—

Ruby: Jesus, you do that every day, Rosie. Do you not think it sounds a bit like a business proposition?

Rosie: In what way?

Ruby: If I wanted to open a joint bank account with Teddy I would say, 'Teddy, would you be interested in opening a joint bank account?' If I wanted to move in with Teddy, I would not say, 'Teddy, would you be interested in moving in together?' Do you see what I mean?

Rosie: Well, I suppose I—

Ruby: That is not the way to broach the subject. And what about marriage? Did he say anything about that? Or about Katie? If you and he get married, will he want to adopt Katie? Did you discuss any of those things?

Rosie: Well, actually . . . no, we didn't even discuss marriage. Anyway, I thought you were anti-marriage.

Ruby: I am, but I'm not the one who wants to get married and who is in a relationship with a man who doesn't. There lies a problem.

Rosie: I never said that I wanted to marry him.

Ruby: Well then, if neither of you feels comfortable marrying each other, go ahead and move in together; that sounds like a fabulous idea!

Rosie: Look, I don't recall hearing anyone saying that Greg doesn't want to marry me, and anyway, that's exactly what you and Teddy are doing!

Ruby: I've been married before and so has Teddy. We both don't want to go through it again. I've

already been there, done that, while this is just the beginning for you.
Rosie: Anyway, it doesn't matter because I told him that I wasn't ready to move in with him right now. It's a bad time, with me trying to settle down in the job and everything, and Katie settling down in the flat. I need to allow a little more time to pass so that Katie can adjust to the whole situation. It's been a huge change in her life.
Ruby: So you keep saying.
Rosie: What's that supposed to mean?
Ruby: You've been in the flat for well over a year now, you've been in that job of yours for a few weeks now, I've seen Katie and she's fine, Rosie, she's very happy. She's adjusted to this 'huge change'. I think that maybe it's *you* who needs to adjust.
Rosie: Adjust to *what*?
Ruby: Alex is married now, Rosie. Move on and make yourself happy!
Rosie has logged off.

Steph: Why didn't Greg ask you to marry him?
Rosie: I wasn't aware that he had to.
Steph: Would you have liked him to?
Rosie: You know me, Steph: if anyone got down on one knee and proposed (on the beach with a four-piece orchestra in the background) I'd like it. I'm an old romantic.
Steph: Are you disappointed he asked you to move in with him and not marry you?
Rosie: Well, I presume if he had proposed it would mean I'd be moving in with him anyway, so I'm really not that heartbroken. I'm lucky to have met someone like Greg.
Steph: Come on, Rosie, you're not just 'lucky' to have met Greg. You *deserve* to be happy. It's OK to want more than you're offered.
Rosie: I've decided to move in with him. We'll take it one step at a time.

Steph: If that makes you happy.
Rosie: *Then* if things are still as perfect between us as they are now, I'll expect the room filled with roses and lit with candles.

Dear Sally,

Sorry I spilled my orange juice on your new dress when we visited a few weeks ago. It is just that when I heard you slagging my mum's new dress I got a shock and my juice went all over you. Just like you laughed to your friend the next day about my mum having me, accidents happen.

I hope your dress doesn't stain, seeing as it was so expensive and all. I hope you will come to visit us sometime in our new house. We are moving in with Greg. It's bigger than your apartment. We had so much fun in Boston when Mum and Alex got new passport photos done for my locket. I'll keep the two of them together in it for ever.

Love,

Katie

PS. My friend Toby says hi and says that he spilled orange juice on his school shirt and it wouldn't come out when it was washed. His mum had to throw it out. It was white too. But lucky for him, the shirt was not as expensive as your dress.

You have an instant message from: ALEX.
Alex: Hi, what you up to?
Phil: I've been surfing the net for hours, looking for the original chrome exhaust pipes on a 1968 Ford Mustang. And do you think I could find the original badges as well as two-tone leather seats for the 1978 Corvette?
Alex: Eh . . . no?
Phil: Exactly, but I don't suppose you want to hear about my problems. How was the Rosie trip? Any more silences?
Alex: Oh, drop it, Phil.
Phil: He he. What's the boyfriend like?

Alex: He's OK. Nothing special. He's not the kind of man I'd have put Rosie with.
Phil: He's not you, you mean.
Alex: No, that's not what I mean. He's not exactly the life and soul of the party.
Phil: Should he be?
Alex: For Rosie, yes.
Phil: Maybe he's a calming influence on her.
Alex: Yeah, maybe. He's polite and friendly, but he doesn't talk much about himself. I couldn't quite figure him out. He's one of those people that don't seem to have an opinion on anything. He would just agree with absolutely everything everyone is saying. It's hard to get a sense of him. Sally and he got along very well, though.
Phil: Maybe he just had a problem with you then.
Alex: Thanks, Phil, you always have such a good way of making me feel better.
Phil: And isn't that why you discuss all of life's little problems with me?
Alex: Yeah. How are Margaret and the kids?
Phil: Great. Maggie thinks she's pregnant again.
Alex: Jesus, another one?
Phil: I'm one fully loaded man, Alex.
Alex: Good to no, Phil.
Alex has logged off.

From Alex
To Rosie
Subject Moving in with Greg?

So I take it you're moving in with Greg? Sally got a letter from Katie during the week, but she wouldn't let me read it. She just said that they have an understanding between them now. I'm glad. Whatever that means.

In answer to your question about Greg, yes, he's a nice man. Not the kind of person I expected you to settle down with, he's very quiet and reserved. A lot older than you as well. He's what . . . thirty-seven?

And you're twenty-seven. That's ten years, Rosie. How will you feel when he's old and decrepit and you're still young and beautiful? How will you ever look into those faded watery eyes and kiss those wrinkly dry cracked lips? How can you rub your hands over the varicose veins in his legs and go running through fields holding hands while all the time secretly worrying about his weak heart?

These are the things you need to worry about, Rosie.

You have received an instant message from: ROSIE.

Rosie: Are you on drugs???

Alex: Only the little pink ones . . .

Rosie: You're a doctor, help yourself. OK, I take it from that attempt-at-being-humorous-but-meaning-every-word-of-it reply that you don't like Greg. I've had enough of your snide comments about Greg. Well, to let the truth be known, I can't stand Sally. Ta-da!

I hate Sally and you hate Greg. Now we have learned that we all can't love each other. Katie and I are moving in with Greg next week. Everything is wonderful. We are blissfully happy. I've never been so in love in my life, blah blah blah. Now stop annoying me and get over it. Greg is here to stay. So what have you got to say to that?

Alex has logged off.

Rosie, Katie, and Greg,

Merry Christmas and a Happy New Year!
Love from Alex, Sally, and baby Josh

To Alex, Sally, and baby Josh!

Warm wishes for the New Year!
With love,
Katie, Rosie, and Greg

Chapter 15

Hello, sis,

Stop worrying! You have me more stressed out than you! Rosie, for the last time, it is absolutely normal for friends not to get along with each other's spouses/partners. Pierre's sister drives me up the wall but that's neither here nor there. Anyway, it doesn't mean that you and Alex are never going to speak to each other again.

The problem with you two is that you're too honest. I can't think of one friend of mine that I would feel comfortable saying, 'I hate your husband/wife' to, and if I even say one minuscule thing to Pierre about how frustrating his sister is then he jumps down my throat and defends her. There's never going to be anyone good enough for your best friend, Rosie. Alex is probably thinking that you could do far better than Greg and you think the same of Sally. Sally and Greg aren't stupid; they probably sense that. Greg knows that Alex was the most important man in your life (he also knows that you once had a crush on him, which doesn't make things any better). And Alex knows that he's been replaced. So both Greg *and* Alex are going to be a bit competitive with each other. This is all quite natural.

Anyway, stop giving yourself a headache with all this stuff, just ring the man or email or write or whatever it is that you two do. By the way, if you don't like Pierre, I don't care. I love him, so keep your opinions to yourself!

Send me your measurements over, will you? And don't lie, Rosie. This is for your bridesmaid dress and if you pretend you're two stone lighter than you actually are and the dress doesn't fit, tough, you have to wear it because I can't afford to get you another one. Do you prefer red or wine? Let me know.

Love,

Your agony aunt

PS. By the way, will you ring Alex and tell him that he and his wife are invited to the wedding? Now there's your excuse to talk to him.

To Rosie,

Birthday wishes from us to you!

Happy 28th – you're catching up on me!

Love,

Alex, Sally, and Josh

To Katie,

YOU ARE 9 TODAY!

Best wishes! I hope you can buy something nice with this!

Love,

Alex, Sally and Josh

From Rosie
To Alex
Subject Great news!

Alex Stewart, why don't you ever answer your phone? I have become best friends with Josh's nanny now and we have both come to an agreement over the fact that you and that wife of yours work far too much. Does poor little Josh even know who Mummy and Daddy are, or are you both happy with him thinking you two are just the nice people who pick him up and cuddle him a few times every day?

Anyway, the reason why I'm emailing you is because I have something brilliant that I really want to tell you and I refuse to announce it to you on a computer! So ring me when you get this message.

Your good advice may have been helpful after all, and I thank you for it!

Ring me, ring me, ring me!

From Alex
To Rosie
Subject Re: Great news!

I am refusing to ring you on the grounds that I am far too angry over your attacking my parental skills. If one more person tells me how to be a father to my son I will explode.

Things are tough at the moment because of my and Sally's working hours. The majority of the time we arrive home when Josh is asleep and I have to stop myself from waking him up just to say hello. We never have the same days off together and we just can't seem to spend any quality time together. It's like we're passing each other in the halls and grabbing quick moments of forced happiness before we run out the door.

It's not the greatest situation for Josh to be in but we just simply can't afford to stop working to be there for him all of the time. And by the way, *never ever* get married.

From Rosie
To Alex
Subject Surprise!

Oh, shucks, you've gone and spoiled my surprise.

From Alex
To Rosie
Subject Re: Surprise!

Rosie Dunne, are you getting married?!

Chapter 16

From Rosie
To Alex
Subject Surprise!

Surprise! What a lovely, lovely way to tell you. I can't have imagined a better way of sharing my delightful news with my best friend.

From Alex
To Rosie
Subject Marriage!

Oh, I'm so sorry, that's great news. Don't mind what I say, I'm just tired and whinging. So how did it all happen? When's the big day? I thought whatshisname didn't want to get married.

From Rosie
To Alex
Subject Re: Marriage at last!

Oh, Alex, you don't have to pretend to be interested in all the little details, it's OK. And his name is Greg, by the way. You've plenty on your mind now so I'll bore you another time. I just want to let you know that the 'big day' won't be so big. It's only going to be a small gathering with close friends and family. Greg doesn't really want anything too OTT and I'm happy enough to go along with that.

Katie is my flower girl/bridesmaid-type person and I want you to be my best man. If Greg is allowed to have one then so should I. Please say yes. Sally and Josh are more than welcome too. Make it a family holiday. I bet you haven't had one of those yet. You can relax and enjoy yourselves because you all deserve it. You can finally spend a few days together as a family.

I won't go into any detail about the proposal; I knew it was going to happen so it wasn't that amazing . . .

From Rosie
To Stephanie
Subject So romantic!

Oh, Stephanie, it was *so* romantic. I had absolutely *no* idea he was going to propose! He took me away for the weekend to this tiny little village in the west that I've never even heard of so I won't even attempt to spell it. We stayed in this charming little B&B and we ate in a restaurant called the Fisherman's Catch. We had the entire place to ourselves. The atmosphere was magical and then Greg proposed over dessert! Then we went for a stroll around the lake and headed back to the B&B. It was low key and quiet but so romantic!

From Stephanie
To Rosie
Subject Re: Romantic

That's funny, Rosie, because I always thought you said you wanted fireworks and romance, rose petals and violins while your man went down on one knee and proposed in front of a gasping and tearful crowd. Greg's proposal sounds *nice* and all, but whatever happened to that dream?

From Rosie
To Stephanie
Subject Fireworks and rose petals . . .

Well, that kind of thing just isn't Greg's style; you know the way he is. It would have seemed silly if Greg hung from a chandelier singing Sinatra while showering red velvety petals over my head (although what a wonderful thought). Besides it's not the proposal that counts, it's the marriage . . .

Ruby: He proposed to you in Bogger-reef?
Rosie: Yes, it's a cute little village—
Ruby: You HATE cute little villages! You like towns, cities, noise, air pollution, bright lights, rude people, and tall buildings!
Rosie: But we stayed in this sweet little B&B owned by the nicest—
Ruby: You HATE B&Bs! You are obsessed with hotels. You work in one. You want to run one, own one, live in one and quite possibly be one. The biggest treat for you is staying in a hotel and he took you to a crappy B&B in the middle of nowhere.
Rosie: Oh, but if you had just seen the little restaurant. It was called the Fisherman's Catch and it had these fishing nets all draped around the ceiling—
Ruby: You starved Katie's goldfish until it floated on top of that stinking bowl and then you flushed it down the toilet. You gag whenever you see people eating oysters (which, by the way, is very embarrassing in restaurants). You block your nose whenever I eat tuna, you think smoked salmon is the work of the devil, and prawns make you vomit.
Rosie: I had a nice salad, thank you very much.
Ruby: You always say salad is for rabbits and supermodels!

Rosie: Anyway, we finished the evening by strolling hand in hand in the moonlight alongside the lake—
Ruby: You LOVE the SEA. You want to live on a beach. You secretly want to be a mermaid. You think lakes are boring, you say they lack the 'drama' of the sea.
Rosie: Oh, please, *stop* it, Ruby!
Ruby: No! You please stop *lying* to yourself, Rosie Dunne.
Rosie has logged off.

From Rosie
To Alex
Subject SOS

Alex, please save me from my family and friends. They are driving me absolutely demented.

You have received an instant message from: ALEX.
Alex: Snap. What's the problem?
Rosie: I don't really want to talk about it. I want to take my mind off them.
Alex: That's fair enough, I can understand that. This is a nice distraction for me too. So why don't you tell me about whatshisname's proposal?
Rosie: OK . . . here I go again. *Greg* took me to a quiet little village down the country. We stayed in a gorgeous little B&B. We ate in a lovely restaurant called the Fisherman's Catch. He proposed while I had my mouth full of chocolate profiteroles, I said yes, we took a walk along the lake and watched the moon shimmering along the water. Isn't that romantic?
Alex: Yes, romantic.
Rosie: That's all you have to say?? Two words on one of the most important nights of my life?!
Alex: Could have been better.
Rosie: How much better? What would you have done to make it so much better? I'm just *dying* to

know! Everyone seems to think they know me so much better than I know myself, so go ahead, humour me!

Alex: OK, that sounds like a challenge! Well, firstly, I would have brought you to a *hotel* along the coast so that your *suite* would have the best possible *sea view*. You could fall asleep listening to the waves crashing against the rocks, I would sprinkle the bed with red *rose petals* and have *candles* lit all around the room, I would have your favourite CD playing quietly in the background.

But I wouldn't propose to you there. I would bring you to where there was a huge crowd of people so they could all gasp when I got down on one knee and proposed. Or something like that. Note I have italicised the all-important buzz words.

Rosie: Oh.

Alex: That's all you can say? One word for the most important night of our lives? I get down on bended knee and ask that you'll spend eternity with me and you say, 'Oh'? You have to do better than that!

Rosie: OK, so that would *also* be a very nice proposal. Did I go on about proposals so much, Alex?

Alex: All the time, my friend. All the time. Anyone who nos you half well would realise that is more or less the kind of thing you have always dreamed about. But a weekend in a B&B sounds fine too.

To Alex, Sally and baby Josh
DENNIS & ALICE DUNNE
Proudly invite you to the marriage of their beloved daughter
ROSIE TO GREG COLLINS
on July 18th of this year

Chapter 17

Dear Rosie,

So you went ahead and did it. You married whatshisname. You looked beautiful, Rosie, I was proud to stand beside you at the altar, and I was proud to be there with you on your special day. I was proud to be your best man, but just as you said at my wedding, I wasn't the best man that day, whatshisname was. You both looked great together.

I got the oddest feeling when you turned your back to me to walk down the aisle with Greg. Could it have been a pang of jealousy? Is that normal? Did you get that feeling on my wedding day, or am I going completely crazy? I just kept thinking over and over in my head: everything is going to change now, everything is going to change. Greg is the man for you, now *he* gets to hear all your secrets, and where does that leave me? It was a weird feeling, Rosie, though it did eventually pass.

I didn't dare talk about it to anyone, especially Sally, because then she would be only too delighted to think that her little theory of men and women being unable to be 'just friends' was correct. It's not like I was jealous because I wanted to be your husband, it was just . . . oh, I don't no how to explain it. I suppose I just felt left out, that's all.

I'm glad Josh finally got to put his feet on Irish soil – well, actually mostly his bum but he's almost there. I meant to bring him home a long time ago but work got in the way. That's funny, I just referred to Ireland as home; I haven't done that for quite a while. It felt like home last week. Anyway, it was good for Josh to be there, and I think Katie was happy enough to mind him all week.

She is you, Rosie. The little girl with the raven-coloured hair and pale skin is the girl I used to go to school with. It was amazing. Even talking to her I felt like young Alex again. Toby kept a watchful eye over me, though; I think he was afraid I would steal his friend away. I felt like I was keeping a watchful eye over him too, because *he* was stealing *my* friend away. I had to keep reminding myself that she wasn't you.

I'm not quite sure how your plan to unite me, Sally, and Josh went. As you could probably tell, Sally wasn't in the friendliest of moods during the few days. I thought the break away would help us, but apparently not. It just gave us a chance to talk to each other too much. And that's not the best thing when neither of you have anything nice to say. I think I can safely say that the honeymoon period is over. We're together nine years now.

Anyway, I hope you and Greg are enjoying your honeymoon and I'm sure this letter will be lying on the mat at home awaiting your arrival. I always thought you wanted to go to an exotic beach location for your honeymoon, I never new you were interested in seeing all the sights around Rome. Although I'm sure they are beautiful, I just thought you were too shallow to care! Just teasing.

Get in touch with me when you get back. Prove to me that at least some things never change.

Love,

Alex

Greetings from Rome!

Hi, Alex. Weather warm, buildings beautiful. But, more importantly, fabulous hotels!

Love,

Rosie x

From Rosie
To Alex
Subject I'm baa-aack!

Just got home a few minutes ago from our honeymoon and I read your letter. You sounded down so I called and guess what? Surprise, surprise, you weren't there. So I'm emailing you once again.

I know I never really liked Sally much, but I want you two to get over whatever it is that's bothering you. It's a big change when a baby comes along – I know that only too well – and I can understand that it's difficult for two people who work harder than anyone I know to deal with a new addition in their lives.

You probably just need time to adjust, but maybe you should go see a counsellor or something. God knows, it took me long enough to accept that Katie was here to stay, as much as I love her. It was, and still is, hard work. So do what you do best and get to work on it.

I certainly don't pretend to be a know-it-all but just stop talking to me about how you feel and start telling Sally. I am always here for you, Alex, married woman or not.

Dear Alex,

I hope you are well. It was good to see you at the wedding. Josh is really cool. Mummy looked lovely and so did you. Me and Toby are fighting. He is ten next week and he thinks he is so cool just because he is a little bit older than me. He didn't invite me to his birthday party and I didn't even do anything wrong. We had a fight last week about whose turn it was to go first on the computer and I went first even though I remembered I went first the last time but I don't think he remembered so he is not mad at me about that. I did not do anything else wrong.

Mum called round to Toby's mum to see why but she does not no either. Toby will not talk to me. I hate him. I will make a new best friend. Mum told me to write to you and tell you because you are my godfather and no stuff about this.

Mum thinks that it is really, really mean of Toby and that I will be motionally scared when I grow up, from the xperience of not being invited to a birthday party. She says you no what she means.

Love,

Katie

Dearest Katie,

Your wise and extremely intelligent mother is correct, as always. I agree that Toby is being terribly cold and calculative. It is an awful thing for anyone to do to a person, to not invite your best friend to your tenth birthday party. I do believe it should be a crime. He is selfish and it is an unforgivable act that will haunt him for years to come, no doubt – maybe even until he is nearly thirty years old, in fact.

I think that there is no punishment bad enough to inflict on him and he should not get away with this. Toby has shown no mercy, has been immature and very very . . . bold. So tell your mother and tell Toby that I shall do my best to make sure that he and I redeem ourselves so that we can walk down the road with our heads held high.

Love,

Alex

Dear Alex,

That was a weird letter. I don't know what it meant but Mum says that Toby is even worse than all the things you said. But she was laughing when she read the letter so I don't no if she means it. I don't think Toby is *that* bad.

You two are weirdos.

Love,

Katie x

Dear Toby,

It's Alex here (Katie's mum's friend from America).

I heard that you're going to be ten next week. Happy birthday! I no you probably think that me writing to you is really weird but I heard that you didn't invite Katie to your party and I couldn't believe my ears.

Katie is your best friend! I no for a fact that your party won't be much fun without Katie there. It once happened to me. You will be watching the door like a hawk, just hoping that she will walk into the room so you can enjoy yourself. Who cares if your best friend is a girl? Who cares if the other guys laugh? At least you have a best friend and, trust me on this, it's really hard to live your life without a best friend, especially if you're in boring school with Miss Big Nose Casey giving out to you all day. If you don't invite Katie then you will really hurt her feelings and that's not very nice.

It's the best thing in the world to have a best friend – even if she is a girl. Let me no how you get on.

Alex

PS. Hope you can buy something nice for yourself with this present . . .

From Toby
To Katie
Subject KNOW not NO

Your mum's friend spells 'know' wrong, just like you. He says NO instead of KNOW. By the way, do you wanna come to my party next week?

From Rosie
To Alex
Subject Dunne women

Very clever, Mr Stewart, but you haven't quite redeemed yourself yet. Us Dunne women are pretty hard to please, you know . . .

From Alex
To Rosie
Subject Done woman

So I see. You're a done woman alright. Well, I have a theory that I wish to share with you. Shall I?

From Rosie
To Alex
Subject Theory shmeory

If you must. I might read it if I have time.

From Alex
To Rosie
Subject My theory

Yes I must, and you *will* read it. OK, if I *had* invited you to my tenth birthday party then Brian the Whine wouldn't have been invited. If Brian hadn't gone then he wouldn't have thrown pizza all over James's sleeping bag and if he hadn't done that and completely ruined my party then you and I wouldn't have hated him so much. If you and I hadn't hated him so much then you wouldn't have had to drink so much in order to be able to accompany him to the debs. If you hadn't have done that . . . well . . . perhaps you wouldn't have been quite so drunk and your darling little Katie wouldn't have been born. Therefore I did you a favour!

And that, Rosie Dunne, is my theory.

From Rosie
To Alex
Subject *My* theory

Very clever, Alex, very, very, clever. But you needn't have gone that far back to accept responsibility for Katie. Here's my theory.

Had I not been stood up by you at the debs, I wouldn't have had to go with Brian the Whine at all. Had you showed up at the airport that day our lives could have turned out very differently.

From Alex
To Rosie
Subject Life

Yeah, that's something I'm beginning to wonder about.

Ruby: They WHAT? They *split up*??
Rosie: Yeah, they're finished. Sad, isn't it?
Ruby: Well, not really, actually. Why did they split up?
Rosie: Irreconcilable differences. Isn't that what people always say?
Ruby: Not in my case. Mine was lazy cheating bastard. So who has Josh?
Rosie: Sally took him and went to stay with her parents.
Ruby: Oh, poor Alex. So come on, spill the beans.
Rosie: Well, I don't know everything—
Ruby: Liar. Alex tells you everything, which is probably the reason in itself.
Rosie: Excuse me; please do not accuse me of being the reason for his marriage break-up. That is very insulting. It was a million little things that all finally blew up in their faces.
Ruby: So when are you going over to him?
Rosie: Next week.
Ruby: Are you planning on coming back?
Rosie: RUBY! QUIT IT!
Ruby: OK, OK. It's sad, though, isn't it?
Rosie: Yes, it is. Alex is devastated.
Ruby: No, I didn't mean that. The irony of it all makes *me* sad; I can't even imagine how *you* must feel.
Rosie: What irony?

Ruby: Oh, you know . . . you wait and wait for years for him until you finally give up and move on with your life. You eventually decide to marry Greg and weeks later, Alex splits up with Sally. You know, you two have the worst timing ever. When will you ever learn to catch up with each other?

Chapter 18

You are one today!
May your special day be lots of fun,
It's not every day a boy is one!
We love our little special boy,
Because you bring us so much joy!
To Josh (and your daddy),
We love you both and hope you have a very happy birthday and Thanksgiving together.
Lots of love,
Rosie and Katie

Dear Rosie and Katie,

Thank you for the teddy you sent me for my birthday. I call him 'Bear'. Daddy made the name up all by himself. He is very clever. I love to chew on his ear and drool all over him so that when Daddy hugs him, it leaves my slobber all over his face. I also like to throw Bear out of my cot in the middle of the night and then scream at Daddy until he picks him up for me. I just do it for the laugh. Daddy doesn't need to sleep. He's only here to feed me and clean my diapers.

Anyway, I'd better go now. I have a very busy weekend with Daddy, I'm being fed at nine o'clock, followed by a burping and then I'm going to try to take a few steps across the living room. I no I can do it. One of these days I won't land on my bum . . .

Thanks for Bear.
Love you and miss you both,
Josh (and Daddy)

From Rosie
To Alex
Subject Happy 30th

I can't believe you're not having a thirtieth birthday party! Or are you having one and you're just not inviting me? I know you've been inclined to do things like that in the past. Jesus, imagine that was a whole twenty years ago. I never thought we would reach the time when we could remember anything happening that long ago. Anyway, Happy Birthday. Have a slice of cake on me.

From Alex
To Rosie
Subject Thanks

Sorry I haven't been in touch, I'm almost ready to finish up my residency here so I can move on to do two more years of cardiothoracic residency program. My one hundred years of study are almost up! No celebrations for me this year, too busy trying to pay back my million-dollar student loan.

You have an instant message from: GREG.
Greg: Hi, honey, how's your day going?
Rosie: Oh, it seems to be one of those neverending days. The hotel is completely booked out this weekend because of the St Patrick's Day parade. There's been a steady flow of big groups arriving all day so I've been constantly checking them in. It has quietened down now, so I'm pretending to be really busy on the computer with reservations, so don't make me laugh, whatever you do, or my cover will be blown.

Well, when I say 'quiet' I mean no one is bothering us at reception. The noise level of the hotel is a completely different story altogether. There's a huge group of Americans in the bar singing along to old Irish songs. Would you believe they got the

Paddy Band into the hotel as a special treat? I've never seen so many green faces and dyed red hair in my life.

Unfortunately some of Bill Lake's family have flown in from Chicago. There are thirty of them so I'm on my best behaviour. Apparently his nephew is a trombone player in the Chicago high school marching band that's taking part in the parade on Sunday.

I'm just dying for the day to end. My face is sore from smiling and my eyes are stinging from staring at this bloody computer screen. I'm thrilled Bill gave me the weekend off! He's such a sweetie. I can't remember the last time I had a Saturday off, or two days in a row, for that matter. Well, it means that for once we can go out tonight and I won't have to worry about getting up in the morning. We can meet up with Ruby and Ted. I was thinking of bringing Katie and Toby to the parade on Sunday – what do you think?

Sorry for rambling on, but I feel like I'm back at school on a Friday afternoon, waiting for the final bell to ring for the weekend.

Greg: Oh, Rosie, I'm sorry to dampen your good spirits but I have to head up north to Belfast tonight. I only found out this morning so it's completely last minute. I'm sorry.

Rosie: Oh no! Why do you have to go to Belfast?

Greg: There's this seminar that's on that I have to go to.

Rosie: What kind of a seminar?

Greg: A financial one.

Rosie: Well, of course it's a financial one. I hardly expect it to be on French cuisine. Do you *have* to go? Will they even notice if you're there?

Greg: No, they wouldn't notice, to be honest, but I want to go. They're quite interesting, you know, and I have to stay ahead of my game.

Rosie: How much more could you possibly learn

about bloody banks? They give you money and ask for ten times more back. That's about it.

Greg: I'm sorry, Rosie.

Rosie: This is so annoying. Of all the bloody weekends Bill gives me off, it's the one you have to go away for. You do know that I will not get a weekend off for another year, don't you?

Greg: I love the way you never exaggerate, Rosie. Listen, I have to go, OK? Talk to you later. Love you.

Rosie: Oh, hold on, before you go, did you see the phone bill this morning?

Greg: What was it like, high?

Rosie: Guess.

Greg: Damn. That's you and all that time you spend on that internet sending emails, you know. I don't understand why you and Ruby can't just arrange to *meet* like normal people.

Rosie: Because no establishment allows us to sprawl across their couches in our pyjamas and smoke. It's far more comfortable at home. Anyway, the price of the bill couldn't have *anything* to do with all those hours a week you spend on the phone to your mother, convincing her she's perfectly capable living on her own, by any chance?

Greg: I somehow think you don't really mind me spending those hours convincing her, my darling!

Rosie: True! Oh, if only we knew a bank manager who could give us a loan . . . how simple life would be . . .

Greg: Unfortunately it doesn't work like that, Rosie.

Rosie: And imagine my disappointment when I found that out after I married you.

Greg: You stuck with me all the same – thank you for that. I have to go now and refuse to give a mortgage to someone, you know how it is. Love you.

Rosie: Love you.

From Kevin
To Rosie
Subject My favourite sister

Hello, my most favourite big sister in the whole entire world. It's Kevin here. Email me back when you get a chance. I'm on the college computer so the internet is free and I wanna ask you something.

From Rosie
To Kevin
Subject Re: My favourite sister

Why do I only ever hear from you when you want something?

From Kevin
To Rosie
Subject Re: Re: My favourite sister

You sound like my ex-girlfriend. What makes you think I want something? Maybe I just want to catch up with my sister and see what's going on in her life. How's Katie? Tell her I was asking for her. How's Greg? Tell him I was asking for him. How's Alex? Tell him I was asking for him. See how interested I am in your life? If you ever need a baby-sitter for Katie just let me know, I'd be only too delighted to help out. Anyway, that's all from me, take care of yourself and keep in touch.

PS. Any chance you could ask your boss for a job for me?

From Rosie
To Kevin
Subject A-HA!

A-HA! I knew there had to be a catch! You never usually care about what's going on in my life. Katie is fine, thank you, so is Greg, and so is Alex. You could see how they are with your very own eyes if you ever bothered to call round. Yes I would love you to mind Katie, thank you very much, but I'm not sure I could trust you after what happened the last time.

From Kevin
To Rosie
Subject Six years ago!

Oh, come on Rosie! That was at least six years ago, I was only seventeen! How could you give a seventeen-year-old male an apartment of his own and not expect him to invite round a few friends? It's only normal.

From Rosie
To Kevin
Subject Normal!

Kevin, you trashed the place. Poor Katie was terrified and I didn't appreciate finding you asleep in my bed with that . . . whatever she was . . .

From Kevin
To Rosie
Subject Water under the bridge

Well, you said make yourself at home . . . anyway, that's all water under the bridge, we're both sensible adults now. (You're getting on a bit – thirty next month!) I would really love if you could help me out. I would be forever grateful and I honestly, truthfully mean that.

From Rosie
To Kevin
Subject You owe me!

Oh, OK, but I'm not promising any miracles. Don't mess this up, Kevin, or Bill will hold it against me and it'll ruin my grand master plan of taking over this hotel.

From Rosie
To Alex
Subject Life!

Christ, Alex, who knew Kevin had learned to walk and talk? I thought he was still at school. He just suddenly grew up. Not that he was ever one for sharing his life stories with me, anyway. He's so secretive. It's people like him the world has to worry about.

Things change so quickly. Just when you get used to something, zap! It changes. Just when you begin to understand someone, zap! They grow up. The same is happening with Katie. She changes every day; her face just becomes so much more grown-up every time I look at her. Sometimes I have to stop *pretending* I'm interested in what she's saying in order to realise that I *actually am* interested. We go shopping for clothes together and I take her advice. We eat out for lunch and giggle over silly things. I just can't cast my mind back to the time when my child stopped being a child and became a person.

And a beautiful person she is becoming too. I don't quite know where I'm going with this email, Alex, but I've been thinking about a lot of things lately and my head is a bit of a muddle.

Our life is made up of time. Our days are measured in hours, our pay measured by those hours, our knowledge is measured by years. We grab a quick few minutes in our busy day to have a coffee break. We rush back to our desks, we watch the clock, we live by appointments. And yet time eventually runs out and you wonder in your heart of hearts if those seconds, minutes, hours, days, weeks, months, years and decades were being spent the best way they possibly could.

Everything is spinning around us – jobs, family,

friends, lovers . . . you just feel like screaming 'STOP!', looking around, rearranging the order of a few things and then continuing on. I guess you probably understand what I mean. I know you're having a really difficult time right now. Please remember that I'm always here for you.

Love, Rosie

Chapter 19

Dear Alex,

OK, so as you probably no, it's Mum's thirtieth next month, and me and Toby are arranging a surprise birthday party for her. So will you come?

So far we have invited Grandma, Granddad, Aunt Stephanie, Uncle Kevin (even though we didn't want to because he scares us), Ruby, Teddy, Toby's mum and dad, Toby and me. That's all so far. Oh yeah, and Greg too if he's here. He's always working and Mum is always giving out to him about it. The other weekend Mum was off work and she was real excited about it all week because she had stuff planned with Ruby and Greg. I no how she feels because I hate school and I love when the weekend comes. Anyway, Greg had to go away again, last minute. Then Ruby called her and said she was sick so Mum stayed in and watched TV with me and Toby, and she let him stay over.

Toby's got this cool new flashlight. It's like the best one you can get. When Mum went to bed we were shining it out our window and it reached all the way up to the clouds and everything, it was so strong. Well, we were shining it across the road and we could see Mr and Ms Gallagher in their house. Toby thinks they were playing leap frog. It was real funny except Ms Gallagher came across the road in her dressing gown real mad at us, and she was banging on the door shouting at Mum. Mum was so mad she said she wouldn't take us to the parade. But she did.

Me and Toby got our faces painted in town and it looked really cool. We even got Mum to get a little shamrock on her face as well and she did, but then she wished she didn't because it started raining and the green, white and gold face paints were running all over our faces. They looked like rainbow tears. Loads of Toby's got in his hair and I rubbed my eyes by mistake and all the green got in. They were stinging so much I couldn't keep my eyes open and I couldn't see, so Mum and Toby held my hands and brought me home. We had to leave before the parade even started.

We were soaking when we got home and Mum's new outfit was covered in the green stuff. The lady that put it on our faces said that it washes off clothes. It doesn't. Toby has had green hair for the whole week in school and Miss Big Nose Smelly Breath Casey isn't happy. Can you believe she is the principal now? Mum says the school must really be desperate. Anyway, when we got back from town we just watched the parade on telly but we only got to see the end because it took us so long to get home because of all the fucking tourists. That's what Mum said.

So will you come to the party? You can bring Josh too. We need more people anyway. Aunt Stephanie can't come because she is due next month and I don't think the pilot will let her fly because she's too heavy or something. Grandma and Granddad are going over to visit her, Pierre, and the new baby if it comes. Uncle Kevin can't come because he's starting his new job as a chef in a new hotel down the country. So it's just Ruby and Teddy, and Ruby says that she can't promise Teddy will be there, because she doesn't like to plan dates with him that far in advance. It's only two weeks, though.

I wanted it to be kinda special for Mum, because she's been really sad again this week. Things have been kinda weird these days. I think it's because the telephone is broken. Every time the phone rings and Mum answers it, no one is there. It happens when I answer it too. It doesn't happen when Greg answers it.

Greg said he would get someone to fix the phone and Mum just spilled her drink on him. I don't really think it's broken. I think that whoever is ringing just wants to speak to Greg and not me and Mum.

It would be good if you came over – you're loads of fun. You can even sleep here but you can't sleep in the spare room because that's Greg's room now, I think. You can sleep on the couch, or I have a pull-out bed in my room. Remember, don't ring because it's a secret and Mum just keeps hanging the phone up without saying hello anyway. Email me if you want.

Love,
Katie

From Alex
To Katie
Subject Re: Rosie's 30th

Thanks for the letter. That's a good idea of yours and Toby's but I won't wait until your mum's birthday, if you don't mind. I'll be over as soon as I can.

Happy 30th, Sister!

Sorry we can't be there.

Love, Stephanie, Pierre and Jean-Louis!

For our daughter

Happy 30th.

Sorry we can't be there. Enjoy your day, love, and we'll see you when we get back.

Love, Mum and Dad

Happy 30th, Sis.

Sorry I can't be there but thanks for getting me the job. I owe you one.

Enjoy the night.

Kevin

Happy Birthday, Rosie.

Sorry we can't be there but we're stuck covering your shift!

Love from everyone at work xxx

To Rosie

I'm so sorry, please forgive me; I have been a complete fool. Please let's put this behind us and enjoy your birthday weekend.

Love,

Greg

Happy Birthday.

Let's get pissed.

Love, Ruby

Rosie,

I'm returning to Boston tomorrow but before I go I wanted to write this letter to you. All the thoughts and feelings that have been bubbling up inside me are finally overflowing from this pen and I'm leaving this letter for you so that you don't feel that I'm putting you under any great pressure. I understand that you will need to take your time trying to decide on what I am about to say.

I no what's going on, Rosie. You're my best friend and I can see the sadness in your eyes. I no that Greg isn't away working for the weekend. You never could lie to me; you were always terrible at it. Your eyes betray you time and time again. Don't pretend that everything is perfect because I *see* it isn't. I see that Greg is a selfish man who has absolutely no idea just how lucky he is and it makes me sick.

He is the luckiest man in the world to have you, Rosie, but he doesn't deserve you and *you* deserve far better. You deserve someone who loves you with every single beat of his heart, someone who thinks about you constantly, someone who spends every minute of every day just wondering what you're doing, where you are, who you're with and if you're OK. You need someone who can help you reach your dreams and who can protect you from your fears. You need someone who will treat you with respect, love every part of you, *especially* your flaws. You should be with someone who can make you happy, really happy, *dancing-on-air* happy. Someone who should have taken the chance to be with you years ago instead of becoming scared and being too afraid to try.

I am not scared any more, Rosie. I am not afraid to try. I no what that feeling was at your wedding – it *was* jealousy. My heart broke when I saw the woman I love turning away from me to walk down the aisle with another man, a man she planned to spend the rest of her life with. It was like a prison sentence for me – years stretching ahead without me being able to tell you how I feel or hold you how I wanted to.

Twice we've stood beside each other at the altar, Rosie. *Twice*. And twice we got it wrong. I needed you to be there for my wedding day but I was too stupid to see that I needed you to be the *reason* for my wedding day.

I should never have let your lips leave mine all those years ago in Boston. I should never have pulled away. I should never have panicked. I should never have wasted all those years without you. Give me a chance to make them up to you. I love you, Rosie, and I want to be with you and Katie and Josh. Always.

Please think about it. Don't waste your time on Greg. This is *our* opportunity. Let's stop being afraid and take the chance. I promise I'll make you happy.

All my love,
Alex

Chapter 20

Ruby: I've decided. I'm putting my Gary on a diet.
Rosie: *You're* putting *him* on a diet? How on earth can you control what your twenty-one-year-old son eats?
Ruby: Oh, it's easy. I'll just nail everything down to the floor.
Rosie: So what kind of diet is it?
Ruby: I don't know. I bought a magazine, but there are so many stupid diets out there I don't know which one to pick. Remember that ridiculous one that you and I did last year? The alphabet one where we had to eat foods beginning with a certain letter every day?
Rosie: Oh yeah! How long did we do that for?!
Ruby: Em . . . that would be twenty-six days of course, Rosie.
Rosie: Oh . . . right . . . of course. You *put on* weight on the third day.
Ruby: That's because the third day was the lucky letter 'C' . . . Cakes . . . Mmmm.
Rosie: Well, we made up for it on the last day. I was bloody starving on 'Z' day; I was practically chasing zebras with a kitchen knife around the zoo. Could have eaten the zoo, I suppose . . .
Ruby: Maybe I'll just invent a diet of my own and give those ridiculous magazines a run for their money.
Rosie: So what's your idea then?
Ruby: Hmm . . . OK, you should only eat . . . whatever food you look like.

Rosie: I bet those magazine diet experts are quaking in their boots.
Ruby: No, really! I think I'm on to something here! Teddy always reminds me of a tomato with his big ripe fat juicy red face. The two hairs on his head that stick up remind me of the stalk. I always feel the urge to stick his head in a blender and mix with vodka and Tabasco. A bloody Teddy. Simon from the office reminds me of a Brussels sprout. He's smelly and . . .
Rosie: Green?
Ruby: No, just smelly.
Rosie: What do I look like?
Ruby: Good question . . . hmm, I think you're a bit of an onion.
Rosie: Why, do I stink and make people cry? Why, do I stink and make people cry?
Ruby: Why did you just repeat yourself?
Rosie: Onions do that, don't they – they repeat on you?
Ruby: A funny onion too. No, I think it's because there are many layers to you, Rosie Dunne, and as the years go by, another one is peeled away. I think there's a lot more under there than people think. So what am I?
Rosie: Hmm . . . a cake. Sweet as sugar with a cherry on top.
Ruby: And fat and unhealthy.
Rosie: Look, Ruby, you invented this diet. If you look like a cake then all you can eat are cakes. Think about it.
Ruby: Yes, I take your point. I always thought secretly that I had a touch of the banoffi pie to me, alright. But it's not a proper diet unless you look like a vegetable or a fruit, and my Gary (although he may have the *qualities* of a vegetable) ain't no fruit or vegetable.
Rosie: What do you think Greg looks like?
Ruby: Ah, that's easy. A bull's testicle.
Rosie: HA! Since when did people ever eat bulls' testicles?

Ruby: It's a tribal thing . . . OK then, a slug. A slimy, disgusting, slow slug.
Rosie: I don't think Greg would eat a slug.
Ruby: Who cares what the cheating bastard eats? What do you think Alex looks like?
Rosie: A Skye.
Ruby: You think your six-foot-tall, brown-haired, brown-eyed, white-skinned friend looks like a chocolate bar with nougat inside?
Rosie: Yes.
Ruby: Now *that's* stupid . . .
Rosie: Well, excuse me, Ms I-Think-Teddy-Has-a-Tomato-Head.
Ruby: Look, all this talk of dieting is making me hungry. I'm taking an early lunch, OK?
Rosie: OK! You cheered me up, Ruby.
Ruby: Ooops, sorry, I wasn't supposed to do that, was I?
Rosie: No, but you're forgiven.
Ruby: Oh good. Bye, honey.
Rosie: Bye . . .
Ruby has logged off.

From Alex
To Rosie
Subject More time?

Alex here. It's been a while since I've heard from you . . . I was hoping you would have been in touch by now. If you need more time, I understand. Please let me no what's going on.

From Rosie
To Alex
Subject Re: More time?

Hey there, Skye! Sorry I haven't written in a while, I've been up to my eyes at work. It's been really busy round here for some reason. Probably because the sun is beginning to peek its big head up again; the country is so much nicer when the sun shines. What do you mean, do I need more time? It doesn't take very long to accept I'm thirty!

Thanks for coming over for my birthday, by the way. It was really sweet of Katie and Toby to organise it, even if you and Ruby were the *only* people there. Sorry I was a bit of a sour puss. I suppose I was just down because I turned thirty and most people were away. It just would have been nice if more people had come, but never mind, it's not the end of the world. You were there and that was good enough for me. I was so happy to see you. You are always there for me, Alex, and I appreciate that. You keep me strong when I don't feel like it.

Anyway, how are things with you? How's Josh? Give him a big huge sloppy kiss and a hug from me.

From Alex
To Rosie
Subject My letter

Didn't you get my letter?

From Rosie
To Alex
Subject Letter?

What's this about a letter? Maybe it's just delayed in the post; I'll probably get it soon. When did you send it?

Dear Alex,

Thank you for coming over for Mum's birthday party and thanks for my present too. She was real sad before you came over but I think you made her happier. I have to go because teacher is looking at me.

From Katie

Dear Katie,

Thanks for the letter. I hope you didn't get into any

trouble at school for writing to me. I'm glad you liked your present. Tell Toby I said hi and that I'll send over that baseball gear for him soon.

How is your mum? How is everything at home? Do you no what a Skye is, by any chance?

Love,

Alex

From Alex
To Rosie
Subject My letter

I didn't post the letter; I put it on the kitchen table in your house just before I left to go to the airport. Didn't you get it?

Dear Alex,

Toby is real excited about the baseball stuff. Things are kinda getting back to normal again. Greg only sleeps in the spare room some nights now. Mum said he's there because of his snoring. I don't believe her because Toby and I put a tape recorder in the room and he doesn't snore. He sleep talks, though! He said, 'Don't send the horses to the rainbow!' It's true, we have it on tape.

Things are kinda OK but not like before. It was nice when you were here. I prefer to stay in Toby's house now. By the way, a Skye is a chocolate bar. It's Mum's favourite. She loves them. She says she would love a diet of Skyes all day. The other day she said she was in love with a Skye then she started kissing it and laughing.

Why do you want to no? Do you want one too? I can post one over if you want, if they don't sell them in Merica. I did that before when I was in England on my holidays and I sent a chocolate bar in the post to Toby because they didn't sell them here and when he got it, it was all melted and stuck to the paper. He couldn't read my letter but I was glad because I missed him when I was away and I wrote some silly things and it was imbarrassing.

So should I get you the chocolate bar? Mum says she can't live without her Skye. She's a weirdo.
Love, Katie

From Alex
To Rosie
Subject My letter

Hi, Rosie. It's important that I talk to you right now. It's about the letter. I wrote some really important things in there and I would love you to read it if you can. Please try and find it.

From Rosie
To Alex
Subject Your letter

Hi, Alex. I searched the house from top to bottom yesterday when I got home from work. No sign of it. Is everything OK? Can you just email me what it said?

From Alex
To Rosie
Subject My letter

Jesus Christ. Rosie, I'll call you in five minutes.

From Rosie
To Alex
Subject Your letter

Alex! You can't call me at work, you'll get me fired! What is this about?

From Alex
To Rosie
Subject My letter

So pretend to be talking to a customer, Rosie! I'm serious, answer the phone.

From Rosie
To Alex
Subject Your letter

Oh, hold on, Greg is online. Before you have a heart attack, I'll see if he's seen the letter.

From Alex
To Rosie
Subject My letter

Don't bloody well ask *him*!

You have an instant message from: ROSIE.
Rosie: Greg, did you see a letter on the kitchen table for me?
Greg: A letter? No, I think there was just your mobile phone bill and the electricity bill.
Rosie: No, I'm not talking about this morning; I'm talking about two weeks ago, the weekend of my birthday.
Greg: But, Rosie you didn't want me around that weekend. I stayed on the couch in Teddy's flat, remember?
Rosie: Oh, you poor soul. Of course I fucking remember. I thought you might like it, seeing as you've been sleeping in everybody else's houses for the past while. I'm not stupid, Greg. Oh, but sorry, I forgot that you thought that I was.
Greg: Honey, I—
Rosie: Don't honey me. Did you see the bloody letter or not? You were home on the Monday just after Alex left.
Greg: No, I honestly didn't see it.
Rosie: Well, there's a reason not to believe you, Mr Honesty.
Greg: Look, Rosie, we can't move on if you don't forgive and learn to trust me again.
Rosie: Oh, go shove your forgiveness up your ass. I

don't have time for another one of these conversations with you. This is very simple. I've got Alex online waiting for me. He left a letter for me. He wants to know if any of us found it. So I'm asking you one more time, Greg, did you see the letter or not?

Greg: No, I promise you that I didn't.

From Bill Lake
To Rosie Dunne
Subject Personal emails

I hope they're business emails you've been sending for the last half-hour, Rosie. We've got a group of eighty arriving in the next few minutes for the weekend business conference in the De Valera Suite. Lots to do, Rosie.

From Rosie
To Alex
Subject Your letter

Alex, Greg didn't see the letter. Maybe you can just write me another one or ring me later when I'm at home and not when Big Brother is watching me on this stupid bloody security camera pointed right at me. Now both of you men leave me alone before I get fired.

From Greg
To Alex
Subject Your letter?

I was told you were online so I hope I caught you in time. I happened to have stumbled across something I believe you're looking for. I would appreciate it if you would stop sending my wife love letters. You seem to have forgotten that she's a married woman. Married to *me*, Alex.

Rosie and I have had our troubles like all marriages

do, but we are willing to put all that behind us now and give it another chance. You need to understand that none of your letters is going to change that. You said it yourself: you had your chance but now the moment has passed you by.

Let's be realistic here for a minute, Alex. You and Rosie are both thirty. You've known each other since you were five. Don't you think that in all that time, that if something was supposed to happen between you two, if it was so *meant to be*, that it would have happened by now? Think about it. She is not interested.

I want no further contact with you again. If you set foot in my house I will be only too glad to show you how unwelcome you are. To save you the embarrassment, I won't speak of the contents of your letter again. And you're wrong, by the way. I do fully appreciate the fact that Rosie is my wife. She is a wonderful woman, loving, warm and caring, and I am so glad she is the woman that chose to spend the rest of her life with *me*. So you can keep on watching her back walk from you at the altar because she won't be turning round.

From Alex
To Greg
Subject Rosie

Do you think your ridiculous attempt to scare me off is going to work? You are a pathetic sad little man. Rosie has a mind of her own and she doesn't need you making those decisions for her.

From Greg
To Alex
Subject Re: Rosie

So what are you going to do if she says yes, Alex? What are you going to do? Move to Dublin? Leave Josh behind? Expect Rosie to uproot Katie, leave the job she loves and move to Boston? *Think*, Alex.

You have received an instant message from: ALEX.
Alex: She didn't get the letter, Phil.
Phil: Oh, bloody hell, Alex. I told you not to put it in one of those damn letters. You should have just told her. I don't know why you can't just use your mouth like the rest of us.
Alex: Greg found the letter.
Phil: The idiot husband? I thought they were finished?
Alex: Evidently not. But it doesn't change anything, Phil. I still love her.
Phil: Yeah, but she's *still* married, isn't she? You're not going to like what I say, and this is just my opinion, Alex, and hell knows you never take any advice anyway, but I wouldn't touch another man's wife. That's just me.
Alex: But he's an asshole, Phil!
Phil: And so are you but you're my brother and I love you.
Alex: I'm serious. The guy cheated on her. He's all wrong for her.
Phil: Yeah, but the difference between now and before is that *now* Rosie knows he cheated on her. She *knows* he's an asshole. But she's still with him. She must really love him, Alex. I'd say back off. Just my opinion but I'd say back off.
Alex: I don't agree with that, Phil.
Phil: Fine! You're your own man; do as you wish. I know you want the best for Rosie but you're being a bit selfish here. Look at it from Rosie's perspective. She's just found out that her asshole husband cheated on her, it must have been hard and for whatever reason she has decided to work it out and stay with him. Then just as she's getting used to that idea, in waltzes you, the best friend in shining armour, proclaiming your love for her. Do you want to confuse the poor woman even more? Look, if the marriage is a disaster, then it's a disaster and in a few months it'll end and Rosie will

come to you. Just don't be the prick that tries to break up her marriage. She'll never forgive you for that.

Alex: So you think I should let it happen naturally? Let her come to me when she's ready?

Phil: Something like that. I'm thinking of starting one of those shows that they have on telly. You know, one of those advice ones?

Alex: You'd have me on it every week, Phil. Thanks.

Phil: No probs. Now, while you go give someone a new heart, I'll go give a car a new engine. Off with you. Do what you have to do.

Alex has logged off.

Chapter 21

From Rosie
To Alex
Subject Letter?

Alex, I searched high and low in the kitchen for your letter, I left no stone unturned and Greg and Katie swear they didn't lay a finger on it so I don't know where else it could be. Are you sure you left it there? We were in such a rush to get you to the airport that morning, maybe you forgot. I checked the spare room you were sleeping in. All I found was a T-shirt you left behind, but it's mine now so you're not getting it back!

So what was in the letter? You didn't call me when I got home from work yesterday. You're really keeping me in suspense, Alex!

From Alex
To Rosie
Subject Letter

How are things with you and Greg? Are you happy?

From Rosie
To Alex
Subject Greg

Wow, talk about a change of subject. That's a very direct question.

OK, I know you can sense that he and I are going through a bad phase and you're worried. And I also know that you absolutely can't stand him, which is really difficult for me because I would really *love* you to see him how I see him.

Deep down, underneath *all* his layers of stupidity, he's a really good man. He may act out far too many selfish thoughts, says all the wrong things at all the wrong times but behind closed doors he's a best friend. I *understand* that he has idiotic tendencies and I can still love him for it. He may not be someone that you feel comfortable sitting next to at a dinner party, but for me, he's someone that I feel comfortable sharing my life with.

I know it's hard for other people to understand what he's like. All you see is an overprotective paranoid mess, but, God, does that make me feel safe and wanted. And his stupidity makes me laugh! We have a long way to go to being the perfect couple. We certainly don't live the fairy-tale marriage, he doesn't shower me with rose petals and fly me to Paris on weekends, but when I get my hair cut, he notices. When I dress up to go out at night, he compliments me. When I cry, he wipes my tears. When I feel lonely, he makes me feel loved. And who needs Paris, when you can get a hug?

Somewhere along the way, without me even noticing, I grew up, Alex. For once, I couldn't take advice from anyone around me about what I should or shouldn't do. I couldn't go running to Mum and Dad and I can't compare my marriage to anybody else's. We all follow our own rules. Taking Greg back was my decision to make and I wouldn't have if I hadn't felt that Greg, and most importantly that I, had learned something. I *know* that what has happened will never happen again and I really, really believe it. Because if I didn't feel so sure about our future, there's no way that I could go through with this.

I have a feeling that's what was in your letter,

Alex, but don't worry about me. I'm fine. Thank you, thank you, thank you, for caring about me so much. There aren't enough friends like you in the world.

From Alex
To Rosie
Subject Greg

And that's all I've ever wanted. For you to be happy.

Dear Stephanie,

So how's the new mummy? I hope you're coping well with everything. I know it's a big change – but a wonderful one. Are you getting any sleep? I hope you are. I always knew you would be a fabulous mother: you always knew just how to take care of your baby sister (and her baby!).

Thanks for all the gory details about his birth, by the way. You're even more wonderful than I thought you were! And no, I don't want Pierre to send over his video tape of the 'magical' experience. I recall what happens only too well . . . Remember they used to show us those videos at school when we were kids to scare us all out of having sex? Well, neither of us was obviously *that* scared. If they really wanted to deter us they should have just shown us the nappy-changing procedure. That would have sent us running off in our thousands to the convent.

You all looked so happy together in the photograph – like the perfect family. Is there such a thing any more, because if there is, my little unit was definitely not in the queue when the title was handed out.

I'm really not sure if I have done the right thing by taking Greg back. It's so difficult to know what decision to make. Christ, Stephanie, I was always the first person to shout out that if my husband was unfaithful there would be no way I would ever take him back in a million years. I always said that was the one thing I could never forgive (well, that *and* abandoning your unborn child) so what am I doing, taking him back?

What am I doing, allowing him to sleep beside me in bed? Why am I cooking him dinner and calling him when it's on the table? This is not what I said I would do. I need all my strength to stop myself from reaching out and slapping him across the face every time he smiles at me.

I thought that sending him packing would be the easiest thing in the world to do, but part of the reason for taking him back was because I couldn't face coping all by myself once more. I just kept imagining me and Katie alone again and I couldn't take it. Now I'm beginning to question my decision. Should I stay with him and learn to love him again, or should I leave and learn to survive on my own, to be independent? I just don't think I can face another tiny flat and one crappy wage for myself and Katie to survive on.

But if I could just *forgive* him . . . if I could just erase the image of his lips kissing someone else's every time he talks to me . . . His touch makes my skin crawl, and I feel so much hate for him it's unnerving. It's hard for my wounds to be healed by the very same man who put them there.

And he's so bloody gung-ho about everything. He's Mr Enthusiastic about us going to see a counsellor together, and he takes a few hours out of his day to talk to me, *really* talk to me. It's all just such a textbook solution of 'how to please your wife after shagging another woman'. Firstly you make an appointment to see the counsellor, being sure to make a song and a dance about the fact you're cancelling important meetings to go, then cook the dinner every day and fill the dishwasher, ask your wife a million times a day if she is OK and if there's anything you can do for her, do the weekly shopping, remembering to include thoughtful little gifts like her favourite chocolate cake or a book that you think she might like, spend a few hours during the day to sit in silence with your wife doing a summary of your day and then discussing in detail how you feel your relationship is going. Do this five hundred times a day, add water and then stir.

And the thing is, the Greg I married would never do all of those things. He would never bother replacing the empty toilet roll with the new one; he would never wash all the food off his plate before putting it in the dishwasher. Everything has changed. Even the small daily routines that make life so comfortable have changed.

If I could find the strength in me to leave him I would, but I'm stuck in this noncommittal limbo. I just want to make the right decision *now*. I don't want to be a bitter old woman in forty years' time, still making snide comments to Greg about what he's done. In order to make this marriage work I need to know in advance that I can, if not forget, then at least forgive. I need to know that the little bit of love I feel for him will grow again, back to the way it was. The one thing that's making me so much stronger is the fact that I know that he won't do this to me again. We've had too many long nights of tears and fights for either of us to want to go through it again.

If Alex lived in this country I would know what to do. All I need is back-up. He's the little angel that sits on my shoulder whispering in my ear, 'You can do it!' It's funny. I'm thirty years old now and I still feel like a little girl. I'm still looking around to check and see what other people are doing to make sure I'm not completely different; I'm still looking around for help, hoping for a quick nudge and a whisper of advice. But I can't seem to be able to catch anybody's eye. Nobody else around me seems to be looking around and wondering what to do. Why is it that I feel like I'm the only person who is confused and concerned about the choices I've made and where I'm headed? Everywhere I look, I see people just getting on with it. Maybe I should just follow suit.

Love,
Rosie

Dear Rosie,

Please do not torture yourself with questions that you don't know the answer to. You are going through a really difficult time right now but you *are* getting on with it, and you do it time and time again. Every knock back makes you stronger.

I can't tell you whether to stay with Greg or not – only you can make that decision – but all I can say is that if there's any love there at all then you should work at it. Every small thing grows when you nurture it, Rosie. Love is just the same. But if that is making you miserable then leave and find something else that brings you the happiness you *deserve* to feel.

Just listen to what your heart is saying and go with your gut instinct and it will lead you the right way. I'm sorry I have no great words of wisdom for you, Rosie, but at least you know that you're *not* alone; other people don't have all the answers to the questions. Sometimes we're all just as confused as you are.

Take care.

Love,

Stephanie

From Rosie
To Stephanie
Subject Silent heart

My heart isn't saying anything and my gut instinct is telling me to go to bed, curl up in a ball and cry.

Note to self:

Do not under any circumstances fall in love again.

Do not under any circumstances trust another human being.

Purchase special Kleenex with a protective balm containing calendula as will then not be mistaken for Rudolph's mother.

Eat.

Get out of bed.

And, for God's sake, stop crying.

From Mum
To Stephanie
Subject Is this working?

I think I've just about figured out this email thingy. Anyway, I just wanted to see if our plans are still in place for your father's sixtieth. He thinks it's a few quiet drinks with Jack and Pauline, so don't email me back on this address because he can read it too. Call me on my mobile. I really would love you to come. It would be nice for us all to be together again and I think it would be good for Rosie. I'm worried about her, she's so upset about Greg that she's lost so much weight. Your father is only two steps away from punching Greg in the face, which won't do anyone any good. Especially not your father's heart. Kevin isn't talking to Greg either, which isn't making life any easier for poor Rosie. However, the more family around her, the better.

Chapter 22

Ruby: OK, whatever diet you're on, I want my Gary to go on it.
Rosie: I'm not on a diet, Ruby.
Ruby: But you look sick and unhealthy; that's exactly the way I want him to look. Unattractive, stick thin, exhausted . . .
Rosie: Thanks.
Ruby: I just want to help, Rosie. Please tell me what's going on.
Rosie: There's nothing you can do to help; Greg and I just have to work this out on our own. Well, me, Greg and Ursula the wonderful marriage counsellor. We've all become such a great team it really makes me weep.
Ruby: How nice for you all. How is the wonderfully helpful Ursula?
Rosie: Wonderfully helpful. Yesterday she told me I had problems discussing my feelings.
Ruby: And?
Rosie: And I told her that made me feel angry and that she could go fuck herself.
Ruby: Well expressed. What did Greg say about that?
Rosie: Oh, wait for this; it's prize-winning. My amazingly intuitive husband thinks that I 'have problems communicating with and understanding Ursula'.
Ruby: Oh dear.
Rosie: Oh dear is right, so I suggested that Ursula and I attend relationship counselling in order to have good communication skills during my marriage counselling.

Ruby: So what did Greg say to that?

Rosie: Well, I couldn't quite hear what he said over the slamming of the car door. It can't have been very positive, though. His nose was flared and he was snarling at me. I'm also thinking of purchasing a larger bed so that there's room for Ursula. She may as well know absolutely everything about us. Maybe she could count how many times I fart during the night or something . . .

Ruby: Is it really that bad?

Rosie: I just can't see how counselling is helping *anything*. Ursula only makes us fight more by forcing us to discuss all the little things that bother us about each other. If we ever start to get along with one another, I can almost *see* her getting worried about her next month's rent. Last week we argued *for an hour* about how much I hate it when Greg leaves a milk moustache on his face purposely just to make me laugh, then when I don't laugh he follows me around the house, tapping me on the shoulder with it still on, until I do.

Yesterday we fought about how it annoys me when his mouth starts to twitch when I get something wrong. If I said the sky was yellow, his top lip would start to do this odd sort of Elvis twitch. It bugs the hell out of me that he can't just *let it go*. He *needs* to let me know in some form or another that I've gotten a piece of 'vital' information wrong. *Oh no*, the grass is green not pink! Oops-a-daisy, what a difference *that* statement makes to our life!

Next week I think I'll bring up the fact that he always wears the silly novelty socks his dear mother buys him. He thinks they're hilarious. Sometimes he just calls her up to tell her he's wearing them. Yellow socks with bloody pink polka dots and blue ones with red stripes. I'm sure his colleagues at the bank think they're absolutely *hilarious*. The wonderfully cool and hip bank manager that wears pink socks, ooh let's all get a mortgage from him! Plus when he sits down, his trousers lift and you can see them from a mile away . . .

Ruby: Wow, and they say you have problems expressing yourself . . .

Rosie: My point is that they just love going into such irrelevant detail. It shouldn't matter whether Greg kisses me on the forehead or on the cheek every morning; the fact should be whether he kisses me at all.

Ruby: So is this bizarre counselling having *any* kind of a positive effect on your marriage?

Rosie: Not really. I think Greg and I would do better without her.

Ruby: Do you think you could both break up with her?

Rosie: Well, we should, otherwise I can't see us still being together by the time Greg turns forty . . .

For My Husband
Happy 40th Birthday, sweetheart.
Lots of love,
Rosie

Happy 40th!
You are now uglier and older.
To Greg
From Katie and Toby

Dear Alex,

I think I'm going to organise a search party. Have you fallen off the edge of the earth? Are you still alive?

I called your mother the other day and she hasn't heard from you very much either. Is everything OK? Because if it's not, I have a right to know. You're supposed to confide in me because I'm your best friend and . . . it's the law. And if things are OK then contact me anyway. I need gossip. It's section two of the same law.

Everything here is as crazy and unpredictable as usual. Katie is eleven now, as you know. Thank you for her present. She is so grown up that she tells me that she doesn't need to inform me where she is going during the day or when she'll be coming home. Unimportant information like that, which a mother apparently doesn't need to know. I thought I had another few years left until she became a monster; saw me as being in the way, interfering and deliberately setting out to ruin her life. (OK, so *occasionally* I do.) The child wears lipstick now, Alex. Pink, glossy, glittery lipstick. She wears glitter on her eyes, glitter on her cheeks, and glitter in her hair; I am raising a disco ball for a daughter. I am now under instructions to knock on her bedroom door three times before I'm allowed to enter, just so she can identify the intruder. (I'm quite jealous because Toby only has to knock once. Greg, on the other hand, has to knock thirteen times. Poor Greg. Sometimes, most of the time, he loses count and Katie refuses to let him in for safety reasons. I mean really, who else could it be at her door knocking thirteen times, or at least *trying* to knock thirteen times?! Although I have become very clever and only knock once sometimes; that way she thinks I'm Toby and lets me in to see the inner sanctum of Katie Dunne. You would expect it to have black walls, no light, scary posters on the wall, but it's surprisingly neat and tidy.)

I'm not sure if she is still writing to you, but if she fills you in on any interesting aspects of her terribly busy and secretive life, please let me know. I'm her mother and that is *definitely* the law.

Everything at work is going well. I'm still at the hotel and I'm the longest-serving employee they have there now. Funny, isn't it? But – and there's always a 'but' with me – I know I've always been obsessed by the inner workings of hotels, but I kind of feel, 'Is this it? Is this all there is to it?' Doing what I'm doing is fine and all, but I'd like to try to move up a bit. I won't rest until I'm managing the Hilton hotels.

Greg says I'm mad. He says I would be crazy to move on from a job with good pay, a good boss and good hours. He thinks I have it easy here and I should be satisfied with that. I suppose he's right.

How is Josh? I would love to see him again. We must make arrangements to meet up soon. I don't want him not knowing who I am. We always promised our kids would be best friends, remember? I don't want to be one of those strangers to him that visit and, once in a blue moon, squeeze money into his hands. Although I very much liked that kind of people myself, I would personally rather mean more to Josh.

OK, so I think that's all my very exciting news for you for now. Write to me, ring me, email me or fly over and visit me. Or you could do all of those things. Just do anything to let me know that you're still walking the earth.

Miss you.

Love,

Rosie

Dear Rosie,

Just to let you know I'm still alive – just about. Sally seems to be sucking all the life out of me these days. We're finalising the divorce . . . it's a nightmare.

So that's what's going on with me. Must go now; have to stick my hands in someone's chest.

Give my love to Katie.

Alex

From Rosie
To Stephanie
Subject Re: Gossip!

Thanks for your letter, Steph. I am absolutely fine, thank you. Everyone is well and healthy; we have no complaints. I feel I've made the right decision about Greg, and from just listening to Alex about the divorce procedure I'm glad Greg and I didn't take that route. At least Sally and Josh haven't moved far from Alex so he can make arrangements to see Josh quite regularly.

My worst nightmare would be to lose Katie. I don't know what I would do. She may watch MTV all day, blare music from her room, ruin my days off by making me go into school to fight with Miss Big Nose Smelly Breath Casey, leave glitter all over the couches and carpets, worry me to death when she's one minute late for her nine o'clock curfew, but she's the most important thing to me in my life. She comes first all of the time. I'm so glad Alex missed the debs and I'm so glad that Brian the Whine was such a boring person. The men in my life may have let me down but the little girl in my life makes up for it every single day.

Dear Ms Rosie Dunne,

I was hoping you would be free on Monday the 16th at 9 a.m. to meet with me at the school. Toby Flynn's parents will also be in attendance. It is regarding the recent results of the summer maths exam. It appears that Katie and Toby have the same answers for all the questions. What jumped out at me was the fact that the majority of these answers are wrong. I have discussed this with Katie and Toby and they insist it is coincidental.

Cheating, as you well know, is considered to be a very serious offence at St Patrick's Primary School. I seem to have a case of déjà vu, Rosie . . . Please ring to confirm your attendance.

Miss Casey

Chapter 23

From Rosie
To Alex
Subject Grown-ups

What are the two of us like? I was going to say who knew we'd be going through so much 'grown-up stuff', but I don't consider you going through a divorce and me trying to pick up the pieces of my marriage is necessarily grown up. I think we both had it pretty much sussed when we were playing cops and robbers in the back garden. It's all been down hill from there!

The weather has been beautiful over here for the past few weeks. I love June in Dublin. The grey buildings seem less grey, the unhappy faces seem brighter. It is so hot here at work, though. The entire front of the hotel building is built from glass and it feels like we're working in a greenhouse on days like today. It's such a contrast to our winter months when the sound of the fat raindrops hitting off the glass echoes around the quiet foyer. It's a pretty sound but sometimes the hailstones are so loud and forceful, threatening to smash through the glass. Right now I'm staring up at a rich blue sky dotted with white candy-floss grazing sheep. It is beautiful.

Convertible sports cars have their tops down and music is blaring, businessmen have been casually strolling down the street past the hotel, with their jackets slung over their shoulders and their shirt-sleeves rolled up, reluctant to get back to the office.

The college students have all seemingly decided to call off their plans to attend lectures to flake out in large circles in the park. The ducks are gathering by the edge of the pond, glad they won't have to search for their own food today. Mounds of soggy uneaten bread float on the surface of the water, waiting to be pecked at.

A flirting couple chase each other around the large fountain, catching its cool spray on their bare arms and legs in order to cool themselves. Couples in love stretch out together on the grass and gaze longingly into each other's eyes. Children use the playground while their parents relax in the sun, keeping one eye shut and one eye lazily focused on their excited offspring, who squeal with delight.

Shop owners stand at the entrance doors to their empty shops, watching the world go by. Office workers gaze dreamily out of the windows from high up in their clammy, stuffy offices, enviously watching the city throb with excitement.

The sound of laughter is in the air, everyone is full of smiles, there's a bounce in their step. The veranda of the hotel is busy with people taking drinks out in the sun: Long Island iced tea, gin and tonic, tangy orange with crushed ice, lime-green concoctions, fruity cocktails and bowls of ice cream. Clothes are being discarded and hung on the backs of chairs.

Cleaning ladies hum softly to themselves and smile while polishing the brass, feeling the sun's rays streaming down on to their faces. Days like this don't come often and you can tell everyone wishes they did.

And I sit here and think of you. I send you my love.

From Alex
To Rosie
Subject Happy!

You sounded happy and very poetic! I've just

returned from a weekend with Josh. He's a feisty little thing now, Rosie. He's running around trying to grab anything and everything from left, right and centre. I was almost afraid to blink in case the room came crashing down around me. But he's in great form and I feel so happy and rejuvenated after the weekend. Seeing him always lights me up, as if a switch is flicked somewhere in my body. I could watch him for ever. Watch how he learns, how he teaches himself, how he eventually finds a way to do things without help from anyone. Josh takes chances; he's braver than I am. He always takes that extra step when he nos he shouldn't. He does it anyway and he learns. I think we adults have a lot to learn from that. Perhaps to be not so afraid and oversensible about reaching for goals.

So I am taking Josh's advice. An eminent surgeon is giving a talk during the week. It's a few days of seminars about a new heart procedure he has developed. I'm going to try and meet him – me along with the other thousand or so wannabe heart surgeons who will be there. Rumour has it he's from Ireland and has moved over here to develop his studies further – and needs some help.

Cross your fingers and pray for a miracle.

From Rosie
To Alex
Subject Mysterious meeting

I have a mysterious meeting with Bill, my boss, next week. I have no idea what it's about, but I'm quite nervous about it. He flew over yesterday in a not-so-good mood and has had a series of secret meetings all day. Lots of suspicious-looking people, dressed in dark suits, have been arriving to talk to him on the hour every hour. I have an awful feeling in the pit of my stomach.

What makes it even worse is the fact that his brother, Bob, is flying over tomorrow morning. They only ever get together to do the hiring and firing. I think that's all Bob does, really. Bill does all the work on their hotels around the world and Bob just spends his share of the money on houses, cars, holidays and women, so I hear. Why is it that people always put women in the same category as cars and holidays, as though we're prizes on a game show? If I had millions you'd hardly hear people saying, 'Jesus, would ya look at that Rosie Dunne. All she does is spend her money on shoes, clothes and men.' Doesn't sound quite right, does it?

I hope they don't fire me. I don't know what I would do. I think I would sleep with him to keep working here. That's how much I love it. Or how scared I am about having to search for a job elsewhere. Or how desperate I am to sleep with a man other than Greg for a change. I love him but, bless him, he's a sucker for routine.

Better go and look like I'm really busy so that they will have absolutely no grounds to fire me. Cross your fingers for me, and I'll cross mine for you.

From Alex
To Rosie
Subject Re: Mysterious meeting

Don't worry, it will all be fine! They have no reason to fire you! (Have they?) You have done nothing wrong since the day you started working there. In fact, you've hardly even called in sick! Everything will be fine. Just about to leave the apartment now to go to seminar. Good luck to the both of us!

From Rosie
To Alex
Subject Re: Re: Mysterious meeting.

You're right. They can't fire me. I'm just being stupid. I am a great employee. They have no reason to. At least no reasons that they know of. I mean, they could never find out about the time I brought Ruby up to show her the penthouse suite. And even if they do know that, there's no way that they could know that we ordered room service and stayed the night. Could they?

Maybe it was the missing bathrobes that they noticed. But they were so cosy and I had to take one home . . .

Or maybe it was the empty mini bar. But I distinctly remember asking Peter to restock the fridge and he owed me one after I gave his parents a Valentine's Day discount in the middle of May. So it can't be that . . . Oh God, this is killing me. I really don't want to go back to working for Randy Andy, and I don't think I have the energy for sending CVs out again. Nor the stress of another job interview.

They only want to meet with me. But Bill didn't smile at me when he said it and his eyes weren't as twinkly as usual. What do you think that means? Oh my God, the new skinny girl has a meeting too today. She's the worst worker ever. She's called in sick more times than she's been in. Probably because she never eats. Lunch breaks are wasted on her. She just stares across the table at your plate with a horrible face on her, as though food is the devil, and she sips on a bottle of water. Then halfway through her bottle she gets full, tightens the lid and leaves it behind.

I'd better start job-hunting, I think.

From Alex
To Rosie
Subject Chill out!

For Christ sake, Rosie Dunne, I love you with all my heart but you need to chill out!

You have an instant message from: RUBY.
Ruby: Oooh, so he loves you with all his heart, does he?

Rosie: Oh, stop reading my emails, Ruby.
Ruby: Well, get a less obvious password, 'Buttercup'. You two are being all flirty with each other lately.
Rosie: No we aren't! How on earth are we being flirty??!
Ruby: You know yourself.
Rosie: Oh please, I thought you were going to make a good point for once in your life.
Ruby: I have one and you know it.
Rosie: We're just getting along like we used to do, that's all. Alex has perked himself up. I think he's happy again.
Ruby: Because he's in lurve . . .
Rosie: He is not in love. Well, not with me, anyway.
Ruby: Oh, sorry, I was just misguided by the fact that he said in his email that he 'loved you with all his heart'.
Rosie: As a friend loves a friend, Ruby.
Ruby: You're my friend and I do not love you with all my heart. Hell, I hardly love Teddy with all my heart.
Rosie: OK then, Alex and I are madly in love and we're going to run away and have a passionate love affair.
Ruby: You see? It doesn't hurt to admit it, does it?
Rosie: Hold on, Ruby.
[Rosie is away from her computer.]
Rosie: Oh my God, celery stick just got back from meeting with Bill and Bob and she's crying her eyes out. They just fired her. I'm next. Shit. I better go. Shit. Shit. Shit.
Rosie has logged off.

Chapter 24

Kevin,

Hi, son. I know I'm not one to write letters, but I'm not sure if you gave your mother and me the correct phone number of the staff barracks. Whenever I call it just keeps on ringing and ringing and that's at all hours of the day and night. You either gave us the wrong number, there's something wrong with your phone, or everybody is working so hard they're not there to answer my calls. I wouldn't like the idea of having to share a phone with thirty staff members. Couldn't you get one of those mobile phones? Then maybe your family could get in touch with you every once in a while.

I hope you're not doing anything daft down there. Rosie really stuck her neck out to get you that job in the kitchen. Don't mess it up like all those other ones you had. This is an opportunity for you now to get a good start in your life. Your old man is sixty now; I won't be around for ever for you to rely on, you know!

It's a shame you couldn't make it home for my retirement party. The company invited the entire family. They really treated us well for the night – treated me well for over thirty-five years, in fact. Stephanie, Pierre and Jean-Louis made it over from France. Rosie, Greg and young Katie were there too. It was a good night. I'm not picking on you, son – just wished you had been there too, that's all. It was an emotional night all the same. If you had been there you would have seen your old man cry.

It's funny how life goes. I spent forty years working for them, remember my first day like it was yesterday.

I was just fresh out of school, all eager to please. Wanted to start making money so that I could propose to your mother and buy us a house. In my first week of work we held a party in the office for one of the old guys retiring. I didn't give much notice to him. People were making speeches, giving him gifts, talking about old times. But all I cared about was the fact that they were making me stay late at work, unpaid, when I wanted to get out of there to propose to your mother. The old guy had been there all his working life, he had tears in his eyes, was really upset about leaving, took him a lifetime to make the speech. I thought he would never shut up so I could leave. I had the engagement ring in my pocket. Kept sticking my hand in my trousers to make sure the velvet box was still there. I couldn't wait for that guy to finish talking.

Billy Rogers was his name.

He wanted to take me aside and explain a few things to me about the company before he left, seeing as I was a new boy. I didn't listen to a word he had to say. He talked and talked like he never had any intentions of leaving the damn office. I rushed him. The company wasn't that important to me then.

He kept on coming back to visit us in the office every week. Would hang around our desks, annoying all the new guys, some of the old guys too, giving advice and checking up on things that were no longer his business. We just wanted to do our jobs. He lived and breathed for that place. We all told him to find himself a hobby. Keep himself busy. Thought we were helping him. Only suggested it out of the goodness of our hearts – that and the fact he was really starting to get up his pals' noses. He died a few weeks later. Had a heart attack on the golf course. He was taking our advice and having his first lesson.

I hadn't thought about Billy Rogers for almost thirty years. Had completely forgotten about him, to be honest. But that night and since I haven't been able to get the thought of Billy Rogers out of my head. Looking around with tears in my eyes, listening to speeches, accepting gifts, catching the new guys sneakily glimpse at their watches, wondering when they could slip away to get home to their girlfriends or new wives or children or whoever . . . I couldn't help but think about all the guys who came through those office doors. Thought about the guys who started off on the same day as me: Colin Quinn and Tom McGuire, guys who never made it to retirement like me. I suppose that's what life's about. People come and go.

So there are no more early mornings for me. I caught up on a whole load of sleep I never even thought I needed. The garden is spotless, everything in the house that was once broken is now fixed. I've played golf three times this week, visited Rosie twice, took Katie and Toby out for the day, and I still feel like hopping into my car, speeding down to the office and teaching the rookies a thing or two about how to do business. But they won't care; they want and need to learn it for themselves.

So I thought I would join the Dunne women in writing. It seems that's all they do. Keeps the phone bills down, I suppose. Let me know how things are going for you, son.

Did you hear about our Rosie's job?

From Dad

From Kevin
To Stephanie
Subject Dad

How are things? I just got a letter from Dad today. Dad writing a letter is weird in itself but what he was writing was even more bizarre. Is he OK? He was talking about some guy called Billy Rogers who died over thirty-five years ago. Make sure he's not losing it. Anyway, it was good to hear from him but he sounded like another man altogether. Not necessarily a bad thing. Sorry I wasn't there for his retirement do. Should have made more of an effort to be there.

Tell Pierre and Jean-Louis I was asking for them. Tell Pierre I'll beat his culinary skills hands down next time I see him! Dad mentioned something about Rosie's job? What has she done now?

From Stephanie
To Mum
Subject Kevin and Dad

Something must be in the water over there in Ireland because I just received an email from your son, my little brother Kevin – yes, Kevin, the guy who never keeps in touch with family unless he needs to borrow money. He was writing to tell me that Dad had written to him and he was worried! Did you even know that Dad could lick a stamp?

Kevin mentioned that Dad was talking about Billy Rogers again. He told me about him too. Is he OK? I'm assuming he is just feeling very contemplative now that he has entered a new era in his life. Now at least he has *time* to think. The both of you have worked so hard all your lives. Now Kevin your baby is gone, Rosie and Katie are gone, I'm gone and the house is finally all yours. I suppose I can understand how it's difficult for Dad to get his head round it. You were both used to a house full of screaming kids and bickering teenagers. When we finally grew up along came a crying baby and you were so good to help Rosie out. I know it was hard for you financially too. Now it's time to treat yourselves.

Kevin mentioned something about Rosie's job; I don't want to call her until I've heard from you about it. She was so worried that she was going to lose it. Let me know.

From Mum
To Stephanie
Subject Re: Kevin and Dad

You're absolutely right. I think your father has a lot

of thinking to do and enough time in the day to do it now. I love having him home! He's not rushing off all the time or thinking about a problem at work that needs to be solved while I'm trying to have a conversation with him. It's like he's all here with me now – body and mind. I felt that way too when I left my job but I suppose it was slightly different for me. I already went part time at work when Katie was born to help Rosie cope. It didn't seem like such a drastic change for me when I eventually left the job completely. But your father is trying to find himself again.

I'm amazed you didn't hear about Rosie's job. I thought you would have been one of the first people she'd have told (apart from Alex, of course), but perhaps she wasn't ready to discuss it yet. That girl has me so worried at times. Honestly, she kept telling me all week that she was going to lose her job, then finally she calls me to tell me that she had a meeting with her bosses and she's got a promotion!

Oh, Stephanie, we were so thrilled for her! I'm surprised she hasn't told you the good news yet, but it was only a few days ago. Anyway, I'll let her tell you herself or else I'll be in trouble for spoiling the surprise. I'd better go now; your father's calling me. We're about to go down to the garden centre. If he plants any more flowers or trees in that garden, we'll have to apply for planning permission for a jungle!

Take care, love, and hugs and kisses to baby Jean-Louis from Grandma and Granddad!

Chapter 25

From Stephanie
To Rosie
Subject Job promotion!

I know you're at work so I won't ring you. Received a letter from Mum today. What's this I hear about a job promotion? Email me ASAP!

From Rosie
To Stephanie
Subject Job promotion

Can't believe Mum opened her big mouth! YES!! The news is true and I'm so excited to get started. The job title is 'Hotel Host', and before you get over-excited like our beloved parents did, it's not the manager's job. I will be the primary source of information for guests to ensure maximum client satisfaction (or so they tell me . . .)!

It was the surprise of *all* surprises. I literally had to *drag* my body into the long conference room where I had my first interview years ago, with my heart banging and my legs feeling like jelly. My body language was all wrong, my palms were sweaty, my knees were knocking and I just kept having visions of being forced to go back to work for Randy Andy until we both became old-age pensioners. I really had convinced myself that Bill and Bob Lake were going to ask me to quietly and calmly return to my desk, gather my belongings, leave the premises and never return.

But they were so generous to me. They pumped me full of confidence as they went through what the job would entail. They said that they were delighted with my 'performance' within the hotel over the past few years (and I really hope they weren't referring to the time when I lay across the piano and sang Barbra Streisand songs after all the residents had gone to bed. Well, you can't blame a girl for trying to live out a fantasy when she can . . .). There they were, telling me I had an abundance of charm and confidence, when deep down I was just waiting for the moment they would break into a smile, look at me as though I was a fool for believing them before telling me the promotion was all a joke. I kept looking round for the hidden camera.

But it seems that I will be moving to a new hotel that's yet to be built (hence all the secret meetings with men and women in dark suits, leather briefcases, gelled hair and no smiles, who have been masquerading through the hotel lobby; it was like there was some sort of bizarre *Matrix*-y thing going on). But if they *are* serious, then my job is to be solely responsible for the running of all aspects of the resort and I'll have to liaise with head office and provide weekly reports. I've never had to 'liaise' before. It sounds sexy and dangerous. Any job that tells me that I have to 'liaise' with the big boys in head office is a winner to me. I can picture myself all dolled up in a cocktail dress at a work 'do' standing in a circle with the other 'suits', speaking in hushed tones about graphs and pie charts and financial reports. If people ask us what we're doing, I can say dismissively, 'Oh, don't mind us, we're just liaising . . .'

Apparently I have a flair for organising and have good communication skills. Anyone who has seen me rushing to get all my Christmas shopping done in the last hour on Christmas Eve knows the truth. But we all have our different ways of seeing things.

From Alex
To Rosie
Subject Congratulations!

I am so proud of you! If I was there, I would twirl you around and give you a great big sloppy kiss! You see, Rosie, things *can* happen for you, all you need is a lot more faith and self-belief and to stop being so negative all the time!

So where is the new hotel? Tell me all.

From Rosie
To Alex
Subject Job promotion

Well, I'm not quite sure of the location of the hotel just yet but I have a sneaky suspicion it's along the coast. Can you believe that I will finally get to work in a hotel by the sea? It will take longer to commute to, but it's worth it to be able to leave the city behind for a few hours every day. I should be out there within the next few months. The resort they are referring to is based around the new eighteen-hole golf course they're building. There will be a gym and pool and more leisure facilities, unlike here, which is in the heart of the city and has nothing but bedrooms, a tiny gym and restaurants. I'm a bit hazy on all the details because they haven't fully informed me of everything yet. They just asked me if I was interested in this new job and of course I couldn't turn it down!

But this entire experience has taught me something. It's taught me that I'm ready to move on from this job. I'm ready to accept a new challenge and, without having any sort of game plan at all, I seem to be moving closer and closer towards my dream. Whoever thought those childhood dreams of running a hotel weren't quite beyond my grasp after all? It's funny because when you're a child, you believe you can be anything you want to be, go wherever you want to go. There are no limits. You *expect* the unexpected, you *believe* in magic. Then you grow older and that innocence is shattered. The reality of *life* gets in the way and you're hit by the realisation that you can't be *all* you wanted to be, that you just might have to settle for a little bit less.

Why do we stop believing in ourselves? Why do we let facts and figures and anything but dreams rule our lives?

But now my mind is changed again. Nothing is impossible, Alex. It was there all the time. I just wasn't reaching out far enough, that's all.

Nothing is impossible. Not a bad statement to come from the pen (or rather keyboard!) of a cynic. Thank you for your faith in me, Alex. I would love to return that hug and kiss to you now! But then again, perhaps *some* things just might be beyond our reach after all.

From Alex
To Rosie
Subject Dreams

Again, Rosie, you're just not stretching far enough. I'm right here. Always have been, always will be.

Note to self:

Dream, dream, dream, Rosie Dunne!

You have an instant message from: RUBY.

Ruby: What on earth is Alex's last message to you supposed to mean?

Rosie: For God's sake, Ruby, *stop* reading my emails!

Ruby: Sorry, I can't help it, but I can assure you that I will continue to read them until you decide to change your password *and* until I find a job that interests me at all.

Rosie: Well, it looks like I'll be changing my password then . . .

Ruby: Ha ha. So come on, I've seen it now, what's he

talking about? What's this about stretching far enough?

Rosie: What do you think it means?

Ruby: I'm asking you and I asked first.

Rosie: Oh, Ruby, don't be so childish. It's simply a friend telling me that he will always be there for me, no matter what, and that he's not that far away at all from me and all I have to do is call and he'll be here.

Ruby: Oh, right, OK.

Rosie: There you go again, Ruby, with the sarcasm! What's your theory now then? I suppose you think it's his secret way of telling me that he loves me and that he will always be there for me and if I just reached out to him then he would drop everything, his new life in Boston, his family life, his great big amazing job, to come rescue me, whisk me away to live in a beach house in . . . oh, I don't know . . . Hawaii, where we would live happily ever after away from all the stresses and complications of the world? I suppose that's what you would interpret it as. You and your sick mind always twisting things, trying to make out as though the two of us—

Ruby: No, Rosie, I really meant 'oh, OK'. That's fine, I believe you.

Rosie: Oh.

Ruby: Are you OK with that?

Rosie: Yeah, sure. I just thought you might have read into it a bit more, like you usually do, that's all.

Ruby: No, that's OK. I believe that he meant it in a supportive friend kind of way.

Rosie: Oh . . . OK.

Ruby: Why, did you *want* it to mean something else?

Rosie: *God no*, I was just expecting you to go on a rant, that's all . . .

Ruby: So you're not disappointed? You're OK with him being your friend?

Rosie: No, why should I be disappointed? That's all he ever was to me! I'm perfectly happy!

Ruby: And you don't want to be rescued and whisked off to Hawaii?
Rosie: Of *course* not! That would be . . . *awful*!
Ruby: Good then . . .
Rosie: Yep, it's great . . . everything's great . . .
Ruby: Good.
Rosie: And the new job will make everything better!
Ruby: Good.
Rosie: And my marriage has been saved and I truly believe Greg loves me more than ever . . .
Ruby: Good.
Rosie: And I'm going to be paid a lot more than before, which is good. They say money can't buy happiness but I'm a fickle person, Ruby . . . I can get that new coat I saw in the Ilac Centre yesterday . . . I'm thrilled!
Ruby: Good.
Rosie: Absolutely! So anyway, I'm going to head off now, got a bit of work to do . . .
Ruby: That's really great, Rosie . . .
Rosie has logged off.

From Rosie
To Stephanie
Subject It's a wonderful life!

Life is wonderful, life is great! I have a good job, just got promoted to an even better one. I have a daughter who talks to me, a husband that doesn't. Only joking! Have a husband who loves me! I have a wonderfully supportive family – mum, dad, brother and sister. I've two brilliant best friends who would do anything for me and who I love with all my heart. I remember telling you years ago just before I started my new job at reception that phase two of my life was beginning. Well, this appears to be the beginning of phase three! Things are looking up for me and I am so happy! I am in a deliriously giddy mood today, high on the excitement of life, I suppose!

From Ruby
To Rosie
Subject Cork?

What do you mean, the bloody hotel is being built down in Cork? And they only tell you now? Are you moving down to *Cork*? I thought you said it was along *the coast of Dublin*? Did they think that piece of information was *irrelevant* to you? For Christsake, Rosie, how are you going to drag your family down to *the other side of the country*?

Do you even want to move? Oh my God, I think I'm going to have a heart attack! Email me back ASAP!!!

From Rosie
To Ruby
Subject Re: Cork?

Oh, Ruby, right now I have a headache. I don't know what to do. I know that I want this job but there are two other people to think about. I'll have to have a chat with Katie and Greg about it tonight. Pray for me! Please God, if you're listening and not busy sprinkling gold dust on all the lucky people of the world, please do me this favour and brainwash my family into thinking of what I want for once. I thank you for your time and patience. You can continue gold-dust sprinkling now.

From Ruby
To Rosie
Subject God

Hello, Rosie, this is God. Sorry to bring you bad news but life doesn't work like that. You must be honest with your family and try to convince them yourself. Tell them of your lifelong dream to take the job that you have been offered and if they are unselfish people they will understand your desire to move to Cork. My popcorn's ready so I'd better leave. I'm already missing the first of this evening's entertainment. I'm watching your friend Ruby's life tonight. Good luck with the family.

Dear Mum & Greg,

Don't worry about us, Mum. Me and Toby will be OK. We have run away because we don't want to be apart from each other. He is my best friend and I don't want to move to Cork.

Love,

Katie and Toby

From Rosie
To Ruby
Subject God

I couldn't help noticing that God logged on under your name yesterday. If you see him around please tell him that if he's looking for drama, he should tune into my family today.

Note to self:

Stop dreaming, Rosie Dunne.

PART THREE

Chapter 26

Dear Alex,

I was so happy when I finally got round to shutting the door on this horrible day. 'It's only a job,' Greg said. Well, if a job is so unimportant then why is he so adamantly refusing to leave his own? It's not *only* a job, though. So they offered me a promotion, but with it they offered me confidence and a little bit of self-belief. To believe that my hard work was being rewarded and I was seen as competent and smart.

But this time I wasn't even given the choice to screw it up myself. That decision was made *for* me. Katie won't leave Toby and I'm not quite hating Greg enough to storm off to Cork in a huff on my own. Although, I'm pretty close to it. God, does that man make my blood boil! Everything is always so black and white to him.

In his opinion, he has a great job here that pays well and I have a good job that pays OK. Why on earth would he want to move to a city where his wife will have a brilliant job and earn great money? Oh, of course, I forgot, they don't have any banks in Cork so there's no way he could ever find a job or be transferred. People just save money under their beds in shoe boxes there.

Plus everything (well, a lot of things, like houses for one) is cheaper down there than it is here. Katie would be able to *begin* her first year of secondary school in a perfectly good school so it's not as if she's being taken out of school midway here. It could all be so perfect.

On the other hand, I can honestly say that her

friendship with Toby is possibly the most important thing to her. He's a great supportive force in her life; he makes her happy and keeps the innocence in her eyes. Children need close friends to help them grow up, to discover things about themselves and about life. They also need close friends to keep them sane, and due to Katie's little disappearing act I now know that her being without Toby, at this stage of her life anyway, would lead to incredible insanity.

Do you realise that they had actually booked their flights to you over the internet with Greg's credit card? They were in the queue to check in at the airport when the gardaí found them! I can just picture them: a little girl with jet-black hair and vanilla skin with no luggage except for a cuddly teddy-bear bag on her back. Beside her, a little boy with messy blond curls, in charge of the tickets and passport details. A miniature honeymoon couple. Someday I will look back on this experience and laugh. After I get over the shock, horror, bitterness and resentment. Probably in my next lifetime.

So I can't accept the job of my dreams because my family won't move with me. Big deal. It's not as though I bend over backwards for them. It's not as though I arrange my life to revolve around them. It's not as though I come home from work tired and still have dinner on the table for them, it's not as though I perform wonderful supportive wifely chores when there's a million other things I could be doing. It's not as though I defend my daughter at school, constantly fighting with the teachers about how she is not Satan's daughter. It's not as though I tolerate Greg's mother for dinner every Sunday and listen to her whinge about how the food isn't cooked right, about my hair, about the way I dress, about the way I have chosen to raise Katie and then have to sit through hours of reruns of her favourite soaps. It's not as though I'm always the one to take a day off work when Katie is sick or drop whatever plans I've made to help people out.

Just as well I don't do any of those things.

But who cares? I get burned toast and milky tea one

morning once a year on Mother's Day as thanks. And that should make up for it, shouldn't it? Greg always tells me I'm forever chasing rainbows. Maybe I should stop now.

Love,
Rosie

From Alex
To Rosie
Subject Rosie Dunne!

I hate to see you miss out on another opportunity. Isn't there anything you can do to convince whatshis-name?

From Rosie
To Alex
Subject Family

Thanks, Alex, but no. I can't force my family to leave their home if they don't want to. They're important to me.

I have to respect Greg's wishes; I don't think I would be too happy about moving away from my job and friends if he had to move due to work. I can't live my life pretending it's just me in the world. But how much easier it would be! Anyway, it's just another missed opportunity.

So enough about me – how are all those lectures going? Find out who Mr Fantastic Surgeon is yet?

Thanks for your support, as always.

From Katie
To Toby
Subject Grounded!

I can't believe we are grounded! *And* on our summer holidays! Our parents didn't have to go all psycho about it! It's not like we ended up going anywhere – we were less than an hour away from home. Hardly worth locking us in our houses for two weeks. I told you we should have taken a ferry over to France or something. In the films, the first places the gardaí always check are the airports. That was where we made our mistake. I've been looking into this and we should have gone to Bus Arás, and got a coach to Rosslare. Next time that's what we'll do.

What do you think Alex would have done when we arrived on his doorstep? Mum says he's not even home, that he's away at some meetings or something, but I think she's just lying to try to prove that our plan wouldn't have worked. I don't think he would have been mad. Alex is cool. But he probably would have called Mum and she would have sent ten million squad cars and rescue helicopters over to get us.

Poor Mum. I'm glad we're not moving away but I feel sorry for her. She was so excited about doing that job and now she's back stuck at that desk where she's been working for years. I feel kinda guilty. I no she would have made me go anyway if Greg had said yeah but I still feel bad for her. She's just wandering around the house looking real sad and she keeps on sighing as though she's real bored and doesn't no what to do next. Just like us on Sundays. She gets up from one couch and moves to another room to sit in another chair. Then she gets up again and moves room, and stares out the window for *ages*, sighs about three million times, moves to another room, in, out, in, out . . . she makes me dizzy just watching her. Sometimes I just follow her around, seeing as I'm not supposed to be allowed in the outside world and I've nothing better to do.

Yesterday I started following her again and she started to walk faster and faster, by the end of it I was chasing her round the house and it was so funny. She opened the front door and ran outside in her dressing gown, teasing me because I couldn't go outside (being grounded and all). But I ran out anyway and the two of us sprinted round the block in our night clothes, me in my blue pyjamas with the pink hearts and Mum in her yellow dressing gown! Everyone was staring at us but it was fun. We ran to Birdie's shop on the corner and Mum treated me to some strawberry ice cream, the highlight of my day. Birdie didn't look too impressed at the sight of us, especially seeing as Mum wasn't wearing anything under her dressing gown, but she flashed her legs at old Mr Fanning, who was there to buy his morning paper. He looked like he was gonna have a heart attack. So at least I got to go outside for a little while.

As soon as we got back inside she continued just walking around the house as if she was in a museum or something. Greg says she's got a feather up her arse. Mum said she'd love to shove a pole up his. He didn't say much for the rest of the day.

Toby, if we had made it to the top of that queue in the airport, do you think we would have gotten on the plane? I'm not sure if I could have left Mum, but I don't think she would believe that now if I told her. She would probably just think I was trying to get out of being grounded, *although* that's not a bad idea. OK, I gotta go!

Email me back before I die of boredom!

From Alex
To Rosie
Subject Family duties!

You and your 'duties' to your family. I just don't want you to be the only person following the rules, that's all.
The lectures are going great. You will never believe who the surgeon is! Your very favourite man – Reginald Williams.

From Rosie
To Alex
Subject Reginald Williams!

Pass me a bucket while I puke. You mean Slutty Bethany's father? Have they come back from the evil past to haunt us??!!

From Alex
To Rosie
Subject Re: Reginald Williams

It's OK, Rosie, take deep breaths! He's not so bad. A very intelligent man.

From Rosie
To Alex
Subject Re: Reginald Williams

What does he do now, hypnotism? Has he been tampering with your brain? So that's why he's been all over the papers here. I have refused to read them out of protest for him and his family's existence. Oh my God – Reginald Williams! So do you think you're in with a chance to be one of the 'chosen few' to work with him, seeing as you were an almost-son-in-law? There's nothing like a bit of nepotism to keep the world a just and equal place.

From Alex
To Rosie
Subject Nepotism!

I think the chances of that happening are fairly slim. I think I sealed my own doom when I dumped his favourite and only daughter!

From Rosie
To Alex
Subject Slutty Bethany

Oh, I don't know about sealing your doom. I think it may have been the *best* move you have ever made.

Come to think of it, I haven't seen Slutty Bethany for about ten years! What is she up to, I wonder. Probably living in a mansion in the hills, counting diamonds and evilly laughing . . .

From	Rosie
To	Stephanie
Subject	Best friends stay with you for ever

Oh, wise and wonderful sister Stephanie, you were right! When I was seventeen you told me that girlfriends come and go but best friends stay with you for ever. I found myself saying today, 'I wonder what Slutty Bethany is doing these days . . .' The exact statement I never wanted Alex to have to say about me. I didn't believe you at the time but I sure do now!! Thanks, Steph. Best friends do stay with you for ever!

Chapter 27

You have an instant message from: RUBY.

Ruby: So you're still here, then?

Rosie: Oh, your words of support are like a breath of fresh air. Yes, I am still here.

Ruby: So you found your daughter, then?

Rosie: Yes, we have her trained to come running back after three whistles and a clap of the hands.

Ruby: Impressive . . .

Rosie: I reminded myself that Alex and I ran off together a few times when we were younger. The first time we ran away because Alex's parents refused to let him go to some theme park to visit Captain Tornado for the weekend. I now understand his parents' point of view because, well, the theme park was in Australia . . . in a cartoon. Anyway, we must only have been about five or six. We packed our school bags and ran away. We literally *ran* away. We thought that was what we were supposed to do, *run* down the road, which was extremely inconspicuous, of course.

We spent the entire day roaming streets we had never been to before, looking at houses and wondering if the pocket money we had saved up that week was enough to buy a house of our own. We even looked at houses that weren't for sale. We hadn't quite grasped that concept yet. As soon as it got dark the two of us became bored with our freedom and a little scared too. Eventually we decided to head back home to see if our protests had made a difference to the Captain Tornado situation. Our parents hadn't even noticed we'd been gone. Alex's parents thought we were at my house and my parents thought we were at Alex's.

I don't know if Katie would have gotten on that plane had she been given the opportunity. I would like to think that I've done a good enough job as a mother for her to know that running away isn't a way to solve anything. You can run and run as fast and as far as you like, but the truth is, wherever you run, there you are. In fact, she tried to tell me today that she loved me with all her heart and that she could never leave me. I thought I sensed sincerity in her eyes and voice but as soon as I reached out to cuddle her, her face brightened and she asked if that meant she didn't have to be grounded any more. I'm afraid she's a chancer like her father.

Ever run away from home when you were a child?

Ruby: No. But my ex-husband ran away from home with a child half his age, if that's any help to you.

Rosie: Right . . . well no, it's not, but thanks for sharing it with me all the same.

Ruby: No problem.

Rosie: So what are you doing for your fortieth, Ruby? It's coming up soon.

Ruby: I'm going to break up with Teddy.

Rosie: No! You can't! You and Teddy are an institution!

Ruby: Ha! That's my point. OK, I mightn't then. I was just thinking of new and exciting ways to change my life. Funnily enough, that was the first one that jumped into my head.

Rosie: You don't need to change your life, Ruby; it's just fine as it is.

Ruby: I'm going to be forty, Rosie. FORTY. I'm younger than Madonna, would you believe, and I look like her mother. Every day I wake up in a messy bedroom beside a man who smells and snores, I trip over mounds of clothes in order to find my way to the door, I stagger down to the kitchen and make myself a coffee and eat a slice of leftover cake. On the way back to my bedroom I pass my son in the hallway. Sometimes he acknowledges me; most of the time he doesn't.

I fight with him to use the shower and I don't mean about who's first to use it – I actually have to *force* him to wash himself. I fight with the shower in order to be neither scalded to a crisp nor frozen to death. I get dressed in clothes I have been wearing for far too many years in a size that makes me physically sick, but that has caused me to lose the will to care about doing something about . . . *anything* – or anything about *something*. Teddy grunts goodbye to me, I squeeze myself into my banged-up rusty old unfaithful Mini that breaks down almost every morning on the motorway that bears more of a resemblance to a car park than a road.

I park my car, arrive into work late again, and get given out to by someone I have been forced to nickname Randy Andy. I sit at my desk where I concoct stories which help me escape the office and I flee to the outside world for a sneaky cigarette. I do this various times a day. I speak to nobody all day, nobody speaks to me and then I return home at 7 p.m. feeling absolutely exhausted and starving, to a home that will never be cleaned and a dinner that will never prepare itself. I do this *every day*.

On Saturday nights I meet you, and we go out and I suffer all day Sunday with a hangover. This means that I turn into a zombie and lie on the couch like a piece of broccoli. The house still doesn't get tidied, and despite being screamed at, it refuses to tidy itself. I wake up on Monday morning to that awful horrible wailing sound of my alarm clock, just to begin the week all over again.

Rosie, how could you say I don't need change?

I *desperately* need change.
Rosie: Ruby, we *both* need change.

For a special friend

May this be the beginning of a truly happy and successful year for you!

Sorry, Ruby, this was the only half-decent card I could find that didn't go on about how your life is almost ending. Thanks for always being there for me, even though you'd rather not be! You're a fantastic friend to have. Let's enjoy this birthday and good luck in your new year.

Love, Rosie

PS. I hope you like your pressie. Never complain of *change* ever again!

This voucher entitles the bearer to ten lessons in Salsa dancing.

Ricardo will be your teacher every Wednesday @ 8 p.m. in the school hall of St Patrick's Secondary School.

You have a message from: RUBY.

Ruby: I'm all salsa'd out! The last time I was in this much pain was when Teddy got that Kama Sutra book for Christmas from the lads at work. I practically had to be fork-lifted to work after the holidays, remember? Well, this time I actually had to take the morning *off* work. Can you believe it?!

I woke up suspecting that I had been in a very serious car accident; then I looked across at Teddy and was convinced we had been. But I forgot that the drooling, sweating and disturbing noises were all part of the Teddy package. It took me twenty minutes to wake him up so that he could help me out of bed. It took me a further twenty minutes to get out of bed. My joints were on strike. They were all just lazily lounging around with their little pickets pitched up, screaming, 'Joints on strike, joints on strike!' The hips were the leaders of this conspiracy.

So I rang my boss and held the phone to my hips so he could hear them too. He agreed with me and let me have the morning off. (Well, he claims *now* that he *didn't* but I'm sticking to my side of the story.)

I never knew pain could be so bad. Childbirth is *nothing* compared to exercise, and Gary was a *big* baby. This is what they should do to prisoners of war when they're trying to interrogate them. Make them take salsa classes. I knew I was unfit but, my God, driving the Mini today was horrendous. Every time I changed gears I felt like someone was hammering away at my arm. First gear – sore, second gear – pain, third gear – torture. I ended up driving to work in second gear because it hurt so much. Not safe or healthy for the car at all but she managed to cough and splutter her way into work, just like her owner.

By the way I was walking you would swear Teddy and I *had* worked our way through the Kama Sutra book. Even typing was a traumatic experience as I suddenly realised that my finger bone is connected to my arm bone, which in some way was pulling on my hamstring, which was giving me a headache. I should have known I would be this bad. When you dropped me off last night I was so stiff I practically had to crawl in the hall door, where my ears were greeted by Teddy and Gary having a mutual grunting session in the living room. I've learned it's their odd little method of communication.

So I left my wonderful intelligent family and soaked in the bath and considered drowning myself. Then I remembered I still had chocolate cake left over from yesterday so I came back up for air. Some things are worth living for.

But thank you for the gift, Rosie; we had fun in the class, didn't we? I can't remember ever laughing so much in my life, which on second thought is probably why my stomach is so sore.

Thank you for reminding me that I'm a woman, that I have hips, that I can be sexy, that I can laugh and have fun.

And thank you for bringing the sexy Ricardo into my life. Can't wait to feel this way again next week. Now after all my whinging and moaning, how do you feel?

Rosie: Oh, fine, thanks. No complaints.

Ruby: Ha!

Rosie: OK, OK, so I feel a little stiff.

Ruby: Ha!

Rosie: Oh, OK, so the bus had to lower the wheelchair ramp for me this morning because I couldn't lift my legs.

Ruby: That's more like it.

Rosie: Oh, the beautiful Ricardo, Ruby!! I had a dream about him last night. I woke up with my top off and my pillow covered in drool. (OK, so, *not really*.) The sound of that sexy Italian voice shouting, 'Ros-ie!! Pay atten-see-on!' and, 'Ros-ie! Stup laffing!!' and, 'Ros-ie!! Get up ov ze floor!' just sends a shiver up my spine. But it was the sound of, 'Vell done, Rosie, *fantabulous* hip action!' that really got me. Mmm, yummy Ricardo with the hips . . .

Ruby: Yes! The hips! Although as I recall, it was *me* he was referring to about the '*fantabulous* hip action'.

Rosie: Oh, Ruby, can't a girl *dream*? I was surprised to see so many men there, were you?

Ruby: Yes! It reminded me of when I was younger at the school discos or the ceilís; I was always one of those girls, stuck dancing with another girl as a partner. There were more men dancing with men last night than there were women with women.

Rosie: Yes, I know, though somehow I get the feeling that was due to personal choice. Although they took the wearing high heels a little too seriously, don't you think? Could you imagine Greg and Teddy coming with us to a class?

Ruby: Oh, that would be a sight for sore eyes! Teddy can't wrap his arms around himself, never mind hug me. By the time he'd get round to doing a twirl, it would be next year.

Rosie: Ha! Yeah, and Greg would probably become so obsessed with Ricardo counting the steps aloud that he would begin to calculate them in his mind, add them, multiply them, subtract the first count from the square root of the sixth or something. Greg, the bank manager and his love affair with numbers. It looks like it's just you and me, Ruby.

Ruby: Looks like it . . . So what's Alex up to these days?

Rosie: He's still hanging around Slutty Bethany's dad, trying to get a job chopping people's bodies up.

Ruby: Oh . . . kay, who is Bethany, why is she a slut and what business is her father in?

Rosie: Oh, sorry. Bethany is Alex's childhood sweetheart and first love, she's a slut because I say so, and her dad is a surgeon of some sort.

Ruby: How exciting – the return of one of Alex' ex-girlfriends. This will be a page turner.

Rosie: No, she's not around any more; Alex is just attending some lectures being held by her father.

Ruby: Oh, Rosie Dunne, expect the unexpected, for once. Maybe this time you won't get such a shock when things don't go your way.

Chapter 28

Aries

The heady combination of Uranus in Aries along with your ruler Jupiter opposing Venus and the sun squaring Pluto means, well, complications.

The new moon brings some light relief – but with a strange twist of fate.

> IRISH SURGEON TO JOIN WILLIAMS
> by Cliona Taylor
>
> Irish surgeon Reginald Williams, who recently achieved success with his much-publicised new cardiac surgery, today announced he would be welcoming fellow Irishman Dr Alex Stewart to the award-winning team. The 30-year-old Harvard graduate says, 'I have always followed Dr Williams' studies with great interest and admiration,' and that he is both delighted and honoured to become a new member of this ground-breaking and, most important, life-saving new surgery.
>
> Dr Stewart is originally from Dublin, and moved to Boston at age 17 when his father accepted a post with the prominent US law firm Charles & Charles. Dr Stewart completed five years in Boston Central Hospital on a general surgical residency training programme before joining with Dr Williams for further cardiac surgery studies. Pictured above (from left to right) are Dr Reginald Williams with his wife, Miranda, and his daughter, Bethany, who

accompanied Dr Stewart to the Reginald Williams Foundation for Heart Disease charity ball last night.

See page 4 of the Health supplement for Wayne Gillespie's report on this new cardiac surgery.

You have an instant message from: ROSIE.

Rosie: Hey, Ruby, you'll never guess what I just read in the newspaper this morning.

Ruby: Your star sign.

Rosie: Oh, please! Give me a bit of credit; do you think I read those things *every day*?

Ruby: I know you read them every day. It helps you decide whether to be in a good mood or bad mood. I can't quite figure mine out today. It says: 'Take the fullest possible advantage of lively financial conditions to seize the initiative at the end of the month. Mars has moved into your sign and you should be feeling full of energy. Exciting new experiences forecast.'

I have never been so broke, exhausted and bored in all of my life. So that's all a load of crap. I'm really looking forward to our next dance lesson, though. Can't believe we're going to be finished this week and that soon we'll be moving into intermediate class. The weeks have just flown by. Anyway, what was in the papers if it wasn't your star sign?

Rosie: Read page three of the *Times*.

Ruby: OK on page three, scanning down through articles as I type this . . . oh my Lord, look at that. I take it that's Slutty Bethany?

Rosie: Should you even have to ask?

Ruby: Sorry, love, but she looks like a normal filthy-rich well-dressed thirty-year-old woman to me, but I'll call her Slutty Bethany if you insist.

Rosie: Humour me.

Ruby: OK . . . Oh look, Rosie, it's 'Slutty Bethany' in the paper with Alex. On page three. Looking . . . em . . . slutty.

Rosie: So I see. Anyway, she's thirty-two. My star sign said that—
Ruby: A-ha! I told y—
Rosie: Oh, shut up with the 'I told you so's' and listen. My star sign said that I would feel light relief but with a strange twist of fate.
Ruby: And . . . ? Mine tells me I'm rich – so what?
Rosie: Well, I'm delighted that Alex has finally got the job of his dreams that he has wanted for so many years, but it's just ironic that it was her he had to meet to get it.
Ruby: I told you to expect the unexpected, Rosie, *and* to stop paying attention to those horoscopes. They're a load of crap.

From Rosie
To Alex
Subject Congratulations!

Heard about your good news. You've made it into every newspaper over here today (I've kept all the press cuttings for you), and I heard you speaking on the radio this morning. I'm not quite sure exactly what you were talking about, but you sounded like you've got a cold. So you can practically bring people back from the dead but you can't get rid of the sniffles.

How's Josh? I rang your mother the other day and he was over with her for the weekend. She put Josh on the phone and I can't believe I could actually have a conversation with him! He's very intelligent for nearly three, a bright lad just like his dad was, absolutely nothing like his mum. He was telling me all about the animals he had seen at the zoo and proceeded to make the noise of every single one of them. I suggested to your mother that she work on the gorilla sound with him as he wasn't saying anything, but she informed me that the gorilla is so depressed he just sits in his cage and doesn't make a sound. So Josh is an impressionist too as well as a clever clogs.

I would love to see him again sometime; I would love to see you. We need to catch up on each other's lives. Tell me something about yourself that the papers, television and radio can't tell me.

Dear Alex,

Rosie here again. I'm not quite sure if you got my email a few weeks ago. I just was congratulating you on your fantastic news. We're all so proud of you over here; Mum, Dad, Steph, Kev, Katie and Toby are all cheering for you. I think Toby wants to be a doctor when he's older, just like you because he'll get to be on the radio and have his photograph in the newspaper. (Plus he revealed he wanted to rip people's hearts out like they do in some movie. I was deeply disturbed by that thought.) Katie is now insisting she wants to be a dance club DJ. You've had no effect on her in that department whatsoever; she'll be in a business that *gives* people heart attacks.

I'm still at the Two Lakes Hotel. Still at reception; still providing the big bad public with a glass roof over their heads. My boss has headed over to the US where he has opened up yet another new hotel so I don't think either of the Lake brothers will be here for a very long time. In their stead they have arranged a series of very sad team-forming experts to come in and teach us how to be at one with one another. Next week the team leader, Simon, is taking us out canoeing so we can communicate outside of a work environment. We're supposed to learn how to discuss our problems.

How can I tell Tania, who also works in reception, that the reason I don't talk to her is because I can't listen to her unnaturally high-pitched voice, that I hate it that she says 'What do you think?' at the end of every sentence, that she wears perfume that is far too strong for a small office, and pink lipstick that sticks to her teeth and that does not and *never will* look good with her hair colour? Steven's morning breath smells of dirty nappies; I love it when he goes on his first coffee break because that means he comes back almost smelling of roses in comparison. Geoffrey has a serious underarm odour problem; Fiona has a serious problem with flatulence – I don't know *what* she's eating. Tabitha nods all the time I'm speaking to her, says 'right' after practically every single word and, even more annoyingly, tries to finish my sentences for me, or join in with my last few words. The really annoying thing is that she always gets it wrong. Henry wears white socks and black shoes, Grace hums the same Spice Girls song every single day, which drives me demented but I always end up singing it to myself when I get home, which causes Katie to despise her old-fashioned 'way-behind' mother, who has no idea of the chart positions of this decade.

They all drive me bloody mad. In fact maybe this canoeing thing is a good idea after all; I can just drown the lot of them. Alex, write back and let me know what's going on in your life.

Love,

Rosie

Rosie,

Sorry I've been so distant recently, but I've been so busy. Still, it's no excuse for not being in touch. You pretty much no all my work news, I suppose, so there's no need to go into that. Mum and Dad are both well, they're still framing every single photo you send them of you and Katie. The place is beginning to look like some kind of shrine to you two Dunne girls.

I have good news! I'll be coming back to Ireland to visit next month. Mum and Dad are coming back too, and Sally has agreed to let me take Josh for the fortnight, seeing as she had him last Christmas. It's been a long time since the entire family has been back together and Mum decided she wanted to be with Phil, his twenty kids and the rest of the family and all her friends, for their fortieth wedding anniversary.

Forty years – imagine. I barely made it to two; I don't no how they did it. You're doing well, though. How long have you and whatshisname been together? Long enough, I would imagine.

I can't remember when I last spent Christmas in Dublin. But soon we'll be reunited, Rosie.
Alex

From Rosie
To Alex
Subject Your visit

That's great news! I'm delighted you're coming home. Would you like to stay over at my house or have you and your parents made other plans?

From Alex
To Rosie
Subject My visit

No, no, I don't want to put whatshisname out. Actually, there's no need for me to be so polite; I hate your husband. So Josh and I are staying with Phil and Maggie and I've booked Mum and Dad into a hotel. Thanks for the offer, though.

From Rosie
To Alex
Subject G. R. E. G.

Hmm . . . Alex, you're going to have to learn my husband's name before you come over. It's Greg. G. R. E. G. Try and remember it, please.

Did I tell you that Ruby and I are salsa dancing queens? I got the first batch of classes as a present for Ruby's fortieth a few months ago and we enjoyed it so much we kept it up. In fact Ruby has surprised me with her talents but I'm secretly sick and tired of having to be the man all the time.

Greg refuses to come to the classes with me but he doesn't mind being taught in our bedroom when Katie is out, our bedroom door bolted, a chair pushed up against it, the blinds down and the curtains drawn. Even the TV must be off just in case an actor or presenter happens to have the magical powers of seeing into people's houses. Well, the whole point is for us to do something fun together but seeing as I'm always the man in class it's hard for me to be the woman at home (and I've *never* been any good at being the woman at home). Then we end up stepping on each other's toes, kicking each other's shins, getting really frustrated with each other, having a screaming match about whose foot was where, whose foot should have been where but wasn't and then storm out on each other.

Ruby's started taking the classes twice a week now but I can't go on Mondays because I have to bring Katie to basketball practice. Ruby does insist that it's not as much fun without me, because she has to dance with tutu-wearing Miss Behave, a six-foot-tall drag queen with the longest legs and blond hair, who's trying to learn salsa for her show, which is on at the local gay club.

Anyway, Ruby and I are really enjoying ourselves, and I find myself looking forward to the next class the minute each finishes. Ruby's delighted because she's losing a bit of weight (she's losing pebbles apparently, not stones). It's nice to find a hobby that excites you and makes you *look forward* to the week ahead instead of constantly dreading days. I hope you're having some sort of life, Alex, and that you're not overworking yourself. Go on any dates recently?

From Alex
To Rosie
Subject Dating?

I might have . . .

You have received an instant message from: ROSIE.
Rosie: I'm all ears now. Anyone I know?
Alex: Then again I might not have . . .
Rosie: Stop it! Who's the unlucky girl? Do I know her?

Alex: Maybe . . .
Rosie: Oh, please tell me it's anyone but Slutty Bethany.
Alex: Well, I'd better rush off because I have to get ready for tonight. Take care, Buttercup.
Rosie: You got a date?
Alex: Maybe . . . then again . . .
Rosie: Yeah, yeah, I get it, maybe not . . . Well, whatever you're doing, enjoy it. But not too much.
Alex: I wouldn't dare dream of it!

You have received an instant message from: ROSIE.
Rosie: Was just instant messaging Alex a few seconds ago.
Ruby: Yeah? Did he say anything interesting?
Rosie: No. We were just catching up on old times, you know how it is.
Ruby: Good for you both. You and Greg have any plans for tonight, then?
Rosie: He's going on a date, Ruby.
Ruby: Who is? Greg is?
Rosie: No! Alex.
Ruby: Oh, are we still talking about him? Who's he going out with?
Rosie: I don't know. He wouldn't tell me.
Ruby: Well, he's allowed to have a private life, isn't he?
Rosie: Yeah, I suppose.
Ruby: And it's good that he's able to finally move on after having his heart broken and going through a divorce, isn't it?
Rosie: Yeah, I suppose.
Ruby: Well, it's good that you feel that way. You're a great friend, Rosie, always wanting the best for Alex.
Rosie: Yeah. Yeah, I am.

You have received an instant message from: ALEX.
Alex: Hi, Phil.
Phil: Hi, Alex.

Alex: What you doing?
Phil: Surfing the internet, searching for a crank hole cover for a 1939 Dodge Sedan. It's a rare car. A real beauty. Just ordered front bumper bar extensions for the 1955 Chevrolet Sedan. It's being shipped in.
Alex: Right.
Phil: Something on your mind, Alex?
Alex: No, no.
Phil: Well then, did you message me for any particular reason?
Alex: No, just seeing how you are. Wanted to catch up with my big brother.
Phil: Right. How's the job?
Alex: I'm going on a date tonight.
Phil: Really? That's good.
Alex: Yeah it is.
Phil: Good to see you moving on.
Alex: Yeah.
Phil: Finding happiness again.
Alex: Yeah.
Phil: Meeting someone new will stop you from working so bloody much.
Alex: Yeah.
Phil: Does Rosie know?
Alex: Yeah. Just was chatting to her there by instant message before I messaged you.
Phil: How's that for a coincidence? Well, what was her reaction?
Alex: Not much of one, actually.
Phil: She wasn't angry?
Alex: No.
Phil: Or jealous?
Alex: No.
Phil: She didn't beg you not to date other women?
Alex: Nope.
Phil: That's good then, isn't it? You've got a good friend there. One that wants you to move on, meet new people and find happiness.
Alex: Yeah. That's good. Good to have a friend like that.

Aries
You're still heavily under the influence of Neptune, the planet that brings you your romantic dreams . . .

You have an instant message from: ROSIE.
Rosie: You're right, Ruby, star signs are a load of crap.
Ruby: Attagirl.

Chapter 29

To Rosie, Katie and Greg

You are invited to my 4th birthday praty on November 18th. I am haveing a magicman. He can make aminals out of balloons. He will give you a aminal for keeps. My party starts at 11 in the morning and there will be lots of candy and then you can go home with your moms and dads.

Thanks.

Love,

Josh

You have received an instant message from: KATIE.

Katie: I look like a goofball.

Toby: You do not look like a goofball.

Katie: You don't even know what a goofball looks like.

Toby: What does it look like then?

Katie: Me. I look like some sort of futuristic human race that got messed up with robots.

Toby: You don't.

Katie: Oh my God, everyone is staring at me.

Toby: Katie, we're sitting in the back row of the classroom. Everybody in the entire room has their back to us. They are NOT staring at you unless they've got eyes on the back of their heads.

Katie: My mum does.

Toby: Look, they're only braces, Katie. It's not the end of the world. Anyway, I know how you feel. When I got my glasses I felt like everyone was staring at me too.

Katie: That's because they were.
Toby: Oh. Could you do me a favour?
Katie: What?
Toby: Just say sizzling sausages one more time.
Katie: TOBY! That is so not funny. You said you wouldn't laugh. I'm gonna be stuck with these stupid train tracks for years now, and it's not my fault they're giving me a lisp. I'll even have them for my birthday photos next week.
Toby: Big deal.
Katie: It's my thirteenth birthday. I don't wanna remember myself in photographs when I'm older as being the one with the two gigantic lumps of metal jammed in my mouth. Plus *everyone's* coming to the party, people I haven't seen for absolute yonks, and I want to look nice.
Toby: Let me guess, you'll be trying to look nice in black again.
Katie: Yep.
Toby: You're so morbid.
Katie: No, Toby, I'm sophisticated. The black suits my hair. It says so in my magazines. But you can wear your ratty tatty shorts and T-shirt, if you like. No point in changing the habit of a lifetime.
Toby: That's what *my* magazines tell me to do.
Katie: No, I *no* what your filthy magazines tell you to do and it's not anything to do with dressing. More like undressing.
Toby: So I'm invited anyway.
Katie: Maybe. Then again . . . maybe not.
Toby: Katie, I'm going whether you invite me or not. I'm not missing your thirteenth birthday just because you're in one of your moods. I just want to see your birthday cake getting all caught up in your braces, oozing out through the cracks in your teeth and then hitting people on their faces when you speak.
Katie: Whatever. I'll make sure I speak to you the most then.
Toby: Who's going, anyway?

Katie: Alex, Aunt Steph, Pierre and Jean-Louis, Grandma and Granddad, Ruby, Teddy and her weirdo son that never speaks, Mum, of course, and a few girls from basketball.

Toby: Well, yippee. What about your Uncle Kevin?

Katie: Does he ever come to anything? He's still working in that posh hotel down in Kilkenny. He said he's sorry he couldn't come but he sent me a card with a tenner inside.

Toby: Well, that's all you want anyway. What about Greg?

Katie: Nope, he's working in the States for a week. He gave me thirteen euro. A euro for every year.

Toby: Cool. You're gonna be rich. Just as well he's working, I hate when him and Alex are in the same room. It freaks me out.

Katie: I no. It's even worse when Mum's in the room because she just spends the entire time running from one to the other like she's a boxing match referee.

Toby: Alex would kick Greg's ass if they were in a boxing match.

Katie: Definitely. Mum would kick both their asses if they even dared. At least now I'll be able to wear the locket Alex gave me without Greg looking at it like he wants to rip it off.

Toby: Oh, he's just jealous his photo isn't in it.

Katie: His head's too big to ever fit in my locket.

Toby: So is there anyone under the age of eighty coming that's not on your crappy basketball team?

Katie: Alex is bringing Josh.

Toby: Josh is four years old, Katie.

Katie: Exactly. You'll have lots in common. Same brain power.

Toby: Oh ha ha, metal mouth. Do you think you'll have any 'sizzling cocktail sausages' at your party?

Katie: You're hilarious, Toby. Well, I suppose my situation could be a million times worse. I could be stuck wearing glasses for the rest of my life like you.

Toby: Hardy har har. I was just thinking, you might not be able to leave the country for the next few years because of the metal detectors at the airports. You could be a real danger to the public. They could be turned into deadly weapons.
Katie: Whatever.

You have an instant message from: ROSIE.
Rosie: My baby is going to be a teenager next week.
Ruby: Thank your lucky stars it's almost over now, sweetie.
Rosie: Isn't it just beginning? And if I had any lucky stars they would be well and truly sacked by now. What's so great about my beautiful baby growing up and become spotty and bitchy while I decay right in front of my very own eyes? The older my child gets, the older I become.
Ruby: Clever discovery.
Rosie: But that's not allowed to happen. Because I haven't even started my own life yet, never mind bringing another one into this world and helping her through her own. I haven't actually done anything of substance yet.
Ruby: Some may argue that creating life is of substance. Anything I should bring to the party?
Rosie: Just yourself.
Ruby: Damn it, anything else instead?
Rosie: You're coming whether you like it or not.
Ruby: Oh alright then. At least Greg won't be there wrapping a leash around your neck to hold you back from Alex.
Rosie: Yeah. I just might be able to hump Alex's leg in peace this time.
Ruby: Here's hoping. So what do I get for the teenage girl who wants everything?
Rosie: Straight teeth, magic spot removal cream, Colin Farrell and an organised mother.
Ruby: Ah, now the organised mother bit I can help out with.
Rosie: Thanks, Ruby.

From Alex
To Rosie
Subject Flight details

My flight is landing at 2.15 p.m. tomorrow. Really looking forward to meeting up with you and Katie again. Will whatshisname be there to greet me too?

From Rosie
To Alex
Subject MY HUSBAND

My *husband's* name is GREG. And no, he will not be there to collect you because he is away on business. He's in the States so you two have luckily swapped countries for the next few days. Let's hope that will be far apart enough for the both of you.

To my wonderful daughter
You're a teenager!
Happy birthday, darling.
Lots of love,
Mum

To Katie
You're a teen today,
Hip hip hip hooray!
It's a joyous day,
You're a teen today!
Greg

You're a groovy Chick!!
Happy birthday, pet.
Love you lots like jelly tots!
Love, Grandma and Granddad

Happy birthday, Glitter Girl!
Take this money and buy yourself an item of clothing

that's not black. I dare you.
Love, Ruby, Teddy and Gary

For my niece
Happy 13th, Beautiful!
Bon Anniversaire!
Love, Stephanie, Pierre and Jean-Louis

To my Goddaughter
Happy 13th, you little adult!
I'm so happy to share the day with you.
All my love,
Alex

You may be a teenager but you're still ugly.
From Toby

From	Kevin
To	Rosie
Subject	Secret visit!

Kevin here. I can't get through to your phone so I thought I'd send you an email seeing as that seems to be all you do every day.

Sorry I couldn't be home for Katie's birthday, but it's absolutely crazy at work. The golf open is being held here this week and all the world's greatest golfers and their dogs and goldfish have booked in. I've been rushed off my feet but they'll thankfully be gone by the weekend. I seem to keep missing the family do's (or family don'ts).

Anyway, the reason I'm emailing you is because I can't believe you kept it a secret from me that you were coming down here for the weekend! Don't even ask what I was doing checking the reservations but it seems that you have the honeymoon suite booked out for the weekend!

Good ol' Greg's a bit flash, paying for all that, isn't he? Anyway, I'm glad you're finally coming down to see me. It's about time. Don't think I've seen you since Christmas. I'll make sure all the staff treat you extra specially, and I'll even tell the lads in the kitchen not to spit into your food.

From Rosie
To Kevin
Subject Secret visit

Sorry, my baby brother, but it must be another Rosie Dunne. I wish it *was* me!

From Kevin
To Rosie
Subject Secret visit

There's only one Rosie Dunne! No, the booking is actually under Greg's name. Shit! I hope I haven't spoiled a surprise. FORGET I said anything. Sorry.

From Rosie
To Kevin
Subject Secret visit

Don't worry, Kev – what day is the booking for?

From Kevin
To Rosie
Subject Secret visit

Friday until Monday. Oh, please don't tell him I told you. It was stupid of me to say anything. I should have used my head first. I really shouldn't have been looking at the reservations anyway. What an idiot Greg is. He should have known I work here.

From Rosie
To Kevin
Subject Secret visit

And in order for him to know where you work you two would need to have a conversation with each other once in a while. Don't worry! Greg's away in the States for the week so I'll be able to hide my excitement from him! I'd better go shopping for a few outfits. That hotel of yours is very classy!

From Kevin
To Rosie
Subject Secret visit

Enjoy it and I'll see you at the weekend. I'll have a look of pretend shock on my face.

Ruby: I have to admit that I'm surprised. That's very romantic of him!

Rosie: I know! I'm so excited, Ruby. I've dreamed of staying in that hotel for years. Oh, I bet the little shampoos and shower caps in the bathrooms are just the most beautiful things.

Ruby: Christ, Rosie, you could open your own shop with the amount of hotel products you've stolen.

Rosie: It's not *stealing*. They're not just there to be *looked* at. Although, they do seem to be nailing down the hair dryers a lot more these days.

Ruby: Just as well you're not strong enough to drag the beds out of the rooms.

Rosie: They'd see me at reception. Although the bed sheets I got from the last hotel I stayed in are by far my favourite.

Ruby: Rosie, you have a problem. Swiftly moving on, when are you being whisked away to the lap of luxury?

Rosie: Friday. I can't wait! I completely maxed out my credit card buying a few outfits for the weekend. I'm so pleased that he's made this effort. Things with me and Greg have reached an all-time high the last while. It's like we're back at our honeymoon stage. I am really, really happy.

From Rosie
To Greg
Subject Coming home?

It's Friday and I was just wondering what time you'll be home? You must be on the plane because your phone's going straight to answer machine. Maybe you can reply via your laptop from the clouds!

From Greg
To Rosie
Subject Re: Coming home?

Hi, love. I told you I'd be here in the States until Monday. I should be home in the evening sometime. Can I call you from the airport for a lift? Sorry if there was some confusion. I'm sure I told you it was Monday and not Friday. I wish it was today, darling, I really do.

How's Katie after her first wild teenage party? I haven't heard from her. I thought she might have thanked me for the present by now.

From Rosie
To Kevin
Subject *This* weekend?

Do you think you could be mistaken about that booking for *this* weekend?

From Kevin
To Rosie
Subject Re: This weekend?

It's definitely correct, Rosie. Greg checked in this morning. Aren't you here?

Chapter 30

From Rosie
To Alex
Subject Whatshisname

Whatshisname is gone. For good.

From Alex
To Rosie
Subject Re: Whatshisname

I'll book flights for you and Katie to come over here immediately. I'll let you know the details within the next hour. Don't worry.

From Rosie
To Alex
Subject Please wait

Just give me a little time before you book those flights. There are a few things I want to tie up here before I leave. And once I go over to you in Boston I'm *never* coming back here. Just please wait for me.

Hi, it's me, Alex.

Look, I'm really sorry but I'm not going to be able to make it out for dinner tonight. I'm sorry to tell you in a letter but it's the best way I no how. You're a wonderful, intelligent woman but my heart lies with someone else. It has done so for many, many years. I hope that when we meet we can remain friends at least.

Alex

Chapter 31

Dear Bill Lake,

It is with great sadness that I submit my resignation. I will remain working in the Two Lakes Hotel for the next two weeks as I'm contracted to do so.

On a more personal level, I would like to thank you for five great years of allowing me to work in your company. It has been an honour.

Yours sincerely,
Rosie Dunne

From	Toby
To	Katie
Subject	Disaster!

YOU WHAT?? You CAN'T be moving away! This is awful! Ask your mum if it's OK for you to stay with me for a while. I'll ask my mum and dad too. They'll definitely say yes. You can't leave.

What about school?

What about the basketball team?

What about wanting to DJ for Club Sauce?

What about your grandparents? You can't just leave them. They're old.

What about your mum's job and the house and everything? You can't just leave it all behind.

What about me?

From Katie
To Toby
Subject Re: Disaster!

I can't change her mind. I can't stop crying. This is the worst thing that's ever happened to me in my whole entire life. I don't even want to go to Boston. What's so good about Boston? I don't wanna make new friends. I don't want anything 'new'.

Oh, I hate Greg so much. You no he hasn't even come home because he's so afraid of Mum. She's scary she's so mad. Even I'm afraid to talk to her sometimes. She screams down the phone at him like a crazy woman. No wonder he's not coming home. She said that if he did, she'd cut off his you-no-what. I'm kinda hoping he'll come home just for that.

It's all his fault we have to move away. It's all his fault Mum is upset. I hate him, I hate him, I hate him.

At least Alex and Josh are in Boston. That's something. I think we're gonna stay with them for a while. So we're really going, Toby. She's not just threatening. She told Greg she couldn't stand to be in the same country as him, never mind the same house. I suppose I no how she feels. I feel sorry for her but I really don't want to go. I just cried all night, Toby. It's so unfair.

Grandma and Granddad keep trying to talk her out of it. We're staying with them tonight because Mum can't stand to be at home. Every time she touches something of Greg's she shudders and wipes her hands. Ruby keeps telling Mum to go because it's where her heart is or something. It's the first time I've ever seen Ruby cry. And Mum cries down the phone to Stephanie for hours every day. Last night I could hear her throwing up in the toilet so I got up and made her a cup of tea. She stopped for a while. She slept in my bed last night. It's only a single bed and we were kind of squashed but it was sort of nice. She squeezed me like I was a teddy.

Mum has started packing her bags now. She's gonna help me do mine in a while. She says she's sorry about moving me to Boston and I believe her. I don't blame her because she's so sad. It's Greg's fault but I haven't really seen him do much to make her feel better.

Mum said you can visit us all the time. Promise me you will. You may annoy the hell out of me, Toby, but you're my best friend in the whole entire world and I'll miss you so much. Even if you are a boy.

We can write to each other all the time. That's what Mum and Alex did when they were younger and he had to move away.

Love,
Katie

You have an instant message from: RUBY.

Ruby: So you're leaving in two weeks.

Rosie: Yep.

Ruby: You're doing the right thing, you know.

Rosie: Funny. You're the only one who seems to think that.

Ruby: I'm the only one who knows how you feel about him.

Rosie: Oh no, I'm not in the mood to go jumping into another relationship. I don't have the energy. My heart feels like it's been ripped out of my chest and tap danced on. I hate all men right now.

Ruby: Including Alex?

Rosie: Including Alex, my father, George the lollipop man, and my brother for telling me.

Ruby: You would have wanted to know, though.

Rosie: Yes, and I'm not blaming him. He hadn't a clue Greg was messing around. Again. The lying little . . . aaaah! I just feel like punching the shit out of him. I don't think I've ever been so angry in my life. The first time he did this I was hurt; now I'm just plain pissed off. I can't wait to get out of this country. I'm glad Kevin told me because I will be the fool no longer.

Ruby: I heard Kevin's in trouble at work. Is it for checking the reservations?

Rosie: No, it's for marching through the hotel restaurant during dinner and punching Greg on the nose in front of his lady friend and the rest of the hotel guests.

Ruby: Good for him. I hope he broke his nose.

Rosie: He did. That's what he's in trouble for.

Ruby: So who am I going to go to salsa lessons with now?

Rosie: I'm sure Miss Behave will be only too delighted to be your partner.

Ruby: I finally get to dance with a man and he wears tights. Oh, I'll miss you so much Rosie Dunne. It's not often in life a woman finds a friend like you.

Rosie: And I you, Ruby, but as much as Greg has hurt me, he's given me an opportunity to start from fresh. I'll be free of him and I'm stronger from it.

I'm leaving next week, Greg. Don't try to contact me, don't try to visit me, I want nothing more to do with you. You have betrayed me just when I had learned to fall in love with you all over again. This won't be happening again. You have thrown it all away but I thank you for it. Thank you for letting me see what it is I married and for freeing me from you.

Whether Katie wants to continue seeing you is completely her decision. You must accept what she says.

Alex: You were right, Phil. She's coming over to me. I just had to leave it and let her come at her own pace.

Phil: Lucky for me I was right! It was a good guess, wasn't it? So did she tell you that she loves you, that she never should have married that idiot and that she only wants to be with you and all that other stuff that they say in the movies?

Alex: No.
Phil: She didn't tell you she loves you?
Alex: No.
Phil: Did you tell her?
Alex: No.
Phil: Then what's she going over for?
Alex: She just said that she wanted to get out of Dublin and that she needed a change of scenery and a friendly face.
Phil: Oh.
Alex: What do you think that means?
Phil: Probably exactly what it says. So you've no idea how she feels about you?
Alex: No. Phil, her marriage has just ended. There's plenty of time when she comes over here to talk about our future.
Phil: Whatever you say, bro. Whatever you say.

From Alex
To Rosie
Subject You and Katie

I'm so excited that you'll be here so soon. Josh is practically running up the walls with excitement. He loves Katie and is delighted about your decision to come live with us for a while. I've a friend who has a friend who owns a hotel and they are looking for a manager. You are more than qualified for the job.

I can help you through this, Rosie. Remember I've been in your shoes. I no how it feels to go through a marriage break-up. I'm here for you one hundred per cent. Moving to Boston may be fourteen years later than you planned but it's better late than never. Josh and I will be here waiting. See you next week.

You're moving away!

Good luck, Rosie. We'll all miss you here at the Two Lakes. From Bill, Bob, Tania, Steven, Geoffrey, Fiona, Tabitha, Henry and Grace

Sniff, sniff.
I'll miss you Rosie Dunne.
Good luck with your new life. Send us an email every now and again.
Lots of love,
Ruby

Rosie and Katie,
We are so sorry that you feel you have to go. We are so sorry that you have reason to go. We are so sorry this has happened. We will miss you both so, so much, but we hope you can find eternal happiness. No more tears for our two girls. Let the world be good to you. Phone us when you land.
Love, Mum and Dad

Good luck with the move. My fingers are crossed for you and Katie. We're all here for you if you need us.
Love,
Stephanie, Pierre and Jean-Louis

Sorry you had to go. Good luck.
Kev

Katie,
Good luck in your new home. I'll miss you.
Love,
Toby

Dear Mum and Dad,
It's not like I'm disappearing for ever. We're only a few hours away. You can visit all the time! We love you so much and thank you for your constant support. This time we need to find the way by ourselves.
Lots of love,
Rosie and Katie

Chapter 32

Dear Rosie,

Before you rip this up please just give me a chance to explain. Firstly, I sincerely apologise from the bottom of my heart for the years gone by. For not being there for you, for not supporting you and giving you the help you deserved. I am filled with regret and disappointment with myself for the way I have behaved and chosen to live my life. I know there is nothing I can do to change or make better the years I acted so foolishly and mistreated the two of you.

But please at least give me a chance to build a better future, to make right what's wrong. I can understand how you must feel so angry, betrayed and hurt, and you must hate me so much but there's not just yourself to think of. I look back on my life and I wonder what have I to show for all these years? I haven't done many things in my life that I'm proud of. I have no stories of success to tell, I haven't made a million. There is only one thing in this life that I'm proud of. And that's my little girl.

The fact that I have a little girl, who isn't even 'little' any more. I'm not proud of the way I've treated her. I woke up one morning a few weeks ago on my thirty-second birthday and suddenly it was as if all the sense that's been missing for the past thirty-two years came to me in an instant. I realised I had a daughter, a teenage daughter who I know nothing of, and who knows nothing of me. I would love the chance to get to know her. I'm told that her name is Katie. That's a nice name. I wonder what she looks like. Does she look like me?

I know I haven't shown any signs of deserving this, but if you and Katie are willing to let me into your lives I can prove to you it won't be a waste of time. Katie will meet her father and I will see my daughter – how could that ever be considered a waste? Please help me fulfil my dreams.

Please contact me, Rosie. Give me a chance to undo all the mistakes of my past and to help create a new future for Katie and me.

Best wishes,

Brian

Rosie: No no no no no no no no no

Ruby: I know, honey, I understand. But at least just look at the other options.

Rosie: Options? BLOODY OPTIONS? I have none. NONE! I have to go. Staying here is not an *option*.

Ruby: Rosie, calm down. You're upset.

Rosie: Too right I'm upset! How on earth am I supposed to try and get my life together when everyone around me keeps fucking it up? When is it *my turn* to live *my life* for *me* instead of for everyone else? I'm sick of it, Ruby. I'm fed up. I have had enough. I'm bloody going. Who is this man? Where the hell has he been for the past thirteen years? Where did he disappear to for the most important years of Katie's life – or *my life*, for that matter?

Who stayed up all night breast-feeding, pacing the halls and singing fucking lullabies so the constant screaming would stop? Who changed shitty nappies, wiped snotty noses and cleaned sick from their clothes every day? Who's got stretch marks and scars, saggy tits and grey hairs at the age of thirty-two? Who went to parent teacher meetings, brought her to and collected her from school, made dinner, put food on the table, paid the rent, went to work, helped with homework, gave advice, wiped tears, explained the birds and the bees, explained why Daddy wasn't around, unlike most of the other kids' daddies? Who stayed up all night and worried when she was sick, taking temperatures and buying medicine, making trips to the doctor or the hospital in the middle of the night? Who missed going to college, took days off work and stayed home at the weekend to care for her? Fucking me, that's who. Where was the bastard then?

And *he* has the cheek to stroll back into our lives after thirteen years when all the hard work has been done, with a little shrug of the shoulders and a pathetic little sorry, just after my husband cheats on me, my marriage is over, I finally decide to move to Boston where I should have been anyway had it not been for that sly little prick ruining my plans, turning my life upside down and legging it off to another country with his dick between his legs.

Fuck him.

This time it's about me, Rosie Dunne, and no one else.

Ruby: But, Rosie, you're wrong. It's about Katie too. She needs to know he wants to see her. Don't punish her for the mistakes in your own life.

Rosie: But if I tell her, then she's going to want to see him. She'll be so excited to meet him and he'll probably let her down again and break her heart all over again. And who'll be the one who cleans up the mess? Me. I'll be the one who tries to mend my daughter's broken heart. I'll have to pick up the pieces and wipe away the tears. I'll have to put on the happy face, shrug and say, 'Ah well, don't worry, my thirteen-year-old daughter, not all men are shits – just all the ones you've ever known.'

Ruby: But, Rosie, it could turn out really well. He may have really changed. You never know.

Rosie: You're right, you *never* know. EVER. And another thing, how can she get to know her father when we're halfway across the other side of the world? I don't want to stay here, Ruby. I want *out*. I want out of this entire mess of a life.

Ruby: It's not a mess, Rosie. Life is far from perfect, for everyone. You're not the only one. There isn't a great big black cloud just hanging over your head and no one else's. It just feels that way. But it feels like that for a lot of people. You just have to make the most of what you've got and you are *lucky* because you have a beautiful daughter who is healthy, intelligent and funny and who thinks the world of you. Don't lose sight of that. If Katie wants to get to know Brian then you should support her. You can still move away, he can come to see you – or if you think it's important enough to stay for, stay.

Rosie: Katie is going to want to stay. Last month, I *thought* I was living in paradise. Life changed in an instant.

Ruby: Well, that's the problem with paradise. Nothing attracts a serpent quite like it.

Dear Stephanie,

Congratulations on the pregnancy! I'm thrilled for you and Pierre. I'm sure baby number two will be a joy as Jean-Louis has been. I'm assuming Mum has told you the news. She's delighted I'm not moving to America any more. Alex isn't. He cursed and swore and screamed every bad word under the sun at me. He thinks I'm giving in again and letting everyone walk all over me so now he's in a huff and won't speak to me. I may have let people walk all over me before but not this time. Katie is number one in my life and my reason for being is to ensure she gets the best chance at happiness possible.

She's been through a lot lately, with Greg, having to move back in with Mum and Dad and then preparing to move again to America. She's been under plenty of unwarranted stress. She's supposed to be worrying about spots, bras and boys, not adultery, moving continents and her father doing a magic reappearing act. None of this is her fault and seeing as I brought her into this world the least I could do is continue the good work I've been doing. She isn't a drug addict, isn't rude, is doing fine in school, has all the right limbs in all the right places and hasn't managed to do anything really stupid with her life. So, with all the awful stories you hear, I think I'm doing a great job.

I'm expecting Alex to burst through the door any minute. I'm sure he has hopped on the first plane to get over here and beat up Brian. I suppose that's what best friends are for. I can't even think about what life 'could have been' like in Boston, without crying. I don't quite know where I should go from here. I have no job, no home and I'm back living with Mum and Dad again. Everything about this house brings back a time when I wasn't happy. I had a wonderful childhood but the years with Katie were so difficult, they're the strongest memories I have of this house – the smells, the noises, the wallpaper, the bedrooms all remind me of late nights, early mornings and worrying.

Anyway, forgive me for not being in contact over the past while but I've been trying to get my head round all of this. I'm trying to make some sense out of the phrase 'everything happens for a reason', and I think I've figured out what the reason is – to piss me off.

When I started school I thought that people in sixth class were *so* old and knowledgeable, even though they were no older than twelve. When I reached twelve I reckoned the people in sixth year, at eighteen years of age, must have known it *all*. When I reached eighteen I thought that once I finished college then I would really be mature. At twenty-five I still hadn't made it to college, was still clueless and had a seven-year-old daughter. I was convinced that when I reached my thirties I was going to have at least *some* clue as to what was going on.

Nope, hasn't happened yet.

So I'm beginning to think that when I'm fifty, sixty, seventy, eighty, ninety years old I still won't be any closer to being wise and knowledgeable. Perhaps people on their deathbeds, who have had long, long lives, seen it all, travelled the world, have had kids, been through their own personal traumas, beaten their demons and learned the harsh lessons of life will be thinking: God, people in heaven must *really* know it all.

But I bet that when they finally do die they'll join the rest of the crowds up there, sit around, spying on the loved ones they left behind, and *still* be thinking that in their next lifetime, they'll have it all sussed.

But I think I have it sussed, Steph. I've sat around for years thinking about it and I've discovered that no one, not even the big man upstairs, has the slightest clue as to what's going on.

Rosie

From Stephanie
To Rosie
Subject Re: Life

Well, isn't that one thing you're all the wiser for? Age has taught you something. That *nobody* knows what's going on.

Hi,

My sincerest apologies for that ridiculous note I sent you last week. Just put it down to a momentary lapse in concentration, I'm a complete fool (as you're already aware) and I have absolutely no idea what I was thinking. But you'll be pleased to no (I hope) that I've landed back on earth with a thump and I'm willing and able to give us another go. So let's not waste any more of our valuable time but get down to the important stuff. Are we back on for tonight?

Alex

Chapter 33

You have a message from: RUBY.

Ruby: So you're still here then?

Rosie: Oh, not today, Ruby, please. I'm really not in the mood.

Ruby: I'm getting rather tired of you, Rosie Dunne. First you say you're moving to Cork, then you don't, then you say you're moving to Boston (again) and then you don't. Then I expect you to finally profess your love to Alex and you don't, so he still has absolutely no idea. I can't keep up with you and your 'leaving the country/ changing jobs/ leaving your husband'-type activities. Sometimes I think you just need a good kick up the behind for wasting all these good opportunities. You're an incredibly frustrating person, Rosie.

Rosie: Well, I'm an incredibly frustrated woman right now. And I'm not 'wasting' good opportunities; it's called 'presenting my daughter with new ones'.

Ruby: You can put whatever name you like on it but at the end of the day a missed opportunity is a missed opportunity. But don't worry; I think there's a lesson to be learned in all this.

Rosie: Please tell me there is *some* sort of reason for all this. What's the lesson?

Ruby: That you needn't bother trying any more, because you're going nowhere. So really, how are you?

Rosie: OK.

Ruby: Are you sure? Oh, come on, Rosie, if my heart

can't take what's happening to you then I can't imagine how you must be feeling.

Rosie: Oh, my heart is broken; stopped beating two weeks ago.

Ruby: Well, it's a good thing you know a man who can heal it.

Rosie: No, no, no, it's the unspoken rule. He heals other people's hearts, not mine. I understand that's the way it is to be now.

Ruby: Here's an idea, Rosie. Why don't you just *tell* Alex how you feel? Why don't you just finally get all of those feelings out in the open, and clear your messed-up little head? At least then he'll know that you're not going over *not* because you don't care about him, but that in fact you love him, more than he knows, but that you need to stay here for Katie. Then that will put the ball in his court. He can make the decision whether to come to you or not.

Rosie: But what about his job? And what about Josh?

Ruby: That's *his* decision.

Rosie: Ruby, I can't. How do I tell him? If we had moved over to Boston I could have sussed things out a little, seen how he felt about me and then told him. He was just out on a date last week, for Christsake – how stupid would I look telling him I love him when he's seeing someone? It'll just be the whole Sally situation all over again. It's too complicated and right now the last thing I'm worried about is which man to fall in love with next. Anyway, he's not even returning my calls. He thinks I've made a stupid decision.

Ruby: Just give him time. He's disappointed how things worked out.

Rosie: I'm sorry – he's disappointed? *He's* disappointed? I think me and the rest of the world seem to be having a communication problem here. Does everyone think that I'm *ecstatic* at these new revelations? I mean, I'm really not looking for sympathy or anything but—

Ruby: Yes you are.
Rosie: Excuse me?
Ruby: Sympathy. Looking for it. Yes, you are.
Rosie: Thank you for decoding that for me. OK, so maybe it would be nice if at least some people acknowledged the fact that my husband has had an affair, my marriage has ended, I'm still a million miles away from Alex and will never know how I feel about him, my child's runaway father is back in Ireland and I HAVE NO JOB! A pat on the back, a sympathetic smile and a bit of a cuddle would be quite nice actually. A few months spent in my bed curled up into a ball, smothered by blankets, in a room darkened by drawn curtains, dressed in a pair of big pyjamas would be my idea of heaven, but unfortunately I can't do that right now because I have a daughter who is hyperventilating over the fact that her father, who she's never met, has come into her life and I need to forget about me and be strong for her. But a bit of sympathy would be nice too.
Ruby: Breathe, Rosie.
Rosie: No, that's how all my problems happen. If I wasn't breathing then everything would be fine.
Ruby: Don't talk like that.
Rosie: Oh, shut up. I haven't got time to kill myself; I'm too busy having a nervous breakdown.
Ruby: Well, I suppose that's good news, kind of. How was your meeting with Brian?
Rosie: OK. He booked a flight over here as soon as he got off the phone from me so it seems he is very serious about his new role of fatherhood. He tells me he's been living in Ibiza for the past thirteen years, where he now owns a nightclub. Providing the highly sexed under-age drinkers of Ireland with a few good binge-drinking memories.
Ruby: Is he all tanned and gorgeous?
Rosie: Never before would I have put the words 'Brian the Whine' and 'tanned and gorgeous' all in

the same sentence. He's pretty much the same, with less hair and more belly.

Ruby: How did you feel when you saw him?

Rosie: I had to muster all my strength to stop myself from punching him. Katie was so nervous about meeting him that she was shaking like a leaf and clinging to me. She was expecting me to be the strong one. Imagine – someone was relying on me. We met him in the coffee shop in Jervis Street Shopping Centre and, I have to admit, as we were approaching his table I felt sick. Sick with anger that the miserable little man who I was going to have to force myself to be nice to for the next hour, and help to become a part of my daughter's life, was the very same person who had caused me so much heartache in the past. *I* had to help *him*. It also felt odd that, as weak as I felt bringing Katie into town on the bus that morning, and as tired, nervous, angry and disappointed as I was to be doing that at all, I realised that these two people needed me to bring them together. So for the sake of Katie's relationship with Brian, whatever feelings of resentment I have for him need to be kept to myself.

Ruby: You've done a good thing, Rosie. It must have been difficult. It will probably be difficult for a long time, watching them grow closer.

Rosie: I know. I have to bite my tongue to stop myself from telling Katie just how much of a hero her father isn't when she tells me about some of the things he has done in his life.

Ruby: What was he like with her?

Rosie: He was even more nervous than Katie so it was up to me to get the conversation started between them. You know, being the strongest out of the three really helped me to see that the decision I made about not moving to Boston was the right one. Katie needed me. They both needed me. He seemed genuinely interested in my life and in Katie's. He wanted to know everything about her and I quite enjoyed sharing our stories from over the years. At first I was telling each story with anger because he wasn't around for any of those situations, and then I realised I was bragging. It perked me up, in a strange sort of way, and made me realise how lucky I've been, as much as I moan and whinge about the responsibility of motherhood. It also helped me see the 'specialness' of Katie's and my situation; we're the only two to share all these memories together. And what we choose to let other people know is completely up to us. If Brian messes up absolutely everything else in my life at least he's inadvertently helped me realise that.

However, unfortunately it's not exactly the best time in my life to have an ex back again. In these situations you're supposed to have become so much more since the last time you've seen them – happy and successful in your life so you can say, 'Nah nah na-nah nah, look what I've done since you've been gone.' A failed marriage, no job and living with my parents did not have the desired effect.

Ruby: None of that stuff is important, Rosie. You should just be glad he's grown up a bit. How long will he be around for?

Rosie: A few weeks and then he'll have to head back to Ibiza for a little while. The summer months are obviously when he's at his busiest. He'll be back a few times to visit Katie, of course, and then he's going to hire someone else to run the club so he can stay in Dublin for the winter. He really seems to be taking this seriously and I'm glad for Katie's sake. Having Brian hanging around isn't exactly wonderful for me, but if it puts a smile on her face then it's worth it.

Ruby: Any luck finding a job?

Rosie: Well, I had just switched on the computer to search the internet when you messaged me.

Ruby: Oh, OK, well, I'll go now and let you become

the responsible parent you should be. By the way, I'm making my Gary come to salsa dancing classes with me. Miss Behave drank one too many sangrias at the summer party last week and went over on her ankle in her twelve-inch platforms. All we could hear was a big CRACK! I turned round and she was on her back with a run in her tights and her wig beside her on the floor.

Rosie: Oh God, did you have to rush her to hospital?

Ruby: Oh no, she broke only the heel of her shoe, and seeing as they are her 'only dancing shoes' she refuses to come to class until she replaces them. Unfortunately they're only available in a store in New York so she has to wait until they're restocked and delivered. So I am without a partner and I won't even ask you because I know you'll say no.

Rosie: You're right. But how on earth did you get Gary to agree to go to dance classes with you? Did you threaten his life or something?!

Ruby: Yes.

Rosie: Oh. Well, I hope he enjoys it.

Ruby: Don't be silly, he'll hate it and shout at me for weeks, but at least he'll be talking to me again. Alright, I better go; I have to buy him a leotard and tights on my lunch-break. I know we don't actually have to wear them but it will be worth it just to see the look on his face when I pull them out of my bag.

Rosie: You evil, evil woman.

Ruby: Thank you. Now go find a job. In a hotel. After all this nonsense in your life, I want you to become the most successful hotel-worker person in the world. No. More. Setbacks. You hear me?

Rosie: Loud and Clear.

Dear Alex,

When will you stop giving me the silent treatment? You must understand that I can't make decisions to suit myself. I've Katie to think about too. It is important for her to get to know Brian. You of all people should know how it is to want and need to be there for your child. Brian has finally realised that he wants to be here for Katie. It's better late than never, as you always say. Some things are.

I think I've stressed my apologies to you on your answering machine but now I'm writing to thank you. To thank you for being there for me as you always have been over the years. For making all those arrangements for me when I couldn't even think clearly. That week, my world was turned upside down and everything that was once secure and solid was uprooted and came toppling down on top of me. Let's not allow your disapproval of my decision to stay to affect our friendship.

Perhaps sometime, someday we can be reunited in the way we planned when we were seven years old. I'm lucky to have a friend like you, Alex Stewart; you really are my moonbeam – guiding the way for me all the time. I don't know how unrealistic the promise we made to each other as children was, to stay together side by side for ever, but we have remained friends from across the seas for over twenty years, and that, I'm sure, is some feat.

I've been job hunting all week. My aim was to try and get a job in a hotel, surprise, surprise, but it seems that as the summer has already begun students and immigrants only too willing to be underpaid have already taken everything for the next few months. The money for these jobs really isn't enough to help me and Katie get back on our feet anyway. I will join in with the insufferable moans of twenty-first-century Ireland in a chorus of 'everything is so expensive these days'. I'm waiting to hear from the council about getting a house but I've been here before and the waiting list is so long.

Unfortunately, my position at the Two Lakes Hotel has been filled. Brian has offered to pay child support but I don't want his money. I managed before without him; I certainly don't need his help now. He can give

Katie whatever pocket money his heart desires but his money is neither requested nor required by me.

There hasn't been a peep out of whatshisname lately. That man is too afraid of his own shadow, never mind of me. I filed for a divorce last week; I need him out of my life for good. I gave him enough love and enough chances but he threw it all back in my face. I would be a fool to stay around pinning hopes on him again. It's not healthy for me or Katie. I'll dance around the streets naked when the divorce is final.

Did you hear that Stephanie is pregnant? She's due in November so all the family are naturally thrilled. Mum and Dad are in great form, always asking for you and Josh, and they're very much enjoying their retirement together. They're actually talking about selling their house and moving down to the country where it's cheaper so they can use the extra money to travel the world together for the rest of their years. I think it's a great idea. They don't need all these empty rooms in the house (apart from when I come home crying to them) and neither of them has any need to be living in the city. But it also means I have to hurry up and find a job so I can move out with Katie. They're not rushing me but they want to put the house on the market so it will sell quickly during the summer. I'll be the only family member living in Dublin then, which I imagine will be rather lonely. Kevin is in Kilkenny, Steph's in France and Mum and Dad will be off on their travels. It'll just be me and Katie. And Brian the Whine.

My friend Ruby is taking her son, Gary, to salsa lessons from this week, which should be funny. You've met Gary, and I'm sure you'd agree he's not the most expressive or emotive person in the world. But it's a good idea, I suppose. Katie and I should do something together. She gets to go out for the day with her father but we never spend any time like that together. We're always just at home biting each other's heads off. I'll think of something good she'll like, maybe bring her to a concert. With Greg in the house I was always the cool mum that came to the rescue, but now with Brian here, he's the cool new dad who runs the trendy nightclub and I'm the boring mum who makes her clean her room. Of course, knowing that Brian has a nightclub has only strengthened Katie's desire to become a DJ. I don't know what we've created at all. Her music just gets louder and louder. Mum and Dad have been so used to silence in the house for the last few years, I think Dad's going to blow his top if Katie blasts her music any more.

Anyway, that's all my news. I'm getting through each day slowly, taking each day as it comes and all those clichés. Please return my calls. The last thing on this earth that I would want to happen is to lose my best friend. Even if he is a man.

All my love,
Rosie

Phil: So you're pissed off because she's not moving to Boston now, because the father of her child, who she hasn't seen for over thirteen years, has come back and wants to get to know Katie?
Alex: Yes.
Phil: Jesus Christ. Who writes your scripts?

Dear Rosie,

I'm sorry, Rosie. I know these have been the worst few weeks of your life and I should have kept in contact. Sometimes I just get so frustrated watching your life but I no I can't control it for you. You have to make the decisions. I wasn't angry at you at all; I was just disappointed for you. I want to see you happy all the time and I new that whatshisname wasn't making you happy. I could see it for years. As crap as it feels right now, not being with him is a blessing in disguise. Anyway, I'll speak more about this over the phone during the week because I could rant about whatshisname for ever.

If I can help you out financially, just let me no, but I'm sure you're just skipping past that line and fuming I've even offered. Still, the offer is there. Business has been going really well lately. Thanks to the diets and lifestyles of the modern world, heart surgery is really in demand. OK, that's not funny.

Speak soon, Buttercup. I no you'll be OK.

Alex

From Rosie
To Alex
Subject Re: Messages

Alex Stewart, you KNOW I'll be OK.

From Alex
To Katie
Subject Catching-up

It's your beloved godfather here. I'm just emailing you to see how you are and to find out how things are going with your dad. Keep in touch. Haven't heard much from you lately and I gather things have been tough. Let me no how your music is going too. Still want to be a DJ?

From Katie
To Alex
Subject Re: Catching-up

SorE this is just a real quick email 2 say hi & that I'm fine tanx. In a rush cos I'm goin out wit Dad in a mo. He takin me to concert in the Point Theatre. He got free tickets cos he nos the band. Felt bad cos Mum already got tickets as surprise for me & her. Said me & her should do more 2gether. Whatever. Don't no wot she's talkin bout we c each other every day. NE way Dad got better tickets so I'm goin with him, and Mum bringin Ruby. They got some crappy tickets down the bak of theatre. Brian is cool. He told me u & him were friends at school & that u went 2 his 10th bday party & that he threw goin away party 4 u b4 u moved to USA. But he said that u & Mum disappeared after first 10 mins. That was a bit rude!

Mum laughed when he reminded her. She wouldn't tell me where u and her went. Where did u go?

Oh here he is now – have 2 go.

Katie: Cool isn't he, Toby?

Toby: Yeah.

Katie: When I finish school I'll be able to move over to Ibiza and work as a DJ in his club. It's so perfect. It all fits in with my master plan.

Toby: Did he say you could work in his club?

Katie: No, but he's hardly gonna say no, is he?

Toby: Dunno. What's his club called?

Katie: Dyma Nite Club. Cool, isn't it?

Toby: Yeah.

Katie: You can come too if you want.

Toby: Thanks. Would you want to live in Ibiza?

Katie: To start off with I would, yeah. First I'd get the experience in his club and then I could travel the world and work in loads of different clubs in each country. Imagine being able to play and listen to music for a living? It sounds like heaven.

Toby: You need to get decks then, don't you?

Katie: Yeah. My dad said he'd get them for me. He's got loads of friends who are DJs and they can get all the best gear for cheaper than the shops. Cool, isn't it?

Toby: Yeah. It's weird – you calling him Dad.

Katie: Yeah, I no. I don't really say it to him, though, just to other people. It feels odd. I expect I'll get used to it.

Toby: Yeah, I suppose. Have you heard from Greg?

Katie: No. Why?

Toby: Don't tell your mum, but me and my mum and dad went out for a Chinese last night and he was there with some woman. He got all embarrassed when he saw me and tried to be all nice and friendly by calling me over to the table and stuff.

Katie: Oh my God. What did you say to him?

Toby: Nothing. I ignored him. I walked straight past their table.

Katie: Good. Serves him right. Did your mum and dad go mental?

Toby: No, Mum winked at me and Dad pretended he didn't see Greg.

Katie: Who was he with?

Toby: Who, my dad?

Katie: No, you stupid. Whatshisname.

Toby: Some blonde. Don't tell your mum though. Has she got a job yet?

Katie: No, but she's been going to interviews every day. She's been in the worst moods EVER lately, banging around the house like the Antichrist. Granddad says that's the way I'm supposed to be now that I'm thirteen. She's such a grump.

Toby: Are you going to the orthodontist guy soon?

Katie: Yeah, Granddad is taking me tomorrow. My brace broke again. Why?

Toby: Can I go with you?

Katie: Why do you always want to come? I've got blisters all on the inside of my mouth and he hacks away at me while you sit there sucking lollipops.

Toby: I like going. I bet you had cornflakes for breakfast this morning.

Katie: What are you, psychic?

Toby: No, it's all stuck in your braces.

Katie: Oh, get a life, Toby.

Toby: I have one. So can I go tomorrow?

Katie: What is your obsession with braces, you weirdo?

Toby: They're just interesting.

Katie: Yeah, about as interesting as this geography test. So come on, what's the answer for number 5? Is the capital of Australia Sydney?

Toby: Yeah, Katie, it is.

Dear Ms Rosie Dunne,

We are pleased to offer you the position you

recently applied for. We would expect you to start in August. Please reply to us as soon as possible with your decision and contact Jessica at the phone number below.

Chapter 34

You have an instant message from: RUBY.

Ruby: Praise the Lord for he is a miracle worker! I love my son, he is perfect, an absolute genius!

Rosie: There's a turn-up for the books!

Ruby: Well, you would agree if, like me, you had just witnessed the rebirth of Fred Astaire. Not only am I in a great deal of pain from dancing like I have never danced before but I am shocked to the very core! As soon as the music started, magic happened!

I mean, Ricardo didn't exactly go easy on Gary, even though it was his first day. He said, 'Rub-ee, zis is ze advanceda classa, Gar-ee vill just have to try to keep up.' And, my Lord, my Gary kept up so much I almost passed out. Ricardo even put on '1, 2, 3 Maria' by Azuquita and you know, Rosie – it's fast, so fast that it had you and me in a slump on the floor halfway through, watching cartoon stars and birdies circle our heads. The way Gary moved was incredible. He looked so graceful, spinning and twirling around the floor with his sweat glistening like a . . . solar system. Ricardo said Gary was a star in the making and that he and I made a great team.

Teddy wasn't too impressed when I shared the good news. Well, I was so excited when I got home that I just blurted it out but I didn't realise that Teddy's fellow truck-driving friends were in the TV room and they were all equally unimpressed. Teddy went even redder in the face than usual and ranted and raved about all male dancers being gay and that I shouldn't be influencing Gary to fancy boys. I told him I was trying to help him come out of his shell a bit, not to literally 'come out'. But the lads wouldn't understand. They think crashing beer cans against their heads, farting (then sniffing the air and laughing), screaming at the football players on TV (as if they would do any better themselves if they got on that pitch), commenting on all the overweight women on TV (like they don't have big beer bellies and haven't let themselves go ten years ago), calling me every ten minutes to serve them more cans of beer (of the fifty-cent-per-dozen variety) and then having the audacity to *lecture* me on what makes a *real* man, the lazy selfish bastards—

Rosie: Whoa, whoa, Ruby, we seem to have gotten a bit sidetracked here. How did poor Gary feel when Teddy and co. had a go at him?

Ruby: Well, the poor lad was so embarrassed that he stormed out of the room, stomped up the stairs and slammed his bedroom door shut.

Rosie: Oh dear, poor Gary. I hope Teddy apologised.

Ruby: Are you demented? Of course he didn't. Gary's display only further showed how 'gay' he was becoming by pulling a 'woman's strop'. But I soon found solace in six delicate fairy cakes with pretty pink icing. So move over Fred Astaire and Ginger Rogers, Ruby and Gary Minnelli are coming through!

Rosie: Minnelli??

Ruby: OK, so I changed my name to something far more superstar-like. Ricardo said he could train us both for competitions. We could even get to travel the world if we're good enough. For someone that considers walking to the end of her garden an adventure, being able to travel would be a real dream. That's *if* we're good enough, of course.

Rosie: Ruby, that's terrific news. What will Miss Behave say when she finds out she has been replaced?

Ruby: I'm worried about that; you know how jealous she gets when I even look at other men, but regardless of what she thinks, I'm bringing Gary all the way with me to the World Salsa Dancing Championships in Miami. You know you need to look beyond the four walls of St Patrick's school hall. *See* the possibilities, *smell* the success in the air, *taste* the rewards.

Rosie: Have you been watching Oprah again?

Ruby: Yeah, that 'Remembering your spirit' part gets to me every time. Maybe Gary and I can be on it someday, talking about how we came from nothing to salsa dancing millionaires just by *believing*.

Rosie: Oh, don't talk to me about remembering my spirit. All I can think of is the vodka I knocked back last night.

Ruby: Not that kind of spirit, you fool . . . Any word on the job front?

Rosie: Well, yes, I received a job offer in the post yesterday.

Ruby: Terrific! It's about time. Is it the one you wanted or the one you didn't want?

Rosie: You've known me all these years and you even had to *ask* that question? Actually it was neither, it's the one I really, really, really didn't want and would only accept if it was the last job in Dublin, if I was being thrown out of Mum and Dad's house on my bum and if Katie and I were so desperate for food we had to lick stamps.

Dear Mr and Mrs Dunne,

Hyland & Moore Auctioneers received your request and we would be more than pleased to act on your behalf for the sale of your home. Thank you for choosing Hyland & Moore to represent you.

Yours sincerely,

Thomas Hyland

You have received an instant message from: ROSIE.
Rosie: Hi, it's me.
Rosie: Helloooo?
Rosie: I know you're there. I can see that you've logged online.
Alex: Who is this?
Rosie: Oh, ha ha, you're so funny. What is this? Let's annoy Rosie day?! Tough luck, I am spilling the beans and sharing the sob story of my miserable little life with you whether you like it or not. OK here I go.

I was offered a job. But I turned it down because I didn't think I was desperate enough to have to accept it. It turns out I was wrong. Suddenly Mum and Dad tell me that they're putting the house on the market *the very next day*, and before my brain has a chance to register what they're saying, people start trampling in and out of the house, nosying through my bedroom, complaining about the interiors, laughing at the wallpaper, turning their noses up at the carpets, talking about which walls they'd knock down, which wardrobes they'd rip out and which of my cuddly childhood teddies they would like to burn in a bonfire in the back garden while they danced around it hollering, with stripes of animal blood on their faces (OK so they didn't say *that*). So then a couple put in an offer of full asking price, can you believe, after only seeing it once! Mum and Dad thought about it for approximately twenty seconds and then said yes!
Alex: No!
Rosie: Yes! Apparently the woman is eight months pregnant and they're living in a very small flat and they need to move house really quickly before the baby is born and has to bathe in the sink and play on the balcony.
Alex: No!
Rosie: Yes! Mum and Dad were really apologetic and everything, but I don't blame them because it's

their life after all, and frankly they should have had to stop worrying about me the minute I first moved out. So all within a matter of days they've sold the house, everything has been boxed up, they bought a house for practically next to nothing in Connemara. The furniture is being auctioned off tomorrow (apart from the pieces I managed to grab), the rest of the stuff is being delivered to the house tomorrow (which is hours away). Mum and Dad have already bought tickets to go on a cruise for two months and they're leaving on Monday.

Alex: No!

Rosie: Yes! This means that I had to call back the people who offered me the job that I already turned down – not too politely, I might add. I had to apologise profusely and try to convince them that I really wanted the job after all. They were really pissed off and said they didn't need me until August. So today Katie spent the day with Brian while I went emergency house hunting.

Alex: No!

Rosie: Yes! Everywhere that was in any way affordable was absolutely disgusting. The apartments were still either too expensive, too small or too far from my job and Katie's school. So Mum and Dad were discussing my personal problems (as they generally do) with the young sickeningly happy couple who are about to embark on blissful family life while butchering my childhood home. And because Mum and Dad had been so speedy and understanding about the whole 'moving out in a few days' scenario, they suggested that I move *into* the flat they just moved *out* of and had decided to rent out.

Alex: No!

Rosie: Yes! But the only thing is that they have already rented the place out for a few weeks to a group of male students so I have to wait until they move out. By which time it will no doubt be disgustingly smelly and dirty.

Alex: No!

Rosie: Yes! So who do I stay with while I wait, I hear you ask. Well, let's see, Mum and Dad have moved to Connemara, as you now know. Kev lives in the staff quarters of the Two Lakes Hotel in Kilkenny, Steph lives in France, Ruby has only two bedrooms and no space for me and Katie, and you're in Boston, which isn't convenient commuting for me. So who is the only other human being in Dublin that I know right now (and don't even think of whatshisname)?

None other than Brian the Whine.

Alex: No!

Rosie: Yes! I am afraid so. I am emailing you from the storeroom of Brian the Whine's rented flat, where I have to stay for a few weeks. How much lower can I go? And that's not even my worst news. I haven't even told you who my new boss is. None other than Miss Big Nose Smelly Breath Casey.

Alex: No!

Rosie: Yes! I am now secretary to the woman we most hated while growing up, the woman who made my daughter's life hell while in school and who is now principal of St Patrick's Primary School, and my boss. Why on earth Miss Big Nose Smelly Breath Casey even hired me is completely beyond me, but she has, and until I find another job in a hotel I won't complain or ask questions. Perhaps she just wants to make my life a misery well into my adult life and until I'm an elderly woman. And speaking of the elderly, she was old when I was *five years old*, for Christsake, and she's still old. The woman has nine lives.

So what do you think of all that? Any messages you want me to pass on to your favourite teacher?

Rosie: Hello, Alex?

Rosie: Alex?

Alex: Em . . . sorry, Alex isn't actually online.

Rosie: Oh, ha ha. Well then, how is his name on my screen and I am typing to him?

Alex: You're not. I logged on using his home computer. I guess his name automatically comes up on your system. I've never come across this little system, it's fun. Sorry, I didn't know you were looking for him.

Rosie: What?? You think I just rant about my private life to all strangers on the computer??? Who is this?

Alex: Bethany.

Rosie: Bethany?

Alex: Bethany Williams? Remember me?

Rosie: What the hell are you doing on Alex's home computer?!

Alex: Oh, I'm sorry, it all makes sense now. Alex didn't tell you, did he? I thought you two told each other everything. I'll be sure to pass on all your little messages to him, though. They were very amusing. Good luck with the new job, Rosie; I'll let Alex explain this one to you. By the way, Alex is working with my father now. He's making good money, doing very well for himself. Perhaps if you're that stuck for money he could give you a loan.

Rosie has logged off.

Chapter 35

Welcome to the Relieved Divorced Dubliners' internet chat room. There are currently five people chatting.

Buttercup has joined the room.

Divorced_1: Screw him, screw'm, screw'm, screw'm!

Buttercup: Hello, everyone.

Wildflower: Wahooooo! You tell her Divorced_1!

UnsureOne: I know, Divorced_1, but that's the problem now, isn't it? I can't 'screw him' any more; he's gone. I should never have let him leave. Oh, it's all my fault.

Buttercup: Em . . . hello, everyone. Is this working? Can you all read what I'm writing?

Divorced_1: Oh, shut up, UnsureOne. I'm sick of listening to you moaning night after night. How is it your fault? Did you drag him into the car and drive him to the hotel room? Did you pull his pants down around his ankles and push him on top of her on the bed?

UnsureOne: Please stop, Divorced_1! Stop! Stop! Stop! No I didn't!

LonelyLady: Oh, leave her alone. There's no need to be so graphic.

Divorced_1: Look, I'm only trying to help. If you didn't do all those things then how on earth is it your fault?

Buttercup: I'm not sure this is working. Hello? Hello? Hello? Stupid bloody computer. Can anyone answer me?

UnsureOne: Well, maybe I inadvertently put him under pressure to do better at his job. You know how things are so expensive these days and the kids always want more, more, more. They were going back to school and the uniforms and books are always so expensive and I kept telling him we needed more money because it was tight and I'm not sure but maybe it *was* my fault, you know?

LonelyLady: Oh, please, Unsure . . .

Wildflower: Oh, I have heard quite enough for one night.

Divorced_1: Look, just forget about him. He's a bastard and that's all there is to it. Screw him.

Buttercup: Well, not that anyone cares, but there was only one kind of job your husband was thinking of that night and it didn't involve a day at the office.

Wildflower: Wahoooo! Welcome, Buttercup!

Divorced_1: You're right, Buttercup, screw him.

UnsureOne: Are you sure, Buttercup?

LonelyLady: I tend to agree with the others, UnsureOne. Welcome, Buttercup. You want to chat?

Wildflower: Please, LonelyLady, every time you ask one of our visitors if they want to chat you scare them away. You sound like you want to talk dirty or something.

LonelyLady: I'm sorry, you know I don't mean to. I just have this horrible habit of driving everyone away.

Wildflower: What are your stats, Buttercup?

Buttercup: My what?

Divorced_1: Oh, everyone look, a chat-room virgin.

Wildflower: Your stats, cupcake – age, sex, that sort of thing.

Buttercup: Well, I'm thirty-two, I'm female, I have a thirteen-year-old daughter and I'm happily divorced.

Wildflower: Wahoooo!

Divorced_1: Congratulations, cupcake. Screw him – that's what I say.

UnsureOne: Buttercup, whose fault was the marriage break-up? Yours or his?

Wildflower: Ignore her, Buttercup. She's riding the 'blame' wave.

Buttercup: That's OK, I don't mind. It was one hundred per cent *his* fault.

Divorced_1: *Quelle surprise.*

LonelyLady: At least you have a daughter, Buttercup, and you weren't left all alone. My husband – well, my ex-husband – left me before we even had a chance to start a family. I don't think it would have been so hard if we'd had children. Then at least I wouldn't feel so—

Divorced_1: Alone, yeah, yeah. Well, trust me it's harder *with* kids. Unfortunately my rugrats are the spit of my husband and when I look at them I just want to strangle the little bastards. Do your kids look like your ex, UnsureOne?

UnsureOne: Yes and no. Some people say they do and others say they don't. I'm not too sure really . . .

Wildflower: Let's not be rude, guys, and introduce ourselves to Buttercup. I'm sixty-two years old, I've five kids and my husband left me last year.

Buttercup: Oh, how awful. I'm sorry.

Divorced_1: HA! No need to be sorry, cupcake. The man had good reason to leave her; she was sleeping with their gardener.

Buttercup: Oh!

Wildflower: Oh, *please*, like you lot never thought of ever doing the same thing.

UnsureOne: Well, my gardener was a woman.

Wildflower: I didn't mean *that*.

LonelyLady: I never would have done something like that to my Tommy. Never.

Divorced_1: Hi, Buttercup. I'm forty-nine years old, have four kids and my ex-husband was screwing his secretary. Bastard.

Buttercup: LonelyLady, what about you?

LonelyLady: I'm twenty-seven, I just got married last

year but my Tommy left me. He just couldn't take married life, he said. One day he just left me . . . all alone.

Buttercup: UnsureOne, what about you?

UnsureOne: I'm thirty-six, have three children and I'm not technically divorced *per se*. We still live together . . . what about you, Buttercup, how did you and your husband split?

Buttercup: Oh, he was seeing a number of different women quite regularly and I was oblivious to it all.

Divorced_1: Bastard.

Wildflower: Well, I believe that we're all put on this earth to have as many sexual playmates as we want.

Divorced_1: Do shut up, you new-age hippy.

Wildflower: There's no harm in expressing my personal view. I don't recall ever attacking your opinions.

Divorced_1: That's because my opinions are always right. So, Buttercup, did you get the house?

Buttercup: No, I got the hell out of there. That was good enough for me.

Divorced_1: I was screwed in the divorce settlement. My ex got the holiday home and I got custody of the kids. What I would give to swap for a few months of peace and quiet in the sun.

LonelyLady: I got to keep the house and it just meant I had to stay here all on my own with rooms full of memories.

Divorced_1: Oh, drop it, Lonely. You sound like a broken record today.

LonelyLady: What? I would stay with Tommy even if he was a shit. I wouldn't care, I just want him.

Wildflower: Ignore her. Her balance is all wrong. The best way to get over one man is to get under another. We all know that.

UnsureOne: I'm not sure that's the correct attitude to have. I certainly have no intentions of sharing a bed with anyone other than my husband.

Buttercup: I don't understand, UnsureOne. You're still married?

UnsureOne: We're not technically divorced. He sleeps in our bedroom and I sleep in the spare room.

Wildflower: UnsureOne, you let him kick *you* into the *spare room* when *he* was the one messing around?

UnsureOne: Oh, is that wrong? I'm not too sure. This is all new to me . . .

LonelyLady: I wouldn't care if Tommy and I couldn't even stay in the same bed. I just want him home with me.

Divorced_1: Sweet Lord, have I taught you ladies nothing at all . . . ? Anyway, Buttercup, where are you living now if shit-for-brains kept the house?

Buttercup: Oh, this may seem a bit bizarre but I'm currently living with my daughter's father.

UnsureOne: The way it should be, I think.

LonelyLady: Oooh, what a wonderful love story!

Buttercup: Oh, no, no, no. Don't get me wrong, there's absolutely no love involved in this story. In fact, I hate him.

Wildflower: Thou doth protest too much.

Buttercup: Yes, I do, and if you met him you would too.

Divorced_1: I wouldn't be sure of that. Ever since this woman hit sixty she's been eating men for breakfast.

Buttercup: Not this one, I assure you, unless you mistake his head for a hard-boiled egg.

UnsureOne: Buttercup, why did you choose that name?

Buttercup: Oh, it's just a nickname my best friend calls me. When we were six we were in a school play and I was Princess Buttercup and he was Prince Moonbeam. He's been calling me that name ever since.

Divorced_1: You're still in contact after twenty-six years??

Buttercup: Yep, we're still best friends.

Divorced_1: You're best friends with a man? Did you ever sleep with him?
Buttercup: Only when we had sleepovers in the non-sexual kind of way.
Divorced_1: Is he gay?
Buttercup: No he's not.
UnsureOne: Well, I think that's beautiful. I mean, I lost contact with my school friends as soon as I left and got married. Leonard hated me having any male friends.
LonelyLady: When I moved from Belfast to Dublin with Tommy I left all my family and friends behind and now with Tommy gone, my friends are all up north and I'm—
Divorced_1: All alone, yeah, yeah, we get the message. Buttercup, is your friend single, what does he do, where does he live and finally is he looking for a hot forty-nine-year-old with four kids? He can take or leave the kids, I'm not bothered.
Buttercup: No, unfortunately he's not single.
Wildflower: Why 'unfortunately'?
Buttercup: Because she's a real bitch. She's his first love from when he was sixteen. I hated her then and I still hate her now. Anyway, he ended up working with her dad in Boston, of all places, and I suppose their love was rekindled.
Divorced_1: And you're jealous.
Buttercup: I am not.
Divorced_1: Yes you are. I can hear it in your tone.
Buttercup: You cannot hear me; we're typing to each other!
Wildflower: What she means is that she *senses* it and, I must admit, I agree.
UnsureOne: But *surely* if you've been friends since you were six and you're now thirty-two, you've both been married once and are now living with other people in different *countries*, then if it hasn't happened by now, it won't be happening at all.
Wildflower: Oh, Unsure, don't be so pessimistic. Soul

mates have a knack of finding their way to one another.
LonelyLady: Does that mean that my Tommy will come back to me?
Wildflower: No.
SingleSam has entered the room.
Divorced_1: Sam!
Wildflower: Wahoooo! Sam!
LonelyLady: Hi, Sam, welcome. How are you?
UnsureOne: Hello, Sam.
SingleSam: Hello, ladies, good to see you all here again tonight.
Divorced_1: Sam, meet Buttercup. She's thirty-two, has a thirteen-year-old daughter and her husband was cheating on her. Cupcake, meet Sam, he's fifty-four, has two daughters and his ex-wife's a lesbian.
SingleSam: Nice to meet you, Buttercup.
Buttercup: Nice to meet you too, Sam.
UnsureOne: So what's new, Sam? Are you happy or sad today?
SingleSam: Oh, today has been a bad day for me.
Wildflower: Oh please! This is supposed to be the *Relieved* Divorced Dubliners' chat room not the Depressed Divorced Dubliners. I'm heading to bed.
Buttercup: I better head off to bed too. It was nice to meet you all.
Divorced_1: See you same time tomorrow night, Buttercup.
UnsureOne: I better put the kids to bed.
LonelyLady: I think I'll watch the wedding video one more time before I go to bed.
Buttercup has left the room.
LonelyLady has left the room.
UnsureOne has left the room.
Wildflower has left the room.
Divorced_1: Well, Sam, it looks like it's just you and me. You put the music on and I'll light the candles.
Click on the icon to the left to print this page.

From Stephanie
To Rosie
Subject Miss Casey!

I cannot *believe* you're going to be working with Miss Casey! Mum told me over the phone and I could barely understand her through all her laughing. She's wondering what her and Dad should do when they receive a letter from Miss Casey while they're in Australia, demanding to see them first thing Monday morning due to your behaviour at work!

Whatever persuaded you to take this job? Have you gone nuts? I never had a problem with the woman personally, but I know that she drove you insane when you were a kid and then again when Katie had her for a teacher! What does Alex think about all this? I'm sure he's got some very interesting views on the subject!

Dear Stephanie,

Well, you, of course, *never* had a problem with Miss Casey because you were Miss Goody Two-Shoes! She loved you and your neat copies and your finished and correct homework and your tidy uniform and politeness!

I probably am nuts taking this job, but to be honest it's the best one with the most attractive pay packet by far. It's Monday to Friday 9 a.m. to 3.30 p.m. which is great, because I had to work all hours and weekends with my last job. It's right beside Katie's secondary school, which means we can get the bus together every day. We're only a few minutes from the flat so I'll be able to escape home for lunch every day. With all of life's other complications these little things will really help me out a lot. I really don't intend working there for very long, just until a job in the hotel industry opens up.

But the main reason for me taking the job is the fact that I have very little choice. I have a week left here in purgatory (Brian's flat) before I can move into my own rented flat, which is a dump. I'm going to need all the spare cash I can get to fix the place up and make it feel like home. God knows, Katie's had so many of them so far. When the Rosie Dunne Hotel Chain buys Hilton Hotels, that's when I can rip up the budget.

Strange things have happened to Katie over the years, but none of them as bizarre as her mother and father living in the same house as one another. What may be a way of life for some children is something for Katie to laugh hysterically at. Actually, it's not as if Brian and I dislike each other, it's just that we know absolutely *nothing* about one another. We are two complete strangers who got together once in our lives (and only for a few minutes, trust me) in a moment I can barely even remember, to make the most incredible thing ever. How could two fools like us create something as great as Katie? When Katie comes home from school and starts to go off on one of her stand-up comedy routines about her day I look at her, I look at him, and think how did *him*, mixed with *me*, make *her*.

With neither me nor Brian working at all, I try to spend as little time as possible here. I stroll up and down Henry Street for most of the day just to stay out of his way. When I'm at the flat I stay in my room or lock myself into the storeroom and send emails all day. You would think that we would share *some* sort of bond or friendship or have *some* kind of relationship. But we're complete strangers.

I still feel angry at him now, but it's a different kind of anger. Before I felt angry at him because he left *me*. *I* had to do everything. *My* social life was ruined, all *my* money was being spent, and *I* couldn't get a job. But now when I look at him joking around with Katie I just think what a waste. That's all he had to do while she was growing up – be there for her and she would have accepted him, as children do, no matter what he was like. I feel angry at him for not being there for *her*. I've finally lost that selfish part of me.

Once again, I don't quite know where I'm headed,

Steph. It seems that every few years I'm shovelling up the pieces of my life and starting from scratch all over. No matter what I do or how hard I try I can't seem to reach the dizzy heights of happiness, success and security, like so many people do. And I'm not talking about becoming a millionaire and living happily ever after. I just mean reaching a point in my life that I can stop what I'm doing, take a look around me, breathe a sigh of relief and think: I'm where I want to be now.

I'm missing something, you know? That special 'sparkle' that life is supposed to bring. I have the job, the child, the family, the apartment and the friends, but I've lost the sparkle.

And in answer to your question about Alex, I don't know what he thinks of my new job because I haven't heard from him in a long time. He's so busy saving more valuable lives and attending charity functions that I couldn't possibly expect him to get in touch with a friend like me. He's far too busy hooking up with 'old' friends. Slutty ones at that.

Chapter 36

Bon Voyage!

I'll miss you both like crazy. Things won't be the same without you but I hope you have a brilliant time!

Love,
Rosie

To Grandma and Granddad

Have fun, send us loads of postcards.

Love,
Katie (your *favourite* granddaughter)

You have an instant message from: ALEX.
Alex: Hello.
Rosie: Oh, so he *is* still alive. Where have you been for the past few weeks?
Alex: Hiding.
Rosie: From whom?
Alex: You.
Rosie: Why?
Alex: Because I'm dating Bethany again and I was afraid to tell you because you hate her with a passion, and then you found out from *her* first, which made things even worse. So I was hiding from you.
Rosie: Why?
Alex: Because I thought you'd come over here and kill me.
Rosie: Why?
Alex: Because you think she's a slut and that she's no good for me.

Rosie: Why?
Alex: Because you're my overprotective best friend and you've always hated my girlfriends (and wife) and I've always hated your boyfriends (and husband).
Rosie: Why?
Alex: Well, because he had an affair, for one . . .
Rosie: Why?
Alex: Because he was an absolute fool and he didn't no how lucky he was. But let's not talk about him any more because he's gone and he's never coming back.
Rosie: Why?
Alex: Because I scared him off.
Rosie: Why?
Alex: Because I'm your best friend and I care about you.
Rosie: Why?
Alex: Because I've nothing better to do.
Rosie: Why?
Alex: Because it's the unfortunate way that my life turned out. Whatever happened made me care about you and yours. Anyway, it's great that I don't have to hide any more.
Rosie: Why?
Alex: Because I've apologised.
Rosie: Why?
Alex: Because I'm tired of not hearing from you and I miss you.
Rosie: Why?
Alex: Because (and I'm now saying this through incredibly gritted teeth) You. Are. My. Best. Friend. But I have to warn you, I'm not going to listen to any of your bitchy remarks about her this time round.
Rosie: Why?
Alex: Because I really like her, Rosie, and she makes me happy. I feel like the little boy working in Dad's office again. And just think, if it wasn't for you getting so drunk on your sixteenth birthday

that you had to get your stomach pumped, we never would have been caught, we wouldn't have been suspended and I wouldn't have been punished so severely by having to file every piece of paper in the world in Dad's office, where, I might add, I would never have met Bethany. So it's all down to you, my dear friend!

Rosie: OH, WHYYYYYY??? Dear God, why?

Alex: Ha ha. I'd better go now because I've got surgery in a few hours.

Rosie: Why?

Alex: Because I happen to be a cardiac surgeon and there's a poor man, called Mr Jackson, if you really must no, who needs aortic valve surgery.

Rosie: Why?

Alex: Because he has aortic stenosis.

Rosie: Why?

Alex: Well, the reasons behind aortic incompetence in general are rheumatic. But don't worry (because I no that you are), Mr Jackson will be fine.

Rosie: Why?

Alex: Because thankfully due to seventy-five years of studying I have learned an operation involving the ball valve prosthesis which will help him. Any more questions?

Rosie: The aorta, it's in, like, the heart, right?

Alex: Very funny. OK, I'm really going this time; I'm really glad we had this discussion and that we've cleared the whole Bethany thing right up. So I'm forgiven?

Rosie: No.

Alex: Great stuff, thanks. Speak to you soon.

Alex has logged off.

Rosie: Thanks for asking about my job, *Doctor*.

From Rosie
To Ruby
Subject Help!

Help . . . help me . . . Oh dear, my head. My poor,

poor head. My even poorer brain cells, they never even had a chance. They're gone. Dead. It's four o'clock in the afternoon and I am bedridden (not exactly half as much fun as it sounds) and bed is where I shall stay for the remainder of my years. Goodbye world, farewell all, thanks for the memories.

And of the ones remaining from last night I shall try to explain to you exactly what I got up to, although there seems to be a heavy mist working its way in from the edges of my brain towards the centre. I'll try to get it all out before I'm surrounded in fuzziness.

After a very frustrating meeting with my bank manager I returned to Brian the Whine's house feeling very deflated, angry and uncertain about my life. I really wasn't in the mood for conversation or company, but sitting in the living room were Brian's parents, who had flown over from Santa Ponsa to discuss meeting Katie and becoming a part of her life. I was already feeling weary and weak and the thought that Katie would have another set of grandparents – even more people in her life she could have known, yet didn't – just really got to me. And I became even angrier by the fact that all these years I knew who they were, they knew well who I was, they had passed me in the street on numerous occasions while I was pregnant, then again when Katie had been born, had heard the rumours that she was Brian's child yet never bothered to make any sort of contact or give help of any kind. The last I had heard of them was that they had sold up and had moved to the sun to help heal Mrs Whine's arthritis.

The conversation was heated, didn't go that well. Let's just say, so I made my excuses and left.

Of course I had absolutely nowhere to go so I just wandered the streets for ages and pondered my life. After a while I decided I hated it and everyone in it (I know, I know – *again*), and seeing as Katie was away safe for the night and Brian the Whine had company, I made my way to the nearest pub and drowned my sorrows.

The bar was really awful actually, but because I was so upset I didn't care. All I saw was a friendly barman and two serial killers deep in discussion at the end of the bar. So the barman saw that I was really upset, and this is real film stuff, but he actually did ask me what was wrong and seemed genuinely concerned. I told him that Greg had ruined my life. (By process of elimination I reached the conclusion that it was entirely his fault.) It just all came spilling out of my mouth, Ruby, all about Alex missing the debs, Brian the Whine, having Katie, missing college, Alex getting married, meeting Greg, marrying Greg, Greg cheating on me, missing my job promotion, Greg cheating on me again . . . I told him about Greg having all those affairs while he said that he was away on conferences and because he was a bank manager I believed that he genuinely had to go to all that stuff.

So then the other two guys down the end of the bar were suddenly really interested in me, saw how upset I was and bought me loads of drinks. They were huge guys, Ruby, over six foot tall, muscles so big they looked like body builders, bald heads, one guy had a tattoo of a severed head on his forearm, but they were so nice! They were really concerned, asked me loads of questions, gave me tissues when I cried and told me I could do better than Greg. I was just really surprised, Ruby. They were kind enough to drive me home and make sure I got back safely because I was in absolutely no state to walk. I pointed out Greg's house as we passed and they seemed really interested and we all gave him the finger. Such nice guys. It just shows, you can never judge a book by its cover.

Anyway I have such a headache so I have to stop typing but last night proved to me that at least there are *some* caring men in the world and they're not just all out for themselves.

Bank Manager Attacked In His Home

A bank manager was badly beaten in a vicious attack and thousands of euro were stolen in a burglary yesterday morning. The victim was forty-two-year-old Greg Collins of AIB, Fairview, Dublin.

The savage raid took place when Collins was awaked in the early hours of the morning by intruders in his home on Abigail Road. The two masked men broke into the victim's home and demanded the bank manager open the bank and empty the safe. Terrified Collins put up a struggle but was punched viciously in the face by the thugs. His nose, which was healing from a previous injury, was further damaged.

A shaken Collins described how he was blindfolded and forced into their van in his pyjamas.

The thugs are believed to be over six foot tall and according to Collins had the appearance of body builders. Although he didn't see their faces he did notice a tattoo of a severed head on the arm of one thief.

The men stole €20,000 and sped off quickly, leaving Collins alone at the bank, beaten and dressed only in his nightwear. The gardaí arrived on the scene moments after the men had left, after the alarm had been triggered.

Collins is unsure of how they knew his address. 'I'm always careful to look out for anyone suspicious following me home each day but I didn't notice anyone that night. It was the worst night of my life – an absolute nightmare,' Collins said, visibly shaken. 'These thugs invaded my home and attacked me. I'm terrified.'

Collins was home alone at the time due to

the recent break-up of his marriage. An investigation into the burglary was underway today but the Garda in charge says it is unlikely they will catch the culprits, due to a lack of leads.

If anyone has any information regarding this crime, gardaí ask that you come forward now.

Photo above: 42-year-old Greg Collins stands outside the bank and shows broken nose.

You have an instant message from: RUBY.
Ruby: You see the papers today?
Rosie: Nope. I've given up on my star signs.
Ruby: Well, may I suggest you purchase the *Daily Star* quickly and cast your mind back to Saturday night?
Rosie: Oh no, did the paparazzi snap me coming out of the pub? Ha ha.
Ruby: Not funny, Rosie. I'm referring to the men. Now quick, look at the paper.
Rosie: What? What men? What are you talking about?!
Ruby: Tabloid newspaper. Now. Quick. Go.
Rosie: OK.
Rosie has logged off.

From Rosie
To Alex
Subject Today's article

It's me, Rosie. Check your fax machine quick! I've sent you over an article that was in the paper today. While you're reading it bear in mind the story of my Saturday night out that I told you about.

Read the paper and tell me what you think. Quick! I need your advice.

From Alex
To Rosie
Subject Re: Today's article

Ha ha ha ha ha ha ha ha ha ha ha ha ha ha ha ha ha ha ha ha ha ha ha ha ha ha ha ha ha ha ha ha ha ha ha ha ha ha ha ha ha ha ha ha ha ha ha ha ha ha.

Chapter 37

You have received an instant message from: ROSIE.
Rosie: Oh. My. God. Alex.
Alex: Yes, Rosie?
Rosie: Are you free to chat or are you busy?
Alex: I'm just doing a bit of work but go ahead.
Rosie: My goodness, life-saving surgery on the internet? Is there no end to your talents, Doctor?
Alex: Apparently not. What's up?
Rosie: You will NOT believe what came through Brian the Whine's door this morning!
Alex: A brick.
Rosie: No!
Alex: A warrant for your arrest.
Rosie: No! Don't say that! Why would you say that?
Alex: Oh, no reason in particular. I was just wondering what the sentence is for people who hire other people to beat up and terrorise their ex-husbands.
Rosie: Alex Stewart, stop that talk right now! It's not safe to say things like that over the internet, you know, and I did *not* do that!
Alex: You're right, the gardaí are probably on a stakeout right now across the road, watching your every move through a pair of binoculars.
Rosie: Stop, Alex, you're freaking me out. The only thing I'm guilty of is a bit of naïvety, that's all.
Alex: A bit? You think those 'serial killer-looking guys' are usually as friendly to lone women in pubs as they were to you?
Rosie: Look, I was drunk, my suspicions were at an

all-time low and my guard was down. In fact, I had no guard. Stupid, I know, but I'm still alive so let's not keep telling me how foolish I was. Anyway, as it turns out they were caring guys. It just so happens that when I came downstairs this morning there was a brown package on the kitchen table with my name on it. Inside was €5,000, can you believe it?! And you said they weren't caring!

Alex: Was there a note inside, or a little thank-you card maybe?

Rosie: Alex, do you not take anything seriously? No, there wasn't any note so it may not even be from them.

Alex: Rosie, a brown package appeared on your kitchen table overnight with €5,000 inside. Unless the postman has a key to the flat I think we can presume it was them.

Rosie: So what will I tell the gardaí?

Alex: You're not keeping the money?

Rosie: Alex, I have a thirteen-year-old daughter, I do not think keeping knowledge of a bank robbery (as well as some of the money) is exactly the wisest thing to do. Plus, believe it or not I have a conscience.

Alex: Well, usually I would agree with the telling-the-truth theory and abiding by the rules but this time around I think you should keep your mouth shut. Firstly, those guys no you are the only person who nos anything about this, they no where you live and can enter your home in the middle of the night without disturbing the neighbours or anyone else inside. I don't think they were giving you this money as a present for a wonderful start to your new life – they don't seem the type.

Rosie: Oh my God, I've shivers up my spine! This is crazy, like a movie or something. But I can't *not* tell the gardaí.

Alex: Do you want to die?

Rosie: Yes, eventually.

Alex: Rosie, I'm serious. Keep the money and say nothing. Give it to charity or something if it bothers you that much. You can make a donation to the Reginald Williams Foundation for Heart Disease if you want.

Rosie: Gag, gag, puke, puke. No, thanks. But the charity thing isn't a bad idea. I think I'll do that.

Alex: Which one will you donate it to?

Rosie: The Rosie Dunne Foundation for Women who haven't seen their Best Friends in America for ages.

Alex: Excellent idea. I'm sure the poor deprived woman will be delighted with your donation. When do you think she and her daughter will be visiting their doctor friend?

Rosie: I already booked them a flight for Friday week. They land at nine in the morning and they'll be staying a fortnight. You're right; giving makes me feel like such a better person.

Alex: Ha! You had this all planned. I'll be there to pick you up.

Rosie: Good. By the way, you *still* haven't said anything about my job.

Alex: Job? You got a job? When? Where? What are you doing?

Rosie: Alex, I've only left approximately 22,496 messages on your answering machine explaining this. Don't you listen to them?

Alex: Sorry. So what's the job?

Rosie: Promise not to laugh.

Alex: I promise.

Rosie: I'm starting in August as a secretary in St Patrick's Primary School.

Alex: You're going back . . . *there*? Hold on a minute . . . that means that you're going to be working with Miss Big Nose Smelly Breath Casey! Why?

Rosie: Because I need the money.

Alex: Wouldn't you rather starve? Why on earth did she hire you?

Rosie: I'm wondering the same thing.

Alex: Ha ha ha ha ha.
Rosie: You said you wouldn't laugh.
Alex: Ha ha ha ha ha.
Rosie: You promised!
Alex: Ha ha ha ha ha.
Rosie: Oh, bugger off.
Rosie has logged off.

Dear Rosie and Katie,
Greetings from Aruba!
Having a wonderful time here in paradise!
Hope all is well with you,
Lots of love,
Mum and Dad

You have received an instant message from: RUBY.
Ruby: Watch out, Ireland, here we come!
Rosie: Here who come?
Ruby: Gary and Ruby Minnelli.
Rosie: You're keeping the name, I see?! What are Gary and Ruby Minnelli up to now?
Ruby: Yes, we're keeping the name and Gary doesn't even mind because it means that he's in disguise and none of his work colleagues or friends will recognise him. The All-Ireland Salsa Dancing Championships are on in a few months from now. A couple from each county goes forward and whoever wins becomes the Ireland champions, then there's the European Championship and the World Championship.
Rosie: So you're going for total world domination?
Ruby: Well, not quite the *world* but Gary and I are willing to take on Ireland.
Rosie: How does Teddy feel?
Ruby: He has no idea and that's the way it's going to stay. Anyway, we haven't even gotten through the Dublin heats so there's no point in causing mayhem and bloody murdering sprees until we get further into the competition. It's on in a few weeks – will you be there?

Rosie: I'm insulted you even had to ask!
Ruby: Thanks.

From Stephanie
To Rosie
Subject Visit

I hope you're keeping well. You're dealing with everything that has happened so brilliantly, I'm so proud of you. I know it's been a tough time and with me being all the way over here I feel like I haven't been there for you like I should have been. If it's OK with you I would love to come over and visit you. Maybe stay for a week or something. With Mum and Dad off gallivanting around the world, unfortunately the rest of us don't meet up like we should, and it must be very lonely for you. Maybe we should go to Kilkenny and visit Kevin. The three of us haven't been in the same room together since I don't know how long. (Don't worry, we won't go to the hotel. We can stand outside and throw eggs at the windows, if you like!)

To be really honest with you I need the rest as well. Jean-Louis is just too much for me right now. He's a bundle of energy and I'm simply not, so Pierre is taking the week off from the restaurant to mind him so that I can see you.

Also, I know that you're at Brian's so I'll stay with a friend – I certainly wouldn't want to upset the happy family! I haven't seen him since your school dance when he arrived at the house wearing his navy tux (I agree with you, it was definitely navy, not black). It'll be interesting to see how he's turned out and I'll give him a piece of my mind too. If you have other plans then feel free to let me know.

From Rosie
To Stephanie
Subject Re: Visit

Of course I would love you to come over. Next week is great; in fact it couldn't be more perfect. You see, Brian the Whine's parents have returned from the depths of hell (and are constantly complaining about the cold here, even though it's the middle of summer and everyone is wearing shorts. Every time I open a window they shiver and pull another blanket around them. Not what they're used to at their private *villa* at all, which just so happens to be a one-bedroom apartment in Santa Ponsa). Anyway, the traumatic thing is that they are staying in this very flat in a desperate attempt to get to know me and their 'granddaughter'. The only thing is, it's the summer holidays and all Katie wants to do is hang around outside with Toby, not inside with two shivering, shrivelled-up whinge-bags.

The flat feels even more cramped than usual with them being here and I feel so claustrophobic. Imagine, I actually can't wait to start my new job just so I can get out of the house. Toby is very funny: he keeps telling me and Katie to be nice to them so we can get to use the apartment whenever we want. So Katie and him keep making them cups of tea and bringing it to them while they're still in bed. I know the boy is only thirteen but he has a point, so recently I started putting biscuits on their saucers.

So you coming over, my dear sister, could not come at a better time. It is both a genius and life-saving idea. Plus I really miss you too! At least I'm going to have a great summer before I start the job in hell.

From Rosie
To Kevin
Subject Steph's visit

Steph is over from France for the week. What days are you off so that we can come down and visit you? We can all go out for a meal or something. We haven't done that for a while.

From Kevin
To Rosie
Subject Re: Steph's visit

That sounds like a good plan. I don't think the three of us have been in the same room together since Mum and Dad forced us to take baths together. I've got Tuesday off, so why don't you both come down on Monday and I'll treat you for dinner?

From Rosie
To Kevin
Subject Re: Steph's visit

Going for dinner sounds good as long as we don't go to the hotel to eat. Knowing whatshisname was there with *her* is enough to put me off it for ever. Stephanie had the wonderfully juvenile idea of me throwing eggs at the hotel to release my anger. Stock up on those eggs, dear brother. We'll be down on Monday to celebrate your good news, see you then.

Invoice Number: KIL000321
Our Reference: 6444421

Fee Invoice

Fee for damage to dining-room windows
of Kilkenny Two Lakes Hotel: €6,232.00
VAT @ 21% €1,308.72

Total €7,540.72

Note to self:

Must always check that eggs are not hard-boiled before throwing.

From Rosie
To Alex
Subject Flight details

My flight is landing at 9 a.m. so don't forget!

Hello from Barbados!

We're having such a ball! The weather is fantastic and we've met lots of lovely people.

Love you both,
Mum and Dad

You have received an instant message from: ROSIE.

Rosie: I'm baaaaack!

Ruby: Oh, so you decided to come home! I'm surprised.

Rosie: Well, I almost didn't. If it wasn't for Brian the Whine and his parents wanting to be my new best friends and ruining all my plans.

Ruby: Imagine, having to think of other people. So how did it go?

Rosie: It was just so brilliant. That's all I can say. Pure heaven.

Ruby: You two get along well?

Rosie: Even better than usual.

Ruby: Did you—

Rosie: No!

Ruby: Did you tell him how you—

Rosie: No! Why on earth would I do that? There's no point. If I did that then I would lose him as a friend for ever and then it would all be a waste of time. He has never suggested to me that he has ever felt that way about me; remember it was me that kissed him the last time. That was embarrassing enough once, never mind having to do it a second time. Anyway, he is already with someone and even if it is Slutty Bethany I couldn't bring myself to do that. We had a really long chat about her, anyway. He took me out for dinner one night to a beautiful Italian restaurant that had wonderful murals of Venetian buildings painted across the walls. The restaurant had two levels, every table was in its own little alcove, and you could only get to them by walking under bridges and arches. It was supposed to have a gondola trip kind of vibe. There was running water tinkling in the background, which was really relaxing although it made me go to the bathroom about ten times. The restaurant was lit entirely by candles all held in big gothic-looking black holders – an insurance nightmare, I would imagine, but very romantic. I think he brought me there to talk about Slutty Bethany and to explain the situation.

It doesn't seem to be that serious a relationship. He said he's enjoying the company after being alone for so long and it's good that she understands his long working hours but they don't see that much of each other and he thinks she understands that it's a very casual relationship. It sounds like he's going to break up with her actually because he got really serious and I thought he was going to cry. It was weird; he said that she wasn't 'the one' for him.

Ruby: And then what?

Rosie: And then Josh rang the restaurant in a right panic, looking for us. He and Katie had been messing around, Katie had fallen and they were convinced she'd broken her wrist. We had to leave straight away but we had finished dessert and everything, so it was just as well. The conversation was finished.

Ruby: Or was just starting, by the sounds of things.

Rosie: What do you mean?

Ruby: God, you annoy me so much, Rosie. Can a human being really be this stupid?

Rosie: Look, Ruby, you weren't there. It's all very well you giving me this advice but I'm the one who physically has to go and do it. I'll tell him how I feel when it's the right moment.
Ruby: When will it *ever* be the right moment for you?
Rosie: When there's the silence again.
Ruby: What silence?
Rosie: It doesn't matter. Anyway, Katie's fine. It was only a sprain. She can't play basketball this week, though, so she's upset about that.
Ruby: Have you pencilled the Dublin Salsa Dancing Championships into your diary?
Rosie: Of course. Katie and Toby are coming too. Has Teddy had a change of heart yet?
Ruby: I can't tell him about the competition, Rosie. If I did he would probably march with his trucker mates to the Red Cow Hotel and protest against men dancing in glittery suits. It's far more enjoyable for myself and Gary if we don't think Teddy is about to barge into the reception hall looking like Homer Simpson on a mission. I'm proud of Gary. I don't want Teddy and his pure ignorance and lack of intelligence to ruin something that has taken years to achieve.
Rosie: Oh, I can't wait to see you two dancing together. I'll bring the camera, so if Teddy ever does have a change of heart he won't have missed the moment completely. So what are you going to wear while you're dancing?
Ruby: Well, that was proving to be a huge problem. I know all the other dancers competing will be baring flesh for all to see but the idea of my outfit will be to cover up as much as I can. Unfortunately, Upsizes don't make sexy salsa dresses, even for my size. Gary was having the same problem. So after Miss Behave got over being in a huff at being replaced, she offered to make us something. She said she's used to 'making women's clothes for people who haven't the nat-

ural figure of a woman'. Worryingly enough, she won't tell us what she's making. But I've told her to steer clear of pink, fluff and rubber.
Rosie: Look forward to it!

Ba'ax ka wa'alik from Mexico!

What an adventure this is taking us on. Hope you're both safe and happy.

Love Mum and Dad

Happy Fourteenth Birthday, Toby.

Hope you like the remote-control car I got you. The guy in the shop said the Rally ones are the best (and they're the most expensive too). I got it for you in the States so I don't think anyone else will have them here. Josh has one as well. That's what I tripped over and sprained my wrist on. They're really fast!

Anyway, here's to another year. Maybe ten years from now you'll be poking at people's teeth. Why you want to be a dentist is beyond me, but you were always weird. I heard Monica Doyle is going out with Sean. Tough luck, my friend.

Katie

From	Toby
To	Katie
Subject	Re: Happy birthday

Thanks for the car. I'm gonna bring it to the crappy dance thing on Sunday. You girls can paint your nails and watch them dance while I drive my car out in the corridor.

Aloha from Hawaii!

I've sent photos of me, your dad and some people that we've met on the cruise. Having a ball. Heading to Samoa and Fiji next. Can't wait!

Love to you and Katie,

Mum and Dad xxx

Ruby and Gary Minnelli!
Good Luck!
I was going to say 'Break a leg' but I don't think it's quite appropriate for the occasion. You will both be brilliant and we'll all be cheering for you.
Love Rosie, Katie and Toby

You have received an instant message from: ROSIE.
Rosie: Congratulations, you Dancing Queen! I'm so proud of you! Are you still glowing from your win?
Ruby: I'm not too sure how I'm supposed to be feeling, to be honest. I really don't think that we should be the winners.
Rosie: Oh, don't be silly! The two of you danced brilliantly. Miss Behave did such a great job on your dress. I'm surprised it was so understated for one of her creations. Black with glittery sequins looked *très chic* compared to all the others. They looked like rainbows on E. Look, you won it fair and square – be proud.
Ruby: But we didn't even get through to the final round . . .
Rosie: Well, it's not your fault the couple who came first were practising out in the corridor. Anyone could have slipped on Toby's stupid remote-control car. It was their own fault. Anyway, her ankle will heal with time. She'll be back next year to reclaim her title.
Ruby: Yes, but technically we shouldn't have won at all, Rosie. Only the two couples who got to the final round were supposed to battle it out. The second couple who were in the final really should have won . . .
Rosie: Yes, but once again that wasn't your fault. It was the woman in purple who tripped over Toby's car (they're very fast, aren't they?), knocking the drink out of Katie's hand, causing the second woman in yellow to slip and land on her backside. That automatically put you through. It's not your fault. You should be delighted!!

Ruby: Well, I am in an odd kind of way. Me and Gary are performing our winning dance in Miss Behave's show in the George.

Rosie: That's fantastic! I'm delighted for you, Ruby. My friend the superstar!

Ruby: Oh, I wouldn't even be doing all this if you hadn't got me the vouchers for my fortieth birthday. Thanks so much, Rosie. And thanks for cheering for me so loudly. I heard you the whole way through the dance. And I'm really sorry you, Katie and Toby were asked to leave the dance hall . . .

Chapter 38

Rosie and Katie,

Magandang tanghali po from the Philippines!

Left the top end of Australia a few days ago. We were in Brisbane and Sydney – very beautiful. Here for a little while, then moving on to China for a few days.

Love you and miss you both,

Mum and Dad

From Rosie
To Alex
Subject Slutty Bethany

So, Alex, did you dump her yet?

From Alex
To Rosie
Subject Mind your own business

Rosie, stop! I'll tell you when I do!

Ni hao from China!

Sorry we're not there to help you with the move. We wish you luck in your new apartment. We're sure it will bring you lots of happiness.

Love, Mum and Dad xxx

Rosie: The place is disgusting, Ruby. Absolutely disgusting.

Ruby: Oh, stop. It can't be any worse than mine.
Rosie: Worse than yours multiplied by one hundred.
Ruby: Such a place exists? God bless you. What's so bad about it?
Rosie: Well, let's see, where should I start? Hmm . . . should I tell you about the fact that it's a second-floor apartment over a group of shops, among them a tattoo parlour and an Indian takeaway which has managed to leave the stench of tikka masala all over my clothes already?

Perhaps I should tell you about the *gorgeous* 1970s green and grey floral wallpaper which is just *dangling* off the walls, and I wouldn't want to forget the fact that there's matching curtains too.

Hmm . . . actually maybe I should start with the brown carpets, which have very curious-looking stains embedded in the pile, as well as cigarette burns and mysterious odours. I think it's been there for about thirty years and has never been vacuumed. The kitchen is so small that when two people stand in it, one person has to back out to let the other leave. But *at least* the water works and the toilet flushes.

No wonder the rent is so ridiculously cheap; no one in their right mind would want to live here.
Ruby: You are.
Rosie: Yes, well, I won't be here for long. I'm going to magically save loads of money and get us out of here.
Ruby: And open a hotel.
Rosie: Yes.
Ruby: And live in the penthouse.
Rosie: Yes.
Ruby: And Kevin can be the head chef.
Rosie: Yes.
Ruby: And Alex the in-house doctor so that he can save the lives of those you poison.
Rosie: Yes.
Ruby: And you'll be the owner and manager.
Rosie: Yes.

Ruby: So what can I be?
Rosie: You and Gary could be the evening entertainment. You can salsa till you drop.
Ruby: Sounds like heaven to me. Well, Rosie, you better get your ass in gear and get this hotel business off the ground before we're all old and grey.
Rosie: I'm working on it. So how's Teddy after the shock of you winning the salsa competition?
Ruby: Oh, he's taking each day as it comes. But seriously, Rosie, I'm finding his behaviour very hard to come to terms with. When he found out we had won the competition and that we were going to perform it in the George he hit the roof. But he must have banged his head or something because the other night he offered to drive us to dance classes, which almost made me drop dead, and he's coming to the gay club on Friday (he's either really proud of me and Gary or he's just tired of me refusing to iron his shirts). Although he's bringing a really large friend of his to make sure no one tries anything funny with him. As if any male or female would try *anything* with Teddy. Anyway, that's enough about me. What are your plans for the week?
Rosie: Well, I start work part time (with the work-experience kids) which consists of printing up the school letters explaining the return dates for the pupils next month, we put the letters in envelopes, stick stamps on them, lick them closed and post them. I don't know about you but I'm enthralled by that idea. But at least it's only for a few weeks and when the kids start back at school then I work full time.

Apart from that I'm trying to make this kip of a place look like a home. Brian the Whine has been very helpful, believe it or not. He's hired out a sander for the day and tomorrow we're going to rip up those smelly carpets and sand and varnish the floors in all the rooms. I'm frightened to think of what we'll find under them. Probably a few dead bodies.

Katie and Toby are having great fun tearing the wallpaper off the walls – well, what's left of it, anyway. We're going to paint the walls white, because even with a million-watt bulb the place still looks like a cave. It needs brightening up and I'm going for the minimalist look, not because I'm trendy and fashionable but because I don't really have that much furniture. I'm going to pull down the old curtains and burn them in a ritual.

My darling brother Kevin was only too delighted to come to Dublin and raid whatshisname's house for all my leftover belongings, which he gladly gave him, probably because he was so terrified of having his nose broken again. I even got the black leather couch which was in the house before I married him but, hey, I deserve it.

Ruby: It sounds like it's going to be lovely, Rosie. A real home.

Rosie: Yeah, now all I need to do is get rid of the smell of curry that's floating around and seeping through the walls of the entire building. It's turned me off Indian food for ever.

Ruby: Now *that's* the best diet I've ever heard of. Live over a restaurant and the smell will make you sick of food.

Rosie: I think you're on to something there.

Ei Je from Singapore!

Having such a wonderful time. We don't want to come home!

Good luck with your new job this week, love. We're thinking of you here as we lounge by the pool! (Just joking.)

Love,
Mum and Dad

You have received an instant message from: ALEX.

Alex: Have you a minute to chat?

Rosie: No, sorry, I'm busy licking stamps.

Alex: Oh, OK. Can I call you sometime later?

Rosie: I was only joking, Alex. Miss Big Nose Smelly Breath Casey has asked me to put together the year's first newsletter so I'm on the school website trying to figure out what happened or is happening that's worth writing about. I'm thinking of putting the fact that I'm working here as the main story.

Alex: How's the job?

Rosie: It's OK. I've been here a few weeks now so I've settled in and it's going OK. Nothing to write home about.

Alex: Sorry I wasn't in touch sooner. I hadn't realised it had been so long. Time has been flying by once again.

Rosie: It's OK. I assumed you were busy. I've moved into my apartment now and everything.

Alex: Oh, gosh, that's right. How is it?

Rosie: It's OK. It was absolutely dire when we first moved in, but Brian the Whine was a really good help. He fixed all that was broken and cleaned what was dirty. Just like a regular little slave.

Alex: So are you and he getting along then?

Rosie: Better. I only have the urge to strangle him ten times a day now.

Alex: Well, it's a start. Any romance?

Rosie: What? With Brian the Whine? You need your head examined. The man was created for scraping mould and sanding floors only.

Alex: Oh. Anyone else in your life?

Rosie: Yes, actually. A thirteen-year-old daughter, a new job and a drawer stuffed with bills. My hands are pretty full at the moment. Although my neighbour did ask me to go out on a date with him this weekend.

Alex: So are you going out with him?

Rosie: Let me tell you a little bit about him first and then maybe you can help me with the dilemma I'm faced with. His name is Sanjay, he's sixty years old, and he's married, lives with his wife and two sons, and owns and runs the Indian takeaway downstairs. Oh, and you'll never guess where he invited me out for dinner.

Alex: Where?

Rosie: His takeaway. He said he would pay.

Alex: So what's your dilemma?

Rosie: Very funny.

Alex: Well, at least you have friendly neighbours.

Rosie: He's not the nicest by far. Beside me there's the owner of the tattoo parlour (which is also below my flat). He's got tattoos covering his body from head to toe. He's got beautiful long black silky hair that he ties back in a plait, and a neatly trimmed goatee framing his mouth. He's over six feet tall, wears leather trousers, a leather waistcoat and big steel-toed biker boots every day. When he's not drilling away on somebody's skin downstairs he's blaring music from his flat beside mine.

Alex: Trust you to move in beside a heavy metal fan.

Rosie: That's where you're wrong. His name is Rupert; he's thirty-five years old, a graduate of the prestigious Trinity College, Dublin, where he got a degree in Irish History and a Masters in Irish Literature. James Joyce is his idol and across his chest is the quote, 'Mistakes are the portals of discovery.'

He's a huge fan of classical music and opera, and at 5 p.m. every evening when he's closing up and cashing up the till for the night he has Brahms' Piano Concerto Number 2 in B flat, Op. 83 blaring out. After that he heads up to his flat where he proceeds to cook the most savoury and delicious-smelling meals and settles down to read *Ulysses* for the billionth time while listening to the sounds of *The Best of Pavarotti* blasting out from his speakers (paying particular attention to 'Nessun dorma').

Katie and I practically know all the words to it by this stage and Toby stuffs a pillow up his shirt, stands up on the couch and mimes along to the music. At least Rupert is educating the children. Katie is going crazy about mixing 'Nessun dorma' into a dance song she's created on her new set of decks. Brian the Whine bought them for her, which made me really angry because I was planning on getting them for her as a Christmas present. But I've made her keep them in his rented flat so that she doesn't disturb my neighbours. Although, to be honest, I really don't know why I bothered caring, with all the other noises and smells going on around us. Oh yes, and did I mention that Joan of Arc is living across the hall from me?

Alex: Ha ha, no, you didn't.

Rosie: Well, this woman (her name is Joan, Mary or Brigid or something) is in her late twenties. She came over to say hello the day we first moved in and when she realised that it was just Katie and me, and that my singledom was not due to the tragic loss of my husband she left rather rudely and hasn't spoken to us since.

Alex: Well, at least she's quiet.

Rosie: Just because she ignores me, the sinner of the apartment block, it doesn't mean she's quiet. Every Monday evening I noticed there seem to be a large herd of elephants making their way upstairs to our level and going into Joan of Arc's flat. After further investigation I noticed that the same twenty people visit every week, all bearing gifts of Bibles in their hands.

My further powers of investigation led me to believe that she was holding Bible-reading groups every week. Now she's put a sign up on the door saying, 'Ye shall walk after your LORD, and fear him, and keep his commandments, and obey his voice, and ye shall serve him, and cleave unto him.' I mean, what does 'cleave' mean? Whoever has heard of such a word?

Alex: Ha ha, Rosie. Oh, I really don't no!

Rosie: You mean KNOW, not NO. You will never

learn, will you? Then down the hall from me is a family from Nigeria. Zareb and Malika and their four kids. And I thought the place was too small for just me and Katie.

Alex: How are your mum and dad?

Rosie: My multilingual mum and dad, you mean? Well, they're having the time of their lives away from all of us. Mum recently celebrated her sixtieth; she sent me a postcard saying, 'Zdravstvuite from Russia!' I can just imagine the two of them enjoying themselves like an old couple from *The Love Boat*. Speaking of the dreaded 'L' word, what was with all the personal questions about my love life?

Alex: Because I want you to find someone, that's why. I want you to be happy.

Rosie: Alex, I've never found happiness with another human being and you know it. I'm separated from my husband; I'm not looking for another victim just yet. Possibly never.

Alex: *Never?*

Rosie: Possibly. Well, I'll never marry again, that's for sure. I'm getting used to my new life. I have a new apartment, a new job, a teenage daughter, I'm thirty-two years old and I'm entering a new phase of my life. I think I'm finally growing up. Anyway, there's nothing wrong with being single. Being single is the new black. You should know.

Alex: I'm not single.

Rosie: Not *yet*.

Alex: No, I'm not. I won't be.

Rosie: Why, have you changed your mind about breaking up with Slutty Bethany?

Alex: My mind was never made up in the first place to be changed, and please don't call her slutty. I never said I was going to end mine and Beth's relationship.

Rosie: Well, it sounded like that to me when we discussed it at dinner last month.

Alex: Yes, well, never mind that dinner. My head was

elsewhere. So what I'm saying is that I want me to be happy with Bethany and you to be happy with someone and then we'll both be happy with people.

Rosie: I know what it is. You just don't want me to be single because I'm a distraction to you. If I'm with a man then you think that *perhaps* you just might be able to keep your hands off me. I know deep down that's what this is all about. I've sussed you out, Alex Stewart. You love me. You want me to have your babies. You can't stand another day without me.

Alex: I . . . don't no what to say . . .

Rosie: Relax, I'm joking. What happened to make you change your mind about Bethany?

Alex: Oh, not back to this again . . .

Rosie: Alex, I'm your best friend, I've known you since I was five. No one knows you better than I do. I'm asking this for the very last time and do not lie. What happened to make you change your mind about breaking up with Slutty Bethany?

Alex: She's pregnant.

Rosie: Oh dear God. Sometimes, because you're my best friend, I think that you're normal, like me. Then every now and again you remind me that you're a man.

Phil: Hold on a minute, Alex. A couple of years ago you were trying to *break up* Rosie's marriage and now you're telling me that you *want* her to meet somebody new?

Alex: Yes.

Phil: Just so that while you're with Bethany, you won't feel *tempted*?

Alex: No! That's not what I said!

Phil: Well, that's what it sounds like. At the rate you're going, I don't think the two of you deserve each other at all.

PART FOUR

Chapter 39

Welcome home, Mum and Dad! (Fáilte go h-Eirinn!)

Glad you arrived home safely and in one piece! Can't wait to hear all the stories of your adventures and see all the photographs.

See you at the weekend.

Love,

Rosie and Katie

Dear Stephanie and Pierre!

Congratulations on the arrival of your new baby girl!

We can't wait to meet little Sophia. In the meantime here are a few little outfits to keep her as trendy as her mother!

Lots of love,

Rosie and Katie

Happy 5th Birthday, Josh.

Lots of love,

Rosie and Katie

Hi, Katie,

Thanks for your card and present that you gave me fro my brithday. I guess my dad told you guys about Bethinny being pregnint. That means I'm gonna have a brother or sister.

Dad is sad because he said all the grils in his life are mad at him. Your mom is, my mom is and Bethinny is too. Bethinny is mad at him cos he won't marry her. Bethinny was crying and saying that dad didn't love her and he was saying that they needed to get to know more about each other before they got married. Bethinny said he knew everything there was to know about her and if he didn't marry her, her dad would be really angry and would fire him.

I think dad should marry her. I want a brother and dad really, really likes his job. I'll fill you and Toby in on more stuff as soon as I can. Cos I'm only here at weekends I miss all the good stuff.

Thank your mom fro my pressent.

Form Josh

PS. Bethinny wants a house in Marthas Vineyard. I've never met Martha and I don't know how she would feel about us moving onto her vineyard all of a sudden but dad didn't seem too happy about the idea. I think he hates grapes.

Dr Williams Rewarded

Reginald Williams was honoured last night at the National Health Awards in Boston. He was nominated through a highly selective process that recognises those who have made major contributions to the advancement of the medical sciences and public health.

This award is considered one of the highest honours in the fields of medicine and health. He was accompanied to the ceremony by his wife, Miranda, his daughter, Bethany, and her newly announced fiancé Dr Alex Stewart, cardio-surgeon at St Jude's Hospital in Boston.

See page four of the Health supplement for Wayne Gillespie's report.

You have received an instant message from: ROSIE.

Rosie: You wanted me to learn about this in the newspapers first?

Alex: I'm sorry, Rosie.

Rosie: You're sorry? You get engaged and you let me read about it in a newspaper? What the hell has happened to you these days?

Alex: Rosie, all I can say is sorry.
Rosie: I don't understand the way your mind works, Alex. You don't even love her.
Alex: I do.
Rosie: Well, that's convincing.
Alex: I shouldn't have to *convince* anyone.
Rosie: Only yourself. Alex, you told me you didn't love her. In fact a few months back you were planning on breaking up with her. Gee, I wonder what happened to make you change your mind all of a sudden.
Alex: You no what happened. There's a baby involved now.
Rosie: That's bullshit. The Alex I know wouldn't marry a woman he doesn't love for the sake of the baby. That's the worst thing you could do to the poor child – raise it in an environment where the parents don't even love each other. What's the point of that? You're not with Sally and things with Josh work out fine. It may not be the most desired position to be in – everyone wants to play happy families – but it doesn't always work out that way. This is ridiculous.
Alex: I'm a weekend dad to Josh; I don't want a repeat of that. It's not right.
Rosie: Marrying someone you don't love is not right.
Alex: I'm extremely fond of Bethany; we have a great relationship and get on well.
Rosie: Well, I'm glad you and your future wife 'get on well'. If you don't think this through properly, Bethany will be another Sally. Another failed marriage is not what you want.
Alex: This marriage won't fail.
Rosie: No, you'll just be miserable for the rest of your life, but that's great just as long as the tongues of disapproving people can't gossip about you.
Alex: Why should I take advice from you, Rosie? What on earth have you done in your life that makes you such an expert on telling me how to

live mine? You lived with a man that cheated on you for years and you kept taking him back time and time again. What do you no about marriage?

Rosie: I know enough not to go racing up the aisle with someone else I barely know or love. I know enough to not allow my life choices to be influenced by my desire for money and power and prestige. I know enough not to marry a man so a bunch of rich people will smile at me and tell me how great I am. I wouldn't marry a man to get my picture in the paper, my name on an award trophy or for some dumb promotion at work.

Alex: Oh, Rosie, you make me laugh. You have no idea what you're talking about. You've obviously been spending too much time in your flat doing nothing but concocting conspiracy theories.

Rosie: Of course, because that's all I do. Sit around my council flat doing nothing, being the poor uneducated single mother that I am while you and your Harvard pals sit in your gentlemen's clubs, smoking cigars and patting each other on the back. We may live in very different worlds, Alex Stewart, but I know you and I'm sick of seeing who you've turned into.

So what would good old Reginald Williams have done if he had learned that his daughter was pregnant and that the fool who was responsible wouldn't marry her? Oh, the shame that would bring on the family, how the people would talk.

But at least now she's got the ring on her finger, and you've got the job promotion, and we can all live happily ever after.

Alex: Not everybody walks away, Rosie. They might in your life, but not in mine.

Rosie: Alex, for Christsake! Not marrying Bethany isn't 'walking away'. As long as you're there for the child then you're not walking away. You don't have to *marry* her!

Alex: Look, I'm fed up with all this, Rosie, with you constantly checking up on me, me having to explain everything to you. You're not my wife or my mother, so give it a rest. Who says I have to run all my life decisions by you, anyway? I'm tired of you nagging at me and moaning at me about people I see and places I go. I can make decisions on my own, you no. I'm a grown man.

Rosie: Then for once in your life ACT LIKE ONE!

Alex: Who are you to insult *me* and lecture *me* when you haven't done a thing right in your life yourself? Just do me a favour and don't bother getting in touch until you have something decent to say.

Rosie: Fine! Well then, I think you'll find you'll be waiting a long, long time.

Rosie has logged off.

Alex: No change there then.

Phil: What are you doing?

Alex: You no what I'm doing.

Phil: Why are you marrying her?

Alex: *Her* name is Bethany.

Phil: Why are you marrying *Bethany*?

Alex: Because I love her.

Phil: Really? Because last time you stepped into the virtual confessional box, you told me you were planning on ending your relationship. Why do you feel you have to do this? Is her dad putting pressure on you?

Alex: No, no, no. There's no pressure. I want to do this.

Phil: Why?

Alex: Why the hell not? Why did you marry Margaret?

Phil: I married Margaret because I love every inch of the woman with all my heart and plan to be with her for the rest of my life, in sickness and in health, till death do us part. She is my best friend, we have five beautiful children and as much as they drive me up the walls sometimes, I couldn't live a day without them. I don't sense you have this with Bethany.

Alex: Not all relationships are like yours and Margaret's.

Phil: No, they're not but the intention should be there at the beginning. Was there the silence thing with Bethany?

Alex: Oh, shut up about the silence, Phil.

Phil: You're the one who's obsessed with it. So, come on, was there?

Alex: No.

Phil: Then you shouldn't marry her.

Alex: OK, I won't, just because you say so.

Phil: What does Rosie say about it?

Alex: Nothing. She's not talking to me.

Phil: How do you feel about that?

Alex: At this stage, I'm so mad at her, I don't care what she thinks. I'm moving on from her. Bethany and this new baby are my future. Can I leave the confessional box now?

Phil: Yeah. Say five Hail Marys and an Our Father, and God rest your messed-up little soul.

You have received an instant message from: KATIE.

Katie: You look very interested in learning about the female reproduction system.

Toby: I'm not. I'd rather figure it out for myself the practical way.

Katie: Oh, funny, but you'll be old and grey before anyone lets you get your hands on them.

Toby: My best friend is a comedienne. You had a salad roll for lunch, didn't you?

Katie: How do you no?

Toby: KNOW not NO. Because I can see the lettuce hanging out of your braces. So what do you want?

Katie: Well, not that you deserve to be asked, but I'm going to the orthodontist again later if you wanna come. You can ask him a million questions about everything he's doing, as always, and annoy the hell out of him. It's so funny the way that vein in his forehead pulsates when he sees you.

Toby: Yeah, I know. Sorry, I can't go. Monica is

coming around to my house to watch the football.
Katie: Monica, Monica, Monica. I'm sick of hearing about stupid Monica Doyle. So why aren't I invited to your house?
Toby: Because you have to go to the dentist.
Katie: Yes, but you didn't no that until a second ago.
Toby: OK then, would you like to watch the football, the sport that you absolutely hate with a passion played by the two teams you hate even more, at my house today?
Katie: I can't. I'm busy.
Toby: You see? Now don't say I never ask you out anywhere.
Katie: How long have you known that I'm going to the dentist?
Toby: All of five minutes.
Katie: How long ago did you invite Monica Doyle to your house?
Toby: Last week.
Katie: My point exactly!

You have received an instant message from: KATIE.
Katie: Mum, I hate men.
Rosie: Congratulations, dear. Welcome to the club. Your membership is in the post. I'm so proud of this moment I wish I had a camera.
Katie: Please, Mum, I'm serious.
Rosie: And so am I. So what has Toby done this time?
Katie: He's invited Monica Doyle to his house to watch the football and he didn't invite me. Well, he did, but only after he new I was busy.
Rosie: Oh dear, he's caught the bug already. Is this moany Monica we're talking about? The little girl who cried all day at your tenth birthday party until her parents came to collect her because her false nail fell off?
Katie: Yes.
Rosie: Oh dear. I hate that child.
Katie: She's not a child any more, Mum. She's four-

teen, got the biggest chest in the school, dyes her hair blonde, leaves the top buttons of her polo shirt open in PE and leans down so the boys can see down her top. She even flirts with Mr Simpson and pretends not to understand what he's talking about in computer class so he'll come up behind her and lean over her to show her what to do.

She hates talking about anything other than shopping so I don't no why she's going to even bother watching football. Well, actually I do no why.

Rosie: Sounds like she's got a case of the Slutty Bethanitis to me.

Katie: What? What do I do about Monica?

Rosie: Oh, that's simple. Assassinate her.

Katie: Please, Mum, for once in your life be serious.

Rosie: I am an incredibly serious woman. The only way to deal with this is to silence her. Because if not, she'll only end up coming back to haunt you when you're thirty-two years old. Death is the only thing for it.

Katie: Thanks, but I'm open to any other suggestions you may have.

Rosie: You said he invited you?

Katie: Yes, but only because he new I couldn't go.

Rosie: My dear sweet innocent daughter, an invitation is an invitation. It would be rude to turn him down. I suggest you turn up on his doorstep this evening, I'll give you the money for the bus to his house.

Katie: But, Mum, I can't go! You know I've got an appointment with the orthodontist.

Rosie: Well, the dentist can wait. I'll make another appointment for you. This is a very important football match, you know. I wouldn't want you to miss it just because of a silly little thing like getting your teeth fixed. Now get off the computer before Mr Simpson catches you and reports me to Miss Big Nose Smelly Breath Casey and gets me fired.

Katie: You wish, Mum. I don't no how you work with her every day.

Rosie: Actually, I'm surprised to admit it myself but she's not so bad. As far as bosses go she's been really, really pleasant. Her name is Julie. Can you believe it? She actually has a first name. And it's a nice, normal name too; I would have thought it was something more like Vladimir or Adolf.

Katie: Ha ha, me too. But is it not really awkward working with someone who used to give out to you every day?

Rosie: Things are a little awkward between us. It kind of feels like she's an ex-boyfriend of mine and we're meeting after years of separation. Every day conversation becomes a little longer, a little friendlier, a little less about work and a little more about life. We've spent so many years arguing with each other it feels odd to agree on things. But each day we talk more and more. Do you know that she thought Alex was your dad?!

Katie: Did she?!

Rosie: Anyway, I told her that Brian was your father and she couldn't stop laughing . . . Actually, perhaps this isn't a story to tell you.

Katie: Wait till Alex hears you saying that you like her. He'll drop dead with the shock.

Rosie: I'll let you tell him, so.

Katie: Oh, I forgot you two still aren't talking.

Rosie: Yes, well, it's a long story, honey.

Katie: People who say it's a long story mean it's a stupid short one that they're too embarrassed and couldn't be bothered to tell. Why don't you talk to him?

Rosie: Because I don't care about what he does any more. His life is his own to mess up as he chooses, and I have nothing to do with it now. Anyway, he doesn't want to hear what I have to say.

Katie: Our neighbour Rupert says, 'Mistakes are the portals of discovery.'

Rosie: Rupert doesn't say that. James Joyce did.
Katie: James who? Do I no him?
Rosie: He's dead.
Katie: Oh, sorry, did you no him well?
Rosie: What on earth are they teaching you at school?
Katie: At the moment it's sex education. It's boring as hell.
Rosie: I would have to agree with you on that one. Anyway, back to Alex: he has just changed as a person, love. He's not the man I used to know. He's different.
Katie: He'd bloody want to be. He was five years old and drooling when you first met him. If Toby is still acting like a fourteen-year-old when we're your age then I'll worry.
Rosie: Well then, as a warning from a woman who knows, be prepared to meet many thirty-two-year-old men who still think they're fourteen.
Katie: Yeah, yeah, yeah. I've heard all this before. Dad's coming home for Christmas, you no. He asked me to ask you if we would eat Christmas dinner with him and his parents. Seeing as it's only you and me this year anyway I thought it would be a great idea.
Rosie: Well, whoopdeedoo. Bring on Christmas Day.

Hi, love,

Hope all is well. It was great to see you at the weekend. Thanks for coming over to us in the west and joining us. I promise the house will be in better order next time you come to see us, but I'm finding it so difficult to settle down after travelling for months.

Settling into a new home, in a new village, in a new county is an adventure for us. Everybody is so friendly here and our Irish is gradually coming back to us. We don't have neighbours as exciting as you seem to have in your new apartment though.

You're my wonderful brave baby girl, Rosie, and your dad and I are so, so proud of you. I hope you know that. You are so strong, you never allow anything to knock you back and you're the best mother to Katie. She's a feisty young lady now, isn't she? She's definitely her mother's daughter. I'm sorry Dennis and I left you at such an important time of your life, it just broke my heart having to leave you and Katie when you were going through all that stuff with whatshisname. But you're a tough cookie and what doesn't kill you only makes you stronger.

It would be such a shame for you to miss Alex's wedding. I was talking to Sandra earlier on and she was telling me that they're planning a very big Christmas wedding. They want to be married before the baby is born, and Bethany doesn't want to be showing too much in her dress. Sandra would love for you and Rosie to be there; they've watched you grow up over the years too. I get the impression she's not a huge fan of Bethany's herself, but she loves Alex and she wants to support him.

Sandra said that Dennis and I are invited but unfortunately we can't go because we are spending Christmas with Stephanie and Pierre in Paris, as you know. Christmas in Paris will be beautiful, no doubt, and I'm excited to meet granddaughter number two! It's such a shame that you and Katie can't come too, but I understand she wants to spend her first Christmas with her dad, and I know she wants to get to know her 'other' grandparents too. I can't help feeling jealous, though, that they'll be seeing my Katie on Christmas Day, and I won't!

Kevin has met a girl, would you believe, and he's spending Christmas with her and her parents in Donegal! It must be serious! I think she's a waitress in the same hotel as him or something, but I'm not too sure. You know Kevin: he's not too good at giving information out.

Your dad says hello. He's tucked up in bed with a nasty flu. He only got it the day you left so you're lucky you missed out on that. He's been very tired since we returned from the trip. I can't believe we're both in our sixties, Rosie. How time went by so fast I'll never know – make sure you savour each day. Anyway, I better go because he keeps calling me. Honestly, you would think he was on his deathbed by the way he's acting!

I'm so proud of my two girls in Dublin.

Love you.

Mum

Dr Reginald & Miranda Williams
invite **Katie Dunne** to join them in celebrating the
marriage of their beloved daughter
Bethany
to
Dr Alex Stewart
at
the Memorial Church of Harvard University
on 28th December at 2 o'clock
& a reception at
the Boston Harbor Hotel
RSVP Miranda Williams

Chapter 40

Welcome to the Relieved Divorced Dubliners' internet chat room. There are currently six people chatting.

Divorced_1: Oh, LonelyLady, just stop crying for one minute of your life and think about your situation. You should be angry, not sad. Repeat after me, I am a strong woman.

LonelyLady: I am a strong woman.

Divorced_1: I am in control of my life.

LonelyLady: I am in control of my life.

Divorced_1: It is *not* my fault that Tommy left.

LonelyLady: It is *not* my fault that Tommy left.

Divorced_1: And I don't care that he did because he is a bastard.

LonelyLady: I can't say that!

Divorced_1: Look, let me put your life into perspective for you. He walked out on you after only six months of marriage, took the furniture, the kitchenware, even the damn bathroom mat, and left you a *note*, for Christsake, so repeat after me, I don't care that he left me because he is a bastard!

LonelyLady: I don't care that he left me because he is a BASTARD!

Divorced_1: Screw him!

LonelyLady: Screw him!

Unsure One: Ladies, I'm not sure that this is a very healthy way to help LonelyLady.

Divorced_1: Oh, shut up, you're never sure of anything.

LonelyLady: Oh, shut up, you're never sure of anything!

Divorced_1: LonelyLady, I didn't mean for you to repeat *that*.
Wildflower: Ha ha ha ha.
UnsureOne: Gosh, I'm not sure anyone is ever allowed to have an opinion in here apart from you, Divorced_1.
Divorced_1: But you never *have* an opinion.
SingleSam: Look, everyone, calm down. Don't be silly, UnsureOne; of course we all want to hear your opinion. How did you deal with Leonard having an affair and leaving you?
Divorced_1: She cleverly moved into the spare room and stopped having a life.
SingleSam: Now, now, Divorced_1, give her a chance.
UnsureOne: Thank you, SingleSam, you're a gentleman. What I was going to say is that I don't believe in divorce. I follow the teachings of the Catholic Church and the Pope himself said that divorce is an 'evil' that is 'spreading like a plague' through society. I, for one, agree with him. The purpose of the family is to be together. And together we shall stay, no matter what happens.
Divorced_1: Well, the Pope was never married to my ex-husband, that's all I have to say to that.
UnsureOne: I'm not continuing this conversation. I don't like your tone.
Wildflower: The Catholic Church believes in annulments, UnsureOne, why don't you get one of those?
UnsureOne: No.
Wildflower: Why not? It's practically the same thing, only the Pope will give his, kind of, blessing to it.
UnsureOne: No.
Wildflower: But can't you at least explain why?
Divorced_1: Because she doesn't want to end her marriage, full stop.
UnsureOne: No, Divorced_1, I just don't think it would be right. For the children.
Divorced_1: What's so 'right for the children' about your husband taking the master bedroom with the

TV and ensuite, forcing you to sleep in the spare room while you stay at home on the weekend and he goes out on dates? Your kids will all get married thinking they're supposed to have separate rooms and multiple partners.

LonelyLady: You let him go out on *dates*?

UnsureOne: Oh, they're not dates. Don't pay any attention to Divorced_1, she's in one of her moods tonight. He goes out on business dinners. I can't very well stop him from doing that, can I? And just because his boss is a woman I don't think I should worry. You wouldn't be at me about this if his boss was a man.

SingleSam: Yes, but, UnsureOne, it was his boss that he was having the affair with . . .

Wildflower: Ha ha ha ha.

LonelyLady: I can understand UnsureOne's reasoning. At least she gets to live with the man she loves, sees him every day, talks to him, knows where he is and what he's doing instead of being alone all day, every day. Who cares if he doesn't love her back?

UnsureOne: You should really work things out with Tommy, you know. Six months isn't enough time to make a marriage work.

Divorced_1: UnsureOne, Tommy *emptied* their bank account, *stole* her engagement ring, *swiped* the furniture, the TV, the CD player, all her CDs, clothes *and* personal possessions and *disappeared*. Why on earth should she want him back other than to point him out in a line-up?

UnsureOne: Because she loves him and marriage is for ever.

Divorced_1: But he is a *thief*. You ladies are nuts.

Wildflower: Well, you know they say love is blind.

Divorced_1: *And* deaf *and* dumb in this chat room.

Buttercup has joined the room.

Divorced_1: Oh good, here comes the voice of reason to sort you lot out.

Buttercup: He's a bloody bastard, you know that? He bloody well married her.

Divorced_1: Oh, well. Screw him.
SingleSam: Did he contact you yet?
Buttercup: No, haven't heard a thing from him since he told me not to contact him.
SingleSam: I thought maybe he would have sent a last-minute invitation.
Buttercup: Not a chance the selfish little—
UnsureOne: Well, you were very rude to him, Buttercup, accusing him of marrying that woman for all the wrong reasons.
LonelyLady: I wish my dad could give Tommy a job promotion. He'd definitely come back to me then.
Divorced_1: Yes, what a wonderful loving foundation to base your marriage on. Very healthy, LonelyLady.
Buttercup: Imagine inviting a thirteen-year-old girl to Boston all by herself. The man has gone insane. That's it; he is officially no longer my best friend.
LonelyLady: Can I be?
Divorced_1: You sad, sad woman.
LonelyLady: What *now*?
Wildflower: But would you have gone to the wedding had he invited you, Buttercup?
Buttercup: Not if he paid me.
LonelyLady: He probably just didn't bother printing up an invite because he knew you weren't going to attend. Invites are very expensive, you know. I remember Tommy and me going through the wedding list together. We were so happy then.
Divorced_1: Probably because he knew he wasn't going to stick around long enough to meet half of the guests.
LonelyLady: That's unfair.
Buttercup: Well, these people are not short of money, believe me, and why else would he invite Katie and not me, if not but to rub it in my face? Smear it right in there like an exfoliating face pack that *scrapes* away at your skin . . . Anyway, I'm almost sure their wedded bliss will be short-lived. He'll be

joining us on this chat room shortly because that woman is evil, I can sense it.
Divorced_1: No, divorce is evil, isn't that right, UnsureOne?
Wildflower: Ha ha ha ha.
UnsureOne: That's not funny.
Divorced_1: All she's done is laugh all night. I think Wildflower has been sampling the wild flower, if you know what I mean.
UnsureOne has left the room.
Wildflower: You're too hard on her, Divorced_1.
Divorced_1: Oh, don't be silly, she loves it. She comes back night after night, doesn't she? I think we're the only bit of adult conversation she has all day.
Buttercup: So did everyone enjoy their Christmas?
Wildflower: I haven't stopped partying all week. It's been great. I've never sat on so many Santa's laps in my life. Anyway, I have to go; I have to get ready for a fancy dress tonight. I'm going as a playboy bunny. Bye!
Wildflower has left the room.
Buttercup: What about everybody else?
Divorced_1: I think I put on about two stone.
LonelyLady: It was, you know, a quiet one.
SingleSam: Television was good this year, though.
Divorced_1: Yeah.
Buttercup: Yeah, I like the Christmas specials.
Divorced_1: Good for occupying the kids too.
Buttercup: Yeah.
SingleSam: Good documentaries too.
Buttercup: Mmm.
Divorced_1: Watched that one on polar bears last night.
Buttercup: I saw that one too . . .
SingleSam: I hadn't realised that all polar bears are left-handed.
Buttercup: Yes, that was interesting . . . and the snails . . .
Divorced_1: They're left-handed too?

SingleSam: No, but they can sleep for three years apparently.
Buttercup: Lucky buggers . . .
Divorced_1: Yes, TV is good at Christmas alright . . .
SingleSam: It's kind of nice to be alone at Christmas, to have a bit of peace and quiet.
LonelyLady: *Total* peace and quiet.
Buttercup: Yes, it's *very* quiet . . .
SingleSam: You know, myself and my ex, we used to have big parties every Christmas, busy all the time, out every night or entertaining whenever we were home. We hardly had any time to ourselves. But this is quite different. No one around. No parties, no guests this year . . .
Buttercup: Same with me.
Divorced_1: Oh, who are we kidding? It's awful; this is the worst Christmas I've ever had.
Buttercup: Me too.
SingleSam: Me too.
LonelyLady: Me too.
Click on this icon to print the conversation.

From Julie Casey
To Rosie
Subject Fax for you

Don't want to disturb you while you're so 'busy' working (how is Ruby?), but a fax just arrived in my office a few minutes ago. It wasn't addressed to you but on reading it I discovered that it could *only* be for you, as which of my other employees would give out *my* fax number for *their own* personal use? I think I can just about make out a 'Form Josh' signed at the bottom. Come into my office and collect it. Oh, and while you're at it, divert all your calls to my office; bring two cups of coffee and a packet of cigarettes in with you.

'Social Lives' by Eloise Parkinson

For those of us who were lucky enough to

attend the wedding of the year (or surely, *at least*, the wedding of the week) we have lived to tell the tale of extravagance, sophistication and splendor that was displayed for the lucky three hundred guests of Dr and Mrs Reginald Williams at the marriage of their daughter, Bethany, to Dr Alex Stewart.

No expense was spared at the wedding ceremony, which took place at the Memorial Church of Harvard University, where vibrant displays of red roses and red candles lined the aisle, like lights illuminating a runway for the exquisite couple to take off to their future life of happiness together.

Bethany, 34, was looking flawlessly stunning, as always, in an elegant white dress designed especially for her by the famous friend-of-the-stars (and mine) Jeremy Durkin. The boned bodice was embellished in ten thousand pearls (and disguised that pregnancy everybody is whispering about). The ballerina-style full skirt, made up of layers and layers of soft tulle, swished as she floated up the aisle on the arm of her proud father, prominent surgeon Dr Reginald Williams.

Miranda Williams looked every bit the perfect mother of the bride in her scarlet red Armani trouser suit, teamed with a fabulous Philip Treacy hat that almost stole the spotlight from her daughter. Catwalk models (and *very* new friends of Bethany's) Sara Smythe and Hayley Broadbank acted as Bethany's two bridesmaids and wore sexy red silk spaghetti-strapped dresses that clung to their barely there curves, half a dozen roses resting between their French manicured fingers. The bride's bouquet was made up of half a dozen red roses and half a dozen white roses (and was caught by none other than *moi*). Her usually flowing long blonde hair was tied back tightly in a French bun that sat low on her head and helped the mother-to-be look every inch the perfect bride.

At the top of the aisle a confident-looking Prince Charming looked down on his princess proudly, dressed in a classic black three-button cut-away coat with white wing collar and red tie, accompanied by a single red rose in his lapel. Everything was certainly 'rosie' on this day.

The extravagant reception was held at the Boston Harbor Hotel where the finest speech by far was made by the best man, five-year-old Josh Stewart, son of the groom from a previous marriage to college sweetheart Sally Gruber.

The day lived up to the expectation (and standards) of 'Social Lives' and it was clear to all who witnessed the newlyweds dancing for the first time as husband and wife that this marriage was for ever. May they live a long, happy, rich and fashionable married life together. As for me, your favorite wedding columnist, I'm off with my bouquet, to find myself a beau.

Rosie,
Happy Birthday, friend.
Another year – here we go again.
Ruby

From Stephanie
To Rosie
Subject Your visit

Can't wait for you to come over and meet Sophia next month. She's excited to meet you too and Jean-Louis is as hyper as always.

Happy thirty-third, sis. No doubt you and Ruby will be out until the early hours.

Dear Alex and Bethany,
Congratulations on the birth of your baby boy.

We wish you every happiness for the future and are delighted that Josh has the brother he wished for!

Rosie and Katie

Happy fourteenth, my little angel.

Have a good night at the disco tonight and remember no drinking, no sex, and no drugs.

Lots of love,

Mum

You have an instant message from: ROSIE.

Rosie: Who is this boy I heard you were kissing and slow dancing with on Friday night, Katie Dunne?

Katie: Can't talk, Mum. Mr Simpson is teaching something extremely important for the end-of-year exams, and it's vital that I listen.

Rosie: Liar.

Katie: I'm not lying. I'm sure it is important, whatever it is.

Rosie: Come on, spill the beans. Who was the boy?

Toby: Hi, Rosie.

Rosie: Oh, Toby, good timing. I was just quizzing my daughter on the mystery man at the disco on Friday night.

Toby: Oh, ha ha. News travels fast.

Katie: Don't tell her, Toby.

Rosie: So it's true?

Toby: Yep.

Katie: Yeah, and Toby was snogging the face off Monica all night as well.

Rosie: Oh no, Toby, not moany Monica.

Toby: Why do you two always call her that? She's not a moan when she's with me.

Rosie: That's because we don't kiss her in front of everyone at school discos. So come on, darling daughter, bond with me and share details of this budding romance.

Katie: His name is John McKenna, he's fifteen, he's in the year ahead of me and he's really nice.

Rosie: Ooooh, an older man.

Katie: I know, Mum. I've got taste.
Rosie: What do you think of him, Toby?
Toby: He's OK; he's on the school football team. He's good.
Rosie: You'll have to keep an eye on him for me, won't you?
Katie: Mum! Now he'll never shut up!
Rosie: Did you have sex with him?
Katie: Mum! I'm fourteen!
Rosie: I see fourteen-year-old girls on the TV who are pregnant these days.
Katie: Well not me!
Rosie: Good. Did you take any drugs?
Katie: Mum! Stop! Where the hell would I get drugs from??!
Rosie: I don't know, but you see fourteen-year-old pregnant girls on TV who are on drugs these days.
Katie: Well not me!
Rosie: Good. Did you drink alcohol?
Katie: Mum! Toby's mum drove us to the school and collected us – when would we have had time to drink?
Rosie: I don't know. You see drunken pregnant fourteen-year-olds who are on drugs on the TV these days.
Katie: Well that's definitely not me!
Toby: What TV programmes are you watching?
Rosie: Mainly the news.
Katie: Well, don't worry; you've lectured me enough to know that it's stupid to do all of those things. OK?
Rosie: OK, but remember, kisses are nice but that's as far as it should go. OK?
Katie: Mum! That's all I want!!
Rosie: Good, now you two get back to your work. I expect you to get As in this subject!
Katie: We won't if you keep bothering us!

Ruby: So what are you going to do for the next two months now that the kids are off school? You're so lucky, getting such long holidays. Randy Andy told me I'd used up all my holidays already, which is ridiculous because all those days were supposed to be sick days. He said there's no way someone could have been sick for sixty-five days of the working year and still be alive.

Rosie: So you can't take any holidays at all? I was hoping we could go over to England on the boat for the weekend. To Blackpool or something.

Ruby: I can now. I told him that if he'll give me two weeks off that I'd mention Randy Andy's Paperclip Company when Oprah invites me on her show to talk about me and Gary wining the World Salsa Championship. What are you going to do?

Rosie: I'm not too sure. Julie mentioned something about being able to do adult courses at the school. She says I should take a course in hotel management like I always wanted to do. Like it's that simple.

Ruby: Why *can't* it be that simple? Look, Rosie, you don't know until you try. Ever since I met you you've been going on about working in a hotel. You're obsessed with them; your home is like a tribute to hotel merchandise. You can barely open the bathroom door for all the stolen mats in the way. I can't claim to understand your fascination with them but I know that working in one is an absolute dream for you.

Rosie: Julie said that if I don't take the course she'll fire me. And she said that when I finish the course she's firing me anyway.

Ruby: You need to listen to her; she's been a good teacher to you over the years.

Rosie: But, Ruby, it takes two years to get a diploma, and it's expensive, and I'll have to work by day and study by night. It'll be tough.

Ruby: Oh, but, but, but, Rosie Dunne. What's the problem? Have you got anything better planned for the next three years of your life?

Dear Rosie,

Apologies for the delay in getting back to you. The past few months have been very busy for Alex and me indeed. Adjusting to married life and a new-born baby all in a matter of months is hard work.

We were delighted to receive your little card and we hope you and Katie are keeping well over in Ireland.

Best wishes,

Bethany (and Alex, Theo, and Josh too)

You have received a message from: ROSIE.

Rosie: You're right, Ruby, it doesn't look like I'll be getting up to all that much for the next two years of my life. Why not educate myself?

Chapter 41

Hi, Mum.

Winter *again*. It's scary how the months fly by so fast. They turn into years without me even noticing. Katie is like my calendar, watching her grow and change. She is growing up so fast, learning to have opinions of her own, learning that I don't have the answers to everything. And the moment a child begins to understand that, you know you're in trouble.

I'm still on my journey, Mum, still caught in that in-between stage of life where I've just arrived from somewhere, have left it well and truly behind and I'm now working my way towards something new. I suppose what I'm trying to say is that my mind isn't settled yet. Still. I mean, you and Dad have done nothing but travel for the past year – you haven't been in one country for more than a few weeks at a time – but you are both more settled than me, and I haven't left for the past year. You both know where you want to be. I suppose that's because you have each other and anywhere Dad is feels like home to you.

I've learned that home isn't a place, it's a feeling. I can make the flat look as pretty as I can, put as many flower boxes on the windowsills as I want, put a welcome mat outside the front door, hang a 'Home Sweet Home' sign over the fireplace and take to wearing aprons and baking cookies, but the truth is that I know I don't want to stay here for ever.

It's like I'm waiting at the train station, busking to make a few quid, just enough to catch the next train out of here. And, of course, the most important thing to me is Katie. Everywhere I am with her should feel like home, but it doesn't because it's up to *me* to make the home for her. I know that Katie is going to leave in a few years and she won't need me like she does now.

I have to set up my own life for when Katie goes. I *need* to do that because I don't see any Prince Charmings coming along to rescue me. Fairy tales are such evil little stories for young children. Every time I'm in a mess I expect a long-haired posh-speaking man to come trotting into my life (on a horse, of course, not literally trotting himself). Then I realise I don't want a man trotting into my life because men are the ones who put me in the bloody mess in the first place.

I'm like Katie's coach right now, gearing her up for the big fight that is adult life. She's hardly thinking of life after me. Sure, she has her dreams of travelling the world and DJ-ing for a living *without me*, but the *without me* part hasn't hit her yet. And so it shouldn't – she's only fourteen. Anyway, she is not up to making her own decisions yet, and I've put my foot down on the quitting school idea.

Although lately I haven't had to force her out of bed in the mornings because of John, this new boyfriend of hers. The pair of them are inseparable; they go to discos every Friday night at the GAA club near where he lives. He's a real GAA man and plays hurling for the Dublin minors. In fact, we're all going to Croke Park this Sunday to see Dublin v. Tipperary, very excited. Anyway, it's tricky for me because I obviously don't drive so I sometimes put Ruby on driving duties. She calls it Driving Ms Lazy. John's mother is a very nice lady, though, and she's kind enough to collect Katie and drop her home some weeks.

I haven't seen or heard much of Toby lately, but I saw his mother at the school when she was dropping off her youngest and she told me he was acting more or less the same as Katie with his new girlfriend, Monica.

I never dated when I was fourteen. The youth of today are really growing up fast . . . (I sounded SO OLD there!) OK, OK, Mum, I can hear you fuming from here. I did become pregnant at the age of eighteen without having a job or education or man, and almost gave you a nervous breakdown, but in some countries of the world that's old, so you should thank your lucky stars that I didn't get started even sooner.

Kevin called up for the weekend; he brought his girlfriend with him. She was very sweet but I've no idea what she sees in him. Did you know that they've been going out for a year now? Honestly, that brother of mine is so secretive; you practically have to beat the information out of him! You never know, there could be more wedding bells in the air for the Dunne family! Tell Dad to get that dirty old tuxedo out of the attic and to brush the cobwebs and mothballs off in preparation. He'll be happy to know he won't have to walk down the aisle this time. (Honestly, he had *me* nervous at my wedding!)

As for my North Strand palace, we might as well have no glass in the windows here at all for all the wind they let in. It's so cold and windy tonight, the rain is pelting off the windows. That lamppost from outside shines directly into this flat. If only it could be moved a bit to the right then it could annoy Rupert instead. Although it does save me money on the electricity. I'm half-expecting Gene Kelly to be outside dancing around with his umbrella. Why is it movies can make everything – even rain – look fun?

Every morning I rise when it is pitch-black outside (and, you know, it's not natural to be up at a time when even the sun can't be bothered to rise), the flat is freezing, I hop from the shower to my bedroom, shivering like hell, I make my way outside where I have to walk ten minutes to the bus stop, invariably in the wind and rain. My ears ache and my hair is normally in wet strings around my head, so I may as well not wash and blow-dry it at all. My mascara is running down my face, my umbrella has blown inside out and I look like a dishevelled Mary Poppins. Then the bus is late. Or too full to stop. And I end up late for work, looking like a drowned rat, having had at least one fight with a bus driver, while everyone else has their make-up, clothes and hair all perfect because they all got out of bed an hour later than me, hopped into their cars, drove to work, arrived at the school fifteen minutes before classes started in time to have a cup of coffee as a relaxing start to their day.

Singing in the rain, my bum.

Notice I'm writing to you today and not emailing and that's due to the guy in the internet café downstairs catching me one too many times staring at him. His face is so scrumptious I feel like taking a bite out of him. I think he's on to me so I decided to stay home tonight. The other reason for me writing is that I'm pretending right now that I'm studying. We both have Christmas exams coming up and I told Katie she needed to take them more seriously. Well, I walked myself straight into that one. So here we both are, crammed at the kitchen table with our books, folders, papers and pens, pretending to look intellectual.

I have so much study to catch up on that I haven't been able to cook dinner all week. So it's been downstairs' delights for the past few days. Luckily Sanjay is giving us forty per cent off our takeaway meals and he's even created a new dish called Rosie Chicken Curry. He sent it up free last night with our order. We tasted it and sent it back down. Just joking. It's basically chicken and curry. All he did was add the Rosie. I'm flattered all the same at the sight of my name on an Indian menu, and it's interesting late at night to hear my name being yelled by drunken men in deep slurred voices. I keep thinking that my Romeo is standing on the pavement below my window, calling me and throwing stones up to awaken me from my slumber. Then I remember that it's Saturday night, one o'clock in the morning, the pub has just closed, drunken men are shouting their special order over the counter and the stones against my window is the rain. But a girl can always dream.

Every time I pass by Sanjay's wife she rolls her eyes

and tuts. He's still asking me out on dates, he even asks me when she's standing right beside him. So I say very loudly that what he is asking me is wrong, considering his marital status, that he needs to have more respect for his wife and that even if he wasn't married I would say no. I say it loudly so that she can hear but yet she stills tuts and Sanjay smiles at me and throws a few poppadoms in the bag for me for free. The man is insane.

Rupert (my other neighbour) asked me if I want to go to the National Concert Hall at the weekend. Apparently the National Symphony Orchestra is playing Brahms Piano Concerto Number 2 in B flat, Op. 83, which is his absolute favourite. It's not a date or anything. I think Rupert is completely asexual and that he just wants some company. That suits me just fine. Plus, the 'I Love Mother' tattoo on his arm would be a real turn-off. That quote by James Joyce on his chest really upsets me too, because Rupert is so tall that when I look straight ahead I'm constantly forced to read 'Mistakes are the portals of discovery.' It's like a sign or something, like Rupert was put in the flat beside me to make me understand the error of my ways. Only I wish the message made more sense than that. Mistakes are more like the potholes of discovery. It's a bloody long bumpy road to discovery, strewn with obstacles and danger. I wish it said, 'Chocolate is good' instead.

Speaking of mistakes, I still haven't spoken to Alex and it's been over a year now. I think this is really it this time. All we've been doing is sending stupid cards back and forth to each other. It's like we're having a staring competition and neither of us wants to be the first to blink. I miss him like crazy. There are so many things that happen to me, silly little everyday things that I itch to tell him. Like the postman this morning was delivering across the road and that stupid little Jack Russell dog called Jack Russell was attacking him again. So I looked out the window and I saw the postman shaking the dog off his leg as he does every morning but this time he kicked the dog in the stomach by mistake and the dog fell over and didn't move for ages.

Then the owner came outside and I watched as the postman pretended that Jack Russell was like that when he got there. The owner believed him and there was pandemonium as they tried to help the dog. Eventually Jack Russell got up and when he took one look at the postman he whimpered and ran away into the house. It was so funny. The postman just shrugged and walked off. He was whistling by the time he got to my door. Things like that would have really made Alex laugh, especially as I had told him all about the wretched dog keeping me awake all night barking, and always stealing my post from the poor postman.

Hang on a sec, Katie is trying to sneak a peek off my page . . .

MASLOW'S THEORY OF HIERARCHY.

Ha ha, that'll put her off the scent. OK, I better go now and actually do some work. See you both soon. Tell Dad I said hello and that I love him.

Oh, by the way, Ruby has set me up on a blind date on Saturday night. I nearly killed her but I can't cancel it. Cross your fingers for me that he's not some sort of serial killer.

Lots of love,

Rosie

You have received an instant message from: ROSIE.

Rosie: Hi, Julie. I've signed you up to be one of my instant message buddies. Whenever I see that you're online I can send you messages.

Julie: Not if I block your name from my list.

Rosie: You wouldn't dare.

Julie: Why would you set up an instant messaging service with me when I am in the next room?

Rosie: It's what I do. It means I can multi-task. I can speak to people on the phone and also do business with you online. Anyway, what is it that you actually do, Miss Casey? All I see you doing is terrorising innocent children and having meetings with pissed-off parents.

Julie: That's about all I do, Rosie, you're right.

Believe me, you were one of the worst kids to teach and one of the worst parents to meet with. I hated calling you in.

Rosie: I hated coming in.

Julie: And now you've added me to your messaging list. How times change. By the way, I'm having a little get-together for my birthday next week and I was wondering if you would like to come.

Rosie: Who else is going?

Julie: Oh, just some other kids that I used to scare the hell out of twenty years ago. We love to gather and reminisce about the days gone by.

Rosie: Seriously?

Julie: No, just a few friends, a few members of my family for a few drinks and a few nibbles for a few minutes to mark the occasion, and then you can all leave me alone.

Rosie: What age will you be? I only ask so I can buy you a birthday card with a number on it. Maybe get a badge for you too.

Julie: You do and you're fired. I'm going to be fifty-three.

Rosie: You're only twenty years older than me. I used to think you were ancient!

Julie: Funny, isn't it? Imagine, I was only about your age by the time you left this school. The kids must feel that you're ancient now too.

Rosie: I feel ancient.

Julie: Ancient people don't go on romantic blind dates. Come on, spill the beans, what was he like?

Rosie: His name is Adam and he is a very, very attractive man. All evening he was polite, a terrific conversationalist and very funny. He paid for the meal, the taxi, drinks, absolutely everything, and wouldn't let me open my purse (not that there was any money in it to spend, given the slave wages I'm paid, ahem . . .). He was tall, dark and handsome, dressed impeccably. Plucked eyebrows, straight teeth and not a nose hair in sight.

Julie: What does he do for a living?

Rosie: He's an engineer.
Julie: So he was polite, handsome and had a great job. He sounds too good to be true. Are you meeting again?
Rosie: Well, after the meal we went back to his penthouse apartment. He lives along Sir John Rogerson's Quay – the place was fabulous. We kissed, I stayed over, he asked me out again and I said no.
Julie: Are you crazy?
Rosie: Probably. He was such a good man but there was just nothing there – no sparkle.
Julie: But it was only your first date. You can never really tell these things by a first date. What did you want, fireworks?
Rosie: No, actually, quite the opposite. I want silence, a perfect moment of quietness.
Julie: Silence?
Rosie: Oh, it's a long story. But last night only proves that you can put me with a guy who's perfect in every way and I'm still not ready. Everyone needs to stop pressurising me – I'll find someone when I'm good and ready.
Julie: OK, OK, I promise I'll stop trying to set you up until you give me your permission to. How's the studying going, by the way?
Rosie: It's tough working, studying and being a mother all at the same time. I end up staying up till all hours of the night, pondering life, the universe and all that's in it, i.e., not doing any work.
Julie: Don't worry, we've all had those days and believe me, by the time you get to my age you stop caring. Is there anything I can do to help?
Rosie: Yes, actually. A pay rise would be a terrific help.
Julie: No chance. How's the saving going?
Rosie: It would be going fine if I didn't have to feed, clothe, educate my child as well as pour rent money into the shoe box I'm living in.
Julie: That always seems to get in the way of things,

that whole looking-after-your-child part. Have you spoken to Alex yet?

Rosie: No.

Julie: Oh, Rosie, you are both being ridiculous. I spent my life trying to separate you two from each other but now the fun is over for me. Tell him Miss Big Nose Smelly Breath Casey has given you both permission to sit beside each other again.

Rosie: That'll never work; he never listened to you anyway. And it's not like we're not in contact at all. Katie emails all the time and I send cards for every occasion under the sun and he does the same back. Every few months I get a postcard from a different exotic country with boring weather reports from him, and when he's not holidaying he's working all hours. So we're not completely ignoring each other. It's a very civilised kind of argument we're having.

Julie: Yes, apart from the fact that you don't talk. Your best friend has a six-month-old baby that you haven't even met. All I'm saying is that if you let this carry on much longer, the years will multiply and before you know it it'll just be too late.

Chapter 42

Dear Rosie and Katie Dunne,

Season's Greetings from St Jude's Hospital.

My wife, two sons and I hope that the year ahead brings you and your loved ones good health and happiness.

Merry Christmas and a Happy New Year from the Stewarts.

Dr Alex Stewart MD

To Dr Alex Stewart

May the coming year be filled with health, wealth and happiness for you and your family.

Best wishes,
Rosie Dunne

You have received an instant message from: ALEX.
Alex: Your card arrived this morning.
Rosie: Oooh, talking to me now, are you?
Alex: It's been long enough. One of us should be adult enough to make contact. Remember I'm not the one who started this in the first place.
Rosie: Yes you did.
Alex: Rosie, no I didn't.
Rosie: Yes you did!
Alex: Oh, *please*! Last year I told you Bethany was pregnant, at which point you went crazy. And, for your information, I proposed to her one night before we went to an award ceremony. Bethany said yes, and naturally being excited, she told her parents at the table (as any normal person would

do). Her father was presented with his award and during his speech he announced that his daughter had just gotten engaged (as a normal proud father would on just learning that his daughter was to be married).

The press were there; they went back to their desks and reported on the evening in time to make the next day's papers. I went out and celebrated my engagement with my fiancée and her family. I got home to bed and woke up the next day to phone call after phone call from my family wanting to no why the hell I hadn't told them I was getting married. My in-box was full of emails from confused friends and I was just about to deal with them when I got an instant message from you.

So I sent you and Katie wedding invites anyway, thinking that even though you disapproved of my choice of wife and concocted pathetic stories about why I was marrying her, you might still have behaved like the friend you claim to be by attending my wedding and being supportive.

So I apologise for the last card you received, your name was on my mailing list, but this particular card was intended for my patients and not you.

Rosie: Wait a minute, I didn't receive any wedding invite!

Alex: What?

Rosie: I got no invitation to your wedding. There was one for Katie alright, but none for me. And Katie couldn't very well go because she was only thirteen and where would she stay? And I couldn't bring her over because frankly I couldn't afford to—

Alex: Stop! Now let me think about this for a moment. You didn't receive a wedding invite?

Rosie: No. Just one for Katie.

Alex: What about your parents?

Rosie: Yeah, they received one but they couldn't go because they were visiting Steph in Paris and—

Alex: OK! Yours wasn't sent there by mistake?
Rosie: No.
Alex: But my parents – didn't they tell you?
Rosie: They said they would love me to go but they don't control the invites, Alex. You never asked me to go.
Alex: But you were on the list. I even *saw* your invite on the kitchen table.
Rosie: Oh.
Alex: So what happened?
Rosie: Don't ask me! I didn't even know there was an invite for me! Who posted them?
Alex: Bethany and the wedding planner.
Rosie: Hmm . . . OK so somewhere between Bethany walking to the post box and the invite actually going in the slot, something happened to my invite.
Alex: Oh, don't start, Rosie. It wasn't Bethany. She's got much better things to be doing with her time than hatching plans to get rid of you.
Rosie: Like doing lunch with the ladies?
Alex: Stop.
Rosie: Well, I'm in shock.
Alex: So you thought all this time that I didn't want you at my wedding?
Rosie: Yes.
Alex: But why didn't you say something? An entire year and you didn't say anything? If you didn't invite me to your wedding I would at least *say* something!
Rosie: Excuse me, why didn't you ask me why I wasn't there? If I invited you to my wedding and I noticed that you hadn't turned up, I think I would at least *say* something.
Alex: I was angry.
Rosie: Me too.
Alex: I'm still angry about the things you said.
Rosie: Answer me this, Alex. Did you or did you not tell me only months previously that Bethany was not 'the one' for you and that you didn't love her?

Alex: Yes, but—

Rosie: And were you or were you not going to break up with her just before she announced she was pregnant?

Alex: Yes, but—

Rosie: And were you or were you not worried about your job when you refused to marry Bethany?

Alex: Yes, but—

Rosie: And were you or were you not—

Alex: Stop, Rosie. All of that may be true but it was coupled with the fact that I wanted to be a part of Theo and Bethany's life.

Rosie: So if you *did* invite me to your wedding and I was *partly* correct on what I said, why did we spend the entire year not speaking?

Alex: Right now what I want to no is where the hell your wedding invite went to. The wedding planner had everything arranged. Unless it was . . .

Rosie: Who?

Alex: Not *who* but *what* . . .

Rosie: *What*, then?

Alex: Jack Russell the Jack Russell. Next time I see him I'm going to wring his neck.

Rosie: Oh, you can't do that.

Alex: I can do whatever the hell I want to that post-nicking little—

Rosie: He's dead. The postman kicked him in the stomach a few mornings in a row completely by mistake (I'm a witness) and one morning he did it, Jack just stopped moving.

Alex: I'm not sorry to hear that.

Rosie: I'm sorry though, Alex.

Alex: Me too. Friends again?

Rosie: I never stopped being your friend.

Alex: Me neither. Well, unfortunately I have to go because my baby is pouring his breakfast on his head and massaging it into his scalp with a look of pure concentration on his face. I fear it may be nappy-changing time again.

For our beautiful daughter

We love you with all our hearts. Here's to a new year.

Happy Birthday, Rosie!

Good luck with your exams in June. We have our fingers crossed for you.

Lots of love,

Mum and Dad

For my sister

You're finally catching up on me, Rosie, which I'm glad of because I don't want to be the only one nearing forty! Best of luck with your exams. You have two months to learn it all – you can get it done. I'm sure you'll fly through them!

Happy Birthday.

Love,

Stephanie, Pierre, Jean-Louis, Sophia

Happy Birthday, Mum.

Hope you like your present. If it doesn't fit you, I'll have it!

Love,

Katie

To a special friend

Happy 35th Birthday, Rosie. I'm working on a new experiment to slow down time. Fancy joining in with me?

Enjoy your day and I hope to see you soon!

Alex

To Rosie,

Happy Birthday again. After this celebration there will be no more distractions. You have to pass these exams with straight As. You can do it and you're my only hope of getting out of here. I'm still dreaming of that job as an entertainer at that fine hotel of yours.

Love, Ruby

You have received an instant message from: ROSIE.
Rosie: Sixteen. My little angel sixteen! What the hell am I supposed to do now? Where's the rule book?
Ruby: It's not like only yesterday she was two years old, you know. You did have a total of let's see, sixteen years' preparation. This shouldn't come as a shock to you.
Rosie: Ruby, you unsentimental witch, do you not feel anything? Are you numb to all emotions? How did you feel when your Gary turned sixteen?
Ruby: I just don't look at things like you do. I don't think much of ages or birthdays – they're just another day to me. They don't symbolise anything but a bunch of definitions and generalisations people have created to make conversation, debates and media discussions. For example, Katie is not going to go off the rails because suddenly she wakes up one morning and she's sixteen. People do whatever the hell they want to do at any age they fancy. Last month you were thirty-five. That means you're five years from forty. Do you think that the day you reach forty you will be any different than you were at thirty-nine or forty-one for that matter? People create little ideas about ages so they can write silly self-help books, stick stupid comments in birthday cards, create names for internet chat rooms and look for excuses for crises that are happening in their life.

For example, the man's so-called 'mid-life crisis' is just a bunch of hype. Age is not the problem; it's the male brain that's the problem. Men have been cheating since they were apes (insert your own joke there), since cavemen times (and again there) all the way up to now, the age of what is supposed to be the civilised man. This is simply the way they were made. Age is not the issue.

Your baby will remain your baby past the point when she has her own little baby. Don't worry about that.
Rosie: I don't want my baby to have a baby until

she's grown up, married and rich. I mean, when I think of the things I did on my sixteenth birthday . . . actually, I can't remember exactly what I did.

Ruby: Why not?

Rosie: Because I was being incredibly juvenile and stupid.

Ruby: What did you do?

Rosie: Me and Alex forged our mums' signatures and wrote notes to school saying we would both be absent for the day.

Ruby: Coincidentally.

Rosie: Exactly. We went to some old man's pub in town where ID wasn't a necessity and we drank all day. Unfortunately it was ruined by the fact that I fell and hit my head, had to be raced to hospital in an ambulance where I received seven stitches and my stomach was pumped. The parents were none too pleased.

Ruby: I bet they weren't. How did you fall? Were you doing some of your funky moves on the dance floor again?

Rosie: Actually, no. I was only sitting on my stool.

Ruby: Ha ha. *Only you* could fall on the floor while you were sitting down.

Rosie: I know, that's weird, isn't it? I wonder how it happened!

Ruby: Well, you should ask Alex. I'm surprised it's never occurred to you to ask him before.

Rosie: Good idea! Ooh, he's online now so I'll ask.

Ruby: It's not that bloody important, but any old excuse to talk to him, I suppose. I'll hold on here and try to make myself look busy while you ask. I'm intrigued . . .

You have received an instant message from: ROSIE.

Rosie: Hi, Alex.

Alex: Hi, there. Do you ever do any work? Every time I log on you're on too!

Rosie: I'm just chatting to Ruby. It's cheaper this

way. We don't have to answer questions at work about the telephone bill. Internet use is unlimited if you pay a monthly charge and, besides, typing makes us look like we're busy. Anyway, I just wanted to ask you a quick question.

Alex: Fire ahead.

Rosie: Remember on my sixteenth birthday, I fell and hit my head?

Alex: Ha ha, how could I forget? Are you thinking of this because Katie's birthday is coming up? Because if she's anything like you, you should be afraid, be very, very afraid. What should I get for her anyway, a sick bucket?

Rosie: Age is only a number, not a state of mind or a reason for any type of particular behaviour.

Alex: O . . . K then. What's your question?

Rosie: How on earth did I fall and hit my head on the floor while I was sitting down?

Alex: Oh my Lord. The question. *The* Question.

Rosie: What's wrong with my question??

Alex: Rosie Dunne, I have been waiting nearly twenty years for you to ask me that question and I thought you never would.

Rosie: What??

Alex: Why you never asked is beyond me, but you woke up the next day and claimed to have no knowledge of what had happened. I didn't want to bring it up; you had brought enough up the night before!

Rosie: You didn't want to bring what up? Alex, *tell me*! How did I fall off my stool??

Alex: I don't think you're ready to no.

Rosie: Oh, shut up. I'm Rosie Dunne, after all; I was born to be ready for anything.

Alex: OK then, if you're so sure of yourself . . .

Rosie: I am! Now tell me!

Alex: We were kissing.

Rosie: We were *what*??

Alex: Yep. You were leaning across on your high stool, kissing me; the stool was very wobbly and lodged unsafely between the cracks of a very old uneven tiled pub floor. And you fell.

Rosie: WHAT??

Alex: Oh, the sweet nothings you whispered into my ear that night, Rosie Dunne. And I was gutted the next day when you woke up and forgot. After me holding your hand while you puked all night.

Rosie: *Alex!*

Alex: What?

Rosie: *Why didn't you tell me?!*

Alex: Because we weren't allowed to see each other for a while and I didn't want to tell you in a note. And then you said you wanted to forget everything that had happened that night so I thought that maybe you vaguely remembered and you just regretted it.

Rosie: You should have told me.

Alex: Why, what would you have said?

Rosie: Em . . . that's really putting me on the spot, Alex.

Alex: Yeah, sorry.

Rosie: I can't believe it. Because I fell, we got caught and I had to stay home for a week while your punishment was to start work in your dad's office, where you met Bethany. The girl you said you were going to marry . . .

Alex: That's right, I said that!

Rosie: Yeah, you did . . .

Alex: Well, I actually said that just to test you but as you didn't seem to care too much I went out with her anyway. That's funny. I had forgotten I had said that! Bethany would love to hear that! Thanks for reminding me.

Rosie: No no, thank *you* for reminding *me* . . .

You have an instant message from: RUBY.

Ruby: Come on, Ms Bumps, I need to look like I'm busy here. You find out what happened yet?

Rosie: Yes, I found out I'm the biggest idiot in the *whole entire world*. Aaaaaaaah!

Ruby: I waited around for *that*? I could have told you that *ages* ago.

Dear Katie,
Happy sweet sixteenth!
Love, Mum xxx

For our granddaughter,
Happy sweet sixteenth birthday!
Lots of love,
Grandma and Granddad

For my girlfriend
Happy Sweet 16!
Lots of love,
John

To Katie
Happy birthday, you pain in the ass. Another few months and those braces will be off. Then I won't be able to tell what you've eaten for dinner.
Toby

For my daughter
Congratulations, Katie. Happy sweet sixteen!
I hope John doesn't try to kiss you!
Love, Dad

Dear Mum and Dad,
I'm never speaking to Rupert again. *Sweet* sixteen my *arse*.

Katie demanded that I give her the money that I would have spent on her present, so that she could go into town and pick her own clothes, which suited me fine because then I didn't have to bother spending sleepless nights trying to think of the 'perfect' gift that she would inevitably hate and hide under her bed. Anyway, she walked into the flat, hand in hand with the big friendly giant (John), beaming from ear to ear so I immediately knew something suspicious was going on.

She lifted her top, lowered her trousers an inch and there it was.

The tattoo from hell.

An awful-dirty-disgusting-very-ugly-I've-just-realised-I'm-beginning-to-sound-like-you-mother kind of tattoo. It sat there on her hipbone, sticking its tongue out at me.

Mum, it's ugly. Mind you, it was bleeding and beginning to grow a scab by the time I saw it. Apparently Rupert said his clients only needed to be sixteen to get a tattoo, which I strongly disagree with so I came downstairs to check the internet. It turns out he's right, but if I could just find some sort of loophole that would allow me to kick his ass . . .

Cute internet café guy asked me if I was OK and he looked really concerned, which I thought was possibly the beginning of something new for the both of us. But then I realised I was thumping the keyboard with my fists so he was probably only concerned about his computer. I have no time for selfish men like that in my life so I've decided there's no chance of a steamy love affair occurring between us after hours on the computer desks. Purely my decision, though.

What makes it even worse is that I was trying to study for my *final* exams and the drilling coming from the tattoo parlour downstairs was really distracting me. What I didn't realise was that I was listening to the mutilation of my own daughter's body.

It was kind of difficult giving Rupert a piece of my mind because I couldn't express my hatred of tattoos without offending him, seeing as he is an actual walking tattoo. It would be like slagging one of his family members.

But the tattoo is the least of my worries. She also got her tongue pierced. Rupert threw that part in for free. She sounds like she's got hot potatoes in her mouth when she speaks. So no wonder I got such a shock when she walked in with a scary look on her face and said, 'Aah, uck at I aa-oo,' and then proceeded to lift up her top. John got one as well but he got a tattoo of a hurley stick and a hurling ball on his hipbone. You don't even want to know what that picture resembles. Rupert drilled the ball too close and on the wrong end of the stick, if you know what I mean.

I suppose it could be worse: they could have gotten tattooed with each other's names. And there are worse tattoos Katie could get than a tiny little strawberry the size of my thumbnail.

Perhaps I'm overreacting?

How on earth must you and Dad have felt when I told you I was *pregnant*?

Now that I think of it, perhaps I should give Katie some sort of award? Anyway, I ought to go back upstairs and face the (very loud, banging) music, plus I need to continue with my studies. I can't believe I've reached my final year. Two years flew by and while it was virtually impossible studying by night, working by day and trying to be a mother at both those times, I'm glad I didn't pack it in the hundred times a day that I said I would. Imagine, I'll have a graduation ceremony! You and Dad will finally be able to sit in the crowd while I collect my diploma in my unflattering robe and hat. It's only fourteen years later than originally planned, but I suppose it's better late than never.

However I won't get to the graduation ceremony if I don't pass my exams so, *no more distractions*. I am going to study!

Love,
Rosie

From Rosie
To Alex
Subject Dad

Something awful has happened. People at work said you were in surgery but, please, as soon as you get my messages and this email, can you ring me?

Mum called me just a minute ago in tears; Dad has had a massive heart attack and has been rushed to hospital. She's in huge shock but she told me not to travel over to her because my first exam is starting tomorrow. I don't know what to do. I don't know how serious it is, the doctors won't tell us anything yet. Can you maybe ring the hospital and see what's going on? You understand all that stuff. I don't know what to do. Please get this email on time. I don't know who else to call.

I don't want to leave Mum on her own, although Kevin is going over to her now. I don't want Dad to be alone either. Oh, this is so confusing.

Oh God, Alex, please help. I don't want to lose my dad.

From Alex
To Rosie
Subject Re: Dad

I tried calling you but you must be on the phone. Just stay calm. I rang the hospital and had a word with Dr Flannery there. He's the doctor looking after your dad and he explained Dennis's condition to me.

What I suggest you do is pack a bag for a few days and get on the earliest bus you can to Galway. Do you understand what I mean?

Forget about your exam, this is more important. Keep calm, Rosie, and just be there for your mum and dad. Tell Stephanie to come home too, if she can. Keep in touch with me during the night.

Chapter 43

Dear Alex,

Coffin sizes can be no wider than 76 cm; can be made of chipboard with approved veneers and plastics for cremation purposes. Did you know that? Ferrous screws are acceptable in small numbers and wood braces will give extra strength but must *only* be placed in the inside of the coffin.

The coffin must have the full name of the deceased on the lid. Wouldn't want to get anyone mixed up, I suppose. The thing that I really wished I hadn't learned was that the coffin should be lined with a substance known as 'Cremfilm', or use absorbent cloth or cotton padding because apparently fluid can leak from a body.

I didn't know any of this.

There were forms. Lots and lots of forms. Forms A, B, C, F and all the medical forms. No one mentioned anything about D and E. I didn't know you needed so much proof to show you were dead. I thought the fact you've stopped living and breathing was a huge give-away. Apparently not.

I suppose it's like going away to live in another country. Dad just had to get his papers ready, get dressed in his Sunday best, arrange his mode of transport and off he went to his final destination, wherever that may be. Oh, how much Mum would have loved to have gone on this particular trip with him, but she knows she can't.

She just kept repeating to everyone at the funeral, 'He just didn't wake up. I called him and called him, but he wouldn't wake up.' She hasn't stopped shaking since it happened and she looks like she's aged twenty years. Yet she seems younger. Like a lost little child who looks around her and doesn't know where to go, like suddenly she's in a whole new place and she doesn't know the way.

I suppose she is. I suppose we all are.

I've never been here before. I'm thirty-five years old and I've never lost anyone close to me. I've been to ten funerals in my life and they were of distant relatives, friends of friends and family of friends whom my life is none the worse off without.

But Dad going? God, that's a big one.

He was only sixty-five years old. Not old at all. And he was healthy. What causes a healthy sixty-five-year-old man to fall asleep and never wake up? I can only comfort myself with thoughts that he saw something so beautiful that he just had to go. That's the kind of thing Dad would do.

There's something completely unnerving about seeing your parents upset. I suppose it's because they're supposed to be the strong ones, but that's not just it. When people are kids they use their parents as some sort of measurement for how bad a situation is. When you fall on the ground really hard and you can't figure out whether it hurts or not you look to your parents. If they look worried and rush towards you, you cry. If they laugh and smack the ground saying, 'Bold ground,' then you pick yourself up and get on with it.

When you find out you're pregnant and feel numb of all emotions you look at their expressions. When both your Mum and Dad hug you and tell you it's going to be OK and that they'll support you, you know it's not the end of the world. But depending on the parents, it could have been pretty damn close.

Parents are the barometers of emotions for children and it has a domino effect. I have never seen my mum cry so much in all of my life, which scared me and made me cry, which scared Katie and made her cry. We all cried together.

As for Dad, he was supposed to live for ever. The

one who could open all the jar lids nobody else could, who fixed whatever was broken, was supposed to do that for ever. The man who let me sit on his shoulders, climb on his back, chase me around while making monster noises, throw me in the air and catch me, spin me around so much that I felt dizzy and fell over laughing.

And in the end without being able to say thank you and a proper goodbye, my final memories of him turn into coffin sizes and medical forms.

I'm still over in Galway with Mum. In the wild, wild west. But it's a beautiful summer and it doesn't feel quite right. The atmosphere doesn't suit the mood, there's the sound of children's laughter floating up from the beach down below, there are birds singing and dancing around the sky, swooping low and catching their fresh meals from the sea. It doesn't feel right to love the world and see such brightness when something so awful has happened.

It's like hearing gurgling babies echoing in the church at the funeral. There's nothing more uplifting than to hear the sound of an innocent child being so happy in a place that people are sad. It reminds you that life goes on and on and on, just not for the one you're saying goodbye to. People come and people go and we know this happens, yet we get such a shock when it does. To use that old cliché, the only certainty in life is death. It's a certainty, it's the one condition of living that we're given but we often let it tear us apart.

I don't know what to do or say to Mum to make her feel better; I don't suppose there really is anything that would accomplish that, but watching her crying to herself all day tears me apart. I can hear her pain in her tears. Maybe she'll just run out of tears.

Alex, you're a heart doctor. You know the heart literally inside and out – what is there you can do when someone's heart has broken? Have you any cures for that?

Thanks for coming over to the funeral. It was so good to see you. It was just a shame that it was under these circumstances. It was good of your parents to come as well. Mum really did appreciate it. Thanks for getting rid of whatshisname too; I really wasn't in the mood to have any discussions with him at the church. It was good of him to come but if Dad had seen him he would have leaped out of that coffin and thrown him in in his place.

Stephanie and Kevin headed home a few days ago but I'm going to stay on for a little while longer. I just can't leave Mum alone. The neighbours are being so good to her. I know she will be in good hands when I do finally leave. I've missed all my exams and by the sounds of things I'll have to repeat the entire year if I do want to complete the course. I don't think I could be bothered doing it all over again.

Anyway, I'll have to go home in a few days as no doubt the bills have been piling up in my letter box since the day I left. I really need to get back before they cut everything off and evict me.

Thanks for being there for me once again, Alex. Isn't it typical of us that it's a tragedy that gets us together?

Love,
Rosie

From Rosie
To Alex
Subject Dad

I just returned home from Connemara to be greeted by an overflowing mailbox. Among a pile of bills was the following letter. It was posted the day before Dad died.

Dear Rosie,

Your mum and I are still laughing from your last letter about Katie's tattoo. I do love it when you write to us! I hope you're over the trauma of your daughter becoming a fully fledged teen. I remember the day that happened with you. I think it hit you before Stephanie! You were always eager to try new things and go new places, my fearless Rosie. I thought that when you finished school you were going to set off around the world and we would never see you again. I'm glad that didn't happen. You were always a delight to have around the house. You *and* Katie. I'm only sorry we had to leave you when you needed us both. Your mum and I questioned our actions time and time again. I hope we did the right thing.

I know you always felt that you were in the way or that you were letting us down, but that's far from the truth. It just meant that I got to see my little girl grow. Grow from being a baby to an adult and grow as a mother. You and Katie are a great team and she is a fine example of the good parenting she received. A bit of ink on her skin doesn't tarnish the goodness or dim the brightness that shines from her. A tribute to her mother.

Life deals each of us a different set of cards and out of all of us there's no doubt that you received the toughest hand of all. But you shone through the tough times. You are a strong girl and you grew even stronger when that idiot of a man (whatshisname, your mother told me to say) let you down. You picked yourself up, dusted yourself off and started all over again, set up home with Katie, found yourself a new job, provided for your daughter and did your dad proud once more.

And now you're only days away from your exams. After all you went through you'll now have a diploma. I'll be proud watching you accept that scroll, Rosie; I'll be the proudest dad in the world.

Love,
Dad

From Rosie
To Alex
Subject Diploma

There's no way I'm giving this college course up now. In the wise words of Johnny Logan, what's another year? I'm going to do these exams and I'm going to get this diploma in Hotel Management. Dad wouldn't want himself to be the reason for me missing out.

It's the goodbye I needed, Alex. What a wonderful, wonderful gift to be given.

From Julie
To Rosie
Subject Staying with me?

So you're staying with me another year then?

I'll allow you, but after that, once you have your diploma, I'm serious when I say I'm firing you. I'm fifty-five years old; I don't have much longer at this job to be waiting for you to fulfil your dreams.

This year the courses will be a breeze, first because you've done it before and second and more important because you have the good wishes and pride of your father behind you. That's the best motivation a person could get.

Do you mind me asking what is it about these hotels that you love so much?

From Rosie
To Julie
Subject Why I love hotels!

I just get this feeling when I walk into really nice hotels. For me they represent everything in life that's luxurious and full of splendour. I love that people pamper you and look after you. Everything is so clean and pristine, so completely perfect. So unlike home – well, my home anyway.

I love that people go to enjoy themselves; it's not so much a place of work as being a host in paradise.

I get excited by the sparkling bathrooms, the big fluffy robes, the slippers and the décor. Where else would you find chocolate on your pillow? It's like the tooth fairy and Santa Claus all at once. There's twenty-four-hour room service and bouncy padded carpets, turned-down beds and mini-bars, bowls of fruit and free shampoo. I feel like I'm Charlie in the

Chocolate Factory. Everything you want is at your disposal. All you have to do is pick up the phone and press the magic number and the people on the other end of the phone are only too delighted to help.

To stay in one is the ultimate treat; to work in one would be an everyday pleasure. When I finish this course I'm automatically placed in a hotel as a temporary manager in training so I just know that there's a job for me at the end of the rainbow.

You have received an instant message from: RUBY.

Ruby: Hello, stranger.

Rosie: Oh, hi, Ruby, sorry it's been so long; I've had a lot on lately.

Ruby: No apologies needed, you know that. How's your mum?

Rosie: Not great. That tear reservoir still hasn't dried up. She's coming to stay with me for a little while.

Ruby: In the flat?

Rosie: Yes.

Ruby: How's that going to work? You don't have any spare rooms.

Rosie: Oh, gosh, it has been ages since I spoke to you. After many days of deliberations with Brian the Whine I eventually gave in and have decided to allow Katie to stay with him in Ibiza for the summer. I must be crazy because no matter how much Brian the Whine assures me that he's a responsible father who will keep an eye on his daughter, I can't stop thinking of the fact that he ran off when he found out I was pregnant and only returned when she was thirteen. I'm not too keen on his definition of responsible. Plus he will be working nights so I don't know how he'll know what she's up to.

Ruby: The good thing about Brian being her father is that he's the owner of a seedy nightclub on the part of an island where he's used to seeing what exactly sixteen-year-olds get up to. He will not want his daughter joining in with that kind of fun. Trust me. Anyway, she'll be on her own, and how much partying can a girl do on her own?

Rosie: You really want the answer to that question? Anyway, John is going to join her for a few weeks and Toby and Monica are going over for a holiday too. But I can't put up too much of a fight because Brian the Whine is good enough to spend most of the year here for Katie and he needs to be over there during the summer. There has to be a bit of give and take, and Katie has never actually seen her own father's home. Also, Brian said he would make sure she gets a bit of experience DJ-ing while she's there, which would be brilliant for her.

Ruby: Have you convinced yourself enough yet?

Rosie: God, does it really sound like that?

Ruby: Yep.

Rosie: Well, without wanting to sound like a complete moan (because we all know I'm not one to moan), this summer is going to be really lonely for me. Even Mum is only staying with me a short while before she's off again. A few people Mum and Dad met while they were on their cruise got in touch with Mum. They're planning a trip to South Africa and they're going to stay for a month. That was the next place Dad wanted to go to. He always used to watch National Geographic and swear he would one day go on a safari. Well, he's going now because Mum is taking his ashes and scattering them with the tigers and elephants. She's really happy with the idea so I'm not going to get in her way. Kevin is a bit upset about it – he wants to have a place for Dad that we can all visit – but Mum insists this is what Dad would want. I don't know why Kev is causing such a fuss. He barely visited Dad when he was alive. I can't imagine him visiting his cremation site every day. Come to think of it, maybe that's what his problem is.

Anyway, Mum doesn't want to stay in Connemara a moment longer on her own, so she's coming to stay with me for two weeks before she heads off. But after that, everyone is gone. Mum, Dad, Katie, Steph, Kev and Alex. I'm all alone and because it's the summer and the school is closed, all I have to do is to study.

Ruby: You think that maybe this is a sign to meet more people?

Rosie: I know, I know. I'm alone by my own choosing. When I was eighteen everyone my age wanted to talk about boys, not babies; at twenty-two they wanted to talk about college not toddlers, at thirty-two they wanted to talk about marriage not divorce, and now when I'm thirty-five and finally willing to talk about men and college, all people want to do is talk about babies. I tried all these coffee morning things; I tried chatting to other mothers as we waited at the school gates for our children. It didn't work. Nobody understands me like you do, Ruby.

Ruby: And even I have trouble with that. You're unique, Rosie Dunne, you're definitely unique. But I'm here for you, and unless me and Gary miraculously become Ireland's Salsa Champions and are whisked off to Madrid for the European Championship, I ain't going nowhere.

Rosie: Thanks.

Ruby: No problem. But continuing with this 'meeting new people' theme, when are you going to start dating again? It's been a few years since you've been in action!

Rosie: Excuse me, did I not go out on a date with Adam, whom you set me up with? Anyway, apart from that enjoyable night with Adam, it's not like dating was ever that brilliant that I miss it.

Ruby: Really?

Rosie: Oh, please, sex with whatshisname was so mechanical. He used to move in time to the bloody bedside alarm clock that ticked so loudly it would keep me awake (at night, of course, not during sex). Sex with Brian the Whine was a mere drunken fumble in the dark so I can't even remember that. I suppose the night with Adam was special, he was different from the other two but I don't think I'll ever meet my Don Juan. I don't really care either. What you don't know, you don't miss.

Ruby: But doesn't what you don't know make you even the teeny tiniest bit curious?

Rosie: No. I have a shit job with shit pay, a shit flat with shit rent. I have no time for shit sex with a shit man.

Ruby: Rosie!

Rosie: What? I'm serious.

Ruby: I just cannot believe my ears. I'm flabbergasted by this news. OK, I'm taking you out clubbing at the weekend.

Rosie: Clubbing? Do you really think bringing me to a place where I am ten years older than everyone is really going to make me feel better? You think young hot-blooded males are interested in thirty-five-year-old, out-of-shape single mothers these days? I don't think so. I think they're interested in women with breasts resting *above* their belly buttons.

Ruby: Oh, don't exaggerate. You're *thirty-five* not *ninety-five*! I met my Teddy in a nightclub, and he may not be Brad Pitt but what he lacks in looks he makes up for in the bedroom department.

Rosie: Really? You mean to tell me that sex is *good* with Teddy?

Ruby: Well, I'm not with the man for conversation, am I?

Rosie: Of course not. But sex was the last thing on my mind.

Ruby: Well, all that's going to change now, so come on, let's go out and have a good time.

Rosie: Honestly, Ruby, thanks but no thanks. I really have no interest in meeting anyone. And if I did what would I do, bring him home to meet my grieving mother sleeping in the room next door?

Ruby: I suppose you have a point, but sooner or later you're going to have to start enjoying yourself again. You recognise that word, Rosie? *Enjoy.* To have fun.

Rosie: Never heard of it.

Ruby: Fine then, we'll go to the cinema again this weekend, but after that I'm putting you back on the market.

Rosie: OK, but trust me when I say I'm only going for the full asking price. And if no one's interested in buying I'm not taking on any renters.

Ruby: What about squatters?

Rosie: Ha ha ha. All trespassers will be prosecuted.

Ruby: I can just picture you standing there with a shotgun in your hand, ordering men off your land.

Rosie: Now you're getting the picture.

Chapter 44

Dear Mum,

Sorry I didn't write sooner but I've been so busy ever since I landed that I haven't had the chance to pick up a pen. It's really hot here at the moment so I'm trying to work on my tan before John comes over. I want to meet him at the airport looking like a complete beach babe!

Dad collected me from the airport, which was a weird experience. Weird to see him dressed up, or I should say dressed *down* in shorts and flip-flops. I didn't know he had legs. You would have laughed if you'd seen him. He was wearing this navy-blue Hawaiian-style shirt with yellow flowers splattered all over it, although he insisted it was black (by the way, I believe you now about his debs suit being navy; he is completely colour blind).

He has an electric-blue convertible, which is pretty cool (he thinks it's black) as I've never been in a convertible before. The island is so beautiful. He lives in a really nice complex just outside the busy part of town and there are about ten white-painted villas that share a swimming pool. There's a really cute guy that lives straight across from Dad, who just swims and sunbathes all day. He's so brown and muscly and such a babe so I spend the entire day by the pool drooling. Dad is freaking out and keeps telling him to put his shirt on. He pretends he's trying to be funny but he looks too angry when he says it.

Toby and Monica are coming over next week, which should be good fun as long as Monica keeps her gob shut. They're both staying in a hotel in town and there's loads of cool clubs around them. But before you go ape shit let me tell you that the day I arrived, Dad brought me up and down the street of bars and clubs and introduced me to all the bouncers and managers. I thought he was doing it so that they'd recognise me and let me in, but when I tried the bars last week not one of them let me in. Not *one*. I thought maybe they hated Dad and were trying to piss him off or something, but yesterday a bouncer from the club down the road came up to Dad's club with his fifteen-year-old son who was staying with him for the summer too, and introduced him to Dad and all the head doormen. Then I heard Dad tell the guys at the door to remember the boy's face and not to let him in.

So I've just been going to Dad's club most nights. Last night I was allowed to stand in the DJ box all night just watching the DJ work. It's crazy over here. Dad's club is really cool. It's packed every night and you can barely move on the dance floor. No one cares, though; it seems the more packed and stuffy a place is, the more popular it is.

The resident DJ is DJ Sugar (He. Is. Gorgeous!) and he was showing me what to do all night and he even let me take over for a few minutes. The entire point was for the crowd not to notice because I wanted to sound as good and professional as Sugar, but I looked up and everyone was staring at me because Dad had a massive camera in his hand and was trying to get people to pose for the camera in front of the DJ box. It was so embarrassing.

I also met Dad's girlfriend. She's twenty-eight, her name's Lisa and she's a dancer in the club. She dances on a podium that's about ten feet off the ground in the centre of the club, and inside a ring of fire in a tiger-print piece of material that she wraps around her body (I wouldn't call it a dress). She's from Bristol and she moved over here to become a dancer when she was my age. She said she worked in a club down the road (which I'm presuming is the strip club) and she met

Dad and he offered her a job (I don't want to know *how* or *where* they met!).

She's talking about bringing a snake into her act next because she bought a new snakeskin costume and she thinks it'll look cool. I told her to dance with Dad. (I think you possessed my body for a minute.) Anyway, Dad thinks she's crazy and refuses to get her a snake and they've been arguing about it all week. I didn't have the heart to tell her that everyone is so drunk in the club I don't think they'd notice if Lisa was dancing with an elephant, never mind a snake. She says she wants to do it so she can put it in her CV. Dad asked her if she was planning on applying for a job with the circus. They're funny to listen to.

I've just realised that you and I have never been on a proper holiday together. In fact, apart from visiting Steph and Alex have you ever been *away* away? You and me can go away next year when I've finally finished school and I'm enjoying my freedom. You'll have finished your diploma by then too so the two of us can celebrate! I hope your studying is going well. At least you don't have me there distracting you from your work. If Rupert blares his music too loud just bang on the floor and he'll turn it down. That's what I do.

I'll write again soon. I miss you!

Love,

Katie

Dear Rosie,

I'm writing to you from Cape Town in South Africa, which is so stunning. The rest of the group are taking good care of me so don't you worry about that. And because they all knew Dennis from the cruise it's nice to be able to talk to them about him and remember the funny times we had. There's another lady here who has also lost her husband and this is her first holiday alone, so we both tend to get teary-eyed together at times. I'm glad she's here because we both understand each other and what we're going through.

I miss Dennis very much. He would have loved this

holiday. But in a way he is here with me. I don't care how nuts Kevin thinks I am, I've scattered your father's ashes. Some into the air, some into the water and some into the ground. He's all around me now. I know this is what he would have wanted. He told me not to let him rot away six feet under or remain in an urn on the mantelpiece. This way he's floating through the air all around the world. Seeing more of it than me now. His final adventure.

Some days are very difficult and I just want to phone you up and have a good cry, but being here is a nice distraction. Not only that, it's a nice place to grieve if you have to. Kevin doesn't understand me at all. He thinks I should be wearing black and visiting a graveside every day like a miserable old soul. But I won't do it. Honestly, I don't know where he gets his way of thinking at all. We have three weeks left and already the gang are talking about travelling some more after! They have a lot of contacts in the travel world so we could get some really terrific deals. I may as well keep spending my savings because it's no good wherever I'm going next.

I hope Katie is getting on well in Ibiza and that Brian is taking good care of her. He seems to have turned into a decent, hard-working man so I wouldn't worry, my dear Rosie. Could you please pass on the enclosed letter for Katie? I wasn't sure of her address.

I expect you're delighted to have a bit of peace and quiet while you're studying. I hope Ruby is leaving you well alone, and not dragging you out for too many nights on the town!

Good luck with the studying, love.

I love you and miss you.

Mum

From Ruby
To Rosie
Subject Bye!

Hi, Rosie, just a quick email to let you know the

great news! Teddy and I got a cheap last-minute holiday to Croatia today. €199 each for a fortnight, including accommodation and flights. How cheap is that! The reason for the price is because the flight is leaving tonight! So I'm throwing all my clothes into my case at the same time as typing this (multi-talented, I know). Do you think it's too late for me to get the perfect beach bod? Maybe I won't eat the food on the plane and we'll see what difference that'll make. Maybe I'll fit into that thong after all, ha ha.

Just wanted to wish you farewell, my friend. I'm sure you'll be delighted I'm gone as you'll finally have a bit of peace to study now. I hope you've fun when Alex and co. come over on their hols, but remember he's a married man now so don't do anything I wouldn't do!!

Take care.

Ruby

Rosie,

Greetings from Hawaii!

As you can see, there was a change of plan! My crazy wife decided that Hawaii would be a far nicer resort than Ireland, why on earth I have no idea!!

The weather is fantastic, the hotel a dream. (I've taken the liberty of stealing a few things for you from my room, which should be enclosed in the package. A shower cap and bath gel all the way from Hawaii! I hope the cap fits.) Restaurants are great too.

You're probably delighted we're not coming over as now you finally get a bit of peace and quiet to study. I hope Kevin leaves you alone and stops annoying you about your mum. I think she's right.

Lots of love,

Alex, Josh, Theo (and, dare I say, Bethany)

Rosie,

Hello from Cyprus.

Weather nice. Hotel nice. Food nice. Beach nice.

Hope you're enjoying your summer of silence and study. (If Steph and the rest of the troop don't invade your home. By the way, we need to talk about Mum scattering Dad's ashes.)

Kevin

Hello from Euro Disney!

Hi, sis, having a brill time. Feel like I'm ten years old! Met Mickey Mouse yesterday and we all had to get a photo with him (as you can see I look slightly star struck. Pierre was a little worried about me). The kids are in heaven. There's so many things for them to look at I think they're going to make themselves dizzy! There's so much to do here that we decided to stay an extra few days so unfortunately we won't be able to go to Dublin at the weekend.

Hope the studying is going well and that you're enjoying your peace and quiet. Don't let Rupert from next door drag you to the National Concert Hall any more. Just tell him you need to study.

Lots of love,

Steph, Pierre, Jean-Louis and Sophia

Hi, Rosie,

I called around earlier but you weren't here so I thought I'd leave you this note. I'm going away for a few weeks with the choir I sing in. We're going to sing for the people of Kazakhstan. We're touring the country and I'm really looking forward to it.

I'm closing the shop, so you'll be pleased to know that there won't be any noise coming from either the shop or the flat while I'm gone. You should be able to study now that we're all away. I've left my key with you in case there are any emergencies.

Good luck with the studying, enjoy your peace and quiet, and I'll see you when I get back. Maybe by the time I'm back you'll have asked that internet guy from downstairs out on a date. I think he likes you – he keeps asking after you.

Rupert

Rosie Dunne,

You have an outstanding bill of €6.20 owed from the last time you were here to use the internet. Please pay it immediately or we will take legal action.

Ross (from the internet café downstairs)

You have entered the Relieved Divorced Dubliners' internet chat room. There are currently no people chatting.

Buttercup has entered the room.

Buttercup: Where the hell *is* everyone?

Chapter 45

You have received an instant message from: TOBY.

Toby: I bet you had a salad sandwich for lunch again.

Katie: How do you no?

Toby: It's KNOW not NO. I can see the lettuce hanging out of your braces again. I'm surprised you haven't taken to eating mashed foods by now, or at least something you could suck through a straw. Solids are a bit of a no-no.

Katie: This time next week you won't be able to slag me any more. For the end of an era has come. The braces are coming off. After three and a half years behind bars, my teeth, my now *straight* teeth, may I add, will be free.

Toby: Well, it's about time. I can't wait to see how they come off. I *need* to see how they come off.

Katie: You don't actually *need* to no everything *before* you study it at college, Toby. The general idea is to learn it there.

Toby: Well, I haven't been accepted yet, have I? I could screw up in my exams and not get enough points for the course.

Katie: You'll get in, Toby.

Toby: We'll see. Have you figured out what course you're going to do yet? You better decide soon because we need to fill out our CAO forms soon.

Katie: The stress of it all. How the hell are we expected at the age of sixteen (and seventeen, in your case) to decide what we want to do for the rest of our lives? Right now all I want to do is get *out* of school, not start planning to get into another one. You're lucky you've always known what you want to do.

Toby: Only thanks to you and your manky teeth. Anyway, you've known what you wanted to do for longer than I have. Be a DJ.

Katie: I can't study that in college, though, can I?

Toby: Who says you have to go to college?

Katie: Everyone. The career guidance teacher. My mum. My dad. All the teachers. God, Rupert, even Sanjay from downstairs said I should go and that he will take care of Mum for me.

Toby: Well, I wouldn't listen to Sanjay because he's got (scary) ulterior motives. I wouldn't listen to the career guidance teacher either, because his job is to take you for a half an hour every week and discuss college courses to his heart's content. Do you think he really cares what you do? Who cares what Rupert thinks, your dad is only agreeing with your mum, and your mum is only saying you should go because she thinks you want to. And don't mind God – as your mum always says, he's only having a laugh.

Katie: But Mum has worked so hard to finally get round to studying what she wants and it's been such a struggle for her. She wanted this opportunity so much at my age and I kind of got in the way and now it's my turn and I've nothing in the way. I think Mum thinks I should be jumping for joy at the idea but it feels more like a prison sentence. Dad said that I could go over to him for the summer again and work in the club behind the bar for a few nights a week. Sugar will train me in on the other nights. He says if I really want to do it I might as well start taking it seriously.

Toby: He's right.

Katie: Well, you don't sound like you're going to miss me too much!

Toby: Of course I won't. If you don't go, then I'm the one who has to listen to you moan for the rest of my life. Look, if your mum knew you really wanted to DJ, seriously, then she'd tell you to go for it.

Katie: I never thought of it like that. Who new we would ever get to our final year, Toby? After all those days of detention, I will finally never have to wear another tie again. For you, dear Toby, your tie-wearing days are just beginning.

Toby: No more double computer class on a Monday morning and I can assure you that if I get into college I will not be wearing ties.

Katie: Brown cords and long hair then, and you can listen to Bob Dylan all day while you're flaked out on the grass, man. I'm actually beginning to think that double computer class on a Monday morning could actually be easy compared to moving away from Mum and Grandma. Oh my God, what about John?

Toby: John has legs. He'll be able to walk on to a plane, sit down, fly to Ibiza or wherever you may be, get off the plane and see you. I noticed you didn't mention me there. Will life be that easy without me?

Katie: Yes, of course it will. No but honestly, aren't there any dentistry colleges in Ibiza?

Toby: Not where you're going, unless you include extracting people's teeth using your fist.

Katie: Well then, I guess it's Ibiza for just me and Dad then.

To Katie and Rosie

Good luck to the both of you in your exams. I'm praying for my girls.

Love Mum/Grandma

To Rosie and Katie

Good luck!

Love, Steph, Pierre, JeAN-LOuiS and Sophia

To Rosie and Katie

My best friend and goddaughter, best of luck in your exams. You will both excel as you always do. Let me no how the first one goes.

Love,

Alex

To Rosie

After these exams can you start going out again? You're becoming an awful bore, and an intelligent bore at that, which is even worse. The quality of conversation with Teddy and Gary is declining week by week, and the other day I was forced to listen to hours and hours of 'discussion' about whether the Aston Martin DB7 is as good or as fast as a Ferrari 575. Oh yes, my family likes to get down to the nitty-gritty and discuss the important things in life.

I know I encouraged you to go for this diploma but if you fail these exams this year and have to repeat I'm giving you the official warning that I have the firm intention of making a new friend. One that won't be so ambitious.

So absolutely no pressure there. Good luck!

Ruby

To Mum

Here we go. In a fortnight we'll both be free.

Best of luck.

Katie

To Katie

Good luck, honey. Thanks for being my study partner. No matter how you do, I'm proud of you.

Love,

Mum

Exam results: Rosie Dunne.
Student number: 4553901-L
Course: Diploma in Hotel Business Management

Recognised by Irish Hotel & Catering Institute (MIMCI) & Catering Managers Association of Ireland (MCMA)

Subject	Grade
Accounting	B
Computer Applications and Data Summary	B
Economics	B
Hospitality Ethical and Legal Studies	B
Financial Control and Marketing	B
Human Resource Management	A
Enterprise Development	A
Languages (Irish)	A
Tourism and Hospitality Industry Studies	A

Graduates qualify for membership of a period of professional internship in the hospitality industry.

YES! YES! YES! YES! YEEEEEESSSSSS! ALEX I DID IT! I FINALLY DID IT!!

Rosie I'm so happy 4 u! Congratulations!

From Rosie
To Ruby
Subject Let's celebrate!

Now we can definitely go out! By the way, Katie is coming out with us too so get your dancing shoes on (of course in your case I don't mean that literally. No one wants to see those scary-looking salsa shoes in a nightclub). She did well in her exams and got accepted to a few college business courses but she's going to stick to her original idea of trying out DJ-ing. Toby got enough points for Dentistry in Trinity College, which is wonderful news so over all everyone is happy, happy, happy!

You know when I was eighteen I missed out on going to Boston and I thought my world had ended. While all my friends were partying and studying I was cleaning dirty nappies. I thought my dream was lost. Never in a million years did I think that I would be able to share this special moment with my teenage daughter.

Everything does happen for a reason. I'll just be so sad to see my baby go away. The day I've been preparing for has finally arrived, Katie is spreading her wings and moving on and I must do the same. I think I might be close to gathering enough money to buy that train ticket out of here.

Rosie Dunne is leaving the station and moving on. *Finally.*

Dear Rosie,

On behalf of all of us here at St Patrick's Primary School I congratulate you on your recent exam results. You have proved yourself to be a true achiever and should feel proud.

Keeping my promise, I am delighted to inform you that your services are no longer required. Your contract with us will not be up for renewal in August.

We are sorry to see you go but you have to. My retirement was one year later than planned but it was worth hanging around to see you succeed. Rosie Dunne, you have been the longest project of my life, my eldest and longest-serving student, and although we may have had a rocky start and an even rockier middle, I am so glad to see you succeed at the end.

Your hard work and dedication is an inspiration to us all and I wish you the very best for the future. I do hope you keep in touch and I would love to see you attend my retirement party, for which you will receive an invitation shortly. I ask that you forward on an invitation to Alex Stewart too.

After years of separating the two of you it would be nice to see you both in the same room again after so many years. I do hope that he can make it.

Congratulations again.

Keep in touch.

Julie (Big Nose Smelly Breath) Casey

Katie,

My baby girl is moving away! I'm so proud of you, love. You are so brave to be doing this. Make sure your dad doesn't forget to feed and clothe you.

I'll miss you so much. I loved having you here with me but I hope I'm welcome to visit you lots!

If you need me, just call and I'll come running.

Lots of love,

Mum

Dear Brian,

This is a huge responsibility. Please take care of Katie and don't let her get up to anything stupid over there. You know what eighteen-year-old males are like – you yourself were one. Keep her away from them as best you can. She's over there to learn, not party and make babies.

Let me know *everything* that's going on with her. Even the stuff she's afraid to tell me. A mother needs to know. Please listen to her and be there for her all the time. If you even sense that something is wrong and she won't confide in you, just let me know and I'll subtly find out.

And last but not least, thank you so much for giving my baby, *our* baby, her dream.

Best wishes,

Rosie

Dear Rosie Dunne,

Congratulations on completing your Diploma in Hotel Business Management.

We are pleased to inform you that your professional internship in the hospitality industry will be undertaken at the beginning of August. Each graduate's employment has been randomly selected and chosen by a computer without discrimination or prejudice. Once a placement has been made the graduate cannot change.

The contract of twelve months is for the position of assistant manager and is to be held at the Grand Tower

Hotel in Dublin's city centre. You are to begin on Monday, 1 August at 9 a.m. For more information regarding your placement please contact Cronin Ui Cheallaigh, manager and owner of the Grand Tower Hotel. The phone number, details and map of directions to the hotel are provided overleaf.

We wish you luck in your new venture and hope it brings you success in the future.

Yours sincerely,

Keith Richards

Hotel Business Management Course Director, St Patrick's Primary School Night Courses

Alex: Very impressive, Rosie. The Grand Tower Hotel? Sounds amazing.

Rosie: Oooh, I know! That's what I thought! I'm not familiar with the hotel, though, are you?

Alex: Oh, you're asking the wrong person, Rosie. Every time I'm back in Dublin some new building, office block or apartment block has popped up where there was nothing. I don't no where anything is any more. You should go down and take a look yourself.

Rosie: Yeah, maybe. After we hung up the other night, I was thinking, and do you know you're losing your accent?

Alex: Rosie, I have been here twenty years. I've spent more years here than in Ireland. My kids are American; I have to keep up with the lingo (Irish expression added entirely for you)! Of course I'm going to lose an accent.

Rosie: Well, you're not so much losing an accent as gaining an accent. But twenty years . . . how did that happen?

Alex: I no, time flies when you're having fun.

Rosie: If you call the last twenty years fun, then I don't want to know how fast time goes by when you're really enjoying yourself.

Alex: It hasn't been so bad for you, has it, Rosie?

Rosie: Define bad.

Alex: Oh, come on . . .
Rosie: No it hasn't, but I wouldn't complain if it became a whole lot better.
Alex: Well, none of us would . . . the job must be exciting for you.
Rosie: It really, really is. I feel like a kid on Christmas Eve! I haven't felt like that for a long, long time. I know the job is temporary and that I'm only in training but I've waited a long time for this opportunity.
Alex: You've waited too long for it. I of all people no how much you've wanted this. I used to hate it when you made me play Hotel.
Rosie: Ha ha, I remember that. I was always the person in charge and you had to be the customer!
Alex: I hated being the customer because you would never leave me alone. You kept fluffing my pillows and lifting my feet up on stools 'for the customer's comfort'.
Rosie: My God, I'd forgotten all about that! I used to try to be like the guy on *Fantasy Island* who looked after his guests so much he would use magic to give them their dreams.
Alex: I don't call forcing me to go to bed at two in the day, tucking me in so tight that I could hardly breathe, a comfort/dream-providing service! I don't no what type of manager you were trying to be but if you behave like that with your real customers then a few of them will have restraining orders taken out against you.
Rosie: Well, at least it was better than playing Hospital. All that game consisted of was you tripping me up on concrete and then tending to me. Mum and Dad used to wonder where all my cuts and bruises were coming from.
Alex: Yeah, that was fun, wasn't it?
Rosie: Well, you have a distorted idea of what fun is. Like the last twenty years, for example.
Alex: Obviously not *all* fun for either of us.
Rosie: No . . .

Alex: Hotels and hospitals. Sounds like some sort of dodgy porn movie.
Rosie: You wish!
Alex: I do wish. I have a three-year-old son who likes to sleep in between me and Beth.
Rosie: Well, I could join the nunnery and I don't think it would bother me in the slightest.
Alex: Oh, I disagree!
Rosie: No really, trust me, Alex. After the men I've been with, celibacy would be like a *gift*.
Alex: It wasn't the celibacy I was referring to; it was the vow of silence that would kill you.
Rosie: Funny. Well, believe me, Alex, there are certain kinds of silences that make you walk on air. And on that note, I'll leave you.
Rosie has logged off.
Alex: Those silences I no.

Chapter 46

Hi, Mum,

Just a quick note to wish you luck (not that you need it) on your first day of work tomorrow. I'm sure you'll knock 'em all dead!

Best of luck,
Love,
Katie

You have an instant message from: RUBY.

Ruby: Well, Ms Assistant Manager, tell me all about it. How's work going?

Rosie: Very, very sl o o o o o wly.

Ruby: Should I ask why?

Rosie: Are you ready for a rant? Because if you're not I'm giving you the opportunity now to get out of this conversation while you can.

Ruby: Believe it or not I came into this conversation prepared. Fire ahead.

Rosie: *OK*, so I arrived on the road the hotel was situated on nice and early and proceeded to walk up and down the street for three-quarters of an hour trying to find the very beautiful and *Grand* Tower Hotel. I asked shop owners and stall owners but none of them had any idea where this hotel was.

After ringing the course director almost in tears and in a complete panic over the fact that I was late for my first day of work, I also succeeded in accusing him of giving me the wrong address. He kept on repeating the same address over and over again, which I told him couldn't be possible because the building in question was completely derelict.

Eventually he said he'd ring the hotel owner and double-check the directions with him so I sat down on the filthy front steps of the derelict building (dirtying the bum of my new suit) and tried not to cry about how late I was and what a bad impression this was making. Suddenly the door of the building behind me opened with a very loud farting noise at the hinges and this *thing* looked out at me. The thing spoke in a very strong Dublin accent, introduced himself as Cronin Ui Cheallaigh, the owner of the building, and insisted I call him Beanie.

At first I was confused by his nickname but as the day wore on it all became very clear. The hinges of the front door were not what made a farting sound; it was indeed the gaseous behind of Beanie.

He brought me inside to the ancient, damp building and showed me around the few rooms on the ground level. He then asked me if I had any questions and I, of course, wanted to know why I was in this particular building and when was I going to see the hotel. To which he replied proudly, 'Dis is de bleedin' hotel. Nice, wha'?'

He then asked me if I had any ideas on how to improve the hotel after my first impression and I suggested displaying the actual name of the hotel on the actual building so as to make it easier for the guests (although not doing so was also a good marketing ploy). I also suggested spreading the word of its existence among the surrounding businesses so they could help advertise the hotel (or at least be able to help give directions to completely lost tourists).

He studied my face very hard to see if I was being smart. Which, by the way, I absolutely wasn't. I'm currently waiting on a sign for the front of the hotel to arrive.

He then gave me a name tag which he insisted I wear. His reason for me having to wear this was so that if customers needed to complain, they would know who to blame. A very positive-thinking man, as you can see. The problem with the name tag (other than having to wear it) was that he appeared to have misheard the spelling of my name over the phone.

I have been walking around the entire week as 'Rosie Bumme'. Something that Beanie seems to find incredibly humorous. Although after he had gotten over his laughing fit he was slightly disappointed. That alone is an example of his level of maturity and the seriousness with which he takes his job and general running of the so-called hotel.

How it has remained open up until now is beyond me. It is one of those beautiful houses that in its time would have been extremely grand but that has been left to rot away. It's probably decaying underneath the floorboards with whatever else is causing the smell.

It was once red-bricked but is now dirty brown. It has four levels and on the underground level, I have now learned, is a lap-dancing club also owned by Beanie. As you enter the ground level of the hotel, you are greeted by a tiny little desk made of dark mahogany wood (as is all the wood in the building). Behind it is a messy collection of former guests' hats, umbrellas and coats that are currently collecting dust.

The walls are wood-panelled from the floor to halfway up the wall, which is a nice feature, and the walls, which were probably once a rich olive-green colour are now more a mouldy green. Small lantern-like lights adorn the walls and throw out absolutely no light at all. The place is like a dungeon. The carpets look like they were laid in the seventies. They're dirty and smelly and have cigarette burns, black patches of stuck-on chewing gum and other stains the origins of which I don't wish to know.

A long corridor leads down to a large bar area, which contains the same dirty smelly carpet, dark wood, paisley-covered stools and chairs and when the sun shines through the tiny, paint-flaking window all you can see is the air thick with wisps of smoke, probably still there from the old man who used to sit with his pipe two hundred years ago.

The dining area has twenty tables and a limited menu. It has the same carpet, but with the added feature of food stains. There are brown velvet curtains, and net blinds; the tables are covered in what were once white but are now yellow lace tablecloths with rusty, food-stained cutlery. The glasses are misty, the walls are white, which makes it the only light room, but no matter how much the heat is turned up it feels cold.

But the *smell*! It's like somebody died and was left to decay. It has since been absorbed into the furniture, the walls and into my clothes. There are sixty rooms. Twenty on each floor. Beanie proudly announced that half of them are ensuite. You could imagine how happy I was to hear that – *some* bedrooms have bathrooms!

Two wonderful women, Betty and Joyce, each about one hundred years old, clean the rooms three times a week, which frankly I find rather disgusting. And given how slowly they move, I'd be surprised if they cleaned each room even that often.

I was also beginning to wonder what kind of customers a hotel like this would attract but it all became clear to me as I worked the late shift one night. As the lap-dancing club finished downstairs, the party continued upstairs. This gave me all the more reason to employ more chambermaids.

The only way someone would find a chocolate on their pillow is if the previous guest had spit it out. The only reason someone would wear the shower cap would be to protect their head from the yellow water that runs through the pipes (though probably safe, I'm sticking to my bottled water).

Last week a radio station rang up to ask if the hotel could be part of a competition they're running – they must have got desperate, or been fooled by the hotel's much swankier-sounding name. I couldn't think of a good enough excuse to say no. People had to write in and explain why they deserved a weekend of pampering in Dublin. They would be treated to a night at the theatre, a meal, a day out shopping and two nights' bed-and-breakfast at a central hotel, all expenses paid. It was great for the hotel as we were advertised all week on the radio and we got a good few guests as a result. Not that any of them knew what they'd let themselves in for.

The people who won had a story so touching that I was nearly crying listening to it on the radio. So I had the honeymoon suite (completely the same as all the other rooms but I told Beanie to put a sign on the door to make the winners feel special. He ended up stencilling it on himself and spent an hour with a black marker in his hand with his tongue hanging out in concentration) filled with beautiful flowers and left a complimentary bottle of champagne for them. I really tried my best with the room, squeezing enough money out of the budget for new bedlinen, etc., but there was only so much the meagre profits could get me.

Anyway, when they found out they'd won, they were so excited they kept ringing the hotel every day before they got here, asking questions and making sure everything was still OK. They walked in the door, took one look at the place and left within fifteen minutes.

Ruby, those people had lost their *home*, the

husband had lost his *job*, broken *both* his legs, lost their *car* and had to leave their village. They had been given an all-expenses-paid weekend and could stay in the hotel absolutely *free* and *still* they didn't want to stay. That's how *bad* this hotel is.

Rosie: Ruby?

Rosie: Ruby, are you there?

Rosie: Hello? Ruby, did you get all that?

Ruby: Zzzzzzzzzzzzzzzzzzzz

Rosie: Ruby!!

Ruby: Oh, what?! Did I miss something? Sorry, I must have nodded off about an *hour* ago when you *started* telling me about your job.

Rosie: I'm sorry, Ruby, but I warned you.

Ruby: Don't worry, I managed to wander off and make myself a cup of coffee and came back when you were talking about olive-green walls and decomposing bodies.

Rosie: Sorry, it's been one of those months.

Ruby: Not all jobs turn out to be what you think they're going to be. Anyway, would you rather be a secretary at Randy Andy Paperclip Co. or assistant manager of the Grand Tower Hotel?

Rosie: Oooh, definitely assistant manager of the Grand Tower Hotel.

Ruby: Well, there you go, Rosie Bumme. Life could be worse then, couldn't it?

Rosie: I guess so. But I do have one other slight problem.

Ruby: Can you tell me what it is in less than one thousand words?

Rosie: I'll try! Alex is coming over for Julie Casey's retirement party in a few weeks and he's bringing Bethany, and they've booked themselves into the hotel for the weekend. You see, I kind of told him that it was really nice . . . and they specifically requested a room with a view. At this stage I'm hard pushed to find a room with a *window* (OK, not *really*) but under the circumstances, we at the

Grand Tower Hotel consider a special request to be a room with a *bathroom*. I mean, view-wise, which do you think they'd prefer, a view of a butcher's or a view of a scrapyard?
Ruby: Oh dear . . .

You have an instant message from: ALEX.
Alex: Hi, Rosie, you're up late.
Rosie: So are you.
Alex: I'm five hours behind, remember.
Rosie: Katie's debs ball is on tonight. She's there right now, in fact.
Alex: Oh, I see. Can't you sleep?
Rosie: Are you mad? Of course I can't sleep. I helped shop for the dress, helped her get ready with her make-up and hair, took photographs of her being so excited on her special night. The night when she will see friends she probably won't see again for years, or never again, despite promises of keeping in touch. It was like turning the clock back to me and Mum twenty years ago.

I know she's not me, she's her own person with her own mind, but I couldn't help but see myself walking out that door. Arm in arm with a man in a tuxedo, excited about the night, excited about the future. Excited, excited, excited. I was so bloody young. Of course, I didn't think I was at the time. I had a million plans. I knew what I was going to do. I had the next few years of my life all figured out.

But what I didn't know was that within a few hours all those plans would change. Ms Know-it-all didn't quite know so much then.

I just hope Katie comes home tonight when she should.
Alex: She's wise, Rosie, and if you've raised her the way I think you have, then you have nothing to worry about.
Rosie: I can't fool myself. She's been with her boyfriend for over three years now so I don't

exactly think they've been holding hands all this time. But for tonight at least, on the night that changed my life, I wish her home early.

Alex: Well then, I'll just have to distract you until she comes home, won't I?

Rosie: If you wouldn't mind.

Alex: So how is our hotel room set for when we're over? I certainly hope the manager can arrange the very best for us!

Rosie: I'm actually only the *assistant* manager, remember, and the hotel isn't exactly . . .

Alex: Isn't exactly what?

Rosie: As snazzy as the ones you're used to when you travel.

Alex: This one will be extra special because my best friend is running it.

Rosie: I wouldn't want to take much credit for the general running of the hotel . . .

Alex: Oh, don't be silly. You never give yourself enough credit for what you do.

Rosie: No, *really*, Alex. I wouldn't want to accept any responsibility for this hotel *at all*. You know, I'm only there a few months. I haven't had a chance to put my stamp on it. I only follow orders . . .

Alex: Nonsense. I can't wait to see it. How funny would it be if someone was poisoned in the restaurant and I had to be the in-house doctor that saved the day? Remember that was our plan when we were kids?

Rosie: I remember alright, and it may not be too far off a possibility. Wouldn't you and Bethany like to eat *out* that night? There are so many beautiful restaurants you haven't been to in Dublin.

Alex: We might. I tried looking the hotel up on the internet but nothing came up.

Rosie: Eh, yeah, the site is being updated right now. I'll let you know when you can see it.

Alex: Great. It'll be weird seeing Miss Big Nose Smelly Breath Casey again. It's about time she retired. The children of the world need a break from her.

Rosie: Her name is Julie, remember that, and do *not* call her by the other name. And she has been very good to me over the past few years so please be good to her.

Alex: I will, I will. Don't worry, I have been out of the house before; I do no how to deal with people.

Rosie: Of course you have, Mr Socialite Surgeon extraordinaire.

Alex: Whatever image you have in your head of me right now, please get rid of it.

Rosie: What? The naked one? You can't tell me to get rid of that.

Alex: Well, whatever image that is, increase the size by ten.

Rosie: Jesus, ten inches, Alex?

Alex: Oh, shut up! So how's your mum these days? Any word back from the hospital about those tests?

Rosie: No, not yet. She's away with Stephanie right now, taking a break from it all, and when she comes back the results should be ready. They really don't seem to know what's wrong with her. I'm really worried. I looked at her the other day and it was as though I hadn't seen her properly for years. Without even noticing it, my mum has gotten old.

Alex: She's only sixty-five. She's still young.

Rosie: I know that, but I had an image of her in my mind and that image was of her years ago. Somehow, since I was young, I've continued to see her like that. But the other day when I looked at her in the hospital bed, she looked old. It was a shock. Anyway, I just hope they find out what it is and fix it. She's really not feeling well at all.

Alex: As soon as you find out, let me know.

Rosie: I will. It's tough having to travel to Galway on my days off. As much as I love Mum, it's a bit of a trek for me. Between working incredibly unsociable hours, travelling to Mum, helping her, I haven't had any real days off for the past few weeks and I am tireder than tired.

Alex: Where is Kevin in all this? Can't he help out, for once in his life?

Rosie: Good question. Well, in all fairness to Kev, he's just bought a house and is in the process of moving in with his girlfriend. If he had more time I'm *almost* sure he would help out.

Alex: Kevin has decided to commit? That's a shock. You should have a talk to him about all this, try to get him to help out a bit more. You can't be expected to do everything.

Rosie: Well, I'm not exactly doing *everything*. Steph is looking after Mum for the week and she's got two kids so it's not exactly easy for her either. (*Looking after* Mum doesn't sound right, does it?) And I don't mind because I want to be there for Mum. She's all alone and I know how that feels.

Alex: You asking for help from Kevin doesn't mean you don't love and want to help Alice. Kev should be told. And he shouldn't *have* to be told.

Rosie: Well, I'll wait until he's settled into his new house, and when that's done, and if he *still* hasn't pulled the finger out, then I'm not holding back. He didn't visit Dad half as much as he should have and I know he's paying for that now. I've never entirely understood Kevin. He likes to keep himself to himself. He came and went from the house and never filled anyone in on what he was doing. Then when Dad died he suddenly thought he could take control of all the plans. Now with Mum being sick he's backed off again. Steph and I have tried to talk to him about it on numerous occasions but there's just no getting through to him. He's selfish, simple as that. Hold on, a coach pulled up outside. Wait while I run to the window and check.

Alex: Is Katie in it?

Rosie: No.
Alex: Oh. She'll be—
Rosie: Oh, *thank God*, there she is. I'd better switch off the computer and dive into bed. I don't want her thinking I was waiting up. Oh, thank you, God, for bringing my baby home. Night, Alex.
Alex: Night, Rosie.

Chapter 47

Mother dearest,

Thanks for last week. It was so good to be home again with you. I missed our late night chats! I bring good news with this letter! Tony Spencer, an English bloke who owns Club Insomnia down the road, was here in Dad's club last night when I was doing my set, and he was so impressed he asked if I'd like to work for him! How cool is that?! He also organises some summer dance festivals so I'll be off around Europe during the summer, playing at those. I'm really excited!

Club Insomnia is a really popular place, and it goes on till about six or seven in the morning. I'll only be on the decks from about 10 p.m. till midnight, just to get started. Tony pays really well, though, and as soon as I get my first decent cheque, I'll send some home to you. I've met a really cool crowd of people over here, who are also just out of school a short while and are doing bar work. Me and three other girls, Jennifer, Lucy and Sara, are talking about renting an apartment together.

I don't no when John is coming over. Ever since he started college in September he's been out all night every night with a bunch of people I've never heard of. He keeps bumping against his phone and accidentally ringing me when he's out, and all I can ever hear are loads of drunken people screaming in the background. It's just been really weird with the two of us. Only more so every time we meet up after weeks apart. It's not the same at all and I don't like it. I thought I'd be with him for ever but the rate we're going I can barely imagine being with him until the end of the summer.

Meanwhile, I haven't heard from Toby in a long, long time. It's entirely my fault because he rang me loads of times at the beginning when I moved over here and I just didn't get round to calling him back. Time just ran away. I keep on saying I'll call him tomorrow but it's been months and now I'm embarrassed. The last time I spoke to him he was having a great time at college, making friends with lots of teeth, no doubt. I'll call him tomorrow, promise I will.

I hope everything at work is OK. I can't believe you got your contract extended. I thought you hated the place. Let me no what's going on there, I'm confused.

Alex wrote to me a while back and told me what happened when he and Bethany stayed in the hotel when they were over for Miss Big Nose Smelly Breath Casey's retirement party. How funny! Didn't you no it was going to be the lap-dancing club's Christmas party? I don't think Alex seemed too disturbed by the sight of red-and-white-fluffy-bikini-clad Mary Clauses dancing around the bar. I can't believe Bethany refused to stay the night. That woman really doesn't have a sense of humour. I don't no what Alex sees in her. I've only met her a few times but she's so uptight and he's so laid-back I really don't see them lasting together for much longer. I can't believe Alex had to tend to one of the guests in the restaurant – was the man poisoned? What kind of food is your restaurant serving?! Just as well there was a doctor in the house.

Anyway, I better go and figure out what tracks I'm doing tonight. Dad's giving me a two-hour set just to prepare me for Insomnia. Lisa keeps trying to persuade me to play eighties music so she can do her flash-dance routine. If it's not snakes she wants it's something worse, like shoulder pads and perms.

When Grandma gets better, you and she should come over to me for a few weeks. There are loads of nice relaxing areas to go to with lovely beaches and scenery; it's not all pubs and clubs. Think about it. Maybe a break would be good for Grandma.

I miss you so much but whenever I'm lonely I just look at the photos of you and Alex in my locket. You're both close to my heart. Always.

Love,

Katie

You have received an instant message from: RUBY.

Ruby: I've been dumped.

Rosie: *What?* By Teddy?

Ruby: No! Don't be silly, that man doesn't know how to put the bins out, never mind dump me. No, the culprit is in fact my adoring son. He has informed me that my salsa services are no longer required and he's traded me in for a younger model.

Rosie: Oh no, Ruby, I'm so sorry. Who's the other woman?

Ruby: Actually, I pretend to be mad but I'm not really. Well, that's a lie. At first I was *really* angry and ate an entire chocolate cake myself – Gary's favourite cake that I had bought for him, coincidentally. Halfway through it I was just angry and then while I was spooning the last mouthful into my mouth I began to think rationally (that's what it does to me, you see). So I devised a plan whereby I was going to invite this 'other woman' into my home for dinner so that I could poison her.

I needed to find out who she was, why on earth Gary left me for her. As it turns out she's only in her late twenties, is from Spain, teaches Spanish at the school (that's where Gary met her, where he works as a custodial engineer), she's thin, pretty and is a very beautiful person.

Rosie: She's everything you would usually hate, right?

Ruby: *Usually*, yes. But this time it's different because she and my Gary have found love.

Rosie: Ooooh!

Ruby: I know! Isn't it great? So I had no problem

stepping aside and hanging up my dancing shoes. To tell the truth, I was thinking of parting with Gary soon anyway. I'm not far off fifty now, I need to dance with someone more my own age, who won't have the energy to be flinging me across the other side of the room. I'm not up to it any more. I'm just happy Gary has finally found someone. Maybe Maria will make him move out of my house and in with her.

Rosie: Would you be upset by that?

Ruby: As upset as I would be if I found a million euro under my bed. The boy needs to realise he is a grown man now and move out. I can't cook him his dinners and clean his clothes for ever. Anyway, enough about me, how's your mum?

Rosie: Not great. It just seems that bit by bit everything is failing on her. Her arthritis has gotten so bad now that she's almost crippled. It wasn't so much of a problem when she and Dad were travelling because then they had the hot weather. Now, though, I don't think cold Connemara is really the best place for her what with the winters there. But she won't move from there. I'm worried for her. She's in and out of hospital with infections and problems with parts of her body that I didn't even know existed. It's as if, when Dad died, her body just gave up.

Ruby: She's a toughie, though, Rosie. She'll pull through.

Rosie: Let's hope.

Ruby: How are things at Fawlty Towers?

Rosie: Ha! Well, I won't have to put up with the place for much longer because I'm leaving at the end of the month.

Ruby: You say that every month and you never do. You might as well just wait until your contract is up next year and then leave. Anyway, unless you actually *look* for another job you're not going anywhere.

Rosie: Between working all hours and travelling back

and forth to Mum, I just don't have *time*. I mean, when's the last time I even saw you?

Ruby: Yesterday.

Rosie: Well, apart from when you drove by me at the bus stop, beeping and waving. Thanks for speeding up, driving through the puddle on the side of the road and saturating me, by the way.

Ruby: We were going in different directions and you looked like you could do with a shower.

Rosie: Whatever. Anyway, it's been at least a month since I've been out properly. It's ridiculous. I have no life. I really want to go visit Katie, and Alex has invited me over to him lots of times but I can't do any of those things because of Mum – not that I'm blaming her, of course.

Ruby: When your mother gets better everything will be a lot easier.

Rosie: She's not *going* to get better, Ruby. She doesn't want to get better. She's just waiting now. She's practically wheelchair-bound at this stage and she's only sixty-six.

Ruby: Get lazy Kevin to help.

Rosie: What would Kevin do? He wouldn't know where to start and I know Mum feels more comfortable with me helping her. Anyway, we'll just have to keep on going.

To Josh

Happy 10th birthday.
Lots of love,
Rosie

To Rosie

Thanks so much for my present and card. It's really cool. Wherever Katie is tell her I said hi. She sends me postcards all the time from different countries and she sounds real happy. She's got the coolest job! I never hear about her old friend Toby any more. I guess they lost touch or something. Anyway, thanks again for the present. I'll be able to buy a new computer game with it.

See you soon,
Form Josh

To Mum

Hello! I'm in Amsterdam. Met a gorgeous guy who picks strawberries for a living. Doesn't speak English but we get along just fine.

Everything here is great. Got loads of gigs and the cafés are nice too!

Love,
Katie

To Rosie

Happy thirty-eighth!

How scary is it that we're so close to forty?! Have a drink for me.

Love,
Alex

Rosie, if you think thirty-eight is bad, just imagine how I must feel, pushing fifty. Aaaah! We'll have a *huge* party. Just you and me invited.

Happy birthday again.
Ruby

Hi, Mum,

I'm in Andorra. Met this gorgeous guy who's my ski instructor, who's trying to teach me how not to break my neck. He doesn't speak a word of English but we get along just fine. Everything is great here. You and I should go skiing some time. You'd love it! The winter festival is going really well, got a few small gigs to do. I'll be home for Christmas so we can catch up on all the gossip! Can't wait to see you!

Love,
Katie

Hi, Mum,

Do you want to stay with me for Christmas? Katie

is coming home and it can be the three of us. I think it would be really nice, you can have Katie's room and I'll set up a sofa bed for her. I'm so excited about the idea. Beanie has given me Christmas Day off so please say yes!

Rosie

Rosie,

I'd love to come over, honey. Thanks for the invite. Can't wait to see little Katie. Not so little any more, I suppose!

Love,
Mum

From Katie
To Mum
Subject Coming home

Thanks so much for Christmas dinner. It was absolutely yummy, as always. It was good for us three to be together again. Just the girls!

Grandma has changed a lot since the last time I saw her and you look tired. I was thinking of coming home for a few weeks and helping out. Maybe I could get a job around Dublin for a short while? I want to help out. (Plus there's the added bonus of meeting up with that guy I met while I was there!)

Let me no.

From Rosie
To Katie
Subject Re: Coming home

Do *not* come home! That is an order! Everything is just fine here. You need to live your life too so you can continue on with your travels, work hard and enjoy yourself! Don't worry about your grandma and me. We're absolutely fine!

I'm really enjoying the job and I don't mind the long hours. It's also nice to be able to go away every week to breathe the fresh air of Connemara. I do have one favour to ask, however. Ruby and I would love to go over to you for a week sometime in February if you could fit us into your schedule. Ruby said she wants to go to a foam party and win a wet T-shirt competition before she's fifty!

Let me know when a good week is for you.

From Rosie
To Steph
Subject Mum

I've a favour to ask. Do you think you might be able to take Mum for another week in February? I'm sorry, I know you're really busy too, but Beanie has finally given me a week off and I really wanted to get over to Katie to check out how she's living these days. I want to meet her friends and see where she's working; you know, annoying things that mothers do.

If you can't then I understand. Perhaps I could twist Kevin's arm into caring about someone else for a change.

Give my love to the family.

From Steph
To Rosie
Subject Re: Mum

Of course I'll take Mum. In fact, I'll go one better and take the family over to Connemara for the week. Pierre dragged me to his mother and father's for Christmas dinner so I think I'm entitled to have my turn!

You deserve a break, Rosie. I'm so sorry you're stuck doing everything. Sometimes I feel like going over there and giving Kev a good kick. I intend to have a serious talk with him when I'm there, and perhaps he may even want to see his niece and nephew for a change.

Have fun with Katie. I can't believe how grown up

she is now, and so much like you! When she stayed with us a few months back I felt like I was talking to you. Enjoy the week with Ruby. I need to spend some quality time with Mum anyway.

From Alex
To Katie
Subject Surprise 40th

I don't no where you are in the world right now, but I hope you're still checking your emails! Seeing as your mum is going to be forty next month and you are going to be twenty-one, I thought it would be a good idea to have a double birthday party. But I was hoping that we could fly you home and surprise your mum with a party?

You can invite all your friends and we can organise all of Rosie's friends too. Perhaps we can bring Ruby in on this too for help? I think she would love it.

Let me no if you think it's a good idea.

Rosie: I'm forty in a few days, Ruby. *Forty.* The big 4–0.
Ruby: So?
Rosie: So it's *old*.
Ruby: Then what does that make me, ancient?
Rosie: Oh sorry, you know what I mean. We're not exactly twenty years old, are we?
Ruby: No, thank God for that, because then I would have to go through a shit marriage and a divorce all over again. We would have to go out and look for jobs, be all uncertain about our lives, care about dating and how we look and what car we're driving, what music we're playing in it, what we wear, whether we'll get into certain clubs or not, blah blah blah. What's so good about being twenty? I call them the materialistic years. The years we get distracted by all the bullshit. Then we cop on when we hit our thirties and spend those

years trying to make up for the twenties. But your forties? Those years are for enjoying it.

Rosie: Hmm, good point. What are the fifties for?

Ruby: Fixing what you fucked up on in your forties.

Rosie: Great. Looking forward to it.

Ruby: Oh, don't worry, Rosie. You don't need to make a song and dance about the fact the world has spun around the sun one more time. We should just take it as a given by now. So what do you want to do for your fortieth?

Rosie: Nothing?

Ruby: Good plan. Why don't we go down to my local on Friday night for one too many?

Rosie: Sounds perfect.

Ruby: Oh, hold on, though. It's Teddy's brother's birthday that night too, and we're all gathering in the Berkeley Court Hotel.

Rosie: Oh, very snazzy! I love that hotel!

Ruby: I know, I think he's on the fiddle again. Honestly, you would think he'd know the gardaí are watching him after he's just got out of prison. Some people never learn.

Rosie: Oh well, would you rather change it to Saturday night then?

Ruby: No! Will you collect me from the hotel and we can head to the pub together?

Rosie: OK, but I don't want to get stuck talking to Teddy's brother. The last time I met him he tried to put his hand up my skirt.

Ruby: He had only been out of prison a few days, though, Rosie; you can understand how he was feeling.

Rosie: Whatever. So what time should I pick you up at?

Ruby: 8 p.m.

Rosie: Are you joking?! What time does it start at?

Ruby: 7.30 p.m.

Rosie: Ruby! You'll have to stay a lot longer than that! I'm not arriving to take you away after only a half an hour; everyone will think I'm so rude!

I'll come at 9.30 p.m. At least that way you'll have two hours.
Ruby: No! You *have* to come at eight!
Rosie: Why?
Ruby: Well, for one thing the party is in the *penthouse suite* of the Berkeley Court Hotel.
Rosie: Oh my God, why didn't you just say so? I'll be there at 7.30 p.m.
Ruby: No! You can't!
Rosie: What is wrong with you? Why can't I?
Ruby: Because you're not invited and they'll think you've a cheek just turning up like that. If you come at eight then you can quickly see the place and then leave.
Rosie: But I want to stay at the penthouse. Have you any idea how much that would mean to me?
Ruby: Yes I do . . . but I'm sorry, you can't stay. Anyway, once you meet the rest of Teddy's family you'll want to leave straight away.
Rosie: OK, but I hope you know that you're breaking my heart – and I don't care what you say, anything in the bathrooms that isn't nailed down is going in my handbag. Actually I think I'll bring my camera!
Ruby: Rosie, it's a birthday party. I'm sure lots of people will have cameras.
Rosie: Yes, I know, but I'll take some photos for Katie too. She'd love to see what it looks like. I was hoping she would be able to come over but she can't. It's her twenty-first birthday a few weeks after my birthday and I was hoping we could celebrate it together but unfortunately it's not to be. Mum is going over to stay with Stephanie again so she'll miss it as well. I was a bit upset about that but she's been so ill lately I didn't want to cause a fuss. I was just glad she said she wanted to go somewhere, even if it was on my birthday.

So it will just be you and me once again, but at least this year I'll get to sneak a peek at the pent-

house suite! I'll steal a few ideas for my own hotel. What a treat!
Ruby: Looking forward to seeing your face, Rosie. See you at 8 p.m., room 440.

Penthouse Suite
440

SURPRISE, ROSIE!
HAPPY BIRTHDAY, ROSIE & KATIE!!

Happy fortieth, Rosie.

I had a wonderful weekend at your party, we really did surprise you, didn't we?! It broke my heart pretending to you that I was staying with Stephanie but it was worth it to see the look on your face (and the tears in your eyes). Alex arranged the entire thing. He's a lovely, lovely man, Rosie. Shame about the wife, though! Do you know, I always thought you and he would get together when you were children. Silly, isn't it?

Anyway, thank you, thank you, *thank you* for being a wonderful daughter and for all of your help over the past few years. Your father would be proud of you. I'll be sure to tell him all about you when I see him!

You are a beautiful young woman, Rosie Dunne. Your father and I did well!

Lots of love, Mum

Chapter 48

Happy seventieth, Mum!

You made it to the big 7–0 and you look as beautiful as ever! We'll have you out of hospital as quick as we can; in the meantime here are some grapes to make you feel *really* sick!

Love you always and for ever, Mum,

Rosie

Hi, Kev, Steph here. Texting as can't get you on the phone. You might want to come to Connemara now. It's time.

Hi, love, get in touch with ur dad asap. He's booked u a flight home 2morrow. I no it's short notice but grandma asking 4 u. Kev will collect u from airport & bring u here. C u 2morrow. Love, Mum

> Dunne (née O'Sullivan) (Connemara, Co. Galway and formerly Dundrum, Dublin 10) – Alice, beloved wife of Dennis and loving mother of Stephanie, Rosie and Kevin; will be missed by her grandchildren Katie, Jean-Louis and Sophia, son-in-law Pierre, brother Patrick and sister-in-law Sandra. Removal at 4.45 p.m. today from Stafford's funeral home to Oughterard Church, Connemara. May she rest in peace.
>
> *'Ar dheis lamh De go raibh a anam uasal.'*

THIS IS THE LAST WILL, dated the 10 day of September 2000, of ALICE DUNNE
Of Boynevyle House, Connemara, Co Galway.
HEREBY REVOKING all former Wills and Testamentary Dispositions made by Alice Dunne.
If my husband survives me by thirty days **I GIVE DEVISE AND BEQUEATH** the whole of my estate to him and appoint him my executor. If my husband does not survive me by thirty days the following provisions shall apply:

1. **I APPOINT** Rosie Dunne (hereinafter called 'my Trustee') to be executor and trustee and appoint her trustee for the purposes of the Settled Land Acts, Conveyancing Acts and Section 57 of the Succession Act.
2. **I GIVE, DEVISE AND BEQUEATH** to my Trustee the whole of my estate upon trust to sell the same (with power to postpone such sale in whole or in part for such time as they shall think fit) and to hold the same or the proceeds of sale thereof on the following trusts . . .

You have received an instant message from: STEPH.
Steph: How's my baby sister holding up?
Rosie: Oh, hi, Steph. I'm not sure. There's an eerie silence in my world these days. I find myself switching on the TV and the radio just to fill the background. Katie had to head back to work; people have stopped ringing and calling around to offer their sympathies. Everything is calming down now and I'm left with this silence.

I'm not quite sure what to do with myself on my days off. I'm so used to hopping on the bus and travelling over to Mum. Life is strange now. Before even when she lay in bed looking frail and weak she still managed to make me feel safe. Mothers do that, don't they? Their very presence can help. And even if I ended up mothering her in the final days, she still was taking care of me. I miss her.

Steph: I do too, and at the oddest times. It's only when you get back to the normal routine of life that you really feel it. I keep on having to remind myself that when the phone rings it's not her. Or when I get a free moment in the day I pick up the phone to call her and then I remember that she's not there to call. It's such an odd feeling.

Rosie: Kevin is still in a huff with me.

Steph: Ignore Kevin; he's in a huff with the entire world.

Rosie: Maybe he's right, though, Steph. Mum has put me in such an awkward position by leaving me the house. Perhaps I should sell it and split the profits three ways. It's fairer.

Steph: Rosie Dunne, you will not sell that house for me and Kev. She left it for you for a reason. Kev and I are both financially secure – we both have houses. We really don't need the Connemara house. Mum knew that so she left the house to you. You work harder than the two of us put together and you still can't get out of that flat. Obviously I didn't tell you, but Mum discussed it with me before and I agreed with her. This is the best way. Don't listen to Kev.

Rosie: I don't know, Steph; I'm not hugely comfortable with it . . .

Steph: Rosie, trust me, if I needed the money so badly I would tell you and we could work something out. But I don't. Neither does Kevin. It's not like we were forgotten about in the will. We're both fine, honestly. The house in Connemara belongs to you. You do with it whatever you wish.

Rosie: Thanks, Steph.

Steph: No problem. So what are you going to do over there on your own, Rosie? I hate you being all alone. Do you want to come over here for a while?

Rosie: No thanks, Steph. I really have to work. I'm

going to throw myself into this job and make it the best damn hotel in the world.

Grand Tower Hotel
Tower Road,
Dublin 1

Dear Mr Cronin Ui Cheallaigh,

Following our visit to the Grand Tower Hotel we at the Department of Public Works are sending you an emergency order due to an imminent and substantial hazard to the life, health and safety of occupants.

After their visit last week, the Department of Building Inspection listed more than 100 code violations including missing smoke detectors, water damage and inadequate lighting.

The bathrooms are noted as being unsanitary, and during our visit rodents were spotted in the kitchens.

According to our records you have received many warnings over the years to improve the maintenance of the building and you were advised to make the necessary improvements in order to keep the building acting as a hotel. These warnings were ignored and we have no choice but to shut you down.

The business on the ground level may remain open.

Please be in touch with our offices as soon as you receive this letter. Details of the Health and Safety Act are overleaf.

Yours sincerely,
Adam Delaney
Office of Public Works

From Katie
To Mum
Subject Your job

I'm so sorry to hear about you losing your job. I no you hated it, but still, it's never nice to have to leave when it's not your own decision. I couldn't reach you on the phone – you've either been on the phone all day or they've cut you off. Either way, I thought I'd email you instead. I completely forgot to tell you that when we returned to Dublin after the funeral, whatshisname called round to the flat to see you.

I didn't want to call you because you were upset enough as it was, so I took a message. He dropped in some post that had been delivered to his house for you and said that he hoped that they would be some sort of help to you now that your mum and dad are gone. He said he understood how you felt, as his mum died last year and he didn't want to be the cause of your loneliness.

He seemed sincere, but who can ever tell with him? It was odd seeing him after so many years. He's really aged. Anyway, I hope whatever is in the envelopes isn't too important but let me no what they are all the same. I left the two envelopes in the bottom drawer of the living-room cabinet.

Dr Reginald & Miranda Williams
invite **Rosie Dunne** to join them in celebrating the
marriage of their beloved daughter
Bethany
to
Dr Alex Stewart
at
the Memorial Church of Harvard University
on 28 December at 2 o'clock
& a reception at
the Boston Harbor Hotel

Rosie,

I'm returning to Boston tomorrow but before I go I wanted to write this letter to you. All the thoughts and feelings that have been bubbling up inside me are finally overflowing from this pen and I'm leaving this letter for you so that you don't feel that I'm putting you under any great pressure. I understand that you will need to take your time trying to decide on what I am about to say.

I no what's going on, Rosie. You're my best friend and I can see the sadness in your eyes. I no that Greg isn't away working for the weekend. You never could lie to me; you were always terrible at it. Your eyes betray you time and time again. Don't pretend that everything is perfect because I *see* it isn't. I see that Greg is a selfish man who has absolutely no idea just how lucky he is and it makes me sick.

He is the luckiest man in the world to have you, Rosie, but he doesn't deserve you and *you* deserve far better. You deserve someone who loves you with every single beat of his heart, someone who thinks about you constantly, someone who spends every minute of every day just wondering what you're doing, where you are, who you're with and if you're OK. You need someone who can help you reach your dreams and who can protect you from your fears. You need someone who will treat you with respect, and love every part of you, *especially* your flaws. You should be with someone who can make you happy, really happy, *dancing-on-air* happy. Someone who should have taken the chance to be with you years ago instead of becoming scared and being too afraid to try.

I'm not scared any more, Rosie. I am not afraid to try. I no what that feeling was at your wedding – it *was* jealousy. My heart broke when I saw the woman I love turning away from me to walk down the aisle with another man, a man she planned to spend the rest of her life with. It was like a prison sentence for me – years stretching ahead without me being able to tell you how I feel or hold you how I wanted to.

Twice we've stood beside each other at the altar, Rosie. *Twice*. And twice we got it wrong. I needed you to be there for my wedding day but I was too stupid to see that I needed you to be the *reason* for my wedding day.

I should never have let your lips leave mine all those years ago in Boston. I should never have pulled away. I should never have panicked. I should never have wasted all those years without you. Give me a chance to make them up to you. I love you, Rosie, and I want to be with you and Katie and Josh. Always.

Please think about it. Don't waste your time on Greg. This is *our* opportunity. Let's stop being afraid and take the chance. I promise I'll make you happy.

All my love,

Alex

Chapter 49

From Ruby
To Rosie
Subject Are you OK?

I haven't heard from you in almost two weeks – that has to be the longest time we've ever spent incommunicado. Is everything OK? I called round to see you at the flat but Rupert told me you had gone to Galway. You just packed up and left without saying goodbye – something must be up. How long are you planning on staying there and why didn't you tell anyone?

Your mother's phone has obviously been disconnected so I didn't know how else to reach you. I understand that you probably just need some time to yourself. Losing parents is really difficult. As much as I complain about how mine were, it was still tough dealing with their loss. I know I joke around a lot but I'm seriously here for you, Rosie, if you need someone to talk to, a shoulder to cry on or even someone to scream at.

I would say I'm sorry that you lost your job at the hotel but I'm not sorry at all. You were better than that hotel; you had bigger dreams that extended far beyond those crumbling walls. Now the world is – once again – your oyster.

Please just let me know you're OK or I'm coming down there myself to check up on you and that's not a threat, it's a promise.

Welcome to the Relieved Divorced Dubliners' internet chat room. There are currently three people chatting.

LonelyLady: The guy from my reading group asked me out yesterday. To go out on a date, like. This weekend. Just me and him. But I just don't know . . .

Wildflower: You don't know what?

LonelyLady: Well, I don't know if I should start dating again. I mean I don't know if I'm ready, being so soon after Tommy and all . . .

Wildflower: So soon? *So soon?* In case you haven't noticed it's been *ten years* since Tommy left you.

LonelyLady: Oh. It doesn't *feel* like ten years.

Wildflower: Well, if you ever stopped whinging and moaning about how lonely you were, you would be able to think rationally about your life. Which guy in your reading group are you dating?

LonelyLady: The *only* guy in the reading group.

Wildflower: I bet the ladies will drop out like flies now. The all-important question for you is, does he have a criminal record?

LonelyLady: No, I checked.

Wildflower: God, I was only joking! But at least you know your TV won't go walkabout when you go to the toilet.

LonelyLady: A luxury which most women don't appreciate.

SureOne has entered the room.

Wildflower: Well, he sounds perfect for you then. I see no reason why you shouldn't go out with him. Good luck with the date.

SureOne: LonelyLady, are you going out on a *date*?

LonelyLady: You say it like it's a disease.

Wildflower: Well, it could turn into one, I suppose.

SureOne: No, I'm just shocked! But in a good way! Congratulations!

LonelyLady: Thank you! Hey, you changed your name!

SureOne: I know. I was granted my annulment. See, I

told you the Church had sense. They agree that Leonard is a complete prick.

Wildflower: SureOne! Well, it's a change to hear that come from you! I'm not quite sure the Church thinks exactly *that* but it's a start . . .

Buttercup: Congratulations, SureOne.

SureOne: Thanks, girls! We haven't heard from you in a while, Buttercup. Where have you been lately?

Buttercup: I've been staying in the house in Connemara for the past few weeks. I've had a lot of thinking to do.

Wildflower: Is everything OK?

Buttercup: No, not really.

SureOne: Do you want to tell us about it? Maybe we can help.

Buttercup: Well, my mother died, I lost my job and I'm afraid to say the words of the 'something else' in case it validates it and causes me to have a nervous breakdown. Because if it becomes true, then it would officially declare the past ten years of my life to be utterly useless and a waste of time.

LonelyLady: But we're all experts on that subject. You know by now that what goes on in this room, stays in this room, maybe we can shed some light on it for you.

Buttercup: Thanks. OK then, here goes . . . I came across a letter that was written just after my thirtieth birthday. A letter that was meant for me but that never made it into my hands. It was from Alex.

LonelyLady: Oooh, what did he say in the letter?

Buttercup: Here's the tough part. He said he loved me.

Wildflower: Whooooah!

SureOne: Oh. My. God.

LonelyLady: No! So where did you find the letter?

Buttercup: Whatshisname returned it to me. He 'didn't want to be the cause of my loneliness any more', he said.

LonelyLady: He had kept it all these years?

Buttercup: Why he would keep it all these years I have no idea. I haven't quite figured that out yet. Although I never truly figured him out at all while I was married to him. I can't really think anything now, I'm in so much shock.

Wildflower: So have you spoken to Alex?

Buttercup: How can I speak to him, Wildflower? Knowing what I know, how can I even *think* of him?

Wildflower: Very easily, I would imagine. He's just told you that he loves you!

Buttercup: No, Wildflower, he told me over *ten* years ago that he loved me. *Before* he got married, *before* he had Theo. I just couldn't bring myself to talk to him. He's been writing and phoning but the thought of that missed opportunity makes me so sick to the stomach that I can't respond to his messages.

LonelyLady: But you have to tell him you know!

Buttercup: I was going to. I was half fearful, half excited. I was going to ring him on the phone and say it to him casually at first to test the waters and see how he felt and then go a bit further. But that morning his annual Christmas card arrived in the post box. With the photo of his wife and two sons on the cover of the card, all wearing colourful knitted Christmas jumpers – Theo with his two front teeth gone, Josh with his beaming smile just like his dad, Bethany hand in hand with Alex. And I couldn't tell him. What would he care now anyway? He's married. He's happy. He's over me, and even if he's not, I wouldn't expect him to jump out of that perfect Christmas photo for me. The possibility of me and Alex being together has faded, just like those old photos of us in Katie's locket.

SureOne: Take it from me, Buttercup, you're right to leave the family alone.

Wildflower: But she *loves* him! And he loves her! And everyone airbrushes their photos these days!

SureOne: What age are you now, Buttercup, forty-two?

Buttercup: Yes.

SureOne: Right. He wrote that letter twelve years ago, before he got married. It's not right to bring it up now. She could break too many little hearts by telling him.

Wildflower: Oh, don't listen to her, Buttercup. You hop on a plane and go to Alex and tell the man that you love him.

Buttercup: But what if he doesn't feel that way about me any more? I've never ever picked up on any vibes from him over the past ten years.

SureOne: Because he's *married*. He's a good man, Buttercup. He follows the rules.

Wildflower: Oh, rules were made to be broken!

SureOne: Not when people get hurt, Wildflower.

Wildflower: Don't let people walk all over you, Buttercup. It's your life. If you want something, you need to get out there and grab it by the horns because no one is going to give you what you want on a plate. Good girls always come second.

SureOne: Good girls have a conscience and that way they can live with themselves. And anyway, we haven't even thought about the fact that Alex's feelings may have diminished for Buttercup over time.

Wildflower: Oh, why don't we just slit her wrists *for* her, SureOne?

Buttercup: She's right, Wildflower. I need to cover all angles before I jump into this head first. God, I feel sick. OK, so what happens if I tell Alex that I received his letter and his feelings have changed? What do I do then? Things between us could never get back to normal ever again and I would lose my very best friend and I don't think I could cope with that.

Wildflower: Yes, but then what if when you tell him how you feel, he grabs you passionately, relieved you finally know his true feelings and the two of you live happily ever after?

SureOne: Yeah sure, in between one messy divorce, child custody court fights, a heartbroken ex-wife . . .

Wildflower: And a partridge in a pear tree.

SureOne: If you can live with yourself by doing that, then by all means go ahead, but I for one couldn't.

Wildflower: But she can't pretend nothing happened.

SureOne: Your friendship will remain strong with Alex and the happiness in his life will also remain intact, just as it did when Alex heard no reply from you all those years ago. He kept on as normal, as though nothing had ever happened.

Buttercup: Why did he keep on as normal? I remember him asking about a letter and I told him I didn't get it. Why didn't he just tell me then?

Wildflower: He could have chickened out.

SureOne: Or he saw that you were in love with your husband.

Buttercup: This is all very confusing. LonelyLady, you've been very quiet. What do you think?

LonelyLady: Well, I of all people know what it's like to feel all alone and there were times that I thought I would do just about anything to find love, *but* SureOne has put it into perspective. Knowing the hurt she has gone through, I wouldn't look for my own happiness at the expense of others. I would carry on as normal, as though nothing had happened.

Wildflower: You three are unbelievable. Learn to live a little. Do unto others as others have done to you. You have all been screwed with by people.

Buttercup: Yes, we have, and as much as I don't like Bethany she has never done anything to hurt me.

Wildflower: Apart from marrying Alex.

Buttercup: I don't *own* Alex.

Wildflower: But you could.

Buttercup: People can never *own* people but whether I can be with him or not right now, the answer is no. Not now. Maybe in another time.
FatherMichael has entered the room.
Wildflower: Ah, don't tell me you're through a divorce yourself, Father?
SureOne: Don't be silly, Wildflower; have a bit of respect! He's here for the ceremony.
Wildflower: I know that. I was just trying to lighten the atmosphere.
FatherMichael: So have the loving couple arrived yet?
SureOne: No, but it's customary for the bride to be late.
FatherMichael: Well, is the groom here?
SingleSam has entered the room.
Wildflower: Here he is now. Hello there, SingleSam. I think this is the first time ever that both the bride and groom will have to change their names.
SingleSam: Hello, all.
Buttercup: Where's the bride?
SingleSam: She's right here on the laptop beside me. She's just having problems with her password logging in.
SureOne: Doomed from the start.
Divorced_1 has entered the room.
Wildflower: Wahoo! Here comes the bride, all dressed in . . . ?
SingleSam: Black.
Wildflower: How charming.
Buttercup: She's right to wear black.
Divorced_1: What's wrong with misery guts today?
LonelyLady: She found a letter from Alex that was written twelve years ago, proclaiming his love for her, and she doesn't know what to do.
Divorced_1: Here's a word of advice. *Get over it*, he's married. Now let's focus the attention on me for a change.
SoOverHim has entered the room.
FatherMichael: OK, let's begin. We are gathered here online today to witness the marriage of SingleSam

(soon to be 'Sam') and Divorced_1 (soon to be 'Married_1')

SoOverHim: WHAT?? WHAT THE HELL IS GOING ON HERE? THIS IS A *MARRIAGE CEREMONY* IN A *DIVORCED PEOPLE'S CHAT ROOM*??

Wildflower: Uh-oh, looks like we've got ourselves a gate-crasher here. Excuse me, can we see your wedding invite, please?

Divorced_1: Ha ha.

SoOverHim: YOU THINK THIS IS *FUNNY*? YOU PEOPLE MAKE ME SICK, COMING IN HERE AND TRYING TO UPSET OTHERS WHO ARE GENUINELY TROUBLED.

Buttercup: Oh, we are genuinely troubled, alright. And could you please STOP SHOUTING?

LonelyLady: You see, SoOverHim, this is where SingleSam and Divorced_1 met for the first time.

SoOverHim: OH, I HAVE SEEN IT ALL NOW!

Buttercup: Sshh!

SoOverHim: Sorry. Mind if I stick around?

Divorced_1: Sure, grab a pew; just don't trip over my train.

Wildflower: Ha ha.

FatherMichael: OK, we should get on with this; I don't want to be late for my two o'clock. First I have to ask, is there anyone in here who thinks there is any reason why these two should not be married?

LonelyLady: Yes.

SureOne: I could give more than one reason.

Buttercup: *Hell*, yes.

SoOverHim: DON'T DO IT!

FatherMichael: Well, I'm afraid this has put me in a very tricky predicament.

Divorced_1: Father, we are in a divorced people's chat room – of course they all object to marriage. Can we get on with it?

FatherMichael: Certainly. Do you Sam take Penelope to be your lawful wedded wife?

SingleSam: I do.
FatherMichael: Do you Penelope take Sam to be your lawful wedded husband?
Divorced_1: I do (yeah, yeah my name is Penelope).
FatherMichael: You have already emailed your vows to me so by the online power vested in me, I now pronounce you husband and wife. You may kiss the bride. Now if the witnesses could click on the icon to the right of the screen they will find a form to type their names, addresses and phone numbers. Once that's filled in just email it to me. I'll be off now. Congratulations again.
FatherMichael has left the room.
Wildflower: Congrats, Sam and Penelope!
Divorced_1: Thanks, girls, for being here.
SoOverHim: Freaks.
SoOverHim has left the room.
Wildflower: Ah, just call me Jane. Right, you love birds, I'm off. Enjoy your honeymoon and I expect to never see you in here again. LonelyLady, good luck with that date. SureOne, enjoy the start of the rest of your life and, Buttercup, or should I call you Rosie Dunne, what *are* you going to do?

Ruby: *What do you mean* you're moving to Co. Galway?
Rosie: I mean exactly that. I'm leaving that horrible flat in Dublin once and for all and I'm moving to Connemara for good.
Ruby: But *why*?
Rosie: Ruby, there's nothing there for me in Dublin. Apart from you, of course. I have had a string of unsatisfactory jobs, have no family there, had my heart broken twice there, have no money and no man. I don't see a reason why I should stay.
Ruby: Well, forgive me for being the bearer of bad news but you have no family and no man in Galway, and no job.
Rosie: I may not have all those things but I have a *house*.

Ruby: Have you gone nuts, Rosie?
Rosie: Probably! But think about it. I have a great big modern four-bedroom house right on the coast in Connemara.
Ruby: Exactly! What are you going to do all on your own with no job, in a four-bedroom house, hanging off the cliff in Connemara?
Rosie: You could be close to guessing!
Ruby: Well, I was thinking very much of you committing suicide so I hope I'm not.
Rosie: No, silly! I'm opening up a bed and breakfast! And I know I've always said I hate B&Bs, but I'm planning on turning the house more into my own mini hotel. And I am going to be manager/owner extraordinaire!
Ruby: Wow.
Rosie: What do you think?
Ruby: I think that . . . wow. I can't think of anything sarcastic to say, actually. I think that's a great idea. Are you sure you want to do this?
Rosie: Ruby, I've never been surer in my life! I've done my research. With my inheritance from Mum and Dad I can afford the insurance. I've asked all the B&Bs around and the place is *crawling* with tourists.

The area is beautiful, the coastline is dramatic and rugged, the boglands have a foggy mysteriousness to them, the sea crashes and whips against the cliffs and I love it. It's just nature and all the elements at their best – who wouldn't want to come here? Who wouldn't want to live here?
Ruby: Well, *I* wouldn't, but I appreciate what you're saying. I think it's a great idea, Rosie. Congratulations, you little genius. I hope that whatever it was that sent you packing isn't going to chase you away any further.

Rosie Dunne will be your hostess in Buttercup House. The building is a modern four-bedroom home approved by Bord Failte, the Irish Tourist Board. All of the rooms are ensuite, centrally heated, and also have telephones. Double, twin and family rooms are all available.

Buttercup House is the ideal location to explore Connemara, and enjoy hill walking, mile-long sandy beaches, sea angling, and fishing in Lough Corrib, Ireland's largest natural inland water mass, a favourite with fishermen for salmon and brown trout. Scuba diving, sailing and surfing are accessible along the coastline.

Connemara National Park is a 2,000 hectare state-owned conservation centre, with mountains, bogs, grasslands and spectacular wildlife. Traces of ancient settlements can be seen, including 4,000-year-old megalithic tombs. There are golf courses aplenty, with rocky hills and ocean inlets providing the ultimate challenge for the keen golfer. Walking, horse-riding and cycling are wonderful ways to explore the terrain, and mountaineering is also popular.

The television lounge is comfortably furnished, with log fire, board games and plenty of books for our guests to relax with after their active days. Traditional Irish breakfast is served in the dining room and the conservatory, which offer panoramic views of the mountains and Atlantic Ocean.

Rates are €35 per person per night.

Contact Rosie Dunne to make your reservation.

From Katie
To Mum
Subject Wow!

Wow, Mum, that looks fantastic! The photographs are beautiful. You've really done so much to the place. You are finally Rosie Dunne, general manager and owner of Buttercup House! I'll come over next week and help with all that's left to do, and we can go shopping for more things to fill this big house! Grandma and Granddad would be so proud of you using the house like this. They always said it was such a waste of space only having the two of them there.

Well done! See you next week.

Dear Rosie,

I just wanted to no if everything between us is OK? You've been sounding a little, well, odd on the phone lately. Have I done something to upset you in any way? I can't think of anything that I may have said to piss you off but do tell me. It seems I have to do nothing these days in order to succeed in upsetting the women in my life. Bethany starts a fight with me if I even look at her. If I have unintentionally done the same to you, Rosie, please let me no.

Bethany is going crazy about organising Theo's tenth birthday party next week. She has invited more of her own friends than Theo's, and Josh keeps stealing my car and driving it around all night with his new girlfriend. She's a sweet girl but I don't no what she sees in my son, that's for sure. He's a mad man. I can't seem to get him to settle down and study (I sounded like my own dad just then). He's supposed to be starting college next September but considering the fact he hasn't applied for anywhere and can't figure out what he wants to do other than drive my car, I'm presuming that he'll be taking a year out before he heads off to educate himself further.

Luckily Theo thinks Josh is nuts. He's actually afraid of him. So we're hoping that Theo can be the son that we can talk about and admit to having. That, of course, is a joke.

Things at the hospital are going well. I'm still doing the same old thing but my life has been made massively easier, due to the retirement of Reginald Williams. I can breathe now without having to explain it. Working with your father-in-law is as advisable as living with his daughter. Joking once again, *of course*. Well, kind of, but we won't go into that.

I have to go now but I wanted to make sure things were OK between us. The brochure for the B&B looks fantastic! I wish you well with it, Rosie. You deserve the best!

Love,

Alex

From Rosie
To Alex
Subject Sorry

I apologise for sounding off with you on the phone. I was a little distracted by a few things that popped up from the past in my life that I was previously unaware of. They were holding me back for a little while, but they've let go of me now and I'm back on course.

I'm ready to move on and spend the next ten years of my life tending to my quest for greatness and happiness. You are more than welcome to stay with me *whenever* you are ready to.

From Alex
To Rosie
Subject Thank you

Thank you very much for that generous offer, Rosie. I'll be sure to take you up on that whenever my wife isn't looking.

From Rosie
To Alex
Subject Flirt

Now, now, are you flirting with me, Alex Stewart?

From Alex
To Rosie
Subject Re: Flirt

Why, Rosie Dunne, I do believe I am. Get in touch with me in ten years' time when your quest for greatness has reached its pinnacle.

PART FIVE

Chapter 50

You have received an instant message from: KATIE.

Katie: Happy Birthday, Mum! How does it feel to be fifty?

Rosie: Hot.

Katie: Are you having another flush?

Rosie: Yes. How does it feel to be almost thirty-one? Any sign of my only daughter settling down, getting a decent job and giving me grandchildren?

Katie: Hmm . . . I'm not sure, although there was a little baby boy playing on the beach making sandcastles this morning and for the first time ever I thought it was cute. It's possible that I'm coming round to the rest of the world's way of thinking.

Rosie: Well, that sounds hopeful. I thought those dreams would have to die, but you've given me hope. Perhaps I can start telling people I actually have a daughter now.

Katie: Funny. How's the B&B going?

Rosie: Busy, thank God. I was just in the middle of updating the website when you messaged me. Buttercup House now has *seven* ensuite bedrooms.

Katie: I no, the place looks terrific.

Rosie: It's KNOW, not NO.

Katie: Sorry, us DJs don't need to be able to spell. OH MY GOD, I almost forgot to tell you! I can't believe this isn't the first thing I said to you! You'll *never* guess who I met in the club last night!

Rosie: Well, if I'll never guess I don't think I want to play this game.

Katie: Toby Flynn!!

Rosie: Never heard of him. Is he an old boyfriend?

Katie: *Mum!* Toby Flynn! *Toby!*

Rosie: I don't see how repeating his name is going to help.

Katie: My best friend from school! *Toby!*

Rosie: Oh my lord! Toby! How is the little pet?

Katie: He's fine! He's working as a dentist in Dublin just like he wanted, and he's over here in Ibiza for a holiday for two weeks. It was so weird, seeing him after ten years, but he hasn't changed a bit!

Rosie: Oh, that's fabulous. Tell him I was asking for him, will you?

Katie: I will. He had lots of lovely things to say about you. Actually I'll be seeing him again tonight. We're going out for dinner.

Rosie: Is it a date?

Katie: No! I couldn't date Toby. It's Toby! We're just going to catch up.

Rosie: Whatever you say, Katie dear.

Katie: Honestly, Mum! I couldn't date Toby – he used to be my best friend. It would be too odd.

Rosie: I don't see anything wrong with dating your best friend.

Katie: Mum, it would be like *you* dating *Alex*!

Rosie: Well, I would think that would be perfectly normal too.

Katie: Mum!

Rosie: What? I don't see the big deal. Anyway, have you been speaking to Alex lately?

Katie: Yeah, just yesterday. He's on the couch again, so to speak. Bethany is tormenting him again. Honestly, I think they're both stupid to wait until Theo heads off to college.

Rosie: Well, they were both stupid for getting married in the first place. You know what Theo is like, though, Katie – he's such a softie. His parents splitting up would break his little heart. But he's going to have to deal with it from Paris at art college, so I'm not quite sure why they feel that will be better for him.

Katie: Well, the sooner the better. They're a match made in hell, I've said it all along. Josh says he can't wait for Alex and her to split up. He can't stand her.

Rosie: Still, they lasted longer than anyone thought they would. Tell Josh I said hi.

Katie: Will do. I better go and tell Alex about Toby. He'll never believe it! Don't work too hard on your birthday, Mum!

You have received an instant message from: KATIE.

Katie: Hi, Alex.

Alex: Hello, my wonderful goddaughter. How are you and what do you want?

Katie: I'm fine and I don't want anything!

Alex: You women always want something.

Katie: That's not true and you no it!

Alex: How's my son? I hope he's working hard over there.

Katie: Still alive at least.

Alex: Good. Tell him to phone me a bit more often. As good as it is hearing from you and all, it would be nice to hear about his life from him.

Katie: I understand; I'll pass it on. Anyway, the reason why I'm messaging you is because you'll never guess who I met in the club last night!

Alex: If I'll never guess then I don't want to play this game.

Katie: That's exactly what Mum said! Anyway, I met Toby Flynn!!!

Alex: Is he an ex-boyfriend or someone famous? Give me a clue.

Katie: Alex! Honestly, you and Mum are getting forgetful in your old age. Toby is my best friend from school!

Alex: Oh, that Toby! Wow, there's a blast from the past. How is he?

Katie: He's fine. He's working as a dentist in Dublin and he's just over in Ibiza for a few weeks' holiday. He was asking about you.

Alex: Great, well, if you see him again give him my regards. He was a good guy.
Katie: Yeah, I will. I'll actually be seeing him again tonight; we're going out for dinner.
Alex: Is it a date?
Katie: Honestly, what is it with you and Mum? He used to be my best friend. I couldn't go out with him.
Alex: Oh, don't be stupid. There's nothing wrong with dating a best friend.
Katie: That's what Mum said too!
Alex: She did?
Katie: Yeah, so I tried to put it into perspective for her by explaining that would be like *her* dating *you*.
Alex: And what did she say to that?
Katie: I don't think she was particularly put off by the idea. So you see, Alex, whenever you get your lazy behind out of that house of yours, you no that there's one woman at least who'll have you. Ha ha.
Alex: I see . . .
Katie: Jesus, Alex, lighten up. OK, I gotta go and get ready for dinner.

You have received an instant message from: ROSIE.
Rosie: Hello, old woman, what are you up to?
Ruby: Sitting in my rocking chair, knitting. What else? No, Gary, Maria and the kids just left and I'm knackered. I can't run after them like I used to.
Rosie: Do you really want to anyway?
Ruby: No, and stiff muscles are a great excuse for not having to play hide and seek 24/7. What are you up to?
Rosie: I'm just taking a break from clearing away all the dust from the builders. Honestly, have they ever heard of the words 'vacuum cleaner'?
Ruby: No, and neither have I. Is it a new invention? How is the new wing looking?

Rosie: Oh, it's great, Ruby, I'll have so much more privacy now. I can stick to my side of the house and the guests can have theirs. I've decorated a room just the way you like it so it can be yours when you stay. Let me know when you can come over. I'm heading off out with Sean tonight.

Ruby: Again? Well, this is really becoming a regular occurrence indeed.

Rosie: He's a lovely man and I really enjoy his company. Even though the house is always full of strangers, I can still feel alone so it's nice to be able to meet up with him once in a while.

Ruby: I know what you mean. He seems a real gentleman alright.

Rosie: He is.

Ruby: I heard that Alex's marriage had ended.

Rosie: Ruby, his marriage barely even started, never mind ended. Unfortunately for him.

Ruby: How do you feel about it?

Rosie: Sad for him. Happy for him.

Ruby: Now you can tell me the truth. How do you *really* feel?

From Katie
To Rosie
Subject Oh, Mum

Oh, Mum.

Oh my God, Mum.

The most bizarre thing has happened.

I've never felt so . . . *odd* in my whole entire life.

Last night was the weirdest night of my life. I met up with Toby and we went to dinner at Raul's restaurant in the old part of town. In order to get there we had to walk up a really steep cobbled stone hill, passing by the local women dressed in black from head to toe, who were just sitting on wooden chairs outside their houses, enjoying the warmth and silence.

The place had only a few tables and as we were

the only tourists there I almost felt bad for intruding but they were so friendly and there was such a good atmosphere. It's not a part of the island that my job allows me to see very often, unfortunately.

The manager of Toby's hotel suggested the restaurant and it was such a good choice because it sat high on a mountain top overlooking the island on one side and the sea on the other. The air was warm, the stars were twinkling, a man played on the violin in the corner. It was like something out of a movie only it was so much better because it felt real and it was happening to me.

We chatted and chatted and chatted for hours until well after we had finished eating and eventually we were asked to leave at 2.00 a.m. I don't think I've ever laughed so much in my life. We continued talking as we strolled along the beach and the air felt so magical! We talked about old times and caught up on new times.

Mum, I don't no if it was the wine, or the heat, the food or just my hormones but there were some forces in motion last night. Toby touched my arm and I felt all . . . *zingy* from head to toe. I'm almost thirty-one years old and I've never felt that before. And then there was this silence. This really weird silence. We stared at each other as though we were seeing each other for the very first time. It was like the world stopped turning just for us. An odd magical silence.

Then he *kissed* me. *Toby* kissed me. And it was the best kiss I have ever had in all my thirty years. And as our lips pulled apart my eyelids opened slowly to see him staring at me, looking as though he was going to say something. And in true Toby form he said, 'I bet there was pepperoni in your dinner.'

How embarrassing.

Immediately my hands flew to my teeth, remembering how he used to always tease me about the food stuck in my braces. But he grabbed my hands and pulled them gently away from my mouth and said, 'No, this time I could taste it.'

My legs nearly buckled from underneath me. It felt so odd that it was Toby that I was kissing but in another way it felt completely natural and I think that's what the odd thing was about it, if you no what I mean.

We spent all day together again today and my stomach is doing somersaults at the thought of seeing him again tonight. My heart is beating so hard the vibrations are practically causing my locket to bang against my chest. I now no what all my friends were talking about when they tried to describe this feeling. It's so good it's indescribable. Dad kept teasing me for walking around with a silly grin on my face all day.

Toby asked me to move back to Dublin, Mum! Not to live with him, of course, but just so that we could be closer. And I think I'm going to. Why the hell not? I'll throw caution to the wind and leap into the darkness and all those clichés, and we'll see where I land. Because if I don't follow this feeling right now who nos where I will be twenty years on from now?

How crazy does all this seem? What a twenty-four hours it's been!

From Rosie
To Katie
Subject Yes!

Oh, it's not crazy at all, Katie! It's really not crazy at all! Enjoy it, love. Enjoy every second of it.

From Katie
To Alex
Subject In love!

So Mum was right, Alex! You *can* fall in love with your best friend! I've packed everything up and I'm heading home to Dublin with my heart filled with love and hope, and my head filled with dreams! Mum told me about the silence she experienced years ago. She kept telling me when I felt that silence with someone, it meant they were 'the one'. I was beginning to think she made it up but she didn't! This magical silence exists!

You have received an instant message from: ALEX.
Alex: Phil, she felt the silence too.
Phil: Who, what, where, when?
Alex: Rosie. She felt that silence too, all those years ago.
Phil: Oh, the dreaded silence thing is back to haunt us, is it? I haven't heard you talk about that for years.
Alex: I new I wasn't imagining it, Phil!
Phil: Well then, what are you doing talking to me? Get off the internet, you fool, and pick up the phone. Or the pen.
Alex has logged off.

My dear Rosie,

Unbeknownst to you I took this chance before, many, many years ago. You never received that letter and I'm glad because my feelings since then have changed dramatically. They have intensified with every passing day.

I'll get straight to the point because if I don't say what I have to say now, I fear it will never be said. And I *need* to say it.

Today I love you more than ever; tomorrow I will love you even more. I *need* you more than ever; I *want* you more than ever. I'm a man of fifty years of age coming to you, feeling like a teenager in love, asking you to give me a chance and love me back.

Rosie Dunne, I love you with all my heart. I have always loved you, even when I was seven years old and lied about falling asleep on Santa watch, when I was ten years old and didn't invite you to my birthday party, when I was eighteen and had to move away, even on my wedding days, on your wedding day, on christenings, birthdays and when we fought. I loved you through it all. Make me the happiest man on this earth by being with me.

Please reply to me.

All my love,

Alex

Epilogue

Rosie read the letter for what seemed like the millionth time in her life, folded it into four neat squares and slid it back into the envelope. Her eyes panned across her collection of letters, greeting cards, email print-outs, chat-room print-outs, faxes and scribbled notes from her schooldays. There were hundreds of them spread across the floor, each telling its own tale of triumph or sadness, each letter representing a phase in her life.

She had kept them all.

She sat on the sheepskin rug in front of her fire in her bedroom in Connemara, and continued to take in the array of words spread out before her. Her life in ink. She had spent the entire night reading back over them, and her back ached from stooping and her eyes stung. Stung from the tiredness and tears.

People she had loved had so vividly come alive in her head during those hours as she read their fears, emotions and thoughts, which had once been so real but which were now gone from her life. Friends that had come and gone, workmates, schoolmates, lovers and family members. She had relived her life all over again that night in a matter of hours.

Without her even noticing, the sun had risen, the seagulls were dancing around the sky, calling with excitement as their meals were thrown around by the angry sea. The waves crashed against the rocks, threatening to come further. Grey clouds hung like smoke rings outside her window still left behind despite the early morning rainfall.

The delicate shades of a newly formed rainbow rose

from the sleeping village, stretched across the wakening sky and fell into the field opposite Buttercup House. A vibrant vision of candy-apple red, buttermilk, apricot, avocado, jasmine, oyster-pink and midnight blue against the grey sky. So close Rosie wanted to hold her hand out to touch it.

The bell from the front desk downstairs rang loudly. Rosie tutted and glanced at her watch: 6.15.

A guest had arrived.

She rose to her feet slowly, wincing at the pain of being crouched in the same position for hours. She held on to her bed post and pulled herself up to her feet. She slowly straightened her back.

The bell rang again.

Her knees cracked.

'Ouch, coming!' she called, trying to hide the irritation in her voice.

She had been so stupid to stay up all night reading those letters. Today was a busy day and she couldn't afford to be tired. She had five guests leaving and four more arriving not long after them. Their bedrooms needed to be cleaned, their sheets washed and replaced for the next arrivals and she hadn't even started making breakfast yet.

She carefully tiptoed between the mess of letters scattered around the rug, trying not to step on the important papers she had saved all her life.

The bell rang again.

She rolled her eyes and cursed under her breath. She was not in the mood for impatient guests today. Not when she hadn't had a second's sleep.

'Just a *minute*,' she called cheerfully, holding on to the banister and rushing down the stairs. She felt her toe hit against the luggage that had stupidly been placed by the end stair. She felt herself falling forward and then a hand grabbed her firmly by the arm to steady her.

'I'm *so* sorry,' the man apologised, and Rosie's head shot up. She took in the man that stood before her, nearly six foot in height, with dark hair that had greyed along the sides. His skin was tired and wrinkled around the eyes and mouth. His eyes looked tired, as would anybody's who had just spent four hours in a car to Connemara after a five-hour flight. But those eyes sparkled and they glistened as the moisture inside them began to well up.

Rosie's eyes filled up also. The grip on her arm tightened.

It was him. Finally it was him. The man who had written the final letter she had read that morning, begging her for an answer.

Of course, after she had received it, it hadn't taken her long to reply at all. And as the magical silence once again embraced them, after fifty years, all they could do was look at each other. And smile.

THE END

There are so many special people who have been instrumental in helping this happen for me.

A huge thank you to my editors Lynne Drew and Maxine Hitchcock. And to Amanda, Jane, Kelly, Fiona, Moira, Damon, Tony, Andrea, Lee and the rest of the fantastic team at HarperCollins for all your hard work and constant support and belief in me.

Thank you:

Marianne Gunn O'Connor, super-agent and friend.

Mom, Dad, Georgina, Nicky and Keano for your love, support, advice, laughter and friendship. You all mean the world to me.

David, for taking every single step of this incredible journey with me. I share it all with you.

After the year that I've had, everyone near and dear to me deserves an even bigger thank you than ever. I'm lucky to be surrounded by such a huge support group, so special thanks to:

Fairy godmother Sarah & Lisa, Olive & Robert, Enda & Sarah, Rita & Mark, Colm & Angelina (ABCD), Dominic & Catherine, Raphael, Ibar, Ciaran & Carmel, Ronan & Jennifer, Eileen & Noel, Maurice & Moira, Kathleen & Donie, Noel & Helen (and families of all!).

Thank you Susana, Paula pea & SJ for keeping me sane (or for at least trying), Adrienne & Roel, Ryano & Sniff – I couldn't have done this without you both, ha ha! Neil & Breda and the Keoghans, Jimmy & Rose, Lucy, Elaine & Joe, Gail, Eadaoin, Margaret. Big thank you Thrity, Gerald & Clodagh, Daithi &

Brenda, Shane & Gillian, Mark & Gillian, Yvonne, Nikki & Adam, Leah BH, Paul & Helen, Drew Reed, Gary Kavanagh (you're not in this one either!), Pat Lynch, Sean Egan, Madeleine Jordan, Michael Ryan, Sarah Webster and her good friend Sister Mary Joseph, Lindy Clarke and the Chinese Chess Team and a huge thank you to Doo Services.

Big thank you to super sub-agent Vicki Satlow.

My very special grandparents Olive, Raphael, Julia and Con who must be pressing magical buttons way, way up there and thank you God who must be helping them.

To everyone who has welcomed my books into their hearts. You've all put a smile on my face and a lump in my throat so I thank you with all my heart.

And finally, thank you, Rosie Dunne, for nagging me all night, every night until your story was told.